Ex Libris

Wareham Free Library

Pieces of Light

Pieces of Light

a novel

Adam Thorpe

CARROLL & GRAF PUBLISHERS, INC.
NEW YORK

First Carroll & Graf edition 1999

Carroll & Graf Publishers, Inc.
19 West 21st Street
New York, NY 10010-6805

Library of Congress Cataloging-in-Publication Data is available.

ISBN: 0-7867-0661-9

Manufactured in the United States of America

for my parents

The days gone by
Come back upon me from the dawn almost
of life: the hiding-places of my power
Seem open; I approach, and then they close;
I see by glimpses now; when age comes on,
May scarcely see at all, and I would give,
While yet we may, as far as words can give,
A substance and a life to what I feel:
I would enshrine the spirit of the past
For future restoration.

William Wordsworth
The Prelude (1805 version Book XI, ll. 334-43)

The panther's child does not fear the night
I can dance all the dances
And my mother eats nothing but the flesh of sparrowhawks.

Patrice Kayo
The Song of the Initiate

'What is this,' said the Leopard, that is so 'sclusively dark, and
yet so full of little pieces of light?'

Rudyard Kipling
Just So Stories

1

The incident with the gorilla remained with my mother for the rest of her life, as certain tiny wounds do on the face. I learnt of it very early, through Quiri, who was about sixteen at the time. We had wandered together up the path into the forest. He stopped at a certain point and took from his pocket a big tooth on a piece of twine. I was five.

'Na whatee dat ting dere?' I asked.

Quiri pointed into the underbrush. He told me that the hairy man was buried there, and it was a place of great power, and that he would batter your head to bits if you forgot his tooth. He picked up two sticks and held them flat to his temples, grimacing. I laughed and laughed. That is one of my earliest memories: Quiri pretending to have his head bashed in by the gorilla spirit.

I asked my mother about it, a few days later. We'd been flicking through *My First World of Marvels*. Gorillas filled one page. They were rather savage looking, with big white teeth and red gums. My mother told me that they were not so tall and savage looking, but that they were very heavy. I wondered how she knew they were very heavy.

'Have you seen one in the forest, Mother?'

She paused, then nodded.

'And did it bash your head to bits?'

She smiled.

'Oh yes, and it took lots of glue to put it back together again.'

I then told her what Quiri had said. Her face had a cloud on it. This cloud came upon her whenever she was about to be ill with her malaria, when my father announced that he must go up-country next week, or when he received a letter from Lagos or Buea that had something to do with a post. It used to come upon her when one of the people she was treating died. It used to come

3

upon her when I would tell her how, when I was grown up, I would build my own house next to the guest bungalow, with a big cage for the beautiful-bird-smaller-than-its-tail that visited us from time to time, pecking at the grain for the hens. I never understood, then, why this displeased her. Worse, it would even come upon her when I mentioned how, at the age of seven, I would make my own canoe and paddle up the reach to my secret hut.

This time the cloud stayed on her face for the rest of the day. I hoped she wasn't going to be ill again.

'Mother, are you all right?'

She asked me to leave her be.

'Is Mother all right, Father?'

He asked me why I had asked. He was in the office, as he always was just before my supper. I knew he wanted to build a big road, but there were too many bridges between one end and the other, and most of them were broken, or not even built, or made of lianas and therefore too narrow for our Bean Tourer to cross.

'Because there's a cloud on her face.'

He told me not to talk like an African.

'I wasn't talking like an African.'

'Yes, you were. I want you to talk good English, or people will laugh at you.'

'Who will laugh at me?'

'People, back home.'

'But this is home.'

'Hugh, you have to realise something. You'll be going home soon, to your own country, where Uncle Edward and Aunt Joy are —'

'The land full of letters and telegrams.'

He hesitated.

'Is Quiri teaching you still?'

I was having lessons in Quiri's language.

'No,' I lied.

My father ran his fingers along his moustache and grunted, returning to his papers. 'I'm going to talk to your mother, Hugh,' he said as I was going out. I stopped, studying the big map pinned to the door, with its rolling hills made by the damp. The road my

4

father was about to build, once the bridges had been sorted out, went up and down these hills. I'm going to feel sick on this road, I thought.

'Oh Hugh,' said my father, rather sadly.

'What?'

'Nothing. Run along now, there's a good fellow.'

My father was a very good father: my happiest times were watching him grunt among bits of the Bean, the bits he rubbed and rubbed with oil to stop them rusting. Although he spent a lot of his valuable time taking the car to pieces and putting the pieces back together again in just the same way, it was the only sensible thing to do, he said: we couldn't have a horse or a pony or even a donkey because this was tsetse country. Each time one of these was brought on the boat, with a lot of trouble and effort, it was bitten and had fever and died, then a huge hole had to be dug.

The first part of his road was the track that went into the forest just behind us. It was decent for ten miles, all the way to the village of Odoomi, because my father had laid logs upon the swampy bits. The Bean made the run at least five times before the heat and damp changed the fuel in some way and the engine stopped. I was sure it was because we had not brought the gorilla tooth, for every other time Quiri had accompanied us.

The story of the gorilla and Mr Hargreaves happened long long ago, before I was born. Other things happened before I was born. There was a big war and my father was in it; he watched ships sink to their masts in Duala harbour. (When we visited Duala one time, we saw these masts with seagulls sitting on them. The masts must be very old, I thought.) He was terribly badly ill with yellow jack and was mended by my mother in England. They came out to Africa together on the big steamer and stayed in Buea, where it's always wet and chilly. Then they came here, to Bamakum, on the Reverend Tarbuck's little steamer, called SS *Grace*. This was a clever boat, my father said, because it had a shallow draw and a flat bottom to take the creeks, and was made of steel plate. There were marks on this plate where a hippo had bitten it – which also happened long long ago, before I was born. Like the Bean, the boat had been taken to pieces and put back together again. The Bean and the boat were like my jigsaw puzzles.

I wasn't allowed to walk into the forest on my own. But the next time I went with Quiri I watched for when he took out his tooth fetish. It was next to a white tree with a wiggly branch and I put that into my head. I thought: when I am seven, I will walk on my own to the village and back with a canvas pack and water-bottle. This was my secret plan. I was not afraid of the forest. Not, at least, of its animals. At night I lay awake and learnt to tell the difference between the cries and calls, when one stopped and when one started. I wasn't sure who each of them belonged to, but I gave them owners anyway: leopard and monkey and mongoose and parrot, gorilla and elephant and bat.

I knew that this point in the forest was powerful. One time, Quiri showed me gorilla tracks, made in the soft mud after a long week of hard rain had cleared to mist, the mist rising in huge clumps and getting snared in the treetops or rolling over the swollen, noisy river. The tracks, he explained, were the spirit of the dead one walking about, visiting his friends and sorrowing.

'Why sorrowing?' I asked.

Quiri put on a complicated expression, as if his thoughts were moving just under the skin. Then he took my hand and led me away, in the direction of the village, away from our home: my father appeared with Mawangu, further down the track. He was on foot, in his bush-boots, finding out about the rain's attack on his track. It had dug new channels, thrown the logs about higgledy-piggledy, cast up heaps of mud, washed out the stones he had tipped into the swampier parts and replaced them with khaki-coloured pools, already bubbling with frogs. In several places there were whole trees fallen across, the ground too softened for their roots to hold. He looked rather miserable, talking to Mawangu – now the 'Odoomi Road Chief'. Mawangu kept his teeth filed to sharp points, so that when he smiled he looked like the mask in the main room. He was smiling now.

'Ah, Quiri,' said my father, as he tousled my head, 'you must appease the rain gods.'

'Ah, Pa,' replied Quiri, 'dis road you never mend.'

'Why not?' I asked.

'Mr Hargreaves done made a very bad ting,' he said.

We were already walking back together. My father coughed and said, 'Quiri, don't talk about it any more.'

We passed the white trunk with the squiggly little branch jutting from it and its one pale leaf waving at me like a hand. Quiri and Mawangu were frowning, each gripping something in their right hand, my own safely nestling in my father's. It was very steamy everywhere, so that the steaminess went into your chest when you breathed. Our faces shone.

Later, in the cookhouse, where I would repair if my mother was busy with her patients:

'Quiri, what must you not talk about?'

He smiled, his back dancing as he chopped the plantains. Augustina was humming, as usual. I shifted on my stool.

'Quiri, who is Mr Hargreaves?'

Augustina's humming stops. Quiri's chopping stops. Joseph whistles and shuts the meat safe. The new *mtoto*, nicknamed Big Baldie (he lost his hair in an infant fever) stirs the foo-foo. Mr Hargreaves, I thought, is a powerful notion (I confounded notion and potion in those days). Then Quiri took my hand and we went together up to the cemetery. The sun was burning through the mist: I felt it strong on my back, like Hercules's cloak in my mother's story. The cemetery was cleared four times a year by the hired labourers my father would bring in for such jobs; they'd arrive on two long canoes and chain up at the jetty, and be ordered about by Mawangu, who'd be ordered about by my father. There were problems about paying them, for someone invisible was ordering my father about, and the money came from that person. In fact, there seemed to be someone ordering that person about, too, who lived in a country that belonged to us, called England, and to which we belonged, because we were English, and to which my parents kept nearly going back before the rainy season. In my father's dictionary, it came after *Engirdle* and before *Englobe*, and contained something called *Presentment of Englishry*, and made me feel chilled – as I felt when we visited high-up Buea on our 'emergency' leaves, or on breezy nights between November and January, or when I was ill.

The cemetery had words in it. My mother was teaching me to read, along with the servants. The people buried in the cemetery were not all English: some of them were German. The Germans were definitely bad: I was frightened of their big, iron crosses sawn from rods or girders, with things called rivets as cross-pieces, and little rusted plaques with nothing on them. They had given my father his slight limp, and punched the mark in his side with some sort of bad magic (though my mother said it was the scar left by the injections for his yellow fever). This made the Germans stand, in my mind, next to the Pharisees, Barabbas, the crowd of Jews, and the Romans. The Romans were both people with helmets and a lot of boring 'pissles', for we read the Old and New Testaments every night, and my mother liked the teachings of St Paul: the Reverend Tarbuck, who always brought me boiled sweets, would test me whenever he visited. I was not a good pupil, but he seemed too tired to mind, ruffling my hair with his blotchy hand and telling me to watch the crocodiles, for they were always hungry, and enjoyed the tender flesh of small boys.

I knew this was true, and good advice, but it gave me nightmares. He said it very close to my face so that I saw my own face in his spectacles. He also had breath that smelt of rotten mangoes and his eyes would look at me rather fiercely. He had a huge boat – the biggest I had ever seen on the river – which had the same name as the little one in my mother's story of how she and my father came here, but which I couldn't make into the same vessel. It smoked frightfully and always seemed to bear one or two white men without hair on their faces who were happy to play cricket with me, or generally fool about with a ball. I loved their visits. Sometimes I'd see them again on the return journey, sometimes not. When I'd ask after them, by name, on a later visit – I didn't forget their names, ever – he would sometimes frown and say, 'Ah, my child, the Lord saw fit to receive him into His bosom.' I imagined the Lord's bosom as a great, moss-covered wall with a cave in it at the far end of the river, into which they had gone. I would have quite liked to see this bosom, but we never went far enough on our three or four trips up-river. I was secretly glad because the bosom had a lot to do with death.

Quiri was now standing right at the back of the cemetery, near the skeleton of the trader's old shed hung with creepers and full of new trees. He looked nervously towards the house, but we were quite a way from it here.

'There,' whispered Quiri, in his own language, 'there is Mr Hargreaves.' Then, in English: 'God done rest His soul, I hope.'

There was a small, upright stone in the grass. The grass was sharp and prickly. The cemetery was due for a visit from the panga brigade, as my mother called them, so Quiri had to bend down and part the grass blades from the stone. Seeds blew in a cloud, settling quickly on my clothes like a shower of arrows. The proper trees began just beyond the shed, enormous white things towering into a grey sky: there was a delicious gloom behind them, which was less hot and held all the creatures that talked to me each night. One of them actually said my name, over and over again: *Hughie . . . Hugh . . . Hughie . . . Hugh . . . Hughie . . . Hugh . . .* I frowned in concentration, determined to read the inscription myself:

John Simkins Hargreaves
1894–1922
Commissioner of this station, 1919–21
May he Rest in Peace

My picture of him was nice. He was like those big playmates who had entered the bosom. He had the same job as my father, funnily enough. I had never thought of anyone else having the same job, here. I'd always thought we were the very first – that even the buildings had been put up by us. I scratched my ankles because something was biting them, but hurt my fingers on the barbed seeds stuck to my socks. Flies settled on my sweat. I had to watch out for tsetse, particularly in the cemetery. And snakes. And tetanus. My mother didn't really like me going in the cemetery when the grass was high. That's why Quiri kept looking nervously towards the house. He was now clearing another stone (the one next to Mr Hargreaves), with his favourite knife: large lumps of moss fell off. There was a small iron cross stuck crookedly into the top with a creeper wound round it. All I could read was *Gil am Northc* and the date: *1893–1919*.

'Massa DO Northcott,' announced Quiri. He then hit his head with his palm a few times, curling his lower lip right over. I knew this meant extreme distress. Then he held his hand around his throat.

'Germans?' I said.

'No no,' Quiri laughed, ''e done get his Winchester rifle an' –' He stuck two fingers in his mouth, his eyes very wide. Then he coughed and took his fingers out. 'RIP,' he added.

My father had two Winchester rifles. He would take one when he went 'on tour', and the other he would leave with my mother. They were for leopards, crocs, or gorillas. Or snakes. Anything, in fact, that might just decide to attack the compound, or someone in it. My mother's chief fear was mad bush dogs. Because of this, my father had put up a fence all around, but it was very hard to stop the forest from clambering over it. He had hammered in big stakes, but had to wait a year for the chicken wire, for some reason. He got very angry about this chicken wire, standing in the canoe and waving some papers about one time. Funnily enough, we and the servants had some chickens, scratching about in the yard, and I was very surprised, when the chicken wire eventually arrived on the traders' rusty old boat (it could go no further than our bay, and once scraped the bottom turning beyond the jetty), to see it in canvas-wrapped rolls, and not in the shape of a hen.

To my relief, this fence made no difference; the number of different droppings left in the house each morning stayed roughly the same. My chief pet was a hen called Stanley with a growth on its neck, but on and off I tended a small python, several lizards, a mongoose, two monkeys, and a baby crocodile, until they upset my mother in some way or other and had to be carried off. My insect collection was never touched, though, and I talked a great deal to the tiny red ants on my wall. They were very clever, and lined up each morning for an inspection by the general. Then they would march off in a column. I called them 'Hugh's Red Coats', but my mother hated them because their friends would pour out of the kitchen tap before the water.

I thought hard for a bit, while Quiri unwrapped the iron cross from its creeper.

'And Mr Hargreaves?' I asked in the end, not really understanding this business with the rifle and Gil am Northc whistling for someone. 'He done himself RIP, too?'

Quiri shrugged. 'He done kill the hairy man,' he said. 'Hairy man done come back an' kill um. Pax. Fair dos. Rain stop play.'

He laughed like a drain for a moment, clapping his hands. I knew that this was not a merry laugh, but something he would do when he wanted to clear himself out of bad things. But when I started doing the same, I was ticked off.

Then he put his hands on my shoulders and told me never ever to tell my parents that he had told me anything at all about Mr Hargreaves.

'Why not?' I asked.

He said he would have to leave, and never come back, because they would be very cross with him. The thought of Quiri leaving filled me with horror. I had never thought that he *could* leave.

There was a long list typed out by my father, a copy pinned to the door of each room, with *DO NOT* doubly underlined at the top. The Reverend Tarbuck called it 'The DO's Catechism'. First was *Forget Your Quinine*, then *Paddle In the River*, then *Touch Any Snake*, then *Go Into the Forest Unaccompanied*, then *Drink or Wash Greens or Face or Hands in Unboiled Water*, then *Fail to Treat Any Bite or Wound*, then *Insult or Swear at or Hit a Servant or Any Other Native for No Just Reason*. Now I headed it in my mind with *Ask Mother and Father about Mr Hargreaves*.

I couldn't understand why, if everything was so dangerous, I couldn't carry around my fetishes as Quiri and the others did. They believed in God, it seemed. At least, they joined in Morning Prayers every Sunday, and were given pieces of bread by the Reverend Tarbuck whenever he passed by, and sang in big voices under the cloth fan that Good Boy Hippolytus, our blind and crook-backed punkah-wallah, would pull vigorously in rhythm, humming along, and said that they weren't worthy to gather up the crumbs under Thy table (a line which always made me feel hungry). Yet they also protected themselves with feathers and teeth and bone and pebbles and twisty bits of wood and flattened sardine tins and broken glass wrapped up in grass and Reckitt's Blue wrapped up in leaves and Ovaltine labels smeared with engine oil from the Bean. As for me, I had to go about naked (though clothed uncomfortably from the top down in clothes Baluti never rinsed properly, so they gave me a rash), with only

Jesus Christ Our Lord around me. He was less visible than the thinnest mist. He was also inside me, like my evening cocoa, but He didn't taste of anything.

I took to cutting out pages from the big Bible and rolling them up in palm leaves, and sticking them in my pockets.

'What do other children do?' I asked, when this was discovered.

We were on the veranda. My mother smiled, rocking in her chair and gazing at the view of our 'bay', with its curtains of forest. 'Certain Christians called Catholics carry rosary beads, others a crucifix. But there aren't any other children in equatorial Africa,' she said. 'Not white children.'

I frowned, but didn't say anything. I wanted her to finish

'You are,' she went on, 'the only white child in the whole of West and Central Africa, that I know of.'

She didn't look at me when she said this, but this was normal. She often stared at a point a little bit in front of me when she was speaking to me. If I moved into this point, her stare would somehow move too, like your shadow did. If your shadow didn't, it meant you were dead.

I leaned against her legs and looked out at the river. I loved the smell of her white dresses, usually: the smell of newly washed clothes and the perfume that the ironing made. But now it held me like a dungeon. I wasn't like anyone else in the known world. This world went one way to the sea, because we visited the Allinsons in Victoria once or twice a year. We stayed in their big cream house next to the Botanical Gardens, rode in their old and smelly hansom cab there or around the town, played on the beach (oh, happiness!), or spent the day up in chilly Buea with its special flowers called roses. The known world the other way stopped at Odoomi: beyond was a for ever and ever of unknown forest rising higher and higher to the sky. Father had said that one day he would take me into there, to swim in the crater lake he had come across on tour. It was not far after the village.

That night I experimented with cinders from the stove, rubbing them into my face. Then I tried my father's blacking, the stuff he brushed briskly but thoroughly into his mosquito boots twice a week.

'What have you been doing, Hugh?' said my mother. 'Go and wash your face. No, wait, I'll do it for you.'

She never trusted me, when it came to water. Anyway, both the cinders and the boot-black bothered my skin, and sweat made white streaks. I was a maggot, an albino, an outcast. The books I looked at were full of ugly little princes like myself, with thin lips and sharp noses, who were bossy and very white. That was England. I looked in the Chambers Dictionary again: 'Presentment of Englishry, the offering of proof that a person murdered belonged to the English race, to escape the fine levied on the hundred or township for the murder of a Norman.' I couldn't understand this. My father came into the room (his office). He was pleased to see me reading his old dictionary.

'My uncle gave me that,' he said. 'Great-uncle James, who I'm named after.'

'Is he dead?'

'Yes.'

'Is he the same as Uncle Edward?'

'No. Uncle Edward's very much alive. He's your mother's brother. He lives in a lovely big house with a big soft lawn to play on –'

I was bored hearing about this house and its lawn. My parents brought it up at the slightest excuse.

'What does *dat* mean?' I interrupted, pointing at the page.

'*That*, not *dat*, Hugh. Show me.'

He read it twice, then explained. So, already, the Normans were more important. The person who ordered about the person who ordered my father about must be a Norman. Normans were the ones who said you couldn't have a fetish. Normans invaded, like leopards, like tsetse flies, like snakes. They had metal helmets with noses, and cruel smiles. I began to be convinced that Normans were in the forest, waiting to murder those of the English race, then put the blame on the English race. I was one of the English race.

Not long afterwards, exploring the North Pole in the horribly airless attic under the boiling-hot corrugated roof, where unwanted things were stored, I found some paintings. These were propped in the corner, and the string that tied them broke at the first tug. They were frightening pictures: they were pictures of Normans, coming out of the forest. On the back of some of them was chalked *Sir Steggie*, and on others someone had stuck a slip of paper typed *J.S. Hargreaves, Property Of.* I bundled them back and scrambled out as quickly as I could, no longer exploring the source of our great river beyond the Lord's bosom, but just wanting a biscuit and a glass of lemonade.

From then on I hardly went into the cemetery, except with my mother after the clean-ups, and Quiri never wanted to take me there. Mr Hargreaves floated backwards into a mist of gloomy thoughts where Gil am Northc whistled for him with his fingers. The German traders were somewhere there, too, but with iron rods for hands and bare little plaques instead of faces. The cemetery was not exactly their permanent camp; that was situated somewhere I couldn't quite place. On certain nights they would all gather there. It was a ceremonial meeting place like the ceremonial meeting places in different spots in the forest (my father told us about these), and everything in it was sacred to them. I knew they were there because the beautiful-bird-smaller-than-its-tail calling my name would go silent, and I could hear the mutterings of their plots and plans over the sounds of the river and the forest. It wasn't the same as the mutterings of the servants around the fire, because the servants were asleep and even Big Baldie (who was also our night-watchman) lay curled up beside his bow and arrows.

Anyway, ordinary weapons were useless against such spirits; their badness crept easily past even my father's Winchesters. But they never invaded, not while I was there. When Quiri had to go away, back to his village for a funeral, for a few days, I persuaded him to give me his tooth fetish. We walked up to a point past the gorilla spirit's place, and then he handed it over with a stern look.

'You no go lose um, small-small chap,' he'd say. 'You go lose um, we go have our heads bashed to bit.'

He told me to listen out for his powerful wolf-whistle in four days' time: I would have to go to him on the path with the tooth. If I didn't, he would be stuck. I handed over the little picture of Jesus, about the size of a large stamp, that my parents had given me after finding the Bible's pages torn out. It was stuck on thick card, and I kept it under my hat. My sweaty skull had rubbed and blackened the picture of Jesus so that you couldn't really see it was Him any more, but Quiri hugged me anyway, he was so pleased.

He was worried about the way a couple of sticks were lying on the path a little further up. I couldn't see anything wrong, but then I didn't know much about evil spirits and their tricks. He spent quite a few minutes studying them, and then walked off down the track with a wave. I was secretly terrified that he would never come back – that he would be eaten by a leopard, or bashed on the head by a gorilla. He'd told me that he was well protected for the forest, but he and I knew that strange things happened; dizziness sometimes came into your head and there was a laugh and it was death coming in as well. There was a spirit that sat in the tree with bloody eyes and long hair and his legs dangled down as long as the longest creeper. Even if he was sitting as high as the highest birds his feet would still touch the ground. If you walked into his legs, they wrapped around you like a snake and carried you up to that horrible mouth.

I watched Quiri run soundlessly away with tears in my eyes, then I hurried back, looking straight ahead. The problem with the sticks had frightened me. Bad ju-ju, perhaps. That day, the forest didn't really welcome me.

At this time I still had what my mother called an *ayah*: she came from the Baptist Mission Station run by the Reverend Tarbuck, on the mouth of the river. Her name was Mosea, and I had never not known her. She always dressed like the Ikasa market women, in bright patterns wrapped around her body and hanging over her shoulders; there was more cloth piled up on her head, like a big turban. But on Sundays she would change into a stiff white skirt and shirt to lead the hymn singing in the sitting-room. I didn't like the Sunday Morning Prayers: I was always put between Mosea and my mother, banging away on the upright piano, and was deafened. The piano was untuneable, despite being looked at for a whole day by one of Tarbuck's cadets. The humidity did something to the wires, and several notes just made a clunking sound. Things were better for me now because I had grown big enough to replace Ndala: his job was to reach into the piano and unstick the hammers that stuck. You had to do it very quickly, and not get your hand in the way of any other hammers that were flying up. I started doing this, standing on a stool, soon after my fifth birthday.

Mosea said something bad about Quiri and he and I couldn't walk together any more. I liked Quiri more than I liked Mosea, because Mosea hung around me a lot of the time looking as if she had swallowed a lot of Baluti's grey lye, which he made out of the ashes from the yard's fire. I reckoned she swallowed this lye to keep her Sunday skirt and shirt as white as possible. She told me a bit about Jesus, and one day she said that she was called Mosea because she was found in a basket floating in the river. I asked my mother about this and my mother said it was true, because some German soldiers had killed everyone else and thrown the children into the river in baskets, like kittens.

This didn't make me like her any more, though. Because of what she'd said about Quiri, I started to make charms against her. I wrote nasty things on scraps of paper and buried them in the earth outside her door. I scattered ash and a few homemade plant potions under her bed while she was in the toilet. There were lots of Sunday School pictures in her room: St Francis with the birds, Jesus among the children or addressing the fishermen of Galilee, Adam and Eve in the Botanical Gardens at Victoria, all coloured badly and covered in spots of mould. A rainstorm washed all the curses into view soon after – but the ink had run, which was why they hadn't worked. The crippling ash potion was swept up into a dustpan. Her hair did not drop out, her toes did not drop off, she did not find her tongue wrapped round her little finger, she did not get so fat she couldn't fit through the door, and no crocodile waddled up at night to make a meal of her.

Instead, I found Quiri squeezing her to death behind the chop-shed, like a gorilla or a snake can do. Then I saw his shy smile, and her frown, and was told by her to go and play with my bricks. I ran to my mother, almost in tears.

'Quiri and Mosea are going to get married!' I cried. My mother was wrapping a bandage around a young boy's infected leg: the smell of creosote and sweat and bad flesh filled her 'hospital' so much I stayed by the hut's door. She looked up and smiled, a fly on her cheek.

'No wonder they wanted you out of the way,' she said.

The young boy's mother, or maybe grandmother, laughed and hit her head. She had big breasts as flat as my father's jacket lapels. She couldn't have understood, because none of the villagers except their Chief knew more than a piece of pidgin. I ran back to my room and wept.

They didn't get married, after all. But Quiri was a little far off from me after that, and seemed to swagger about. He usually went bare-chested, and he had often made the muscles under his breasts jig up and down, to make me laugh. Now they seemed to roll like the river did sometimes, when something monstrous called the Big Beef passed, pushing out a wake that slapped at the new jetty on its concrete pillars. My father said that it was probably an effect of currents, but when Quiri slowly rolled his muscles up to his neck-bone in the weeks after he'd hugged Mosea, I couldn't help thinking of the Big Beef, and its waves disappearing under the jetty.

My parents soon forgot about Quiri's bad influence. I liked to press my pink hand to his chest, and feel my fingers moved one after the other by the iron rods of his muscle.

'Are you old, now?' I asked.

He smiled, showing his crooked front teeth. They always had a grain stuck between them, that he would flick with his tongue.

'Hey, small-small chap, you done be cheeky, heh?'

He lifted me up wriggling in the air, and did a bounce-bounce. I flew up and down, each time landing in his huge hands. We were near the cemetery, and I scampered up to its broken iron gates and stuck my tongue out at him through the bars, wiggling my ears.

'Mr Hargreaves, he go coming for get you,' I yelled.

Just at that moment a bird crashed out of the bushes next to me and I hid my eyes. Then I pulled my canvas hat over my face for extra covering. Quiri came up, laughing.

'Massa Hargreaves, 'e no go worry me atall,' he said.

He was holding something in his shorts' pocket, I could see that. I snatched at his wrist and pulled and the hand came out because he wasn't ready for me. The thing fell into the soft undergrowth. It was a fob-watch like my father's old one, but with no glass and only one hand. He cuffed my head and picked the watch up. We examined it together. He told me that it had been the property of Mr Hargreaves.

'Did he done give um for you?'

Quiri shook his head. 'In his bones,' he said. 'Tick-tock, like dis heart. But heart done be broke. He done be a dead chap, long-long time. End of over.'

'You took um from Mr Hargreaves when he done be dead?'

Quiri nodded and pulled a face. 'No fine for telling time,' he murmured.

He put it back in his pocket.

'Is dat ting for protecting you, or for go getting power from dat dead man?' I asked.

He didn't reply. His glistening face was thoughtful for a while, so I copied him. The sun beat up off the ground and filled my head while I sat on my heels, as Quiri was doing; I felt as if my head and my feet were from two separate bodies. I shivered. The two separate parts of me were now joined by a coldness, like the butter floating in the water jars. I blinked and felt my head growing longer. Quiri seemed to be making me fly through the air again; in fact, he was carrying me. I was either very hot or very cold. My mother's voice and face stuck up both very near and very far away, like the enormous head of a pin. I was in bed, shivering all over, with my head bashed to bits. Then I was melting into pure wetness. My mother's voice and hand soothed me, my father boomed, things rattled and tick-tocked. Of course it was the fob-watch that had possessed me: I saw it, at one point, coming up through the floor as if the floor was liquid. It was huge, and the hand was spinning round very fast. I screamed. I think I saw people crowding the end of my bed, very far away.

'The fob,' I screamed. 'Mr Hargreaves!'

It was probably the German traders. They tortured and killed, I'd heard Tarbuck say: he was saying it again, but laughingly, and they were all coming out of the cemetery now, taking the fort. I had no fetish anywhere near me. I was melting away like butter, dragged by my feet into the bosom of the Lord of Life where

Hargreaves and Gorilla am Northc were waiting, making the river ripple as they whispered and muttered about Normans and Englishry and long leaves.

I woke up in the night and asked for Mr Hargreaves's fob to be taken out of the room and given back to Quiri. I saw it being carried out by the members of the panga brigade. It looked very big on their shoulders, and their knees were buckled. Then I got better. When I stopped feeling queer, I felt as if I was looking through dirty, speckled glass. When I closed my left eye, this went. The malaria has done something to the eye, I thought, but if I tell them they might take it out.

My mother was a good nurse. I was soon well enough to walk outside for a bit each day. I went to see Quiri. He told me that Pa Arkwright had asked him for the fob-watch, and that he'd been very lucky to have kept his work. He might not even have had something called a recommendation. He never told me anything secret again. We'd walk up the track into the forest, but mostly in silence or while talking about nothing. He held my hand, threw me about, played bat and ball, and found new pets for me, but never told me any more secrets.

While I was convalescing, Mosea read me Bible stories, over and over. I quite enjoyed them. Some of them I knew already from our lessons, or from the Sunday services, but quite a few were new to me. I closed my eyes and easily pictured the scenes: Joseph with his brothers, the parting of the Red Sea, Isaac and Esau's night voices, the cool night roofs of Jerusalem.

Whenever she came to Moses in the bulrushes, she read it very proudly.

These stories walked between the ju-ju talk and hid some of it. One day, still feeling a bit weak and so staying in bed, I asked my mother again about Hargreaves.

'Did he shoot himself?' I asked.

She shook her head and laid her hand on mine.

'Hugh, darling, where did you learn that sort of thing?'

I shrugged. I just knew it. I was nearly six. For once, her eyes sought mine. They were very dark, my mother's eyes, exactly the colour of her hair. She'd told me about her great-grandfather, who was Jewish and a travelling merchant from Persia and had married a blonde haberdasher and settled in London. It was this ancestor, she said, who had passed on the dark eyes and hair and skin.

'Mr Hargreaves,' she said. She looked away, out of the window. 'Oh, he thought he was invulnerable.'

'What's invulnerable?'

'The African warriors in the early days wore special shirts or waved fetishes about or bathed in water some witchdoctor had put a spell on, and they thought no bullets could touch them. They thought they were invulnerable.'

'But they might have been.'

'They weren't, Hugh. Not against those horrible machine-guns.'

She stared at a place on the coverlet next to my hands.

'Mr Hargreaves thought the same,' she said, very quietly.

'Against a machine-gun?'

She shook her head, then waited again. What for, I didn't know, but her eyes kept flitting on to my face, as if I had to give her a signal. She sighed, then she left the room. I had learnt more, but not much.

Another clue, a week later. The harmattan was starting to haze the sun with its fine red dust, but the outside was still sweet after weeks in my room. I liked to visit the chop-shed when Joseph was in there, choosing tins for meals. He was down at the end, in amongst the desserts and sugars. Ants were everywhere, as usual. The lamp was perched next to a row of big square tins covered in dust and cobwebs. There were about twenty of them, stacked three high. Their labels, stained with age, showed a lion lying down, with flies around its head. It looked dead. *Tate & Lyle's Golden Syrup*. I tested a rusty dribble on the side with my finger. It was delicious, a bit like honey.

I asked Joseph about it. He chuckled and drew a hand across his sweaty face.

'Na nyama-nyama ting,' he said.

Nyama-nyama didn't mean yummy, it meant 'bad'.

'Na poison?'

'No,' he laughed. 'I go tell you, small-small chap, an I go lose my work you say Jack Robinson.'

'Is it to do with Mr Hargreaves?'

His face quivered, as if I had hit it, and he looked fearfully towards the door. Then he turned his back on me without another word and fiddled about again on the shelves opposite. Yes, the Lyle's Golden Syrup had something to do with Mr Hargreaves. That's why no one had touched it. Without really thinking, I seized one of the tins and ran with it out of the chop-shed. Joseph shouted after me.

My mother was down by the river. A canoe was drawn up, and a few boxes of medical things were being unloaded on to the jetty. The tin felt enormous and rather heavy in my arms. She saw me and gave me her usual tired smile, then appeared to jump back as if something had hit her.

'Where did you get that?' she said, in a trembling voice.

'From the chop-shed. Can we have some for lunch?'

'No!'

She pulled the tin from my arms and threw it into the brown river. The man on the canoe had to duck. She looked at her hands in disgust. They were probably as sticky as mine. The stickiness was dark. It must be very strong ju-ju medicine, I thought. The moment reminded me of the time my parents had shouted at each other one evening, and my mother had thrown a bottle of my father's gin into the river. Gin, explained Quiri, was strong medicine but made you too happy. Perhaps Lyle's Golden Syrup made you too happy.

'Is it like gin?' I asked.

My mother, still trembling by the river's frothed edge, turned and let out a wild laugh. It must be like gin, I thought: she's too happy. The man had finished unloading the canoe and was waiting for his dash. My mother bathed her hands in the river and gave him some cigarettes and a few pennies. He paddled off and she sat on one of the crates. It was marked with a red cross and had 'Stag Brand Surgical Dressings × 150' stamped on the side. She looked around her slowly, at the forest, at the river, as if they were about to gobble her up. Her face was very sweaty from moving around too much.

We weren't supposed to bathe our hands in the river. But now she was pressing them against her face. The water was calm enough, near the edge, to have Billy Harzia's snails in it.

She asked me to sit down next to her, on the crate. She put her arm round my shoulders and pressed me against her side. This was quite unusual. She never touched me a lot.

We didn't say anything. She smelt as spicy as everyone else this morning. I wanted to bury my face in her armpit, where the big dark patch had crept up to her shoulder. Instead I said, 'Did Mr Hargreaves kill himself with Lyle's Golden Syrup?'

'Yes,' she said.

It was poisonous. I would die, obviously. I wondered whether to tell her that I had tasted some, but I didn't want an emetic.

Then she sighed and said, 'I'm going to tell you. After a long time away, he came back. At least, Mawangu, I think it was, saw him standing by your window. You were in your cot, still, just two or three months old. He wasn't in a very good way. Mawangu said hello, but Hargreaves – Mr Hargreaves ran into the cemetery. I was told he was there, but frankly, Hugh, I was frightened. Your – your father was away on tour. I was on my own. I told the servants to come inside. We watched the poor fellow from your window. I held you in my arms, very tight.'

She stood and twisted her hands together and then sat down again.

'He looked like a wild man, a wild man of the woods. Like Ben Gunn the maroon. He was behind the cemetery, picking leaves and rubbing them on his face and bare arms and legs. Then he gave a shout and broke into the chop-shed. Anyway, it wasn't locked. I knew exactly what he wanted, and didn't do anything about it.'

'Did he want a tin of Lyle's Golden Syrup?'

'Yes. Nothing else would do, you see.'

'Was he mad?'

'He had gone to seed, yes. Or gone to bush, as your father says. The fellow believed in ju-ju, Hugh. This is why you have to be very careful of paganism.'

'Did he eat it all in one go?'

She laughed, but emptily.

'He rubbed it all over him. He stripped off in front of the chop-shed, rubbed the stuff all over him, and ran off into the forest. I didn't stop him. I should have done, but I didn't. Sloth, pure sloth.'

I knew what sloth was from Mosea: not getting up in the morning was one of the deadly sins. I nodded. My mother must have been in bed.

There was a long pause, as long as the stretch of the river took to change itself from end to end. I was lost in the swirls of mustard-coloured water, seeing Mr Hargreaves rub himself all over with that rusty sweet stickiness. When I looked back at Mother, she had very wide eyes and they were staring at me. Her mouth was small. She's pretending to be an insect, I thought. A fly or a beetle. Before I could pretend to be a bird eating her up, she took my face in her hands and held it, like a woman holds a bowl to lift it on to her head. Perhaps she's going to lift my head on to her head and walk about with it, I thought.

'Your eye,' she said. 'Giddy aunt.'

I kept my mouth closed, which was difficult, because it was squashing up between her hands. My jaw hurt a bit.

'Something wrong with your eye. Don't do that with it. Stop it.'

I blinked hard, once. The blurry shapes were no better. They covered her face in spots. Also, my eyes were filling with tears. Her face swam in a pale blur.

The hands fell away and my face felt very wide for a moment. My jaw still ached. I pretended to scratch my cheek to stop a tear going any further down. I wasn't really crying. Anyway, she wasn't looking, she was wiping her face on her handkerchief and I waited for a bit. I couldn't bear not knowing what had happened to Mr Hargreaves, in the end.

'What happened?'

'What?'

'To Mr Hargreaves?'

'He was dead. Extremely dead. At least his bones were. When we found them out there. Quite by chance, a long time after. Your father went with two or three of the servants and cleared up.

23

We gave him a decent burial, about a month later. The Reverend Tarbuck presided.'

'A month later?'

'Yes. It took a while to contact him, and the boat was being refitted. But it wasn't urgent, was it? We kept the remains in a trunk, in the chop-shed.'

My mother bowed her head. She was either laughing or crying, I wasn't sure which. She sighed and squeezed my hand. Then she wiped her eyes on the handkerchief and stood up. Without saying anything more, without even looking at me, she walked away up the slope, up the steps, and disappeared into the house.

I tried to carry one of the crates, but couldn't shift it more than an inch or two. I wanted to help her. I wanted not to upset her. Finding out what had happened to Mr Hargreaves had upset her. I stared out at the brown, swirling river, with the curtain of forest on the far bank falling to a thick black line just above the water, and thought about the tin of Lyle's Golden Syrup sacrificed to the crocodile god. The memory of the sweet stickiness now made me feel sick, and I spat it out. But at least I hadn't rubbed it all over me. It was obviously a magic juice that slowly swallowed you up, and spat out your bones. Tick-tock. And fob-watch.

That night, we said our prayers together, as was usual: we said a little prayer for Mr Hargreaves, and one for poor Mr Northcott, and I invented one for our houseboy Mr Henry, who had stepped by mistake on some dry leopard's dung by the path and was now feverish (though Mother said it was nothing to do with the dry leopard's dung). I lay awake for a long time, even after the creaks and murmurings of my parents had settled into silence. The prayer seemed a very weak thing, against the night. My name was not being called. There were many other noises, but that night I couldn't sort them out: I had a great fear that the bones were not those of Mr Hargreaves, despite the fob-watch caught in the ribs. He might have killed someone else and placed his fob-watch there deliberately so that he could boast about his ju-ju powers when he came back. Quiri had told me a lot about cheats, tricking people into thinking they were powerful sorcerers, able to come back to life and so on; it was hard to tell what was truth and what was a lie, sometimes, until it was too late. By the time I drifted into hot dreams, I was quite sure that Mr Hargreaves was still alive, roaming the forest in a Norman helmet, ready to feed on members of the English race.

Sir Steggie, looking in at my window.

The river was a very strong thing in my life. I would gaze at it for hours. The forest didn't touch the river, except when the river was full: then the lower branches would dip and sway in the current, and one felt the land might be taken away like a giant lump of moss. Otherwise the foliage ended about a foot above the water, in a straight line that marked where the water usually rose to. Between this line and the water's muddy surface was deep shade. The bank could not be seen.

The forest seemed to float on this black stripe of shade, all the way to where the reach curved out of sight, either side. Everything that lay beyond the reach's bend was exciting and magical and mysterious, even though I had travelled up there a few times. And because the three or four traders that passed each year would be full of talk about gold and diamonds, I pictured a glittering place even further up, where the water frothed over a river-bed streaked and encrusted with treasure, and the forest was full of natives covered in precious and fantastic ornaments instead of cowrie shells and brass rings.

I was reading a lot about this sort of thing, of course, in books by Stevenson, Baroness Orczy, Blackmore, Henty, Rider Haggard. There were no playmates of my age to pull me from the pages, even if I didn't quite understand them. They were mostly my father's books, with an oak tree and *Ex Libris J.F. Arkwright* pasted in the front. And the tales I heard from the servants – of monsters, spirits and snakes with jewelled heads, of witchdoctors and sacred trees, of warriors and gourds and precious plumes – merely heightened my belief in the realness of this world just beyond my own.

The river wasn't evil, though it had evil mists and evil insects and evil crocodiles. We never stepped on a canoe without a gun.

The river's mists were more evil in the old days. Even now, they smelt like bad eggs when they were thick enough. It was Charlie Moore who explained to us why they were more evil in the old days. He was an old trader who had survived thirty years in very remote parts. One year he was rich, the next he was poor. Right now he was poor. He was bald and had a scar running from the corner of his mouth to his ear; the stitches were so badly done by a drunken army surgeon that you could count them. He asked me to and I counted fifty-one. He said it was made at the storming of the Oba's palace in the old kingdom of Benin. They'd rushed in and found crucified slaves on trees, slaves pegged to the ground alive and eaten up by ants, pits full of bodies, and altars dripping with blood. There was so much blood its smell made you giddy. My eyes grew wider and wider, but I kept very silent: my parents tended to forget me, when they had a visitor. Moore swallowed a good mouthful of his pink gin and wiped his stubble. He had rubbery yellow skin that looked as if it needed ironing. Then he told us about the German traders and how he remembered seeing a pile of native bodies where the chop-shed was. The Germans would get drunk and torture and kill any native they thought was a thief.

'Bloody mad-house,' he said. 'Bloody lunatic asylum. And then the Belgians.'

I knew about the Belgians. King Leopold chopped off native hands if their owners grumbled about growing rubber.

'I don't think our slate is totally clean,' said my mother.

'Whose is?' said my father.

Mr Moore said that the world came down to two things: money, and the world of fools that kept taking it away from a chap. But my mother told him that it was his fault because he kept playing cards. I don't know how she knew this, but people seemed to know about each other without meeting each other before.

'Dog eats dog,' he replied. 'Dog eats dog.'

My mother got up and walked away, looking upset. The cane chair made funny noises without her weight, as if it was pleased.

My father said, 'Hargreaves.' Mr Moore nodded and looked at me for a moment because I was leaning forward with my mouth open. So he knew things, too. My mother came back, fanning herself with a *Vogue* magazine. It was the one that said 'Christmas

Gifts and Winter Sports' on the front under a picture of a woman so thin I kept thinking she was a spiral of smoke.

The old trader stretched out his legs and looked up at the roof.

'I don't recall a veranda,' he said.

'My CO predecessors,' said my father. 'We improved it. The whole house is new to you since Fritz times, surely.'

'Same building.'

My father shook his head. 'Pure Public Works Department. Unmistakable. Cross between an army hut and a cheap villa.'

Mr Moore made us walk round to the side of the house facing the forest. He pointed to the badly rusted netting and the windows' warped and swollen frames.

'Tell me, little man – why is the netting rusted on this side, and almost not at all on the other?'

I shook my head.

'Age,' said Mr Moore, placing his big hand on my canvas hat and squeezing my skull. 'These windows are older. Pre-war. It was your PWD fellows pierced the windows in the river side.'

'Surely there were windows there before,' said my mother. 'It has all the view.'

'That's where sickness comes from, Mrs Arkwright. Malarial vapours, miasmas chock-full of fever. No man with sense puts windows in the river side.'

'What nonsense,' said my mother. 'We're hardly going to advance medically in Africa unless we sort out fact from fiction.'

But, I thought, you're always going on about tainted air. Perhaps tainted air is not the same as a miasma, and it was a mosquito bite that nearly killed me with malaria. I suddenly found myself in the air, just like the day the fever started.

'Ah,' said Mr Moore, putting me on his shoulders, 'fact and fiction are just what Africa makes sure you can't sort out, Mrs Arkwright.'

He galloped about the yard with me, whooping: he was a horse, and I was a Canadian Mountie, and the river was full of Indians. We spent the rest of the day playing cricket. Tarbuck had recently given us a complete set. It really belonged to the young cadet my mother sometimes talked about, who'd been on the SS *Grace* when it had brought my parents up the river for the first

27

time. He was a charming, good man but had died of blackwater fever a few months later. The bats were warped, but you could still use them. There were two for children, and two for adults. Tarbuck told us that the object of the donation was to fulfil the poor fellow's aim, and spread the game of cricket through the native populace. His name was marked neatly on all of the equipment: *Herbert E. Standing*. His spirit was dressed all in white, very tall, and remained at the end of my bed with a straight bat all night and every night, in case Sir Steggie should come.

From when I was five my parents would tell me what a big boy I would be when I was seven. So now and again I would talk to my parents about my plans.

'When I'm seven, can I go with Tarbuck up-river, and see the cannibal village?'

'They aren't cannibals any more,' my mother said.

'But they eat Jesus!'

'Hugh, that's naughty to say that.'

'But can I go when I'm seven? You keep saying what a big boy I'll be, when I'm seven.'

'You *will* be a big boy. A very big boy.'

Then she would look almost tearful, and I wondered for some time if I was going to die on my seventh birthday – be sacrificed in some way. There were quite a few villages in the area where human sacrifices were carried out, as there was at least one group who ate people because – like crocodiles – they liked the flavour of human meat. There were also those who ate captured warriors as they ate leopards – to become braver in battle. Quiri told me that in his village the Devil woman ate snakes – especially the black mamba, if it could be found – to become better at telling who had done something wrong, for snakes were famous for their cunning. In *our* village, I thought, we eat a man-god who is made of bread, and drink his blood, which is made of claret. The grown-ups did, anyway: I would do the same (like the cannibals) when I was old enough, apparently.

I asked Quiri if there were villages where they sacrificed children. He nodded, frowning. Then he slapped his thigh and laughed. I felt a bit sick. I asked him then if the children were told that they were going to be sacrificed. He stopped laughing, pouted his lips, and frowned again. He shook his head. Then, my heart beating horribly loud and fast, I asked him if it was decided early on, maybe years before, even when the child was a baby. He told me that there were signs, and one of the signs was a lot of questions about sacrifice.

Then he was called to go in by Joseph, and I was left to ponder, kicking stones into puddles or at the hens in the yard: the sky was awfully grim, but it hadn't rained all day. I was six years and six months. It was now September. I went into the house and asked my mother, who was unpacking some thick steel syringes in the office, if I could go with Father to Ikasa on the long canoe, next May, if the rains weren't too heavy. She seemed rather shocked.

'That's rather a long way away, Hugh! You are a little planner, darling. Like your father.'

My father was hammering away outside, doing something to the Bean's engine, 'taking advantage of the dry', as he'd put it. There was something about my father that annoyed my mother, apart from his evening gin (which made him cross, not happy); perhaps it was this planning thing.

'But can I, Mother?'

'I think that should be all right, Hugh.'

My father went to Ikasa once a month. He picked up telegrams there, and urgent supplies, and chatted with the Chief, and resolved disputes. My mother occasionally went with him, but she didn't like to abandon her surgery – or, perhaps, me – to the *ayah* or the other servants.

'But you musn't get in the way. Just watch, and be good. Why wait until May? You're big enough now, I think. I'll ask him.'

I nodded calmly, and she looked disappointed with this reaction.

'And can I go with him to Crater Lake the November after that, when the rains have stopped?'

She blinked hurriedly, as if I was blowing my breath directly into her face.

'The November after that?'

'Yes. When the road's better.'

'Why not this November, darling? I'm sure he'd be happy –'

'I'm planning things, Mother, like Father does, with his thing on the wall and all the numbers. I have to know if I can go in a year's time, when the rain has cleared up, and the track's better.'

She stayed looking at me for a bit, as if trying to read my thoughts. I put a cloud· over them. Quiri could still read them behind a cloud, like he could tell what the moon was doing even in the covered months of the rainy season. Not being Quiri, she gave a little sigh and brushed her forehead with her forefinger, as she always did when she was secretly agitated.

'It's a road, darling. Your father likes to call it the Main Road.'

She stared at a point just in front of me and then dived back into her box and talked about syringes, and serum, and how even the needles seemed to rust, and how the suppliers had got some lint 'specification' completely wrong.

'But next November,' I said.

She stopped, her hand covering the big red cross on the lid of the box.

'I'm sure that'll be fine, Hugh,' she said, in an oddly high voice, looking not at me but out of the window. She was fibbing, of course: I could see that.

Then I said, 'For my eighth birthday, I would like a fishing basket, to put in the little rapids like the Africans do.'

The rapids were a cluster of rocks at the furthest point of our clearing, where the water jetted and frothed for a few yards. The servants had caught fish there in their cone-shaped baskets, which they left tied at night. She smiled uncertainly and brushed her forehead again. She seemed about to say something: her mouth opened, then she smiled again, blinking quickly at the floor by my feet.

'So I can fish when I'm eight,' I went on, 'when I'm big enough, by myself.'

'Oh, Hugh,' she said, 'I don't know about that.'

There was a horrible silence. I couldn't bear it any longer. I turned on my heel and went straight to my room. I thought, lying on my bed, trying to cool my face with a book: something terrible is going to happen to me just before the big rains start. My seventh birthday, on April the fifteenth, will come just before the thin drops start to fatten. I am going to be sacrificed on my seventh birthday, like the pale-skinned pure boy a nearby village used to leave out pegged to the ground for the leopard spirit, once a year.

I was loved by my parents and the servants, but Quiri had once said: I know a place where the most loved person is given to the gods, for nothing less will do.

But we are Christians, I thought. Then, with a terrible lurch in my stomach, I'd remembered the lines that were said each Sunday, in the main room of this very house: 'And he gave His only-begotten son, most beloved of the Father . . .'

My mother was at the door. She came and took my hand. My heart was pounding. I hugged her.

'Has someone told you, Hugh?'

'No, no, no,' I wept.

'I have to admit it. You can't stay here, not for ever. We're going to England, next year. Our long leave. Together, darling. You'll be seven. We'll be going to Uncle Edward's, and his very nice house, with a big soft green lawn, and woods, and –'

'What kind of woods?'

'Oh, English woods. Bluebells, and foxes, and primroses, and lovely trees, dappled light, nightingales, all that sort of thing. You'll be able to breathe there. No malaria, no tropical fevers, no frightful ants or snakes or crocodiles or jigger flies or tsetse flies or ju-ju or goodness knows what else. It's civilisation, Hugh. Your country. You can roll about on the lawn, without worrying about it. There'll be lots to do, and lots to read and learn. School. Children. You'll enjoy it so much.'

'Then you aren't – I won't be sacrificed?'

She seemed to jump in my arms; then rested very still, but with a hardness in her body that I could feel against my chest. Her breath was in my hair, moving it slightly: otherwise I might have thought she had suddenly died. Each breath hit my scalp in a warm gasp. I had made my mother cry. This made me suspect that the English trip was a story. My mother was being forced, as the mothers of the loved ones in the villages were, and as the Virgin Mary was, to give up her son to the gods. I felt so powerless that I never brought the subject up again, and made it disappear into the deepest shadows of my own mind, where I could not think about

31

it except when it crept out in the middle of the night, as the most powerful of the malign spirits usually did.

About three months before my seventh birthday, when the rains had slackened, I accompanied my parents and Quiri on a short bush tour. The Bean had never started again, and the spare parts it needed never turned up, or were always wrong. Instead, three BSA motorcycles, used by despatch riders in the last war, had arrived. They'd come down the river, perched on three dug-outs, because the final bit of the track between us and Ikasa was still a swamp. They had long, graceful handlebars and slim fuel tanks and curvy saddles but could take on the roughest or most liquid ground. The wheels were strange: they each had a smaller metal wheel attached to their spokes; my father pointed out the brake-pad that clamped to this inner wheel and squealed the machine to a halt. I wanted to hear the engines explode into life, but it took a fortnight to clean and oil and adjust them. My father was always very thorough. The bits were unscrewed in a heap of spanners and rags, and I worried that the three cycles would end up like the Bean, already tangled up in creepers beneath its tin awning.

Then one day, as we all watched, my father strapped on his thickest leather puttees and bush-boots, and kick-started one of the cycles. He crouched by the engine for a few minutes, changing its roar to a growl, and then its growl to a trembling throb, before mounting the saddle and moving off rather uncertainly, his boot descending a few times and slithering on the earth as he picked up speed. The chickens scattered, terrified. When he appeared again round the corner of the main building, we all laughed and cheered. He sped past with a look of great concentration.

I was so happy, I jumped up and down and Quiri did a little dance next to me. When my father finally wobbled to a stop, he was grinning from ear to ear. The machine smelt deliciously of Castrol oil, and made the air above it move around, as the air did sometimes off the river or the roof on burning days. My mother then had a try, on her machine. She had bush-trousers on, like my father, and her hair was drawn into a tight bob. She found the bike very heavy, and it took her some time to move more than a few yards without her boot kicking the ground – but she was soon riding calmly round and round, frowning as much as my father. I chased after her, but she was too fast for me, even though the machine seemed to be lumbering its way along.

There was a sudden cheer from the servants, and I saw Quiri setting off across the yard, his engine coughing like a tubercular. I ran towards him and made him swerve and take a light tumble. He put me on his lap and we chugged around together, slowly increasing speed until the river, when it was next to us, flowed the other way.

A chair was made, which could be bolted on to the back of either cycle; it was no more than a cushion in a basket, but it was *my* seat, my place. We thumped and smoked and throbbed our way, my father and I, until he was certain I wouldn't tip him over. I was very happy – even if my view was the back of his bush-shirt, stained with sweat in a big dark shape I made faces out of, or islands full of treasure. I could cling to his big belt, or waist, or to the sides of the pannier, and sometimes lay my head against his hot, wet back, feeling its spine rub against my ear as we roared about, my knees drawn up high and my feet vibrating on the wire guard that curved over the fan belt.

The day came when we set off up the track to Odoomi, the servants who were left waving us goodbye. Our plan was to spend a few days there and in the two or three neighbouring villages, and then to go north a little further to the lake my father had already seen and swum in, dark and calm in its crater. Boxes on the back held our equipment and supplies: we were travelling lightly.

When the little caravan started to make its way up the 'road', I was so excited I forgot to worry about the gorilla spirit, though my own personal fetish was in the small canvas pack on my back. This was a grease-paper packet containing a holy wafer 'borrowed' from Tarbuck's tin; a feather which I persuaded myself was from the beautiful bird; a river pebble in the natural shape of a crocodile; a tiny bone found near Hargreaves's grave, and a miniature woodcarving made from a fallen branch of the sacred ebony tree that grew near Quiri's village, given to me by Quiri for my sixth birthday. He said it was carved in a trance by the chief

33

mask maker of the area. It showed a skull, in the shape of my mother's egg-timer, but flat and shiny. It was supposed to be worn around the neck. It was by far my most precious belonging.

I had already visited the village several times, and the children greeted me warmly, crowding around my chair and helping me down. The people here went about naked except for a glistening cover of palm-nut oil and some ornaments. I knew the Reverend Tarbuck didn't approve of this, but I didn't really notice it. The unmarried women wore a belt of beads around their waist, while the married ones tied a square of the same beads to it, hanging between their legs. The men wore ankle-bracelets of leather, a line of beads around the head with a feather or two stuck in, and a twine of liana just beneath the chest. The only other decorations were patterns on the bare skin, burnt in with sticks from the fire. These were done, my father said, at different stages in life. They were mostly on the face, the stomach, and the forearms.

Quiri had told me what some of them meant: the half-moons, the dotted squares, the banana-shapes, the circles-within-circles. I knew which youths had been told secrets, which women were married, and which parts of them had been ill or infected. Everyone had the same thick line across their cheekbones as Quiri had. The mark of the snake, he'd said: the mamba. The mamba protects little children. I felt uncomfortable again at my unmarked, pink face: I am a fat white grub ready for the birds. The flecks of pink on many of the faces were (I understood from Mother) smallpox scars: underneath the ebony lay this pink flesh. Perhaps, I thought, I was missing a layer of skin, and their pink palms were where that layer had been rubbed away.

The children tugged at my clothing, wanting me to play with them. I was still a bit deaf from the growly roar of the motorcycles, but the children's excitement was even louder. I nodded and smiled and felt princely and weak at the same time. The roofs were thatched and pointed, with entrances that made even me need to duck. The Chief's house was a bit bigger and with a low fence of woven liana around it; my father told me that in this compound the Chief heard the people's complaints and dispensed advice, like a native DO. He was small and plump, with a moth-eaten robe of leopard skin (I was worried about that) and a

34

crown of feathers that came over his eyes. He held a snakeskin rod in his hand, which no one else was allowed to touch on pain of death. This was drummed into me before we set out. The village council met under a huge acacia tree; tame bush dogs slept in its shade, and hens scratched about everywhere.

We slept in a hut behind this tree. The hut was kept for visitors, and it was bare except for a gourd bowl of what I thought was milk in the corner. Quiri told me that it was millet paste mixed up with boiled water. We each had to take a sip, and it was cool and refreshing. The water in the big red gourds outside was for us to boil. A fire was smoking in front of our hut; we ladled the water into a pot and left it on the fire. The smoke kept away most of the mosquitoes, once dusk fell, but we put up our mosquito nets anyway because there was a deadly beetle that lived in the thatch and liked your sleeping smell so much it dropped on to your head. The hut had been very carefully swept, but Quiri checked the earth floor for jiggers.

All around us the forest spoke, and a bright three-quarter moon rose. I made it huge and blinding with my father's heavy field binoculars. There was dancing, and the fetish woman waved feathered twigs at us behind a wooden mask with white eyes. It came down to her belly and made her invisible to evil spirits. The dancers' feet shuffled and stamped, helping the sun roll through the bottom of the earth, waking the ancestors up. My mother's fly switch swept in front of her in time to the beat of the drums: if I closed my eyes, I could float off the stool and come back again without her noticing, for the drumming held me up in the air with its pounding palms. We sat in a big circle of all the people and ate plantains and millet porridge and sweet mangoes and (unless I was being teased by Quiri) grilled mamba meat with fearsome pili-pili powder sprinkled on it. At my father's request, the Chief ordered his drummers to tell the next village that we were coming. They drummed the words and the words were carried off into the darkness like the heartbeats heard through my mother's stethoscope. Quiri had told me you could sometimes feel the earth's heartbeat in your feet. It was carried into the light on the backs of cicadas, where it spoke to men and kept the trees growing. The reply was so faint that my father's bad ears couldn't pull it out from between the night calls of creatures and the endless sizzles of cicada. But it was a welcome, the Chief said.

I dozed against my mother as the adults discussed matters of local importance, each seated on stools carved with grimacing faces. My father was always nodding seriously when I woke up, his face flickering in the fire like a god's. I had played hard with the children, showing them the rules of cricket (those I knew) with my rubber ball and a couple of thick sticks. Big gourds served as the wickets. I was watched from the corner of a hut by Herbert E. Standing's spirit, accompanied as it always was by the sweet smell of linseed oil. I made a century, and bowled three wickets. He clapped each time, but reminded me that the aim was to teach, not show off.

In my dreams, to which I was carried by my mother, my camp bed became a boat, full of my playmates, sailing over the treetops with a glorious throbbing roar. I woke, once, in the middle of the night. My head rested on my canvas pack, which held my fetish packet. Quiri, sleeping outside, no longer had the fob-watch – but I didn't even think of Sir Steggie marauding beyond, such was my complete happiness, hearing my mother's gentle breathing, my father's grunts, and thinking that life was going to be full of such days, stretching before me in their smoky richness for ever.

We took a week to reach the lake; more village parleys, feasts, firelit dances and cricket; more bumping and roaring along the track, through dense forest, the patter of light rain on thatch, morning mists caught high in the treetops as we climbed higher and deeper and further into paradise. By the time we took the path up the ancient volcano's side, I had almost forgotten my old life. We had seen none of the creatures I had wanted to see: no elephants, no gorillas, no leopards. But I had a creature more precious than any of those, resting in my pocket. We had passed a group of hunters with bows and arrows, crouched at the bottom of a huge grey mahogany tree next to the track. They were not surprised to see us. Quiri talked to them over our chugging engines and he told us that they knew, from the drums, we were in the area. Pieces of light fell on their naked bodies and gleamed like ashes off a fire. One of them was holding something tiny in his hand. It was something they had caught.

'A galago,' my father said, who spent as many hours as I did studying his animal books.

'*Galago senegalensis*,' I added.

My mother giggled. The fact is, I had always wanted to see one. It was tiny, with huge eyes and hands like a very old man's. There was another one, even tinier, clinging to its back. The bigger one was dead. It was the mother. The hunters had shot at it with their sharp little arrows. It had fallen, but the baby was living. This they regarded as a special event, and wished to take the baby back with them, to have its tiny head for the top of a fetish stick. I gripped my mother's arm and pleaded with her not to let them do this.

'I'll look after it. Please give them dash!'

There was a lot of bargaining, but the hunters wouldn't budge. The tiny creature's huge eyes met my own eyes and I felt that if I did not save it I would die as well. My father started to lead me back to the motorcycles, his arm on my shoulders. I broke away and ran back to the hunters, unstrapped my pack, and found the fetish packet.

The skull amulet was in my hand before my parents could take me away again.

Quiri muttered fiercely, 'No, small-small. Hugh-boy, no!'

The hunters looked at his face and then nodded at me and we swapped the bushbaby for the amulet. Quiri shook his head, frowning. Then he walked away, back to the cycles.

'Hugh,' said my mother, 'that was a pretty carving. Quiri will be upset. It probably cost a lot of his savings.'

The tiny creature lay in my palm, clutching my thumb. It wanted the fur and smell of its mother. Its miniature body trembled. The gods had made the eyes first, then forgotten about the body. When they remembered, the flesh had grown old and shrunk, like an old rind. But they used it anyway. That's why the eyes looked so young and gleaming and big, while the rest was so small and shrivelled and old. All it needed was milk, my mother informed me. We said goodbye to the hunters and found some milk in the food box. We punctured the tin and poured a little into my palm. The bushbaby wouldn't touch it, but trembled and clutched my thumb even tighter with its long fingers. I began to be worried about it.

37

'It's extraordinary,' said my father. 'Like a tiny homunculus, not like an animal at all.'

'I'm sorry, Quiri,' I said.

Quiri couldn't say what he really wanted to say, not in front of my parents, but his eyes told me clearly that I had done a dangerous thing, to cast away something so powerful on strangers. He was far more worried than hurt. So we were both worried.

We reached the lake as twilight was spreading across it. It filled the crater to just short of the brim. The brim was hidden by a great thickness of forest. My father knew that the side where a small sandy beach had grown was free of bilharzia, but not the other side. We weren't to swim beyond the centre. The path ended on the beach, and we propped our motorcycles up and collected kindling. I sat by the fire and stroked my tiny friend. (I knew it was a he, though my father wasn't sure.) He looked about him with terrified eyes. The lake was mysterious, dark, and beautiful, and I showed it to him. It appeared all tiny in the two liquid globes of his eyes.

My father was already swimming, setting out with strong strokes in his striped bathing suit. The light caught only his ripples, slowly widening in golden circles over the dark surface of the water. The forest rose straight from the lake all about, but there was nothing beyond the topmost tree but the evening sky, in which the first stars and the first fireflies were fighting each other. The moon had not yet risen. We were at the top of the world, it seemed. The lake was perfectly circular, but not at all like the pond in the Botanical Gardens in Victoria, or the little boating lake in Buea. My father had explained to me, on the path up, how the volcano had spat out fire and ash and roared and thundered long long before, before I was born, in the time of the dinosaurs, when Africa had been part of the Americas, and nothing even resembling a homunculus was walking the earth. Then it had died, the volcano, and slowly the rain, the incessant thundering rain, had filled its blasted hole inch by inch, and the forest had crawled back up and over its laval rim, until this perfect, lovely scene presented itself for our delectation and enjoyment. I nodded. My father didn't often explain things in such an excited way. He was proud of this spot, I think: he said he was the first

38

white man ever to have seen it, and that it was the jewel in his big tangled mop, which was bigger than Wales. He christened it, that night, Charlotte's Lake.

Quiri paddled, and my mother bathed in the shallows, but I (like Quiri) could not swim, and I had my tiny homunculus to look after. The three of them made the lake dance with golden and blue light, but my monkey friend could only mourn his mother. I couldn't do anything to comfort it: all its short life had been spent in a place of leaves, fur smells, and safety. I imagined its home as a hole in the tree's trunk, grassed and comfortable, where it would curl with its mother and suckle. I talked softly above the splashes and shouts of the bathers. They were laughing together: Quiri was settled to his neck, splashing my mother, who squealed and splashed him back. My father was further out, kicking the water to a froth, and singing a silly ditty. Their voices echoed back off the crater's brim, or lost themselves among the stars that thickened each time I looked up. I talked to my little forest child, offering a round pool of milk in my palm, or stroking its shivering back with the tip of my giant finger. It clutched my thumb so tightly I could draw its hands down to the milk; there was a moment when its tongue came out, and then it was drinking.

I would have shouted out the news, if I had dared. But any movement, any sudden noise, made the little creature frown and look anxious. I wondered how anything so delicate could survive in this world, and then how anything so delicate and lovely could be made from forest and water and sky, which were such broad and deep and dangerous things. Did it have its own spirits, its own fetishes, its own holy wafers, its own prayers? Did Sir Steggie want to drag it off into the night? I thought of the hunters, but felt against them no real anger. This was because I had my own bamboo bow and arrows at home. I had already shot at cockroaches, spiders, rats, mice, and the plump frogs in the shallows of the river, pretending they were lions or rhinos or crocodiles or the Big Beef of legend that made the waves slap at the jetty and at the hulls of the canoes as it passed.

The little galago had its hand on its mouth, its eyes wide above the long fingers, searching for something it might recognise. This is how Mosea was, I thought, after the missionaries had taken her in. This is how I might feel, if cannibals or a crazed leopard or a mad gorilla or some drunken ivory traders were to set upon us all, or if Sir Steggie were to drag me out from under my net one night, and I were to find myself quite alone in a world I didn't know, still alive but in a living death of loneliness and fright.

I looked out at the lake: it was darker now, quite inky-blue, the colour of my father's ink with which he wrote his letters. The three I prayed for most each night were calm, enjoying the coolness of the water in the warm air. The stars were growing thicker, the last flush of sun quite green above the brim beyond my father's pale form, as if the forest was leaking into the heavens. Perhaps the lake, in its depths, harboured a Big Beef, or crocodiles in the shallows, hidden in the darkness. We would have heard those by now, surely, coughing and roaring. My father had told me that there weren't even fish in the lake: only waterborne insects, bilharzia snails by the far bank, some amphibious lizards, and a crowd of frogs with bright red cheeks. In the sand there were no tracks, except our own: I wondered why not, why no animals came to drink here. The galago was lapping at the milk again, one hand clutching a fold in my skin. Its body tickled my palm, as my mother's finger used to tickle it when she went round and round the castle long ago. I kissed my new pet's head. No ticks or fleas could live on such a tiny thing.

'I'll look after you for ever and ever,' I murmured.

That night we stayed up late, gazing into the fire, with the moon turning the water to milk where it lapped out of the brim's shadow. I thought of the gourd bowl left in each of the huts we'd stayed in, and its cool drink. Quiri had told me that in the beginning there was nothing but a round gourd. It filled the universe. Everything was held by it: all time and space. The bottom half of the gourd became earth and fire, the top became the sky and water. When the water trickled down the sides of the gourd to the earth, fire burst out, lightning crackled, and all living things grew. Our ancestors smiled in the light of their fires.

The crater lake was the bottom half of the gourd. All things had started here, obviously. Quiri sang soft songs he knew from his village. He called them thinking songs. He also sang a few hymns. My mother sang some jazz songs that I already knew from our wind-up gramophone, jigging about as she did so; my father made us laugh with his music-hall ditties, and made my mother cry with his songs from the war. My little bushbaby looked about him for a while, then fell asleep against my chest, against my heartbeat.

Far out on the lake's water, I thought I saw tiny white splashes, as if someone was lifting a handkerchief to wave goodbye, over and over.

When I woke in the morning, with the sun just winking over the brim, I found myself in the camp bed, under the net. The bushbaby lay on my chest, under my hand. I smiled and stroked it. But its fur didn't quiver any more. Its body was cold. Its eyes had dried up. It had somehow trembled and shivered its tiny heart to pieces while I was dreaming.

I'd dreamed that I was swimming without any problem across the wide waters. The starlight and fireflies were scattered around me like grain for the hens, and there was nothing under my body but a big gloom, and silence.

My mother played the station's gramophone records on Hargreaves's machine – which had Northcott's initials carved on the side. She had some of her own records, too: hissy jazz tunes that made her jerk about instead of taking an afternoon nap. She would always play them on her own, in the main room, with the shutters closed. When I got up once and peeped on her through the door, she was quite cross. In the villages, everyone danced together, in a line. When I told her I wanted to learn her dances, she said they were 'private'. On my sixth birthday, however, she taught me the 'Shimmy', the 'Missouri Walk' and the 'Twinkle' as a present. We would then, every so often after supper, dance together as the warped records bumped and shouted. She called it our 'revel', and it left her looking as if she had stood out in a rainstorm.

Oddly enough, it was those jazz tunes that echoed in my head for months after my arrival in England, rather than the forest noises they somewhat resembled.

Did my mother tell me, clearly, what was to happen?

Two months before my seventh birthday, my mind still ringing with the pleasure of the trip to the crater lake, I found my mother 'sorting out' my room. She had two large trunks, and was filling them with my clothes.

'What are you doing?' I said.

She looked up. 'You know we're going to England, Hugh.'

I did know, but the trip existed beyond the wall I had put up between the fact of being six and the fact of being seven. I had never trusted it. I thought it was a yarn spun to hide the awful truth. The gods wanted me, as they wanted all children – only to return them with a different name, and the marks on the cheeks smoothed off. They wanted me just as one of them – the Father, the Chief – had wanted Jesus back. My parents were powerless against the demands of the gods, as a person is powerless against the daimon that possesses him, and makes his face white with spittle (I had seen this in one of the villages, on our trip, during a ritual dance), until someone hits him with a palm branch.

My big mistake was to have given the skull carving away: Quiri told me that it could suck in evil, that it could be held against bad situations to come as a hen's cut throat is held against a snake-bite, absorbing the poison. He had discovered (I think through Mosea) that I was to leave the station before my health was broken further. He had told this to the mask carver – an old and very powerful man – and the mask carver had made that fetish after a day and a night's reflection, in semi-trance. My mother was right: it had cost Quiri quite a bit of his savings. The fetish was not only to protect me from further malarial attacks, but also to prevent the bad situation from taking place.

'Why didn't you tell me before?' I asked, when I had found my mother packing my clothes.

Quiri shrugged. It seemed I only had to carry it about, for the mask carver had told it what to do, holding it against his lips and murmuring.

I wondered about finding the hunters again, but it was at least four days' travel by motorcycle along complicated paths, once the 'road' was left. I had secretly brought the bushbaby's tiny corpse back with me, and buried it under a brick near where my mother was trying to grow some pretty shrubs against the house. I asked Quiri if the bushbaby's spirit might have entered my heart, against which the animal had died. Quiri nodded.

'Possible,' he said, in his own language. 'Now you can think on the animal, and make yourself a home for its spirit, to put in your pocket. Then it won't get angry inside your heart, and tear it, for taking away its mother.'

I did as he suggested: I sat by the river with a lump of red, rather smelly mud and squeezed most of its moisture out. Then I fashioned what was in my head. It was perfect clay – the natives used it for their pots and platters – and it moved easily under my fingers. I pinched out a nose and a great mouth, and jabbed in some eyes with my thumb. It looked more and more ferocious. A tongue came out; it was rude. Its mouth was wide open, drawn right back to meet the ears. I laughed, and imitated what was staring at me from my hands. If a crocodile had emerged at that moment, I might have frightened it off.

I left the head to dry, in the shade of the house. It was too big for my pocket.

'That's an ugly thing,' said my mother, when she saw it.

'It's screaming,' I said.

Quiri said that it wasn't enough.

The next day, he beckoned me into the chop-shed. He had some white paste in a gourd, and he made me strip off my shirt and marked my skin in thick lines of white with the heel of his hand. He laughed: one could hardly see it against my white flesh. On a grieving family in one of the villages, it had looked as if their bones were showing on their skin. Still, it would make my sorrow bearable, he said. Then he brought out a sharp knife and some ash from the stove in a tin and made me bend my head over.

There was a crackling noise on the nape of my neck, and small hairs sprinkled on to my shoes. I felt a sharp, cold pain, and flinched.

'Stay still,' Quiri ordered.

Blood dripped down my neck and hit the soft earth floor of the chop-shed. I knew what he was doing. I was happy with it, but I started to cry, silently; this must have been the kaolin paste bringing out my grief. I felt the ash being rubbed in as one feels an ointment being applied; it stung, and I had to bite my lip. My chief worry was my parents: but Quiri hid the wound with my hair, which was rather urchin-like at the time.

43

Because I couldn't see it, even in the mirror, he drew it for me: it was a cross in a circle, the four points meeting the rim. He explained that this was the symbol of Yolobolo, the powerful creature in the forest that no one had ever seen, but was very like the little man-thing I had found.

Part of Yolobolo's power was that he held a great secret. One day, Yolobolo might tell it to me.

The dull ache of the cut mark kept me awake through siesta time, and my mother wondered why I had a stiff neck. But I shied away from her nurse's enquiring hand. In any case, they couldn't do anything about it, now: even if they washed out the ash (I had to avoid any rain, Quiri said) there would be something, however faint, left.

That night, I insisted on washing myself; my mother took it as a healthy sign of maturity. I closed the bathroom door and stripped off. The kaolin stripes had rubbed mostly away from contact with sweaty clothes. I made splashing noises with my hand in the tin hip bath, washed my feet, and donned my nightshirt without touching the kaolin marks or the wound. My neck throbbed. The ash seemed to be burning into my throat and ears. I knew all about the dangers of infection. I had broken one of the *Do Nots* – although ash was, I seemed to remember my mother telling her patients, as good as boric acid.

But, whatever might occur to me after my seventh birthday, I was now prepared.

I didn't refer to the coming trip, as a result. Anyway, my mother became cloudy and anxious in the fortnight before my seventh birthday. I slept in an oddly bare room; she had started packing too early. The rains also started too early, in the second week of April. A storm cracked the sky and the resultant downpour continued for three days. My father reckoned that it would beat a fellow to the ground, if he didn't keep running.

Gloom settled in the rooms, barely lifting from morning till night. Ironshod horses cantered over the roofs, and the evenings were thick with flies and mosquitoes, apparently sheltering. The river swelled and tugged at the lower branches. A huge tree came down on the opposite bank. It was eventually swept away along with the thick detritus of leaves and logs and putrid matter pulled from up-river. I looked out for jewels; either there were none, or the view was too blurred and mist-laden to see them. The distinction between air and rain was lost, as was the distinction between water and ground in the compound.

Quiri was delighted; he was sure that Yolobolo had asked the Creator to bring the rains early and stop me leaving. Then it brightened on the fourth morning, and only a light drizzle swept across us. There was a whole day when there was no rain at all: the sun battled through mist, burning my forehead and nose bright red and drying up the smaller puddles. My mother came into the main room, where I was reading on the sofa. She was wielding some scissors. She stood on the leopard-skin rug with the big snarly head. My father had spent a week tanning it in the yard, and Quiri said that its spirit would come back for it one day.

'Time to look smart, Hugh,' she said.

I fled the room, knocking a brass tray off the mantelpiece above the fireplace we never used. I heard the clatter behind me as I ran across the yard towards the forest, towards the track to Odoomi.

My dream was to settle with my parents and Quiri beside the crater lake: to build and thatch a mud-walled hut and swim each day, explore the forest, descend to the nearest village for a game of cricket once a week, take part in feasts and dances and important rituals, to have myself marked as the others were, to marry a fertile and beautiful wife and bring forth a crowd of healthy children, to die an old and wise man, to feel the twine of my life cut and to float away to join the other ancestors, my empty body to be buried in the floor of the hut next to my parents, just as the villagers of those parts buried their dead, in their own homes, under their dreams.

One of Quiri's greatest fears was that he would die childless, and roam the forest as an evil spirit. This became my chief fear, too – though if I were to be sacrificed to the gods, as we saw the hens sacrificed in one of the villages, this would not matter, as my spirit would join them as Jesus's did (He was obviously still a child, the Son on the Cross).

England, in those last weeks, became a place I associated with this fear of dying childless.

I wasn't sure why. When I was about three, I remember asking my mother if I could have a brother or sister. She laughed and said that I was quite enough trouble. Then, soon after, on a return from a bush tour, my father had fallen ill. I went to see him, at some point. He was asleep, but his breathing was funny; I couldn't keep count, his gasps were so quick. His face gleamed like the enamel bowls we had a lot of in the cookhouse. His mouth was open, with small drops of yellow spittle at each corner. My mother placed a cold wet towel over his forehead; this steamed slightly. When he recovered, he was bad-tempered and old-looking for a long time, his moustache grey and his hair thinned, and he drank more gin after sundown to make himself feel better.

A year or two later, watching him fiddle about with the Bean, I asked him the same question about brothers and sisters. He wasn't in a good mood, and told me gruffly that he couldn't make them. When I asked him why, he blamed Africa, swearing at her and hitting the Bean's rusted mudguard with his spanner.

'She stops you working, you see.'

'Like the Bean, you mean?'

'Like the blasted Bean, yes.' He gave a big laugh. 'Twelve hp, she was. Now she's zero. Like me.'

I didn't ask about brothers and sisters any more. In the last weeks there, I thought quite a lot about my father's bad illness; I reckoned it had stopped him making children, as a week of thick mist had stopped the Bean's engine for good.

That day I ran away from my mother's scissors, coming to a halt well out of sight up the muddy track, I thought again about what he had said that time, crashing his spanner on the mudguard, and how important it was that I didn't die and leave my parents to roam around evilly after their own deaths.

I felt the soft rain on the nape of my neck and covered the scar with my hand. Surrounded by the huge, dripping trees of the forest, my indoor sandals hidden in a warm puddle, I invoked Yolobolo in the way Quiri had taught me: *Kan wak, si-pap bobo, bolo yol nga.*

The rains had washed all the animals away; there was a great silence behind the drip-drops of the rain off the big leaves.

I said the magic words again. I wasn't saying them properly — and anyway, I was a little white grub, ready for the birds, my skin nude except for the one unsealed mark and some smears of kaolin. I'd asked Quiri how children were made, recently; he'd said something about heads of rats caught in traps, that made them swell their cheeks and spit. The trap was the woman, the rat the man. He'd laughed, and told me I was too young to ask.

That was it, I thought: my father had lost his rat, as I had lost my galago and a tiny lizard I'd caught last week, which had left behind only its tail in my room.

I felt the mark on my neck with my finger; it was bumpy, and smooth, though still a little sore. I didn't feel like running away to Odoomi, and then the crater lake, without my fetishes. It was in weather like this that Sir Steggie woke up, because he thought it was night. And a little further on the angry gorilla spirit was waiting. I thought of all the childless men and women who had left their spirits behind, ready to do mischief, and remembered what Mr Moore had said about the heap of bodies here in the German times. They would not have been prayed for; their spirits were scattered through the air, moaning. The shreds of mist in the trees might be them – headless, like the slaves of Benin. The air was clamping itself to my back. Because I had run, my shirt was wet with sweat as much as rain. Anyway, it wasn't raining: the droplets in the air were mist. Now and again they stuck together and you could see them.

I loved this heat, this moisture, this warm mist. I loved the smell thickening from the ground, that the first heavy rains brought in their wake, sweeter than any other time. I feared England's cold, suddenly. I pictured it as a sharp blade, like my father's cut-throat razor. How was I going to survive a season when everything died, when the branches were stripped of leaves and nothing grew at all? The pictures of winter in my books reminded me of my worst dreams of skeletons and ghosts.

I cried, helplessly, alone on the track, when I thought of that. Hard edges and points would squeeze and prick me from every angle. My blood would stiffen as the hen's had on the stone in the courtyard of the village. I would miss these trees; the other servants agreed with Quiri that the trees protect you. Their roots suckle the ancestors, the trunks suckle us, the leafy tops remind the gods to send us rain. Did England have such trees? The thin track

47

was wide to me, at that age; it had cut through these gigantic, protecting creatures and left a tangle at each side difficult to penetrate or to see into.

It was my father's great achievement, and I felt it was also mine.

The sun burned again through the mist. Pieces of light appeared in the gloom, as if they were solid bits of a puzzle. As I heard my mother running through them, towards me, shouting my name, I looked northwards, towards the Crater Lake, and made the picture – the track, the tangle each side, the huge trees and the spotted gloom under them – enter my head for good.

'Heavens above, they can take you as you are,' said my mother, hugging me tight. 'Little urchin.'

She cradled my head in her hands and looked at me. I didn't think she was going to take my head off this time.

'Grace,' she said.

'What?'

'Grace. Just that word. Will you always remember that?'

'Like the Reverend Tarbuck's boat?'

'Yes. Yes, like the boat.'

I can't remember what it means, I thought, apart from saying grace. I'll have to look it up. I saw the steamer with its black funnel, surrounded by smoke.

She was searching my face for something. For grace, perhaps. It was something holy, I knew that much. Was grace the same thing as graceful, which my father kept saying African women were, when they walked around with pots on their heads? I tried to put on a graceful expression. But she frowned and said in a small voice that there was something wrong with my eye again. This time she wasn't squashing my face with her hands, just holding it. I knew there was something wrong with my eye, but I hadn't told anyone. Just recently it had bothered me even more with its blurry spots. Crying must have brought its yellowness out.

'When I had my fever,' I said. 'It did something to my eyeball.'

Then I was suddenly seized with the idea that this might stop me going to England. I exaggerated the condition immediately.

'I mean, I can't really see through it.'

My mother's slight frown dropped into a look of utter horror. I was so surprised that I backed away, my face slipping from her hands. She was now clasping them together, with that horrified stare fixed on her face. Because I honestly thought that going blind in one eye meant that I could stay, I couldn't stop myself beaming from ear to ear.

This broke her stare, but turned it into something cross. She seized my hand and almost dragged me to the house, where my father had a look at my eye and grunted a bit. Then she disappeared, to lie down, and I was told not to disturb her. I could hear them muttering together for a while, but no change was made to the plans.

The next day, I looked up the word 'grace', and found so many meanings for it that it blurred into a simple sound, like a charm in Quiri's language. (I used it in the same way, therefore.)

My mother's strange reaction still strikes me as a watershed; after that moment on the path, we were never quite as close. Sometimes, in England, during those few years that remained to us, I had the strange impression that she was looking at me with a slight shudder. This, far from making me distance myself from her, made me try to please her all the more. I wanted to win back whatever I had lost on that hot, misty afternoon in the forest, on my father's 'road' (of which there is now no sign on any map I can find).

The picture I took in my head there is still very clear, however. As it turned out, and unknown to me at the time, it records the very last moment of what I sometimes think of as my golden age, before the Fall.

2

The wave rose very big behind the ship, then broke its crest just under the keel so that foam tumbled over the hull until only the mast showed. The mast rocked and righted itself and showed the prow waiting for the next crash. I crouched and let the wave splash against my face and then waded in until I towered over the boat, a single vein running through my bronze body from neck to ankle. I rained stones upon the *Argo* until the crew begged for mercy. The next wave tumbled it over and over and knocked even me to my knees – the harsh water suddenly over my head and sucking me under until it decided to push me up the black sand instead, where it was more interesting to be Robinson Crusoe than Talos.

I stayed lying on my tummy with my feet in the foam. The coconut shell was thrown up next to me, bereft of its bamboo mast and leaf sail. Mr Allinson appeared in the distance, waving his cane and calling. I saw through one eye (my bad one), that he had started to run. He came up puffing and panting through the spots, holding on to his pith helmet.

'Hugh!' he shouted.

I didn't move; I had only just been washed up. I had many years of solitude before Friday came.

'Oh God,' he groaned.

He sat on my back and started to squash my ribs against the ribs of the sand.

'Ow, ow,' I said.

'Never *ever* do that again, Hugh,' said my mother, afterwards. 'You know Mr Allinson has a weak heart.'

There was a real storm that night, which kept me awake. I watched it from the bedroom window with my mother. As usual, we could only see anything when there was a sheet of lightning.

She thought the palms looked lunatic. The breakers had broken away from their usual positions and kept moving on towards us, but they always gave up at the last moment, smashing to pieces and being dragged back only inches from the sterns of the dug-outs lined up on the beach. The land was just stronger than the sea, thank goodness. The night sky boomed and cracked and made the floors judder. My mother held on to my hand and kept talking about the sea as if it was a patient with a high fever. I saw it as healthy, sinking all the ships that were to take me away from Africa. I put my other hand in my pocket and held my fetish tight and asked for this to happen, but saving those in peril on the sea when the decks disappeared under them.

The Elder Dempster liner appeared like a white palace around the edge of the bay in the morning. It crept past the calm palms and hooted. Black smoke sank down behind it and stayed in a long lumpy line. It had a giant bayonet sticking up in front, as if it was on parade. I watched it from the dripping veranda and thought: that ship is stronger than anything else.

'Thar she blows,' said Mr Allinson. 'The SS *Abinsi*.'

He had his hands on Lucy Allinson's shoulders. She was thirteen, and hadn't been out to Africa since she was four. She kept saying to me, 'We're going back together,' but I was only going, not going back.

Well, England might be exciting, I thought. I'm not going to be sacrificed. I'll make pals, like in the books. And play cricket and laugh. You get used to the cold. I'll carry around Yolobolo's mark and feel safe. School worried me, because – eager to know what it was – I'd read *Tom Brown's Schooldays* the previous month. I didn't want to be held in front of a fire or be someone's slave.

'I'm no one's slave,' my father would say, when he was cross with HQ.

When he'd waved goodbye with the servants from the station jetty, he'd looked as if someone had pinched his nose very hard. Halfway across the bay, with its water chuckling past the canoe's hull a few inches from my elbow, my mother had said, 'Look, Hugh!'

She was pointing at my father; my father was saluting. Quiri and Mr Henry and Joseph were also saluting. Augustina and Ndala and Baluti and Big Baldie were not waving any more. For some reason, my father had brought out the gramophone player with the huge horn. It was now playing the National Anthem, blown across to us over the forest's shrieks and whistlings.

'That is most unfortunate,' said my mother, almost to herself. She gripped the two sides of the canoe and seemed either anxious or cross. 'If that is your father's idea of a joke —'

'Don't worry, I'm not going to stand up,' I said.

She looked at me as if surprised, and then laughed. But I was being serious. The long dug-out was crammed with our cases: we had to be careful. At the other end, after the rowers, stood Mawangu, with a gun. He was a very good shot. He knew exactly where to hit both a hippo and a croc. He had to be standing so that he could see if a croc or a hippo was on its way. I studied my mother for a moment. That same cloud had come down over her face. I had the oddest feeling that I wasn't ever going to see our home again; I had not asked any questions about this. The trees were already sliding between here and there. The river was brown and full, and carrying us quite quickly, and the rowers had barely to row.

I turned and lifted myself up a bit, forgetting.

'Hugh, sit down!'

I think she thought I was about to jump in and swim back, but I needed to see the forest beyond the buildings, to burn it into my mind so I would never forget it. I sat down and screwed my eyes shut. I had taken a sort of photograph again: I could see it down to the trees sliding across, shutting it off. I wish I had taken one of Quiri. I settled down again.

Then: 'We *are* coming back, aren't we, Mother?'

Her eyes flickered to the water and back again to my face. 'Of course, Hugh,' she lied. 'Eventually. We'll plan things later. It's going to be so exciting for you, darling.'

The two days in the Mission Station were strange. The Reverend Tarbuck, who was rather ill and out of sorts, kept coming up to me and tousling my hair, staring at me with tears in his eyes. At other times he would be talking quietly to my mother under the big acacia, turning round as I approached and giving me a look that was not so pleasant. This again awoke my suspicion that I was to be sacrificed.

'Come into the cemetery with me,' he said, on the second morning. 'I want to show you something.'

'No,' said my mother. She looked either anxious or cross, again.

Anyway, I ran off and hid. After that, he stayed most of the time in his house.

I thought about this as I waved goodbye from the big ship, very high up, standing on a box so that I could see over the side. Why hadn't I hidden like that in Victoria, even on the wharf with all its huge crates and logs and bales? I was told that this ship was a mail steamer, but she carried much more than letters. Lucy was waving next to me, and my mother was blowing her nose behind me. Lucy's parents had pecked her on the face like hens, saying goodbye. Mr Allinson had pumped my hand.

'So long, Mr Crusoe!' he'd boomed.

Now everyone was growing smaller and smaller, until we couldn't even see their hands above their heads. The hooter groaned, as if leaving was a big effort. I had never seen so much metal in my life, and it was only rusty around the bolts, the million bolts that kept it all together. When the sun shone, the ship was almost too hot to touch.

I tried to spot the Ndian estuary, or even the Mission Station, but we were too distant, a long way past the creamy breakers. Only Mount Cameroon stayed recognisable for a while, with a head of grey cloud like a toadstool. Then it dwindled into the mist. This mist shut us off from the solid world half of the time, letting us see land only in glimpses, or when we pulled in at a port.

Lucy was very happy when the wind no longer brought the smell of my home, a few days later.

'I can jolly well breathe now,' she said, leaning back in her deckchair.

I studied Lucy's face.

'What are you staring at?' she snapped.

'You,' I said. 'You were crying. What you done cry for?'

She repeated my last sentence and laughed. 'Golly, you're a native!'

'I know why you're crying,' I replied; 'you're missing your parents.'

She snorted, and wiped the tear from her cheek with a fling of her hand. Then, looking out on the water, she said, 'I don't miss them at all. I don't miss anyone. So there.'

I looked at my hands, noticing how delicate hers were. My fingers were marked with tiny cuts and scratches, and the skin was rough. Quiri had said that all these marks, if they stayed, meant things; the thin red scar above my eyebrow, where I had fallen against a stone aged two, meant that my secret eye had woken up. The adhesive bandage on my second finger had come off, leaving a paler band like a ring.

In the evenings, all the men wore different coloured cummerbunds and laughed loudly above the piano and the noisy glasses. My mother would appear for a bit, but mostly I'd play chess with Lucy. She wanted to get to Bathurst because she liked the deep blue cummerbunds best. I liked the red ones from Sierra Leone. The only men to come on at Bathurst, however, stayed in Second and Third Class, where we didn't really go. One of them would walk up and down the deck muttering to himself, with a completely yellow face and bald head and stubble. He said rude words, according to Lucy. She called him Dracula, but his teeth didn't stick out. Later, she told me he had died suddenly in the night. He was an up-country trader. Maybe he's infected all of us, she said, and we'll become a ghost ship.

Sometimes I forgot the black smoke behind us was ours, and thought it was lifting out of the water to chase us and suffocate us. It gave me a cough. Lucy said I wouldn't like London. When I asked why, she said that it was full of 'pea-soupers'. This made me worried, because typhoid made you have a pea-soup stool, according to my mother. If someone staggered in from the forest with a pea-soup stool, she would order me and all the servants to keep inside. If the person died and no one came, the body would be wrapped in a sheet and buried very carefully.

The humid air had been left behind. Now I might float up like a bubble, if I wasn't careful. I couldn't sleep. I went to my cabin window and looked out into a soft breeze. A darker line must be the Tropic of Cancer, I thought. Or maybe the coast of Senegal, because Senegal came after the Gambia. The sea was like the night river with all the far forest swept away like a big lump of moss. The moon settled on the sea in pieces that were pressed into spoons and then sank, while directly below me the phosphorescence sped off and sped off and made me so giddy it was like going to sleep.

Although it was mostly calm, my mother kept being sick in her cabin and Lucy kept sitting in corners with wet cheeks.

'Leave me alone,' they'd both say.

England was cold, like the flat-iron when Augustina wasn't using it. It was as smoky as Africa, but the smoke had a sour taste. Liverpool was associated in my mind with the word 'liverish', one of my mother's words. So the sight of the port made me feel a bit ill. (The same thing happened when I'd look at the drawings I had done or the books I had read just before my malaria attack, ages before.)

There was more of a swell, as we approached, than at any other time in the whole voyage, and my mother was sick. She was a very bad sailor and kept saying she wanted to die. Lucy had been ill, but with a fever. She emerged looking bone-white, as if her face had been rubbed with kaolin, and stood beside me at the rail, with a purple shawl around her shoulders. She was smiling, lifting her face up to the sunlight. There were big boats and smacks and cranes and a glistening, slippery-looking wall that seemed to slide forward and hit the sea in plumes of spray. It was sunny in bits, and when the sun went in so did all the colours: even the sea was just grey. Its shallow and dirty dullness wallowed and slopped about the breakwater. Each of the concrete blocks tumbled down on it bore a curved iron handle, like the handle on a suitcase. There were bottles on the waves, and rusty tins, and scraps of paper imitating the seagulls that were seated amongst them. I wondered if the water here was English, and whether, if you took some away in a little bottle and poured it into the ocean off Africa, it would dissolve like quinine or float about for ever and ever like a tinned gooseberry.

'Ah, dear dear England,' said Lucy. 'Pro patria mori.'

The ship hooted but it sounded jollier now. There were tiny people on the long wharf, all white. Some of them were waving as they grew. None of them had pith helmets or Bombay bowlers; many of the men wore the funny type of hat I had seen in pictures, with no brim except for a bit in front. Others wore what I knew was called a 'trilby', from my *Child's Illustrated Dictionary*, though I had never seen one before. There were no parasols and nobody dressed in cream flannels or skirts. Most of them had covered their bodies in long, dark coats, so it was hard to see. I had my thick coat on, but I was used to it. I'd worn it for the last three days, coming out on deck. It no longer hurt my neck or weighed down my shoulders.

Bicycles and cars went up and down behind the people, or even between them, and there were flat trolleys scurrying about, and horses and carts, and a donkey with blinkers. Even the stevedores weren't black. It was as if someone had peeled off their skin under their singlets and caps and beards. Only the dirt and grease made black streaks on their glistening muscles. I saw this as they grew almost to human size. They must be very cold, I thought.

Now even my mother had joined everyone else on the deck, her hand cold in mine. She had on the same sort of hat as the women down there, curving down so you couldn't see her eyes from the side, even looking up at her as I was. It had a little red flower in its band. Some of us were waving, and there were whistles and rattle-noises from the people on the wharf, but generally everyone was silent on the ship, as we slid to our berth. Big blue-and-white letters passed us in reverse order, painted directly on to the wall: *Elder Dempster Lines Berth 2*. The wall plunged down to a hiss of dirty foam like the suds after Baluti had done the laundry, and there were mad gulls daring the gap between metal and stone.

I could see houses now, beyond the huge sheds and cranes of the dock. They were low and all the same, one after the other moving up the hill and facing others also the same – and more even beyond them, still the same, more of the same than I'd ever seen in my life, all smoking. Their roofs were neither thatched nor of corrugated iron – though there was a lot of corrugated iron on the dock's sheds, as at Victoria, and around a big square of rubble.

The houses that were all the same were not white or cream but very dark and dirty looking, and crept up the hill as if they felt shy. There were big chimneys dotted about, smoking blackly, and strange buildings stuck on to them that looked as if they had fallen sideways like a set of dominoes, with hundreds of windows set in their high walls. These buildings had letters painted on the roofs, or on their tall chimneys. They must be factories, I thought, for I had seen a picture of a factory in Father's *Complete Encylopaedia*. They were far bigger than I had expected.

I found I was gripping my mother's hand. I was searching for forest, but saw only fields and some small, puffy trees. I was also searching for big white cars and narrow laughing ladies with furry collars or nothing on at all, splashing in a pool. I'd seen these in my mother's copies of *Vogue*, which arrived now and again in the dug-out, along with bales of *The Times*. But the pool, liverish though the water was here, was nowhere to be seen.

A vehicle I recognised as an omnibus with Dewar's on its side passed between two buildings, followed by another with Saxa Salt, which was our salt. This excited me: both because I knew the name so well and the fact that it appeared on something I had always dreamed of riding on. The big chains on the ship rattled and men shouted and there was a knock under our feet.

'We're here,' said my mother. 'This is England, Hugh darling.'

'Thank goodness for that,' said Lucy. 'Absolutely top-hole ching bong spiffing.'

She often said things I couldn't understand, when she spoke at all. She looked bigger in her cape and shawl. Perhaps she'd grown in three weeks. I wanted to say something, but nothing would come. It was only then that I started to feel really homesick. It started in my stomach, and climbed eagerly into my head. It was a sort of panic, but beaten out on a very low drum and hummed slowly. There were pictures in my head – turned from everything I had known and loved – but continually breaking, like the beads of a kaleidoscope. The only one that stayed fixed was the last view of our coast beyond the fluttering strip of white that was all we could see of the breakers, the sky loaded with long dark clouds like logs.

The sharp smell of my father's spine-pad hanging off the back of his chair rose for a moment over the fishy stink of the docks and the boat's huge funnel. Then it disappeared, like a vapour. My mother was always complaining about the air in Africa, saying it was 'tainted' or 'putrid' – she particularly disliked the smell that came off moist skin and from grown-ups' armpits, describing it as full of 'foul matter'. I quite liked it, but never said so. Now I missed it badly, as I missed the smells of vegetation and cooking and rotten wood.

Tears were dripping off my chin, but I made no sound.

'Isn't it exciting, darling?' shouted my mother.

Lucy nodded, but her cheeks were wet again. That made me feel better.

The gulls screeched above us, eager to offer me a lift home on their huge wings, mile after mile after hundredth mile. There were no canoes about the ship, to throw pennies to and watch the hands in them flower or the glistening backs curve into the water and come up as grinning heads. There was only the dull, dirty water, full of bottles and paper and tins. This is where the Normans preyed on the English race. This is where the person who made my father anxious and sometimes angry lived. This is where Mr Shakespeare and Mr Tennyson and Mr Kipling and Mr Henty and Mr Haggard were Bound in Cloth and had All Rights Reserved. This is where Blind Pew tapped and the Black Spot was caught and Long John Silver swung his crutch. This is where all our tins, newspapers and bottles came from, to be used up by us and buried in the pit behind the cemetery or handed out to the villagers that visited.

'This is where, Hugh, you're going to live,' my mother was saying, her arm around me. 'An English boy in England, with an English family and English friends.'

The fat man with the black umbrella, standing next to Lucy, turned and smiled. I noticed that for the first time on the three-week voyage he had changed his panama for a little straw bowler and was clothed in blue-and-white stripes, as if it was not cold.

'Jolly good show,' he cried, 'and here's to the old country.'

He drew out from his blazer pocket a small gun and pointed it into the air, then shouted, 'God Save the King!' It was one of those wooden guns with an iron pin and trigger that you could buy in Victoria, dating from the German days, or even before. I was never quite sure whether they were real or not, whether the natives had ever used them against the Maxim machine-guns. He pulled the trigger. The gun made a dull clack. You could only just hear it above the bustle of the ship's berthing. He laughed again, wheezily, and my mother joined in. She seemed to be awfully relieved about something.

We took a train to London. England, I noticed, was full of what Lucy called 'fag-ends'. Every time I looked at my shoes there was a fag-end next to them: on the cobbles, on the slabs, on the metal grilles, on the carpet of the carriage. Father had said that I must kiss the earth when I arrived, like William the Conqueror. But William the Conqueror was a Norman, and there was no earth to kiss.

Lucy's face was still drawn and pale, but smiling. The steam in the railway station reminded me a little of the mists off the river and in the forest. I closed my eyes against the hisses and whistles, and it helped. When I stumbled and had to open them again, the sun was pouring through the station's glass roof and our shadows rippled on the fog.

I almost wetted my pants as the train jolted into life; this was the only thing I had really looked forward to, but it wasn't at all like the little plantation train the Germans had built before the war, with its open carriages. This journey was made in a room my mother described as 'close'. She opened the window and I thought the smoke would pour in but it didn't. I had to go to the lavatory but couldn't do anything when I saw the ground rushing past through the hole. The lavatory had the worst stink I had ever known.

Next to my mother again, I pressed my forehead to the window. The other people were reading, or dozing. The land rushed past nearby but went slower further out, as if it wasn't very interested. There was not very much forest and the trees were in puffs of very pale green. They looked as if they might be easily torn, like my mother's best silk stockings. There were trees that were all white. 'Is that snow?' I cried, very excited. Lucy laughed and said it was blossom. She looked around at the other people as if she was shy, suddenly. They all looked at me for a moment and then went back to reading. There were more of those shy-looking houses climbing in chains up and down hills, then approaching us so close we went through their back gardens and nearly ripped their washing off the lines.

I wanted to please my mother so I fixed a grin on my face and kept it there for the whole journey. Poles whipped past and Lucy tried to count them. There were cows and sheep in the fields, and horses and men and machines, but each thing was taken away before you got used to it. I kept my hands under my thighs so long that my skin bore the imprint of the woven seat cover, and I wondered whether it would ever go. A big car at a level crossing had a man in it who waved just too late to wave back, but I waved at some boys on a bridge who didn't. The air in the carriage was worse than on the smoky deck of the boat, but its sourness made me think of the SS *Grace* passing my home.

My mother looked at me and I tried to be full of grace.

When we arrived in London the hard ground seemed to edge away each time I set my foot down. Dust filled the air, sourer than the harmattan. The sun's beams shafted into it, making a kind of yellow mist through which everyone hurried incredibly fast. My mother and I were too slow: even Lucy was slower than anyone else, getting knocked and scowling at people. We had very little luggage: the rest was being sent on to Uncle Edward's. I imagined Uncle Edward as peeping out from behind a great hill of crates and trunks and hatboxes.

The man helping us with our suitcases was black. I wanted to ask him to stay with us, but he was shouted at by someone else and hurried off. Omnibuses were everywhere, now: they rumbled and growled outside the station, each window framing a face like a photograph. I was surprised to see that most of them had roofs on the upper deck. We took a chugging taxi to the hotel, to my disappointment. It was as though the sea's waves had turned into bonnets and hoods and hubcaps and all those in peril were swimming for their lives between them. There were only about three horses, which surprised me: in the photograph of Piccadilly in my bedroom at home, there were lots. I kept swallowing but the taste stayed in my mouth. My throat was dry. It was only when we were in the hotel lobby that I realised Lucy had gone. I told my mother.

'But Lucy got out at Chelsea. She said goodbye to you. Don't you remember? You are a funny boy!'

Now I remembered, but not very well. I saw her melting into thin air like those vampires did in Dracula's castle. Melting into the endless streets and faces and shouts and rumblings. I suddenly missed her. She had been a bit of Africa, a bit of Victoria. She probably still had black sand in her pockets, like me.

Our room had a tiny iron veranda that looked down on a straight reach of street that never stopped flowing past. When we went down into it, I noticed certain differences. Shoes clicked here. Pidgin never came out of people's mouths. There were so many words properly printed on walls and doors and cars and buses that I couldn't read more than a bit of each one, but some of them stayed for ever: *New 'Yard' Sensation, Permanent Wave 25/- Full Shingled Head, Old English Maple Furniture FURNITURE*, and lots of high Toilets with the *i* missing on their signs. There were even men carrying words on them, in front and behind, and a lot of the words were very loud. The dust and grit and dryness had given me a kind of asthma by the third day, yet it had drizzled without stopping on the second. The real houses went up and up and were as grey and black as rocks, but at least they stayed still; the vehicles were also like houses but they moved. I struggled to move without losing my mother's hand but it was hard. When we had to cross the road she chose a spot and said, 'Here we go, hold tight.' But she held *me* so tight that I dreaded crossing the road because it hurt my hand so much.

Perhaps only one thing swept away my fear long enough for me to be excited by it. We'd shopped and 'popped in' to friends and relations, we'd eaten in something very new called a 'snack bar', we'd wandered between waxworks with glass eyes like the eyes of our leopard-skin rug or the masks in the villages, we'd seen a film on a screen ten times bigger than Mr Tall's white sheet in Buea, and we were about to go to the zoo. Then the weather turned suddenly colder, and people scurried about in their long funnels of coats, feet and head protruding at each end, looking bad-tempered and even whiter. My mother said we'd have to spend the afternoon in a theatre instead of going to the zoo, because I had a throat and it was spitting.

The theatre was called the Gaiety. It was like the cinema, its seats covered in something strangely agreeable to rub, called red plush. The long red curtains opened and real people with huge feathers on their heads started to sing and jig about in front of a town with lots of pillars. Then the colours changed and the floor underneath them started to turn and the town turned into a desert with palm trees and camels and a far-off pyramid.

'This is Ancient Egypt,' my mother whispered. 'There's the Pharaoh.'

Now we were in a golden room. Golden masks bumped about around a gold throne. I closed my eyes and opened them again. It was very like a dream but it wasn't. It hadn't cost us very much because it was the afternoon and called a matinée, which means 'morning' in French. I presumed that while all this was happening in front of my eyes the rest of London had stopped still, but I heard a faint grumble all around which I thought might be traffic, and a tinny bell passing very quickly, which I reckoned might be a fire engine. It was like when you dream, I thought: your dreams go on without the rest of it. Long curving horns blared and the golden room started to fall down. It turned into a big tent where soldiers were shouting and then into a courtyard where a real fountain dribbled. A woman was crying and then a man came in and she was happy and they sang a song, and then lots of people came on and sang, raising their arms at us and waving like on the jetties and wharves. I thought of my father and the servants and wondered what they were doing right at this moment. The theatre wasn't very full, but the laughter was quite loud and the clapping even louder.

'Did you like that?' my mother asked. London started up again with a big crash just as the attendant pushed the doors open for us. I nodded. Ancient Egypt was in Africa. It was too loud to say anything.

'Well, don't sound too enthusiastic,' said my mother.

So I made sure I didn't, even though something golden was flowing through me from head to foot.

The next day we went to the zoo. Everything wanted to be let out. They all want to go back, like me, I thought.

'It smells beastly,' I said, and my mother found that funny.

I pressed my nose to the bars all the same because the animals at home made sure they weren't seen easily, or at all.

'Goodness me, there's the leopard, Hugh.'

The forest was full of leopards, but this was the first one I had ever seen alive. It was like the skin my father had spent ages tanning, but with something stuffed into it that rippled and then stared at us. The cold wind blew across it and it shivered. I shivered, too.

'It is rather frighteningly huge, isn't it, darling?'

There was something called the Leopard Society at home. I had no idea what this was, except that it was even more frightening than a leopard. I knew that my mother was thinking about the Leopard Society, looking at this shivering creature on its concrete rock.

There were other odd things: it was very odd not to see a pith helmet or a Bombay bowler, or mosquito boots, or fly switches, or no more than a handful of black people. I still couldn't sleep properly without a mosquito net between me and the night. Night didn't really happen, anyway: lights blazed inside and outside. The tall drooping gas ones were lit and snuffed by a funny little man in a black cape, with a long pole, who whistled like a bird early in the morning. Before then, instead of the night calls of the forest, I heard only the rumble of a storm that never came and the calls of car horns and klaxons, and strange, high shouts that sounded like the beginning of a dance. There were no drums. There were no murmurings of servants around the fire. The light in the middle of the room made everything cruel-looking; my mother instructed me not to put my fingers in the holes in the wall. I knew this from the Allinsons, who had a generator. Instead of the smells of river and forest and rain, there was a sickly sweet scent of beeswax and mothballs and old carpet, and that same sourness from the street that came in through the window and lay on your tongue and tickled the back of your nose.

'Isn't London extraordinary,' said my mother, collapsing on the bed after a long tour of several very big and never-ending shops that turned out to be one shop, called Harrods. (Horrid Harrods, I was thinking.) 'Isn't London quite, quite extraordinary. Do you know, Hughie, I feel quite bush. I feel quite the native, marvelling at it all for the first time. And it's so wonderfully *cold*. Oh, come here.'

She put out her hand and I lay down next to her and cried. I wanted the river, not the jumbly street below. I couldn't get used to the idea of things passing the window, continually on their way to somewhere else. Nothing ever stopped, though it always sounded as if it was about to. What were all these people hurrying off to do? Even in Duala, which I had visited once or twice, one somehow understood what everyone was doing, however bustly they were. I should have brought the bones of the bushbaby with me. I thought of it curled up under the brick in the wet red earth of the compound and cried even more. Quiri was wrong: the spirit had stayed in the bones, I was sure. And the bones were far away and all alone.

I clung to my mother as one clings to another in a flood. The flood slowed us both, though my mother was becoming too fast for me. Her fingers were stroking the back of my neck. I stiffened.

'Darling, you've got the most enormous bite.'

She made me turn my head, worried by the possibilities. Her fingers crackled at the nape of my neck. I heard her breath being drawn in, hissing between her teeth.

'Oh good God,' she said. 'Oh, that's appalling.'

She wasn't really addressing me; I felt I was asleep. She made me tell her the truth about it. When I did, she nodded and looked decided about something.

That evening she wrote a letter to my father, but I wasn't allowed to read it. I sent a card of Buckingham Palace, with *Please give my love to Quiri and the others*, as a PS. The next day she took me to a skin doctor who pronounced the mark 'indelible' – unless I had a painful operation which ran the risk of infection. I had already decided that if my mother tried to get rid of Yolobolo's sign I would jump from the window into the street four floors below.

We went to Griffiths McAllister in Regent Street and I was very glad to see khaki tunics and shorts and bush-boots, hurricane lamps and cholera belts and Bombay bowlers, even if the place smelt very sweet and stuffy. My mother bought some shirts and trousers and a Union Jack. Our flag had looked sad on its rusty pole as my father saluted our departure. My mother washed the flag every week, but mould had damaged it. When she took it down, every Sunday, she would tut at the green patches on the cloth. By the time of my departure it had been washed too many times and the red had completely disappeared. It looked like a map of a hilly and forested place, not a flag. The new one was big and bright and the man serving agreed with my mother that the colours were fast and the cloth durable, stroking his hand over it as if it had to be calmed down.

It seemed wrong to me – that she might well return with a new Union Jack, but without me.

I lay on the big bed with my card as she was writing her letter and thought about this. I thought of myself as wrapped up in the flag, smuggling myself back home. I had read somewhere that when a sailor died in battle they wrapped him in the Union Jack and let him drop from the side into the sea. I wondered whether they had done this with the dead trader on the ship, but my mother had said that a young man had told her he was a chap 'gone to seed', so they probably hadn't.

There might be a mistake; they might think I'm a sailor's corpse and let me slide into the ocean, wrapped up in the flag, before my mother knew it.

The light bulb in the lamp hanging from the middle of the ceiling was giving me a headache. I was amazed to see no insects – not even a moth – fluttering around it. I counted the windows on the photograph of the Palace. My mother kept glancing at me from the little table, where she was writing her letter. I felt like a piece broken off something, but I wasn't sure what. I wasn't sure whether this piece was me and my mother, or just me. My mother and I, I corrected myself. Lucy had teased me about the way I talked: she said it was 'out of date, like an old book'. Lucy was staying with a friend in Chelsea, then was bound for her aunt's in Twickening, or Twickingham, or something, and then 'horrid school'. I'd probably never see her again. She had to see a special doctor, someone who knew all about tropical diseases. So did I, even though I didn't have a tropical disease. I also had to see someone about my eye. It was much worse, in London. I tested it against the pale net curtains.

'Are you all right, darling?'

'Yes. What are you writing?'

'Why don't you look at the Meccano set I bought you?'

'What are you writing?'

'Just saying *Hello, we've arrived safely*, to Father.'

'It's taking you a long time, just to say that.'

I closed my eyes and saw again the trees sliding across the view of home over the bay's waters. In front of it were millions of white faces with hats on, bustling and jerking about. However much I tried, I couldn't get rid of them.

I was saving my Meccano for later, but I gave up and tried to build a crane. The hotel carpets were annoyingly thick, and it kept falling down, and I lost some of the tiny screws. I prepared for bed and my mother read me a story, then left me to sleep. I imagined her downstairs in the hotel lounge, chatting gaily as she did on the ship when she was feeling well enough, a graceful glass in one hand, a cigarette in its ivory holder in the other. A strange, sickly light came in through the thin curtains blown by the summer breeze, along with the grumbles and shouts and boomy roar of the city. I touched the mark on my nape, then noticed Herbert E. Standing billowing in the curtains. The air sucked them flat and he was left by himself for a moment. The sweet scent of linseed oil filled the room. He was holding a bat, so warped that he could have scooped water with it. I smiled, and then had a sudden, dreadful fear that he had changed and become evil, that he would approach and batter me to bits with the bat.

Instead, he started to cry, his face rumpling like a piece of cloth. I watched him, trying not to move or show any expression on my own face. I wasn't sure whether he was crying for himself, or me. I had left the cricket set at home. There'd been no point in taking it, if I was coming back. Anyway, the cases were full to the brim.

'Sorry about the cricket set, Mr Standing,' I said, quietly.

The curtains rippled and he was gone. I could hear rain on the glass of the window. The smell that came up was like the baby of the smell that came after storms at home, and it sent me immediately to sleep.

I knew, the moment I arrived at my uncle's house (a couple of hours in the train from London), that I would never escape it. There was a gate, a laurel-hedged drive, and then the huge house, sideways on. As the old-fashioned trap turned and bumped past the blank brick wall, I resigned myself to the rest of my life. I thought: Yolobolo's secret won't be known for a very long time. I won't be going back to Africa.

Then these thoughts dipped and swirled and disappeared into the flood of life like scraps of paper.

My uncle came out, and then my aunt. We alighted from the trap. My uncle paid the driver a penny and called him Stan. Stan scratched his mutton-chop whiskers and flicked the horse into motion. The wheels ground away across the gravel and my uncle was tousling my head.

'Well, well,' he said, 'the very spit.'

He looked at my mother and laughed. She gave him a cross look. My mother was always telling the servants off for spitting.

Aunt Joy had no hat on, just very short hair that curled up to touch her cheeks and a spotty dress that stopped at the knees. She had heavy shoes on, and in between was a lot of sunburned leg. I could smell the house through the open door; meat and beeswax mainly, much like a lot of open doors in England, I'd noticed.

'Hello, dears,' said my aunt, wringing her hands. 'And how's our African boy?'

She gripped my face and kissed me on the nose. I was so surprised my mouth fell open. Her palms were very cold. I wrested my face away and stepped back. They were laughing, all three of them. Uncle Edward had his arm around my mother.

'You look astonishingly well, dear sister,' he said.

I thought my mother looked pale and drawn after our stay in London, but didn't say so.

We went into the house, a red-faced maid called Susan puffing like the branch-line train as she carried our suitcases behind us. From the outside the house was nearly as enormous as Buckingham Palace, or at least as big as our hotel in London. Now

70

suddenly it was all shadowy corners and big pieces of furniture and curly rugs tripping me up, as if the inside had been washed badly and had shrunk.

I stumbled about after the adults until I was shown my room. It was up two flights of creaky stairs. When I looked out of the window I was surprised to see a huge lawn with trees at the end, and bright green fields beyond those, rising to a crest with funny grassy bumps on. I hadn't had time to notice the garden at all, before we went in. This wasn't the same garden as my mother had put into my head, but it didn't matter. The big trees around, one of them a sort of dried-blood red, cast big shadows on the grass, which was very smooth and the green of my father's folding card table. The sun was low in the sky. There were white and blue butterflies, and tall spiky flowers like furled flags, and a few of those special ones called roses, like at Buea. The green fields stirred in the breeze and I fancied for a second they were lakes or even seas, so like waves were the shadows that passed across them. The sky was paler here, though almost cloudless; everything was paler, in fact. Even the shadows falling across the lawn were paler than the shadows in Africa. It reminded me of the washed-out Union Jack on its post in the station.

My uncle gave me a humorous card to pin up above my bed: it showed what he called a 'piccaninny' with big red lips and a fat belly standing in a mess of banana skins. His white eyes were rolled up, looking at someone – an adult, obviously – out of the picture. Printed across the bottom in large black letters was: *I ain't seen yo' bananas.* The child had a blue ribbon tied around his middle, with a big bow behind, like the gifts for people my mother had bought in Harrods. His belly sagged over this ribbon. I didn't understand the point of this card, but my uncle pinned it up anyway, laughing.

After my room in Africa, my room in England was quite small and narrow, but not at all dark; there were two windows with diamond-shaped leading, each with a sill wide enough to sit on. There was a small lamp with a blue china shade on the bedside table, and a ceiling light with a buff shade made of some animal's skin, as thin as card. The cupboard was huge, with squeaky doors and a lazy latch that would go to sleep halfway through the night

71

and let the doors swing open, terrifying me. I worked out that this meant that the floor, if not the house, was on a slope.

There were two framed pictures in the room; one of a ruined church on a cliff and the other of a girl with a bucket grinning in front of a gate. At first I thought this picture was as real as the paintings of Sir Steggie back home, but after running my finger over it I realised it was printed, like the pictures in the magazines. There was a large rug on the floor, faded but with dark patterns I could use as roads for my Dinky cars. Around it was a dark sea of oak planks which I could use for the racing cars because the planks were going the right way. My uncle was proud of these planks: all the wood in the house, he said, was oak. I liked the colour of this wood, and its smell, and the fact that it stayed calm and unchanged: in Africa, anything made of wood buckled or split or was eaten by insects.

We visited the garden before supper. The air was full of midges, gilded by the light flickering in rays out of the trees at the side of the garden. Our shadows were very thin and tall, getting ready to sleep and fatten themselves in the big shadow of night. I wondered if the spirit in my shadow was aware of the coldness of the lawn, of the thinned and cooler air here in England.

The dying sun wasn't as red as at home, and neither was the sky. We entered a wood at the bottom of the garden; there were two woods, in fact. One was what my uncle called a beechwood, and the other was next to it but fenced off with wire. My uncle called this the 'wildwood', saying it as one word, but it didn't look terribly wild to me. Its trees were a mixture of thin and fat, short and tall, young and old, and there was a lot of thorny stuff on the ground, and some thread-like creepers with pinky-red flowers looped from the branches. We went into the beechwood, though.

'Oh, an English wood!' said my mother, as if she had just received it as a present.

I found the inside of it rather bare; someone had swept it. There was no mist, and the sun fell into the wood in bright shafts I could put my hand in and out of, as I'd done with Mr Tall's magic lantern's beam. The trees were oddly thick and most of them curved a bit, finishing not very high above us. I was amazed at how the leaves, if they were caught in the sun, glowed, like lumps of wood on Baluti's fire when a gust blew across it. I realised quite quickly that in England a forest had very thin leaves, and its roof was nearer to the ground. One didn't feel giddy looking up. There were no cicadas, and only a few birds singing, and the earth was dry underfoot, smelling very sweet. Then the trees ended suddenly at the field, which I gazed upon as if I had reached the end of the world. I couldn't believe its size, nor its colour. It was malachite green with bright spots of red and yellow and blue, and I wanted to walk into it. But I wasn't allowed to. One day soon I would sneak out and let the green stuff (my uncle said it was ripening barley) close over me as I swam through it, for I could not believe it was not liquid in some way. Yet it rustled, as dry things rustle, as dry beans rustle in a gourd.

'They make this into beer and food, Hugh,' said my mother.

'It used to be sheep, do you remember?' said my uncle.

'Yes,' said my mother. 'Things change.'

'Are there snakes in the grass?' I asked.

They all laughed, especially my uncle, and he made a joke I didn't understand.

My aunt sneezed, and for that reason we had to go back. Crossing the lawn, my mother told me that we would see some sheep tomorrow, when we went to fetch the milk. The lawn no longer had our soul-shadows bumping along it, because it was twilight, and the grass had turned bluey grey. The wildwood was a dark lump in the corner. Being a shy boy, and still hurt by the laughter, I didn't ask my uncle why there was a fence around it. I imagined my mother playing on this lawn, as a girl, but it seemed too long ago to be real. I was gripping the fetish packet in my jacket pocket. I didn't yet know what spirits were lurking; the tiny forest my uncle called a beechwood struck me as a rather empty, echoey place. But no one can know, as Quiri put it, what milk a gourd contains until it is split.

I felt my life narrowing, despite the newness of things. My mother was busy that summer, organising her medical supplies and so forth, and I spent much of the time running about in the garden, alone. I was absolutely forbidden to enter the wildwood. I accepted my uncle and aunt as parts of the whole, and the whole was England. England was neither bad nor good, but couldn't be helped. I found the children introduced to me mostly puzzling; their ways were not strange so much as not very interesting. I could never find out what their symbol was, so I reckoned that nobody here had one. Some of them were strangely rough — pulling my hair or jabbing me with sticks for no apparent reason. My chief desire was to ask them about the spirits of the woods and fields, and what measures had to be taken when one walked in the countryside; only one boy, a little older than me, could tell me. He said that there were fairies at the bottom of his garden, and he left them acorn cups and beds of moss. He also said that there was a ghost in his cellar. He said it with such seriousness that I thought at last I had found someone who knew about these things. But then, with the same seriousness, he told me that he had discovered five diamonds in a hole behind the village church, and had killed ten black knights with his catapult, and that he had a very serious disease which anyone could catch by eating grass. I was just then nibbling at a grass blade, so I felt that he was a tease and not to be trusted.

A boy whom I liked, called Cecil, peopled the woods with pirates. His house was in a nearby village called Fawholt (the one we lived outside was bigger, and called Ulverton). At the end of his garden was a much larger wood than ours; in it, down a windy path, lay a pool with some drowned trees. A stream fed it. It was black and probably (he informed me) bottomless. I was sure there were powerful spirits there, and collected a silvery stone lying on the edge of the water. He saw me doing this and teased me, because he thought I'd thought it was precious. I told him why I'd pocketed it: I also said that I needed some of the clayey mud to make a fetish.

'What's a fetish?'

'It's something that's full of power and protects you.'

I thought of something my mother had once said.

'It's like the bones of saints in a little bag or a badge with St Christopher on it. And you know the Great Plague?'

'Course I do. And the Black Death. You had big boils in your armpits and died really horribly.'

I nodded; as far as I was concerned, everyone died rather horribly.

'Well, they held bunches of sweet herbs and flowers, especially roses, up to their noses. It stopped the fever coming into them.'

'No it didn't, stupid,' cried Cecil. 'That's just what they believed, and it wasn't true!'

'Well, that's what a fetish is.'

'There isn't any Black Death round here, stupid.'

'No, just evil spirits, probably. This is a strong place.'

He came nearer to me, a little frightened, and asked me what an evil spirit was, exactly. Was it the same as a vampire, or Frankenstein, or the Hound of the Baskervilles, or the headless fellow who haunted the crossroads where the gibbet used to stand? No, I said: there were lots of different types. Many of them were those of people who died without having children, others were those who had died far from home, so they couldn't find their way back to join their ancestors under their house. Many were of animals whom someone had stupidly killed, or of trees stupidly cut down, or of guardians placed outside a village to protect the departing traveller, which had been smashed or broken by a stupid enemy. I said how strange it was that there were no feathered figures or carved heads embedded with teeth outside any villages here; everyone must go about frightened and worried all the time. There were also types like Sir Steggie.

'What's Sir Steggie?' Cecil asked.

I smiled, and threw a pebble into the pool. The plop made Cecil jump. We watched the ripples travel very slowly out until they rocked a small white feather near our feet.

'Sir Steggie,' I said, 'is the enemy of Yolobolo.'

I had never thought of that before, and was surprised at my saying it. But I knew it was true. I knew also, then, that Sir Steggie had followed me, somehow. Maybe he'd hidden in the hold, in our big trunk. *Property of J.S. Hargreaves.*

The trees round about shivered in a gust, and Cecil asked me about Yolobolo. Before I could reply his mouth snapped shut and he cried, 'You're pulling my leg something rotten, aren't you? I don't like you!'

He then ran back to the house, leaving me alone in the wood.

For a moment I was frightened – very frightened – but I held my finger to the mark on my neck and concentrated, shutting my eyes tight. The thin English air, very sweet and dry, barely covered me, but the sun shifted over my eyelids and I felt the chill of fright leave. Cecil had populated the pool with pirates, and they all had names: Nasty Cabbage, Black Jack, Sammy Scar, Rotten Rednose, Bloody Bob. When we were together they had filled my vision, armed with cutlasses and sporting big black beards – we beat them off with sticks and our catapults, sinking their ships with stones from behind our cover of raked-up leaf mould. Now there were no pirates, and there never had been. It had been a game. But the spirits were still there, both good ones and bad ones, waiting, cautious of me for the moment. Somewhere close, in the shadows beyond the pool, was Sir Steggie, looking for his fob-watch.

I walked back to the house without showing him my back, despite the protection of my mark. Yolobolo was not in England, that was the trouble. I was his ambassador – to use a term of my father's. I would need all my wit and cunning, and the protection of my mark and my fetishes, to survive in this hostile land.

Then, as I was thinking these thoughts, emerging on to the lawn, Cecil's mother appeared and told me to come inside for a word.

'Do you believe in God?' she said, standing by the dining-room table.

'Yes,' I said.

'Do you believe in Jesus?'

'Yes,' I said.

'Then what is all this nonsense you have been frightening Cecil with, Master Hugh?'

Cecil's mother had huge teeth and flaring nostrils. Her skirt came out from her waist as if it had a wire basket inside it. Everything about her was big except for her fingers, which were long and thin. She was the wife of the Vicar, and the house was called the Vicarage.

'I don't know what you mean,' I said.

Cecil appeared in the shadows.

'He's a pagan, Ma,' he said.

'Well, he seems to have been unfortunately influenced, in Africa,' said Cecil's mother. 'It is hardly surprising. Despite all our gallant efforts, there are still dark spots to be brought into the light. I will talk to your mother about it, Hugh.'

I frowned. I would never have talked about spirits to the Reverend Tarbuck, on his visits, because I knew he didn't believe in them. I had learnt, at home, to be careful of what I said. But even when I was not, it didn't seem to matter; my parents liked my stories about the forest, they liked what they called 'native yarns', and what I had said seemed to flow off into the day like a branch taken by the river. Here, however, the branch got stuck, and created swirls of yellowy foam.

Once my mother had left, and I knew the betrayal was complete, I stopped talking about spirits or fetishes or powers, or anything to do with home, or the forest. It was as if the cloud of chalk and grit left by her departing taxi had stopped up my mouth in some way. She'd left hurriedly, somehow, giving me only the briefest hug, and I ran after the car the moment I knew what was happening. I ran up the lane as far as the orchard, and its windfalls were already heady and sweet. Then I tripped over on a stone and cut my knee. If it had been Stan and the trap, I might have had a chance.

We went back to carbolic and plaster, toast and tea. My aunt had brought out her mulberry jam. This, apparently, would make up for my mother leaving me for good. She spread it thickly. (She was never to do so again.) The label on the jar was marked *Autumn 1928*. I was still in Africa, when that was bubbling in the pot. The jam was both a comfort and a cruel joke. I made up a charm to make her mortally ill, that night, using some of the ingredients I had used against Mosea. They looked tired and withered, here in England.

I had further distractions, of course, to fill the empty room in my chest. My aunt and uncle had many visitors: bit by bit the idea crept up on me that my uncle was quite famous, amongst certain people. These certain people passed through the house, talking a lot. They were mostly young men, many with spectacles and beards, and some in strange gowns or cloaks, as people wore in England in days of yore. There were also women with amazingly long hair who smoked all the time and always had a glass in their hands, and women with short, almost stubbly hair who didn't. My head was tousled by these people until I had a headache, or imagined I had. My mother had cut my hair carefully, so that it lay over my nape. I don't know what she had told my aunt, but my aunt didn't say anything about my odd haircut. All the other boys I met had their necks exposed, their hair beginning well on to their skull.

One morning, I realised that a small part of me was ashamed of my mark. That small part was squeezed into a lump of earth from the beechwood and thrown into the field's stubble.

Each Sunday my aunt and I – but never my uncle – went to church. My uncle had lost his faith in the war, my aunt told me, as we walked up the lane. 'His *Christian* faith, at least,' she added, widening her eyes in a peculiar way. Maybe he had another faith, I thought. The services were no more interesting than those I was used to at home, but during them I always felt an overpowering desire to go back there, to see my parents and the forest and chat to Quiri. Then a deep sleepiness would come over me, which could last several hours, or even into the next day. I was always introduced as 'our little nephew from the colonies', or 'our charge from the Dark Continent' to people my aunt didn't know very well. The Vicar would take my hand in the church porch, bowing down as if to kiss it. I always feared I would have my hand sucked up into his large, frog-like mouth, so I tended to remove it quickly from his clasp. This always made him laugh, his big white gown flapping about his arms and giving off smells of mothballs and my uncle's drinks' cabinet. My aunt called him Reginald, but my uncle called him The Vic, even to his face.

There was a Christmas party at Christmas, for children. I was instructed by my uncle to take lots of mistletoe and give each child a sprig. It came off the apple trees in the little orchard behind the crumbling summerhouse. There was some problem about this, between my aunt and uncle, and I wondered if it was because the white berries were poisonous. I went hugging my mistletoe nevertheless, with my aunt, but the Vicar took it all away and it never came back. When my uncle asked me if I had handed out the mistletoe, I said yes, because my aunt had told me to, adding that it wasn't a lie because the Vicar would hand it out himself, later. My uncle patted me on the head and said that if ever I saw the same stuff growing on an oak tree, I should tell him. He would give me a shilling reward. My aunt pursed her lips and wagged her finger.

'Edward,' she said, 'that's enough.'

'No it isn't,' he replied, in a very stern voice, his words booming over my head: 'it's not nearly enough.'

'An interest is becoming – something else,' said my aunt. 'I won't have it becoming something else.'

'And why not?' boomed my uncle.

My aunt glanced at me. I didn't want to leave the room. She looked at my uncle. 'You're too clever for that,' said my aunt, steadily.

My uncle boomed with laughter. He went back to his books – or so my aunt told me. She then said, at the kitchen table, 'You musn't take any notice of him, when he does these things.'

I nodded. I had no idea what she meant, but I was feeling too sleepy to bother to find out. I went up to my room and cried for Africa and for my mother and father.

The next day I received a long Christmas letter from my mother, written three weeks before on her new typewriter. It mentioned all the servants except Quiri. My father was very well, she was very well, and the Reverend Tarbuck was not very well. A fellow in Ikasa had shot a twenty-foot croc. The weather was cool and agreeable (which meant very hot compared to the weather here, which I was having difficulties with), and it hadn't rained for a whole week. The dispensary was better equipped than ever, and she was training a native, a very clever girl from Ikasa. She finished with lots of love and said how much she missed me but she had forgotten to sign it. Where *Mother* should have been was a blank.

Outside it was midwinter. The world had been sucked of all its juices by some dragon who lived underground. The trees had worried me when they began to lose their leaves, a month or so earlier; they were like some of my mother's patients whose hair fell out after certain fevers. I knew this was to happen, because I had read about it. I had read quite a few poems on the subject, and my mother had told me about the four seasons before we'd left. All the leaves fall at the same time, she'd told me. Then they come back at the same time. It's not like our forest, where things fall and come out all through the year. In winter, in England, there are no butterflies and not many birds, and some of the animals sleep. Bees and wasps sleep, and even flies disappear. The grass doesn't grow, and there are no flowers, and the trees are just branches and twigs. The night falls early – around teatime.

'*Tea*time?'

I found the thought frightening.

'It's a rather wonderful season,' she'd said, and sighed. 'Muffins. We toast muffins and drink warm wine with cloves in it.'

Now here I was in England, in my room, looking out upon a winter landscape, and I hadn't yet had a muffin, let alone warm wine. My uncle thought that this particular time, when the days were very short indeed, was extremely special. He told me out of the corner of his mouth, when my aunt was talking to Susan by the back door, that we had to persuade the sap to rise up and return into the branches, or else the spring might never come, and the earth might plunge into eternal winter. In former days, he said, we'd sacrifice a young man or woman, and their blood restored the earth, feeding it. I nodded. I think he was trying to frighten me, but I was used to the idea of sacrifice, human or animal. The Reverend Tarbuck told me that certain tribes could not be dissuaded from their pagan ways. One tribe, who lived further down the river from us, would throw into the river a young albino girl, once a year. Now they threw in a white goat, thanks to his efforts. The elders said that this would not work, but the fish were just as plentiful that year, and no one was eaten by a croc. I didn't tell my uncle about the Reverend Tarbuck's merciful doings.

The fact is, I didn't tell my uncle anything about Africa – nor my aunt. They weren't interested, for a start; they called it the Dark Continent or the White Man's Grave, and used the same terms for the natives as some of the traders always did, and as Mr Tall and the Allinsons sometimes did, and as my father did just once, when he was very angry about something.

My uncle would say, 'How's my little nephew from nigger-dom?' and then laugh a lot, tousling my hair. He was a large man, but not very tall; he had bushy ginger eyebrows, gingery hair on his hands, and pale eyes. He was not like my mother at all, except for the lobes of his ears, which were also pointed. He had been very good at sport, my mother told me. He'd been a Rugby Blue at Oxford, just before the war. I saw him as a young man with a blue face and blue hands holding a ball. Then the war had crippled him. I didn't think of my uncle as a cripple; his hands were huge and firm, he had no scars, he didn't limp, he wasn't swollen up or twisted and didn't run about legless on a little wheeled tray with leather straps on his knuckles, like they did in Duala. But apparently the war had stopped him being a sportsman, because he had been very upset in some way. My mother said that it had made him old before his years, like a lot of the young men she'd looked after in the sanatorium in Hampshire.

The war and winter were linked in my mind; this was because my father would now and again tell me how he was jolly glad his war had been mostly in Africa because in Flanders it was damn parky; there were no trees, and if there were trees they had no leaves on them. You were either frozen and miserable or wet and miserable.

'At least in Africa it was warm and miserable,' he'd chuckle.

I reckoned, looking out on the midwinter garden with its blackened branches, and the midwinter fields of dark mud disappearing into mist, and the one misty blank of sky, that this was how the war in Flanders must have looked. No wonder, then, so much blood had been poured into the earth!

Just before she left, my mother and I had tried, together, to catch the first falling leaves. It was a very difficult game. We ran about on the edge of the wood or jumped up and down under the big copper beech, but I scored only when one landed by chance in my hair. We raked a load up and lit a bonfire. (My mother enjoyed helping in the garden, 'complimenting', as I thought she put it, the weekly visit of old Jeremiah Jessop.)

The wind had dropped. It was a very grey evening, the last in September, and you could hardly see where the smoke ended and the sky began. I expected flames to leap up, like an erupting volcano, but they didn't. Whitish smoke rose in a fat column, buckling only when she jabbed the heap with her rake, to let the air in. The smoke joined the huge umbrella of sky, merely smudging it above the house if one looked carefully. It was queer, how whitish smoke could smudge a darker sky. That night my clothes and hair smelt of smoke, but it wasn't the sharp, sweet smoke of home – of the night-watchman's fire or the drumming villages along the river or in the forest.

A month later, on a gusty day, I stood on my own in the beech-wood and watched amazed as a great plundering took place overhead: Flint's treasure chest of doubloons and double guineas and moidores and sequins rained down slowly through the sunlight, as far as the eye could see. No one came to gather it, and I played the treasure hunt on my own – the voice among the trees and the death of Merry and the saving of Jim and Silver, and the counting of the gold in Ben Gunn's cave – until dusk.

And not much longer after that, it seemed, a violent squabble of angels took place in the yard of the heavens.

'Look,' my aunt urged, leading me to the porch, 'look at this, Hugh!'

The downy feathers fell past my open mouth, sinking to silver on the doorstep and on the stone path, but clinging even more whitely to the grass. Gradually (but only when one turned one's gaze away), the earth became the sky. It was more than a hens' squabble; the sky itself was crumbling, like our ceiling had been at home before Father mended it. I was dressed up from head to toe and stood, sweating like a pig under scarf and balaclava and woollen coat, in the middle of the lawn. I was never allowed to stand out under rain here, because the raindrops weren't warm; the snowflakes were even colder, but I was still allowed to stand under them, for some reason.

When they stopped, and the world had been turned to show its grieving insides, my aunt called out to me, 'Play in the snow, Hugh, like normal boys do. You're not Mowser.'

Mowser was the cat; she'd felt the snow and shaken her paw as if she had scalded it. I kneeled down and scooped out a lump. I was starting to shiver.

'Not on your knees, Hugh!' my aunt cried. 'You'll get lumbago!'

I heard her, through the open door, remonstrating with my uncle; the word, I thought to myself, was 'exasperated'. My mother had used this word on several occasions, in relation mainly to the servants. I stood up and left a trail of footprints, making big circles that joined up with each other. I made a face like this, staring up at the sky. I sensed my aunt and uncle watching me from the kitchen window, and hoped that this was what other boys did in the snow. But I had to remind myself that this wet, cloggy stuff was what I had seen pictured on Christmas cards.

Passing the beechwood, I glanced up at the trees. The evergreen shrubs of the garden had shrunk to my aunt's woolly tea-cosies (she made them for orphans), but the trees were as finely spun as spiders' webs. My aunt then decided that I was muddying the lawn (which I was), and could only play on the paved part by the back door. This reminded me of the yard after Augustina had plucked a hen for supper, though the iron smell of the snow put a wall between me and that picture. It had all gone by the morning, and everything was crying. It made me think again of what Quiri had said when he'd smeared my face with kaolin: without this, you will cry too much and for a long-long time.

Compared to snowfalls to come, it was pitiful, but for someone who had not climbed Mount Cameroon (like my father had) and seen the magic substance sprawled amongst the boulders of her peak, it was still a miraculous thing to recall, once vanished.

As were the frosts I had already seen, for they were even more like grieving. My mother had read me stories about the Frost Queen, and I was thrilled to see, one morning in late October, that she had breathed strongly upon the world. At first it looked as if everything had been turned to stone, but when I went outside, surprising myself with the air's sharpness, I saw how the frost coated only the top of each twig, or leaf, or post. It looked as if the frost had fallen from the sky, and that each thing was staying absolutely still under it, waiting for the mortal danger to pass.

I wanted to keep watch that night and see it fall – perhaps from the Frost Queen's very mouth – but my uncle told me that I wouldn't see a sausage.

'I don't want to see a sausage,' I replied. 'I want to see the frost fall.'

My aunt told me that if I went on like that, I wouldn't get anywhere in life. But my uncle was chuckling as she was saying this.

I went out again after lunch. It was still frosty where the shadows stayed. I found my mother's pair of gardening gloves on the coal bunker, and tried to put them on, but they were as hard as the hands of the plaster nymph in the drawing-room. My breath smoked and my cheeks tingled. I took my glove off and felt them: my cheeks had shrivelled up, like old apples.

I wandered on to the middle of the lawn, muttering to myself as usual. I was Wolfe at the head of the Louisbourg Grenadiers, charging the French line. A shot had just shattered my wrist when there was a shout from the house. My aunt appeared in the doorway.

'Hugh, off that lawn at once!'

Maybe, I thought, the lawn was a frozen lake I might suddenly fall through. I walked back to the house carefully.

'Even your uncle is forbidden to walk across the grass in frost,' she said. 'It breaks the blades. Just think of it as brittle, Hugh.'

'What's brittle mean?'

'Oh, like glass.'

She must have been brittle because a year later she was dead. It was too long after my charm to make me connect the two.

One morning in January 1931, I scraped at the ice on my window and spotted a dark track of footprints curving over the frosted lawn, ending up in a huddle by the wire of the wildwood. My uncle was in there, I thought, and my aunt is not here to scold him for breaking the grass. The funeral had taken place, in Ulverton, just after Christmas. I had been a boarder at Flytings Preparatory School only a year, but it seemed like ten. I was sent to Flytings for the start of the Easter term, joining the school a term late. I had no idea that schools and farms had the same year; it took two weeks for me to discover this.

Flytings was very like my uncle's house, only bigger and filled with boys. A term had made them very sure of themselves. I stumbled about and didn't know where anything was or what any names meant, and couldn't understand why everyone else knew so much, so quickly. Only a few had been tutored at home until now. There were several boys in my year from the British Colonies, but the ones whose fathers worked in West or Central Africa had not been out at all. Either they had boarded at a nearby Pre-Preparatory from the age of four or lived with relatives. The last were like me, I realised with a shock. One, whose father was an officer in Kano, had lived with his mother in his grandmother's big house in Dorset. This upset me.

The whole year passed in that place like the onset of a fever that never quite takes hold. I did not cry once. I never tried to run away, either. My mark was discovered on the second day, but I said that I had sailed the seven seas as a cabin boy, and been tattooed like a stevedore, in Malabar. Incredibly, all the boys around me believed this was true. After that, I had to tell them a tale of my sea-dog days every night in the dormitory. This earned me some respect, but not very much: I was still bullied rather badly. If the story wasn't exciting enough, I was turned out of my bed and hit with pillows. My fetish packet was kept in the inside pocket of my jacket, and I was terrified that that would be discovered too, one day.

It was very difficult to be alone long enough to make charms or curses; even the lavatories had no doors on them, and walking by yourself in the grounds was not allowed. But when one of the worst bullies died of pleurisy one weekend, very suddenly, I felt rather guilty.

Some of the teachers had been in the trenches, like my uncle; these were either very nice or very nasty, but nothing in between. There was one who was a poet, and felt our bottoms in a funny way when we went up to his desk to have our books marked. He was soft and friendly, and apart from the bottoms thing and the fact that he picked his nose while he told us about the Latin poets, I liked him. Our headmaster was a war hero, one Captain Dene, a very tall man with a trembling head. One day a vice-captain gave me my shoes, which I had left out of their locker, and told me to see Dene after Tea. I had had this dream, ever since my arrival, that I would be called to see the headmaster one day and be told that my mother was missing me so much that I could go back to Africa immediately. I was so excited I ran the wrong way in the rugger match that afternoon.

There was a queue outside his study, and I joined it. None of us talked because a vice-captain was watching us. Boys went in, one by one, and came out biting their lips, their faces crumpling. I could hear a faint, light noise through the door as I edged closer, like a sheet of paper being torn top to bottom. I did not quite link this to the idea of beatings – probably because I knew I was not about to be beaten, even though no one was asked to see Dene after Tea for any other reason.

When I went in, Dene didn't say anything about my mother or say anything at all. He was looking at three sticks one beneath the other on the wall, and whistling. This whistling was the sign that Dene was 'on the warpath'. It was always five notes long and sounded like the signals on the short-wave of a wireless. I thought: the three sticks are the three canes the chaps all talk about, that draw blood. He chose the thinnest cane. It was of green bamboo, like the bamboo in the forest in Africa. Quiri made sticks from it, too.

When I came out, I had to stand for the rest of the day, hiding my waddle as best I could. One of the boys said, 'What did Dismal want?'

'It was about my mother, who's in Africa,' I said.

'Has she copped it? Mine has, years ago.'

'No,' I replied, thinking quickly. 'She wanted to know whether I had enough tooth powder.'

The boy found this very funny, and told everyone else. That night I was surprised to find my tooth-powder bottle empty. When I pulled back my sheet and blankets, there were a lot of sniggers from the other beds. The tooth powder was spread like snow over the bottom sheet. Instead of being immediately angry, I was immediately worried: my aunt had told me that unless I used tooth powder on my teeth every day, they would rot and drop out, one by one.

I never mentioned these things in my letter home. We were

86

allowed to write once a fortnight. I always said things were jolly fine, and hoped things were jolly fine in Bamakum, too.

My mother returned on leave a little later than she had done when with me, the year before. The thought of seeing her soon had made me very nervous; I'd ticked off the days of school in my *Schoolboy's Pocket Diary 1930*, and now, at Uncle Edward's, I ticked off the days to her arrival. When there were only fourteen left, at the beginning of July, I sailed in my mind past the long African coast, watching its forest and twinkling bays dwindle to one long beach of white sand – leaving the Canaries behind, leaving Casablanca, leaving Lisbon for the final choppy stretch past Land's End towards the port of Liverpool. This is how I got to sleep each night.

When there was only one day left I disembarked and took the London train, clutching my fetish packet in its dry, brittle banana leaves and willing my mother's safety and happiness.

I knew all the times of the rickety branch-line train to Fogbourne. We waited on the platform in front of a poster for Sutton's Seeds, my uncle and aunt and myself lined up like the three steel milk churns next to us. I thought how funny this must look. The train was late; if it hadn't been for the old porter with his newspaper and trolley at the other end of the platform, I might have believed it was not coming at all.

Too anxious to stay put, I wandered off to look at the red traction engine parked in the station's yard. Stan and his trap were waiting, too, next to my uncle's new Lanchester. Stan was snoring across the passengers' seat. It was hot. I wished I could go to sleep like Stan. Then I heard the signal on the other side of the tracks clack into a new position. There was a distant hoot, and the sky was smudged with smoke above the trees on the edge of the cornfield next to the station.

I ran back just before the train came into view, the rails clicking and singing and telling us all how merry life is when things you expect come. And it did come, black and huge around the bend, clacking and whistling far too fast to stop. There was a big hiss and a cloud of steam, and the carriage slowed to a halt with its last door opposite us.

The stationmaster strolled up and opened this door. An old lady

87

in a flowery hairnet stepped down, helped by the stationmaster. This was not my mother. Then another door opened, and an elegant man with a cane and a small leather case stepped down, looking about him as if expecting someone. A woman came running through on to the platform, in tears, and hugged the man.

'There there,' I heard him say, 'there there, Marjorie.'

Then just when I was looking at this queer sad couple walking away, supporting each other and talking, my mother must have appeared, for my uncle said, 'Here we are!'

When I looked, she was already standing on the platform, at the engine end of the carriage. It was as if she had not stepped down, but had always been there. She waved to us in a funny way, polishing the air in front of her face. We started to walk towards her. The porter was unloading some cases I recognised. I was between my aunt and uncle, having to walk fast to keep up with their grown-up pace.

'Hello, all,' said my mother.

She looked very tired, and had tiny wrinkles around her eyes; I didn't remember these from last year. She kissed my aunt and uncle on the cheek, and then bent down and put her hand around the back of my head. I don't know whether she meant to feel my mark, but feel it she did, and it made her face go like the field at the back of the garden when a wind darkens the corn for a moment.

Then she smiled again, through her tiredness. There were tiny black dots on her forehead, which I knew were smuts from the train. She smelt very much of trains and a little bit of eau de Cologne and also of unhygienic armpits.

'Hello, darling,' she said. 'Have you been a good boy?'

I thought of the beating, and blushed. Africa lay over her skin like a veil. Even when she kissed me on the cheek, the veil stayed, and my Englishry couldn't break through it.

'Was it ghastly?' boomed my uncle.

Was what ghastly?

We walked over to the car as my mother peeled off her white gloves and told us about the journey. Much of it went over my head, to do with times and people in London I hadn't heard of. Stan and the trap had gone. The traction engine was still there, awaiting someone's orders. The queer sad couple had gone, too. My mother's cases were belted to the back of the car, and the box strapped on to the roof.

We drove back very slowly, my mother in the front with my uncle. This disappointed me: I wanted her in the back with me. Instead I had my ailing aunt, sucking Altoid Mints for her carsickness. Perhaps because she always sucked them for this purpose, their sharp, sweet smell made me feel carsick. A certain bend beyond Fogbourne lifted this sickness into my throat. I gripped the handle and started to wind the window down.

'No, dear,' said my aunt in my ear, 'your mother's been in the tropics.'

The car swayed like a ship with its heavy load, and my aunt's mints made the air thick. I leaned my cheek against the glass and tried to catch a draught coming from a round ventilator in the front. I was stifling, breaking out in a sweat, and my uncle had his pipe in his mouth, puffing hard. The mint and the smoke and the leather of the seats, and something stale from my mother's coat in front of me, made me feel even sicker than did the swaying motion of the car. I couldn't believe my horrible luck. I had never noticed the zigzag weave in the bristly carpet between me and my mother's seat before. I couldn't stop even though my aunt was yelping and I was saying *sorry, sorry.*

'Oh, how disgusting,' shouted my aunt.

The doors were opened and my mother helped me out, though my body was still in spasms. My uncle and aunt were cross. The fact that they were cross, and I was weeping with humiliation into my mother's handkerchief, made her take my side. I had been sick on the route between Fogbourne and Ulverton, just where it goes up on to a very bare ridge. My mother and aunt and uncle were being cross with each other in the middle of the dusty road, the car's cut-off engine ticking as the sun beat down. The downs rolled away on each side, dotted with sheep but shadeless. A lark sang high up, directly above us. One of the problems was that there was no water in the car to drink, only water for the car's radiator, which I had once tested secretly in the garage and spat out.

'You were sick in Father's car once, if you remember, Edward.'

'He didn't have a car until 1914.'

'Well, you were sick in something – I remember it all over my shoes.'

My aunt said, 'He could have said. If only he'd said. What a welcome.'

'Oh, don't fuss on my account, please,' said my mother. 'I am his mother, after all.'

There was a brief silence. Flies buzzed.

'Attracting attention to himself, yes,' said my aunt.

I wandered off up the road. The sun was pleasant, away from the petrol and oil and sick smells of the car, and those awful voices. There were crickets singing in the grass. I wondered whether I could trap one and keep it as a pet. I heard someone coming up behind me. There was a hand on my shoulder. My mother's face appeared above me, then dropped down to mine.

'Don't worry at all, Hugh,' she said. 'But at least take off your shoes and trousers.'

She sounded even tireder than on the station platform, but her cheeks were red. I took off my shoes and trousers by the car while my uncle's bottom protruded from the door on my aunt's side. He was settling some oily rags on the carpet. Aunt Joy had her pinched look on, or perhaps she was just sucking hard on a mint.

'I'd walk if we were nearer,' she murmured, as if only to my uncle, who was emerging with a grunt.

'Oh, do pipe down,' he snapped, his face sweaty and strained, wiping his hands on his handkerchief. 'For God's sake, pipe down.'

As I stared at the footprints across the frosty lawn some six months later, I thought of those words of my uncle's. *Oh, do pipe down.* She had certainly piped down now. Well, we all piped down, eventually. The only mystery was when, and where. (That was – is – the mystery of my mother, of course.)

'Have you been a good boy, Hugh?'

That question again. I thought of the rippled *Do Nots* on the doors in our house, and of Mosea's pictures of Jesus in her room, straining to be released from their pins. But being good in Africa was not the same as being good in England.

We were sitting in deckchairs on the lawn; at least, my mother was sitting in one – I was perched on the end of the other, as I didn't like the way deckchairs hugged you and made it hard to jump up. I was forbidden to sit on the grass, and no one had brought out a rug. It was the second day of my mother's leave. I was sure that the tiredness covering her would soon melt away. I considered her question, staring at the grass. Even from here, we could hear the tick-tock of Uncle Edward's excavation up on the ridge, at the bottom of one of the mounds. It made me think of Long John Silver, of course, though Uncle Edward's aim was not treasure. He was a friend of Mr Keiller's, who was a well-known archaeologist in the area and had come to Sunday lunch with us a few times. Mr Keiller had shown us an object so like the amulet fetish I had exchanged for the galago that I blushed with shame. It too was shaped like an hourglass, if a little fatter and made of chalk.

'Now there's a mystery,' he'd said. 'No perforations, so it wasn't hung.'

My uncle had turned it over in his hands, but my aunt had tutted.

'Not at the table,' she said, 'not while we're eating, Mr Keiller.'

She'd said this as she might have said it to me, only this time she was smiling, and Mr Keiller smiled back, saying how sorry he was to be a bad boy, tucking once more into his roast beef and potatoes. I thought of this incident now, and how my uncle had told off my aunt after the famous archaeologist had gone: 'How dare you treat such a distinguished man so,' he'd shouted, 'he's not Hugh, y'know.'

'Have you been a good boy, darling?' said my mother again, in just the same way, as if I hadn't heard the first time.

'Yes,' I said.

'And are you happy, with Aunt Joy and Uncle Edward?'

I continued staring at the grass. My mother was asking these questions in a very tired voice. The voyage had been long and there had been a storm off the Canaries. Aunt Joy had suggested (but in a firm voice) that I didn't 'bother' my mother too much for the first few days. 'You don't want to make her ill, do you?'

No, I didn't. If I told my mother the truth, she might 'have a turn'. It would certainly bother her. I was so deeply unhappy, especially at Flytings, that if the truth broke surface it would be as horrible and bothersome as the Big Beef itself.

'I'm perfectly happy,' I replied. 'It's all quite jolly. Especially now you're here.'

My mother smiled, running her forefinger over her forehead. I knew, then, that she didn't believe me about being happy.

'It's a simply lovely place to grow up,' she said. 'And Aunt Joy always wanted children.'

'She can have her own.'

'None arrived,' she said, softly. 'No one knows why. It sometimes happens.'

I blinked quickly at the trees, which were gusting slightly, to turn them into a film. I was making a film of Unknown Africa, in the footsteps of Cherry Kearton. My Aunt-who-couldn't-have-babies reckoned I had a 'tick' – but I had never heard of a tick that made one blink, and she never tried to remove it as I'd had them removed from my scalp at home.

'Mother,' I said, 'how's Quiri?'

She was blinking now.

'Oh,' she said, 'jolly fine, I'm sure.'

I wanted her to say, 'He sends his love,' but she didn't. Perhaps he'd forgotten about me.

She had closed her eyes and very soon, her face full in the sun, her mouth opening slightly so that the bottom lip shone, she 'dropped off'. I moved the parasol, with some difficulty, to shade her – feeling naughty because my uncle said that the sunlight was very good for you, like water full of vitamins. I had always been taught to fear it, and was glad when my mother and I were in the parasol's shade. I desperately wanted to lay my head in her lap; the last time I had done this was when my father took a photograph of us both on the veranda in Bamakum.

I looked anxiously towards the house. It looked more than ever as my uncle described it: 'A cliff of granite pretending to be a home.' The parts my uncle had added on after the war, with black beams and white plaster and leaded windows, which he called 'Shakespearean', looked as if they were the bullied servant of the central block. This bulged out either side of the front door and central windows in two big bays that went all the way up to the roof, covering all angles of attack. Always, when I looked at the house from the garden, I imagined my aunt to be looking out at me. Even after she was dead. Only in the wood did I feel safe and unwatched. I would imagine the house to be Mordred's castle, and lay siege to it, or charge it on my white charger, firing arrows with rubber suckers on the ends. My uncle took no notice or laughed and said I was so knock-kneed it must be rickets, and my aunt's spirit was too feeble to hurt me.

Now, with my mother breathing gently beside me on this sunny lawn, the house seemed to be bearing down upon us like a big tank. It was an extremely cold house, even in summer, and my aunt was never seen inside without fingerless mittens at this time. Then I remembered that she was up with my uncle at the excavation, for she was keen on old things, and was very excited when he had returned a few days before with an amber bead.

I laid my head on my mother's lap and she stirred.

'No, James,' she murmured.

I kept very still, in a rather uncomfortable position against her legs, my own curled on the grass, wondering why she had said my father's name. After some time, during which I too dropped off, I heard voices from the wood, and broke away from my mother's lap.

'What have you been up to?' cried my aunt, coming up to us over the lawn. 'Your face!'

I felt it: it didn't seem very different. My mother was waking up.

'We mustn't tire her out, now,' said my aunt.

'I'm all right,' said my mother. 'I'm not an invalid.'

My aunt stiffened, because she often called herself an invalid, but my mother didn't know that.

'Did you find anything?' my mother asked.

My aunt waved a small cloth bag in front of her face, like the conjuror at the village hall. 'Pottery and bones,' she said. 'Pottery and bones. Nothing older than Romano-British, *as yet*.' She said 'as yet' as if she was warning us to behave. Her nose was burned red.

There was something I didn't like about my uncle's latest

hobby. The previous week I had watched him cutting into the turf around the tumulus, where the ground dipped slightly, and had stood in the wrong place when he'd tried to peel it off. He called this 'penetrating the turf line', but it reminded me of the sick man who'd walked all the way to my mother's 'hospital' with flaps of skin hanging from his legs, the flesh white and full of maggots. The sods of turf were over a foot thick and very heavy, but I managed to heap them up to one side, their grit painful under my nails. I wasn't allowed to use a trowel, so I sat on the slope of the mound above the ditch and watched my uncle's bent back, shielding my eyes against the glare off the chalk.

It seemed a very dull and slow thing, archaeology. He scraped away for ages and then scooped the little pile of chalk he'd made into cloth bags. He took these back at lunchtime and spent the afternoon in the garden 'riddling' them through a wide sieve, as they riddled corn in the little tumbledown farm at the end of Maddle Lane. He'd set up a hose to wash the finds, and the tiny stream snaked over the lawn and made mud patches which upset my aunt.

The bits of bone and pottery were like something off one of the mixens in the village, but I accompanied my uncle each morning in the hope of finding treasure. The farmer who owned the field, called Jack Jennet, would pass by with the same hope; my uncle had already paid him something for the use of the field, though the crop had not been touched, and had had to promise him a bit of the treasure if any were found.

This was odd, because my uncle had said that he wasn't looking for treasure, only a pig, a ram, and an ox.

I had walked on my own once, in the spring, to the tumuli, with a pack of Bovril sandwiches and a Thermos. It had taken some time because I was Jack McLaren, sailing up the coast of Cape York desperately hunting for a site for his palm plantation. The two tumuli were Simpson's Bay, its beach just where my uncle was now cutting long white scars – and my aboriginal friends were not happy about it. I had to play this game to make the place exciting: the fact that the bits of rubbish he called 'finds' were very old did not make them magical. In fact, I was glad I felt nothing for them, for the little bones reminded me of Mr

94

Hargreaves on his way to becoming Sir Steggie, and at any moment I expected a fob-watch to be found. The bones were mainly of deer, however, and the Romans lived before fob-watches were invented.

My mother and I packed up the deckchairs and followed my aunt inside, as the gusts had dragged a large cloud in front of the sun. I checked my face in the mirror: there were red ripples all down one side where it had been pressed against the folds of my mother's dress. If they stayed, I would look like the boys in the villages we had visited on the way to the lake, except that there were no circles or waves, nothing carved carefully by a knife. But the patterns would not stay: as I touched them, they already seemed to be fading. I thought: if Quiri were here, he might be able to tell me what they meant; according to him, all marks that the days and nights made on your body were like words, and said things, even if they vanished after a few minutes.

My aunt crossed the hallway and saw me.

'Admiring yourself, Hugh?' she said.

She disappeared into the kitchen with a chuckle and I heard her and my mother talking. I looked at my hands. The lines on my face looked like the lines on my hands. I thought of the story Quiri had told me many times, which his mother had also told him many times, for it was also her favourite story. It was the story of how the human race came to have lines on its hands. I didn't like the story, because it was mysterious and very sad when you thought it was going to be funny – you felt tricked each time, and each time, when it came to an end, you looked at your own hands. You couldn't help it. One day, I would tell it to someone in England. Maybe even at school, in the dormitory, I would tell them that one instead of the wild yarns they forced me to spin.

My name was being called. It was tea with the rest of the special cream cake my mother had bought in London, on her way down. My aunt spread newspaper at one end of the kitchen table and we admired the 'bits and bobs', as my mother called them. They were the bigger bits, and on one of the 'sherds' there was a wavy pattern. My aunt became very excited when she saw a tiny blue bead in the crumbs of earth, but it turned out to be a hundred and thousand.

95

'You didn't do that deliberately, did you, Hugh?' said my aunt, in a playful but annoyed way.

'No,' I replied.

'No what?' said my mother.

'No, thank you.'

They both found this funny, but I had been daydreaming.

'Manners maketh man,' said my aunt.

I wiped cream from the corners of my mouth with my hand.

'It's not for want of trying,' she added, to my mother.

My mother said she had to go and unpack her last things, and have a little nap. I went off to play and came back into the kitchen when the Indian gong rang, for supper. My mother was there, looking better; she and my aunt had a glass of sherry each, while I ate my buttered egg.

My uncle appeared at the outside door, with several bags of finds.

'Ah, cake,' he said. 'Jolly good. Joy always makes ours.'

It had been left out for him, with a colander over it. He wiped his hands on his trousers and ate the last slice in three mouthfuls standing up, sucking the cream off his dirty fingers. My aunt tutted at the crumbs on the floor.

'I'll sweep them up,' I said.

'Oh, Huggins,' said my mother.

I took the dustpan and brush off their hooks in the scullery and swept up the crumbs around my uncle's boots.

'Thank you very much, most obliged,' said my uncle, in what my aunt called his 'caustic soda voice'.

'Is this cheek,' my aunt asked, 'or is it willing?'

I stood up. 'What do you mean?' I said.

'I'm sure it's willing,' said my mother. 'I used to encourage this sort of thing. It doesn't do to rely totally on servants.'

'We don't,' said my aunt.

'I didn't say you did, Joy.'

'No, but Hugh has not been noted for his helpful ways before.'

I looked at my aunt, who was smiling horribly, and wished her in Hades (we'd started Ancient Greek at school).

'Throw the crumbs on the lawn, Hugh,' she said. 'There was a coal tit there this morning.'

'I hope you've been helpful, Hugh,' said my mother.

I left the room. My uncle snorted. 'You've missed one there, old boy,' he shouted after me.

I jerked the dustpan on to the grass but most of the crumbs fell on my shoes, caught in the laces and lace-holes. An evening cool was just emerging from the lawn, and the sun was tangled in the lowest branches. My face was burning: I must have played about on the lawn too long, but my uncle would approve. It was nice to stand out here for a few moments, knowing that my mother was behind me, in the kitchen. It was almost more delicious than actually being with her, because when I was with her it was too real.

I went back inside. My uncle was explaining why he was grumpy: he had found terrifically old stuff mixed up with quite old stuff. The broken bits of pottery looked all the same to me, spread out on the table, but he explained that the levels had got mixed up over time, one sinking into another, burrowed by worms and rain and badgers and rabbits, so that nothing was clear, and hundreds or even thousands of years were all muddled together.

I thought of the hundreds and thousands on the cake, when he said that, mixing with real amber beads. I noticed that his hands were no longer white, but dark, as if he was now digging into earth.

'You should come to Africa,' said my mother.

She poured me a glass of milk. It was as warm as when I'd collected it from the Jennets' farm this morning, but only because it had been boiled earlier.

'No, thank you,' said my aunt.

'Talking of times being mixed up,' my mother went on.

My uncle grunted. 'I thought it all broke down out there. Into one great rotting compost, what? Trees, masks, ju-ju huts, district officers –' He gave a barking laugh, which was a sign that he had just made a joke.

I didn't like the idea of my father becoming compost. (The compost heap in the garden smelt of old fruit, and was teeming with woodlice, creatures which reminded me of Sir Steggie.) My uncle always made this sort of joke when he was in a bad mood. I bit into my bread and was pleased to see that Herbert E. Standing stayed on guard by the door, pale and glimmering in his cricketing togs beyond my aunt's head.

'Do wash your hands, Edward,' said my aunt. 'The boy's eating.'

'You mean Hugh,' laughed my mother.

It wasn't a real laugh, it was to cover up the crossness – which still came through, just as the fish taste of cod-liver oil came through the square of chocolate I was allowed after it.

'There isn't any other boy in the room,' my aunt replied. 'Unless you regard dear Edward as a boy, which I quite frequently do. *A little boy*,' she added, in a hoarse whisper.

From the way she was blinking, I knew that she had had 'a touch too much'. (I was fairly sure that this referred to sherry but had never seen her sip more than her 'thimbleful'.) My uncle brought his dirty hands down on to the table. He had very large hands, and my glass rocked enough to ruin my experiment, which was to see how much of the inside of the glass I could keep clear of milk. This meant drinking from the same spot every time and putting the glass down very carefully, so that the milk's film was kept to the area under my lips, like a white cloth being drawn up.

'Sometimes,' said my uncle, in a voice I had expected to be loud, but wasn't, 'I regret the passing from this world of the practice of human sacrifice.'

'It hasn't quite passed,' said my mother, gaily. 'Not quite.'

My uncle stopped glaring at my aunt and blinked at my mother, as if she had slapped him on the cheek, or tweaked his beard (he was starting to grow it at this time). Perhaps this was something to do with the fact that she had spoken gaily when his own voice had been like a big leopard prowling through the bush.

'It hasn't?' said my uncle, frowning.

'Listen,' said my mother, 'I won't go into details here, but suffice to say that lycanthropy is alive and well, and so is the use of the *borfima*.'

'What the blazes is a *borfima*?' my uncle asked. 'And for the benefit of my dear wife, you might explain lycanthropy, too.'

He was smiling now, but not because he was happy. Aunt Joy

98

said, 'I know perfectly well what lycanthropy means, Edward. A lot of bilge about werewolves.'

'Leopards, in this case,' said my mother, making me jump in my chair. 'I will explain *borfima* when certain petysonolee.'

Whenever my mother said 'petysonolee', or a similar nonsense word, with her mouth going in and out, it was what people said in France, and was a way of talking outside me. As a result, I was looking forward to visiting France.

'Very well, message taken,' said my uncle. He went to the sink to wash his hands.

'Not in the sink, Edward,' said my aunt.

Surprisingly, he went off to the bathroom without saying a word, looking thoughtful. But then he always did what Aunt Joy told him to do, in the end.

He came back, scrubbed and changed, with a whisky in his hand. My mother nodded to me at the same time as my aunt did, which made my aunt giggle in a rather painfully high-pitched way, like a bat squeak. I drained the cocoa I'd made myself, pecked my aunt and uncle goodnight and kissed my mother (not that I defined the difference as such, it was an instinctive thing), closed the kitchen door behind me, and pretended to mount the stairs. The stairs were wooden, wide and creaky, and couldn't be descended even on tiptoe without announcing someone's presence. So I remained on the bottom stair and walked on the spot, carefully fading out my steps until the right number had been reached.

The keyhole in the kitchen door was large enough for sound-waves to travel through unimpeded, and once my ear was settled against its chill iron frame, I might as well have been in the room.

I knew this word *borfima*. I had reckoned it was a horrible illness, which was boring, because there were so many of those. It had cropped up in conversations between my father and people like Charlie Moore, but was always followed by a French word and a glance at me. I believed it had something to do with the Leopard Society, too.

There was some mumbling, and the sound of a glass being set down, then: 'Sierra Leone,' said my mother, as if in reply to someone. 'Actually, it's a bundle, a little package of things, a sort of medicine.'

'A medicine or a fetish?' came from my aunt.

'Fetishes are medicines of a sort, dear,' said my uncle, sounding weary. 'The Enos of the spirit world.'

His barking laugh, a mumble from my aunt, then my mother's voice again: 'Now hold on tight. Here's the official recipe, known right across equatorial Africa.'

There was then a strange, wavery sound, and I momentarily changed my ear for my eye; in the egg timer shape of the keyhole my mother was waving her hands about, like she did when she danced to her jazz records. I listened again, wincing at the cold of the metal on my ear: '. . . point of needle, grain of rice; blood of cockerel, small crow's feather; dust of trampled ground and cockerel's crop; skin of human hand and bit of human liver; portion of testicle and strip of cloth from menstruating woman –'

'Good God!' came from my aunt.

'Not finished yet,' said my mother.

'Go on, go on,' cried my uncle. 'Eye of newt and baby's wotsit, I suppose.'

There was a little pause.

'You've put me off,' said my mother, in a normal voice. 'I can't think. Have I mentioned the skin? From the palm, the sole of the foot, and the forehead. Then the whole lot is wrapped in leaves and anointed periodically with oil.'

'Palm oil,' said my uncle.

'No,' said my mother, 'oil boiled from the fat of a human intestine.'

'Whose, might we ask?' said my uncle, jovially.

'This is the important bit,' said my mother.

'Oh crikey,' said my aunt.

'You are,' my mother went on, 'a handsome boy or pretty maiden strolling back from school, when the bushes stir and out leap what look like leopards. But these leopards have human faces above their spots, and their claws are three-pronged knives. Your only consolation is that none of you will be wasted.'

'Good grief,' said my aunt again, after a pause; 'I mean, how can you bear to live there?'

'Fascinating,' said my uncle, 'quite fascinating.'

'*Borfimas* are outlawed, of course,' my mother went on. 'As are leopard-skin costumes and three-pronged knives and membership of anything resembling a Leopard Society. About twenty years ago it got particularly out of hand, and a Special Commission was sent out from England. They hung nearly a hundred leopard men.'

There was a long silence, in which I could only hear my own heart beating, exactly as Jim Hawkins's did behind the apple barrel on the ship.

'And what is the point of all this savagery, all this awfulness?' said my aunt.

I heard my uncle murmur something.

'Vital Force, my foot!' my aunt cried. 'It's superstition and savagery!'

My uncle was very keen on this Vital Force. His excavation was something to do with it. (I had recently shown my uncle an advertisement for rhubarb tonic, in which Vital Force was also promised, but he'd only looked cross.)

'If you carry the package around with you, it makes you very powerful and rich,' said my mother. 'Everyone goes in fear of you, in case you use it against them. However, if the oil goes off, or isn't replenished, the *borfima* will turn against the owner and destroy him.'

'How do you know all this?' asked my aunt, in a suspicious way.

My mother made a noise that might have been a chuckle. 'Oh, we keep our ears to the ground. And there are books, Joy. *Human Leopards*, for instance, by one of the Special Commission chaps. I forget his name. And quite a bit is being done in the field by ethnographers – you know, earnest young men in round glasses with dog-eared copies of the *Golden Bough* –'

'No,' my aunt insisted, 'I mean why should you *need* to know all this, my dear Charlotte?'

There was a short pause. The clock in the hallway was tutting at me. My neck was stiff. My ear felt as if it had frozen to the keyhole. But I didn't want to move an inch until the answer had come.

'A few months ago,' my mother said, so quietly that I was

hurting my ear to catch her words, 'I had a patient with a frightfully ripped-up foot, from a village not very far away. When I asked him how he'd come by such a nasty injury, he said that he'd caught it in a trap. What kind of trap? I enquired. A leopard trap, he replied: it caught my paw and when I pulled it out the pad was left dangling, Missus Medicine.'

Another pause. I felt slightly sick, and wanted to go to bed.

'Lycanthropy, dear,' said my uncle.

My aunt must have been looking puzzled. I heard a glass being set down on the table and the scrape of a chair. Looking through the keyhole, I saw the big buckle on my aunt's skirt. I made for the nearest door, which led down to the cellar. The kitchen door opened as I was closing the cellar door, and I stood trembling in the darkness for a few minutes, until the stairs had finished thumping and creaking.

The darkness behind me, down the stone steps, was terrible. Leopard men crouched with iron claws, waiting for me to move, while Herbert E. Standing glimmered only fitfully between, like the faulty electric lamp by the bus-stop on the lane. I knew, then, as one does know these things, that Sir Steggie was in England, making for this house. I had no fetish packet in my pocket; its crumbling form was under my pillow, where I most needed it. But when I thought of my fetish packet, I could only see the nightmarish stuff of a *borfima* – as I could only think, looking at the cross in the village church, of Benin's slaves hanging headless in a stink of blood. The cellar's invisible stairs were very steep, I knew that; I was not allowed on them for that very reason. There was a maid in the Vicarage who had died falling down the same sort of stairs. Cecil had told me, and he had seen her ghost in its pinny many times, moaning between the cobwebs and bottles of wine. She was there among the leopard men, now, holding a three-clawed knife and grinning. (Cellars were all the same, to her.)

I scrabbled for the latch and lifted it rather hastily.

'Wawa,' came from my mother through the unfastened kitchen door, as I tiptoed past it, 'wawa, wawa!'

She sounded as if she was conducting a voice exercise, which she did before singing along to the jazz records at home. Either that, or she was turning feverish and slightly mad. At least my uncle was laughing.

I crept up the stairs, using the edges. Safely in my own room, I realised that it was the same word my father would use when something bad happened, usually to his road. When the Bean 'packed up', he stood next to it and shouted, 'Wawa, bloody wawa!' – which made the servants grin. I'd asked him one day why he said 'wawa', like a baby crying.

'It's an acronym, Hugh.'

'What's that?'

'It's when you only say the first letters of words. Look.' He wrote it out for me.

W A W A, or: West Africa Wins Again.

Why was my mother saying it, now? Why was she imitating my father like that? For she had caught his voice, the exact way in which he said it, like the foghorn on the Elder Dempster liner. I lay on my bed and flipped the torn piece of wallpaper next to my pillow, as I usually did when thinking. I desperately wanted my father here, suddenly. (He was to come in a fortnight's time.) I didn't like my uncle laughing with my mother, like that. It was queer, thinking of them as brother and sister, running and laughing across the lawn in a time so long ago it was before the war.

I fished under the pillow for my fetish packet and gingerly brought it out on to the sheet. I had, just before leaving, replaced the grease-paper with banana leaves. These were now yellow. Tarbuck's wafer, the green feather, the crocodile-shaped river pebble, the tiny bone, the palm leaf, and the penny stamp wiped against the chain of one of the BSA motorcycles – lacking human flesh or oil or blood, they seemed suddenly weak. I chewed some nail off my thumb and spat it in, then pondered on how best to draw blood. I had a wobbly front tooth: I could tie it by a thread to the door handle and yank it out, then spit bloodily on to the 'bits and bobs' that still smelt of home. Either that, or I would prick my finger – but that reminded me of the Wicked Queen in *Snow White*, and any decent amount would hurt. I covered up the fetishes again and held the packet in my hand, closing my eyelids and bringing back the picture I had taken on the track a year before, down to the last blot of shade and spot of light on leaf.

I had to be careful not to drop off and grip the packet tight in my dreams. Only the rubber band kept it from falling apart completely, the leaves were so brittle.

I ran out of the house when the horn blared. There was a strange man alighting from the car. He waved at me.

'Hello, Hugh!'

My mother was looking at him in the same way as I was, but holding his hands as if she was about to be swung round. 'Goodness gracious!' she was saying.

'It's your Pop!' cried the man. 'It's your dear Pa done come!'

It was my father, but he was thinner, and his moustache had vanished. Where his moustache had been was a shadow of grey skin and a boil just under the nose. When he kissed me, I missed the bristling hairs and their smell of pipe tobacco. My uncle pretended to be frightened and my aunt said how like Douglas Byng he looked, which made everyone laugh except my father.

'Was it because of the boil?' I said, showing him my room.

My father laughed.

'It's not a boil,' he said. 'It's a family heirloom. A minor defect in the perfect model.'

He winked at my mother, who stood in the door.

'Then it can't be perfect,' I pointed out.

My father tugged the knees of his trousers and rested his elbows on them, bending down to look at the thing I had made out of my uncle's old wooden bricks.

'It's the Maharajah's palace,' I explained. 'It's the biggest palace in the world.'

'Yes,' said my father, straightening up, 'your grandfather had just the same, or so I believe, somewhere under his enormous beard.'

'Then why haven't I got one?'

'Count yourself lucky, old boy,' said my father, gazing out of the window.

'Did you know about it, Mother?'

My mother grimaced. 'If I had, I would have run away screaming,' she said.

I turned to my father. He was grinning, so she couldn't have meant it.

'So why did you shave it all off?'

'Did you want me to leave half?'

I stamped my foot and a tower fell off the palace. 'Oh, you know what I mean!'

'Sometimes,' smiled my father, tousling my head, 'you feel like getting rid of things.'

I couldn't get used to him without his moustache, especially as he would scratch his top lip as if the itchiness was still there. Also, the photograph I had on my bedside table, taken in Victoria on one of our trips, was more familiar to me than the real face.

After a week at my uncle's, we drove off in the hired Riley to Bexhill, with a green fishing net sticking out of the rear window. We had a small suite of rooms in a large hotel overlooking the beach. The hotel smelt of warm rubber and gravy and was full of shrivelled-up little palm trees and pictures of aeroplanes. It had an alcove full of 'reading matter' and jigsaw puzzles, where I liked to sit on rainy days (there were many that summer) and devour numbers sometimes older than I was of the *Magnet*, *Tiger Tim's Weekly* and even *True Detective Mysteries*, while my mother helped me with a 500-piece of Scott on the *Terra Nova*, though half his face was missing.

On certain evenings my parents left me in order to 'jig about' downstairs. My mother would stand at the door of my boxroom in a long black dress and say, 'Don't run away, darling,' with a little wave, her green malachites swinging from her ears like bell-pulls, filling the room with her scent so that it stayed after she had gone.

The band's music came up as a tinny drone, over which the sea washed and the plumbing gurgled. I made the best of the disappointing shells and pebbles, as I did of the several occasions we drove off to a sandy beach. I was happy, but sad underneath; I wanted my parents as they were in Africa. Here, they were smaller and neater, with dry-looking skin, and had a lot of what my mother called 'silly ding-dongs' over my head. These were about things I could never find interesting enough to follow and there-fore understand. Sometimes I felt, looking at them both in their deckchairs on the crowded beach, that they were as real as the straw-stuffed figures one saw on the edges of fields at home that made the yams grow well. Those stretched-out bodies under their beach hats held the spirits of my mother and father, but the real gods were far away. As for the other people on the beach, I found them unpleasant looking and loud. Their red faces and scrawny legs poked from striped costumes as tight as the skin on a snake. I wanted the sea to wash the beach clean, and leave me alone with my parents, as I was on the beach at Victoria in what seemed like another life, where the ocean chased you across the black sand like a friend until the sun dropped, its round red ball lost again for a night in the furthest and deepest waters.

Sometimes, out there, we had done as the natives did, and stayed on the beach after dark. They lit candles in jam jars and tins, that flickered here and there as far as the eye could see; I thought of them as firefly kings, and the circle of natives their subjects. Ours was a bright paraffin lamp, its flame shivering in certain warm gusts that never quite put it out, and we had rugs to sit on.

We'd eat chicken legs with the Allinsons and watch the ocean showing its foam here and there when the moon came up. The rest of the sea was a gleam, or a solid darkness. Low moans of songs would waft from the scattered groups of natives, whose silhouettes crouched or waved their arms about or walked on the spot, as if they were cold. My mother said they were pagan services, but my father agreed with Mr Allinson that they were palm-wine 'binges' because he'd seen them still there at dawn, with empty bottles all around them, fast asleep.

'Maybe it's both,' I said.

The adults laughed: I count that as my first joke, though it was accidental (they didn't usually laugh when it wasn't).

My mother had bought me a little drum in the market; to her surprise, I took it with me wherever we went that holiday. Because the natives around their candles generally had a drum or two, and played it, so did I. I was quite good, I think, using all my fingers and the side of my thumb as I had seen the others do, weaving rhythms by ear.

Mr Allinson, who kept his Bombay bowler on even under the stars, said, 'Goodness gracious, he's gone bush.'

After he had drunk a lot, he told me to start drumming again and ordered Mrs Allinson to dance. She had also drunk quite a lot, but told him to shut up. I carried on drumming and Mr Allinson tried to drag Mrs Allinson into the middle. She started shrieking.

'Dance, woman, dance, blast you,' Mr Allinson was shouting.

My mother told me to stop drumming.

'Shall we go home?' said my father.

Mr Allinson's Bombay bowler rolled across the sand towards the sea and I ran after it. Looking back from the glimmering surf, I saw Mr and Mrs Allinson scuffling silently together like shadow puppets in front of the paraffin lamp. They might have been dancing, if there had been more than the surf booming.

The following morning, my drum's taut skin had a tear in it, as if someone had tried to poke around inside it. My mother said she would buy me another one, but she didn't. I continued to drum on any hard surface to hand, but I was banned from doing so at table, and the habit wore off. In Bexhill my mother bought me a tin whistle from a stall which sold buckets and spades and rubber balls whose bright colours came off on your hands on hot days. The tin whistle was very loud and piercing in the room, and someone in the hotel complained. I imagined this person as a tall, thin shadow at the end of a corridor, waving an arm.

Everybody else seemed to go back by train; we sped home, as we had come, in the hired Riley, because my father wanted to 'taste' the decent English roads. I had to sit very straight, with my head up, to see out of the window. The clouds of dust prickled my eyes. My parents were 'bickering' in the front. Flytings loomed after the weekend like an illness and was already invading my tummy.

However, I had a big plan for tonight: I would first of all beg my parents, on my knees in their bedroom, to take me home with them, on the steamer. I would work at my lessons very hard, By Correspondence (I had read advertisements about this in the paper). If they refused, then I'd become a stowaway. This was not yet more than a blurred idea, with the darkness of a big trunk in it and one picture of me popping up on deck, smiling sweetly, past the Canaries, the warm ocean wind blowing my hair into wild shapes.

As the countryside made my eyes flicker, leaning forward in the Riley, I gripped the seat's leather in front and thought about Captain E.R.G.R. Evans. I had just read his chapter in my *Heroes of Modern Adventure*, a big fat book my mother had tried to dissuade me from bringing on holiday. He and his two companions had marched fifteen hundred miles across the Antarctic through fierce blizzards, over endless ice, in freezing temperatures, pulling a four-hundred-pound sledge. Evans had scurvy, Lashly and Crean were at the limit of their endurance, they ate biscuits soaked in paraffin. I turned the rolling Hampshire hills into a wilderness of crevasses and broken ice, narrowing my eyes against its glare. Crean had left sick Evans with Lashly in the tent, walking the last leg alone to seek help. Eighteen hours without a halt, on the very edge of the world, after a march of hundreds of days, all alone with the endless horizon.

My parents' bickering turned into the far cries of penguins, and then into silence, as I slogged on, step by step, with only my shadow and the groan of my snowshoes in the ice to accompany me, towards whatever relief might lie in the midst of that mighty, frozen land. Something brushed my cheek: a sandwich, in my mother's fingers, at the end of my mother's arching arm, passed back without looking (to look back made her feel sick).

'Hugh? Are you there? Huggins?'

It was ham, which I detested. As I was taking it, the world moved backwards and the seat socked my face, tumbling me into the tight gully between the front and back. I was upset by the fact that the sandwich had fallen on to the carpet and opened, the ham slice flopping out next to my nose. Blood spotted the bread's whiteness. Blood was falling from my face. Some sort of pig had squealed – the sound had stopped, but I was only hearing it now.

'Bloody cat,' said my father, 'bloody damn cat.'

'Oh dear,' said my mother, 'oh dear.'

She sounded as though she was about to cry. We had all knocked our heads, and were all dripping blood from our noses.

My father had cut his lip on the steering wheel, my mother had struck some knobs on the dashboard. We got out of the car and saw the troughs made in the road by the tyres, their rubber smeared white where it had gripped. The car was facing the opposite verge, but there was nothing else coming. I'm afraid I was crying, though my nose didn't hurt that much. Perhaps it was the cat, which lay perfectly intact further up the road, as if it was sleeping off the shock.

My mother hugged me. Her dress smelt of the hotel room's mothballed cupboard. My father picked the cat up by the tail and laid it on the verge, slapping his hands afterwards as he always did when he'd carried out a difficult task. Then he dabbed his mouth again, and I looked up at the sky and dabbed my nose, and my mother dabbed hers and mine. My mother was giggling: it was apparently funny, the three of us dabbing our faces with hankies, even though we only had trees and hedges to watch us.

Then she said, 'Poor cat. It might have been adored by someone.'

I was careful to keep my mother's hankie, saying I still needed it. As soon as we got back to my uncle's, and the privacy of my own room, I cut out the bloody part and put its red circle, folded tightly, into my fetish packet.

'Give me the heart of a lion,' I murmured, 'and the cunning of a snake, and the astonishing pluck of Captain E.R.G.R. Evans.'

I was holding the packet against my chest. It seemed to move in my hands, like the brown monkey's paw jerking in the hand of its owner in a story I'd found in the hotel's bookshelves, and which had not left my head. Quiri had once told me that fetishes were not for wishing upon, unless you were a sorcerer. I also remembered that, unless the blood was replenished, the *borfima* turned against its owner, like the monkey's paw in the tale. I felt I had taken a wrong step, on which there was no going back.

I sat on the bed and put the fetish packet under the pillow. I felt more like Captain Scott than Captain Evans, and thought of that half face in the puzzle. Because the tablecloth underneath was red, it had looked as if Scott had been horribly injured. There was a soft knock at the door. I grunted, chin in my hands. My mother stepped in, with a clean set of pyjamas and a glass of milk.

'Sand between my toes, I've got sand between my toes,' she said, in a sing-song voice.

I decided to wait till tomorrow before pleading with my parents. The knock on my nose had given me a headache, and I was feeling suddenly weak and tired, as if the whole of the rest of my life from now would be a great burden, to be hauled over broken ice and around dark chasms of crevasses.

The next morning I asked my mother to cut my hair. It was thick with salt and took three washes to clear it. I was always worried when it came to having my hair cut, but no grown-up ever thought my mark was anything but dirt, or a bruise, or something inherited at birth. Mr Hassingham, the oily-haired barber in the village with a missing finger, thought it was dirt. He pointed it out to Aunt Joy, but my mother must have talked to her because she didn't say anything to me afterwards. The school barber, a bald man called Jardine who claimed to be related to the England cricketer, thought it was a 'birth defect'. He'd arrive on a silver bicycle with his scissors and things in an old Red Cross case on his back. I recall him very clearly because he was full of tales of the England side; I both liked him and feared him as his razor scraped at my nape.

On my first holiday back from Flytings, my aunt herself cut my hair. She used her sewing scissors in the kitchen, leaving the back just long enough, but sharpening it to a tail. Through the year, she'd collect the fallen curls in a paper bag; as soon as the first rosebud showed, she hung the curls in bunches from the stems, or threw them wildly over some of the bushes, to keep off the deer. It was my smell, she said. I helped her, rubbing my hair between my fingers so that it came alive, then scattering it over the budding shrub.

'Not that one, Hugh!' she'd shout. 'That's for display in the Hortics! They won't give me a prize if it's full of your off-cuts!'

These special shrubs she covered with a fine netting. My hair mostly worked, which was a shame; I wanted to see deer wandering through our garden at night, taking the blooms one by one in their mouths, leaving only a shivering stem. It excited me, to think of deer living nearby. I only saw them a couple of times, from my window very early in the morning – their tawny shadows leaping across the field's ploughed lines and up over the crest which just hid the Atlantic Ocean, not more and more of England.

It was as my mother was cutting my hair, after our return from Bexhill, that my uncle found what he was looking for.

The ditches he'd dug were quite large and long and deep by now: at the bottom and along the sides there were large chunks of chalk, a bit like rough-hewn Lotts Bricks, a set for giants. There were three of these ditches, curving round the tumulus like a bone necklace; they were, in fact, following the old ditch, which my uncle said had been filled in over the millennia. I was very proud of the little wooden sign at the head of each ditch, because I had painted the names on them, red on white: *Segment A, Segment B, Segment C.*

At first it was quite hard to see the skeletons, but my uncle pointed them out to us, in Segment B. My mother and my father stood either side of me on the edge. My scalp glowed and tingled from the wash and the cut, the feel of my mother's strong hands. My uncle was standing on a plank in the ditch, his sunburned face split into a wide grin.

'There's the pig,' he said, pointing, 'and here's the ram.'

I saw what I knew were ribs, mixed up together – and the twirly horn of a ram.

'Tell us more,' said my father.

'It's *Suovetaurilia!*' said my uncle, with his hands on his hips and his legs wide apart, sounding as if he was greeting somebody with that name whom he hadn't seen for a long time.

I thought that *Suovetaurilia* (which was obviously Latin) must be very well known, whatever it was. My father said, 'Something to do with a bull, Edward.'

My uncle said, 'What a fine classic you are, James! Never knew you had it in you! A sacrifice, my dear chaps! A pig, a ram, and an ox! The classic sacrifice of the classic world! Only here we're talking about pre-classic Britain!'

Every time my uncle said *classic*, it sounded like a pistol shot.

'Where's the ox?' my mother asked.

My uncle blinked a bit. 'You always have to have everything at once, don't you, Charlie?'

My mother laughed.

'Um, how many years before Rome, exactly?' asked my father.

My uncle waved his hand about. 'This is a primary level,' he said, 'so we're in the Neolithic – *early* Neolithic, what's more. A good two thousand years before all those awful bloody straight roads.'

'How on earth did you know it was there?' asked my mother, not telling him off for swearing.

'I didn't *know*, Charlotte, I *intuited*.'

'Oh, come on, Edward!'

'I did!'

He was bouncing his pendulum in his hand. It was like a large teardrop, and was made of crystal. I'd seen it go round and round, as fast as a carousel, under his stiff hand.

'Oh *that*!' snorted my mother, 'then they must be two-a-penny.'

I wanted to ask what 'intuited' meant, but there seemed to be an argument going on between my uncle and my mother, and my uncle was just opening his mouth again.

'But hang on,' my mother interrupted, 'you've found an awful lot of bones, you know. You were probably bound to find a sheep and a pig chucked in. Not counting the non-appearance of the ox.'

'In the same ditch? Buried whole? Just as in *Suovet* –'

'They probably roasted them on a spit, Edward.'

My uncle flung up his arms and made an angry sound, almost a roar: 'Sometimes, Charlotte my dear, I want to do to you what I used to do to you!'

My father turned to my mother, with a faint smile on his lips: 'What *did* he used to do to you, darling?'

My mother frowned. 'I can't think, James. He was such a sweet, kind, thoughtful brother to me.'

Then she smiled, as if she'd won. In the stories she'd told me of her childhood, Uncle Edward always seemed to be bashing her up, or teasing her, or playing practical jokes. I frowned, a bit puzzled. The sun came out and we had to shield our eyes from the glare off the chalk.

My uncle joined us up on the edge; I had wanted to go in, but for the moment nobody else was allowed to – not even my aunt. He was wiping his hands on a cloth. 'I've always wanted to find a sacrifice,' he said. 'A real one.'

'There are false ones, are there?' enquired my father.

My uncle stopped wiping his hands and looked at my father with a twisted-up face, which might have been because of the sun in his eyes. 'You know damn bloody well there are, James,' said my uncle. 'You and I were in the biggest one of the lot.'

He threw the cloth down and walked off, as if he was very annoyed. I looked up at my mother. Because I'd just had my hair cut, my neck and back were itching. She'd carried out the scissors by mistake: they were in her hand like a knife.

'The war,' she said, but so quietly I had to read her lips, as I had to do when she asked me for something across the tea table while my uncle or aunt were talking.

The following evening, I knocked on my parents' door while they were dressing for dinner. It was a special dinner, because it was the last one before their return home. I was in my pyjamas, and had already kissed them goodnight. My father was pulling on his new white trousers; he was very proud of them. We had gone together to Walters of Oxford at the beginning of his leave, where he had bought the trousers, a white dress coat, two spine pads, mosquito boots, and two hurricane lamps.

'Look at this,' he said to me.

Instead of buttons, the trousers had a 'zip', like I had seen on bags. He pulled the zip up to his waist button.

'Very American,' said my mother, making her eyebrows darker and thinner at the dressing-table mirror. 'I never thought I'd live to see the day, James.'

She turned to me, with only one eyebrow painted, like clowns had. 'Your father's a fuddy-duddy, you know, Hugh.'

'What's a fuddy-duddy?'

'Someone,' said my father, 'who doesn't like to throw out the best of the old for the worst of the new.'

I dropped on to my knees, as I had always planned to do. My mother was looking at my father's reflection in the mirror, and didn't notice.

'That's much too pat,' said my mother. 'New things scare you.

You're scared of things like jazz, you're scared of the wireless, you're scared of talking films –'

'Nonsense,' said my father, buttoning his dress shirt, 'it's a question of taste. Talking films are vulgar. I do not want to hear a fairy or an Emperor talk with an American accent or any other accent, for that matter. People talk too much, anyway, and mostly nonsense.'

He was taking his collar out of the drawer, breathing as if he'd just been running. 'Nothing scares me,' he went on, 'except the little man in round glasses on the Clapham omnibus, with his packet of weedkiller. And the smell of garlic.'

I opened my mouth, lifting my hands into the right position, flat together in front of my face.

'Why garlic?' laughed my mother.

My father, his shirt dangling over his trousers, leaned on my mother's chair and gazed at her in the mirror. Because I wanted to know why he was scared of garlic, I closed my mouth.

'Mustard gas,' he said, quietly. 'It blew over us while I was having my little stint in Flanders, before the blessings of Africa. The damn stuff smelt of garlic, and vice-versa.'

'Of course,' sighed my mother, 'you don't need to tell me.'

He kissed her on the cheek and stood up straight again.

'Hugh,' he said, in a different sort of voice, 'I expect you to be a good boy at school, and to write us once a week.'

He was looking up almost at the ceiling, attaching his collar stud. My mother was pressing a lipstick against her mouth. The room was puddled in light and full of a sweet, grown-up smell that normally started when I was in bed. I swallowed. I realised my hands had dropped and that I was sitting back on my heels.

'I'm not going,' I said, in a thin voice that was not really mine.

I was looking down at the nearest foot of their bed, poking out from under the green-and-orange coverlet. The foot was shaped like a claw, as if waiting to rip apart a passer-by.

'I always used to say that,' chuckled my father, unexpectedly. He was tying his tie, still looking up at the ceiling. 'Always used to say that, before the off.'

I could see him in the mirror, where his face looked skew-whiff beyond the back of my mother's head. This was swapped by her face with a bright-red mouth, and I looked away, surprised.

'Hugh,' said my mother, 'we've had a lovely time together. It won't be long –'

'Nine months,' I said.

'It goes very quickly, Hugh. For some children, it's two years or even more –'

'I want to go back –'

'Don't be ridiculous!' snorted my father.

My mother said 'Ssssh!', then: 'You're not unhappy at Flytings, are you?'

She looked both anxious and annoyed. I heard my father sigh, impatiently – perhaps because he had been told to shush. Or perhaps because of me. I wanted to leave the room, because my parents were not quite my parents. Perhaps a sorcerer had called their names from the side of the path. I stood up. Now I had a very strong desire to throw myself upon their bed, but their bed was spread with their clothes, wrapped in cellophane. My mother had bought a roll of cellophane in Oxford, to my great excitement. The man in Walters of Oxford had then told her that cellophane and Africa did not go well together, but she'd said that that was true of everything.

My mother stretched out her arm, so that her fingers rested on my elbow. The nails were very shiny, as if they were under cellophane as well.

'Hugh, you remember that little white girl called Primrose, whose parents ran the Mission Station on the road to Duala?' I nodded. (She had spent much of the party at the Allinsons' pulling my hair.) 'Well, she died of a fever at Christmas. Africa and white children do not go well together.'

'Like cellophane,' I murmured.

'What? Speak up,' said my father. 'I won't have things said under your breath.'

My father was not usually so short-tempered with me here, but perhaps that was because I had spent the holidays striving with all my might to be a very good boy.

'Like cellophane,' I said, louder.

'What?' my father snapped. His nose was still red and peeling, from our seaside holiday. His nose had never been burned like that in Africa, though when he'd had too much gin and was cross with everybody and everything, it looked as if it had been.

I found myself back in my bedroom, where I lay on the bed and tried to weep. I forced tears to come, as if I was squeezing my face like a lemon. The end of my visit to their bedroom was unclear in my head, as if I was seeing it all with my good eye shut. I had walked out and slammed the door, but between my father's 'What?' and my walking out there had been some other things said. Both my parents had talked at the same time, about school and duty and selfishness and fever, but my ears had gone deaf, filling with a kind of brown water.

It was better to keep things secret, I thought. It was better not to breathe a word of what you felt, because then it was always before and not after it, when it was already too late and Long John Silver and Israel Hands and George Merry and the rest were aboard, waiting to cut you down like pork.

Very bad news is broken in stages, however abruptly. I once heard a friend of my uncle's liken it to evolution, making a sort of nihilist joke. I was about fifteen when he said this: perhaps precociously, I ignored his nihilism and referred him to the beaten-up messenger in *Antony and Cleopatra*.

'It's partly selfish, this tact,' I said.

We were in deckchairs on the lawn: the man was very thin with a straggly moustache under a pointed nose. He had dirty fingernails and was some sort of priest in a hessian ballgown, eating nothing but a gruel of knotweed, dock leaves and nettles at teatime.

'Hugh's a scholar already,' my uncle said.

The friend made a face. 'Scholars can't see their noses for their fat bottoms.'

'I have no desire to see my nose,' I replied, 'were it long enough in the first place.'

I wasn't normally so spirited; something seized me that afternoon and I rode on a fiery chariot, witty perhaps for the first time in my life, fencing an adult with an assured arm. My uncle was amused, and maybe proud: at least, he made no apology for me.

The very bad news about my mother certainly evolved, rather than broke.

Sometimes I think it began as early as when she first disappeared up the lane and I tripped over by the orchard. There were three more leaves (she couldn't come in the year I was ten) and each one repeated this disappearing act. I didn't chase her any more, of course; I would stand by the gate and pretend to wave cheerily, or on the station platform if she was leaving for London. But the night I was given the bad news, it wasn't those moments I dreamt of, or even the bush; instead I saw her being swallowed up again by Pottinger's Mill, knowing in my dream that its big doors opened on to a bottomless and lightless cliff.

The real thing happened during her third leave in 1931. I was nine. One morning she said she wanted to go for a 'stretch'. This meant a decent walk. Often she would go on a walk by herself because she needed to read poetry, and she would take a thin book out of my uncle's library. If I asked her afterwards if she'd liked the poetry, she looked shy, or even cross, and said I musn't 'examine' her. My uncle reckoned she didn't even open the book; I heard him say this when he was putting one of them back. This was probably because my mother didn't like Miss Edith Sitwell, and my uncle did.

So I leapt at the idea of walking with her, this time. We hadn't been alone very much on this leave, since she was away a lot shopping in big stores or staying with old friends from school or the sanny; I was allowed to accompany her on one or two of these trips, but I hated shops and most of her friends had children younger than me.

I asked her if she needed some poetry and she thought I was teasing her, but laughed anyway. We set off and to my dismay she wanted to see what the old mill called Pottinger's looked like these days. It was an abandoned mill just outside the village and was full of bats, but it wasn't that that scared me; it was the boys with shaven heads who used it as their base. They weren't really a special gang because all the boys in the village used it, off and on. If they were there, they threw stones at you and yelled out that they were going to capture you and tie you head-down on the mill-race. I told my mother that I didn't want to go past the mill but she didn't seem to hear me; she was a few paces ahead with her hands in her skirt pockets, looking worried about something. It was very hot, even by the river, and the river was so low the grass that waved about underneath was now withered on top. We carried on up the overgrown path along the bank and even here it was dusty. I prayed to God and Yolobolo that the boys wouldn't be there today. I had bad butterflies. All that was left of my fetish packet were a few crumbs of palm leaf, the penny stamp stained with chain-oil, and the red circle cut from my mother's bloody handkerchief, kept in a matchbox: the tiny bone, the pebble, Tarbuck's wafer and the feather had been lost through the disintegrating banana-leaf wrapping. I hadn't brought the matchbox with me.

We crossed the slippery little bridge with the missing planks you could fall through and came out near the mill. The millwheel had a bird standing on it and weeds dangling from its hub. I couldn't hear much over the sound of the mill-race, but the water kept turning into shouts and jeers. I knew the very last miller had heard voices from it shouting at him to jump in and that's what he'd done, but no one had seen his spirit except Mrs Jefferies, who also said that she had seen an angel in the church.

The path went round the front of the mill with a weedy yard between; my mother said she remembered it being full of waggons with fat sacks. I tried to speed up, but my mother was dragging her feet. The mill looked huge. She said she remembered it working as if it was yesterday, it made a big booming noise and now it was quiet. She said it was like a Constable. I tried to see it as PC Cox, but I couldn't: he was thin with such long legs that when he pedalled, everyone said, his knees would deliver uppercuts to his chin (I'd not seen this myself). The mill made paper in her grandfather's day, she went on, but she only knew it as a corn-mill, full of grain and powdery meal that turned her black eyelashes white.

That's my great-grandfather, I thought. It seemed queer never to have met him, and he wouldn't even recognise me if I stood in front of him and stuck out my hand. She had stopped, now. She probably wanted to go inside: that had been my chief dread. I stopped as well, trying to invent a good excuse. Then a stone landed at my feet. At first I thought a bird had dropped it. I didn't want to tell my mother, for some reason. She was still looking at the mill.

'There's somebody in it,' she said.

Then there were shouts. I wanted to run away but my legs were stuck. They might capture us both and tie us to the mill-race with our heads down in the water. We'd drown together. I saw a shaved head bob up at one of the windows and then out of the big black entrance a boy appeared. He was running towards us through the weeds and grass and waving his arms.

'He's going to capture us,' I said, but not loud enough.

Before I could do anything about it, he had reached my mother and was shouting at her and actually tugging her sleeve. I wasn't sure what he was saying, but she understood the local accent better than I did. I knew the boy by name: it was Reggie Cullurne, he was older than me but shorter and his voice was still high. He would call me a toff in the street but never touch me. Now he was capturing my mother. I looked up and down the path and in the grass and weeds for something to use as a sword, as I had just been reading a long poem about Sir Galahad. When I looked up again, with a knobbly stick in my hand, my mother was disappearing into the big black open door. It was a door big enough for waggons and tractors to pass through without touching.

I waited a few moments and then walked towards the mill. I'd thought of going for help, but remembered Sir Galahad and decided it was better to die than to leave my mother at the mercy of the gang. I walked quite slowly. No stones were thrown and nobody ran out to capture me. The mill was even bigger and there were bunches of weeds in the brick walls. A notice next to the door said *Private Property, Keep Out. By Order.* The big dark door was around and over me and then it was all black.

Into this black there rose a shaft of golden light full of hay dust; I began to see furry ropes hanging in loops like liana, tall ladders with rungs like sausages, a huge hook hanging from the beams. There were some heads, shaved for the summer or for lice. They were on top of bodies standing in a circle: with a start I realised that they were the village boys. I came close but they didn't notice me. I thought: if they've sacrificed my mother, I'll tear them to pieces one by one.

In the middle of the circle stood my mother. She was holding a boy from behind so that his head dangled forward. Her hands were under his arms and she was bent back. I knew the boy: it was Ted Dart. He was slow and thin and got croup and made a noise when he breathed; I wasn't afraid of him. Now he'd had a fight with my mother and my mother had won. I didn't know what to do with my stick. One of the boys asked if he was 'a goner'. My mother bobbed Ted Dart up and down and he gave a great shudder and hacked badly. Sputum dribbled from his mouth. The air was full of dust. The shaft of sun made it look like a church and my mother was the Virgin Mary, not Guinevere. Ted Dart was Jesus. He looked up blinking and said, 'Larks. Blimey.' Everyone laughed except me.

Because she'd saved his life (it wasn't croup, he was 'asthmatic' and had had a 'crisis' from the mill's dusty air), I thought the boys would stop calling me names in the village, but they didn't. Ted Dart's mother came round with a basket full of onions and some homemade biscuits. My mother told her that her son ought to be seen to in London because she'd heard a leopard growl. This meant that his windpipe was inflamed. I never liked meeting Ted Dart after that; he still growled without meaning to and I felt as if he was going to jump on me and claw me to death, but instead he would smile and say, 'Your old mum's a shiner.' She wasn't old, of course. I ought to have appreciated him being nice about her but I didn't: I started wishing that I could have asthma and would imagine collapsing on the lawn with a crisis in front of her, wheezing and growling. I listened to my breath but there was nothing, not even a purr.

My uncle was always very absorbed in his work, so I spent a lot of time, when at the house, hanging about Susan or Jeremiah Jessop, or the new red-faced cook called Mrs Stump, or watching the various workmen who came and tinkered with odd bits of the house – 'keeping the ship afloat', as my uncle put it. Much of my knowledge of the wider world came from these people: most of them had never been further than Netherford. Anyway, my spirit was not here but at home, and home was somewhere I could not find on the most detailed of the maps in my uncle's study, or in the Geography classroom at school. Not even the river was marked, let alone its creeks and bays and villages – but the brambled seep that marked the end of my uncle's garden had, so he claimed, been mentioned in an Anglo-Saxon charter some thousand years before.

One day, testing a new wooden-handled penknife in the orchard up the lane, I found that one half of my apple had just two or three little withered seeds in it, while the other was crammed tight with fat ones. And this is how I was divided; one half had all the seeds and lived in Africa, the other half was being 'occupied' by me in England, as Gauls 'occupied' forts. I didn't think this at the time, exactly, but I knew that not all of me lived here. But this 'here' was too strong to unstick from, like this side of the mirror was too strong to unstick from. So when I woke up morning after morning and didn't find myself back in my room at Bamakum – where I could have called there 'here' – I'd have problems not crying for a few moments.

Most of all I wanted to rest my head against Mother's chest, because it said the name of my home: *bamakum, bamakum, bamakum.* I heard it once through her cotton shift, the first time I had a fever. Ted Dart must have heard it, too.

Letters from my parents had arrived quite a lot at first and then not so much; sometimes if I hadn't heard anything for two months, I would wonder whether I had ever really been in Africa, except in some long dreams. When you were in a dream you didn't know it was a dream.

My mother was ill, or well; my father was ill, or well. Quiri was never mentioned in the news of the servants, though I sent him postcards of local scenes. Joseph had died, suddenly, falling on to a pan of sweet potatoes he'd been carrying across the yard. Mawangu had lost a finger when chopping a new pole for the flag with his panga. Baluti, the laundry boy, had run off into the bush one day, after a row, and had never come back. My mother found all this 'very trying', on top of the 'awkwardnesses' that 'emanated' from the Colonial Office. My mother was very successful in her medical work, and my father's road was 'coming along' despite the usual setbacks, but the 'CO bureaucrats in London' didn't approve of their staying beyond the period they felt was 'the statutory maximum' for this kind of station, which was as many years as I had when I left Africa. I didn't quite understand all this when she wrote this sort of thing to my uncle, but I'd always ask him to read his letter out after I'd read mine (which was usually too short). He never let me read them myself, and I noticed (looking at his eyes) that he would skip bits. Then the letters would disappear, probably into his locked desk. He wanted my mother to tell him more about African customs, which were beginning to interest him.

He only ever really frightened me once, and this was to do with what my mother wasn't telling him enough about. Now and again Mrs Stump would come and take me to church, 'for your own good, Master Hugh'. This amused my uncle. He had a worm-eaten crucifix in his study and one Sunday, standing in the garden, I plucked up courage to ask him why, if he never came to church, he had a cross in his study.

'It reminds me of something very important,' he said.

'Love and forgiveness,' I suggested.

'No. It reminds me that the gods want only your nearest and dearest.'

'What's your nearest and dearest?'

'Sacrifice isn't sacrifice unless you miss what you're sacrificing. A sheep is pathetic – unless it's your last sheep and you're starving. God gave His only begotten Son. He didn't really, because God is an invention, but Jesus knew the ropes. He outwitted the gods at their own game and they've never recovered.'

I didn't really understand this thing about Jesus and the gods, but I pretended I did.

'Who would you sacrifice, then?'

'All depends on what I wanted from the gods.'

I thought for a moment.

'To make the wildwood spread faster.'

He gave a little start. I knew he thought of the wildwood as a sort of seed, the seed of the great forest that was going to cover

Britain from end to end, as it did long ago before farmers cut it all down – except for the bit in our garden. That's why I wasn't allowed in.

'That's a good example, Hugh. I would have to please the gods an awful lot, wouldn't I? Yes, in that particular case, I would do as your Africans do. Nearest and dearest. Give my favourite child, or my wife, or whatever.'

'You haven't got children, and Aunt Joy's dead.'

He looked at me steadily, puffing on his pipe. I felt my stomach go queer.

'That leaves me,' I added, trying to turn it into a joke.

'What?'

'I'm your nephew. I'm next.'

He nodded almost without moving his head, still staring into my eyes, as if I had sparked off a train of thought or given him the start of an idea. Then he gave a sigh through his nose, blowing out smoke, and looked away. We were standing by the unweeded tennis court, which he was wondering what to do with: it had no net and the white lines had disappeared under clover. The high wire-netting around it had come down in places and there were lots of twigs and branches stuck in the wire from the gale a few weeks before: they looked like hands and fingers. Aunt Joy had held tennis parties here, even though she was mostly too sickly to play. I suddenly blushed, aware that I might have said something rotten: if I was next, then who was just before me? I saw Aunt Joy in her white frock and cardigan turning round and staring at me, as if the net was in place and the tennis party was real. I began to say that I hadn't meant what I'd said, but my uncle was already walking away in big strides towards the house, from where the smells of Mrs Stump's roast were drifting.

From that moment a part of me was always waiting to be leapt on – at least until I was old enough to see what nonsense this secret fear was.

One day a letter came from my parents, saying their tour had been 'renewed' again for another three years. Although the time between my leaving Africa and that day was also three years, and seemed like a whole life, I was still afraid that they might leave the station before I had a chance to return. I couldn't imagine

Bamakum without my parents there. I began to think of my stay in England as a 'tour', and that it was 'statutory', renewed by some unseen bureaucrat. 'Statutory' made me think of statues. I was stuck in a kind of block of marble, and couldn't find the hole that would let me out. This block of marble grew thicker with thick clothes, and although I felt the cold more than the others, I would deliberately underdress. When I think of my English childhood, I think of cold – which seemed to start inside me and work out to my nose and my fingertips and my chapped knees.

I would go down to the village only about once a week, to buy sweets and run little errands for Mrs Stump or my uncle, or to post my letters to Bamakum. I liked to post them myself, imagining them setting out on their long voyage and finding it hard to believe that they would end up in a canoe paddling into the bay in under a month's time. The village stores were run by a young woman called Gracie Hobbs, who smelt of flour and gave me 'a little something' extra each time; seeing her lean towards me on the counter, with what my uncle would call her 'full figure' squashed against the polished wood, reminded me of the women in Africa, and I had no problem imagining what was under her sweater. Apart from the Post Office in the square and the village stores and of course the church when Aunt Joy was alive, I didn't know Ulverton itself all that well; even if I took bread to feed the ducks in the pond, I could only do it when there were none of the crop-headed gang about. There were quite a few lanes that I had never been down at all.

Because children were hardly ever invited to the house, I read a lot and walked a lot and played on my own a lot. The centre of my island was the beechwood, but it included the orchard on one side and a long rough coomb beyond the two mounds in the Jennets' field. To go to the Jennets' farm, which I did often because I liked Mrs Jennet's byre-smelling friendliness and the shuffly warmth of the cows and pigs, I had to pilot the SS *Grace*.

There was no Aunt Joy now to tell me off; my uncle hardly noticed me. Because my mother couldn't come at all one summer (something to do with accompanying my father on a 'grand tour' into the northern parts of the country, which were said to be 'remarkable'), I spent the whole of my longest holidays constructing a cabin in the beechwood. I called it my 'cell' because my favourite poem in Latin lessons was by a man called Alcuin: he was leaving his 'holy cell' which was surrounded by apple trees and fields full of herbs and blossoming streams and white lilies and red roses and singing birds. It reminded me of Bamakum when I read it, even though we had none of those things except the birds. Alcuin was sad, too, because of leaving: 'O mea cella, mihi habitatio dulcis, amata,/Semper in aeternum, o mea cella, vale.' Building my own cell out of planks and branches and old leaves and grass stopped me thinking of the fact that my mother would never see me being ten years old, because she wasn't due to come until I was eleven. (My father had promised to come, too. He hadn't seen me being nine, either.) She'd written to me at school a few months before that, telling me the bad news (although she was excited about the tour); I was quite 'cut up' when I read the letter, and had a mild return of my malaria as a result.

Strangely, I was much more cut up then than when my uncle told me the much worse news less than two years later.

Although I saw or at least talked very little with my uncle at this period, we went along together now and again to the village hall to see another type of 'touring': these were actors, and they were 'touring' plays. My uncle had started a mumming troupe, and wanted to see how the 'pros' dealt with the hall. I saw my first Shakespeare play there the same summer I was building my cell; *A Midsummer Night's Dream* was going to be performed in the hall's garden, against the birch saplings, but rain forced it inside. Despite the rain, it was very hot and crowded. It had the same effect on me, however, as the golden show my mother had taken me to in London. At the end, the thin one called Puck stepped forward in his long green slippers of felt and said, in a soft voice, 'You have but slumbered here.' My uncle was snoring, and this made people laugh. But I wasn't embarrassed. There was a man next to the stage with a big glass jar in front of him, filled with water, and a pulley above it, like my Meccano crane, dangling a metal cone; when he lowered the cone into the water, the lights went down very slowly. Somebody was playing a gramophone record of soft violins at the back: as it rustled and moaned, Puck's face disappeared without moving, a green-gloved finger to his grinning mouth, until darkness swallowed him up.

We were the last to leave, because Uncle had to 'take a recce' of their technical equipment and scenery. I couldn't believe that the back of our slumbering and its magic dream could be full of so many nails and strips of wood and primed canvas and ugly things like hinges and hooks. The junk spread around the floor turned out to be the very same gorgeous things Puck and the others had held, and a rather rough fellow in a cloth cap, who was talking to my uncle about 'running flats' and 'stage screwing', was slouched on the throne of the king, smoking a cigarette.

I thought: if life is so much jollier and brighter on a stage, why do we ever come off it?

I decided where my own stage was, in the beechwood; a flat area falling quite abruptly into a natural hollow, where I imagined the faces looking up at me over the lip, out of the coppery-silvery mould. Through the quiet of afternoons, when it wasn't raining and I wasn't finishing off my cell, I acted on my own and out loud in a sort of hoarse stage whisper almost drowned by the rustle of my feet on the leaves. I used a spare volume of the Complete Works of Shakespeare my uncle had given me from his library. There was a picture of Shakespeare's house and a portrait of Shakespeare with long hair and a debonair moustache, looking rather cross. The book said it was 'To Henry Irving, who, by his fine intellect and splendid accomplishment, has, for many years, illumined several of the great plays of SHAKESPEARE throughout the stages of England and America'. There was a 'Biographical Introduction' that began: 'There is no name in the world of literature like the name of WILLIAM SHAKESPEARE.' It said he knew woods very well and also human nature, and that he wasn't Bacon. There were photographs of Mrs F. R. Benson playing Miranda, Mr Lewis Waller playing Brutus under little coils of greased hair like the postman's, Mr C. Croker-King playing Slender in striped tights, Mr A. S. Homewood playing Florizel in a leopard-skin skirt lying in Perdita's lap played by Miss Irene Rooke in long white muslin, Mr Gordon Craig in what I thought was the same leopard skin playing Arviragus, and so on. I used these photographs as my guide, to help me know how to stand, to use my arms, my hands, my legs, my face, and how to use the few bits of costume I carried down. I took every part and scared the jays now and again when my voice screeched instead of staying quiet. In the soft light falling between the grey trees I saw the air of Sicilia, of Arden, of the park in Navarre; the trunks became the columns of palaces and castles; a toadstooled stump bubbled into a cauldron crouched round by witches played with my fingers crossed. Then everything was swept away on one still and misty morning for a blasted heath in a storm. I had a toy recorder and when music was needed I blew on it softly, always variations of 'Greensleeves'. The only properties I had were a wooden sword and a battered old chair from one of the sheds, which served as everything from throne to hill to tavern bench. I mostly forgot about the faces in the hollow, or the fact that I was on stage at all. I played favourite scenes many times, and knew them by heart, page after page after page.

I kept my props in the cell, which I repaired each holidays. It stood a little way off between three grey trunks of beech: I also had a little lamp in there, and some *Boy's Own* annuals wrapped in cellophane. Sometimes I would sneak out very early, just before dawn, and read 'with devout lips', pretending I was Alcuin. Mostly, however, I was Ralph Rover on his coral island, or Colonel Fawcett with a pair of binoculars in Bolivia, or David Balfour in a Jacobite hideout. When I saw my mother again the following summer, I couldn't show her my cell, or even tell her about Shakespeare. This was something to do with the fact that she hadn't been around when I'd started both those things. My father was wearing a trick mask to make himself look old, but it turned out to be his real face; he'd lost a lot of his hair. Just before I went to bed, he told me how big I looked. For the whole day I'd been waiting for my mother to hug me; she'd only kissed me once on the cheek as she'd kissed my uncle on her arrival, but now I realised that it was because I was big that she couldn't hug me tight to her chest. I'd either have to have a crisis or be very ill with a fever.

We went to Bexhill again for a few days and it was sunny and bright. When we were on the beach one morning, my mother said there was something wrong with my pupil, that even in the glare it was big, it must be letting in too much light. She took me to an ophthalmologist in London, who said that it didn't matter how much light went in, because I could only see it a tiny bit. She wasn't pleased with me for hiding my eye's near-blindness; she mumbled something about a curse, but she often said things were a curse. My father went back early and the days were easier; I enjoyed the late summer on the lawn alone with my mother, playing cards. She said how nice it was that I was big enough now to entertain her. But when she looked at me, her mouth had lines down the sides which stopped it smiling properly. This must be what happens when you get older, I thought.

My uncle read the whole of Miss Edith Sitwell's *Gold Coast Customs* out loud one evening, and afterwards she said it was so like a chant that she thought my uncle might take off or turn into a worm. I sat there too frightened to speak: it was like the Witches in *Macbeth* but worse, and was full of things about bones and Death and blood and white masks and leopards that brought back the moments in Bamakum when I had lain awake thinking Sir Steggie or the cemetery spirits or the monster with long legs or the Big Beef or the members of the Leopard Society would come and drag me away. I didn't want to upset my uncle, so I kept a smile fixed on my face. My mother looked at me and said that I mustn't ever put on that silly face again. The lines by her mouth were very deep in the gaslight. But on the lawn they would vanish from time to time, even in the lovely late sun of September, when she was playing cards with me and telling me about her childhood on this same grass. It wasn't the same grass, I thought, because it kept being cut.

She laughed sometimes, remembering, but never as much as she did when we went up to London together, just before she left. She bought clothes for Africa – white lightweight things and a long, cherry-red coat for chilly Buea – and then we had tea in the Langham Hotel after a children's concert in the Queen's Hall opposite. She pointed to a woman with a nose like a beak, sitting in the lounge, and said, 'That's Edith Sitwell, won't Uncle Edward be excited when we tell him.' Edith Sitwell was dressed all in black and covered in huge necklaces and gold brooches and rings; she reminded me of the way the girls looked when dressed for their special ceremony in the villages around Bamakum. I said this to my mother – that Miss Sitwell looked as if she was waiting to be 'circusised' (I thought it was to do with circuses, a special test like tightrope walking) and to my surprise she laughed so much that we had to leave quickly before anyone noticed. For the rest of the day she kept giggling suddenly, without warning. It was as if my comment had made her drunk.

By the time of the very bad news, I had acted right through every play in the Shakespeare book, and was starting again on the Island of strange noises. It was chill and echoey in the wood, and for once the book felt too heavy for my wrist. The leaves were frosty and Prospero had just made his long speech to Miranda while sitting on them, her head in my lap. I was now trying to contort my body as the deformed Caliban and the book refused to stay open in that position. My muscles ached. I heard cars arrive, and loud voices between guttural laughter. I closed the book and wandered back to the house, my basket of costumes banging against my knees.

The jolly Germans had arrived, members of something called the Thule Society. My uncle was keen on them because they were pagans, they liked astrology and standing stones and celebrating the important bits of the year that had been forgotten. Most of them were men. They drank a lot of beer and wrote in funny letters called 'runes'. They taught me some German words, calling my uncle's winter solstice celebration a 'Julfest'. This always involved a girl dressed all in red with blood-red make-up smeared on her face, who had to fall down on the lawn near the bonfire. The local mummers then waved their arms about and hopped around her, and she got up again. Then my uncle plunged a big fat stick into the ground and shouted out his poem about trees and sap and so on. I didn't understand how this saved us from winter going on and on, especially as the girl was usually Alice Punter, the chief mummer's daughter, who always giggled between her sticking-out ears, but apparently it did. This year she had scarlet fever and so they used one of the German women. She was a big wobbly girl with blonde plaits and a big voice and spoke quite good English. She let me watch her 'making' her plaits, and wrote out for me where she was from: Schleswig-Holstein. Her nickname was 'Queen Gunhild', which she didn't seem to mind, because Queen Gunhild was a very great and strong queen of the Norse peoples a thousand years ago and they'd found her in a deep bog and people went to see her in a church. There was a chance Queen Gunhild might come back, she said, to put things right. Her real name was Ingrid. She did the dance very well, not giggling at all, though the red costume was too tight for her and she looked like a pork sausage. Later, around the fire, she let me drink some of her punch and I realised that it was the kind of warm wine Mother had mentioned at home. There was plum cake, but no muffins. They had the same idea about an eternal winter as my uncle, but gave it their own name: 'Fimbulwinter'. They told me stories from the Brothers Grimm without looking, and stories about Loki and Wotan. These were full of frost and fire, of hideous black shapes whistling though the air, of wolves and winds and worlds drowning in blood. Wotan was one-eyed, which made me like him, and was the most powerful of all the gods. Yet Loki finished him off in the Ragnarok, the last great battle which had something to do with Fimbulwinter. I was never quite sure whose side they were on, Loki's or Wotan's, because when the story-teller described Ragnarok and the burning of heaven, his voice went high and excited, and the eyes of the listeners shone in the firelight as if delighted by it all.

Some of them put on a play the day before the celebration: it was called 'Scenes from Faust by the great Goethe', and the bad one called Mephistopheles wore a little cap on his head and a big false nose; this made everyone laugh except my uncle. It was all in German, but I enjoyed it anyway – mainly because Mephistopheles was funny and horrible at the same time, limping about crookedly and even 'letting off' at one point. The little cap was, I realised, like the one Sir Henry Irving wore as Shylock, in my Complete Volume. Perhaps Goethe was as great.

But my uncle stood up at the end and in a quiet, stiff sort of voice said that he was very disappointed and walked out. Someone sniggered. The group never came again after that – it was my turn to be disappointed.

'Why were you all upset by the play?' I asked him, as we stood by the ashes of the bonfire. It was damp and cold and grey. I saw winter as a thimble over a warm flame, putting it out. It was Christmas in two days, though.

'They had promised not to be rude about the Jews.'

'Was Mephi-thing a Jew?'

'Yes. They have all the right ideas and interests and think Hitler is a vulgar little fellow, then they go all Teutonic and silly, especially when drunk, and are nasty about the Jews.'

'Mother's father was a Jew.'

'He was indeed. I'm half-Jew and they don't even like those.'

'And quarter-Jew?'

'Not even sixteenth-Jew, Hugh.'

He thrust his shooting stick into the ashes. They made a little cloud, as if there was still heat down there. My head was freezing, because hats prickled me. I felt like burying my scalp in the ashes. It was Christmas in two days. I wanted Mother and Father so I could go into the room with my stocking. As it was, I didn't have a stocking. Uncle didn't even believe in presents. All we had was a Christmas tree and lots of mistletoe. He believed in the Druids and that's all *they* had. It was lucky that Mother and Father usually got things sent – including a hamper from Fortnum and Mason's full of stuff, some of which I quite liked – and that friends of my uncle gave me 'a little something' when they called round. Also, Mrs Stump and Susan made sure we had a proper Christmas luncheon and a box of crackers, though my uncle called them 'gewgaws' and always 'absented' himself by the time we were starting to pull them. Then Mrs Stump and Susan would go home and have another Christmas meal at dinnertime. This was why, I decided, they were rather fat.

He went on: 'I don't mind them going on about *specific* Jews, especially when they're bankers and businessmen, but I don't like this general thing. It's childish. They're not coming back, not all at once anyway. People go queer in groups. Never join a society, m'boy. Bang your own drum.'

I burst into tears. It was the mention of the word 'drum'. It made me think of the drum I'd had on the beach in Victoria, which someone had ripped. My uncle was astonished: he'd never seen me cry before. But I couldn't stop it. It was coming up from the ground, up my legs and into my eyes and nose and mouth. He mumbled something and went inside and got Mrs Stump to come out and see to me. She blamed the Germans, the over-excitement and the punch they'd made me drink, silly fools. One or two of them had pinched her bottom. She giggled, though, when she said this, so I knew she was pleased.

Her giggle went higher and higher. I wasn't sure whether we were inside or next to the bonfire, but someone must have lit it again because I was very hot. The giggling went on even when I woke up in bed, in what might have been my room if it hadn't been made of rubber, pressing me down. People came and went, mostly with cold hands, and wolves ran in packs past my bed very silently on their way to swallow the moon.

Among the people was my mother. She might have had cold hands too, but she didn't come near enough to touch me. In fact, she stayed on the threshold, by the open door. She said 'Darling Hugh', then the words twisted up into a question, panting among lots of hands that were reaching up behind her. She wore the bright red coat we'd bought together in London three months earlier. It was going to be for Christmas in cool Buea and she'd said it was 'almost vermilion, it will clash with the hibiscus'. The shopkeeper had laughed. I saw it going into the cellophane and wondered for a moment whether we were back in the shop. Then she was in it again.

There was snow in her hair. It was melting, the big white flakes silvering at the edges, and some lay on her shoulders and on her broad lapels. It was a 'fancy' coat but her hair was loose, as if it had fallen from its grips. She must have been running for her hair to have been loosened like that: all the respectable women I knew had it bunched up around the ears and pinned to a small hat. In fact, she had no hat on at all: this worried me. She was always particular about a hat in cold weather, saying that one caught a cold by the head.

I tried to say something, but my words were balloons tied to my mouth. She was stage-screwed to the threshold: I wanted her to come in and give me a cuddle, or stroke my forehead. I looked at her feet to check them for screws. She had on her heavy shoes-for-England, and they were muddy. Her ankles went up a little way and then stopped at the hem of her coat. This was definitely my mother. But there was snow in her hair. Maybe she'd just come off the top of Mount Cameroon, walking down quickly all the way to me. My curtains were drawn; through them came a metal light that might have been snow. The thought of snow was pleasing, since I felt extremely hot. Then a kind of yawn in white rose up from my bedclothes and tried to smother me. The door was closed: my mother was gone, the hands or hand had pulled her away. There followed a terrible, echoey shouting, which might have been issuing from my own throat, and screams, and suffocating smells. My uncle's face appeared, and that of the doctor with a crab-apple on the side of his nose, and then a nurse with smiles and an ice-cold flannel.

I have no precise idea of the hours or even days this all took, but I know that I was very seriously ill with pneumonia at one point, and the voices around me were deep and sober. I found myself in the corridor, opposite my mother's bedroom door. The door opened and there was an arm with a frilly wrist balanced in her old doll's house. The hand must be stage-screwed to it, I thought, or it wouldn't stay horizontal like that. I looked along the arm and it finished by being attached to Mother on her knees, not looking back at me but at a piano in her fingers. Then her face turned. It was not very jolly, not happy to see me at all. In fact, it was frightened. I was sucked away.

When I was better, a couple of weeks before my uncle broke the news, I decided not to mention my visions of Mother, as I had not mentioned Herbert E. Standing or the fear of Sir Steggie over the last four years. I felt older and wiser after the illness, somehow, and was convinced that my mother's spirit had visited me. It reinforced my old beliefs, that had been gradually fading in the English light. I knew very well that fever gave rise to hallucinations; I had suffered from vivid visions at home, and my parents as well as visitors had impressed me with their malarial experiences. I had once watched my father moan as imaginary spiders attacked him in his bed, and heard a sick trader gabbling about a blue-and-red kite falling through the floor. Then there was the legendary story about the consul who thought he was a poached egg, and you had to pretend his chair was a piece of toast. But I chose to forget all that. What do I think now, some thirty years later, in our humdrum world of Omo and gramophone records and take-over bids? I do not think, but feel. I feel an immense sadness that my three words trapped in their balloons did not reach my mother's ears, for everything I wanted to say to her was in them.

'*Mother, please stay.*'

'Hugh,' said my uncle, 'I have some worrying news.'

I had been better for two weeks, but I still felt weak, and couldn't leave the grounds because I was more infectious now than when I'd had it. I gripped my cocoa, on the way up to an early bed, and stared at a knot on the kitchen table. His hands were trembling. They were large, hairy hands, and I fancied sometimes that I was Jack, trapped for ever in the ogre's castle. He was already drinking quite heavily at this time, and was studying his mug of beer as fiercely as I was studying the dark swirl in the table. The wall lamps sputtered in the silence, giving off not only their harsh, chalky light but a smell of gas. My uncle hated electricity, though the village had been wired up three years earlier in a blaze of lamplight.

'Your mother,' he said.

I swallowed loudly, and found my head to be making tiny, jerky movements all by itself, like my headmaster's at Flytings.

'Rather bad news, Hugh.'

The pauses were there for me to fill. She was very ill, of course. A lot of people, not just black people, died out in Africa, where I had my home. My uncle took a gulp of beer and wiped, not his mouth, but his forehead. It reminded me a little of my mother's old gesture. I thought of my father, and how worried he must be. I pictured him sitting by her bedside, frowning. I hadn't breathed for a little while but my body did so automatically, letting it out with a quick sigh. My uncle looked at me, then. His gingery eyebrows, thicker and wilder with age, looked like the thatch over some of the cottages' windows along the lane. I thought of the ogre again. His mug was made of beechwood and leather. He had a dark leather jerkin over his worsted shirt, and thick brown corduroy trousers, baggy enough to pass for plus-fours at a distance. This was a costume (I thought of it as such) quite recently put on, as were the white cloaks he wore on certain days, and the intricate sandals, and the long plum-coloured cape he'd go to town in. It reminded me of both the shepherds and the kings in the Nativity Play that fat Mrs Beeching would put on in the village, or of the courtiers disguised as rustics in some of our dramatic efforts at school, which I went along with; they were usually scenes from Shakespeare or Milton's *Comus* or the whole of one of the Roman plays (I'd pretend not to have the lines by heart at first). I knew it was not a costume, however, but a serious thing, as I knew these were not lines from a play.

'Is she quite ill, uncle?'

'What?' he grunted.

I cleared my throat and repeated the question in more than a strangled murmur.

'Not exactly, Hugh,' he said. 'It's rather worse than that.'

Strangely, I didn't think of death, then. I imagined the word 'worse' as a suitcase full of nasty things, spiders and poisonous fungi and rotting hands and powerful, wriggling curses – the sort of things I had seen under fever in the weeks before. But death, final and cold and definite, didn't emerge to wipe it all out. I frowned.

'Can't think,' I said, as if my uncle had just posed me a cryptic teaser from the newspaper, or of his own invention. I shivered, without meaning to: it was a cold house, away from the fireplaces or the stove. I was in my dressing gown, but the open door ushered in the frigid air from the hallway. I fancied, just for a second, that my mother was waiting for me there, and that if I didn't run to her this instant, she would leave without me, and for the last time. But my feet in their slippers refused to move.

My uncle stood. My cocoa was scalding my fingers slightly and I saw that my hands were trembling, spilling it. He came over and took the mug from me and put it on the table. I thought that he was about to hug me tightly, as once or twice he had done over the years, but instead he leaned back against the table and crossed his arms, studying my knees. I felt them go weak, and their bony backs found the rickety chair by the door, with its usual offering of torn envelopes and bills. I sat in a rustle of them, not caring. I looked down at the floor. There was a spent match stuck in the greasy join between two boards.

'The fact is, Hugh, you're going to have to be a brave chap, from now on. Your dear mother has disappeared, into the jungle. Just like that. God knows why, old fellow. She's been missing three – no, four – weeks now. Enquiries made by your father and others, in the villages or whatever, have yielded nothing. Not a single clue. I think we have to presume, dear boy, that she's never going to come back. Never. I think we should proceed on that basis. Yes. Definitely. Yes. Come on now, chin up.'

My eyes were filled with tears, but they weren't the tears he thought they were. I was immensely relieved, even joyous. She was not dying from fever, or drowned, or eaten by a croc, or just stark dead. She wasn't *dead*, that's the thing. My uncle's shadowy form disintegrated as I blinked, light splintering from the wall lamps and dazzling me as the river would in sunlight at home. Of course Mother would come back, eventually. She had gone to the crater lake. She had gone to paradise and soon she would be back to take me there, too. I had no doubt about it at all. We would live together on the shore in perfect love and harmony, for there were no crocs in the deep, black water, and England was beyond imagining there.

I felt my uncle's heavy hand on my head and wriggled free. I must have been smiling, because as I ran up the stairs he shouted after me, 'My, you're a queer little fellow, Hugh!'

His voice was more fearful than amazed – the only time I ever heard it like that, high-pitched. He was certain she was dead but I was certain she wasn't. I lay that same night with my cold sheet taut to my chin, plotting the gentle curve of my existence with her in the coming years in a hot, green paradise by the lapping waters of the crater until sleep lapped over me quite easily too.

3

Saturday, 4 September

Hamlet – still green and fresh after eight weeks. My actors are like racing-drivers: the roar of lethal passion is icily controlled by technique, formal gesture, the second-to-second changing of gears, liquid oratorical movements, a precise dance with danger, with inward heat and explosion and death. Alan G. went *chalk-white* at the sight of the Ghost tonight, as Betterton once did. It has taken him – us – twenty years to arrive at that blenched face. Blood draining right out. *Yet no loss of control*: the hand gestures still precise, not a metrical beat muffed. Audience quite hypnotised. Sheer enchantment. Will I ever be as happy again? As now, writing this in the empty theatre, my cheeks still smeared with their make-up, with their kissing joy? All these silent seats. All that sound suspended, not quite gone.

Tuesday, 7 September

Nothing but boxes for the last two days. Turned down offer to front a series for the BBC on the 'Great Tragedians'. I cannot delay the book any longer. Awful day of meetings, admin., minor balls-ups. I felt like one of those nineteenth-century actors who watched Charcot's patients for examples of *hysterica passio* – only the patients were all around me, fussing about nothing. Snatched lunch with Linus F., who asked me if my actors were *literally* possessed. Of course, I replied, but they also know it and control it. Without technique, they would either look ridiculous or go mad. He is writing a biography of Garrick and can't understand how I've managed to make the old style work. But Garrick replaced the old style when it was hollowed of all meaning, mere stiffness and declamation. I have pumped the blood back in, the vital spirit. He nodded diplomatically. I got so excited that the tall menus couldn't take the wind from my gesticulations.

Wednesday, 8 September

Clearing the study. Found at Sumerian level my childhood memoir rolled up in a ribbon, like an old map. First few pages missing: begins *in medias res* with the 'gorilla incident' – never quite sure what that was, in the end. Thirty-odd years ago I was writing about my life thirty-odd years before that – and in thirty years' time? I will be a hundred.

Listless interview with the *Telegraph*. They'll get it all wrong.

Thursday, 9 September

Morris called. Appalled by how much I am not throwing away. And I thought I was being ruthless.

I would give the rest of my life (after the book's done) to stand among the apprentices and artisans and dusty soldiers in the Globe in 1604 and watch, say, *Othello*. I think I would still be surprised and astonished by what they did with it – for all my efforts, my fidelities. Morris called me an obsessive, when I admitted this. 'Isn't Shakespeare our contemporary, like that Polish guy said?' Shakespeare is a monster, I replied, a monstrous genius of the past whom we strive to comprehend from inside whatever tiny present we inhabit. Put it another way: we wade towards him through thick time. It is a battle against time. A terrible battle against time.

Friday, 10 September

A throat from the dust off the tops of the books, which leaves permanent spots. Morris said should use a feather duster regularly. Enormous yellow skip almost full by teatime. Jamming things in on my tiptoes, was chatted to successively by a red-faced Irish woman, a Cockney bag-lady, a dapper little Indian and a wrinkled African-Caribbean with white hair. Like a bad sketch. These people have all lived around here for years yet we only talk when I'm leaving. When it's safe to, I suppose.

Saturday, 11 September

Last night of *King John* and big party after. I gave a speech that made everyone cry – 'Ripe for exploits and mighty enterprises,' etc. John G. on very good form, told a couple of Larry jokes relatively new to me. Got back inches before dawn with Diana changing lanes each time she roared with laughter at something I'd meant to be serious. Old memories. End of an era. Feel suitably frayed. Or 'overripe', as Ronald Watkins used to say of himself when I was still firm and green.

Thumped the skip as I passed and it sounded hollow. By dawnlight from my window it is. Even the awful polka-dotted lampshades. I feel *dispersed*.

Sunday, 12 September

Mostly asleep in my bed in a strange, bundled-up place that was until yesterday my dear home. A dream: I am in New York, in an abandoned block-turned-theatre, watching a famous hippy theatre group taking all day to set up, the show changing as members have rows and leave, or new ones join. The name of the group is *Swan God Feel Like Missionary*, but I persist in calling it *Swan God Merein Missionary*. I am desperate to be given a part, the teeniest-tiniest part.

I will miss London, yet I can't wait to tear free. Of course I might even come back for good. Though a cottage in the country, a sort of Pascalian existence full of *pensées* and pruning, has its lure.

Monday, 13 September

Two large wheezy men in fluorescent overalls came and carted everything off to Morris's huge attic in between police-like conversations on a mobile phone. The flat looks even more estranged from me, empty, walls much less white than I thought – except where the furniture's blocked the pollution. The panic of being in your own home without the means to make a cup of tea. Fifteen years and the only familar note is next door's mindless dog, yet not a day has passed that I haven't wished its painful death. My last entry here, on my knee, looking out at the top of the turning linden. *O mea cella, vale.*

Later. Writing this in the hotel in the village, late. Dropping the keys off at the estate agent was definitely the pulling of the anchor. Train down with two large suitcases and my box of reference books opposite an area sales manager for Spud-U-Like and I said I didn't, though she was young and bonily attractive.

Taxi to the village. Looks as if someone's run off with the real thing, leaving a fake. The Old Barn Hotel where once the Jowett rusted, full of chickens, has carpet for wallpaper and lavender pot-pourris everywhere, though home-owned and friendly: pleasant room up in the beams overlooking the square, church tower, glimpse of the mild downs. The country is so fresh, but always looks as if it's been rather indifferently waiting for you. London never does; you have to hop on as on to a moving train.

The house broods as ever: a maiden aunt in rictus of sexual fervour or slow, agonising death. Most of its windows still blocked by Aunt Rachael's strips of carpet and squares of lino: she used so many nails it looks like stitching. Garden a scramble to explore. Aunt Joy's champion rose bushes a mess of blown thorns, summerhouse a clump of nettles and a sandwich of window-frames. Beechwood glorious in the setting light. The cows in the same old field next door (but not the same cows) all huddled in a line the far side – as far away from the house as they could get, it looked like. Sensible, sensitive creatures. Though the wildwood's fence is down I didn't go in, just hovered on the edge. Conjuring *her*, as she was.

Then – this is absolutely true – *a sudden, pungent smell of wild garlic.*

Isn't it much too late for ramsons?

The key worked in the back door and I ventured in as far as the stairs. Trod on a few sweetpapers, but otherwise saw very little and had to grope, stupidly without a torch. The sitting-room appears to have a hole in the window so I suppose recent visitors have entered by that. Musty smell and droppings of rodents everywhere. A bottle of gin, empty. Chilly place, still. Could hear Aunt Rachael say, in that sodden, tobacco-blasted voice, *So here you are.*

Not literally, of course.

Awful night full of wrong trains. Groping for a piss I brained myself on one of the beams, once high up in a dusty darkness.

Visited the house again with my pocket torch and this time made it to 'my' room. Pulled away the lino from the window and the old view appeared but as if it had come back from the dry-cleaner's not quite the same: garden, woods, field, tumuli like two breasts on horizon, blank white sky. The house is stripped bare but on peeping into the attic I saw where it had all gone to or not been removed from: a choppy sea of junk. I have to confess to a vague feeling of being watched, throughout.

I will just tell someone to open a plug and empty out the junk, swirl it away. I don't even want to see it.

Pitter-patter of rain out of a white sky. Leaves dropping, rain dropping. They've stuffed a bungalow into the orchard, but a few of the trees are still up one end, all mossed. Returned here with a wet collar and am ensconced again in this lounge, alone. Fake log fire but old comfy chairs and an antique school desk on which I'm writing this. Lots of time for you now, dear fitful diary. Hotel frigid but comfortable. So far in my sorties I've met no one I once knew but then I've not sought them out. Village Stores still there, new butcher's, Bint's Bakery now something called England Made Me with squadrons of lead farm animals in an elegant whatnot, old grain-measurers, mahogany stools, swathes of printed throw-overs hung like a harem: always shut. People passing almost recognisable and then turn out not to be, or are much too young though not young at all. The warty old pavement in front of the Post Office almost frighteningly familiar down to the last fissure, but about to be ripped up, from the look of it.

Reading my childhood memoir like watching a man and his son fishing on the opposite bank. Forty was such an awful age, but then things got going and I didn't think about age until about last week. Did Dr Wolff ever read what I wrote, in the end? Wet, steaming red earth of Africa: smell it as I read. Otherwise, it's all happened to someone else before recorded time.

Netherford Public Library just the same with colourful posters and carpets instead of lino but people looking like they've drifted in from the bus-stop. Aunt Rachael's solicitors have vanished in the intervening twenty years since her death. Too lazy or tired to find out why. Can't even recall why the will wasn't enacted immediately. Some turgid legal reason with no one bothered enough to push. Am I bothered enough now? But hardly a day has passed over the last twenty years when I've not pictured the place 'deteriorating', as estate agents put it.

Took my shoes off and pretended Reference was all a wing of my *château*, then detected awful smell from my shoes which of course I washed in the bath last month. Someone came up to me thinking I was someone who was dead, but not Hugh Arkwright. Someone he knew personally, drowned in grease. In grease? Or did he mean Greece? Reminds me of a friend of Jean's who really did think I had died but quite a few years ago. Convinced he'd read my obituary. I think the same about Bernard Levin, then he pops up again.

Browsing, fell upon a thick report of Keiller's Windmill Hill excavation. Ah, I remember Keiller. He came to dinner at Ilythia several times, with dirty fingernails. Gained his fortune in marmalade, Aunt Joy would say, which made me think of him as sticky. She kept pronouncing his name wrong, it came out like 'Killer' and Nuncle would tell her off in front of the poor chap. She was so pale yet she blushed so deeply, like an electric ring. Drawing of chalk phallus on one page that I'm sure I remember turning in my little hand. Shaped like an hourglass or a pair of testicles. Made me feel peculiar – today, I mean, looking at the drawing. I would hear Nuncle and him rumbling on about witches through the study door, but he wasn't in any way creepy.

Thought inevitably of the book, though Morris advised me not to until after Italy. A fortnight here, some six weeks among the cypresses working through Bulwer, Heywood, Greg, Granville-Barker *et al*, then David's cottage in Cornwall until sheer loneliness drives me to finish. Of course it must be done: otherwise after my death there'll be no blueprints. But I hate writing. Like being a composer but having to tune the piano, too.

Had a drink in what was the New Inn, now officially the Never Fear – its old nickname. The disgruntled locals now call it the New Inn, of course. Interior completely unrecognisable: could have been in Chertsey. Ghastly soft music like an airport. This man I took to be Indian at the bar said, 'Hello Mr Arkwright. I know you. I knew Mrs Arnold, too. The *second* one, that is.' He said the last with a sort of leery grin on his podgy face. He wasn't Indian at all but a coalman, semi-retired, dyed dark by his trade. He delivered coal to Aunt Rachael for many years and they always shared a pot of tea. My eye-patch usually gives me away like this. Didn't know him from Harry, and can't even remember his name now. Perry? Potter? Another old boy claimed he knew me as a nipper, so I pretended to recognise his sunken cheeks and warty nose. One had the feeling this happened every day and they'd all been slumped there in silence since I left in my teens a few hours ago.

Everyone was in general agreement that the house was 'troubled'. Troubled! What a marvellous word, an old worn penny still circulating in this God-forsaken place, and tendering nothing beyond it.

Thursday, 16 September

Breakfast near enough to another area sales manager for him to engage me in enthusiastic talk. He was in frozen foods and had an earring. I said Bejam made me think of mortuaries and he looked ever so surprised. Lonely, I think. He calls it 'chilled food', which is worse.

Interview in the *Telegraph* as if dictated by a tipsy secretary while I was out. Under the sub-heading *Authentic Bard: The Man Who Came in from the Globe*, I am referred to as 'the infamous director who sports a piratical eye-patch and believes in humours, vital spirits, and actors learning lifeless hand gestures by rote – because that, he firmly believes, is how it was done in Shakespeare's time. While admittedly different, even strange, his efforts haven't enchanted everyone: tourists, for instance, are staying away in droves, and that's got the Arts Council very worried indeed.' Headless chicken sort of journalism, but it still

145

has such a debilitating effect. What will happen when I'm not around to reply?

A Damascus moment followed from this, however: while over at the house, still irritated, suddenly saw it as a sort of brain, balancing the more muscular practicals up in Eilrig Lodge. A fine reference library, dorms, intimate performance space on the usual lines, lectures on Elizabethan acting from renowned specialists, seasonal courses on rhetoric, wit, rhythm, the science of gesture, theatrical decorum, court manners and so forth, lovely garden and good meals, retreat weeks for harassed actors, with cornettos and crumhorns (or even the odd Jacobean masque) on the tended lawn. The Eilrig Foundation's a charity and we could say it's for 'young people' with our hand on our hearts. The local authority will fight it but who cares about them? I'll phone Barry about it tomorrow. Pull out the plug and sluice away the junk, everything to do with that past. What an unhappy place.

Found an old cigarette card on the stairs: Betty Nuthall, Wimbledon star of around 1930! Must have been mine, once. Didn't notice it yesterday. She's playing around the baseline with bobbed hair, sexy white stockings, loose blouse; a neat hedge and glimpse of mock-Tudor beyond, but no leaves on the trees. As if someone had propped it on the top step, just for me.

All the wallpaper's the same except some dribbly stuff in the 'morning-room'. Scared by a bat floundering in front of my face for a moment in Mother's room.

Friday, 17 September

Interview over the phone for *Kaleidoscope*. Interviewer 'A man in all the world's new fashion planted/That hath a mint of phrases in his brain', but without Don Adriano's panache. He kept saying I was turning the clock back and why? I said I'm not turning the clock back, I'm taking it off the wall and mending it. He drawled the word 'musical' as if he meant the noun, not the adjective, and quoted my enemies who claim my theories are built on inhibitions and I said that's absolutely right, early acting is built on control and inhibition as early instruments are built from seasoned wood. It only encourages me to write my book as a sense of

146

mission, like Tyndale's Bible. Finished with my favourite: 'As M. Clemenceau said, passing a pretty girl at the age of seventy – Oh, to be sixty again!' He laughed, aged I should think thirty.

Barry thinks my ideas feasible in terms of the conditions of the will but it means putting the Social Services appointment off until late next week. He said he'd 'sort it', anyway. I hope they don't smell a rat. Their disturbed youngsters can find somewhere else to disturb, surely. I suppose I'm flying in the teeth of Aunt Rachael's post-mortem intentions but draw succour from the thought that a Historical Performance Research Centre (working title) would go so completely against Uncle E's desires. Like sitting on his face, to use a yobbish expression.

Am I mad? No, just ripe for mad exploits.

Organised a handyman to clear the garden, but he didn't turn up. Gorgeous, sad time of year, this, hazy with bonfire smoke: leaves falling, conkers bulging from their gourds like blind eyes staring up at blue sloes, red hawthorn and beechmast and scudding swift skies. Rather cold today. Stripped elderberry bushes and ate the berries raw as I did sixty years ago. Crab-apples on same old gnarled tree at lane's corner. Walked through the beechwood at bottom of garden and on into the field: stubble freshly burned and one of the tumuli badly scorched. Lots of equally cindered crows above it, still with bad throats shouting 'hodge-podge', as of yore.

Country feels empty off the roads, these days. Just the odd machine doing something agricultural, and distant high-powered noises. Stood on the charred left tumulus for a bit. The shallow depression around it presumably all that remains of Uncle E's trench.

After supper, took a moonlit walk to the house. Pungent sludge of windfalls in the orchard on the lane made me feel sick. House like a great black cliff against the moonlit sky. Thought I could hear more bats so stopped myself going in. No whiffs of wild garlic on the lawn or anywhere else. Defied my own silly fears just by walking about in the garden with my back to the mournful old face. Bloodshot eyeball watching me through a tear in the lino, of course.

Writing this in bed. Obscurely excited. It must be the project, or the fact that I dared myself and won.

Saturday, 18 September

A good breezy walk over the open downs, *at least* seven miles. Touched when a bent old man in front of the shop said, 'Hello, Hugh boy.' Identified himself as Jimmy Herring, the pimply clerk in the Post Office who'd save me first-day stamps – and suddenly quite obvious under the wrinkles and creases, as if all that he needed was a good airing. A few threads of belonging, though I never felt I belonged. *Some* good times here, mostly when Mother came back on leave. The memoir makes her oddly remote: when I think of her these days she's almost stiflingly close, as if my head is buried in her skirts. Starch and woodsmoke and sweaty legs. I think when I was forty I still felt betrayed by her leaving us so abruptly.

Lunch anyway at Pottinger's Mill *aka* the Mill House Restaurant, pricey-posh. Strolled there by the old muddy path now officially entitled 'The River Walk', with stone or metal sculptures covered in graffiti called things like *Isopod 2* next to fogged-up display boards of herons, otters, obscure waterfly, etc. Didn't see any, of course, and therefore felt let down.

Ate desultory *poulet basquaise* quite possibly on the same spot Mother saved Ted Dart in asthma attack by holding him like Jesus but no identifying points – huge picture window where door was, false walls, hired bric-à-brac, not even a case of 'thereabouts'. Weedy yard now full of white gravel and smart cars. Recognised by discreetly cultivated couples, but by staring back at them I clearly *wasn't* Hugh Arkwright, despite the eye-patch. Not all ship's cooks with peg-legs and parrots are Long John Silver.

Sunday, 19 September

Sudden momentary conviction on the loo that I should forget the research centre idea and simply hand over the house as agreed. When I told Barry about sluicing away the junk, he went on about me being entitled to the 'chattels' – but I *insisted* I didn't want to start burrowing. If there's a chest of doubloons up there then let Oxfam have it, or whoever. Certainly the terms of the lease mean the place has to be empty. Feel pushed about by this damn will – presumably not Aunt Rachael's aim. Just that I shouldn't have the house, only the responsibility of handing it over to the Good Cause. Can't say it's vindictive, exactly.

Anyway, let the Good Cause be Shakespeare. The English poetic drama. Nothing finer, in the end.

The revolution's intelligence HQ.

Nuncle will be writhing in his grave. Or wherever in the wildwood his ashes landed on that gusty wet morning. I think he really did believe it would leap over the fence and smother us all under its melancholy boughs, smother our silly chatter and din, the moment his burnt offering touched the mould – and it hasn't spread an inch, just grown scruffier at the edges. Rather an attractive notion, Britain as one great greenwood, when I think about it! Oh dear. Morris asking me once why I loathed my uncle so and me saying I might tell one day – on my deathbed. I told Dr Wolff, but that was different.

Missed church service, wandered about around the graveyard looking for Aunt Joy's stone and two more ancients on a bench greeted me as if I'd been away a week. They've usurped names belonging to rough lads from my past, big crop-headed bullies who've just stayed here, growing older and older until the choice *not* to not leave has gone and soon they'll be part of the wind.

Good roast for lunch. Friendly couple run this place: Jessica and Roger Marlow. Told me she was a fringe actress, once. Lovely throaty laugh.

Passing posh country residence that used to be a tatty farm off the Fogbourne Road, I saw a youngish man in the garden peeing into an immaculately clipped privet. He had a three-piece suit and tie on. Swing on the lawn but no sign of kids on this lovely day. All packed off to school, leaving him free to piss with abandon into his privet.

Monday, 20 September

Organised another handyman-gardener, one John Wall (of the unpleasant Wall clan, though he said there was only his mother). 'Hello, Mr Arkwright,' he said, as if he knew me from somewhere. He has a limp and is pasty-faced and looks as if he's about to snigger all the time, but I think it's shyness. He likes to use weed-killer and wants a big sit-up mower to tackle the lawn but I put him right on the last two counts. He's about forty but could be a barely-pubic fifteen (especially his voice, poor thing), and I guess he's gay but has never been allowed to realise it and so remains with Mum accumulating hang-ups. We found cob-webbed tools in the main shed but I don't know if he'll use them. I said if he wants to hire a motor-mower that's up to him, but I have no car. All I want is the garden to be de-jungled so that I can see things more clearly. These people are always in love with technology, anything that smokes and makes a big noise.

I stood in the attic for a while. Vaguely recognisable bits and bobs, like lines from long-ago reps. Some African souvenirs dumped by Father on his ignominious return: masks, stools, skins of snake and crocodile and the big leopard pelt he spent weeks tanning, an awful job. Something terribly creepy about old animal skins, too bestial by half and completely dead and vanquished but still grinning.

Beyond the decades' broken furnishings spotted one of the big bamboo-ribbed trunks we'd had in Bamakum. Locked. I think it was there not long after Mother left us. The dust was awful every time I lifted something and my ankle-bones are bruised. Nothing induces me to 'sort it', and anyway it would take weeks. No leaks in the joists and no bats, only mice which I don't mind. So the roof's intact. Perhaps what we need is a big pyre.

A pint literally to lay the dust in the Never Fear and to take soundings on John Wall. A man in braces said he'd heard I was to get John a big sit-up mower and something called a bush-cutter. 'Oh dear,' I replied. A hairy man with as high a voice as Wall said that the trouble with John boy is that he thinks he's Damon Hill and then Braces made a jerky movement with the flat of his hand on the bar, growling. Everyone laughed: the jerkiness was the limp and the growl a racing car. Thirty years ago it would have been Graham, not Damon. With another cripple to rag.

Told Jessica Marlow I would stay an extra week. The villa's free all autumn.

Sitting on a bench in the square, studying the pond's ducks. A disturbing day, as they say.

Popped into the village stores this morning and Marjorie Hobbs was behind the counter. Actually she's now a Rose, married one of them a generation back and come through to widowhood without my seeing. Same pleasing pre-war smells of wax polish and dry goods, and still all basically dog chews, woven name-tapes, metal hairgrips and mopheads, plus the usual tinned groceries and some feeble-looking greens. Fluorescent bits and bobs for kids but otherwise no concessions to progress. Remembered how I used to fancy Marjorie's mother when I was pimpled and now the little daughter in ribbons is a fat fifty-odd. An old bird hunched up in a basket chair by the door leading off to the living quarters but I didn't make the connection. Marjorie said she had seen me pass the window and how was I doing?

'It's Mr Arnold, Ma,' she called. I mumbled Arkwright but saw that Gracie was responding so went over to her and shook her hand, all soft folds of skin yet bony like a little bird's. She has the same twinkles for eyes, but everything else has gone as it was based on a sort of yeasty plumpness, leaning her full chest on the counter and smelling of split peas and tea as she strained to hear my blushing thruppenny orders.

Of course I've seen her since, but how many times have I been back in the last fifty years? A handful, and not at all since 1974.

Gracie genuinely pleased to see me – I am still the little boy. We somehow got on to Mother. She liked Mother, called her 'handsome' and 'a proper lady'. This doesn't mean posh, it means charm and treating the shopkeeper as a person. No mention of Uncle E. Then she leaned forward, whispering. I didn't catch it at first: her false teeth loose, my ears going. Something about walking. My mother liked walking and was deaf? Was staying where?

'I saw your dear mother walk, the day of her death.'

'What?'

'I did. I saw her walk. The same day.'

I nodded as if she'd told me the price of bacon was up. My hand was gripped in hers.

'How did she look?' Daft question, but Gracie replied, 'Famous.' Serves me right.

Reflecting on it now by the pond. The most moving fact is that Mother is still present in the collective memory. Much more important than the fact that it's all whimsical nonsense. *There was no death*, for a start. I'd have asked more daft questions but Gracie started to choke on a cough and Marjorie ushered her away into the shadows. One truly wonders if it is less tiring to be a duck than a human.

Wednesday, 22 September

Guardian article by Emma Murphy fine except for a sudden veiled attack on our use of boy-players, as if we're denting the feminist cause in the name of authenticity. Even the early music brigade would admit that a decent treble beats a decent soprano in terms of limpidity and poignancy. Our boy-players are expert virtuosos after five years at Eilrig; if choir schools do it, so can we. Then they grow up and are as finely honed as any opera-singer.

She also mentioned the new Globe going up, as if I had something to do with it. I had said that if it had been erected anywhere else, I might have done – but where it is will mean block-bookings by Americans and a lot of compromise. Like the RSC not getting the hell out of Stratford, despite all my efforts. I don't *believe* in spirit of place. Not a word of this appeared, of course.

Have just read that nasty paragraph again. It's a little like that chap from the lighting union who went on in the name of his members about our sticking to steady 'daylight', whingeing away about our usual absence of effects bar the winched awning and the flaming torch. As if keeping some truculent Sparks happy is more important than honouring Shakespeare.

I wrote a letter after breakfast and then tore it up. Other more pressing tasks. Mainly wandering about the house and imagining its new role. Have removed some of the looser coverings from the windows but the dust is too awful. Let it rest in its gloom until we're certain.

So here we are.

Spent the rest of the day on the phone to all the people who have to be activated if the new project is to work. Andrew Barnes said that the Lottery is going to reap a windfall for the arts. I said we've always been a nation of wasters and spenders: it'll just mean everywhere will be covered in scaffolding and closed.

Late drink in the Never Fear marred by a big slow man in a smelly flared suit producing little squares of paper on which he wrote apothegms in laborious block capitals. My pockets are now full of them: YOU CAN STAND AND TAKE THE PISS BUT EVERY TIME YOU SHOOT YOU MISS, and so forth. GIVE INSTRUCTIONS TO A WISE MAN HE WILL BE YET WISER AND TO A FOOL IT IS WATER ON COLD STONE. Perhaps he meant to be threatening, but otherwise he never said a word. No sign of our leery coalman, thank God.

Thursday, 23 September

Rain, rain, rain. Depressed and strangely exhausted. Suddenly no deadlines, no opening nights. No strung terror that it won't be ready or any good. Just the fear that without me the enemy will close. What was it Pascal said about each one of us being everything to ourselves, because when we die, the whole dies with us? That is the illusion, anyway.

Dreams about Mother, droll rather than pleasant or sad. She gives me used-up ration-books and there are sirens and she disappears, that sort of thing. I showed her the searchlight this morning (which turned out to be the sun through the curtains), and she was impressed, but I kept looking out for the Junkers over the Humber. She left us six years before all that nonsense.

This comes of reading the childhood memoir, which I finished after lunch. Stops abruptly at the bad news. Seems like another life, another person. But I'm behind the same mask, playing the same story. On looking out a few minutes ago through the streaming blur I saw a chap in cricketing togs sheltering in the bus-stop and assumed, before I could check myself, that it was Herbert E. Standing.

He's gone, now.

Ten days here and it feels like three, I've achieved so little. Have made appointments in London for early next week. *Hamlet* is sold out for the run: appreciative Japanese tourists who are used to Noh, probably. If only Burbage or someone had preserved it all like the Shogun did at exactly the same time. Alas, we have no equivalent of Zeami's *Kadensho*. Seven books on how to achieve the 'flower', that mysterious and supreme beauty of performance. My own effort is merely a shoring of scattered fragments with the glue of intelligent surmise. A 5,000-piece puzzle left out in the rain, scattered through the dark woods of neglect.

Today dank but not raining. Showed Barry and Andrew Barnes around the house. John Wall has made cursory inroads into the tangle, but both came in only their prissy city shoes and Andrew wore his long cream gaberdine – which of course got spotted the moment we entered the house, groping about with my little torch. I didn't prise away any more lino and carpet doping as there are broken windows and it would invite natural and human invaders. Anyway, Andrew and Barry agreed it was only feasible if the place was gutted.

What a place to be a boy in, they said. Not sure whether this meant that I'd been lucky or unlucky.

Have made new living arrangements for myself. Wanting to avoid that mute Dr Johnson in the Never Fear, tried the Green Man at the far end of the village. Except for the neon strips, hasn't budged an inch since it was my occasional furtive haunt just before the war. Buttoned horsehair seats, Player's floor mats, bedraggled dartboard, bleach-and-beer smell, fat tabby curled on a bentwood chair. Farm-labourer types in camouflage jackets, no music. Ted behind the bar in Roy Orbison specs and cardie has to be since my era. It came up that he had an attic room which from time to time had been used for guests – workers on six months' contracts in the area, etc. He did a decent breakfast. One of the customers said he should get Maisie to do the fried eggs. Ted didn't like that – mumbled an explanation that his wife did the breakfasts when this was a proper 'inn' but she went and 'let him down' – *i.e.* ran off with a lover, I presume.

We went up to have a look and it really is a garret but not without charm, split in two by a thin partition. The bathroom's just below on a floor otherwise populated by empty numbered rooms. The deeper room has only a tiny skylight – Ted said he'd find a lamp. He also reckoned he had a solid table somewhere and a little cooker, otherwise the furnishings are what one used to call humble and the floor is joyfully to boards with only a frayed rug. Will pay half what I'm charged at the Old Barn and it'll feel less hotel-like, more like digs. David confirmed the villa's free through the winter. I told Ted I'd take the room to November and then we'd see.

Saturday, 25 September

A lacklustre day scribbling ideas about the research centre. I took the deposit to Ted and to check if the place was quiet in the evenings. The awful coalman and John Wall were in there, playing darts. They seem to know each other. I mean, they seem to be friends. Even in the pub John Wall looks as if he's never had to fetch his own slippers. Morris's gay-detecting radar (or gaydar!) would bleep feebly next to him but I don't suppose the poor chap himself has any idea.

I couldn't avoid them, of course, and the subject of the house came up. The coalman's name is Frank Petty. 'However, I am knowed as Muck.' I'm not surprised. He went on again about 'nice Mrs Arnold', and then had the cheek to ask me 'ezackerly what relation' she was to me. Again with that horrible leer. I can't *imagine* that there was anything between them, even twenty-odd years ago – the man is like a little tub with a flat gristly face and a swollen mouth in which his front teeth are so worn as to be virtually missing. Tiny eyes, reddish from drink and weather and some tainted vehemence. Smells of public lavatories and fox-holes. Mind you, age does awful things. I replied that she was my uncle's wife, and no blood-relation of mine. Then this preposterous wink, and a snigger from John Wall. I am not trowelling down any further: Aunt Rachael was a sad, bitter mystery to me. Leave well alone.

More on the house being 'troubled', however. John Wall threw a dart into the upper division but it dangled from a loose piece of felt. 'That counts,' he said. Coalman Muck, turning to me, said,

'Hark at the old boy, he reckons that counts.' I replied that it would if it didn't fall, whereupon the man stamped hard on the floor and the damn thing fell out. To my surprise, John Wall calmly lowered his score without counting the offending dart. Muck clearly felt uneasy and turned to me again; 'Fair, weren't it, Mr Arkwright?' I said that I reserved judgement, as Mr Wall didn't seem to mind. Muck then pointed his dart at me and said, 'That's what all clever chaps say. That's what you'd say about your bogyman, *Mr* Arkwright.'

'What bogyman?'

'The Red Lady.'

'The Red Lady?'

'That's the bogywoman,' said John Wall.

Muck threw his dart angrily into the bull and was so flushed with his success that the bogywoman vanished as quickly as she'd appeared, to my relief. Something about its name made my heart's little flame flare up for an instant, as if I knew it from my childhood. But I'm sure I don't.

Sunday, 26 September

Stood at the back during the Family Service and tried not to think too much about ghosts. The fragments of medieval wall-paintings are wonderful, I'd forgotten how wonderful they were. We have something to thank the German bombs for, since it was a bomb that cracked the whitewash. Maybe I only saw them that one time, when the plaster was still all over the pews. Fewer hats, but even more old ladies, including Gracie. Insurance policy, I suppose. Eager kids making a lot of noise, harmless sermon on beasts. Do beasts have souls? That has always struck me as Christianity's fault-line. The fat, jolly vicar hopped over it with aplomb and kept to pandas.

People looked at me but I slipped out afterwards, wandering between the graves again. No official death and nothing to bury, even. Mother, I'm talking about. Somehow the plot in Ulverton churchyard never marked with a stone, a memorial stone. I have no idea where this plot was or even is, perhaps it was mythical or used up by some complete stranger: we somehow never gave up hope and then forgot. No sign of Aunt Joy's, though I'm sure it was near the kiss-me gate into the paddock.

Spotted Gracie between the stones, with a bunch of flowers. Herbert Hobbs's grave, of course, space on it left for her. I mentioned this business about Mother's plot – felt empty-handed with nowhere to go. She mumbled something about singing carols. 'That's when I saw your mum, clear as day,' she said. On the way back from the village carol-round, as far as I could gather. Mother always loved carols. I wanted to cry.

The junk is in layers, every time I move one thing, another appears or falls out of it. They must have got rid of much less at the auction than I realised. Kept stopping at the thought of a bat about to flutter out blindly towards my face. The thought worse than the deed. I know they're protected and all that, but have a horror of their fat little bodies and complicated rodent faces, let alone their leathern wings. Not even sure what I'm looking for, but you never know.

Monday, 27 September

Slept until ten. Almost missed breakfast: charred kidneys.

A long walk to clear my head in indifferent milky weather, returned via the house. No sign of Wall though half the lawn is cut.

Begin to see the bones of the exploit flesh. Once the windows are unblocked and the nettles and brambles cut away from the walls and front door, it will blink and open its eyes and breathe. Had no heart to go inside and anyway left the key in my room.

Tried to penetrate the wildwood and remembered the strict injunctions of Nuncle not to. Stood on the edge where the old wire fence lay rusting in nettles and stared for a little while, thinking. Then I walked deliberately in.

The scratches still painful on my ankles and knuckles, though I didn't get very far. A fat, familiar face passed me in the square on my return and I beamed back and of course it was the Vicar in a polo-neck. Had never heard of any of us Arkwrights or even Arnolds, yet gave the impression that he had considered our souls all week. I mentioned the two plots and he said that he'd get his parish clerk to look up the relevant documents. The Vicar's name is Oliver, Eddie Oliver. Sounds like an extinct music-hall act, with whistling solos and imitations of animals. The type Ulverton Village Hall used to host. He mentioned something about a Mrs Prat and mummers, when he understood that I was 'on the stage'. Vicars are much too hassled by life and death to concern themselves with earth-changing characters like me.

Unbelievably, *the* Mrs Prat (whose name fits her like a hat) accosted me in the village shop about an hour ago. That damned eye-patch again. Planning a traditional Xmas festivity with mummers, folk dances, etc. Could I pop in to give a professional hand with the mumming play? Now and again? Reminded me that my uncle had started the Ulverton Folk-Life Society. I looked steely and said that if I were to help, it would be in my capacity as a theatre professional, not as Edward Arnold's nephew.

She took that as a yes and thanked me profusely.

Evening: Bush-telegraph, my word! A Malcolm Villiers, the director of operations, has just phoned and invited me to tea on Thursday. Sounded nervous and/or depressed. Told him that Hardy's proof of an authentic village folk ritual was the bored, miserable look of the participants. He chuckled and sounded jolly.

Do-gooding is just that: it does one good.

Took a deep breath and mentioned the Red Lady to the agreeable Jessica Marlow before supper. It's because I can't get rid of this flary little flame in my chest, every time I think about her (the Red Lady, not Jessica). She said I should meet Ray Duckett, the local history man. She's got his book on Ulverton's ghosts somewhere; will lend it to me. Duckett, she added, is very ill with cancer in a private nursing home outside Netherford. He's bound to pass away minutes before I reach him.

An unsteady centenarian on stork-like legs entered the bar and it was none other than old Moon, the strapping blacksmith whose anvil used to vie with the church bell. He's stone deaf. The yard's now an up-market garage, but still Moon's. Perhaps he'll just go on and on, his heart wrought in iron.

Am rather drunk.

Writing this in Morris's spare room with that gorgeous rumble of London below. Rumbling river of life.

Arrived at Paddington in a fluorescent-jacketed bombscare and everything terribly loud after the country. Everyone shouting over unoiled moving parts. Throbbings, stinky smells, the air stinging the eyes. Cypriot taxi driver bawling his opinions. But a relief. Unpleasant sense that back there in the country everything's paused, waiting for me. Even the leaves not dropping or even trembling. Even Mrs Prat of the flowery cravat not bearing down on anyone. Everything just suspended and waiting for me to come down the road as if back from the war. Like my uncle did, apparently. Actually walking down the lane in uniform and dusty face, backpack, wheezing from the gas and not in possession of all his marbles.

Interrupted Morris installing the Internet – which is just more displacement activity and will end up being taken over by the disturbed, but he disagrees and thinks it's the most important advance since Gutenberg. Tried Arkwright, Hugh: forty-two entries. Fourteen for some baseball player called Hugo 'Choppie' Arkwright Jr, the rest a mixed bag of adulation and nastiness, mostly out of date, and mis-spelling Eilrig. We went to an Italian with tiles as green as old Burkett's the poulterer's in Brompton Road and talked of that old drab half-lit London, whether it was better than the bloodshot star-shell frenzy of today's. Decided it was because now we're old and less able to jig about.

Three olds, look.

Morris spent his first night ever here in the long-gone Cavendish Hotel, but I couldn't remember where I'd stayed with Mother, only that it was near Peter Jones – where only four years later I went shopping with her for the very last time, buying that fancy red coat for Buea. Twirling in front of the mirror between all that stifling cloth and saying she was tired of looking 'bush', she was going to look 'fancy', but would it clash with the hibiscus? Such a happy image, and the shopwoman saying how lovely she looked. I don't suppose she ever wore it. Of course she never wore it. She vanished before Christmas, just before their Christmas up in chilly Buea. Morris let me talk because he was just as sloshed. He told me that I never talk about my mother. He has decided to abandon his hair to whiteness and it makes him look blacker and very dignified, like an ambassador. I said the great shock on arrival in this country was the milling multitudes of white faces. Morris recalled Missouri and his childhood just like a Faulkner novel, the Americans so awful and unbelievably racist while in Africa itself the English were racist in a weak well-meaning way, but the effects were in the end the same. I do understand now why he never went back apart from falling in love with a Cambridge chap, and perhaps why he's my closest and most loyal friend. Mutually loyal. He reminds me of my friend the servant called Quiri sometimes, whose servantness was like an irritating obstacle and Morris has done away with that. Quiri is probably dead now.

Wednesday, 29 September

Feeling horribly furred up inside, had to spend the whole day meeting people individually or in meetings trying to stir up enthusiasm. Much emphasis from everyone on 'youth', 'multi-ethnicity' and of course 'accessibility', which I keep thinking means having ramps. Dan Hartley questioned my record on blind casting which is absurd, I have never once picked an actor for a role on account of his or her colour and he's confusing critics (attacking our 'authenticity' on just this basis) with our own policy. Imelda Tupp (pure coincidence) then pointed out that my Othello was a white actor blacked up and I said, 'Exactly, Ms Tupp, and my Iago was of Asian origin, the brilliant Nadeem Rafiq.'

Want sometimes to say shuddup very loudly but these people hold me in their sweaty palms. Always the implication that one is guilty and on trial to prove it, with nothing registered of one's achievements that doesn't fit into one of those silly little boxes on the forms. They have never liked the fact that I only use actors who've been trained in Eilrig which Bill Saynor, that awful old potato-faced pseud, keeps calling the All Right Method. The only clever idea he's ever had, yet he's up there at the top doling out the dosh, with immense powers to create and destroy.

Now I'm back in the dark, quiet countryside with murmurs from the hotel bar below and an owl that sounds as if it's been wound up. Odd swish of a car. Feeling a bit drained and old. The moment your back's turned! New young bucks who are *deliberately* letting rip at our achievements; if they take over in a few years or so at the RSC we'll weaken our hold there and will again be seeking our own space.

The Research Centre shall be another little flame at the heart, keeping our blood clean and scarlet.

Thursday, 30 September

Social Services meeting in Netherford's new overheated council offices. Much humming and hawing *re* feasibility of turning Ilythia into home for maladjusted youths (money, basically) and still awaiting architect's report, so we have a bit of grace. Kept mum in meeting but had already warned Brian Padmore, the jolly but ineffective solicitor here, that I was considering setting up my own project, charitably within the terms of the will. Row of neckties like bellpulls facing me, plush room furnished by racked-up rents. Emerged feeling jaded and dull, like them. These places cast a malign spell.

Tea with Malcolm Villiers. Lives next door to John Wall and his mum, one half of same double-cottage. Jed the bilious gamekeeper had it in my time, patrolling woods now criss-crossed by public paths behind the new private housing estate. The spirits of him and his mucky little spaniel must be having a fit.

Malcolm a nice shy chap with a beard and the usual roster of views to go with it, but we didn't fall out. He's divorced with a little girl whose presence was in the withered flowers in a jam jar on the kitchen table and some rather disturbing paintings. He blamed his neighbour for his marital breakdown: some extraordinary story about Wall's father falling ill and being treated with Chinese herbs by Mrs Villiers. They then fell out over an incident with the Wall's vicious little dog until Jack Wall came back one day covered in blisters and with streaming eyes, demanding to see Mrs Villiers. She stayed with him until he was taken off to hospital and he died there the next day. Whereafter she was regarded as a murdering witch and under that pressure their marriage fell apart. Wall Senior was a nasty piece of work and a well-known badger-baiter. The official verdict was arsenic poisoning. Malcolm relieved to hear that I hadn't heard it already and I think by telling me he was pre-empting false versions. It was probably rat poison carelessly used against some harmless woodland beast. Country ways haven't changed, I said.

Our conversation revolved otherwise around Nuncle, for whom Malcolm has an unhealthy admiration. Most excited when I told him about *I, Nubat, of the Forest People* as illustration of just how childishly dotty Edward Arnold was. He wondered if he could get hold of a copy and I told him it was very rare. He looked shocked suddenly at something over my shoulder and on turning round I saw John Wall staring in at the window.

He entered and told us that his mother had 'taken a fall'. Malcolm groaned and looked fed up so I went round and sure enough Mrs Wall was bleeding profusely from her nose and forehead, swearing like mad at her son as he came in. Plop, plop, plop went the blood on the table's oilcloth: dark red on green. I dabbed her with a wet flannel and was struck by whiffs from her cardigan of expensive perfume. Big telly blaring, cheap fittings, lino below and bare bulb above, yet fundamentally the house is a mirror-image of Malcolm's, which is put to pine and a cosy scatter of antique junk, rugs, etc.

John Wall looked on benignly as his mother swore at him and then the two tottered off down the lane to the doctor's, she not changing her boots or donning a coat. Dark blots all over the table and the floor – I had half a mind to clean it up. But didn't. Malcolm said on my return that it happens regularly and it's probably somehow John Wall's doing. My hands still smell of the woman: sour and sweet. There really is so much blood in the forehead, right against the bone.

Agreed to look in on mummers' rehearsal, Saturday. For my sins.

Friday, 1 October

Maybe the howling of wolves at a bomber's moon, but have unearthed something rather startling. To mix a metaphor.

On my way to the house, popped into the doctor's surgery (bright, like a kindergarten, with no horrible maps of the body's regions these days) and checked up on Mrs Wall's welfare; receptionist amused that I'd bothered.

Saw thick smoke from the lane and thought the house was on fire. John Wall burning leaves in the garden. No mention of yesterday, so I didn't hang about but disappeared into the attic and put away some bits and bobs using cardboard boxes from the shop. Seeing Wall had gone home for lunch, I went down once more to the wildwood's edge.

Pungent smell of wood garlic, no doubt about it. Rich and vegetative and profound, like nothing else, not even much like French cooking. Have confirmed in flower book here just now in the hotel lounge that wood garlic or 'ramsons' (*Allium ursinum*) is over and done with by July, like the bluebell. (Aunt Joy always called them 'ransoms', I remember.) The smell was in a sort of invisible cloud which after a few minutes had passed away. I walked back and forth along the ferny edge in the rain but there was nothing.

Went back for a spirit-summoning Scotch in hotel bar and Jessica came up very excited with Duckett's book, *Ulverton and Her Ghosts*. Crudely drawn illustrations of ghostly shepherds with lamps, big black dogs, skeletal shadows, etc. However, the passage on Ilythia and the Red Lady so shook me that I ordered a double. Here it is.

Further up the lane, past the old apple orchard, is a large, rather gloomy house, long empty, once the home of the well-known author and mystic, Edward Arnold. I remember him as an eccentric old man, sporting in all weathers an old tweed smoking jacket and a bamboo-handled umbrella – which would stay rolled even in rain! He died in 1965, and was survived for several years by his much-younger widow, a recluse in chronic ill-health. I believe the property has now passed into the hands of Arnold's nephew, the theatre personality Hugh Arkwright [*sic*]. The house is called 'Ilythia', the nameplate still legible on the gate.

An empty house is as inviting for ghosts as it is for wasps, as we have already seen. But 'Ilythia' – the name of an obscure Greek goddess, in charge of child bearing – is certainly haunted, and was so long before the shutters went up [shutters?]. Apart from the odd but unconfirmed sighting of lights burning in the windows at strange hours, several people have seen a ghostly lady walking in the grounds – but only, apparently, in snowy weather. In each case, immediate investigation has shown no footprints. She is dressed in a red coat, with black hair, and has the peculiar quality, for a ghost, of having a dark skin. Both Miss Eva Oadam and Mr Frank Petty maintained that her skin was tanned, as if she had been sun-bathing. The late Miss Eva Oadam saw a bright-red coat gliding over the lawn on a snowy day in the early 1970s, though she also saw an accompanying pair of bloomers and three hovering brassières – I am tempted to conclude that a washing-line might have played a role! Mr Frank Petty's report is more interesting: in his own words – 'I was delivering coal to the late Mrs R.S. Arnold, when I looked up from the bunker, where I had just emptied my sack. I saw a woman – certainly not Mrs R.S. Arnold – walking across the lawn. She was at some little distance from me, and it occurred to me then that she might be the so-called Red Lady. I didn't feel frightened, but unfortunately the coal dust made me cough, and she vanished, as if I'd startled her. She must have the hearing of a deer! She'd been walking towards the wood at the bottom of the garden, across thick snow. The snow was undisturbed, however: the only prints on the lawn that I could see were those of birds. I didn't talk about it to Mrs Arnold, for fear of causing her alarm, as she was of a nervous disposition.'

Another witness, Mrs Enid Bradman, saw a red-coated lady walking down Crab-Apple Lane during snowy weather, probably in 1982, but cannot recall whether it was in the vicinity of the Arnold house or nearer the village centre. She was already aware of the previous sightings.

Mrs Grace Hobbs (who runs our general stores), says that she believes the ghost to be that of Mr Arnold's first wife [sic], who died at the same time as Mrs Hobbs's sighting, which took place in the early Thirties. The first Mrs Arnold spent much of her time in Africa, which might account for the tanned skin; she eventually died out there in mysterious circumstances, many thousands of miles from her home. However, there are various anomalies in this case. First, Mrs Hobbs saw the ghost, not by the house but in the snow-covered lane, gliding swiftly towards the gate. Secondly, it is usually someone very close to the deceased, and not a bare acquaintance, who receives a vision of the person at the moment of his or her death. Thirdly, the ghost in such a case does not usually return.

I have not been able to track down any other witnesses . . .

He then 'field-tests' the snow theory himself, crouching behind a bush on the lawn, but is merely troubled by cold and the whining of his dog. Of course the dog has to whine.

Jessica tells me that Enid Bradman died last year after being pushed over by a mugger, and was full of tales. But what a nice woman – she saved the old barn from being demolished, for a start. Mugger never caught, but they think it was someone local. She trod on so many toes. That's one thing I won't be doing, I said. Mugging, or treading on toes, Hugh? I do like Jessica, I really do. Maybe Enid Bradman's something to do with Herbert Bradman. Nuncle was very keen on him – almost as dotty, as far as I recall.

Anyway, I need to see Gracie again. I'm sitting here at the sloping desk with my heart flaring and my forehead sweaty like a frightened, excited little boy.

I need to ask her about the redness of the Red Lady. Whether it was close to vermilion. Whether it would clash with the hibiscus, as it were.

Jessica wondered when I would be staying to and I confessed that I was moving to the Green Man next week. She seemed relieved not sad – there's a big party of geologists coming and it looks as if they're under-booked, so I've had to hurry Ted up.

Went into the Green Man to see Ted and again Mr Muck and John Wall were there. I don't know how but the tale of Jack Wall's demise came up. Muck whispered to me conspiratorially while John Wall grinned inanely yet with cunning in his eyes that arsenic had been found on Mrs Maddy Villiers's fingers and that she'd actually been arrested! Released for lack of evidence, apparently. One can see why this was left out by Malcolm but then what else was left out?

Muck was a bit past it on barley wine, drawly accent even drawlier, but I did mention his 'sighting'. He said it would cost me a glass of same to know more. I relented, of course. He then gave me an idiolectal version of his appearance in Ray Duckett's book, but with no extra facts. I thanked him. There was a pause, and he said, leering at me: 'Oh yes, we have some fond memories of young Mrs Arnold, don't us, John?' John nodded, beaming. 'I expects you do, too, Mr Arkwright,' the coalman added. There was something so horrible about his look, the way he eyed me then, that I felt physically sickened and had to bid them a hasty goodnight. I find their company more irritating than picturesque and will be coldly polite from now on. No reason why John Wall shouldn't continue doing his bit for me, however.

Saturday, 2 October

Rehearsal in the village hall, still a corrugated tin shed lined warmly inside with waxy wood, but painted green, not brown. Spare the details of the pudding of a ritual drama that Malcolm's struggling to produce, except that he's throwing in dollops (or wallops) of a Sword Play, a Wooing Play, and a Hero-Combat Play and stirring hard. Mrs Pratt (apparently with two *t*s) introduced me as 'terribly famous', and everyone (including me) chortled with embarrassment. Felt so sorry for Malcolm as the débâcle proceeded that I invited him to dinner at the Old Barn.

We talked theatre history, over the candles. Or theatre prehistory: hobby-horses rooted in centaurs, mumming in fertility rituals, all that misty-moor stuff. He mentioned that in Nuncle's *Harmonies of the Primitive* there's a photo of the Ulverton mumming troupe and the hobby-horse has a leopard skin draped on it. This is apparently because the Babylonian centaur was always depicted on vases and so forth with a leopard skin and wings. Uncle Edward dispensed with the wings, I said, because wings have a habit of falling off.

Malcolm didn't smile over his vegetarian quiche. He wants to resurrect the leopard-skin practice. I didn't say anything about my find in the attic – even though it must be the same skin. Instead I told him that this was a falsely exotic touch by my uncle, that no real mummers' troupe in this country would ever have sported such a thing. I also repeated my assertion that most of what Edward Arnold wrote was second-hand tripe. He asked me over the pudding why I hated my uncle so much, just as Morris had asked me once. I gave a flustery sort of non-answer and we ended up talking about something else – music, I think. He teaches music and a bit of drama in various primary schools but with no great enthusiasm. He whinged on about everyone believing teachers are lazy whingers and I stopped myself making the obvious comment. A middlebrow touched with leftish views, which makes him think he's radical: Mozart less 'relevant' than a rap song, Shakespeare an old dud, kids better off with a triangle and a couple of tom-toms than a violin. I'm amazed he talks to me at all.

Sunday, 3 October

Mother's birthday. The day before the Feast Day of St Francis, we were reminded by Eddie the Vicar. A great number of little birds in the air but not much song yet. She'd have been easily still alive, not yet a hundred, a dear withered old thing with twinkly eyes. I wish there were candles to light in parish churches (but anyway they're mostly locked). I did offer up a prayer in Holy Communion, and relished the taste of the wine. Perhaps it isn't just wine. The arguments about this remind me of the arguments about the actor and his part. Passion is not less passionate for being feigned. One can be both possessed and in possession, both the mask and the face behind. The wine can be both plonk and blood.

Joined the coffee and biscuits afterwards in order to corner Gracie but was cornered in turn by Eddie, clearly thrilled by my zeal. I almost found myself in charge of hymn-books for the next few years, or something, but at least he introduced me to a snorty, snuffly little man called Mr Quallington – the parish clerk. Mr Q said he was terribly busy but at some point we could 'go through' the old sextonian documents for the whereabouts of the two plots.

He made it out to be the greatest of chores. An ex-schoolmaster, is my guess. Gracie gave me the slip.

Afterwards I felt a sort of ancestral loneliness, unrelieved by walking (grisly grey weather, mashed-up leaves everywhere) or by reading. If I'd had children, then I would still have them, however ghastly or unsympathetic they'd turned out to be. Like Tom Everett's daughters. Walking the Heath with someone calling you Daddy, gentle remonstrances, arm in yours, *leaning* on you at least.

Should I let a girlfriend happen? Someone of Jessica's strength and maturity and jolly smile, easy ways, straightforward beauty? There are women who like old and difficult men who are gifted, have power. Play the sage.

But then I would be spoiling whoever I plucked, a ghastly parody of my one and only love. The old goat who spoiled it now played by me, buffoonishly. Can memory – a memory – be blighted in the same way? I have expended so much energy on dividing those golden memories of her from the Fall, and it has worked so far. She is two different people, and now she is dead anyway. Long dead. Her beauty can hang intact in my head and along my arms while her blighted second self can be decently buried.

Old goat? He was only in his early forties, then. My mother was not even that, she was thirty-nine when she left us. If she left us. This still seems old, because even to my boy's eye she seemed physically younger, almost like a young girl, with the smooth skin of a young girl. Might have been to do with the soft, humid air of the out-station. She had shadows under her eyes and a thinness – but that was fever, that was Africa.

Watching a mother and her son over lunch today at the Mill. She rotund and wobbly, big laugh, probably has enormous house and dogs; he about ten, assured, probably at boarding prep, perhaps his birthday, but blue around the eyes and wearing a baseball cap over what looked like baldness. Maybe mortally ill.

I'm reminded by the childhood memoir how Mother never looked at me properly. This must have been because she knew she was going to lose me to England. Easier for both of us: buckling down her maternal instinct as cargo was buckled down in the steamer's hold. She wasn't the reserved type, otherwise. Jigging about to all those records. Laughing with the men at the Club in Victoria. Kissing Father.

But if England had been replaced by Death, she might have looked at me as the mother in the restaurant kept looking at her son. I did nearly die, of course, that time – that winter of snow. And that was the time she disappeared.

Good God.

I don't believe in ghosts. No I don't.

Later. Very pleased to be here, in Ted's attic room, out of the hotel and into something I can call my own domain. He has found me an old table, an old round pub-table he removed years ago because it had accumulated obscene graffiti. He thought I wouldn't mind and I don't. There were obscene scribbles in Pompeii. He brought up the 'lamp' very proudly and it was one of those glass columns full of tumescent fluorescent ectoplasm that make me feel sick. And far too dim. Perhaps he thinks I have ultra-violet sight under my eye-patch (or knows I was an observer in the war). I thanked him, anyway.

The room smells of bleach, nicotine and underarms beneath the beer because Ted's cleaning lady has only just done it. Ted is pleased to see me installed, but is nervous about breakfast, I can see that. *Joe the Gelatine Was Here* pencilled next to the door: the whole place, even the rooms below, occupied by a film crew shooting a documentary a few years back that I never even noticed. He said they drank him dry, sounding nostalgic. Not my thing, I'm afraid, I said.

Have made enquiries about Ray Duckett: he is installed in the Hazeldell Rest Home just south of Netherford. Am in no hurry. If I hurry I will screw things up.

Screw what up?

My investigation into the mystery of the Red Lady, of course. Good grief, sounds like something Wilkie Collins might have put on in his drawing-room, for the delectation of the ladies. Or *Now Showing at the Criterion Theatre.* Six-foot letters in red on a black background, all over London: THE RED LADY MYSTERY. To what have I descended?

Anyway, I look upon this room as the show's headquarters. Its sloping ceiling reminds me that it is an attic and I feel nicely high up. There is another attic less than a mile away and perhaps that holds a clue of some sort. There are suitcases and boxes and the big bamboo-ribbed trunk and piles of papers, mostly newspapers, and African souvenirs. So far I have found nothing.

But archaeology, I remember Keiller saying, is 99 per cent mud and boredom and wet winds up one's back. Much like theatre.

Feel I am sitting here piloting a craft that is pitted against the great lump of the other thing, that if I tear open that lump I will find what I am looking for. Quite seriously, dear diary. But I can't set it down yet. Not in so many words. I do have a few grains of superstition left.

Monday, 4 October

Wrote postcards this morning: there is only one of Ulverton – the main street with lots of Ford Cortinas and women in dumpy coats and head-scarves. One of the coats is bright red, of course.

Went straight to the house after lunch, straight up to the attic, and then couldn't bend over for indigestion. First things first, and first things are in there. I have of course made inroads but now I am more alert because more *convinced*. Found a pile of Mother's warped gramophone records, mostly jazz, mostly cracked or broken in their paper sleeves. That might be a clue. I don't know. I'm no detective. My heart is my magnifying glass: I thought of that while up there, coughing on the dust.

Finally cleared a path to the big trunk. On the way I found the fetish box, the one that looks like a stool or a drum. Father bought it off some trader. Said to contain many powerful fetishes. A lid but jammed tight, cloaked in cobwebs. Pandora's Box, Mother called it.

The trunk had an Elder Dempster label on it with a picture of the steamer behind some palm trees and on the label was not only our name but a very faint date in ink: December 21st, 1933. I nearly passed away, of course.

This is the most likely date for Mother's disappearance, around the solstice. Midwinter in England. Sap right down. Hardly any light. The blurred stamp over the date was of the port authorities, perhaps in Victoria. When I was a boy here I was forbidden to go up to the attic, as I was forbidden to go into the wildwood. The truth seems to be dropping into my hands. The trunk was locked. Horribly, thoughts of Ginevra entered my head. Climbed for a joke into a trunk on her wedding day and years later, when it was opened, was found as a skeleton in her wedding dress. Ginevra! Ginevra! Ginevra! the bridegroom had called, running up and down the corridors. Now he too was long dead.

There was a creak behind me and to my horror my torch-beam found John Wall's head. I thought for a moment it had sort of rolled there – that it was just resting there after decapitation. So pasty. Then a sheepish smile broke across it. The rest of him emerged from the trap-door while I controlled my annoyance and made some joke about the junk. On clambering back I tripped over the leopard skin and its big skull flopped into view, snarling at us both.

He was most impressed and offered to clean the thing for me, then carried it down on his back. For all his weedy appearance, he did this without apparent effort, the big furred head bumping on his greasy hair. Laid out on the kitchen table it looked rather fine, for all its dirtiness and moth holes. Most of the claws are intact, as are all the teeth in the upper jaw. No lower jaw, being originally a ritual costume in its untanned life. Whiskers mostly bent or broken, alas, which would have upset Father.

He insisted its use was never sinister, never for murderous practices in a leopard society, but how could he have been sure? Still loath to touch the fur, even though musty and cobwebbed now.

John Wall took it home to clean it – he has cleaned many skins. No doubt.

I left the label where it was. I'll only lose it to the cleaning woman here. How shall I open the trunk without a key? Force seems wrong. Bad throat from the dust. I need a brandy and Jessica's ordinary cheeriness.

Awful dream: entering some sort of warehouse or church and stumbling on Nuncle with a butcher's knife, pleaching some complicated basket out of human flesh. I pretended I hadn't noticed, I was so terrified. Woke up with the sweating realisation that not only do I own the rights to his forgotten works, but that I have never more than dipped into them – as one might dip into the *limus niger* of the Styx, I suppose. Certain early passages have stuck only because I had to endure their interminable repetition on those wireless-less evenings of my youth.

Breakfast alone in the big back room full of gaunt cupboards: six fish fingers along with fried eggs, cereal, toast, served by the pimply youth who helps Ted behind the bar now and again. Can Ted keep this up? He appeared at one point and I expressed my admiration. The table is all by itself in the middle of the room, the pool table pushed to the side, and I feel like Louis XIV. Pimply Adrian, bleary-eyed and not very bright, clicks across the floor for ages before he gets to me. Or so it seems.

Mrs Pratt sidled up to me in the street this morning and suggested I'd upset Malcolm, apparently by not leaping up and down with admiration at the mummers' rehearsal. Then I bumped into Malcolm himself in the shop (no sign of Gracie) and he did seem morose. He said he had tracked down a copy of *I, Nubat* through a specialist friend. What was I supposed to reply? He asked me how I reckoned drama had actually started and I replied that since there is a blurred line between drama *per se* and metaphoric gesture, one could trace it at one extreme back to the casting of petals on to the Neanderthal graves and at the other to the strutting about of the shamans. Between the loo rolls, Persil packets, hot-water bottles and crummy greens, the discussion felt ludicrous, and since we were both holding wire baskets I also felt obscurely effeminate. Asked me to tea again tomorrow and I said yes, scarcely believing it's a whole week since the last time. Caught a glimpse of us both looking short and swollen in the huge fish-eye mirror above the door and had a stupid thought: *this is how the dead see us.*

Went to the house armed with a screwdriver but of course it

was the wrong size for the trunk's screws and I fouled one of the heads. On trying to lever the left lock away from the wood the cheap tool actually snapped in two. I measured the screws with a bit of paper and then, on hearing John Wall's strimmer or bush-cutter starting up, retired from the fray. I don't want him coming up here again and anyway I had a spat of breathlessness like last month – it's nerves and over-exertion and irritation.

Looked in on Mother's room again.

Wednesday, 6 October

Completely ridiculous but on arriving in Netherford at the hardware shop I couldn't find the bit of paper I'd marked the screw size on. Bought an expensive complete set and, on the advice of the helpful owner, a fierce-looking sort of jemmy with a claw at one end. Then to the library where I gazed on micro-fiched pages of the local paper for 1930 to 1935 and found some interesting stuff on Edward Arnold in the *Ulverton* column, written mostly by his acolytes. The Thule Society visit in 1933 is mentioned, along with the midwinter ritual.

Copied it and also confirmed the weather for late December 1933: basically, there was snow and a lot of it. On a sudden whim I checked when the Manor's carol-singing jaunt had taken place: it was on December 23rd in very fine crisp weather followed by a high tea. Gracie must then have seen Mother on December 23rd at about 7 o'clock in the evening – if she left no later than anyone else. Perhaps if the stamp on the label, showing George V's smudged head over the date, was not of the Victoria port authorities but of Liverpool's, then Mother, with her trunk buckled in the hold, arrived on the Elder Dempster steamer two days before. Anonymously. In disguise, perhaps.

It fits. Her son was very ill. It fits. Her son wasn't very ill when she set out, but maybe I have the dates of my illness completely out. Maybe I was ill in November. Maybe that particular Thule Society visit, after which I collapsed, was another year. Memory is a patchwork of unreliability, after all. Why otherwise would she have left Africa in such a hurry?

And what on earth happened to her once she was here? Because

– I have to remind myself – she *disappeared* and for *ever*.

Working backwards, then: Father's bush tours were generally three weeks or longer in duration, so it's quite possible that she vanished or made off around December 1st and the servants were lying, all of them, on her instructions. I know they loved my mother and my father had already started drinking too much. Anyway, not much baksheesh would have sealed their lips or persuaded them to fib.

I've been reading what I copied out in the library and one article in particular troubles me.

It dates from December 14th, 1931, and is only initialled. The opening is harmless enough: justifying ritual as a sharing in the 'daily miracle of existence' via references to Wordsworth's 'motion' and 'spirit' rolling through all things, and the native belief that 'everything partakes of the same essential mystic reality'. No quarrel with that, though its dark side is nowhere evident: trees with designs on you, spirits behind every bush, ancestors waiting to enter your head. I was about ten when I first started reading Shakespeare and reckoned that the tragic vision might have something to offer over animism (not even Nuncle's cod sort). It explained my loneliness. Morris says I should write my Life and put all this in but I'm still shy about it, still nervous of being watched or overheard through the trees.

Anyway, the piece then advertises Edward Arnold's own 'ancient ritual', one of those winter solstice things to encourage the sap back up: the mention of the 'resuscitation' dance performed by the village mummers around a bonfire, 'in which a young lady, dressed all in red (the symbol of life), is ritually "killed" and "revived" (all volunteers welcome, skull guaranteed unbroken!)', brought it all back, of course. No recollection of this specific one – they've mostly rolled into a muddy mass flitted over by long white gowns and flames and leering faces. But that mass is vivid enough and of course there again is a red lady. A Red Lady. Nearest and dearest. Oh God.

Well, what *would* he have stopped at for the sake of that blasted wildwood? Absolutely nothing, probably. Absolutely nothing. Agamemnon killed his own daughter for a fair wind. Abraham and Isaac. His only begotten Son, all that. Something so precious it can't be counted. If the stakes are high enough. Oh dear God. One great rustling greenwood on the back of it. 'I'd have to please the gods an awful lot, wouldn't I, Hugh?' Yes, they'd have been pleased all right, Nuncle.

But the wildwood hasn't budged an inch!

Stop this. Leave it.

Have organised my visit to Ray Duckett's 'rest home' for tomorrow morning. Cliff's Taxis will take me there and back. I won't tax him, I told Jessica. Just as long as he can still talk.

Tea with Malcolm a tense affair since I was in no mood to lavish lying praise on his efforts. He said he felt a complete failure and started to needle me about my method, finding it restrictive, anti-creative, anti-political and so on. I didn't feel like fencing and just answered by rote, head whirling like a dervish with other thoughts. His *coup de grâce* was to accuse me of being antiquarian, so I said, 'Well, I've always hated quarians.' He just blinked. I don't think he has much sense of humour. Then seeing the sun beaming through the window, we went out for a walk. Caught up short by the sight of the leopard skin hanging on John Wall's washing-line.

Malcolm's mouth fell open and so did mine. The thing was very striking against the dull bricks of the cottage – as shiny as silk and the spots inked so clearly the Ethiopian had clearly just pressed his fingers to it. The head dangled morosely but the teeth were shining and the glass eyes flashed in the sun – they'd been filmed with dust and filth before. It was very much a crucifixion. I told Malcolm the story of David's little girl in Umbria, who pointed to a roadside rood and asked why they'd hung that man up to dry – but he didn't laugh like everyone else does, he was too overcome by the sight of the skin. It was like a gift from the gods, he said, it was uncanny, he'd been wondering how to get hold of a leopard skin just that morning. When I pointed out that it was the same one as in the Arnold photograph (mentioned over dinner), he made a sort of strangled noise. Had to explain how it had ended up on John Wall's washing-line and then fibbed: 'I'd intended it to be a surprise, of course.'

He turned instantly happy, like a little boy given a new bicycle.

Thursday, 7 October

Horrible. Absolutely horrible.

[*No further entries*]

4

Dear Mother,

So here we are.

I'm doing jolly fine, on the whole.

I've had a spot of bother but it's passing. The people here suggested I write about what happened, since I can't talk about it.

Dr Wolff suggested the same years and years ago, when I was feeling a bit down. But it's *my* idea to write to you like I used to write to you from school, telling you about the week, what I've been up to.

They're very pleasant and helpful, here. You would get on with them. The funny thing is, this place is how I always pictured your sanny in Hampshire, where you met Father. I think back to those days, often. There's a big lawn and many trees. I have a very well-appointed room looking out on the car park, but I can see a bit of the lawn if I squash my face against the glass. The window only opens at the top. That's the way it's made.

When I take a stroll, I'm always thinking you're about to appear down a corridor or from out of the trees on the lawn, pushing Father.

I'll tell you what happened, in order. How am I getting on? they say. Quite well, I signal.

I prefer not to talk.

You're listening to me now, but I'm not sure you're absolutely hooked. There are a lot of coughs. I'm still sweeping the stage, but I'm not a clown.

Since I saw you last, I've been very busy. I can't tell you about all that, not now.

I used to keep a diary. Then I stopped it.

I think I'll start where I stopped it. This was about a year ago, now. During this year I've also stopped talking. I'm worried that if

I open my mouth to use my vocal chords, quite another sound will come out. This is the effect of shock. There's a word for all this. They use this word here, instead of the other word.

Dysfunctional. That's it.

I think it was a Thursday. I think it was. I'm getting stuck already.

Your ever-loving son.

Hugh

Rain.

Dear Mother,

So here we are again, again.

As you write, things will come back to you, they tell me. Exactly as Dr Wolff said. Exactly as when one writes one's diary. I hope nothing comes back that I don't want.

I have to write in the present tense. This helps, they say. It's like watching a play. You don't perform plays in the past tense, do you?

It is a Thursday, yes. Early October.

I'm in this big blue car.

A Rover, with leather seats. I'm being driven to an old people's home on the other side of Netherford. I'm feeling carsick, as usual. It's all these mini-roundabouts. I ordered the taxi, and the taxi driver's called Cliff. He has stubble instead of hair and keeps an eye on me in his rear-view mirror. He tells me he has not always done this, he used to be a mechanic on oil tankers. He misses the sea.

How much do I put in? They say the details are important, but I might go on too long. I might lose you before the very bad thing.

We're inching down the High Street. You'd recognise Netherford High Street, except for the Victorian lamp standards; they're new. Most of the old shops have gone. There's no one to carry your provender in brown paper bags to the boot of your motor car or the back of the cart. You will not see a single horse or donkey or sheep or cow. No smell of farms on market day.

Oh no, there's John Wall! I mention him in my diary, which

I've left out on the table for you to read, along with the bundle. Don't look in the bundle yet. That's for afterwards. Read my diary now, while I'm having my lunch brought in. Food is quite good here, but it's not to my taste. There are too many vegetables.

Had a look at it? Good. Back to John Wall. He's waiting to cross the road, he's just next to my window but it's not wound down. I look the other way, then he starts to limp across. Everyone looks stronger than him, here in the town.

Hazeldell Rest Home No Exit. It's red brick, maybe twenties, with a fat boiler-flue giving off smells of boiled cloth and bake. Just like school. Through a window I see rows of melamine tables set to nothing but sugar-dispensers. Inside, in the hall, there's a table with dried flowers in a vase and a strip of cardboard asking for old or laddered tights to stuff draught excluders with – it takes hundreds to make a crocodile, apparently. That's all I can recall at the moment. This awful woman bustles up, with a navy jacket and a pan-scourer perm. She's the chief, she's, she's Mrs Stanton-Crewe, that's it. She treats me as if I'm a client, just about ready for this place. I tell her I'm here to visit Ray Duckett, who I haven't seen for ages. (A lie, I haven't seen him ever.) I musn't be shocked by the change, she says, especially if his teeth aren't in.

'Don't teeth make a difference, Mr –'

'Arkwright. Hugh Arkwright. I've always found teeth very useful, yes.'

Ray's room is stuffy. What big teeth he's got, too big and white for his withered face! Mrs Stanton-Crewe whispers to me that I shouldn't sit too close. Will he eat me? She wrinkles her nose and taps it, then leaves.

'Don't know you from Adam,' says Ray, from his huge easy chair. I wave my copy of *Ulverton and Her Ghosts* and he smiles. I sit on a stool by the window and explain why I'm here. The Red Lady business. His sick face lights up even more and he finds me in the book: almost a footnote. He spits into a spittoon and says that his saliva tastes like shampoo and he's not supposed to swallow it. Then he goes on about my uncle, what an honour it is to meet Edward Arnold's nephew. Don't be too surprised, Mother: Ray Duckett is an expert on old folk-customs, local myths, standing stones. These are the people who think a lot of Uncle Edward and his books. I suddenly realise that only one leg is emerging from Ray's dressing gown. Its slipper has *Detroit Fever* stitched into it in bright yellow.

His eyelids are closed, stretched like chewing-gum. He's about my age. He does smell as if he's rotting away. Yes, we're a slosh of stagnating juices and our hearts are made of fire, a little flame that death blows out one day. There's a picture of kittens playing with a balloon above the melamine chest-of-drawers. It'll end in tears, as Aunt Joy used to say.

Bony elbows on bony knees, the sick old man looks all nobbly, like a bat. He opens his eyes again and I ask him about the Red Lady.

Yes, Gracie Hobbs and Muck are the only two living witnesses of this particular ghost. Yes, Gracie's sighting must have been around 1933, in the bad snow, but he didn't know that it was the night of the carol-singing round. Call me Ray. Are you sure no one else is likely to have seen it, Ray? No one still living, no, sorry. Not to my knowledge. It's not surprising you want to check, Mr Arkwright, given the ghost is the ghost of your aunt.

Hugh, please. If the ghost is of anyone, it's of my mother. But your aunt was the one who died out in darkest Africa at the time of the sighting, Mr Arkwright! No, it was Edward Arnold's sister and she didn't die, she just went missing. Her married name was Arkwright. *Who was my mother!*

He covers his face. He's trembling.

'That's bloody awful,' he says. 'I'm known as the recording angel.'

I was often taken for my uncle's son, I say. I was his ward from the age of seven. Someone must have misinformed him. When did your aunt die? 1930. (The footsteps in the snow, curving off towards the wildwood. I saw these from my window, not long after she died. I don't think I ever told you, Mother.) Did she ever wear a red coat, Mr Arkwright? No, and her hair was bobbed, short and grey.

He's talking of ghosts, of course. I don't tell him that I don't believe in ghosts.

'I'll have to check in my notebooks. Oh deary me.'

Notebooks?

Some wicked goblin sits on my tongue and makes me show an interest in the notebooks. My head is in a muddle. You and Aunt Joy are becoming, horribly, one person, and somehow running around as Aunt Rachael. (Not *Rachael*, no, she's safe!) The notebooks are back in Ray's cottage, Bew's Lane. 'I can show you where to find them,' he says. 'If you give me a lift.'

'Am I allowed to?'

He shrugs.

Then he gets dressed. That is to say, I do as a nurse does and help him get dressed, breathing through my mouth. He has a sweat-shirt under his dressing gown with the word *Venom* on it, and a lunging snake's head. He taps it and says, 'My son in California. Don. Backing musician. He's done very well.' He growls when he breathes. It reminds me of Ted Dart. You saved Ted Dart's life, Mother. Remember? How many lives did you save, in the end? Quite a few, I imagine. Better to save lives than take them away, in most people's books. Don't ask me about my record.

'Sick of this place,' says Ray. 'Depressing.'

I express a doubt that he's up to an outing. From his smile I have the awful feeling that it's more than an outing, that outing is not the right word at all. I should have stopped then, of course. I should have walked away and headed straight for Italy, not stopping at Go. There are some things one really shouldn't know. And no one would have died. I'm sure they wouldn't have died and in that horrible way. The leopard head bouncing

Fresh sheet. I've had a low two days. Better, now. Get on.

Downstairs, I tell the nurse that I'm taking Ray out for a drive. You see all these little lies, Mother? But I want to see the notebooks. I'm on the scent, even in the middle of all that carbolic and decay. Cliff sweeps us both away and the nurse in the porch waves to us from behind the wheelchair until the hedge hides her. Ray gives a throaty cheer. Then there's the shock of something cold and dry against my knuckles.

'I'm glad it's Cliff,' whispers Ray. 'Cliff understands us oldies on the edge of life.'

183

Sorry – can't remember anything else about the journey. Except Ilythia suddenly appearing behind her Scotch pines, then vanishing.

The cottage is old and pretty, a brick path up through foxgloves and love-in-a-mist to a crooked oaken door with big old nails in it. Probably the place you and I visited once, Mother, to have tea and scones with Mrs Stump's sister smiling in a woollen crossover, the room packed with dark furniture. Now it's lighter and full of books. You'd like it.

'Hello, home,' says Ray. He sits in the largest chair. We light the fire. He watches the flames. I'll bet that's what he misses most, I'm thinking. We can only find camomile teabags so Cliff leaves thirsty.

Ray points out the shelf. There's a row of red and black notebooks. Above them are his published works. One of them is called *Brick Kilns of North Wessex*. No stone unturned, as they say! I fill two Tesco bags with his life's work. I could burn them, I'm thinking, in a big blaze. Isn't that awful, Mother? The things one thinks. They (I mean, the experts here) say it's to discover one's limits. Have something to bounce off. It's because Ray is watching me with such a vulnerable look, as I pack his notebooks, that I think this awful thought.

He doesn't want lunch. I pop out for a cheese roll and munch it in front of the fire. He's dozing. I flick through some of his books. Well, he's not a great writer, but someone's got to track the little things. When he wakes up, I ask him what time he wants to go back to Hazeldell. He tells me he's staying the night. I knew it! Small lies lead to bigger lies. I phone the Home and tell them he has to stay because he's had a dizzy spell. The young nurse says she'll tell the boss. She sounds a bit worried. It's now mid-afternoon.

'Want anything for supper, Ray?'

'I'll tell you what I want. Hedgerow fruit, freshly picked. And a bran loaf. If you can stretch to it. If it's not too much bother.'

Bother. I thought he was going to say 'an egg'.

Back in my garret, I begin to look through the notebooks for any more signs of you.

I'll explain the system now. The black notebooks are called

Magpies, the red notebooks are called Robins. The Magpies steal anything that glitters, the Robins pick through this hoard by theme, with the page reference of where it was found in the margin. There's a redbreasted notebook entitled *Spooks, Etc.* After an hour in this I dig up Gracie's story. First recorded in *Magpie 1973–4*. So I go back to this first scrawl, written in the open with a frozen hand in the scuffed black notebook.

I'm so disappointed. In all that primordial scribble there's not one new fact. I read the entry several times, because it's muddled up with a ghost on a gate and the ghost of the German pilot who crashed his Me. 109 in Stiff's field, but the most important fact is clear.

Gracie *did* mean you, Mother.

It was Ray who muddled Arnold and Arkwright when rewriting the scrawl neatly in the Robin. He then jumped to the conclusion that you were Uncle E's 'first wife', when he typed the passage for the book. Too many women, I suppose.

He was very concerned to find out who Mrs Rachael Arnold was, though! There's a cross-reference to a page in the Magpie for 1978–9, next to Aunt Rachael's name in the Robin. But it's dusk and I'm fretting about Ray, so this reference doesn't get looked up. Why should it? It's you I'm pursuing, Mother.

I think it's at this point I go out and garner Ray's supper. Hedgerow fruit, remember? Yes, it must have been at this point. As I write, a lot of things come back, grow clearer. As the experts here said they would. This is the point of it all, for me. Although I must say I'm beginning to feel very close to you, talking to you like this. As I used to do at school, writing you letters. You were at my shoulder, then. You're the other side of the room now, like a spectator at a play. But I still feel you are closer to me than when I was a boy. Whether you like it or not.

I pick blackberries and hazelnuts along the Gore path. It's good to know they're still there. As I do so, I begin to think it's all nonsense. I've put the yellowing label from the trunk in my socks drawer. I put Gracie and Muck in there too and that's it, that's all my conjecture's based on. Neither Gracie nor Muck seem quite of this world. I'm picking the blackberries and dropping them into a plastic bowl and remembering how Father told me once about living men who are actually dead. They are killed by a sorcerer but given the appearance of life for a short time, until something ordinary like a cold or an attack by an animal kills them. Father told me about this in his study: the corrugated map, the rust-spotted typewriter, the fan you could work with a string on your foot, the heat.

'Why does the wizard do this?' I asked him.

'To cover his tracks, of course. No one can trace the false death back to him.'

Clever, isn't it? Like dropping bombs.

When I eat a blackberry off the hedge, I eat all the months behind it. The squirrels have plundered the beechmast in Harry's Wood. All the squirrels were red in our day, weren't they? I pick quite a few hazelnuts, though. Nuncle (I started calling him Nuncle when I was old enough) held hunter-gathering feasts in his Maglemosian period and I wrote the labels in italics: *Honeysuckle, Juniper, Elder, Black Bryony, Dogwood, Hawthorn.* On the second day everyone would throw up. He'd flap about in his long hempen cloak shouting, 'Soft stomachs, soft heads and soft stomachs!' No one ever actually died.

His Maglemosian period was at its worst after you left us. But even before you left us, I do remember you telling me how the trenches had made him suffer so much, that a time before history offered him a way out. Years of a blasted wasteland might urge anyone to dream of endless forests, Hugh — even to dream that a small patch of neglected woodland in a country garden could seed it all, Hugh!

So he must have been quite Maglemosian even before you went.

I return to the village and buy Ray's bran loaf. It's around now that one of the mummers called Sally, in a self-knitted sack, says she hopes to see me at the rehearsal and that she's heard about the leopard skin. Oh dear, I think, John Wall still has it. I would have forgotten! This is why I'm in John Wall's garden a few minutes later, talking to his mother. Her forehead has stitches in it. We're talking next to the chicken coop, full of plastic cartons and tins. She tips out some vegetable scraps from a bucket and tells me that John isn't in.

'Will he be back before nine?'

'He's up at the house. The funny one. Finished my husband, but it en't finishing my son, if I can help it.'

'My house, you mean?'

The chickens lift their claws in disdain around the vegetable scraps. I don't blame them.

'How did it finish your husband?'

She gives a big snort. It could mean anything. I ask about the leopard skin. She gives a smaller snort and leads me inside. The kitchen's cleaned of her blood. While she's upstairs, I poke my head into the front sitting-room. The parlour, in your day. It's odd, it's full of little rugs – no, dead cats. There's this big monument of a crazy-paved fireplace and all these dead cats draped everywhere. Then my eye gets used to the light and I see that the cats are a lot of skins: every field and woodland creature you can think of, Mother. Badger, mole, rabbit, stoat, fox – even an otter! He's nailed huge black glossy wings above the fireplace and the bushy tails of squirrels next to the Swiss clock. There's a big black badger's claw dangling from the door handle. The room smells like a long-shut theatre wardrobe and mouldy woods.

Scalps, I think. Shrivelled heads. Power. Ah, yes. Power.

Nothing big enough in the shadows to resemble a leopard. Nothing with spots. A creak on the stairs. I whip my head back.

'It en't up there.' She's eyeing me suspiciously, scratching around her stitches.

'I need it rather urgently. It's for a costume.'

That's all for now, phew!

>   With lots of love,
>   Hugh

A few days later. Spitty.

Dear Mother,

I'm still in John Wall's house, with Mrs Wall, where I left off. The TV's on, showing a circus act. She watches it for a moment, as if I'm not there.

'You'd think they'd get cold, wouldn't you?'

It might not be a joke. I watch the trapeze artists in their sequined swimsuits as if it isn't.

'You don't want to go out in it,' she adds. 'Catch y'death. Took all his clothes off down to his knickers and put it on. You Jane, me Tarzan. Silly bugger. Looked like that Jackie Collins, I told him. He didn't like that. Just like that Jackie Collins. Weren't the right thing to say at all, were it?'

But she smiles, thinking about it.

'Chased me right round the table here. Could scarce catch my breath, silly bugger.'

I think at first her hands are catching invisible midges. But it's a clawing movement. She's miming.

'He's upped and sold her, anyway,' she snaps. And sits down with a bump, wheezy, rubbing her thighs.

'Sold her? The leopard skin?'

'He'll tell you it were pinched. Cabbaged off the line. Butter wouldn't melt an all that. Feller in Fogbourne, taxidermite chap. Stuffed crows, people are so bloody daft. That's what I reckon. He's upped and sold her.'

'I hope not,' I say. 'I do hope not. I certainly didn't ask him to. I'll be at the rehearsal in the village hall tonight at nine o'clock. If he could deliver it by then –'

Thump thump and screams. The clowns. Doing things with boxes.

'Go on. Give him the boot, then.'

Her stitches look like black flies. I can imagine her going on for ever and ever, soiled and undead. She's getting me to give him the boot because she's afraid of my house. Afraid of the house!

Well, I can't blame her.

Ray is in his kitchen. He's made himself a pot of tea. The metal crutches lean against a chair. I have to move them to pour myself a cup and I'm ashamed to say that I find their weight and their warm black pads rather repulsive. I could lift one up and batter him over the head with it – such an onion-like head with its wisps of white hair. What an awful thought! I'm sure everyone has them, Mother.

'We're in trouble,' he says. 'The son's phoned the Home. He

can sue 'em. Supposing I pop off here. They're not happy. You might have kidnapped me. Have you kidnapped me?'

We laugh about it, but I'm worried. And the son is on his way. Ray starts to feast on the blackberries, straight from the tub.

'I have to spend the night here,' he says. 'Or I'll go nuts.'

The son turns out to be blond and pudgy. 'Hello Piers.' 'Hello Dad.' I introduce myself and pour him a cup of tea. He drops his car-keys on the table; the key-ring is a large plastic fish, like you see on the backs of cars belonging to an evangelical sort of Christian, Mother. He rubs his hands briskly and asks his dad how he's getting on. A crutch begins to fall, but Piers catches it by the pad. Even he looks a bit repulsed. (I bet Jesus didn't.) At some point there's an argument about when Ray should go back, because Piers is here to take him back. It's to do with personal insurance. Piers takes a punch at his father! – but is just looking at his watch, it's all right. I suggest staying the night, if that would help. Piers looks at me. His eyes are too small for his head.

'I've got a house meeting at nine,' says Piers. 'Chipping Norton.'

'I never wanted to stay in that dump in the first place, did I?' Ray growls.

Piers keeps quiet. The fish key-ring on the table looks as if it's gasping.

So that's how I end up staying the night in Ray's cottage.

'See you, Dad. You haven't even got your beeper thing, have you?'

'No, and I haven't got Jesus either.'

Piers leaves, all pink and tense. I'm thinking, as Ray chunters on, that the one in California has the better deal. There's a photo of two small boys on the fridge. Another of a toothy woman in a scarf by a lake, windblown in boots. That must be the mother, now dead. I have no photos in this room. I didn't want any, it's not worth it, I'm here for such a short while. In for a service, as I joke. Top notch people. One of them was trained by Dr Wolff, who I came across thirty years ago! They've all heard of me, in one way or another.

I can't stand Ray's company any longer, to be frank. (I'm back in the cottage, Mother.) He's chuntering on about Piers, and the crutches seem to be growing taller. There's a bad smell and the kitchen is rather poky, with crookbacked black beams. It's like being inside a spider's web. I've never been good with ill people, as you were. And Ray is so ill, he's dying. I can see Death's mouth stretching its jaws behind him, ready to snap in a few days or weeks. Or even hours. I say I'll be back to put him to bed. He seems pleased to be left alone. Ray is somehow sticky, I reflect. One gets stuck on his threads. It's all this snooping about of his.

There's a big party of student geologists in the hotel restaurant, and I end up sitting next to two of them. They're conducting field work in some old quarry nearby. My fingers are stained purple from blackberrying, theirs are pallid from grubbing in the chalk. Jill and Tim, that's it.

Jill is very attractive, Mother. She has a Brum drone but she also has It, as you would say. I didn't know what It meant when you said that, but now I do. It means that someone is stirring your golden syrup – or even turning up the little flame in your heart, in rare cases.

I explain to them why my fingers are purply.

'Ooh, chuck him into a bog, quick,' says Tim.

I express surprise.

'The season of death'd be perfectly recorded. Last meal. The sludge in his peat-kippered duodenum would be full of pips. Dead useful to our palaeo-ecologist colleagues in a few thousand years.'

That's how these people talk, like I talk about theatre. Tim spent the summer not far from Eilrig, bobbing up and down in the heather, collecting midge remains from a Highland bog. His big windburned face is grinning away, but Jill tells him to shut up. Did I know that downland chalk is 1,500 feet thick? That no one really knows why? And so on.

Now I'm in the churchyard, Mother. I've a few minutes to kill before the rehearsal at nine. There's moonlight on the grave-stones, their silica winks a sort of blueish white. The dead prefer moonlight, because they can open their eyes. Then a shock.

Aunt Joy's name, as if she's reciting it over the telephone.

Joy Crystal Arnold, née Unsworth, 1889–1930. Not where I thought it was at all. Next to it is a little square stone laid flat with nothing but *Dawn* etched in, but there are fresh flowers on it.

Aunt Joy's slab is bare, except for the shadows of branches shifting about in the moonlight. I'll have to bring flowers. I can hear that little clearing of her throat – a tic, really. Do you remember, Mother? The black Scotch pines moan and whisper like shingle or sad ghosts. Standing by Aunt Joy's grave, I feel cross that I can't bring you a bunch of flowers. Really cross! There are empty plots and I think: I must find out where yours was. Even if it's been taken by someone else, I must find out. Then I think: well, I can buy a little plot for you and put a memorial stone on it. Otherwise, when I'm dead, there'll be nothing. How awful. Only a legend about a ghost, fading in turn. Nothing.

Not a trace.

'Please please *please* listen. Hugh has come here especially. We're incredibly lucky to have him. *Please.*'

But the Man-Woman, the Witch and the Bold Slasher would not be any better were they to listen to what I'm telling them. My approach is dependent on rules. They don't know any of the rules. And there's no leopard skin. Malcolm thinks it's my fault, but doesn't say so. I don't tell him that John Wall might have nicked it. Mrs Pratt's very tall son spends his time tapping the chair at the back with his knuckle. Sally the Fool is always desperate for a fag. The depression that rises from mediocrity descends on me, it's infectious, a sort of miasma. I recognise a face or two staring from the Village Hall Founding Committee photograph, 1928. Was I really alive, then? And can they all be dead, now? You must have known them.

Ray has hobbled up to bed by the time I get back. Tufts of white hair show above the blanket in the dim light of his bedroom. His grunts sound as if someone's thumping him. Doesn't he need a pain-killer against the gnaw of cancer? His teeth float in a glass of pink water: why are they grinning so gleefully at me?

A book lies on the bedside table, pressed open at an underlined passage I know by heart from sixty years ago:

I will sit here on the turf and the scarlet-dotted flies shall pass over me, as if I too were but a grass. I will not think, I will be unconscious, I will live.

I'm always telling the people here that the best cure for the blues is a walk in a graveyard. A walk through the works of Richard Jefferies is also to be recommended. The book is a first edition of *Field and Hedgerow*. It is over a hundred years old. I'm sure it has another hundred left in it. Piers has got it now, I suppose. Or sold it along with all the other books. You don't recognise it, Mother? Oh. I know you liked novels, magazines.

I'm lying on Ray's sofa, under a blanket. The firelight flickers on the walls, the books, the old crooked beams.

I'll fill in my diary last thing. What a full day! Full, because I'm doing things I did not do in London or Scotland. I did not babysit dying men, muse in churchyards, rehearse hopeless amateurs, or chat up student geologists. It's good for me, I think. I pick up the black notebook and read the passage relating to you.

Closing my eyes, I mutter to myself that I don't believe in ghosts, therefore I don't believe the Red Lady was a ghost. It's like a charm, a magic formula. But I'm not sure what's emerging from the green smoke, you see. What monstrous form.

Being thorough, sieving the grains of earth one last time for a tiny amber bead, I read the Robin entry again. There's still that cross-reference next to Aunt Rachael's name. It's in another black notebook, the Magpie for 1978–9.

I pick it up and turn to the appropriate page. A sort of dark shaft runs through me from head to toe but I take no notice. It isn't always a warning.

Horrible. Absolutely horrible.

How high does my horror mount? Up to the sky and beyond. A searchlight's beam goes on for ever and ever. My horror goes on for ever and ever. But it's not like the horror that is to come, Mother. That horror fell out of the sky and hit me on the head, burned me to a shell. This one's precise and focused and goes up and up. It picks out the words one by one, as we used to pick out the tiny silver Dorniers from the black sky. I even copy the words down.

Of course I don't have them on me. Only the odd phrase has stuck.

But here's the gist.

It's March, 1978. Ray is out walking. He meets Muck ('Frank

PETTY') trimming a dogwood hedge in Gumbledon Acres, tying up the branches to dry for kindling. Because Ray is heading for Wot Tor, Muck recites those lines Jeremiah taught me sixty years ago. I'll give you Jeremiah's version, only slightly different from the one recorded by Ray:

> Thee be lookin a bit shart o' breath, Richut.
> I hev a-bin tearin up Wot Tor, Willum.
> I dunno, Richut – thee tells I what tor 'twere.
> Why, I telled thee straight – Wot Tor 'twere I were tearin up.
> Then I deddent catch ut, Richut: thee'll have to be a-tearin up ut agin.

Ray gives Muck a tip and then Muck delivers the filthier version. This is something that has stuck, Mother. Oh yes.

> Thee be lookin a bit shart o' breath, Rachel.
> Why, I hev a-bin tearin up Wat Taylor's willum.

Muck doesn't say if Wat Taylor or Rachel were ever real people. But he receives another tip.

Ray notes that the name 'Rachel' is a kind of leit-motif in these sorts of verses, but not Wat. He then lists all the possible village Wats (a certain Wat TAYLOR was killed at Ypres in 1918), and all the possible Rachels, including Rachael Arnold. Now comes the interesting bit, if you're interested in horrible things. He has found out that Mrs Rachael Arnold's nickname was 'Rampant' – and, in one really obscene cluster of jokes, 'Randy' (he doesn't repeat the jokes). Against this startling fact is another cross-reference, to a page in the Magpie for 1982–3. Much research by Ray in the 'tap-room' of the Green Man has established that this nickname is not due to marital infidelities, Mother, but to a certain incident dating from around 1940, several years before the said Rachael was Edward Arnold's wife.

I paraphrase, as briskly as possible.

In 1940, a young poacher by the name of Jack Wall, in the

woodland attached to the Arnold property up Crab-Apple Lane, was up a tree when he spotted a couple of naked youths coupling 'like Adam'n Eve'. He says the girl was Ransoms Rachael, though he didn't know her at the time. The boy remained obscured by her, though various names are put forward (not recorded). Ray notes that Randy probably derives from Rampant which probably derives from Ransoms. Why Ransoms? Jack Wall takes him to the spot in question. The damp hollow is full of wild garlic − or ramsons! Ransoms is a corruption of ramsons. Ray sounds very pleased with himself for unearthing the original nickname, as well as its provenance. One can see him displaying it in a glass cabinet, a nasty little lump, a relic. The toffee found in the murdered child's mouth, that sort of thing. The recording angel has passed, and we are full of grace.

There, that's better. It's amazing what can be done when one puts one's mind to it. That's been the philosophy of my whole life.

I'm going to have to fill you in, Mother. I haven't filled in anyone else about this. About Rachael, I mean. (Not Aunt Rachael, not Mrs Rachael ARNOLD. That's where Ray DUCKETT went wrong.) It's top-secret. It always has been. At least, that's what I thought. Top-hole secret! So I sit on Ray's sofa in the cottage feeling rather low and confused. There's this old forgotten theatre character called the Changeling. He has drooping hands and a stupid expression, a bit of a simpleton wearing a dunce's cap, in whiteface. I sit on the sofa as the Changeling, the notebook slides from my hands, the clock chimes midnight.

I do allow myself a little chuckle, when I think of the name Jack WALL. The first Shakespeare play I ever saw. The play in the play on a midsummer's night. *That vile Wall which did these lovers sunder* . . .

Pure coincidence. An old Ulverton name. You must remember the Walls. Jack Wall's son is John Wall.

That's all for now. Isn't life busy when you put it down? One thing after another! Hope *you're* keeping busy.

Your ever loving,
Hugh

A few days later. April showers. A few flowers on the spiraea outside. Don't they call it Bridal Wreath?

Dear Mother,
    I'm doing rather well.
    Then I switch the light off: the clock has just chimed midnight. It's ugly, with plaster foxgloves around it. This is the first of my bad nights. Jack WALL is at the chink. I wake up, disturbed by the feel of his eyeball and a soft laugh, but it's only the clock pinging. I wonder where I am for a moment, as I do sometimes here – it's quite normal. I'm cramped and chilly on the sofa. After ages being awake, I drop off and dream I'm stuck in bottomless chalk. There's a bog, with Ray having his throat cut on the edge of it. Spots of his bright blood spatter the black bog and turn into Jackie Collins, who is the goddess. And I never knew! I try to keep her as Jackie Collins but she's also Mrs Wall. As long as she's not Rachael, I think. I'm dressed in a dinner-jacket, but the others are in anoraks or skins. They grunt and heave Ray into the bog, holding him down with a stick. Then I'm the one being held down with a stick. The goddess is sitting on my chest. She's almost you, Mother, but with a black, wrinkled face. The goddess turns into a swan, then a wise man in white muff. The man is saying 'Sir' and trying to throttle me. Another man in white stands near me in a living-room I do not recognise. I try to sit up, but am pressed back on to the cushions by my executioner.
    'Just relax, Mr Duckett, while we check you out. We're the ambulance.'
    I'm not Hugh Arkwright. That was all a dream of a few minutes. I'm really Ray Duckett. Then I wake up properly.
    'Sorry, I'm not Ray Duckett,' I say, my voice rather hoarse.
    The man has hairy wrists and chilly fingers. There's a smell of something like Brut. He blinks stupidly for a few seconds. I sit up, his strong hand sliding from my jugular. The other one looks about sixteen, with bright ginger hair curving into unfashionable sideburns.
    'Come on, Mr Duckett,' the first one shouts, as if I'm a long way off. 'Easy does it.'

'I'm not Mr Duckett, I'm Hugh Arkwright. Mr Duckett has only one leg. I've got two. He has two eyes, I've got one.'

My eye-patch is hanging from the chair next to the sofa. I get up and strap it on.

'There.'

Brut asks Ginger if those specifications were given. Ginger shakes his head and says something quietly as I'm slipping on my shoes. My ears have always made up for my missing eye and I catch the words *not altogether there.*

'I'll show you who Mr Duckett is, right now,' I growl.

I push past them and run up the stairs, slipping on the loose runner and banging my knee. The men must have been sent by the Home. No trust in this world.

I knock on Ray's door and open it. The tufts of white hair have gone. Mother – imagine coming into my bedroom in Bamakum early in the morning and not finding me gurgling in my cot. You were always afraid of some beast snatching me off, so Mosea said. Ray's bed is horribly neat, as if it's never been slept in at all. Ray's shoe is missing from where I placed it under the chair, and his coat and the crutches have disappeared, along with the Jefferies book. And the teeth. I think of suicides who, before they throw themselves under a train, remove their coat, fold it neatly on the platform seat, and adjust their tie. Then I think of what Tim said. Last meals. Pips. Shards of bran bread. I'm sure Ray knows all about bog bodies.

'Oh, fuck.'

The other two poke their heads in and look around as if checking for spare seats in a pub.

'Looks as if your one-legged chappie's done a bunk,' says Brut.

'Hopped it,' says Ginger.

They disguise chortles by coughing.

'Come on, Mr Duckett,' Brut says.

I feel a hand on my forearm. A walkie-talkie in Ginger's top pocket crackles. I snatch my forearm away as if it's been scalded, but I know it's hopeless: I'll be taken to the Home and the awful Mrs Stanton-Crewe, while Ray is dying on some grassy hummock. Perhaps even Mrs Stanton-Crewe will say, 'Hello, Ray.' I'll be like Lady Glyde arriving at the Asylum in your favourite novel, Mother. I'll look at the label on my shirt and see Ray's name stitched in. I'll be the Man in White. It would take so little to disperse Hugh Arkwright on the wind, as dreams are dispersed by daylight. As you would be dispersed without me.

I shake my head free of this rubbish and think again of the underlined passage about grass and what it means: Ray has wandered off on to the open downs to become as unconscious as grass, to sink into the waves of turf for ever. It'll all be my fault, of course: headlines in the local papers, phone ringing, my age asked for twenty times and still printed wrong. Arkwright spelt Arkright or even Awkward. Food for my enemies!

I nod and agree to come along. I think, I think I then find some excuse to go into the kitchen – to lock the back door, that's it.

'Want your night things?' Ginger's pointing into the bedroom. 'Thank you,' I reply.

I leave them both folding up my, I mean Ray's pyjamas and go down into the kitchen. There's an empty milk-lined glass on the table and the back door is not quite on the latch. Ray sneaked out this way: there'd have been no need to pass me. So I follow him.

Cold morning air in my throat.

A wobbly gate at the end of the little overgrown garden; it leads straight on to the sunken footpath that runs the length of Bew's Lane from the school to finish somewhere high on the open downs. I'm sure we walked it together. On the other side of the hedge lies Gumbledon Acres, nibbled into these days by bungalows crouched behind thick blue hedges. We used to picnic there in the meadow and gather its flowers for pressing, Mother. Once or twice at least.

I aim for the downs, the limber supple sea of the open downs. The path is churned up but stiff with cold, and sunk between its banks. Crisp packets caught in the dogwood hedge, that arches over and stops the frost from falling out of the air. So no footprints, no nicks of crutches.

Perhaps he never existed, not outside my body. What a silly thought. Perhaps I'm following myself.

The notebook. This drops on to my head, as it were. How can Hugh Arkwright dissolve so easily? Muck, I think. Frank PETTY. When I think about him and Duckett talking together all those years back, somewhere up this path, I feel Hugh Arkwright very solidly in my veins. The gristly muck-faced goblin cutting the blood-red twigs for fardels. Ray burrowing again, snooping, poking his nose in.

'Randy' is horrible. Absolutely horrible. Randy Rachael. It won't leave my head. Ransoms Rachael is not too bad. But Randy is horrible.

And Jack WALL's eyeball huge and bloodshot at the chink, watching, looking down through the branches, poaching that most private and secret moment and hanging it up like a skin for all to snigger at. I might as well have no clothes on, jogging up the path. Flayed, that's how I feel.

I'll tell you all about it when I'm ready, Mother. It's a bit of an off-day, today. We all have them. But I'm doing well, on the whole.

A woman with a dog. The dog hurtles forward and treats me as the prodigal son. It's a big white thing like a vulgar rug, to go with vulgar furnishings and a giant television, and has clawed paws heavy enough to hurt. The owner evolves into Mrs Pratt.

'Hallo, Mr Arkwright, what a lovely morning,' she pants. 'Rollo! Off now! He *so* loves people, he's *quite* daft.'

I ask her if she's seen anyone on her walk this morning. Only the Stiff girl with her paper-round, taking a short-cut. Most inadvisable these days. Once one could walk anywhere, without fear. Now children are kept at home, and even home isn't safe. You've been jogging, Mr Arkwright!

Said as if it's something astonishing, with a prod of the finger.

'If you see Ray Duckett on your travels, tell him there's an ambulance waiting for him, Mrs Pratt.'

I shoot off again. The hedge's troupe of greenfinch bursts out twittering in front of me, like an ambush. I'm already short of breath. He can't have got *this* far, surely! Swinging like a monkey!

I hit the top of the path. Through the gate is the field I remember as the turnip field. Now it's spread to harsh stubble. With determination one can go miles swinging on a pair of crutches, even dying. He's fled to the downs. The downs aren't what they were, Mother — the broad grassy sward's more than a bit moth-eaten these days, more than a bit torn up – but there are still a few rough-enough spots to lie in, to become turf in.

As I cross the old turnip field, I start to shout his name.

'Ray! Ra-ay!'

But I'm rather out of breath. I should have stopped and walked back. Then the absurd thing about to happen wouldn't have happened. I wonder if I should stop here? I mean, stop at the stubble and turn back? As I stopped my memoir for Dr Wolff at the very bad news about you?

Cowardice. I've got both legs, after all.

There's a bare field beyond, I can see it from here, from halfway across the stubble, my ankles pricked through my socks. The far field is bare to its light drills. To its winter grass and its dragon's teeth. But these must stay put for a while. Oh, I wish I was in Africa now. I'm planning to take a trip out there, to our old haunts, Mother. To Bamakum, if there's anything left of it. Father's road. Odoomi. The crater lake. Charlotte's Lake. You'll come with me, of course. Just the moment that I'm completely on my proverbial feet again, up and running again, I'll be out there. The minute I'm one hundred per cent.

I'm going to do something rather fun, rather pleasant. I'm going to take us out there now. Buea, you always liked Buea. Let's book in to the Mountain Hotel. Pleasant climate, when it's not misty or raining. Once ensconced there, I can fill you in on some missing years. Otherwise nothing after the stubble can possibly be understood as it ought to be. Least of all to myself.

So here we are.

The mountain is clear today, and one can imagine snow on its peak. I would like to climb it, or at least a part of it, in this rare sunlight. Instead I will sit on the veranda and write to you slowly and gracefully, while you visit people. Mr Tall, for instance. The Allinsons. The jungliness of a life requires such discipline, such stamina, as Father used to say, staring at his road – the rope-bridge dangling into the torrent, the smashed sleepers, the liquid mud shining between the trees. Such discipline, such stamina. And then Time grows over it so quickly, doesn't it? What a pleasant climate. It's the altitude. Soon we can go on to Bamakum, when we're adjusted.

That's all for now. Let us enjoy Africa.
Your ever-loving son,
Hugh

Weather clearing. Cool breezes but sun hot. Mr Tall and the Allinsons and the others are all dead. Peak hidden.

Dear Mother,

I'm glad you found my childhood memoir intriguing, and that parts of it made you cry. Blow your nose now and I'll carry on.

War broke out when I was seventeen. I had a place at Oxford, rather young, but I lied about my age and entered the Forces. I did this mainly because Uncle Edward was a pacifist, even though he wanted the end of civilisation. I was getting on badly with him at this time. Up to now, my years here had been divided between school and a house I had the right to shelter in. It wasn't home. Home was Bamakum. I travelled there in my head, reliving certain days while my fetish packet crumbled and its contents were lost one by one between dormitory boards or under lonely hedges.

My mark remained, more like a big bruise than a tattoo: you didn't have to worry so much about it! I was teased for this at Randle, but I invented more tales about my time as a boy sailor (I knew *Treasure Island* and a lot of *Coral Island* by heart). Randle wasn't my favourite period. I won't go into details, Mother. I wrote you quite a few letters, even knowing you wouldn't get them for the moment. I never let myself think that you wouldn't get them at all, not ever. I never posted them, though, because Father would have been upset to have seen your name.

I spent the holidays mostly on my own, reading or cycling around the countryside or walking up on the downs. No friends came to the house, and I was hardly ever invited out: Nuncle couldn't be bothered with this sort of thing, he was too deep in pan-Celtic mysteries and numerology and what we call these days the 'para-psychological'. The house had no neighbours. Nuncle and I might as well have been separate tenants in the same house. My mature reading had started with Stevenson and Kipling,

Ballantyne, Buchan, the sea-tales of Conrad, then proceeded through all of Spenser, Milton, Scott, Dickens and so on, to the French of Balzac and Hugo, and of course the Latin and Greek of the ancient poets. (I took after Father, you see.) Through the quiet of afternoons in the beechwood or sometimes in my room on rainy days, I continued to act on my own and out loud every single play by Shakespeare. I also read new writers like Lawrence and Forster and Woolf and all the English Romantics, and had a pocket Housman I took with me on walks. I tried to write myself, of course: poetry after Keats or Drinkwater, prose after Henry James. I still saw the countryside – the wood, the pool, the meadows and pastures and the free, open downs – as inhabited by spirits. But they were getting more and more literary, I suppose. And Nuncle was becoming more and more interested in African beliefs, in animism and fetishes and ancestors, the survival of the dead. He poisoned these things for me, so I let them fade away.

I was thought of as wilfully shy or even cold by his friends – they kept suggesting that I be sent to somewhere like Summerhill or Forest School, to run about naked on lawns with overweight adults and learn from flowers and trees or sit on long-haired poets' laps – be forced to, that is, as I refused to do this at the house. But Nuncle wasn't bothered enough to change my school.

His crowd overlapped the minor members of the Bloomsbury set, whom I dreaded. They shouted 'penis' at odd moments and asked me what I thought of the fusing of the body and the soul or of homosexual love. 'Not very much,' I would say, and run off. On the fringe of this set stood a Jewish painter called Ernest Katzen. Almost all his paintings were stored in a warehouse in the war, and the warehouse received a direct hit. So he's completely forgotten now. Please don't think you should have heard of him, Mother.

In the summer of 1937, my uncle held a week-long 'symposium' on the Kabbala and Biblical theosophy. Katzen was there to give a talk. He wandered about the house and grounds in a dark suit, looking lost behind a brindled goatee beard. I wasn't then a great fan of modern art, but I liked his paintings: a bit like Chagall, I suppose, seen through smog. But the art world at that time did not approve, and Nuncle's crowd were so snooty about them when they were hung up in the morning-room for the week! This made me like them more.

His daughter interested me, too. She drooped about the lawn in a long lacy dress, smoking madly through a long ivory cigarette holder, and wore a broad fedora with a long veil attached to it. The veil (and maybe the dress) was her grandmother's, I think. I was fifteen. I reckoned that she was not much older, though she behaved as if she was.

The weather was very fine, and all meals were taken outside, at a row of wobbly trestle-tables borrowed from the Women's Institute. One of these collapsed, pinching Nuncle's fingers in its folding legs so badly he screamed. I had to go and fetch the antiseptic cream and plaster for the cut. Copies of his magazine, the *Scarab*, littered the house. It was the most boring magazine I had ever come across, full of numbers and bits from the Bible or badly drawn plans of the pyramids, with overexcited contributions from people like Charles Williams or A.M. Ludovici. One issue had a drawing of an African mask on the cover, very like our mask at home.

I mostly kept to my room or roamed the wood, spying on the chattering throng with my new binoculars. There was a tall, debonair German with a bronze pin on his tie featuring a tiny swastika. 'It goes,' insisted my uncle, 'the right way, the way of the sun, of creation, of light.' Hitler's went anti-clockwise, the way of Kali and dark destruction – but the Jewish group, led by Katzen, complained and the man was packed off on the second day, threatening us all and waving his arms about – 'Just like Kali,' someone said. I recognised him from the visit of the Thule Society years before, and was rather sorry, as that visit belonged to the last moments of my life before my illness, before the bad news about you. It seemed a different life, that one, going on on the other side of a heavy drape.

On the same day this man was sent packing, my roaming binoculars found Ernest Katzen's daughter. She was part of a group talking excitedly, I assumed, about the expulsion, but she looked bored by it all. She floated across to an empty space and lay on the grass, leaning back on her elbows, taking the sun on her uplifted face. I shifted away from a blur of foliage and crept forward to the very edge of the wood, concealed by a young spindle tree. She had taken off her hat and veil, and her raven hair, burnished in the late sunlight, hung thick and loose behind her like a tumbling stream. It wasn't at all like the cropped or curled styles of the older women on the lawn. It was, I suppose, like yours, Mother, when you let it out of its pins at night, when you got up in the morning. Her dress hung open at her neck. It was cut low. She had a generous bosom.

My binoculars stayed on her for ages. She wore no shoes, and her feet were very arched – they matched the curve of her waist when she stood. Her chin was rather sharp, but I liked it for that. It was teasing. I was struck by her resemblance to one of the actresses photographed in my old Shakespeare volume. Oh, Rachael was the most magnificent creature. So overcome was I that I fled to the other end of the wood, where I thought long and hard about love, about the different types of love.

You weren't dead, then, Mother. I was patient, I was full of faith. I knew that the moment I gave in to my father's and uncle's lack of hope, you would never reappear. Father had returned a year or two after you left us. Need I tell you that he was all but broken? Quite bald, and with a pronounced stammer? I wonder what broke him. Africa, I suppose. You going off like that.

Anyway, he was now confined to a desk job in the Administration's offices in London. I visited him from time to time, in his tiny Bayswater rooms. I'd no heart to ask what had happened to our home, to the little cluster of huts between the forest and the water, to the concrete PWD house that looked like a face, to your bush 'hospital', to the servants. To Quiri, especially. But the out-station did not matter so much to me, now – it was the forest behind that mattered. In there was the pearl that did not tarnish. Of course you would come back.

Whenever I asked him for details about your disappearance, I'm afraid he just looked very gloweringly at me, his lips pursed tight. Then he would go into a long, silent gloom. So I stopped asking him, and we hardly talked about you at all. Don't be hurt.

As the week progressed, Rachael Katzen began to pearl, too, in my head. And not just in my head.

I hid my Meccano set. I gave away my Lotts Bricks.

In the day, I kept my curtains drawn. At night, I didn't sleep very well.

I was quite often on my belly by the wood's edge, trying not to mist my bird-watchers' binoculars as I breathed. One day I brought my box camera with me and took a photograph of her.

I did not talk to her or even meet her eye, not once. I learnt her name only by studying the list of guests in the kitchen, while Mrs Stump moaned on about the vegetarians: three of them, could I imagine, only ate carrots – one had 'em boiled, one had 'em raw, one had 'em sliced into slivers. 'I'll sliver *them*,' she added. *Katzen, Rachael: will eat anything.*

The voice had come to me mingled with others; though she mostly looked sullen, it was high and cheerful. Now and again she attached herself to her father, putting her arm through his. They looked very foreign together, and this pleased me. The rest of the gathering were clumpy and stiff and bespectacled, despite some priestly capes or Babylonian robes. She was like a sylph amongst them, in comparison.

My voyeur's photographs were hopeless: a large area of grass in the foreground, a few blurry figures dotted about, and the gaunt cliff of the house beyond. The figures were so tiny, it was hard to distinguish Rachael at first. When I did, she looked plain, even through the magnifying glass, as if my crudely ground lens had distorted her. I tore the photographs up, sadly.

I did not see Rachael again for two years. Meanwhile, I was not wholly uninterested in that side of things, Mother. I lacked conviction, that's all. The boys at school panted over naughty postcards of women naked but for suspenders or boots or furs; I had seen women naked but for a sheen of palm oil, and for real! The vicar's daughter had been the object of my attentions for a while, mainly through the local tennis club, its brand-new grass courts breaking into my solitude with hearty cries, flushed faces, and warm lemonade on a burning bench. She was a magnificent player, was the vicar's daughter. Nuncle, in a rare spasm of interest (I must have returned looking particularly miserable one day) asked how I was getting on, and I said that she 'regularly thrashed me'. He found this very droll, repeating my comment to his friends for years afterwards. Through this girl's brother I was roped into the same croquet team you used to play for, Mother. I spooned with my partner (a doctor's daughter with a contraption on her teeth) after a mixed match in a nearby village. We crouched behind a shed sticky with creosote. I could taste the metal on her contraption but it didn't matter. I got as far as her underthings, which she told me she'd knitted herself. This put me off. That's all.

Then there was the seminar on the esoteric tradition in European painting. Uncle Edward hired the village hall for a week, for the lectures. Rachael came with her father. She'd dropped the veil and seemed firmer and less sylph-like, but just as lovely to my mind. I certainly hadn't forgotten her, had I? Now, slipping out from the village hall during my uncle's tedious speech on Blake and the coming apocalypse, passing the rows of pale faces, I saw Rachael getting up, as if to follow me. We had already exchanged a polite greeting over cakes and tea in the house, our eyes finally meeting like Dr Livingstone and Stanley in the huge forest (that was how I saw it, anyway). Stepping outside, my nape tingled as it had never tingled before: I didn't dare look back. Should I close the door behind me? It had always had a difficult bolt, the wood was warped. Could she have been getting up because she saw me leaving? I let the door swing wide.

She appeared, closing the door behind her. I automatically and too quickly offered her a cigarette through my fierce blush, which twilight hardly hid. To my great surprise, she said she would share mine.

You're the only one I'm telling this to, Mother – the only one I've ever told. You've no idea how painful all this is to me, and how blessed. I hope it's not too chilly for you on the veranda. Soon we can move inside and sit before the hotel's roaring log fire, as we used to do each Christmas, pretending we weren't in Africa. I do like writing to you. It is terrible what lies and frauds people can conjure up, and so meticulously. I'm thinking of that bundle there, on the table. I brought it out with us. You can open it when I've finished writing to you. The demon did it, in order to destroy me. I believed it for a while.

Rachael Katzen and I were leaning against the village hall's corrugated-iron wall, terribly coolly. I was Winterbourne and she was the very pretty Daisy Miller, but it wasn't quite Rome, was it? Tin huts would be very familiar to me soon, though I didn't know it then: it was 1939. This date is as unrepentant as 1914, Mother. However, war was not yet declared, the evening was brooding and sultry and full of peace, with Europe's cities intact in our thoughts, if we ever thought of them. I noticed small beads of sweat on her bare shoulders. She seemed even lovelier this time. She was nineteen. That seemed very much older than seventeen. She was matchless, she was fiery, she knew everything about London and its life. I sometimes think you must have been very like her when you were nineteen.

When she gave me back my cigarette, the felty pad of the filter tasted faintly of violets. 'Violated by violets,' I thought, blushing deeper still. It was, I think, the scent of her perfume invading my taste buds, because her full, red lips needed no lipstick. I coughed as the smoke hit my lungs for the first time in my life – I had always held the smoke in my mouth, before. I handed the cigarette back to her. What would she taste on it? Something pleasant of me, I hoped. Had I used my tooth powder this morning? I felt I'd known her for ages, despite my nerves: we'd been childhood sweethearts on a coral island far away, or in a book we'd walked out of as living beings, or in a play they'd played in the theatres of Greece and Rome.

'London must be jolly good,' I said, my voice cracking.

She took a deep drag and didn't cough, then let me taste her violets again.

'Dull,' she replied, 'so flat. Full of pompous little poets boring you in smoky pubs, most of them either terribly religious or terribly Marxian. I haven't found one who actually fought in the war, the one in Spain I mean. I'm going to Paris, the minute I can, and paint. I want to sit and drink Vermouth on the pavement, and watch humanity pass. You can't stay in a country where you can't drink on the pavement. When they do, in London, on a hot night like this, they look so nervous, like naughty little boys and girls sipping their lemonade. I like the new sandwich bars, all that steel and neon light. I pretend I'm American. I go to the quick-lunch counter and drawl.'

She gave a quick giggle. I had no idea what a quick-lunch

counter was, but I was impressed by her boldness. I hadn't let the smoke past my tonsils, this time, and my voice came out loud and clear over the drone behind the wall. (The droners were faded, old, in specs. There was already a pact of youth between us.)

'You want to be a painter, like your father?'

'Not like my father, please. Like myself. I want to paint people in snack bars, just as they are. Slums, railway stations, hospital waiting rooms. What are *you* going to do? You look much older than you were last time, by the way. And just as sad. What's wrong with your eye?'

'I can't see through it.'

'An accident?'

I didn't want to tell her that I'd had it for years, and that she couldn't have been very interested in me last time, or she'd have noticed it, so I nodded. There was a pause. She was looking at me straight.

'Nelson,' she said.

'Lady Hamilton,' I replied, looking at her right in her slate-grey eyes, in the one moment of my life when I have matched my own desire to be charming, witty, and a bit of a rake. The one moment, ever! I was astonished at myself: it was as if I had suddenly become a man. Suddenly a man. Quite suddenly. All my Lotts Bricks tumbling and vanishing out of sight for ever. My Meccano set.

That's all I can manage for today. Besides, the mosquitoes are biting. Such a lovely deep, thick thick dusk.

Your loving son,
Hugh

Fresh morning. Peak clear. View over the forest magnificent, wisps of mist rising like white smoke. Bright geckos everywhere, stuck then slithering. How do they stick and then slither? Pock, pock, pock of the red tennis-court.

Dear Mother,

Hope you slept well. I slept well, most of the time.

I smoked my cigarette coolly as she smiled at me. The metal of the wall was hot against my back. I knew that I was handsome, desirable, and jolly brilliant, even if I knew underneath that I was none of those things.

'Do you hate your uncle?'

This question surprised me. I'm afraid I choked a little on the smoke. Clapping broke out behind us, through the closed door. I chucked the cigarette at my feet and ground it into the grass as I'd seen chaps do in the village.

'I think I'm going for a walk,' I said, thrusting my hands into the deep pockets of my white baggies and looking out at the fields. 'If you want to come.'

She did, and we took a stroll around the back of the village, avoiding the areas that might harbour the crop-headed type. It was dusk, but still warm. I felt as if I was playing truant. This elated me – it was like the odd time I'd cut class in Randle and wandered alone in the woods and fields that were only really glorious then, as if they belonged to no one else, as if they were all part of my own private kingdom. Glow-worms abounded near the river. We tried to catch one. I touched Rachael's hand as the light pulsed inside it, then pretended to put one in her hair. We were giggling. We were still giggling when we passed a young, wizened, asthmatic young man, holding a pail. I gave him a bold 'Hello, Ted.' I told Rachael that you had saved him in a mill, once. She asked me if I missed you, because she'd heard the tragic story about my mother. I shrugged my shoulders. Of course I only shrugged my shoulders to impress her, Mother. This evening, you see, I was a man. This shrug did impress her, I think. I hope you don't take it in the wrong way.

We sat on the river's edge and watched the trout rise. I caught one for her – it was easy, there were so many of them, but she insisted I threw the flapping thing back. Everything I did was easy and controlled: the world had been created – the twilight fields, the darkling trees, the twittering birds, the river and the cottages and the ivied mill, the trap-maimed badger glimpsed limping up the bank and wobbling along its crest, the early stooks and haystacks – it had all been created just for us, for our courtship, for me to impress my lovely companion with. It was like the glimpses of wall and tree and hut behind the actors in my Shakespeare volume, only this was not nailed and sized and painted, it was real and rustling and sweet with summer and dusk. I was suddenly unashamed of my connection with the village, of my non-reading days spent bicycling and butterfly collecting or whatever, dipped deep in fantasies of the past and the future in which I was always impressing you, Mother, with some record feat, or talking in a husky whisper to my guardian angel in his cricketing togs. Rachael kept murmuring something about Proust, her eyes appearing to be kindled by my knowledge of the places we walked past. I was extremely well and happy, oh yes, so happy and well, drinking deep draughts of that summer evening and its sweet smells, convinced that the rest of my life would follow suit in one gloriously uncorroding season of Rachael, glow-worms, and heady summer air.

We did not kiss, or anything like that. Oh no. Something, some yearning not to puncture the perfect tissue of my love, prevented me from any ungainly lunge of the sort which had pressed my hands upon the doctor's daughter's hand-knitted brassière. I could not imagine even holding Rachael Katzen's hand. Each accidental touch of the fingers was enough.

There were drinks afterwards, in the morning-room, the new French windows open on to the garden. Nuncle had that afternoon placed candles in old lamps and hung them from the branches, with my sullen help. Soon the nattering stopped over the nut-roast portions and elderberry wine and the different kinds of vintage English apples in straw-lined baskets, and those who were staying went to bed. Rachael and I wandered about the garden, admiring the stars, and talking. I can't remember what we talked about. It was probably twaddle, Mother. Marvellous philosophical twaddle, perhaps shadowed by the Nazi menace or perhaps not. When she yawned, and turned to go in, she told me that this was the nicest evening of her life.

'I'm jolly glad,' I said, 'because it's the nicest evening of my life, too.'

All night I lay awake wishing I had either said something more interesting, or had gazed into her eyes a bit more as I'd said it. A kiss was beyond imagining.

The next morning, I accompanied Rachael and her father to

the station in the tatty trap still driven by a very doddery and deaf Stan. Well, he was cheaper than a motor-taxi, and I knew that Rachael and her father were poor. The seats were frayed raw, and a cushion on one of the arm-rests was missing, but Rachael thought it was Proustian again. I told her Quiri's story of how the human race first got lines on its hands – you remember it, Mother. As we swayed and jolted, and I reached the point at which the grandmother clutches her grandson by the hair to save him from the water's grip, my finger touched Rachael's palm. 'The grandmother tugged, but the lake tugged harder, and she felt his hair slip slowly through her hands and down, down, down he went. All she was left with were the marks his hair had made on her palms.' Rachael looked at her lines – just as I would always do. I was still touching her palm, the movement of the trap making my fingertips stroke her skin. When our eyes met, I thought my chest was going to explode. But her father was squashed in with us, so we couldn't kiss. 'What a sad story,' she murmured. I waved to her as she waved from the carriage window, slowly engulfed in steam, and I bounced back on Stan's trap as gay as a lark, singing aloud when we crossed the open downs. The result of my jollity was a bruised coccyx, but I nursed its discomfort like the dropped button of hers I found down the trap's seat. It had fallen from her blouse during the ride and Stan let me search for it when we got back. It was a top button, from the hollow below her throat. It smelt sweet, probably of the skin of her throat. I kissed it and kissed it and kissed it and kissed it, and nearly swallowed it by mistake. It lost its faint sweetness under this assault of my mouth.

Then war. As thick as the black smoke from the train. This war was just as bad, and even bigger, than the one you knew, Mother. Although I wasn't yet eighteen, I volunteered for the Observer Corps, pretending I was born in 1921. (Anyway, they couldn't have cared less, they just nodded me gratefully in.) To avoid being an officer, and in obeisance to my youthful socialism, I also pretended I hadn't been to public school. I reckoned that I wouldn't kill people in the Observer Corps and that it wouldn't be too much like the loathsome OTC at Randle, but I would still manage to annoy Uncle Edward. He didn't seem to care less either way. And I did become an officer, in the end.

Rachael and I wrote to each other every week. At least, I wrote every week. She was up in Coventry and I was down in London, sharing a circle of sandbags on Parliament Hill with a short-sighted milkman. His spectacles were so thick, he had to take them off when observing because the binoculars kept striking their lenses. And I was one-eyed, though my scratch medical passed me. Things were very chaotic, Mother, in those early days of the war. It was like putting on a huge play at the biggest theatre in London without any rehearsals or very much money. An inspired, improvised frenzy. Our dogged rivals, throbbing along in their straight, Teutonic lines, simply couldn't cope.

Then Rachael came down to London just when I was moved up to Derbyshire for a whole star-gazing winter on a seachlight battery. I'd watched the searchlights skimming the heavens over London, skimming them free of silver splinters with a pillar of light equal to some hundreds of millions of candles, and thought: that's for me. Rachael had a secretarial job in His Majesty's Stationery Office in Kingsway, which she would always call (deliberately I presume, at the top of the letter) His Majesty's Stationary Office. She would usually pen her letters, though. Sometimes mine were a trembly scrawl from the cold that froze us up on Mam Tor, as that first winter was rather a hard one, something of a *Fimbulwinter*. (I did wonder, at times, whether it wasn't *the* one.) There were periods when no fresh supplies came through and we fell back on iron rations, but there was never a missing mail. The motorcycle emerged from a blizzard, once. Letters were more important than food, you see.

We never actually declared our love. But it was there. I started to read Proust in English, but the lack of action was too familiar; I preferred to devour the sixpenny dreadfuls that the troop officer had stocked up on. I recognised some of your favourites, Mother: *The Love Pirate, Unconventional Molly, Passions of Straw*. Strange, to find them here, not warped or blotched with damp and squashed beasties – I'd imagined yours as unique! I began to improve my French with a 'Teach Yourself' course, dreaming of moving to Paris one day with Rachael. I would read her Proust in the original while she dabbed and scraped ordinary life on to canvas. A garret above an echoing *cour*, the sweetness of love and life, of ordinary days of peace. And what would I do? Oh, vague ideas of being a writer. Sitting at a *café* table and writing short novels with long long sentences. All my ideas were vague.

I was well known, on the station, for murmuring Rachael's name as I scanned the empty skies. When Venus rose, showing her motley, teasing me with her restless red and blue glitter, I wanted to shout my sweetheart's name, but only ever murmured it. Then one day I saw the big white letters on the searchlight's drum, the paint dribbling obscenely down the metal: they spelled RACHEL, of course. It was the searchlight's new name, its misspelling like something crippled. The others made filthy innuendos whenever it was my turn to polish Rachel's huge black drum or wipe the glass eye free of bird's-muck (the only enemy fire). But I also had the notion that if we were attacked, and the searchlight wrecked, the real Rachael would suddenly collapse, stark dead.

Such superstitious nonsense. Either one's brain mossed over with this sort of thing or one became overwrought and mistook Orion's Belt for a trio of Dorniers. Also, I had continual mouldering thoughts of Rachael dancing with Spitfire pilots in fleece-lined brown-leather flying suits. All I had were my words. They seemed so feeble. (But of course words aren't!) Each time I spotted her round hand in my name on the envelope, I was as glad as when I saw yours in my name at school, Mother, on the letter bench. Your handwriting was similar to hers.

I did not leave Mam Tor for three months, but I can't say that it was all that miserable up there. My astronomical knowledge improved, as did my muscles. Rifle drill, gas drill, predictor bearing and angle drill, until they were drilled into our sleep. Every metal item, from the grandest ragbolt to the catch on the Lewis gun, lubricated and cleaned to perfection. Silhouette identification, messing fatigues, site cooking, guard duty, the laying-out of kits and bedding and the digging of ditches – but still the days weren't filled high enough, so we mended crumbling drystone walls. The locals didn't thank us, for we never saw one local on that blasted heath – not even a king and his fool.

What else? Well, we descended once a week to the village three miles away with our pockets full of pennies to make phone-calls from the tiny grocer's. I would phone Rachael, of course. It didn't always work, the chat was quite often interrupted by the operator telling us not to hog the line, didn't we know there was a war on? We carried soap and towels down with us for the bath in the cavernous vicarage, and treasured our sixpences for the pint in the village pub – an old crookbacked lady's front room. She also had a wireless set, which cheered things up. A Lance-Bombardier not much older than me fell in love with the postmistress, a widow with six children, so he spent his leisure hours carving little planes out of matchwood. In March I crushed a finger under a keystone, and was invalided out for a month. Thus was my early war, Mother. Not much like Father's, I suppose.

But at least I now sported an eye-patch. Although my eyeball hadn't yet started to rot.

I was going to skip it, but I believe you might want to know how I got my eye-patch, Mother, as you were always very concerned for my bad eye.

Well, our station consisted of a single searchlight, as was normal that first winter of the war. Mam Tor was a steep-sided hump with broad views over more of the same bare moorland. Very few trees. A single-track metalled road hugged the bottom; from certain angles, in the wet, from further along the peak, the side of Mam Tor looked like a face. She had a sharp nose and a great, guffawing mouth. From where I would look at her, a gorse twig gave her a hand – a claw, really. More like a claw on a shrivelled arm. I'd take a walk on my time off and talk to her, sitting on a flat slab of granite and keeping the twig in the right sight line.

Then I started to speak to her. Perfectly normal. People speak to flowers, to trees. When she began to reply to me in a kind of nursery-rhyme gibber, with the wind shivering the shock of sheep-wool she held in her claws, I approached my troop officer and told him all about it. He nodded, puffed a little on his pipe, and asked me to show him the face. We walked to the flat rock and I showed him the correct viewing position. He squinted, grunted, closed one eye, and after a few moments started to grin like a little boy. 'Remarkable,' he said. 'And how do you see it without closing yours, Arkwright?'

'Sir?'

'You see it with both eyes open. The twig goes double, in my case. It's too close up.'

'I have only one eye, sir. One that works.'

He was so surprised, he dropped his pipe in the tussocks. He apologised and we began of course to talk about Africa, about hearing voices, about curses and spells and whether there was a spiritual entity in Nature. He was quite a bit older than me, and had a bad strawberry mark across his face which he liked to pretend was the result of the early blitz on the Firth of Forth: I reckoned that this was a birth-mark and it had made him the reflective man he was. He'd been something in a borough council, wasn't married, and was northern enough to call the underbrush 'scrog' and his mother 'Ma'.

Well, Mother, it was through this man that I went into theatre, I suppose. He knocked his pipe on the rock and suggested that on my day off, instead of wandering over the moor, I organise a concert party. There were a round dozen of us on this site, and the loneliness and routine boredom had caused quite a few quarrels already. We weren't slipshod, so he couldn't be distributing ginger – but this wheeze creased two birds with one shot: the crow of my dottiness, and the vulture of tedium.

Dottiness is dangerous in the Forces, of course. Especially in wartime. Quite unacceptable, in fact. But wars make one dotty. Now there's a conundrum. You must have come across some very bad cases, Mother, in the sanny. Chaps rendered quite bonkers, trembling all over. All that noise. It's the saddest, most dangerous thing.

I'm feeling slightly too tired to carry on for now.

Keep well, dear Ma,

Hugh

Rain. Mist right up to the hotel's gates. But the hawkers stay put along the drive. Definitely a day for the fire. Even the hibiscus droops.

Dear Mother,

I was writing to you about my concert party. I know you love concert parties. I talent-spotted that evening. We had a fellow imitating a courting frog, a tubby homosexual who'd play hymns on his piano accordion, a stammering Geordie with a remarkably rubber face – and myself, with quite a bit of Shakespeare by heart as well as most of *Treasure Island*.

By the end, after a lot of rehearsal, everybody had something. The short private crouched in half a paraffin drum and spun it very fast, another blew 'Tiger Rag' on his tissue-covered comb, a tattoed ex-docker was a crooning Mrs Bagwash in a curtain, the frog told a love story. The troop officer judged the show too ribald for the local villagers; despite our measly spending power they didn't really like us, believing we attracted bombs. We rigged a curtain up in the mess hut and played to ourselves and a ragged ewe called Piles (after our C-in-C, General Sir Frederick Pile). Piles had taken a liking to our rations and no one arrived out of the buffets of wind to claim her. No one arrived at all, most of the time.

I was so happy, when the curtain fell and Piles bleated and we clapped ourselves. So happy.

We played again whenever anybody appeared out of the mist and snow – signalmen, an electrical engineer, the odd truck driver. I suppose that's where my public career really began, Mother; up on that lonely moor, not in the beechwood's hoarse and solitary echoes or later in the flashy lights of London, and certainly not in those bawling performances of the Roman plays at school, where I always seemed to be someone called Perfidius, murdered early. The voice from the laughing face stopped, and I clipped the claw with wire-cutters, just in case.

It was February. The concert parties had lost their glamour. We were preparing a 'clean' version for the village, but its ninety inhabitants were not an audience to look forward to. The besotted Lance-Bombardier perfected a speech from *Romeo and Juliet* and insisted we rig up the wireless in the village hall for a dance after the show, French chalk ready in his mess tin to sprinkle over the floor.

One night, when I was on duty, scanning the clear, coldly glittering sky, the troop officer came up to me with a mug of tea.

'Arkwright, I need to say something to you.'

'Listening, sir.'

The sky's blackness hung above us, a black dome of black iron punctured like a chestnut pan; beyond the tiny holes lay a blazing heaven, burning out all impurities, forging us into steel-eyed angels, winged, in cricketing togs.

'If you don't mind me asking, why do you close your blind eye when on watch?'

'Because it sort of gets in the way, sir. The doping on it isn't quite sealed.'

'As long as you don't get the wrong one, like Nelson did.'

It was the hundredth time I'd heard this joke, but I chuckled dutifully. I sipped my tea and warmed my mittened hands on the mug.

'A spot of warmth is all one needs, eh, Arkwright? Just a spot. Without that spot, one feels somewhat abandoned. Maybe death's just having no spot of warmth.'

He held his mug close to his face, looking up at the stars. The steam would soon freeze on his eyebrows, I thought. Now the inside of my chest was warming, too. The letters of the name in white paint glimmered next to me, where the base of the searchlight's drum sloped. The officer's steamy breath (his name escapes me, I'm afraid) mingled with the steam from his mug as he spoke. 'Isn't it tiring, keeping it closed?'

'I suppose the side of my face would feel rather pained, sir, if the cold hadn't prevented me feeling anything whatever in that region.'

He smiled kindly on my youthful pomposity, and then sighed. His breath wreathed into my own. 'Rather hit-and-miss, our war, isn't it, Arkwright?'

'Do you mean I might miss something with this eye, and hit something with that, sir?'

He looked faintly embarrassed.

'With respect, you're mistaken, sir. My other eye has perfect vision, and my ears, of course, are unusually acute.'

'I was thinking of the problem of depth.'

'I have depth of vision. I don't know why or how, but I have it.'

The mark on my nape tingled under the harsh collar of my troop shirt. I reckoned my uncanny ability to read depth came from the mark Quiri had burned in. 'The spots in my bad eye get in the way,' I added. 'It's better to get rid of imperfection completely than let it trouble something perfect, don't you think, sir?'

'Arkwright.'

'Yes, sir?'

'If I didn't know you already as an unusually earnest chap with an odd way of phrasing things, I'd say you were ragging me. But I do know you. So carry on, carry on. Who knows? Maybe this'll be the night for an illumination.'

'Thank you, sir.'

It wasn't, of course. We imagined SLs all over the country catching tiny silver splinters in their sights, while we caught bats. Bats are all right out of the light, but not in it. Their crumpled little faces made the Lance-Bombardier scream. In fact, there was very little night bombing in those early months, and we were the norm. We exposed our beam every time we heard anything, sweeping it about in that clumsy manner our night-fighters were to find so annoying, but the target was never hostile, Mother!

The little hall was packed for the show, and we gave it everything. Afterwards, during the dance, we all got drunk, the Lance-Bombardier ended up sobbing on the chalky floor and we lost our way back. I won't go into details, but no great harm was done. Sometime in the week that followed, returned from his supply run on his motorbike (a BSA, like Father's in Africa), the troop officer handed over a little packet. I opened it. Inside there was a little purse with a leather thong. When I took it out, it turned into an eye-patch.

'Less strain, Arkwright, less strain.'

It was a fatherly gesture. I appreciated it. I wore the patch spasmodically at first, thinking I looked silly. It appeared in our final performance for a couple of new chaps, sported by my Blind Pew, and I found that my headaches dissolved behind its shield. My present patch is its grandson, Mother, an exact copy of a copy of that first one, which eventually frayed and became irritating to wear. I've lost the eyeball since then, of course.

No enemy plane passed over Mam Tor in all my four months. But a moment's lapse of concentration would bring them screaming out of the sky, we each knew that. On a clear morning, blue and cold, the murmuring wind was definitely a pack of Dorniers, flying too high for binoculars. The grass throbbed its far engines, granite boulders on the crests winked their perspex. Everything conspired to cheat you, you see! I was glad to break my finger, in the end – to be looking into the Thames on Waterloo Bridge, waiting for Rachael. Who came down the length of it and kissed me, just like that. A proper kiss. The cold of Mam Tor hardly out of my lips, hers so warm.

Then another kiss in the back of a throbbing bus, then another in the cinema with the newsreel flickering in the corner of my eye: smoking tanks, salutes, so many men. London was a strange place, that April: a lot of dangling gas-masks, not much black-out doping, a few clumsy daylight bombs gingering us up. We expected gas again, Mother, not fire. So the coaly sprawl was still intact, but neurotic and melancholy. I was neither. I was full of moorland air and Rachael. I was full of a soldier's confidence. Grassy whispers and starlight were now the noise and dazzle of London, her pubs and night-clubs and cafés, her theatres and cinemas and smoky chattering rooms.

I stayed with Father in Bayswater, sleeping on the couch; he had two tiny rooms reeking of gin and cheap cigars in a boarding house full of high-class prostitutes. I won't upset you with details, with the decline, the stooped shuffle, the bad nights when he thought I was his friend – the one who died of yellow fever before your time. I *think* that's who he thought I was. I assumed so, when he screamed out and crouched in terror, not letting me touch him. But it was a cheap service flat providing breakfast, lunch and tea; even the coal fire was laid for him, so he wasn't too neglected, Mother. The prostitutes I bumped into in the passageway seemed bubbly and kind-hearted. Times were good, I suppose. I was invited for sherry by one of the younger ones and she'd tell me about her elderly clients – stockbrokers or MPs or businessmen. She never did the military, she said. Her room was full of antique furniture and silver plate. She talked about fetishes, for which she charged double – some clients liked her to wear boots, or a trilby, or a foxfur wrap. I told her in turn about African fetishes – something quite different, I explained. Rachael laughed when I recounted all this, a little drunk, but she didn't like to come into the house in case someone mistook her for a tenant. We would kiss around the corner and then I would leave her. 'Back to your whores,' she would say, laughing. 'No, back to my daddy,' I'd reply. I had my obligations, Mother.

The Colonial Office gave Father a back windowless room with a brown carpet, a dismal fireplace and a tower of old maps to colour and update by hand. It was useful for me as a base in the day, now and again. His maps were beautiful: stretches of the White Volta, the hills of Adamawa, the estuary of Rio del Rey, that sort of thing. He had to colour in the tin workings, banana plantations, groundnut farms, fisheries, railway depots, roads. I think, Mother, he was happy in his way. As long as he had a clean collar and a tie, and his beard was not too sprawling, the Colonial Office put up with him. He was not the only broken man there. But he didn't talk. Not even to me. He grunted and whispered when he had to, but he had no conversation. He showed me a map of our old area, that he'd coloured recently; it was mostly green bush with a lot of blue squiggles, but a careful scarlet thread marked his road between Bamakum and Ikasa. I knew it was a lie, that what stretches he had laid were mostly swept away or tangled over, but I didn't say anything. He looked at it very proudly, with tears in his eyes. I asked to see a section that included the crater lake. The map wasn't where it should have been, in the big wooden cupboard, but in his personal drawer along with his lunch and biscuits and keys. He unfolded it as if it was Flint's map, looking shifty, saying how he had the right, he had the right. The lake was like a pool of bluebells in a wash of beechen green. Its name was in meticulous white italics, an inch above. *Charlotte's Lake*, it read. I squeezed his shoulder, but neither of us could say anything.

I spent as much time out as possible, exploring galleries and bookshops and museums. Rachael worked her long hours in the HMSO and looked tired, less fresh and vivid than she had done in Ulverton. But she was still the most beautiful girl I had ever seen. She took me to the Harem club, or the Wheatsheaf next door, places like that, full of chattering poets. We saw Dame Edith Sitwell at the Sesame Club, Mother, rustling about in black satin, her face even whiter, her fingers encrusted with rings. This sight made me tell Rachael a bit more about you. That was on my birthday. We drank champagne. I momentarily forgot that I was not nineteen.

She said I would meet Augustus John at the Wheatsheaf. Augustus John flirted with her madly, she claimed. It was a scream. Instead, we spent a smoky evening with Elizabeth Smart, Tambimuttu and Charles Gray, ending up in Gray's rooms in Howland Street. He always had these long ribbons of red cloth dangling from his overcoat, symbolising some sort of saving fire – they were infamous, anyway. He noticed my bandaged finger in its splint and wrote a poem on the wounded hero, while the doe-eyed Tambi flirted with Rachael, and promised her the next cover for *Poetry London.*

'The trouble is,' I said to her, afterwards, a little worse for wear, 'I'm looking for something more than nicer, lonelier versions of my uncle's friends.'

'Why don't you like him, Hugh?'

'Who? Tambi?'

'Your uncle.'

'Don't I?'

I was leaning on her arm as we turned into a side alley, and she fell against a coaly brick wall, laughing.

'What's funny?'

'You'll spend your life looking, won't you? With your funny little searchlight.'

'So much for Augustus John. Anyway, he's a dreadful old flirt, like Bluebeard. I don't want to meet Bluebeard. I don't even want to meet Tom Eliot.'

'Kiss me again.'

I kissed her for a long time. She no longer tasted of violet drops! Eventually she separated my lips from hers and wiped her mouth, the dark eyes shining.

'Rachael Katzen,' I murmured.

'Rachael Katzenellenbogen, originally.'

'That's better. It lasts longer.'

She laughed, holding my face in her hands. 'The Katzenellen-bogens were fine shoemakers in Danzig. I still have family.'

'Haven't they left?'

'No. I expect they'll all be killed. Then it'll be our turn.'

I didn't know what to say to this, because things did look grim that spring: we were all expecting a mass gas attack at any moment. But the odd thing is, I felt very well and happy, Mother. Mam Tor had frozen me, then revived me into a different person. This person made witty remarks in pubs and clubs, had Rachael Katzen as his sweetheart, and didn't care about the morrow. This person was no longer a boy.

Then she said:

'What do you want?'

'Apart from spending the rest of my life with you?'

She nodded, grinning. There was a gaslight burning softly over our heads. Even then, this was unusual – it reminded me of Ilythia. Searching for a clever answer to her question, this picture came into my head, of a lonely moorland path. I was stumbling on it, in pursuit of someone always just where the mist began to thicken. I won't say who that someone was. You know who it was. I wanted to cry – it was the alcohol, really – and I scratched the mark on my nape, fiercely, so that my collar popped open under my tie. How could I be so miserable, with Rachael so close? I thought: if she vanishes – run over by a bus, stolen by some tangle-headed poet, killed by a German – what would I do? Kill myself, of course.

'Hugh?'

Tears were gleaming on my hands; it wasn't the rain, because it wasn't raining. A late bus chugged past, a couple of men in Homburgs wheeled their stretched shadows over us, someone cried out from a window, there was a waft of gravy smells from a vent near us. Near the vent was a high-heeled shoe, very white, the heel sticking up like a nose. I couldn't stop myself crying. Yet I'd just kissed the girl I loved, whose face I saw in the heavens whenever I searched them for the enemy. Her hand, rather cold in the night air, was on the back of my neck, stroking me, a cigarette in its fingers. I could feel the filtered end of the cigarette rubbing my mark. Ash, I thought. If she turned the cigarette round, and laid its burnt end on my nape, she might destroy my mark. I might begin again, from the ruins, with her as my angel.

I was abandoning you, Mother, for a girl I scarcely knew! I'm
so sorry! I'm so sorry!

Let's call that a day.

Your ever-loving son, your only

Huggins

Hot wafts of air from down there, where Victoria lies. Birds very noisy.
Also cicadas. Tss tss tss. Very disapproving little creatures. I love the
waiters here, their gloves as white as Edith Sitwell's skin.

Dear Mother,

I reached back and gripped her hand with the cigarette in it,
tried to turn it round. In the confusion I smelt that foul smell of
singed hair, and felt a brief pain near my jugular. The cigarette
landed in a puddle.

'What are you doing? You've hurt my fingers. You're drunk.'

'I'm going to be an actor.'

'What?'

'I'm sorry I hurt you, darling. I'm going to go into the theatre.'

'What are you gabbling about? It's after midnight, they're all
closed by now! Why are you crying?'

She was holding her hand, looking perplexed. Then she began
to smile. She was used to people behaving oddly. She liked it. I
think she liked to be tested: she was adored by all her father's
artistic friends, and by her own chums, and she wanted something
more. She liked me, in the end, because I was not easy; because I
came from somewhere else. I wasn't difficult in the way a lot of
Bohemia was difficult, deliberately exaggerating their despair,
their little ecstasies around pots of bitter beer and bad wine. I
didn't pose, I didn't exaggerate, for all my faults. My eye-patch
was real, not rakish.

'It's what I'm going to do. Because it's so incredibly hopeless.'

She frowned, her face pale under the gaslight. I thought of
Private Chamberlain in his metal drum, rehearsing for hours until
he could spin it, and started laughing.

'It's so incredibly hopeless, I can't fail!'

'What's hopeless?'

'My chances of being something, in theatre. Who'll take a one-eyed actor?'

She understood, I think, and held me. I buried my face in her thick hair. It smelt of coal. The city mumbled around us. It was quite intact, then. The gas-flare chuckled above us. I watched it chuckling and fluttering in its glass like a little imp beyond her hair. I wanted to show her my country haunts. Somewhere in one of my haunts, we would do It together, I knew. Not before, not here, where gas might drop on one. There was something dirty about doing It here, in London.

Anyway, Nuncle had insisted I see him in my month's leave. I told him about Rachael, rather triumphantly. Despite the various meetings and seminars and 'ritual celebrations' he organised, he was lonely. The German mystics of the Thule Society had mostly turned into Nazi sympathisers. His old friend Rudolf von Sebottendorff, founder of the Thule Society, had raised funds for the fledgling National Socialist Party back in the twenties. He was a jolly, elegant man with a pendulum just like Nuncle's; I'd been on a long scramble with him in and out of the vast ditches at Avebury, years before. He and Nuncle never stopped discussing astrology, numerology, and Jewish mysticism. Without von Sebottendorff's money, without the early help of that large, elegant fellow laughing among the standing stones, the Party might never have grown and the Holocaust might never have happened. Do you remember him, Mother? One thing leads to another.

So Nuncle looked worn and lonely and rather old, when we arrived. That soon changed. It changed, I think, within minutes of Rachael arriving. Blood returned to his cheeks. He plumped up. Then he shot off to lead a dowsers' walk until nightfall, leaving us sipping our tea in the kitchen.

'Fascinating man,' said Rachael.

What had he said?

We went for a walk ourselves. I wanted to show her my haunts. I taught her to make a walking stick out of buckthorn, showed her badger runs and badger latrines, crouched to the stink of a foxhole. She was suitably appalled at Jed's gibbeted crows and stoats. I prepared a picnic around Mrs Stump's immobile groans

223

(her arthritis, my uncle, the shortages – you know old Stumpy-Grump, Mother) while Rachael licked precious butter off her fingers and tried not to giggle. I rescued my aunt's bicycle from its crotchety rustiness so that we could wobble out together on to Furzecombe Down and touch the Kissing Stone on its tumulus – that worn old cross supposed to bring luck in love. I told her that somewhere around here, perhaps where we were standing on the open downs, the Danes had fought the Saxons of Alfred's army all day long around a lone thorn bush. We found a suitable clump of gorse and tussled. This could be It, I was thinking. But she flopped out of my arms and rolled on the ground and asked why there was always war. 'Ask my uncle,' I said. 'He blames the farmers.'

'Oh, that,' she said, chewing a stalk. 'Poppa goes on about that, too. He's a very clever man, is your uncle.'

We spotted sparrow-hawks, surprised rabbits, chased early burnets and pretended to be the swallows we saw swooping out of a barn, swooping out and over the lovely and lonely sky-naked downs. I was glad they weren't forest any more. We could run down and over them for ages, as if completely free.

I lay flat out on my belly, watching her chase the butterflies with my boyhood net: each detail of sheep-nibbled grass, of stitchwort and tangled vetch and a stumbling ladybird on a fern-leaf beyond my chin, seemed blessed and vivid, as if everything pig-headed and stiff-necked in the world had been dashed to pieces by Rachael's litheness and laughter and dark-eyed beauty. When I raised my head the sward swept away into fold upon fold of open curves covetous only of the sky's blueness – as blue as the hedge-sparrow's egg we found in its little nest and kissed for luck as we wended our way back to the village, but paler than the blue-violet drifts of bluebells in the woods and copses.

Each copse looked so inviting. These might do for It, I was thinking. But none of them was quite right. We'd leave our bicycles on the chalky verge and penetrate the copse almost on tiptoe; the trees were still so tender in their new leaves that any sound might scatter that cloudy light, those malachite necklaces of shadow – and there was always a jay that clattered and screamed and made her jump, however quietly we went in. None of them would do. I even secretly tested certain spots for softness by walking on them in a little circle, while she was picking bluebells, but either they were soggy or rather open to the open downs. The copses were too small. Someone might peep.

We came out of Swilly Copse with her arms full of bluebells. 'Ugh,' she said, 'my hands are all sticky –' 'Sssh,' I interrupted, 'look up and shut up.'

I wasn't being rude: it was what we'd say on Mam Tor. Look up and Shut up. But she was confused for a moment. Then I pointed, all my nerves on alert, despite myself. My hairs bristling.

A white vapour trail left by a scintillating speck, a far-off drone more like a motor-boat on a lake than a plane; I checked it through my old bird-watching binoculars. Then I laughed – laughing so helplessly I rolled on the grass while Rachael crawled around me.

'What's so *funny*?' she pleaded.

'The first sight of the enemy I've ever had,' I explained, wiping my eyes. 'The very first sight. The very very first sight.' I leapt to my feet suddenly and hopped up and down, shouting like a madman: 'Seen. Bearing 290. South-west. One Heinkel 111k. At 10,000. Expose the beam! Angle 18! Put a beam on her! Engage the fucker! Engage her! Disperse the beam! Dazzle her! Bring her down! It's my bird! It's my fucking bird!'

I felt much better, afterwards, as I stood there panting. The speck had disappeared. It was probably packed to the bulkhead with bombs ready to shriek down on the motley patchwork below, so it was just as well it didn't hang about, I suppose. Rachael had dropped all her bluebells in fright.

We reached the beechwood from the Jennets' field. In those days there was a hawthorn hedge, remember? Its corymbs were tipped with white, ready to burst into flower against the dark leaves. I told Rachael that the hawthorn is called the may because it flowers on May Day. 'But how does it know?' She was serious, I think. I said that we should come back here tomorrow to see if this one had followed tradition – the next day was May Day. We decided to set out just before dawn, to watch the sun rise on the blossom. To go a-Maying, and gather garlands in the old manner. That's how I put it.

'What else did they do, Hugh?'

We were right in the beechwood now, near the hollow with the old fungal log. It didn't feel like a theatre, now. My old hermit's cell, a little way off, had crumbled to a rotten plank or two and a dark little mound of compost that was once the grass roof. 'To quote that blind old puritan bore, Milton,' I replied, '*Hail! flowery May that dost inspire/Mirth and youth and warm desire.*'

She laughed, her eyes twinkling in the dappled light. She had never looked so lovely. We kissed for a long time on my old stage, but there were no rows of faces in the hollow, gawping up. There was no one. No one! The theatre was dark! The beechwood was empty but for the dumb beasts! Let all the woods be empty but for the dumb beasts!

That's all for now, Mother,

　　With all my love,

　　　Hugh

Cold.

My dearest Mother,

I can't always be with you. The people here say that I must go back to England. So here I am again. The spiraea is now in full flower. One can order books. There is a reading group. It's extremely comfortable. I hope Africa is not too hot, even in Buea. I will join you soon. You are not to go home without me.

For dinner, she changed into an elegant, old-fashioned tube dress of satin. It had probably belonged to her mother. She had never known her mother, which seemed almost ridiculous. One could imagine the mother, though, from the dress: she was thin and boyish and haughty. With Rachael squeezed inside it, the dress looked extremely provocative. Nuncle showed her a special attention that evening, over Mrs Stump's roast – yes, overdone as ever! He stuck on his bearded wise man look and charmed with the eyes, their two globes as darkly polished as the scarab ring on his finger. They kept settling on Rachael. This young woman by my side, dressed in satin, looked impossibly lovely. She was all, everything to me, every speck of creation from the first star of the first morning to the last flea on the last fleece. Everything was made better by her. Everything sang. Everything.

'Do you know why the month of May is called May?'

'I know why the hawthorn is called may, Mr Arnold.'

She looked at me and squeezed my hand under the table. Nuncle took no notice of what she'd said. What an old goat – over forty, for God's sake!

He told her why May is called May. Ovid says it's because the Romans sacrificed to Maia on the first day of the month, and I recited the appropriate lines in Latin. Neither of them took any notice. 'Maia's the mother of Mercury,' I added; 'that's why the mercury goes up in May.' I can't recall whether anyone laughed, but I do know that Rachael asked Nuncle if that's all the Romans did on the first of May, with a straight face that hid the most delightful squeeze of my fingers. My heart hammered. Why not the beechwood? Yes, why not the darkened stage itself, where so many love scenes had already passed?

Nuncle blinked, unconcernedly, and took a mouthful of Mrs Stump's succulent bread-and-butter pudding. He spoke with his mouth full. He ate like a peasant.

'Sacrifice is the most potent practice of all, Rachael.'

'Doesn't it depend on what you sacrifice?'

'Hitler's jolly fond of that word, isn't he?' I added, feeling we were sparring with him. 'He wants to sacrifice everybody but himself. I suppose that's pretty potent.'

Uncle Edward ignored me. Sometimes whole days had passed in my boyhood when he would avoid addressing a single word to me, using Mrs Stump or Susan as a medium. He had to be left to think. Did you know this? I felt like a ghost. I was annoyed at myself now for feeling hurt again.

'The Romans made do with a pig or a ram or an ox. Their predecessors understood the gods and gave them a young virgin. Or many young virgins, all at once.'

My face was aflame, I'm sorry to say. I sighed, knowing what was about to be said. He only ever said about three things, Mother, endlessly embroidered on.

'And we whites have persuaded the African that throwing a

young virgin to the crocodiles is less efficacious than using the nearest old goat –'

I chuckled behind my blush. There was one old goat I would dearly love to sacrifice.

'Hugh will tell you all about that.'

'No I won't.'

'His father is one of those whites. The poor African gods have to put up with goat meat, these days. The blood of poultry. No more young virgins or succulent albinos for the gods. Oh no. It's all goat's meat and agricultural officers and democratic elections, these days. That'll put Africa on the right path, won't it, Hugh? But I have my doubts, Rachael, I have my doubts, with all those hungry gods about.'

I said nothing, of course. Rachael left my fingers gripping the napkin on my knees. She rested her chin on her fingers and flashed the kind of smile I'd seen in Fitzrovia, when Gray was describing his red ribbons of cloth as the flaming torch that would save the universe. It was a smile of patience in the face of fools, but it only encouraged them. It only pleased them. She said that sacrifice was completely irrational, like the loon in Camden Station shredding sweetpapers into his top hat. It doesn't mean anything, it's an illusion. So if it came to choosing between a young virgin, a goat, and a communion wafer, she would definitely choose the wafer.

She was eloquent and intelligent: Nuncle's showy twaddle was bringing out the best in her. Rachael was well used to his sort of provocative bore.

The bore was unstoppable.

'That doesn't take into account the mind-matter principle. Energy flows uninterrupted between mind and matter, between hoof and flower and hair and hands and the great caverns within us, between the stars and your thoughts, between your thoughts and the growing tree. Where is the edge, the limit? Where do our minds stop? At the bone of our skulls? At the rainbow-coloured aura around us? At the furthest stretch of our helpless hands? Surely not! Surely not!'

He was thumping the table with the flat of his hand. I looked at Rachael. She was magnificent, staring him out, completely undeterred. The wine from Nuncle's cellar was old and strong: I had never seen such good wine, here. I tried to stand up, to break the spell of the table, but my knees tangled with the tablecloth and I fell back abruptly in my chair. Perhaps the wine was drugged. Rachael did not turn her head to look at me, but kept her gaze fixed on Nuncle's face. Magnificent! Nuncle leaned forward until the candle was only an inch from his big nose. He passed a finger slowly through the flame.

'Tomorrow is Beltane. Sacred to the old Celtic god, Belenos. The first day of summer, as Imbolc is the first day of spring. On Beltane a small griddle cake was cooked and broken up. Then it was shared out like a child sharing his currant bun. There was a fire lit upon the temenos. If your portion of cake was burnt, you were thrown into the flames.'

'Charming!'

'Later, in less vigorous times, the victim had only to jump through the flames –'

'That's progress!'

'– three times, in devotion to the threefold mother goddess of the giving earth. D'you see?'

His finger passed through the flame three times, slowly. His eyes had never left Rachael's face, though he'd ignored her interruptions. She must be so uncomfortable, I thought. But she is used to it.

'What do we do these days?' he went on. 'Warble songs from the top of an old tower, with the odd dance around a maypole. Summer must be born in fire, don't you think?'

'I do hope this summer won't be,' said Rachael.

'Then we'd better be feeding Belenos jolly smartly. Or there'll be fire from the heavens, raining down on our ungrateful, neglectful heads, out of the stars we no longer read.'

'Don't worry, Rachael, I'll be back on duty by then.'

She didn't seem to hear my joke.

'Out of the stars? Do you think they'll be attacking at night? What a horrible thought – while we're all asleep.'

'Night bombers are not at all likely to be a threat,' I assured her. 'Germans like the sun, they like to see England stretched out beneath them under a clear sky. We'll drive them higher and higher, until they're out of our range at 15,000 feet. They can't get correct aim from that height.'

'The Teuton likes to see flames blaze out of the darkness,' Nuncle said, as if I hadn't spoken at all. 'Ragnarok, the triumph of frost and fire, that's what sleeps in them. The end of the gods, even of one-eyed Wotan, father of them all. The wolf swallowing the moon, the serpent blowing poison over the world, heaven burnt to cinders, all that. Night, winter, the birth of the Reich from the ashes. Except that the horribly vulgar little idea of the Reich won't be born from the ashes, of course. The tiny green shoots will be trees, my dear.'

He glanced at Rachael with a glistening roll of his eyeballs.

'Trees. And a handful of people among them.'

'You, for instance?'

He smiled. I was numb with boredom, knowing all this twaddle off by heart, all this guff about the wildwood being a chip off the great block of forest that would rise again after some apocalypse or other – spread out from Ilythia and engulf the country! I could feel in my head the heavy roll of the searchlight as we angled it, hear its ratchets squeak, the soundless blast of its beam. Closing my eyes, I was up on Mam Tor again. If only I had engaged something hostile. If only I'd had something to impress her with.

Oh God, Mother. Nuncle did go on, didn't he? In his growly bass. I can't imagine he was ever a piping boy, running about the garden with you. Now he was going on about the obscenity of electrical illumination, how it has banished our species from a primal pleasure: darkness, and the flicker of flame upon darkness. 'Have you noticed how trees come alive in firelight? Grow even bigger? One of the gains of this ridiculous war has been the black nights. Do you know our little local story?'

His eyes twinkled again as they looked at Rachael. She shook her head, of course. He told her about his friend Herbert Bradman, who under cover of the black night, had pissed into the ditch under the crab-apple hedge on his way here. 'There was a sort of furious groan. Herbert shone his torch into the ditch: two well-known young lovers, Jimmy Oadam and Annie Hobbs, lie there spluttering and half-naked. "Next time you choose to tup in the ditch," Herbert remarks, "make sure you tell me first." "Us weren't tupilatin'," comes Jimmy's reply, "us were jus tekkin' cover." '

I laughed with them, to cover the fire on my face. We shared some more black-out stories. For a while it was quite pleasant.

'Anyway, I think the German is very practical,' Rachael said, finally. 'They're not going to drop their bombs at night, with all the problems that entails, just because they want their crews to participate in some sort of huge fire festival.'

'It's inevitable,' Nuncle replied. 'The Teuton's soul will not recoil from it, as other nations might. Before the year is out, the wondrous terror of the night blaze will be upon us: none of us has ever dreamt of the like.'

'Not even you, Mr Arnold?'

I think she was tipsy, Mother. The twaddle continued. I was desperate to walk with Rachael in the garden, but the twaddle was holding her attention. It even continued into the hall. Eventually Nuncle kissed her hand and said goodnight, at the bottom of the stairs. 'I have seldom enjoyed a conversation so much as ours this evening, my dear girl. If you were the young virgin our ancient ancestors had chosen one May morning, long ago, to lay in the earth alive, there would have been no more winters to appease, I'm sure.'

'Oh, for God's sake, Uncle!'

Rachael looked startled: Uncle Edward merely tilted his head with a shy smile and disappeared up the stairs. I snorted my impatience and suggested to Rachael we walked out in the garden. We took a shawl and scarf off the hook in the hallway and left by the French doors. We had linked elbows, walking on the lawn like old-fashioned lovers. I apologised for the evening. She asked me what I was apologising for. Her weight, which was being taken by me so much that I had to watch my step, removed itself a little. One could tell the angle of the searchlight's drum, without looking, from the pull on the wheel at the end of the long pivoting arm: Rachael was angling away from me. The shrubs loomed in the moonlight rather menacingly, and a tawny owl hooted from the wildwood. I wished I hadn't drunk so much: the old vintage was invading my stomach, loosening my bowels. The lawn felt spongy.

'My uncle talks twaddle,' I said, firmly. 'It sounds impressive, that's why people like it —'

'The Fitzrovia crowd, for instance.'

'Yes, the less perceptive among them.'

'Not necessarily, unless you think Mr Coomaraswamy imperceptive.'

'All right, the Indian intellectual finds something familiar, but I know my uncle —'

'You're too close. I mean, you're too emotionally bound up with him to look on his work with detachment. He's saying some very important things.'

'Have you actually read anything?'

'No, but Tambi's shown me bits, and my father —'

'Read it, the whole lot. By the end you'll not only be screamingly bored, but convinced of his fraudulence. My mother talked more sense than her brother, and she was just a nurse, with no pretensions whatsoever.'

'She kept her place, did she?'

I stopped, letting her arm go. She was smiling. I'm afraid I felt angry — an absolutely terrific surge of anger on your behalf. It came from nowhere.

'That's not fair,' I said, between gritted teeth. 'That's not what I meant.'

'I'm sorry . . .'

'And what's more, she didn't. You know she didn't.'

'I *don't* know, Hugh!'

My anger went. My lips still felt white, but the anger went, just as quickly as it had come. *Tu whit whit* went the tawny owl, moving swiftly now. Rachael was looking towards the wood, towards the sound — perhaps slightly afraid of the moonlit garden, the humps of trees and the ogreish shrubs, all whispering in the night breeze. She held her shawl closed at the throat. Her lips shone like blue glass. I could either shut up, or continue. 'Well, yes, you do know. She didn't keep her place at all. She ran away. That's not keeping your place, is it?'

'I didn't know she ran away. I thought she just sort of vanished.'

She clicked her fingers and gave a little giggly snort. I wanted to giggle, too. To laugh and roar and roll on the ground. It was like wanting to be sick.

We were crossing the lawn towards the beechwood. My heart started pounding because I reckoned that It could happen now, even if it wasn't quite May morning. Then she suddenly veered towards the tangle of the wildwood. Her step quickened as she talked. 'Do you feel angry sometimes, that she ran away like that? Or even if she didn't run away, even if she just — I mean, do you feel very cross but you can't tell her off? Because I do. I feel so angry with my mother for dying when I was so young. I can't remember her, not a thing. I feel ever so cross but not at God, no. At her! Poor thing! She couldn't help getting a chill, could she, in some draughty railway station or other, waiting for my father? And I'm not even angry at him for being late, or the train, or whatever caused the delay! And what do you think of that, Hugh?'

'I don't know. I've never felt it.'

This was a white lie, Mother. I'm sure I had felt anger, but couldn't precisely recall it. We stared into the wildwood. I was thinking more about It than about you, I'm afraid. I put my arm around her shoulders, but she slipped away.

'I'm talking!'

'I know you're talking —'

'She left you, didn't she? She dropped you off here like a piece of baggage and went back to Africa.'

I stood, frozen with a sort of horror.

'Who told you?'

'Mrs Stump. In the kitchen.'

(Mother, Mrs Stump must be forgiven. She was a simple soul. Anyway, I don't think she ever put it like that. Tell A you find B a little trying and A will tell C that you find B absolutely impossible — and so on.)

'Oh, she did, did she?'

'Yes. In so many words —'

'Damn Mrs Stump. Ever heard of sacrifice? My mother wasn't exactly working in luxurious conditions. To most people, life out there, in the bush, is a pretty good definition of hell.'

'Anywhere can be hell,' she retorted. 'There was once a man

who arrived in Bristol and thought it was hell – suddenly, just like that. And as the carriage took him towards the town centre, he imagined all the people were pointing and saying: Look at that poor soul, he's bound for the deepest circle.'

I laughed, despite myself. Sometimes I had thought Ulverton was hell – or school was, or the whole of England.

'Anyway,' she went on, 'as for sacrifice, I've always had a soft spot for Cain. He only sacrificed vegetables. It's all very well burning the fat of the lamb, but what about the lamb?'

Now I stopped laughing. You can see why, Mother. I looked across at her. She was in profile. Unutterably lovely in the moonlight, which made her dark hair so very black and silver at the same time.

'I admire my mother', I said, 'and cherish her memory. That's all.'

'You admire her, but admiring something doesn't tell you much. I admire Hitler's capacity to fool a whole nation that he's not utterly doolally.'

Was she very drunk, or just a neurotic? Amazingly, this passed through my head at the very moment I wanted to take her in my arms for ever and ever. At the very moment I decided I would like to marry her. She was beating you over the head, Mother, tearing you into horribly bloody strips – yet I had never desired her so much!

I stepped towards her. She stared at me defiantly. All I could say was, in a high voice – how unfortunate a comparison! Then I caught a glimpse of Nuncle's shadow in his window, cast huge and wavery by a bedside candle. Perhaps he was watching us.

'But I don't find it very surprising, Rachael.'

'What?'

I stared at a straggly oak in the wildwood, ivy gleaming in the moonlight all the way to the topmost branches.

'What do you mean, Hugh?'

Then I looked back at Nuncle's window. The shadow had gone.

'I don't find it very surprising that frauds can dazzle to that extent. There's such a thing as – as hypnotic influence. And the

234

ability to drag out into the bright light what otherwise intelligent people have hanging about in their darkest, deepest caverns.'

Rachael snorted.

'I hope you're not comparing your uncle to Hitler, and me to the German masses, just because I found the harmless things your uncle had to say rather intriguing. If you don't mind me pointing out, that is a jolly unfortunate comparison, too, given my blood.'

'You were the one who brought up Hitler –'

'Of course I wasn't for a moment comparing your mother to that horrible monster. Whoever do you think I am? I'm sure your mother was admirable, like mine. Even though yours was a nurse in darkest Africa and mine was a singer in tatty music halls. Is it true what they say, by the way?'

She giggled, crooked her arm through mine, and moved towards the house out of the trees' stretched shadows. The moonlight glared on the white tassels on the front of her dress. If I were to pull them, would the dress open? Or were they just decorative? She was angled towards me, now. I could kiss her, and then I could start to pull them. I could slip my hands right inside.

'Is it true, Hugh?' she asked again, squeezing my arm against her ribs. Love and desire floundered deliciously in my throat; I was quite breathless, as if I'd been running a long way.

'Is what true, my darling?'

'That he only has one – you know . . .'

'My dear love, his lack of an essential miniature sandbag explains this whole ghastly show. But I refuse to donate the essential article just to stop the war.'

I stared at her glaring white tassels, then started to pull at them with both hands. I'd forgotten to do the kissing first.

'What are you doing, Hugh? You'll break them!'

They were purely decorative. One came away in my hand. She was quite annoyed. I offered to mend it. The lawn spread glaring around us, our shadows so utterly black and long and lively. We were caught right in the middle, like a pilot in a beam. The wavery shape, again, in the window. I hurried her off the lawn as if it was some ancient arena full of ghosts, full of tainted dangerous air. We kissed briefly on the landing. 'Until dawn,' I whispered, holding her tassel as if it was some sort of love token. She frowned and plucked it from my hand, then disappeared into your old room.

> With all my love,
> Hugh

Still obliged to stay here in England. Not long! Pottery classes. I can make nothing but lumps. They think I'm processing my pain (whatever that means), but I say they're just lumps. Pain better today, anyway.

Dear Mother,

I hardly slept, and had confusing dreams. Splashed my face from the bowl and jug in my room, and staggered with a headache to Rachael's door as the first birds erupted, dawn pretending to be windows. Night is like a mist, at that hour, which every move of the head clears a little, then lets fall, then clears, then lets fall, then clears, then lets fall – and so on. Until it's suddenly light. Who's to say, then, one hasn't created that light oneself?

Lights! Lights!
Lights!

> With best wishes and love,
> Hugh

April drizzle.

Dear Mother,

I'm doing generally very well. I must say it does me a lot of good writing to you. When are you coming to visit? I'm tied up here for quite a while. I think I'm well on the way to talking again.

Knock knock. No answer. I opened the door. The room had barely changed since you'd last used it – and you used to tell me that it had hardly changed since your childhood. In front of the doll's house lay a tiny divan and a miniature sewing machine; Rachael must have played with your doll's house. I put them back immediately, of course.

Rachael lay fast asleep in the narrow bed by the window; her

236

head was turned from me, and her black hair lay like black flames on the pillow. It might have been you, dear Mother, lying there, returned from the shadows of the forest, its bits and pieces of light. But it wasn't. I touched her shoulder, shook it gently. She mumbled something, turning her face towards me. Your bedside lamp burned gently under its tulip glass. Rachael had said that the gas brackets made her feel sick, but the darkness of the country bothered her, even when the moon had risen. So I found the oil lamp in the cupboard and filled it.

Next to it, on the bedside table, there was a file full of papers and a copy of the ARP Handbook No. 1: *Personal Protection Against Gas*. She'd told me she was proof reading the new edition for the HMSO. The sight of this made me feel low, for a moment, as did the mournful, baggy stare of her mask, dangling from the bed-end. I saw now that she was frightened of the gas in her room, though she didn't say that; frightened of the smell it puffed out when it was turned on or off – or even of its bleached light. Much more of it could fall from the sky and burst anywhere at any time, wafting over rush-hour crowds so that they all fell gasping in a wave. Perhaps some shells had burst unseen in wintry woods, sopped up by the cold wetness, only coming up now. And which type would it be? Lewisite? Mustard? Chlorine? Phosgene? Or something non-lethal like bromobenzyl cyanide (whose acronym was BBC, to Nuncle's delight)? Well, we'd taste it and guess, like apple tastings in the village hall. For now, it was time to go a-Maying.

When she opened her eyes briefly, it looked as if she'd been crying. I kissed the eyelids gently when she closed them, and felt the eyeballs moving under the silken skin, under my lips. She told me it was much too early to wake her. The old pillowcase had left the impress of its lace edging on her cheekbone; I stroked the place and told her it was dawn.

The dewy lawn was cold underfoot through our canvas shoes. The birdsong was deafening. Rachael yawned and shivered.

'Where's the sun?'

'There. There's the earth coming up,' I said, pointing.

'You are strange.'

'I'm not. I'm just a Copernican.'

237

'The sun's coming up. I can't see it as anything else.'

'It takes practice. I trained myself in Derbyshire over a lot of dawns. You have to deceive your eye with the truth. Now I don't see the sun coming up. I see it staying still while the earth's tilting.'

'Well you're the only one in the world to see it like that.'

She snuggled against me. The new light touched her face. The bright orange disc was the huge eye of a god, and we were descending past it. It approved of her beauty.

We walked through the grey, echoing beechwood, not yet shafted by the sun's rays. My old stage was dark. There were scurryings everywhere. The hedge of may was still spotted all over with buds. I said we'd have to wait for the sun to warm it. Rachael seemed disappointed; the magic hadn't worked. She touched a bud, as if its little packed fist might spring open. 'Come on, you,' she said. The air was sweet and somehow stippled with warmth, though it was still cold. (You would say in Africa how much you missed May mornings in England, Mother. You know how they are.) 'Come on, you!'

'There's no hurrying Nature,' I said. I kissed her. Her mouth was still soft from sleep. If a single flower had been out, I would have done It there and then. She was ready. My whole life might have been different. The very bad thing might not have happened, so many years later, because one thing leads to another. But the bud stayed tight and shut.

'Holloa!'

Waving at me from the other barrow: silhouette identification, her arms stretched out like wings, breaking as she waved. I'd seen one of ours waving its wings like that, then folding its arms into flame, then exploding somewhere over the suburbs.

The field was still in the wood's shadow below us. Closer, around the barrow, there were spatters of chalk and flint: maybe Nuncle had been digging again. Or maybe it was rabbits. Cowslips in the tough corn. I could pick her a cowslip. Her silhouette was so slender against the burning light, on the round swollen mound. If the earth tipped much further, she might fall into the fire behind her.

I shouted, pointing to the next crest about a mile away, its smooth edge ruffled only by an oak clump. In between lay a heathy coomb, full of sarsen stones that looked like a big flock of sheep, but I had never seen a single real sheep grazing there. It was always in shadow. A heath-dwelling giant had gone for a walk to see his downland mate, I told Rachael, when we were standing on its edge. It was a wet day, and he had a lot of the heath on his boots. A clump of it fell off just here. 'He must have been a big giant,' she said, 'to make such a deep footprint.'

There was something else odd about it, if you remember, Mother. (Did you go there as a child? Or did I show you?) A giant cat had clawed its near side. An enormous beast, the king of all the cats, a big beef the size of a house. Maybe it was Nuncle who told me. It had to have somewhere to sharpen its claws. So the side was scored with belts of grass between the bracken and heather. Some of these grassy stripes kept going all the way down to the bottom. It was hard to tell from the top which was which. It was like a game: sometimes you won.

'Did you used to play here as a boy? It's a bit spooky. I'm sure there are some sheep down there. They're just asleep.'

'Not very often. Well I did, sometimes. I pretended it was the plateau on Treasure Island. The oaks over there were where they found Allardyce.'

'Was he the maroon?'

'No, that was Ben Gunn. Allardyce was the skeleton.'

She didn't say anything, just breathed so I could hear it. Maybe she wasn't used to walking and running. Or maybe it was something else. I turned to go back, to head back for the beechwood before the sun came up too much and the rest of the world woke up. People would be doing things in the fields any minute. Horses and motor cars and the smell of bread. Gun oil and men baling out up there.

'I want to see if those are sheep.'

'They're not, I promise.'

She was starting to go down.

'Wrong one!' I shouted. I showed her another grassy strip but had remembered wrongly – it was ages since I'd been to this place; we ended up struggling through a heathy thicket of bracken and heather. When we reached the bottom, she started picking leaves and thorny bits out of her stockings and the hem of her coat. The frost lay over everything like a veil. There were one or two gorse flowers out. There were some rabbits at the far end, creeping back.

'They look so sinister,' she said, looking at the strange rubble of sarsens. 'Did someone put them here?'

I told her about them, as you told me once.

'You mean they were just left here by the ice?'

I nodded. Why did she have problems believing it?

'But you can see patterns in them, the way they're set out, squares and rows and things, like a big game of chess.'

'Well they're rubble,' I said. 'Completely haphazard. More like a game of marbles.'

She climbed on to one of them, a large brown-grey hump that curved up to a point about six feet high.

'How did they farm here, with these in the way?'

'I don't suppose they did. Anyway, it's too heathy, the soil's poor. Maybe it was pasture.'

She pointed to the stripes of heather and grass on the slope.

'What are those?'

'The clawings of a giant cat,' I said. 'Prehistoric.'

She shuddered.

'Horrible.'

She believed me, now. When I fibbed, she believed me.

'Actually, I think they're strip lynchets, except strip lynchets are normally horizontal.'

'Strip what?'

She was giggling on top of the stone, quite high up it seemed to me. The stone was wobbling slightly, despite its enormous size. I told her to be careful. 'Why? Is it going to fall down after millions of years? Look! I'm Amy Johnson! I'm going to disappear into thin air! Wheee!'

She was making fun of me on the top of her stone, holding her arms out wide. The more the time passed, the harder it was to summon up the pluck to do It, to make the first proper lunge, to go beyond a long kiss. Now she was on top of a huge wobbling stone, saying she was about to disappear. The stones had children stuck in them. There used to be a village beyond where the rabbits were, and an old witch called Anne Stile had led the children here to dance to the Devil. When she heard someone coming, she covered the children and herself in stone. But being a forgetful old crone, she couldn't remember the undoing spell. If you listen carefully on certain nights, you can hear their high little voices and the voice of the witch herself – she's pleading with you to go to her house and bring back her spellbook. It's on top of the cupboard, between the Condy's frog fluid and the broomstick oil. Was that what you told me, Mother? Don't tell me you made it all up! Because I don't believe you made it all up! Rachael was standing on the very witch's stone itself: you could tell from the way it curved up into a sort of hood! It would swallow you up by the ankles as the witch tugged you in, that's what you said! The Wobble Stone. The Witch Stone. Oh, my God. It was actually leering at me. All its wrinkles were a leer on a face. Hit it before it does harm. Hit it, hit it!

Have to dash now.

I'm well.

    With love and very best wishes as ever,
    Hugh

Showery intervals. Leaves out everywhere.

Dear Mother,

Sorry I've been out of touch for a bit. Ups and downs, but generally fine now.

One of her canvas shoes was overlapped by a rough fold and the wrinkles in the stone were leering at me. Ha ha ha. That's why I went over to her immediately, seized her around the knees and lifted her off as she shrieked. I almost toppled over with her.

'Youch,' she said, freeing herself. 'My foot. It's got cramp.'

She shook it. The shoe seemed loose. I wrapped her in my arms and hugged her tight. Her heart beat quickly under the light coat – I could feel it. A buzzard wafted beyond us, mewing, as if suddenly there was a strong wind beyond the coomb. For a moment, while Rachael was snuggling into my neck, I imagined us being transported into a past before war was invented. Before

241

the time of the gods. I couldn't see anything but stones and gorse and grass and sky, you see.

Her body softened against me. My lips tasted salt on her throat. I took her face in my hands and looked. She kept her eyes closed, but her cheeks were shining with wet, and her lips seemed bruised. I asked her why she was crying. She said she didn't see anything when she looked ahead. I didn't know what she meant. It was chilly in the coomb. But she didn't want to shift when I tried to move her away. Maybe she was turning into stone, as in your childish story.

'They're overrunning everybody like rats,' she said.

'Who?'

'Oh God. So it's true what they say about the AA Defences!'

'What do they say?'

I sounded hurt, I suppose. 'Never mind.' She gave a long, sad sigh.

'Do you mean the Germans?'

'No, I mean the rabbits, dimmo. Why is everyone so calm? They've not got family in Danzig, that's why – they don't know what beasts can do – human beasts! Well, just wait until they're prowling about in your lovely village, when your house is their billet and –'

'It's not my house.'

'Oh, you and this thing about your uncle! It's so obviously because he's brilliant, isn't it?'

I flushed so deeply I thought my ears would go up in smoke. Even my hands burned. My knees felt like a schoolboy's against my baggies. I broke away from her and started walking away, hands thrust in my pockets. She caught up with me halfway up one of the claw marks.

'All right, Hugh?'

'No. I thought we were going a-Maying.'

'We are!'

She was panting from the climb. I was panting from fury. Oh, I was so furious!

'I didn't realise you were into the sacrifice of young virgins. You should've said. He'd have been so touched. He'd have made a really big pyre and said some really brilliant things you could have slobbered over before having your throat cut!'

I was stopped and staring at her now. Well, she was dragging on my arm, and the climb was quite steep. The sun hit her from behind and burned in her hair. Her face was in deep shadow. I think it was smiling. She hugged me. I hugged her back, incredibly tightly. The slope made us fall on our bottoms. This was It. But she pushed me off.

'Not here, Hugh.'

I sat up, looking round. There were rabbits watching us, down there. It was rather exposed. I was torn between not caring less and a feeling that the sun was dazzling us to make us a target.

'Haec statius est tacitis fida cupidinibus,' I panted.

'I will lay waste your fort with a huge army?'

'Almost. Let's find a wood.'

I scrambled up, taking her hand, and we ran straight for the beechwood. Oh glorious world! Trampling over the young corn, food for the nation at war! Throwing cowslips over her!

At the may hedge. It was not yet in the sun. Its corymbs were about to burst. White, white, white. Foaming up the edge of the beechwood. Almost there. I picked a bud anyway and swallowed it. God knows why. I almost choked. I had to hawk it out. She was laughing so much. The cool warm world one great pool and every gesture stirring its naiads. Sweet May. Sweet sweet May of youth.

Your loving son,
Hugh

Quite warm. Lawn being mown.

Dear Mother,

It's not easy to write to you about certain things, but I must.

The beechwood wouldn't do. As soon as we plunged in, I realised this. It was full of faces. They had watched me perform my plays and one couldn't blame them for being intrigued. Their Elizabethan ruffs and hoods and hats poked out from every root and bole and branch. Fairies flitted here and there, not all of them good. Lost princes and melancholy clowns, too. I had peopled this wood so many times, to keep myself company. A goodly company! Henry IRVING was strolling about, keeping an eye. And William SHAKESPEARE himself was leaning against a tree, chewing on a goose-quill. You see my problem, Mother. No theatre is ever really empty. No isle is ever quite silent.

So I aimed for the wildwood, Rachael dragging on my hand. 'It's all right! It's all right!' I hissed. Perhaps we would have seemed very intent to anyone looking on – to Nuncle, for instance, as we flitted over the wedge of the lawn separating one wood from the other. I don't know, I can't remember how we arrived, only arriving, plunging into the deeps. Clambering over the chicken-wire and plunging into the deeps.

It was so quiet, so shadowy, so safely tangled. Such a safe spot for shy lovers. And then the poem goes on:

> Pervixi; neque enim fortuna malignior unquam
> Eripiet nobis quod prior hora dedit!

Did you know this poem? Petronius wrote it. He killed himself because he knew Nero was about to order him to.

> I have had my day, but bad luck in the future
> Shall never be able to take away from us
> What past hours have given!

Yes it can. Oh yes it can. Unless you kill yourself first, before Nero calls you in.

With all my love and affection, dear Ma,
Hugh

Inclement weather. Radio prattling next door.

Dear Mother,
The next day, we said goodbye on the platform at Euston Station. Even through the smoke and steam, her neck still smelt of wild garlic.

'See you jolly soon,' I said.

My sick leave was over. I was going up to Hull. I squeezed on to the train and managed to lean out of the carriage. Our fingers were hooked until the last moment. I ignored the filthy remarks from my fellow passengers. The train shoved me against them and I caught a kitbag in my stomach. Fuck fuck fucking fucker – usual Forces thing from around me, but no violence. I scrambled back to the window. Her face was a tiny garden in a waste of khaki, a garden of white lilies like Campion's in the song. Her hand waving in its cream glove like a seagull. Then nothing but steam and smoke and the shrieking of a tunnel.

Your affectionate son,
Hugh

Someone says there's been a frost.

Dear Mother,

Too short, they suggest. They're helpful, generally. Spots of bother.

War experience. Everyone wants to know. It's the eye-patch. I lost it off Malabar, I tell them. Boy sailor. SS *Abinsi*. Pirate vessel rammed us. Sold off as a slave. That's interesting, they say. They find everything so fucking interesting. They're just trying to get me to open my mouth instead of using a pen. I'll tell them I'm a poached egg, if they're not careful. But they'll only come in with a chair and say it's a piece of toast.

Otherwise, to be honest, things are quite pleasant.

I haven't touched Rachael for fifty-four years – not since our fingers were unhooked that time. Or is it fifty-five? I've lost count, this end. I've touched Aunt Rachael once. A handshake after your brother's funeral, 1965. Love, Love Me Do. A small squeeze, then separation. She was drunk and chain-smoked unfiltered King Size. She had bags under her eyes, her whole face had collapsed, her hair was a mess of grey, she was dressed in black slacks with white crumbs on them. What was I supposed to do? Quote Petronius again?

Rachael and I were too busy saving civilisation, that was the trouble. Once we'd saved it, then we would go to Paris – if Paris was still standing. So I was saving Paris, I suppose. While I was up with an SL battery in Hull, as a very junior NCO, she left the HMSO office and trained to be an RAP nurse. Our leaves never combined. A year passed. She was lightly injured in a Baedeker raid on Guildford. The Humber was brilliant with flame, too; we wrote to each other in the red glow from burning cities. It was all very exciting, Mother. Then one May night in 1941 – the second night of heavy raids – our light engaged a Junkers 88 coming over too low, too big, with what looked like flashes of fire in its port engine. We could taste Hull's black smoke in our mouths. Nuncle was right, you see; the night attacks had begun in the summer before. But while the rest of the world crouched in darkness, we showed ourselves in bright sweeping columns. Look, here we are, down here! The fighters came like moths would come to our Tilley lamp in Bamakum, killing the light with their wings. It was a long way from the hushed boredom of Mam Tor. I didn't mind in the slightest, as long as Rachael lived. If I didn't live, then I wouldn't know, so it wouldn't matter.

'It's been shaken up, sir,' said the Lewis Gunner. 'It's losing height all the time.'

He was in the gun's swivel seat and I was standing next to him, about to hand him a mug of tea. He was holding the gun nearly vertical, the back rim of his helmet digging into his coat. Red-headed Alf Jellicoe, from Brierley Hill. I had no idea where Brierley Hill was, he always said it as if I should know. The Midlands, from the way he spoke. Alf's eyes were very bright in the glare.

I ran over to my SL a few yards away and told my crew to hold the bird, whatever. One of the men had time to grin at me. 'Save a drop for me, will you, sir?' I was just nineteen, he was forty (though they thought I was twenty, of course). Yet the 'sir' came out loud and clear. It was like being the school prefect again, but with grown men fagging for you instead of boys. I found the tin mug still in my hand, steaming into the air; I must have run over with it, gingerly, looking the nancy! I flung it away – and then the plane banked and dived towards us, as if it had noticed. Its glass nose flashed, dazzling us with our own light. The thing was absurdly large. It was like a bomb-site crane suddenly beginning to lean over you, too heavy to right itself. 'Here she fucking comes!' Within seconds it was so close I could see the hatches in its belly swing open. They were laying prehistoric eggs. Tyrannical lizards of fire.

I stood, unable to move. Heads and shoulders disappeared into the emplacement. Belly down! Someone was yelling an unintelligible and unnecessary warning which turned out to be me. I flung myself, not into the emplacement, but on to the flat and open ground, clutching my tin hat and wanting to scream still more – screwing up my eyes so tight that they ached, my face thrust so hard downwards that the tiny stones in the dried mud embedded themselves in my cheek and cut my lip.

Or perhaps that was the nasty man who jerked me by the ankles. Then a great heat and brightness, a wind, a noise of ten thousand waterfalls plummeting. Crashing. Down very far. Silence. Plummeting. Down very far. May hedge blossoming white NOW! Hot. Pale pink-tipped petals. A white hand, waving. All on its own.

Seconds, but lasting years. Billions of years, as the volcanoes roared and belched and the sea broiled. Now I was tiptoeing about on its cooled lava and calmed shallows. Those seconds weren't the only time I'd heard them, surely.

Out of breath, somehow, and on my back, and not where I was. So many billions of years. Everything was much further off. Maybe this was hell, because there was fiery spitting and black smoke, thick rubbery stenches. Through the smoke appeared a stick with tangled wires, spitting and blazing at its root, set black against a further fire. Was that the Devil with his fork? There were ashes like tiny glow-worms in the air, settling on my hands and face. I don't remember any human sounds: the odd silhouette running and gesticulating, but no sounds. It was up to me to make the sounds. SL 05K. What did that mean? My mouth. Grit glued my tongue. Up into the dull red sky rose this huge shining pillar, so tall it made me dizzy. It never ended, it travelled on into desolation, into the vacant spaces of night. This pillar had something to do with me. Its name was Rachel. No, that was a long time ago, where there was frost, not fire. Then there was a wood. Then there was Rachael.

'Sir?'

A man with a bloodied head. Pulling the pillar about was a big shining bird. I pointed. The man shouted and ran away. The bird's nose was made of glass, in which I could see heads and shoulders and a hand. That is the blowfly's brain, I thought, and the big black crosses on its underwings are its lungs. I stumbled and staggered back to the Lewis gun. My legs knew this was a Lewis gun, and that Alf from Brierley Hill had disappeared – that's why they had moved the rest of me. But they didn't know where Brierley Hill was. Could I ever get to Brierley Hill? There was something bulky smoking on the ground near the bucket seat. I stepped over it and sat. My trembling hands knew what to do, too – they grabbed the gun and swivelled it so fiercely the butt hit my ribs.

I swore, but the awful pain cleared my head. I knew who I was, and why.

It was back. The Junkers 88 was back. It had bombed us and now it was back, shrieking and rattling out of its tight bank, levelling towards us, the searchlight's beam flashing off its propellers, off its swelling windows, turning the smoke from its port engine to carved marble drapery. I shouted something very obscene and pressed the trigger. As I did so, I realised that my tin hat had gone. My skull was a blown eggshell, like the type you made at Bamakum for Easter, painted in bright colours. And my life was shaking, suddenly. I was a pair of baggies without their braces. I had to hold myself up.

The glass cabin on top of the Junkers shattered, throwing out tiny diamonds or particles of ice. It was more like ice, I think, but scintillant in the sheer light. Could this be to do with me? I sent more bullets up to it and, amazingly, it responded. It shuddered, it took bits off itself, it opened its vital parts. It was helpless, completely helpless. Bits of the fuselage tore off and rolled through the air like strips of skin, a tiny hand poked out, little flashes appeared around the belly as it passed overhead – I was shooting up vertically into its soft belly. I was burying myself inside it. I was travelling up with the bullets and burying myself inside it, guiding myself in, jabbering and groaning and shrieking. Or perhaps the plane was making all the noises. Then I remembered to breathe.

I disgust myself as much as I disgraced myself then. You know what I mean, Mother.

The Junkers came down in fields beyond our vision, and the fires lit by its incendiaries crackled too loudly for us to hear the explosion. My face was spattered with its life's glycol. The pilot was recovered with a bullet in his head. I wasn't officially given the bag, but my crew disagreed. That was more important, in daily terms. The celebrations were soured by the casualties. The smoking heap by the gun turned into Alf Jellicoe. A grinning skeleton smeared with fat turned into the plump, jolly cook. A lazy No. 4, sleeping by the burning canteen, left half of himself stuck to the ground. Five other men were brought out of the canteen alive; a blazing hut, broken into from the back with crowbars, yielded two more, scorched and sobbing. Communications and electricity were restored within hours, and a damaged SL on a neighbouring site repaired within a day. My ribs had been badly bruised. I had to rest in my little room for the next two days, its shattered windows covered over with cellophane which a strong wind off the Humber kept blowing out of its tape or flapping loudly all night. I had plenty of time for reflection, but I didn't reflect. I simply lay there half breathless all the time, with the whole lot running through my head over and over again.

I wrote to Rachael the next morning. I had something to impress her with, now. And I was proud of what I had done – the men made sure of that. They exaggerated my role in the fury of not having the bag allotted to one of the crew, as the HAA that had first winged it were given the chalk. The plane would have gone on losing height and come down in the open sea, even without my bullets in it. Yet I killed the pilot. The crew might have baled out. It might have pancaked and settled on the swell, burning under its pall of oily smoke – but not as a crematorium. Those German boys would now be tending their tulips and taking their grandchildren out for a creamy cake in some neat *Kaffeehaus*. Yet if they hadn't been shuttlecocked by the AA guns, they'd have dropped bombs on Hull and its people. Don't tell me, Mother, unrolling your lint, that I did wrong.

    With much love, your loving son,
    Hugh

Grey, but I am enjoying the cricket on the radio.

My dearest Mother,
    I have lied to you. They say I musn't lie. One can lie by omission. This will not process the pain. Am I in pain? Not at all, Mother. That's their expression.
    I crushed my finger on Mam Tor because I cheated – one cannot cheat with drystone walls. One has to dismantle and start again.
    Anyway, I must go back a little and fill you in, now, or the rest will fall down. I do apologise. It's because they want to know about my war experience.
    First of all, she wasn't a 'young virgin', though she was young.
    Second, I must not give you the impression that she left in any way dazzled by Nuncle. I'll explain why.
    We emerged from the wildwood and skipped across the lawn – the first time I'd ever skipped across the lawn, I believe. There were dead leaves in our hair, green patches on our coats. Nuncle had gone out. Later, he found us lying on the grass, side by side under the blanket, by the copper beech. He towered over us, a silhouette against the sun, and said that lunch was served. He reminded me of a dolmen.
    We ate ravenously, and talked about the weather. Uncle Edward seemed elsewhere in his head. I certainly was. I felt like a god, an exhausted heroic god. Then he perked up.
    'Are you proposing to be eaten by a Frenchman, my dear Rachael?'
    'I'm sorry?'
    'You smell of garlic – most pleasantly, I might add. Your clothes, not your breath.'
    I coughed, in a sort of nervous spasm. Rachael was very cool.
    'We walked through a mass of it, in the wood,' she said.
    'Of ramsons,' I added. 'Wild garlic.'
    'I know what ramsons are. Aunt Joy used to call them ransoms,

and I was always correcting her. I hope you didn't break any stems. Flowers scream when they are cut or trampled, you know.'

'We were very careful,' Rachael fibbed. 'I love flowers.'

'The human digestive system is quite remarkable,' Nuncle went on, ignoring her. 'This beef we are eating, for instance, is not much different from human flesh — it's certainly just as demanding for our juices to break down. Now tell me: why does the human body not eat itself? Why do the oesophagus and the intestines not consume themselves, even when famished?'

Rachael gave a little shudder, I was pleased to see.

'There,' Nuncle went on, 'there is the answer. Because the thought revolts you.'

'There are chemicals involved,' I said. 'Our linings are covered in something unpleasant, an inedible protection —'

'Bah! It is mind over matter. Cannibals eat their own species because it tests that capacity, and thus strengthens it. It is a homoeopathic remedy against weak will.'

'Are you suggesting we eat you for supper, then, Mr Arnold?'

He was taken aback, I could see that. But he came back very quickly, breaking into a crooked smile.

'For my vital parts to slide down your throat, my dear girl, would be counted among my greatest pleasures.'

She flushed furiously, even though it was said lightly, followed by his wheezy laugh. I started to talk about the garden, which had been rather neglected since Aunt Joy's day. This hooked him, since he liked to give the impression that he knew everything there was to know about the vegetal world.

Afterwards, outside again, Rachael reckoned that Edward Arnold's brilliance had its odd side. I bid her communicate that to her friends in London who admired him from afar.

'They're all vegetarian pacifists with dirty little beards and pebble glasses,' she said. 'I can't wait to tell them about his views on eating meat.'

'I thought they were your friends.'

'They declare that the future's with us, quote Edward Carpenter or D.H. Lawrence or Gandhi or someone, and look smug. I can't take anyone seriously who goes about in sandals, for a start. And their nut cutlets give me tummy-ache. As soon as

Hitler's over here, they'll be finding something in his sort of purity. I'm sure he only eats carrots, to make him see in the dark. Anyway, at the very least he shares with them an absolute hatred of pleasure —'

'That's a bit unfair —'

'No it isn't. They're like the Reds. How can anyone not think Stalin is just as horrible as Hitler? Because they all want someone to collect them together in a big mass and tell them what to do. If they need a Daddy, what's wrong with their biological one?'

'I don't think Adolf hates pleasure. He just has some very peculiar tastes, and he's unleashed those tastes on the rest of us.'

She looked at me. We were walking up Crab-Apple Lane, past the orchard, and the light was shredded by the overhanging boughs, falling like confetti on her face.

'You're making a connection again, aren't you?'

'What connection, my sweet?'

'Between your uncle and Hitler.'

I hadn't meant to make it, but I was happy with her interpretation. I shrugged my shoulders and squeezed her waist.

'Look at the blossom,' I said.

Some of the old, twisted apple trees were flowering on the outlying boughs. The bole-wood moulded into limbs towards the ground, as if each thick trunk was made from a hugging circle of men and women. I told Rachael that the wild apple and the wild rose were related, but no one sees this because the apple flowers are gone by the time the wild rose blooms. She said this was like family, that she thought something like this every time she saw a photograph of her mother. 'If I walked up to her in the street, she wouldn't know me.'

I wondered to myself if my own mother would recognise me from the timid little boy she left. What do you think now, Mother? Would you recognise me now? This elderly gent? This seasoned pirate of life's seas? This maroon?

'There's a whole line of hundreds of people who were born too early to know us,' I replied. 'Complete strangers, and yet they're all our blood.' I didn't want to talk about mothers, Mother.

'I talk to her, of course.'

'Do you?'

252

'Don't sound surprised. You're very English, do you know that?'

'What?'

My body had been coursed through with something beast-like and fine, that morning. I took her statement as a rebuke.

'Am I? Well, I am English.'

'I don't know what I am,' she said. 'All this, apples and wild roses and the lane and so on, it's all so terribly English, and it's what we're supposed to be defending from the barbarians and all that, but it's a sort of picture to me, it's not really inside me.'

I felt discomfited. The lane and its green shadows were so familiar, it was as if she was stepping outside me, saying this.

'I wasn't even born here,' I pointed out. 'You were.'

'So what? I wasn't born with earth in my mouth.'

I laughed. I loved her so much, her jumpy ways, her sparkle. She lit a cigarette and we wandered about the orchard and then we took the path to the river. We watched the sun dance around our fingers, submerged in the cold rippling water, and imagined ourselves in Eden. Anywhere can be Eden, as anywhere can be hell. You don't have to be born there. I hope you're not in hell, Mother. We splashed our faces and held wet hands and kissed. I could taste the vegetal water of the river on her cool lips.

Your affectionate son,

Hugh

Brighter. Cricket still on.

My dearest Mother,

I was at RAF Waddington in 1942, though I was still in the Army. Rachael's letters were full of her new life as a nurse, but short on *amore*. Her father was very ill, mainly from losing all his paintings in a raid: when she wasn't nursing soldiers, she was nursing him. I'd tried to travel down to Guildford on a rare leave, to meet her for a dinner-dance, but an air raid put paid to a stretch of the track; the train was maroooned for ten hours in the depths of the Fens, and I had to hitch a lift back in a truck.

My first proper sortie over Germany was in May: I thought to myself, I haven't seen Rachael for two years! My teeth rattled by four Merlin Rolls-Royce engines, gut fear, and the cracks of hostile ack-ack, I felt my first doubts about the whole thing. She must have changed, hardened – her letters showed this. Then the letters stopped and she scribbled terse postcards, fitfully, right through until February 1943. One of these, to my surprise, was of the Ulverton white horse, and postmarked locally. 'One of your uncle's pacifist meetings,' she wrote, vaguely. But her father had died over the winter. (His death had been a relief, she'd said – as the end of a raid is a relief even when there is nothing left but rubble.) The horse galloped queerly into my thoughts: it was one of Nuncle's favourite walks, along that crest.

I wasn't unhappy, though – not then. The aerodrome was a breezy sort of place, and not just literally. Only on fog days or after a heavy loss did the breeziness leave us, and we drooped like the windsocks could droop. Meanwhile, everything on land crouched – even the planes themselves crouched, until they left. Even the giant metal sheds and hangars that made your voice ring like a god's. It wasn't a cowering, it was like a cat about to spring. One cannot leap high without crouching first.

Anyway, we were in obeisance to the sky. The aerodrome was only the bottom of the sky, in the end. The detritus that accumulates.

I sometimes pretended I was at university – where I should have been, of course, if Hitler hadn't intervened. It wasn't so different, I imagined, except for the uniform and the windy spaces and the fact that the drop-out rate was rather alarming. I never knew who I wasn't going to sit down to breakfast with any more, from one day to the next. It could be my best friend, or that chap who ribbed me about my bad eye. Sometimes I would think it was more like an old people's home, full of folk very close to the end of their days but who happened to be not much older than schoolboys. You forgot who'd gone: our shaved napes look too much the same from the back, over the same tunics. Grins lingered in the air like Carroll's cat, voices hailed you in the thrum of a loose sheet of tin as you walked into the wind. No one died, usually: they vanished. You'd wait for the stragglers. The stragglers landed. There'd be a pause, a long pause, but the sky refused to yield my good friend, went on refusing until dusk. Went on refusing while the bombers were making ready yet again in a medley of winking lights and throbbing steel.

Or sometimes the lost one did come back, terrifically late – and we'd all rush out and watch her limp closer and closer. 'That's him! That's David! Good God! Well done!' Smoking like a train. Very low. Clearing those damn trees, those telephone lines, that blossoming hawthorn. Silent watchers, preparing their cheers. Wheels bumping on England, England skidding. The smoking wings bouncing, the great fuselage careering. A bit of flame, there. Oh no. Oh dear me. He's lost it. He's lost it. The ugly disappointment, the wretched distress. Better to just vanish, in the end. Better to let the wind swallow your ashes.

We were raided ourselves, once or twice. I realised again how the biggest blast can leave only a hole in the ground and a black *V* on the nearest wall. From the air we were a big clean handkerchief called central Lincolnshire with a tiny red initial sewn in at the corner. But the cities we were targeting were not like that: they were embroidered densely all over with a stitch so tiny and intricate that a careless prick of a pin would cause irreparable damage. We pricked and pricked, again and again, deliberately. I hardly ever considered that embroidery as anything but an industrious pattern of swastikas. It wasn't schools or houses or hospitals, it wasn't the cosy *Kaffeehaus* on the corner or the chanting *Kindergarten* or the sumptuous gallery or the packed theatre. It was either factories or docks or the enemy. It was vengeance. It was crippling their means of production and bringing them to their knees. They were evil, Mother. Please don't look at me like that. A bullet cannot be stopped by a naked hand. Don't say to me: 'You wouldn't even kill an ant, Hugh. Instead you would *talk* to them. You wouldn't even kill one of those wretched *ants*.'

Was it my fault I was born when I was born? I never asked to leave Eden. You know what I am talking about.

I'm cross, now. I'm full of blistered babies and charred old women. Why should I write to you, anyway? You never write to me!

Hugh

255

Hot. We lost the cricket.

Dear Mother,
  Sorry. I'm doing very well indeed.
  I was the only air observer with an eye-patch. Technically, I shouldn't have passed the tests, particularly the judging of distance, but I did. I scored highest in pretty well everything – I always had done. I can't explain this; I was nicknamed 'Sonar', for a time. Perhaps it was Quiri's mark. I've never felt a lack of depth in what I see, but I don't remember what it was like before. Perhaps I am imagining this depth.
  I was intensively trained in reconnaissance and gunnery. The body and soul of reconnaissance, according to our instructors, was 'a spirit of restless inquisitiveness'. To this end, small dramas were enacted on distant hillsides for the delectation of our binoculars, guns were fired that we might recognise their different tunes, and we were finally placed alone in a dark room with an aircraft gun to play with and a small table to write upon. Over my heart I sprouted a single wing – I could feel it beat, dear Mother! Officially an air gunner, sitting in the front turret blister in the very snout of the plane, my main job was to spy upon the enemy's ground defences, to scribble down a description of what exactly was trying to drop us. I was a hybrid, a sort of Air Army chap. I rather liked that.
  I always took one of Rachael's letters up with me. If she hadn't written lately I would take up one of the old letters, carefully folded in the hip-flask pocket of my tunic. Over my tunic I had my brown leather flying suit, fleeced with wool. I wore it dashingly open, imagining her watching me as I strolled across the concrete to the bomber. As soon as we were aloft in the freezing cold, I zipped up. I'd made a lot of sorties by this time, with no more damage than a peppered aileron or two. Enemy ack-ack through perspex was a familiar sound, a bit like drunken cavalry picking their way over gravel, or like God coughing in a cathedral, or like a walk across frozen snow. Statistically, the chance of going down was about five per cent these days – the three-month shindig over the Ruhr had been particularly costly,

but we were now about to hit Hamburg. This was, in fact, the first sortie of an epic production that was to roll for five months.

As I said, I always took up one of Rachael's letters. Others took a teddy bear, a lock of a girlfriend's hair, a shiny pebble, a snapshot. One bomb aimer had the dried larva of a caddis-fly preserved in a matchbox. Another had a spatter of russet hair in a locket: he said it was his girlfriend's armpit hair. Well, these were all one had to hold up against the Gorgon stare of fatalism. Sometimes this fatalism was a steady river you knew would bring you safely home; at other times it was just as steady, but ended in a chasm, into which the river plunged a horribly long way down through pitch darkness. Neither prayers nor fetishes made the slightest difference, of course, yet we all used them. One chap, a friend of mine, very calm and collected, had this thing about Berlin – he'd tremble all over, when it was a sortie over Berlin. And that's where he bought it, in the end.

The letter had come in the evening, as I was preparing myself in my tiny room – the officer's privilege. There was a cupboard, a chair, an iron bed with a red blanket, a shelf for my books, and a thin brown rug. An orderly knocked, handed over the letter, took my empty jug of water, and left me to my business.

I recognised the bold blue-violet hand on the envelope immediately. She hadn't written for a month, and now it wasn't a postcard but a letter. My heart oozed rather than hammered, as it did whenever I spotted the long silky-orange gleam of the Ruhr out of the night's blackness. Not that I wasn't already nervous, as I always was just before a 'performance' – the same looseness of the bowels, the same shortness of breath. Stage-fright for the play whose principal character was Death. One wag had written a sketch for a concert party I'd produced in which a bomber-crew, bald and toothless and trembling over their sticks, sang a song in wavering falsetto called 'Nobody Told Us It Was Over', of which I recall only the last verse:

> Nobody told us it was over,
> We could have been sitting in clover,
> Now we are ninety in '99
> And still dropping our pants on the Rhine!

The next night, they went down, all of them.

I tucked the letter in my tunic. I was too fidgety to read it now. But I'd take it up with me, to read as we were coming back. This assured me, somehow, that we would come back. I was particularly fidgety because the Hamburg defences were expected to be lively. My job was to dissect that liveliness, for the sake of future sorties. I would have to put the letter out of my mind.

It was a terrific sunset, blood-red through my window, which faced west and let soldering beams in to fire the buttons and belt buckle of my tunic and bronze my leather flying suit. I was twenty-one, Mother. I think you'd have thought me handsome, the job well done. Can I be forgiven for squaring my shoulders and turning a little in the light, imagining myself as Odysseus before the high ramparts – spotted leopard's skin over my shoulders, ornate shield on my back, splendid greaves on my shins clipped with silver at the ankles, bronze and enamelled cuirass on my chest and a nodding, red-plumed helmet instead of my cap? After all, Homer had made an SL of Agamemnon in the passage that I had declaimed (in English, in my own toughly trochaic school translation) for a concert party up in the Hull battery:

> From the bronze he wore flashed beams
> High into the distant sky, where
> Hero and Athene thundered –
> Answering, by that salutation,
> Golden Mycenae's King.

Within half an hour I was inside our own Trojan horse (all rivets, fuel and duralumin rather than wood), clambering over the bomb-aimer's panel, opening the stiff bulkhead door, tugging open the two turret doors, gripping a bar in the roof and swinging myself into my tiny nutshell of a kingdom, soon to be looking out on infinite space, the view that a clear night gives us of our imaginative limits. We shudder and groan aloft, the intercom babbles and clicks, we are one of a multitude, a great dark flock in the night around us. The crew are experienced, confident, motley: the captain is Canadian, the navigator Jamaican, the bomb aimer from Orkney. The rest of us are English, not all in our twenties – the rear gunner is forty tomorrow, we have a cake made in the shape of a turret, candles for guns, a party planned. *Many Happy Returns, Reg.* He was a stocking salesman before the war: we have a sketch involving bare legs and ladders, barely rehearsed but it'll go down well.

I check the letter, suddenly fidgety, by placing my hand in my pocket. A certain military discipline forbids me to take it out, now.

We bank tight, turning towards the North Sea, the Dutch coast, and I muzzle myself with my oxygen mask. The Canadian sergeant likes to bank tight, he likes to show the night what an extraordinary machine he is moving through it, how strangely manoeuvrable this great galumphing monster is – we've looked down half a dozen factory chimneys on training runs over Leicester, we've written the name of his girlfriend in the clouds – but this turn presses my left ribs against one of the ammunition tanks between which my seat is squeezed, and I softly curse him, and as softly ask God to forgive me.

God is with me only, I might add, on a sortie. Mine is a gerrymandering belief (the cramped corridor of the Lancaster was later replaced by the cramped backstage of a full house, Mother). Nothing must happen to the pilots. Least of all a bullet in the head.

I have a notebook on my knees, a pen in my top pocket, an orange lamp shining dimly over my shoulder, and two guns at eye-level which are, like the spar on a ship, the leading point of the huge bulk of it all – only these stick out from the snout like a tiny, vicious sting. Their handles remind me of our motorcycles in Africa: when I twist them the turret rotates, taking the guns with it, and if I wish to spit fire into the night I squeeze the triggers on the grips. There's even a smell of Castrol; if I close my eye, I can see the river going the wrong way, feel Father's soaked back. But I'm not meant to close my eye, I should be peering out and scribbling. If an enemy fighter rears into view (God forbid) I will fire at it. Otherwise I must note everything I see, and try not to think about dying. I can just make out my face, like a dim harvest moon in the dark. When I need clearer visibility, I switch off the lamp. Then the fireworks outside make my face loom and hiccup, half-missing behind its mask.

259

We are over the sea. There are only a few lights. The odd pinprick, the odd little necklace on the coast. I wish we were over the famous forests further south, cooler after the day's heat, sweet with pine sap, full of animals scurrying through the darkness! I am envious of these last, suddenly, despite the danger they are always in, the fear they feel. I shift in my seat, roll my head and shoulders a little at the first twinges of cramp. We are a strange-shaped house, a stretch of fetid rooms throbbing through the air – the bomb aimer under me, the pilot behind, long passageways and poky attics. Someone found a rat, once. The rent's due, goes the joke. So where's the services, then? When's luncheon served, eh? When's tea? Where are the whores?

My elbows on the perforated tanks knock minutely as the metal vibrates: to write I have to lift them clear, or my writing will look like the note Father Christmas left me once, thanking me for the carrot and the 'dram'. Aunt Joy wasn't so bad, really. You never did that. You found Christmas strange in all that heat, but you'll point out that we had sagging decorations on the ceiling and strings of paper angels draped over an acacia cut for the occasion. So my thoughts drift as we appear to drift lazily over the North Sea – once called, in happier days, the German Sea. Crouched in a cold our altitude has created, far in my little cell from the sweet July warmth of England, I drift.

What does this 'England' mean? What did Rachael mean by saying I was 'so English'? I never saw England until I was just seven. Everything I knew, everything I loved, was far away. Now I am encased in metal and bolted perspex, flying through the air to bomb a city, in the name of this England. How did I arrive by this? The mark on my nape tingles. That's a good sign. But when I think of the fetish packet crumbling away to nothing years before, my stomach contracts with fear. These thoughts and reactions are nothing new. In this extreme case, when I start to imagine imminent extinction, and the horrible impossibility of it – or, worse, some slow-dying agony of flame – I call on my guardian angel, Herbert E. Standing. He stands behind me, a tall white figure crouched by the lamp, a vague cloud in the glass that curves in front of me, whose blister we occupy like infinitesimal parasites in the eye of a gnat. This is how things are. I cannot change them. (Did I ever wonder why, in that orange-tinted dimness, his togs stayed white? Don't ask awkward questions, please. I have to concentrate.)

There are pulsations in the distance, old gold and wild-daffodil-yellow. I wonder for a moment why there are so few orange wild flowers, and try not to. We are banking again, less tightly this time, and Pete's drawl announces that we are almost over our target. I hear Dom the Jamaican navigator behind him, maybe making a joke. He has a reputation for bringing luck, though some of the men don't believe a black can navigate. When a new fellow said this at the top of his voice in the mess, triggering a general laughter, I lost my temper and we tussled, losing my cap and a button. (He didn't have time to nurse a grudge, since he was lost in a raid the same week.)

The sea, a dim gleam where the lights pulse, suddenly contracts, is pinched by the darker coast. I swallow with difficulty, and I wonder again how my faithful heart copes with such an acceleration, such an oozy pounding. It is a healthy, strong heart, according to my medical. No one on this plane has anything but a strong heart. The first burst hits that organ before it hits my brain; it is underneath us, cracking like an ice sheet, deafening me through the din of the engines. Have they found our height? The city is fitful ahead, sprinkled with tiny dots of light, as if careless citizens are lounging and smoking in the streets, giving away their positions. One forgets the scale. Suddenly, red and blue dazzles, swings, makes pillars like sunlight through deep dark pond water. I scribble madly, then coolly. The red and blue might be an illusion, an optical trick.

Possibly white searchlights in air disturbed by rising heat, I write. The end of an evening, warm night air, the beer halls stacking their chairs. Glow-worms nestle beneath, then go out. Those are our bombs, I think. Not this plane's bomb. My stomach hasn't yet declared that we are dropping, losing altitude, daring the sweeping arbitrary claws of their defences – to lift free afterwards as if the two tons of blockbuster were what had been dragging us down out of the clean air. Under me, under the ribbed plates, Steenie MacLean from Orkney would have opened the panel by now, staring into the chasm, lining up his crossed wires like a sniper.

Instead of a buttoned chest – a geometry of streets through perspex, Flint's bearings guiding us to the precise spot. Yellow and orange sprinkle themselves over the ground, like a stage Devil scattering thunderflashes. These are guns, firing at us. I jot the details as the barrage rocks us, makes us a little tipsy. I am on my stream of devil-may-care, my mind hovering somehow on the edge of my body. The fleeced high collar of my flying suit irritates me; I press it down, bang my elbow on the tank. We descend abruptly, so abruptly my stomach is left behind as when a motor car takes a humpback bridge too fast. For a teeth-chattering second or two, I think it's something to do with my elbow hitting the tank, then that we've been hit. But the barrage is too low and too high to worry us. We are at 13,000 feet. The firework display is no lower than 14,000 feet, but there is more quite a bit further down . . . at, say (I screw my eye up), 10,000 feet. I spot the silhouette of a bomber – one of ours – sliding fleetingly between us and that far-down mass devotion of fire. She trails a little ribbon of sparks she won't ever be able to get rid of, like an animal's hurt, perplexing.

We've caught them napping, though: no fire control, they're just sending everything up as it comes, trusting to a thickness, a wall of fiery splinters, flame itself, the last convulsion of the gods. They are carving the air into dragons and worms, frothy billows, sharp spears and panic-making wolves, all sheathed in gold, all tumbling about and crashing into each other, seeking our dark, ominous shapes and sometimes striking home to the heart where the glycol seethes or blundering into an aileron, the hard rivets of a wing, the blister that shatters into particles of ice. I think of the jolly men of the Thule Society, looking up from the streets below at the hideous shapes rushing through the air behind one-eyed Wotan, Wotan the furious, the terrible, the wise – the little open-mouthed boy in England now the rider of the skies behind his twin guns, Wotan himself! Ach! He's come! The night of the gods has come at last and heaven shall be scorched to cinders, friends! Their little round spectacles flashing. A wind age, a wolf age, the age of Thule. But we are the ones with the fire! Ha haaa!

We're hit.

I know it because it's happened once before. Five per cent.

Someone has to fulfil the quota, a few eggs have to shatter in the back of the cart. Oh, dear God and Jesus. Oh, Herbert E. Standing, save us. Oh Yolobolo. *Kan wak, si-pap bobo, bolo yol nga.*

This is how it has gone, in those few seconds: the plane converged on itself, like a lung contracting, attempting to pop its bolts. Then it ejaculated with a shudder and a screech. Then ivy shot up from the ground, wrapped itself around the fuselage, and tugged. We are now fighting this for a moment, my hands gripping the surface of the tanks so hard on either side of my ribs that the palms will still have a chessboard of holes when we land at Waddington. Then the ivy snaps and we roar free, straight into what looks like an ogre's face constructed from fire. The fire streams over us, and is gone. I am blinded, I have to blink. Our bombs are dropped. Quite quickly, just like that, without the usual ostentatious feel. Steenie's voice crackling in my ears. *Still will we be the children of the heather and the wind . . .*

We rise, a few tons lighter. I'm seeing the ghost of the face in my eye, now blue, now purple, now a black hole cut out with scissors. I should be observing. How do I observe my own death? The picture of a tiger jumping through a hoop of flame slides into my mind, an old picture from a child's encyclopaedia belonging to you, Mother. The thought of you fills my head and my heart as Pete the captain tells us, in his soft Canadian drawl, that we have been hit. We've been hit at the back. I think of Reg the stocking salesman, manning the rear gun. I think of our tail. If the tail's damaged, it might drop off. Then we will twist and spin like a child's toy. Where will I have my grave? Down which chimney will I look?

We are banking, not too tight. Now I see Hamburg, very clearly. The harbour burns. Troy is torched. Dolt. This is not Troy. This is like Cologne, Essen, Dortmund. This is like Coventry, Hull, London. I have done this before. I have even been in a plane that has been hit before – perforated by splinters where it didn't matter. Tonight I feel doomed. The rule is: if you feel doomed, you are inviting doom.

Now I cross-examine the new sounds in the beast, peering at them, gnawing my lip under the mask, as if I am in a classroom, as if I am trying to hear what it has to explain, what calculation it is summing up. A knocking. There is a distant knocking on the hull, beyond the usual throb, as if a stowaway wishes to climb out. There is also someone playing a flute, winsomely, rising and falling, as they'd play flutes in the afterlife, lacking body. We stagger a little, then right ourselves. The intercom is silent. There are no crackles, even. It is dead. No drawl from Pete, no jokes from Dom. They've lost their helmets. I visualise cables dangling, electric wires frayed to a dandelion head. Yet my own lights still wink. I smell, very faintly, something bitter, like the burnt bottom of a fried egg, a witch torched at the stake – what? Why that? Some of you are concerned, intoned the chaplain last week, at the thought of going down while you are killing. In for the kill. Wounded mice and birds attract the hawk. At that very moment they come. Did I bring them? I take my motorcycle handles and fire round after round at teases of wings and tails, at sheer shrieks and wails. Nothing happens either to them or to me. They pass close enough to touch, able to burst my blister with a single round. And then they are gone.

I think of them as a band of harpies in a vision. Perhaps I fell asleep. But I saw, through the little holes in the tanks, the ammunition juddering into my guns, and the guns are hot. My hands are black from the grips. There is something wet on my face. It is blood, on my forehead. A nick on my forehead is bleeding profusely, considering the size. I start to laugh. How did anything cut me inside this glass dome? How did anything reach me in this nutshell, where I alone am king?

My hand reaches for a handkerchief and instead finds the letter. We are over the sea, now, flying low, low enough for me to unbutton my mask. Are we losing height? The dark, glandular sea is invisible on this moonless night, apart from the odd wink of a boat, a necklace on the coast. Beaches, children in the sand. Will they be out tomorrow morning? I doubt it. Barbed-wire and guns, a proper sandcastle stiffened to concrete.

I open the letter. I am afraid that if I don't, we will lose height so rapidly we will crash. I have considered clambering out of the turret and up to the pilot's cabin, but have dismissed it as somehow treacherous and meddling. Pete will see day, Dom will guide us. I know them well, they're good at their job: when these beasts were new and still being put through their paces over England, I accompanied Pete in the cockpit – we went very low, some telephone wires loomed up, should we go under or over them, Hawkeye? (Hawkeye was my other nickname, I liked it.) Pete has a sense of humour which will see us on to the smooth concrete of Lincolnshire.

I take off my gloves and read the letter through spots and thumbprints of blood. The blood is red in the orange glow, but the blue-violet ink has turned black. A trick of colour complementaries. I read it again, swearing in a whisper. Then I laugh, a manic howl of a laugh, like a wolf. My lamp is hit by my outflung hand and I have to right it. It still burns – the bulb has burnt my palm.

She doesn't know why it is happening. She is bound on a river. It is her fate. And other such rot.

I look out of the window as one looks out of a window in a train, cupping my chin in my good hand. I now know, for certain, as if Herbert E. Standing himself has squeezed my shoulder to assure me, that we will make it back. Because, for the first time, I do not care if we don't – at least, not for my sake.

Of course we got back. Chaps cheered. The rear gunner's turret was missing, apart from a dangling ammunition tank. That had been the knocking sound. Scythed clean away, it had taken Reg with it. 'Life ends at forty,' someone remarked dolefully, walking away towards the mess hut.

Nobody knew what to do with the cake, of course. The cook brought it out, embarrassed, with a knife: he'd taken a lot of trouble. I couldn't cut it, anyway – I'd blistered my palm on the bulb. The mid-turret gunner was too busy swearing to himself to help, and the others were walking away. As for me, I didn't know what to do with the letter. That night they showed some silent comedy shorts; a dollar bill sticks to a robber's hand and he can't release it. Whatever he does, however hard he flaps it, the paper bill sticks. But whenever anybody passes, he hides it in his pocket. I'd torn up the letter into confetti, appropriately, but it stuck on my hand all the same. It would always be there, I thought, however hard I try to flap it off, or hide it inside my heart.

They thought my tears in that dark flickering hut were for Reg. Well, perhaps they were, perhaps they were.

The marriage was some sort of nature ceremony in the wildwood, Mother. Trampling wild garlic to pulp. I didn't go. I was too busy saving the world (as I wrote to Nuncle) from the likes of him.

Your affectionate son,
Hugh

Very hot. Sultry, even. Window only opens at the top, of course.

Dear Mother,

A hag's face, horrible, in the hedge.

It's not you, don't worry. It pops up.

War experience passed, well done, ten out of ten. But tell your mum the rest, they say. Right up to the very bad thing? Yes. You're on course. Don't wander.

Where was I? In the stubble. Rather older. Ankles pricked.

Still hunting for Ray, remember? So I start shouting his name. Now I'm off the stubble and in a bare field, huge, newly sown from the look of it. Deserted but for a scatter of birds on its drills, further up.

Ra-ay!

Ra-ay!

Bloody man. Wild goose chase. He'll be up there, on that hill, Effley Long Barrow, wherever there's long grass. There are still a few tufts left on the torn-up downs, here and there. I'm striding beside a high beech hedge kept back by chicken wire. One, two, one two. Swinging the arms helps.

Ra-ay!

Ray-*chul!*

That certainly wasn't me! So shocked, I've stopped. The only movement is from a sabre-toothed machine on a track way off, heading for a metal barn. I lean against the hedge and its chicken wire. Who's teasing me? The pot-potting of guns, hoarse crows, chugging magpies. Could have been a magpie. Rae short for Rachael, anyway. I could have been shouting for her.

266

So that's why I end up saying her name to myself. Why not? It's totally normal. I've read something unpleasant, in Ray's hand, last night. You can't blame me for trying to recover her, get back our secret little joy from the poachers and slanderers.

The flock of feeding birds doesn't rise, not even when I project the name straight at them. RACHAEL! Maybe I'm only mouthing it. Awful thought. They're annoying me, now. I'm practically shouting it but they're still not budging and the field and sky swallow up my shout. Nothing afterwards, no echo, not even a sigh. There's this far-off blast furnace working without cease – but that's traffic, that's not her breath in my ear.

Hoarsely whispering her name again, over and over as I walk, one for each step, a stage hiss – though there's nothing to fear, no one in sight, no living thing but the birds on the drills, the open downs going on and on. Pigeons, they look like. One of them alights. No, is alighting, wings spread wide, not more than a foot from the soil. I never knew pigeons could hover, like humming-birds. The other contemplating the seed, it seems, before stabbing. Only my shoes are moving, appearing one after the other beyond my stomach. Maybe everything else has stopped, too. I look up at the clouds but there's not enough wind to move them, not visibly. Even the machine's seized, in front of the metal barn. There are sounds, but they don't count. When time stops, spirits can be summoned. They slip in and out between one moment and the next, I suppose.

You never know.

I stay very still and look at the ground, saying her name quite loud, my body bent over, hands on thighs. I probably look as if I'm about to be sick. Picture her face, as it was. Her loveliness. Say her name, again. Picture her face. Summon her, summon her, summon her up, cancel the slander, get her back as she was. Pigeons still frozen. But something catches my eye, something in the hedge.

A face.

The face of a hag. Utterly hideous. Green and mouldering. She's come straight from it, I've pulled her straight from it, the earth still on her.

Oh. Oh no.

'Mornin', Mr Arkwright.'

The face melts into a leer I recognise. The man, the coalman, Muck. He's leering – no, grinning – behind tatters of green plastic hung on the chicken wire. A steaming thermos-cap in a gloved hand. Perhaps he didn't mean me to see him. Perhaps it was all my fault.

'You were miles away there, Mr Arkwright. I could see that.' My face hot.

'Looking for Ray Duckett,' I reply. Hoping my heart, flailing around in my throat, will be thrown back into the deeps of my chest. He must have heard. Thank God the names are homophonic.

'He's not been along here, Mr Arkwright, and that's a fact.'

Still grinning. Front teeth worn away almost to the roots, nutty and purple-veined skin, a great disc of a face, tinted glasses. Belgian Army camouflage jacket, hood over his ears. A canvas stool next to his boots, with a packet of Jaffa cakes and the thermos. A gun on its canvas casing in the leaf-mould between us: F.A.P. painted on in white, not *Muck*. No dribbles on the letters.

'Shooting?'

'That's right, Mr Arkwright. Pigeons.'

My fists clench. Thank God the chicken wire with its fake plastic bindweed stands between us. Turn to the field. Still alighting, the pigeon, wings spread wide. Bobbing slightly in the breeze.

'And those?'

'They're dead, Mr Arkwright.'

Ah. Dead.

Impaled on a wire, like an office toy. Mouldering invisibly with the others, about thirty of them. Not feeding, not alert for danger, not ready to scare and wheel, even at a gunshot. Crude and obvious, now, in awkward positions, like a child's lead miniatures spread on a thick carpet.

'Decoys,' I say.

'That's right, Mr Arkwright. Decoys.'

I turn with a glare but he's dropped the grin; he's seadog serious, knows the ropes, wants to show it.

'Thousands of 'em, yesterday. Very few today. Bin 'ere twenty minutes, bagged a couple. I'd have had three, but one got up an flew away when I come over.'

'He fell from the sky?'

'Dropped like a stone. Creased the skull, I reckon.'

Duckett must have passed more than twenty minutes ago. Hours ago, maybe.

'What's the gun?'

'Twelve-bore. Bagged hundreds yesterday. Strange, that. The field was crawling with them. A carpet. Very few today.'

Divert him. Put on a mask. Play the boss.

'They learn from bitter experience, Muck. Or maybe they smell death when it's near. Do you eat them?'

'I do it for the sport, Mr Arkwright. My bit of indulgence. Sell 'em for the cost of the cartridges. Mainly to Belgium, Holland. They like our pigeon over there. Keep one or two for the pot, as it were. For the *oven*, Mr Arkwright.'

His face beams through the steam of his tea as he sips it. A little king in his den, plumed by the green and yellow beech leaves, veiled by the green tatters of plastic. The fanged machine's trundling back along the track, away from the metal barn. Point it out, ask him what it is, keep him chatting, mollify him, because I somehow have to persuade him that what I was saying was something else.

'That there tackle's for handling the hay rolls, Mr Arkwright.'

Ah, I see, not a digger, not as savage as it looks. Men and women with pitchforks in my day, helping them up at the Jennets'. So did he, mind, but a little younger than me. One of the brattish boys who threw the hay about, squealing.

'Sorry if I was miles away, Muck. I was rehearsing a play.'

'A play, Mr Arkwright?'

'Yes. I have written a play about – my uncle. His early years, and so on. I was rehearsing the lines.'

'A lot of words in your play, are there?'

Don't rise.

'As many as there are living birds in the sky.'

He chuckles softly.

'And what's up with Duckett, then? In your play, is he?'

Look at him straight.

'He's gone missing. We're all very worried about him. If you spot him –'

'I won't take a pot-shot, Mr Arkwright. Don't you fret. I'll tell the others, too.'

'The others?'

He waves a hand towards the field, bounded on three sides by a raggeder version of his covert. Either he smells, or there's a fox nearby.

'There's a couple of others over there. Dougie Barret and John – John Wall.'

The field as still as its hedges, pure regulated tilth. Three guns trained on it, three pairs of eyes behind the sights. Me the fool gesticulating and shouting far away on a vast stage. And my cries? Wasn't I just shouting for Ray? But John Wall and Muck will compare notes. The bursting servant of Midas, whispering the truth to the reeds on the river's shore and with every gust of wind the reeds whisper of his ass's ears. You used to tell me that story, Mother. It was your favourite story, wasn't it?

John Wall is no doubt keeping his telescopic sights on us, or I'd pay Muck off. Wall knows already, of course. It was his father, after all! Young Jack the peeping poacher. Sniffing the crushed ramsons, afterwards, like his dog. Poaching my warm and trembling treasure – stuffing its skin, nursing it, bobbing it up and down in the pub like a glass-eyed puppet, raising cackles. I turn to Muck. He's happily munching a Jaffa cake.

'Can't offer you one, Mr Arkwright. Holes ent big enough, see.'

He gestures at the chicken wire, but something lewd beats in the air. Maybe a wink behind the tinted glasses.

'I'd better be off. Ray Duckett is in extremely poor health. Might have made his way right up there this morning. On crutches.'

I point to the hill and its copse, the flock of lifeless birds scattered between, like grit in the eye. The one hovering is still hovering, its stretched wings streaked with white, white marks on all the throats. Ring dove, of course. Father reciting the lines at dusk on the veranda, the bush a crescendo, his regular joke: '*The moan of doves in immemorial elms,/And murmuring of innumerable bees!*' I hear the click of a gun. Muck is checking his cartridges, snug inside the breech. He lifts his face, grinning again.

'Hopes as you bags yours, Mr Arkwright. We'll keep our eyes peeled. I've helped Mr Duckett quite a bit in my time.'

A far white figure, like an angel, is coming towards us across the stubbled field. Herbert E. Standing never stumbled like that, flapping his hands about. I nod briskly and leave. The path goes straight on through a gate, which means I can avoid John Wall.

Into the next field, I stop to wipe my face. Something has spattered me with glycol again. The angel's now out of my sight line, flitting behind the hedge.

I climb up the slope. There's a stretch of long grass and I plunge in, up to my chest. A gun-shot from the field below. You could hide a massacre in here. I shout Ray's name and push on through, the dry grasses sounding like the sea and then even more like supermarket trolleys being stashed in the car park – of all things! Not very Jefferies, I suppose. No. Rather as a woodpecker sounds like snoring, your light snoring in the hot afternoons, Mother, mouth open, on the bed, me at the door, gazing on you.

Breaking out sweatily to where the hill rises clean between the odd nest of hawthorn, I see a white blur down there around where Muck surprised me. Brut. Or Ginger. Not Herbert E. Standing.

Oh, the fun of the chase! The Black Spot, the Black Stone! I reach the top of the hill and am utterly spent. Jelly legs, throat sore, face a mask of heat now chilling, like the old fevers. I feel a bit sick, too. The angel at the fork stands like the stubborn type of white hunter in Africa, refusing khaki – and I'm in the shadows of the beech trees, camouflaged. Now he's climbing towards me. I lope quickly and quietly to the stones of the long barrow, adjust my eye to the black, crawling into the chilly cave with care in case Ray's face lies under me.

Empty.

There's a gnawed bone on the damp floor, a bit of cellophane, sweetpapers, the wriggle of a condom. A withered mistletoe entwined around an oak branch, laid like a wreath. The grass-cutting rota for Effley parish church, *Ratsbane* written across its crooked type, its innocent names.

Outside, the angel leans panting on the information panel, looking like von Sebottendorff giving his lecture on astrological co-ordinates, my uncle and a couple of others nodding eagerly. This could have been theirs, I'm thinking. The wind age, the wolf age, comic-opera types in black leather strolling about. The green barrow dozing on like a decrepit old dog, regardless.

Brut's no longer living up to his name; he should be called Sweaty. He's standing over me, getting his breath back.

'You led us a merry run, Mr Duckett.'

We return the longer way, avoiding the drilled field. He talks about golf, as far as I recall. Duckett must be dead. An unseen ambulance yelps as if someone's stepped on its paw. All I have to do is ask the first person I know to say who I am. If they say, 'You're Ray!' then I'll know I'm mad. If you know you're mad, you're not mad. If you know you're dead, you're not dead. If you know you're a leopard, you're not a leopard.

That's all for now.

Your affectionate son,

Hugh

Still hot. Water shortages. Lawn yellow. Very high sky.

My dear Mother,

We pass three or four people but all of them are strangers to me. Strangers to Ray, too, because they don't say, 'Morning, Ray.' If I'm not Hugh, that is. Sweaty Brut steers me bodily into Bew's Lane, so no popping into the Green Man or the Old Barn or the shop. I mustn't run off again or he'll have a heart attack; can happen even to ambulance men.

The ambulance has gone. 'Where's he gone, then?' says Sweaty Brut. He looks around him in the middle of the lane with his hands on his hips, like a morris-dancer. The door of the cottage opens. It's Jessica Marlow. I'm on the little brick path. She asks me how I am.

'I'm fine, I lie. 'What's happened?'

'What do you mean, what's happened?'

'To Ray.'

She doesn't say, 'Um, *you're* Ray, Ray,' but, 'Oh, Cliff Trindle took him out for a drive.'

'A drive?'

'First thing this morning, apparently. Those seeds will be hell to get out of your jumper. Did you want to see him? He'll be back soon. They left very early, I'm told. Goodness knows where they've gone to.'

Sweaty Brut comes up and I ask Jessica to tell him who I am. She'd heard Ray was back and wanted to see him, she knew where the key was hidden. Ginger returns in the ambulance, having done a little tour looking for us. Brut tells him who I am — it's official. Ginger eyes up Jessica but it's me she plants the kiss on, leaving.

When Ray comes back in the blue Rover, there is a small reception party: Ginger, Sweaty Brut, and myself. But you cannot tick off a dying man. His eyes are shining with delight.

'I saw it,' he says. 'I saw the sun rise behind Silbury Hill. I saw the stones of Avebury go blood red. Now God can have me whenever.'

Cliff grinning, shaking his stubbled head.

'Good for you, Ray,' I say. 'Your notebooks were most revealing.'

The ambulance doors close. I wave. No one waves back, as far as I can see.

I return the notebooks to the cottage. Well, I can hardly burn them.

After a nap, I make up a sandwich and pack my claw-thing and screwdriver. I want to go to the house, Mother. You know why I want to go to the house.

I pick up some fruit from the trays outside the shop then try the door. Damn. The old *Ever Ready* sign's half-pulled to 'Closed'. I pop a pound coin into the lobotomised head of the RNIB Sooty and wait: it ought to have been open five minutes ago, on a Friday.

Muck emerges from the Never Fear, guffawing loudly. A knot of crop-headed kids are fooling about on the long bed of orange sand left by the pavement-layers. They make rude noises and he swears at them. Dr Johnson of the apothegms has followed him out in his usual flared suit. They're heading my way. I feel I know what the guffaws were about.

Halfway up the lane, I sense he's following me. The dart of something red, behind a beech trunk. But the sunlight and shadows are so confusing! There. And again there.

Well, I make Ilythia's gate almost at a trot. I want to get to the woods, I don't care which one. Halfway across the lawn something breaks away from the wildwood. It's John Wall, holding a gun.

He walks towards me, dragging his foot, and my face starts to burn. He'll still have the smell of the field on him, the covert. That sly, knowing smile. I prepare my firm, neutral mask when suddenly he jerks, starts to yell, waving the gun, shrieking. Shrieking at me to gerroff, to gerroff and out, to scarper bloody quick or else. He's gone mad, and he's armed. Camouflage jacket, khaki balaclava, the works. Maybe he's already been killing! Stranded in the middle of the lawn, I drop to my knees and crouch, knapsack held in front of me, my heart wild, as he runs yelling towards me, waving his gun.

There's cat-calling from the house, behind me. I glance back. Three of the crop-headed youngsters give us the finger as they run off, one in a sports-type hooded blouson, red as a postbox.

John Wall waving his fist just next to me.

'Trespassin', Mr Arkwright. All they understand is a gun, these days. No discipline.'

I stand up, brushing my trousers, puffed again. 'They followed me from the village. Just fooling about. Thought you were waving your gun at me.'

'I wouldn't do that, sir.'

The familiar half-smile, a thinner version of Muck's. Am I in hell?

'I hope you weren't shooting in my wood, John.'

'Vermin.'

'You *were* shooting in my wood.'

'Cleanin' it up, see.'

'Like father, like son . . .'

Am I snarling? Yes. Yes yes yes, Mother. I am snarling. John Wall looks frightened! Well, my face has twisted up, my poor

274

teeth are exposed to the gums. It happens to all of us, mostly when we're alone. I'm feeling very cross all of a sudden, you see. I'm puffed. I've had enough. The filthy notebook business is trampling delicate things in my head. 'Listen, you can't just go killing things in my wood. There's no such thing as vermin. No such thing! If there is such a thing, then humans are vermin too. In fact, I think there are more verminous humans than verminous animals.'

Or words to that effect. Enough to make him step back. I'm aware of my fierce scowl, and lose it. John Wall screws his eyes up as if taking it over and looks towards the point where the youngsters disappeared. He's not scowling, he's reflecting. Perhaps I didn't frighten him, after all. 'Wonder what them lot were about, stalkin' you like that?'

'Having fun, I should think. Didn't *you* do the same sort of thing at their age?'

His eyes settle on my face, locked there for a second. Then he sort of brushes past me, towards the house. The limp distorts his body today, hips as if on cogs under the jacket. The one left by the Pied Piper, the lonely limping boy, dragging behind the others as the rock shuts on them, shuts him out.

The gun's canvas case bounces on his back next to a brace of ring doves, hung by their necks.

I disappear into the wildwood.

Your loving son,
Hugh

Dull.

Dearest Mother,

When I emerge, wiping my mouth, John Wall is a silhouette against the brightness. That was the whine that ruined my picnic. A pullulating strimmer strapped to his body, stinking of diesel smoke, he's slitting into the long grass and bracken, the hidden fence ringing against the blade, sending out sparks. He has earphones on. Then he sees me and silences the machine, takes his earphones off, goes on about hiring the thing at his own expense from the Manor's gardener. He calls it a 'bush-cutter', not a strimmer. Is there bush in England? Not now, surely.

I say I'll refund him, of course. The earmuffs are from a mate in the army.

'A gunner, see. Tanks. Big historical display tomorrow, Salisbury Plain. Panzers, Churchills. If you're interested. I've got all the books.'

Eyes gleaming – but no sign that he knows what I think he knows, no suggestive stuff. I leave him to it, saying I'll be in the house, not to be disturbed.

'Sortin' private matters out, then?' he calls after me.

I turn round. That stupid, knowing grin again, the shadow of Muck's! 'I'm clearing junk. Sentimental interest only.' This said to expunge any scent he might have of valuables.

Now he actually *winks*, Mother!

'Comprendo,' he says. 'Mum's the word.'

Muck told him everything this morning, over sips of the thermos, both men snorting and sniggering. I can tell.

'Thank you,' is all I say.

His eyes linger on mine. Some mercenary motive stirring in him, perhaps. Say nothing. I walk away towards the house. The bush-cutter starts up again. Its diesel stink is foul, but there was no scent of wild garlic in the wildwood today.

I drop the latch on the kitchen door and give myself a moment to recover. Then I walk up the stairs, flashing my torch, heading for the attic. So John Wall has books. I walk along the corridor in the gloom, past your room – and in the moment before I see the crouched shape I'm rolling over it as if over a barrel!

The fetish box rolls to the edge of the stairs, lingers a little, then drops down step by step, thump thump thump, as if too old to flee any faster. I retrieve it in the hallway, where it's lying against the front door, next to an old umbrella leaning there. Aunt Rachael's, I presume. The two look as if they're waiting for me to take them for a walk.

The fall has loosened the base of the fetish box, not the lid. I had never planned to open it, but its leaking cinders smell of Africa. I cradle it in the gloom of the hallway, fumbling at the base. Then there's a shuffle the other side of the door, a low mutter, a grunt – and the bush-cutter bursts into its demonic shrieks again.

I flee up to your room, Mother. A corner of the lino that covers the window is loose. I work my hand under it and the length, rotted by the rusty tacks, comes away as I pull. It smacks on the boards, chivvying dust out in clouds. Light shafts in, marbling the air in long columns.

The trick base is still jammed. I take my claw-thing from the knapsack and work the gap wider, splintering the wood slightly: it's one solid tree-bark, smoothed and patterned at the flick of a blade with diagonal herringbones, as on prehistoric pots and urns. Pandora's Box, you called it. The base falls on the floor and I look inside.

The scent of burnt wood is overwhelming, Mother. So much of Africa suddenly pouring out that I have to stand up. John Wall's on the lawn just below, belted to his bush-cutter – my shadow catches his eye. He waves as I duck.

The box's interior is very dark, full of cinders. My hand comes out patched with black, holding something quite large, sharp and white and curved.

A talon.

I lay it on the boards, again reach in. A small honey-coloured bowl turns into a skullcap.

There's other strong medicine, Mother: a frontal lobe with a red tint to it, bits of redheart, an iron ring, a miniature version of the box containing more wood cinders. My hand is black, now. I'm thinking: the sorcerer sat with his initiates, making this, somewhere in the last century, in the deep bush. And no one's touched them since! Or can say what they mean! The eyes of the sorcerer in the firelight, the drums and feathers and shivering limbs, the fireflies on the edge in the darkness and the beasts' eyes in the deeper darkness beyond. Oh, I hear the frogs from the brown river and the crickets zizzing over and over with the hot flannel of air on my face, so comforting, so close, as I rest it on your lap and watch out for crocodiles on the slip of silver beyond the land, Mother.

Your lap, smelling of clean laundry. Infinite breadth and softness. But something taut in the soft legs, as if you might

277

suddenly turn evil and devour me. Yes, I used to fancy like this, Mother: that you and Father were imposters, that you were only pretending to be sweet and good so as to lull me into dropping my guard. That this was a long contest between us, already a thousand or ten thousand or a hundred thousand years old. It might be at this moment, with your hand slightly tense on my head, my head given to your lap in the evening darkness, that you turn into the croc you really are and gulp me up.

Your loving son,
Hugh

Cooler. Leaves blowing about.

Dearest Mother,
I'm much better now, thank you.
I'm in your bedroom, still. My head is lying on my own black hand. Some of the cinders have spilled out, and I scrape them together to put them back. In amongst them is a tiny slip of paper.
There are three lines typed on it. The type is uneven. Just like Nuncle's old machine, that he would bash on day after day.

The centre
Never gives
Seven answers

I count the fetishes.
Seven.
I stand and go over to the window. I recall Father telling me again how the great fetishes were passed on from chief to chief. That when the chief has to fight, he would open the fetish box in front of his warriors and rub its cinders on his forehead, making himself invulnerable. I see in the glass my black-smudged face. The great gongs that sounded the gods. That summoned the end of one's enemies.
I gaze through my face at the garden. October was always the month it retired gracefully, leaving the stage to the trees and their

burnished colours, bringing out the rake to scratch its way across, finishing in smoke. I half expect to see Aunt Joy clipping things down there, in her blue gardening apron. The whine of the bush-cutter as it slices away at the brambles by the front door, as if John Wall is attacking the house. Next week he will come with a giant hoover for the leaves.

The centre! I'll show Nuncle the centre.

The Hugh Arkwright Centre. Oh yes.

I'll sit on his face.

Study weeks on Bulwer, conferences on Heywood, Gayton, Bacon, summer fortnights on Galenic medicine, courses on metre, gesture, the humours – the lot. Masques on the lawn, crumhorns over dinner, a huge library. Eilrig the training ground, here the intelligence HQ. Body and brain in fusion. Colossus.

Can't recall how long I stay by the window, nursing my vision. The next thing I remember is turning the forehead in my hands, its red blush clear in the light from the open window. I'm thinking of Nuncle's boiled skull smeared with ochre in its glass case at the funeral. This one's too small and modest to be Nuncle's, I say to myself, smiling. And anyway, he planted the note!

Mother, I think it's around now that I have my detestable thought. Or rather, when my previous detestable thought to do with you, Mother – I mean the Red Lady and midwinter rituals and sacrifice and the wildwood and Nuncle's thing about nearest and dearest, about having to please the gods an awful lot for the wildwood to spread over the kingdom into one great greenwood, into thick and impenetrable bush, all those horrible connections lumping into one thick wet thought in my head (I don't wish to spell it out, I have a violent distaste for this sort of thing, I want to keep it a lump!) – when that abstract thought hardens into something very solid in my hands. All it lacks is your hair.

So I drop the skull-part with a clatter on to the boards. The thing rocks upside-down, like a fat-lipped laughing mouth in a fun fair. It's all I can do to put it back with the other things, seal the base.

I certainly can't open the trunk today.

John Wall literally bumps into me outside, at the corner of the house. I remind him as calmly as I can about the leopard skin – that it'll be needed this evening, at the village hall.

'I'm your man, Mr Arkwright.'

Steady eyes, then he yanks the bush-cutter into roaring life, making my face quiver.

Now I'm back in my cosy garret, making tea. Yes, that's right. It's almost dusk again. I'm still nursing my exciting vision as a means of forgetting the detestable one – watching Ilythia turn and become beautiful in my head, hearing the crumhorns, the metrically perfect renditions, the murmuring scholarship, the gaiety and precision of it all!

That'll do. There's a samba concert given by the local primary school, any minute. I want to be at the other end of the grounds.

Your affectionate son,
Hugh

Drizzle.

Dearest Mother,

Hope you're well, etc. I am.

Dozing off, I'm late for the rehearsal, it's already underway – I think a broom fight between the Witch and the Fool, stage-boards groaning and banging, something like that. How can I remember everything! A big brown-paper parcel lies on the table, addressed to me. John Wall left it on Malcolm's doorstep with a cleaning bill meticulously itemised in red, the sloping signature taking up half the page: *I remain, cordially yours, as ever, John Leslie Wall (Mr).*

'Taken you to the cleaner's, has he?'

Malcolm's been saving that one up. He turns and tells the horse to get a move on. 'Can we have Derek, too, on this one? We've got Derek now,' he adds, quietly. 'Beelzebub. His mum died last week, so he's a bit fragile. Give him lots of oomph.'

Derek appears to the sound of a roaring waterfall (the cistern has not been changed, then) and shakes my hand breezily. He's still in his work suit, Rotarian badge on his mauve lapel, not a hint of grief or mourning.

'Hope it doesn't make me sneeze,' he says. 'Blimey, it's *enormous*.'

I tear at the paper. The great head snarls into view. The paws fall out with a thump on to the table. John Wall has somehow enlarged it.

'Big beast, in its time,' says Derek.

Young Gary and younger Mark whistle and wow. Jenny and Sally pull faces above their saggy jumpers. (I don't think I've introduced you to the cast, Mother, but you'll catch on.) Little Rebecca gives a brief lecture on the Siberian tiger and the fact that there are only four hundred and thirty left and it's the biggest cat in the whole world. 'School project,' whispers Jenny, wreathing me in stale tobacco. She has completely yellow teeth. Derek, Gary and Mark are marshalled into hobby-horse position and we drape the skin so that the head closes on Derek's large skull and the bulk of the rest covers Gary. Mark doesn't know what to do with the tail, and giggles, pulling it like a bell.

'Fuck off,' Gary says, muffled voice cracking into the upper register.

Derek peers out as if at a slightly tricky committee meeting. The leopard's maw is about to close on his head and swallow it whole. His fingers absently stroke the paws dangling either side of his shoulders; they must feel like teddies, like his old teddies.

'Is it OK?' he asks. 'Rather uncomfortable, to be frank.'

I'm sure it is, but I wouldn't know, would I? No.

Malcolm says it looks fantastic, then explains why it's so important – the centaur is the earliest hobby-horse and in classical art it's often depicted sporting a leopard skin. I think of Arviragus in my old Shakespeare volume, and Florizel's skirt. The ancient shamans of Indo-Europe, Malcolm continues, were the first performers – they travelled in trance on their hobby-horses to meet with the gods and bring back the Asclepian cure. 'We the Ulverton mummers are in the same genetic line as the first actor.' He looks around. I'm not sure he's convinced, though.

The real hobby-horse has by now uncoupled its three vertebrae and Derek bears the skin alone like a chief – or maybe the skin bears him! Its savage grin and glassy eyes move whenever he moves his head or scratches his ear. It looks as if it's weighing us up, calculating the distance.

'Did centaurs really exist, then?' asks Jenny, face screwed tight, perplexed. 'I'm *dying* for a fag,' she adds, turning to Sally.

Malcolm says that they were a mythical creature of the imagination or rather the deep psyche – and then confuses us further by mentioning birds as traditional trance vehicles. Eagle-feathers on the shaman's drum, Icarus, something about Jung. Nuncle stuff, really.

'Like the native Americans,' says Sally. 'All those big head-dresses. It was symbolic, really, wasn't it?'

Because Malcolm's playing the Doctor, riding in on the trance-horse (groan from Gary), Hugh will be directing, which is 'an incredible treat'. Malcolm can't stay on and the three parts of the horse cannot move together. I tell them to enter and they don't enter. Then Derek enters on his own, asking if it's now. This happens too many times. It has never happened to me before. Every time they're on, they giggle and snort and the leopard skin ends up in a heap. It's somehow wrong, what they are doing to it. There is no control.

I say this. Malcolm picks himself up and shouts at everybody. Derek blinks at him and nods fervently. The leopard agrees with him. Or maybe he is agreeing with the leopard. 'Director's tantrum,' says Jenny. 'I'm off for a fag if I'm not needed. It's too bloody hot in here.'

'Sorry,' says Malcolm, addressing me, 'but I don't like wasting your time.'

I shrug. His comment has attracted hostility towards me, I can feel it, I can feel the tiny iron filings all over my skin. Every production is a little country, complete with its own scapegoat, Mother.

Jenny goes off for a fag, Sally disapproving because Jenny is pregnant. From the door, smoke draughting into the hall, she asks how Rebecca's German measles is getting on. It's past the dangerous stage, Sally reassures her, or Rebecca wouldn't be here. I express surprise that German measles is dangerous.

'For pregnant women,' Jenny corrects me from the door.

Sally looks up at the ceiling, sighing as if blowing out a flame in her hair.

I've had a flash, Mother, there in the draughty hall. My life is passing in front of me. It stops just when you appear at my door that time I was very ill – in England, not Africa! Snow in your black hair. That coat, red as a berry. Not coming any closer, no.

Then I travel to *your* door and see your sudden look of fear, kneeling in front of the doll's house, all over again.

And later, maybe a week or so later, up on my feet once more: 'Why can't I go out of the grounds for six weeks, Susan? I'm not sick, now. I'm feeling jolly fine.' 'The doctor says as you're more infectious now nor you were when you were poorly, Hugh boy.' But you must know all about scarlet fever, being a nurse, Mother.

'Hugh?'

'Ah, yes, quite so.'

Everyone looking at me.

I make my excuses and go straight to the surgery, which was open late but is now just closing. I catch Alan Scott-Parkes as he's locking his consulting room. He's a taller version of his father, with the same look of someone only doing this because he likes to tell people the worst. He's ten years or so younger than me, we never knew each other. He's never even heard of me – the waiting-room's all back-numbers of *Hare & Hound* and *The Sporting Life*. I tell him I used to come to his father as a boy and that his father had very cold hands. I was petrified of his father, actually. Did you know that, Mother? The son frowns – the same chilly blue eyes.

I have a simple question, purely academic.

Your loving son,
Hugh

Still dull. How many shades of grey are possible? I've counted fifty.

My dear Mother,

I go straight from the surgery to the Old Barn. It's the geologists' last night, they're leaving tomorrow. I'm regaling them with the creakiest stories of the boards. Jill is lots of loose hair, all

283

shampoo and bath-salts when I lean to hear what she's shouting. I'm a bit overwrought, perhaps. It's all these detestable thoughts. Well, one detestable thought, Mother. All it lacks is your hair.

I pop my other question of the evening. Jill and Tim only know that skulls used to be tinted red with ochre, and that ochre was in use at least half a million years ago. That's not what I want to know. They ask down the table; their tutor, a big bespectacled man of about forty-five, rather merry already, tells me that it stood for potency.

The lad next to him feebly hoots, then goes bright red. The table's gone quiet, listening: the tutor's so many places away from me that he's having to bellow. 'The skull's lost its life-blood along with the flesh, so they replaced it with red ochre! Maybe they reckoned ochre was the earth's life-blood! It looks a bit like veins, when you see it in a cliff! Its use goes back at least half a million years! The first expression of something symbolic, you might say! All right?'

The other tutor, an ageless woman with straggly ginger hair still wet from the shower, adds that the most famous example of a painted skeleton is the Red Lady of Paviland.

The Red Lady! My heart congeals.

She continues in an unattractive falsetto – she doesn't have to bellow. The Red Lady was really a man. Giggles. The famous William Buckland dug him up. He reckoned the rubble of glaciation was caused by the Flood. 'And he thought these rufous bones were of a Roman lady with a fondness for rouge. In fact, they were of a vigorous young man of the late Palaeolithic, some fifteen thousand years further back!' The assembled students laugh obediently as she chortles. What on earth can link these two Red Ladies, one of which was a man? Somebody's birthday produces a cake with *Sedimentology Rules OK* iced in green over an actual flint, which has sunk part way into the sponge. Squeals and raunchy in-jokes: the pin money of youth but how soon it's spent! How soon, how soon!

I kiss Jill gallantly on the cheek and leave. She catches up with me at the main door and hugs me for rather a long time. Soft flesh, thick curls: a smell of honeycombs and musk-rose and sweaty joints and wine. I quote some Shakespeare, God knows what.

How can I remember everything? Her father died when she was small, that's my reading of it. Why else go after old men? Out on the pavement I find a long coppery hair in my mouth.

I'm back in the Green Man's yard by about ten o'clock. Ted catches me sneaking upstairs and insists I have a jar on the house. No idea why, but we're as tiddly as each other. The bar is full and its smokiness thrusts me into having a cigar. I don't see either Muck or John Wall. It's clamorous and packed but I'm sloshed enough to be tolerant. An ex-sailor tells me he was sunk in the Falklands conflict, jumping fifty feet into an icy grey swell.

Meanwhile I've found the link between the two Red Ladies: Ray Duckett. He'd have christened the ghost, making a sort of scholarly homage. Threads, threads. They'll end up weaving a pall.

The bar help on Friday night's a New Zealander with a pony-tail, called Nick. He tells us a horrible yarn, as if tuning in to my thoughts. I only mention it, Mother, because it led to the best spontaneous joke I've ever made. It might not be to your taste.

Some Israel Hands of the high seas, a mate of Nick's on a freight ship bound for mainland China, would draw his evening tipple off a pickling vat in the hold: a free glass of pure alcohol from its drainage tap. One night, instead of the booze, a black tentacle of hair appeared, dangling from the tap's mouth and dripping alcohol on to his shoes. He checked in the vat and saw, at the bottom, curled in the inch of liquid that was left, the naked body of a young Chinese girl, preserved like an onion for burial in her homeland.

'How did it taste?' someone asks.

'Nice and sweet,' Nick replies, showing a yellow tooth.

'Schnapps for chaps,' comes out of me, somehow.

I make my exit at that high point with the gales of appreciation blowing in my ears. The echo is still blowing in my ears when I finally drop off into dreams of entanglements in seaweed and hair.

Before I drop off now, shall I tell you what I asked Dr Scott-Parkes, Mother?

I asked him if scarlet fever is dangerous for pregnant women. Yes, he replied, even in these days of antibiotics − the streptococcus bacteria, you see. And pneumonia? Even worse. Why, do you know someone at risk?

Yes. Very much so, Doctor. But I think it's much too late, now. Much much too late. Isn't it?

Your affectionate son,
Hugh

Blowy, terribly blowy. All the leaves off.

Dearest Mother,

I've started painting classes again. Quite enjoying them. So far I paint only grey blobs, but they say that's fine. If I only want to paint grey blobs, that's up to me. Think of it as a process. I've got forty-nine more shades to play with, after all.

You can order books. Thank God, because the library's not quite up to scratch. What are we without books, without writing, Mother? Mute, like me – a muteness of bits and bobs, big stones, enigmatic mounds and bones. The ceremonies between the upright sarsens thousands of years ago (not Nuncle's weedy frauds) all dispersed, every last feather and fire of them, into the stars. We don't know what they thought inside those skulls, not a flicker of what they thought. A few pots and axe-heads. No sounds. Not even the loudest shout, not even the booms of drums given no quarter. How satisfying. What luck. As you can see, I'm rather well, now.

Get on.

I wake up (it's Saturday morning) with another hair in my mouth – my own white one – and I'm not smiling. Nauseous headache, horrible taste, stiff legs. A dream about Jill, who showed me her new antique shop in the middle of the orchard, called Latin Remainders, a bungalow stuffed to the gills with overpriced junk. For £39 I bought a turnip watch in a presentation box that included a wax recording of Edward Arnold, manager of the machine-tool factory, congratulating the retiring worker on his productivity. As Jill showed me the wax record in the lane it became very heavy and we dropped it, or it became elastic and bumped against the tarmac – it cracked, anyway, and there was a lot of bellowing which turned out to be a delivery man outside, shouting at his mate over the rattle of drink crates.

On the way to buy a paper and draw money from the tiny Nat West sub-branch with its hairline opening hours, I spot Gracie Hobbs hobbling out of Shirley's (the village hairdresser) with a fabulous and strangely opalescent coiffure, like the inside of a conch.

'You tell 'em,' is all she says, gripping my arm and then crossing the road to the shop. I trot after her. 'Gracie,' I pant, 'I want to ask you something.'

'What is it, Harry?'

'Hugh, but never mind. Mr Arnold's first wife. My mother.'

'That's right, it's only natural. That's what I tell 'em. It's only natural.'

Must be exhausting for Marjorie, I think, and shine the brightest beam I can into the fog. 'You saw the ghost of my mother, Gracie. She had on a lovely new red coat. Was it snowing? Was their snow on the ground? Were those nice fluffy garlands for Christmas hanging in the square, just there?'

She peers at me. The fog is Time, and I'm on the wrong side. Mrs Pratt approaches with a lolloping teenager at her side, all sleeves, sex indefinable.

'The very same day she died,' Gracie says. 'And that's official.'

'Snow?'

'Bright as a button, white as a sheet,' she confirms. ' "O Come, All Ye Faithful". Those Aladdins, swinging on a chain. Not that we needed 'em, but you can't go doing a carol round without the old lamps, can you? Not the same but you never know. It gets dark so early. Ronald squeezing me on "The Holly and the Ivy". Can't have been tiddly on the mulled, as that were after it. Even that time.'

Words to that effect. She gives me a great wink as she turns to go and is nearly run over. Mrs Pratt bustles up and witters on about sleeping policemen, while the indefinable appendage looks as if he's planning a break-in while they are. It must be her younger son.

'Dominick,' says Mrs Pratt to her son, 'please learn to say hello. A little charm gets you a long –'

I'm already turning away.

There's a message from my old friend Morris, at the news-agent's-cum-Post Office. This old-world custom displeases the grumpy chap behind the grille. He shoves a scrap of paper into the coin-tray and says something a sudden burst of bell-ringing drowns. The note reads:

Message for Mr Hugh Arkright residing in Green Man. No Arnold on elder Demser passenger lists from November to January 1933. Could she have travelled freight? Hell to get hold of. Have put them in post. Thule dates for 1933 are December 17 to 21 in Visitor's Book. Also hell to find in your boxes. Phone soon. Good luck. Love Morris.

I return to my room with the note. Sorry to spy on you like that, Mother. All in the course of duty. You might have travelled incognito, I'm thinking. You might even have embarked from somewhere like Calabar, where none of the port officials would have recognised you. And the crew? You might have taken a boat new to you, or perhaps you were in disguise on the SS *Abinsi*. Keeping yourself to yourself, with a different cut, you would only have *resembled* Mrs Arnold, who was much jollier and such a dashed good dancer, too, what?

There are many other suppositions running through my brain as I pack my tools. Nothing quite fits, but bobbing among all of them is a tasteless remark of Nuncle's after the war, when I met him at Father's funeral: 'What a pity you took fire to those poor people of Hamburg, my dear boy. Freya doesn't like them cooked.' I feel I'm in league with you, Mother, that I'm stretching out a hot hand to you, and you to me. By the time I get to the attic, I'm sweaty. Rushing about as usual.

I set up my torch and move a huge valve radio in mottled brown plastic away from the little skylight. The trunk sits like an upturned boat, sparred with bamboo: when I blow on it, the dust is trapped by the cobwebs. I make short work of one of the locks with the claw-thing; the lock's anchor in the lid of the trunk has been loosened by woodworm and the metal spike pulls out quite easily. The other tongue is firmly fixed, and I have to use my steel teeth (Ted's hacksaw, actually). It takes an hour and a lot of my breath before – oh, bliss – the rusty iron divides.

Your call, Mr Arkwright.

The lid is stiff, opening only with jiggles and a heave that leaves me breathless.

Green inside, all green. Humpy green, like pasture, like the open downland before it was ploughed. Green canvas. Ants didn't like it, did they? They liked everything else but not green canvas, so our beds and soft chairs were covered by it. Now the heady smell of old cloth, mothballs and the must of damp. On the canvas lies an envelope, right in the middle.

Yes, Mother.

I recognise your writing, the sort of blue-edged envelope you would always use. It's addressed to Edward Arnold, Esq., Ilythia, Ulverton. Holding the torch close, I can just make out the date on the blurred postmark: 1931. The letter arrived here, yes.

The trunk has already been opened, then. If only to place this envelope inside.

Nuncle has been here before me!

I glance over my shoulder, cast an eye on the shadowy attic. I feel him watching, you see. The demon watcher. Some degraded form of my life touches me. It has such cold fingers, I shudder.

The envelope is open, and contains a letter. With fumbling hands, I remove the letter and unfold it. At first glance, no more than the usual chattiness, Mother. I'll read it properly later, put it aside. The dates are now confusing me; the trunk was sent from Africa in 1933, but my uncle has placed a letter inside from 1931. I feel like that excavator friend of my uncle's who found, digging for King Sil's grave deep inside Silbury Hill, a bottle of nineteenth-century port.

I lift away the canvas, lighter than I remember but still awkward, still a weight.

A hideous, flesh-peeled face.

No, a pair of tiny shorts. Tiny trousers. Tiny socks. A tiny jacket and two tiny hats. All neatly folded on top of the spotted wallpaper you ordered one year, but which slid off the sweaty walls. Of course. The evidence. I hadn't expected anything quite so obvious, I hadn't thought of baby clothes as such (being a man,

289

perhaps, Mother), but the surprise of there being no surprise is so odd it's almost frightening.

So, I think, staring into the trunk – she fled Africa with my sibling in the pod! And she never liked to talk of my birth, it was so difficult and dangerous. My half-sibling, I presume. Someone native, even?

Scandal.

This is what I'm thinking, kneeling in the gloom, Mother. I'm terribly sorry. And then it gets worse.

Unless she came here to England to get rid of it!

That quite upsets me, for some reason.

But she wouldn't have packed the clothes, idiot, if she'd been wanting to get rid of it! And beneath the infant clothes there are more clothes, less tiny. I have never seen any of these before.

A layer of brittle wallpaper, then more clothes. Know us, some of them say – those I hated wearing. A pink nightshirt with a lace collar. A bright blue felt jacket. A solaro bush-shirt that gave me a rash. The others are indifferent, then three or four shirts say: know us too. You liked us. You were glad we came back from being pummelled on the smooth stone in the yard, still warm from the charcoal iron. You know who folded us, too: Baluti, the laundry boy. He would always turn our sleeves up and over the chest, so that we looked as if we were praying. We were comfortable and you liked living in us. Remember?

All the shirts are praying dutifully. My white shorts, my long bottle-green trousers. Clammy feel on my thighs, the difficult way they buttoned, the bloom they'd make on my knees if Baluti hadn't rinsed out all the Reckitt's Blue. Oh, the thin strip of red cotton that served as my tie. Oh, a faint violet stain on a tropical jacket where my new pen burst in the heat. You were annoyed about that, though it wasn't my fault. Oh.

The last layer of clothes: the ones I'd not yet grown out of at seven years old but which were too tropical for England. An abandoned air to them. Helpless, still praying. The trousers laid on their side as if indisposed only for a moment.

Under these are shoes.

Each pair wrapped in oil paper, the oil paper we swaddled things in when green canvas was not practical. My tiny blue baby shoes in wool, my first leather pair, my sandals of untanned leather from the market in Ikasa, my white cricket shoes, my scuffed bush-boots. All the heels well worn. Deformed by pressure, like the Cheshire bog-body's face that Tim drew the other night on the paper cloth. Mouths and noses and eye-holes, squashed by sixty years of pressure.

These are phantasmagoria, compared to the hands I see behind them, laying them down just where in turn I'm lifting them from. Only you would have done this, Mother, setting down my wardrobe in levels of age, like sedimentary rock! This would not have been Father's thing, nor Baluti's, nor any of the other servants'. Mother did this thing, I'm thinking. Sorted my clothes out. This is what rather moves me, up there in the attic. Not the things themselves, not my things, I'm not moved because they are mine. I see you as if you're underwater, reaching up as I lift them from their place and stack them neatly next to me. Our fingers almost touch.

Beneath the shoes, halfway down now, under a roll of oil paper, lie the books. Illustrated annuals from the 1920s; my dog-eared *Treasure Island*, Kipling's *Rewards and Fairies* and *Just So Stories*; Orczy, Pearson, *Dr Jekyll and Mr Hyde* with the frightening pictures; Hodgson Burnett, Henty and Rider Haggard and others now forgotten; my child's encyclopaedia; my 'Empire' atlas, my *Heroes of Modern Adventure*; my leather-bound and gilt-tooled *Beauties of Shakespeare*; my scruffy *Lamb's Tales* with bookmarks of broad dried leaves, the torn school history book and a few cloth-bound poetry anthologies clamped and bowed to their own fossilised damp. And so on.

This layer affects me more. I had always imagined myself as embedded in a great heap of my own books out there, defying the shadows of ignorance and loneliness with words. But I can't think of a single volume of my own that is not here, and there are less than twenty!

The books smell so much of our house in Africa, Mother; the time between doesn't so much telescope as feel scanty. Everything I have achieved since peters out. If no one touches this house, then the wrack in the attic will survive me. And the wrack is really junk, old junk lying unmoved beneath the pitter-patter of rain and birds and mice, while the world dissolves not only my person, but my influence.

This is what the books do to me, up there in the attic.

And what lies beneath the books? A corrugated layer of newspaper, from September 1931, loud with forgotten quarrels, diplomatic crises, floods and fires, defunct furniture stores and fashions. The sun will set at 9.06 pm over the smoky rumble of London, the jazzy lights will dart in the puddles as the heels cross them on their way to see *Escape Me Never* at the Lyceum, and I can't tell anyone about Hitler, about the Reichstag, about what is to happen soon.

As I can't tell myself, crouched there in the attic, what is to happen soon.

You must know all about this, though. You must be mouthing warnings all the time.

And what is the newspaper hiding?

Toys.

My furry animals. Oh yes. My big red tin car. My lead farmyard set, my jigsaw puzzles, my trick tightrope-walker, my clockwork train, my building blocks, my sailing-boat, my Napoleonic rear guard, my model of the Crystal Palace, my framing kit. The cuddly animals are small and uncuddly. They are the unwanted ones, the ones I abandoned; I was allowed to take only two to England, remember? I chose my broken-armed teddy and my fat, frayed dog. You promised to replace everything I had left behind. Mostly, you did. Perhaps this was a means to protect yourself – if I had taken everything and left nothing, it would have struck me earlier, the fact that I might not be going back for years. Or at all! At no point do I ever remember you admitting that I wouldn't be going back for years, or at all. Don't go away, there's worse to come. I mean, you must be strong, Mother. There are so many wicked people in the world, so much calumny and lies. I just want to say that you slid away from that responsibility, rather as you slid slowly from my life after the very bad news. The way your eyes used to slide

Get on.

Under the farmyard base, sawn by Father out of Whale & Co. chop-boxes, there's a toothy face grinning up at me.

Oh.

Massa Hargreaves, 'e no go worry me atall.

The torch falls with a clatter as I step back in fright.

Don't step back in fright, Mother. You packed the trunk, after all. And please don't think I'm taunting you. I'm not taunting you. I'm just writing you all my news! When I was beaten at Flytings or Randle, or something really rotten was done to 1e by an older boy, I never told you, did I? The people here say I must now tell you everything, however unpleasant. Because by telling you, I'm telling myself. Think of your mother and you as processing the pain together, they say.

What an extraordinarily unfortunate remark. But they don't know, do they? They don't know the half of it, do they, Mother?

Your affectionate son,

Hugh

Chilly. (But the heating's always on too high. It makes everyone sleepy and safe, I suppose.)

My dearest Mother,

I'm holding the farm base like a shield against a Medusa. I am, in fact, stooped and as still as stone. Ridiculous. I know what it is now, without looking again. I look again with the torch.

The mask. A worm-holed Babinga mask, from up-country. Dan the Devil. That was my name for it. Dan the Devil. Still snarling at the world. It was lying quite peacefully under the clothes, in the darkness, until the torchlight woke it and it snarled out of instinct, not spite.

Father brought it back on one of his trips, didn't he? Oh, you don't remember? Fancy that. While he was away I'd had the most awful dreams. One of the servants – Mr Henry, I think – said that what I needed was a horrible mask to frighten away the bad spirits that were taunting me. What I needed was Father, but I believed Mr Henry. You were very busy with the dispensary at the time, there was some sort of epidemic. I asked to have the mask and it was hung next to the bed and the nightmares stopped. Then the mask itself began to bother me. I had toothache, from my second teeth; the mask had given me the evil eye as I lay asleep, mouth open, breathing softly beneath it.

It was taken down and appeared above the drinks cupboard – to frighten away light-fingered tipplers, went the joke. *Now* do you remember? Good good good. It still belonged to me, of course. Father reckoned it was a masterpiece and very old and valuable. He did know about these things, didn't he?

I hold it up in the attic and agree with him. Its midget's bulbous forehead presses down upon an alcoholic's eyes – like Father's towards the end, I'm afraid. Have I told you about his end? It was sweet, it has to be said – one of the prostitutes, from the room across the passageway, held his hand, and he looked at her and murmured your name. He couldn't really see anything of course. I was there, wiping his brow, rather choked. I thought you'd want to know that.

The eyes are cut deep above a square mouth. The mouth is huge and angry and filled with teeth, their ivory sharpened to a point precise enough to sever flesh, like Mawangu's teeth. And do you remember the extraordinary nose, feline almost, nostrils stretched and creased by the snarl, set right up between the thin baggy eyes? A big hollow bowl of a head, really, the tassels of hide dangling from the chin like Nuncle's late Confucian beard. The decayed twine stuck around the inside edge proving it was worn, that it wasn't a wayside terror on a post. You never liked it, did you? What's the point of having something nasty-looking on the wall, James? Missing the point completely, if you don't mind me saying.

I lay it down with care, as one does with antiques. It stares up, rigid, like the corpses in the war. Or my face in a pond. I'm touched by the fact that whoever packed this trunk remembered that this mask really belonged to me. Would Father have remembered, in his grief, or even without it? I think to myself: no, not likely. I hope you didn't pack it only because you wanted to *get rid of it*, Mother.

Your affectionate son,
Hugh

Dull again. Michaelmas is always dull, though. Here it's even duller, despite the entertainment.

Dearest Mother,

They insist I carry on. I hope they know what they're doing. I had a spot of bother but I'm much better now.

I will not talk, however. I preserve that right. One does not have many rights. Why the fuck should I talk, anyway? No other beast talks. How sensible.

I'm thinking hard, up there. I haven't the foggiest idea why you've packed this trunk with my things. I sniff a touch of rue. Hm. Whose, though? Only one or two of the toys could have interested me at the age of eleven. The books had mostly been replaced by new, unwarped copies. Nuncle never told me about the trunk, and I wasn't allowed up in the attic, under pain of losing a month's pocket money. If the scrawl on the ticket is correct, I was ill when it arrived. If it arrived with you seated next to it in Stan's trap, and you then vanished here in some way I am yet to fathom – of course he wouldn't have told me! It was as good as out of sight, out of mind, up here. Yet why the envelope and letter, placed so carefully on the top – the rest untouched, shifted only by the swell of the sea-journey, the handling on the docks, the slow train, Stan's badly sprung trap?

You see why I got myself a little worked up, up there?

I crouch on my knees and run my hand around the sides for any last tiny thing, like a child with its Christmas stocking. In one of the bottom corners my fingers hit something, concealed in the lurid shadows thrown by the torch and by its wrapping: an oil paper parcel on the oil paper lining of the trunk.

The trap sprung. Snap.

I undo the string by rubbing it against the metal teeth of Ted's hacksaw; in the process I cut my thumb, but not severely. The oil paper reveals a bundle of typed, carbon copies. Your letters. To your brother and sister-in-law in Ulverton.

You kept copies of all your letters, for your planned account of your life on the station – for a nursing journal, was it? You couldn't trust that your news would be saved by the recipient and you were right: not a single letter of yours has survived – outside the trunk. I read the first immediately, and am gripped. It appears that they are the chronological survival of your earliest time in Africa, before I was born. Perhaps they will take me right through to the mystery of your vanishing. I scrabble, hands trembling, to the last letter at the bottom of the bundle: its faint blue date disappoints me profoundly. It is later than the first by only five months – April 1921 – and written from the Mission Station on your way to Bamakum. Would you have written twenty or more letters to Uncle Edward in five months? I notice something scribbled in pencil across the greasy paper wrapping, perhaps in your own hand: *Not in order. Sort through!*

It is at this point, before I have even asked myself why these letters should have ended up in a trunk otherwise dedicated to me, or considered who that pencilled command was addressed to, that I hear a footfall somewhere below me.

And then another. Someone is climbing the main stairs, betrayed by the booming hollowness of all empty houses.

I switch off the torch and keep very still. John Wall probably lied when he said he was off all day at the tank demonstration. The clothes lie spread across the green canvas next to the empty trunk. I am holding the bundle of letters in my hand. The rustly copy-paper would be enough to give my position away, were I to tuck them back out of sight. In the near-darkness, in that forest of junk, between branches of chair legs and boles of carpet, I feel like a little animal when the big beasts stalk or the python slides soundlessly through the tangle. I am as terrified of discovery as I once was of death in the rumbling bomber. Oh yes. Exaltedly so.

The mask is watching me, the image of something hung up above the piano in the English Club in Victoria. Father and I noticed it together one Christmas. It was a night photograph, taken by means of a low wire tripping a flash. A pair of eyes dazzled by the glare into two shilling pieces dragged slightly in a blur of shock, lips drawn back to a wavy glint of teeth, the phantom of itself behind it. This was the moment the night had exploded in the trees, thrusting this most secret easy languishing man-creature into light, into reason, into a world of dress collars and pink gin and Gilbert and Sullivan. Having no name for itself, it's given a name. Gorilla. Or King Congo, in the Victoria Club. Because of your thing about gorillas, you didn't like to look at it. I did.

I crouch on my haunches thus for far too long; my legs are even stiffer. Age is unavailing, Mother. You won't know about this! It pours over the breakwater of morning exercises and brisk walks, it batters and shreds bone and muscle, yet it is so *silent*.

My face is the flash-lit gorilla's, showing all its teeth. I'm tense, you see, as the stairs creak. We stood under the big wobbling fan and Father told me about evolution, pointing at the photograph, using words like 'stagnant' and punning phrases like 'brains stopped play'; drawing a strange parallel with a private branch-line he knew whose grass whipped the little train's undercarriage, and that ended in an abandoned cocoa-plantation and its rusting sheds from the time of the Germans. As we hominids flashed past the poles, faster and faster, clacketty-clack. No buffers in sight, not yet.

There's grit under my palm. It's black sand from the boat.

Whoever it was on the stairs has gone down again: a light step, perhaps a woman's, but not Wall's because his foot drags. Nerve gave out on seeing the long corridor and its shadows, probably. Should have locked the kitchen door behind me, I think. There's a far thump and the attic door creaks in sympathy. Whoever it was has left. Yes, I hear through the skylight a far-down sneeze. A man. I hurry down to the kitchen and bolt the door from the inside, just in case. Hold the stockade, pieces of eight, Job Anderson at the middle loop-hole. Just as well the windows are mostly blocked. When they're not, I duck to pass!

Up in the attic again, I flutter through the dates on the letters and, yes, they are not in order – but they only go up to May, 1922, and there are only ten of them (the rest is bills, memoranda, scrawled accounts). The first was written soon after your arrival in Africa in 1920. Precisely the period that *doesn't* concern me, ending just as my clothes start! As I start!

— Then it occurs to me that maybe this is all my life, from even before the womb. If the female carries a finite number of eggs from birth, then I was in you from the beginning. From when you arrived in Africa and when you were working in the sanny and even before, from when you were running about and squealing on Ilythia's lawn. Oh yes. Ah yes. Or even before that, wheeled out in your perambulator to gurgle at the shadows in the leaves above, while your big brother crawled about with his wooden ducks long before the first war.

Even then I WAS INSIDE YOU.

I smile at this, feeling the weight of the letters: I was closer, I realise, than ever *he* was.

Ah yes.

    From your loving son,
      Hugh

Weather better. Crisp. Crisp and clear.

Dear Mother,
    I'm fine, now.

Unpleasant article in the paper, should never have been shown to me. Drew a parallel between Artaud and myself. Artaud was a famous French theatre man who went bonkers, really bonkers. Nevertheless, having drawn this parallel, the journalist then uses a quote from the poor chap to harangue me: Arkwright has 'a fetishistic superstition for the past'. But I know that quote, it comes from Artaud's rejection of modern costume! If I meet this journalist, I will challenge him to a duel, as in Pushkin. 'Who's Pushkin?' he will say. A duel to the death. I did unspeakable things to the cutting. I can do unspeakable things to him, too. I can do unspeakable things, full stop. As you can see, I am a bit angry. The people here have been excellent, on the whole. They want to give me a vegetable patch.

I pack everything away again in the trunk and close the lid, then use one of the big sheets of brown oil paper to wrap up the letters and the mask. I go down to your room and wrap the fetish box into the same huge bundle. I can't possibly leave anything valuable here. It's an awkward overgrown child in my arms.

I stand stiffly and there's a sudden gust of cold: the window is swinging petulantly back and forth, the heavy morning breaking into a squall. I must have left it open yesterday: the rain has darkened the floor beneath it in a precise curve. Careless. Closing the window, I see a piece of red moving in front of the wildwood.

Let me embarrass myself: it was the little service tree in full autumn crimson. But in my silly haste, I cracked one of the panes.

The parcel's huge crackly looseness is hopeless. I need string. I'm downstairs in the hallway, wondering where to find string or twine, when I see the front door handle turning, the door itself shivering to thumps from outside. The old umbrella topples over, shredding its cobwebs. I see a scarfed pirate the other side of the door. Nuncle's bearded skull. John Wall and his gun. The door opens a few inches, sticks on the floor.

I dive for the nearest door, the one down to the cellar, and close it behind me just as the other bursts open. I sit there, panting, on the stairs, holding my awkward child whose oil paper coughs each time I move. Blood from my hand trickles down my wrist, so I suck it. A muffled voice – a man's – says 'Hello?', but too timidly to recognise. I can't even say that it's not Nuncle's.

I am stuck ten minutes or so, in that darkness. The person out there thumping about for ten minutes, all over the house, perhaps looking for spoils. Then the gleam of a torch under the door sends me scuttling down to the bottom. Everything falls out, the fetish box bumping and rolling down to the bottom again, the mask and the letters only just caught by my arms. The door opens and the torchlight flashes in, me pressed to the shadows and filled with such, with such a pure thrill of terror! Wellington boots coming down a few steps, flashes catching crates, rows of empty bottle stands, the blade of an old bacon slicer. My heart very loud in my head, the fetish box lying next to a hooped wooden cask. Torchlight shivering through dust, catching the tips of my shoes, the rough earthen tiles, the white cobwebs. Nuncle never wore green wellies, no. John Wall wears army boots.

Then the flashing retreats and the door closes. The front door closes, too. I bolted the back door, of course, that's why the intruder had to try the front. Like the attic door, the cellar door creaks in sympathy. The house knows everything that happens. It always did.

I flash my own torch round. A pile of old crates, empty wine bottles, a broken bench. Remember the cellar, Mother? Given real light, the tiles would sprout grass again. The cellar of the old Jacobean farmhouse your granddad demolished, living on, the must of dust and age gravitating down. Nuncle kept his wine here, and then it had a mad rat. The mad rat meant that I couldn't go down, not on my own. Much later it became, so I understood, a shelter in case of nuclear war. The mad rat happened around the time I first saw Rachael during that symposium, in 1937. The door was always locked, but I was used to that.

I clear the cobwebs from the crates. They're full of bleach, judging from the peeling labels. Aunt Joy's hygiene fetish, perhaps.

My heel catches a stiff rag. But it's not a rag.

It's the mad rat, stretched on the tiles, mummified in all its plumpness, its fatted-up folds! Must have died in a summer of drought. Next to it, something that makes me step back in absolute horror, knocking the cask so that it collapses into a flower of staves, the hoops clattering at my feet.

A bigger head, just the head, all tiny pointed teeth in a glare of pure agony.

And another one, a much smaller rat, curved taut beside the mother. A family group. The mother and the child, in their agony of hunger, ate the father. That's it. That explains the plumpness, and their deaths. Don't you think? One never really knows, one can only suppose.

I can't touch them. The mummified fatness and the shocked, agonised head appal me. The head especially, looking as if it still can't quite believe it! Just thinking of them lying unchanging in that pitch darkness appals me to nausea even now, Mother. Even now.

Outside there's an indecisive squall; I have to cradle my bundle like a refugee with all his worldly goods. I need string. There are the ruts of a car in the grassy gravel. I'm amazed I didn't hear it – the clop of the door, the splintery growl. The cellophane shell of a cigarette packet, just peeled, blows to my feet: Brian Padmore smokes like a chimney. Litter-bug! There's no dustbin, and I have to stuff it in my pocket where it expands, crackling. That very good idea of mine will be presented by Brian Padmore in

Monday's meeting. It really is a very good and increasingly exciting idea, but it doesn't quite smother the detestable one.

The two outhouses escaped the auction: there are good tools in the wooden one, but no string. Trays full of withered little testicles – scrunchlings, of course. The other shed is of brick with a solid wooden door: another locked area in the old days. The lock's screws are half out of their holes and my claw-thing finishes the job. I find some greased twine in the debris of harmless junk and also Aunt Joy's bike, still haughty in its rust, the pannier loaded with clogged tins of Trojax enamel paint. There's a big dark bottle of rat-killer on the shelf – definitely 1930s from the besuited and rat-like operator on the label. I smile, picking it up. So much for the empathy with the animal and vegetable kingdom, the railings against chemicals. The tin is sticky.

I clear the bicycle of cobwebs and wheel it out. It has the most dreadful squeak! The deteriorated rubber pumps up, amazingly. I place the package in the pannier and squeak into the village, wondering whether the last bottom it took was Rachael's that weekend in 1940. I think I hear flames, but it's Brian's cellophane crinkling in my pocket as I pedal. The spitty air refreshes me.

I carry on squeaking two or three miles towards Fogbourne, despite the package. No old men on bicycles, these days – ah, except me! The parcel thumps slightly when I go over bumps or pot-holes: I try not to think of the tinted forehead inside it – but when I do, I feel strangely comforted. As if I am in unique possession of something vital to me, once more. Then a horrified nausea. Then the comforting warmth again. Malcolm passes me in his car, looking anxious, and I wave. He slows as if to stop but doesn't. I think I upset him, leaving the rehearsal like that, as if in a huff. I wobble back into Ulverton, startling everybody with my squeak. Look, I have been away over the sea, on the wastes of ice in company with Captain E.R.G.R. Evans. You do not know me any more.

The parcel goes straight into the wardrobe, unopened – even for the letters; I've only an hour before the next wretched rehearsal. A generous single malt oils my naked thoughts, whatever they are. I don't remember exactly. You can imagine, dear Mother: dark shapes in fog, confusion. I reach into my pocket for a handkerchief and open my damn cut again on a folded piece of paper. This is the letter on its own, that was placed on the top. I read it straight away, dotted though it is with my blood. It's dated November 28, 1931 and is full of Bamakum news, though you have only been back from England for a month. I can't distinguish it from others I received at the time. I hear your light, cheerful voice, smell the warm pungencies of Africa. You mention halfway through how 'jolly' a time you had in England, describing various excursions and visits to friends (none of which I recall, so they must have happened without me). Then you say something I find odd. I've got it in front of me now. What do you think of this?

'Africa smothers you with all sorts of hot and shadowy thoughts, as if one is lightly fevered all the time. The matter we talked about will go on getting more difficult, each time I visit it's more difficult, he gets bigger and bigger and it's as if there's a sort of – O, I'm frightening myself just putting it down like this! (Can *nothing* be done about that eye?) I have stripped his old room to the bare walls and put it all in a trunk: I meant to do it straightaway, after he'd left, because guests aren't very fond of the big spiders in the hut, it seems, but the months and then years slip by like water. I'll either bring the trunk with me one time or send it on its own. James believes the trunk just to be full of Hugh's things: look carefully and you will see different. I enclose the key now, in case. James finds everything of mine, in the end, and the ants will only carry it off on their backs. I feel – O, so released! Is this the meaning of your "propitiation", dear Edward?'

Well, Mother? I'm sure you don't recognise it, do you? Nuncle put it in, remember.

The rest of the letter returns to gossip. I pour another malt and reflect: What is the difficulty? Parting, of course. Why is she frightened? I grow bigger and bigger and she feels time slipping past 'like water', time for ever lost, until she will no longer know me. Why does she feel released, propitiated? Because she has severed her obligations, by stripping her African home free of me. The competition of her instincts has been smothered. Mental imbalance will follow.

Or in other words (I know the language now) – she will become dysfunctional. She will not be able to process her pain. I pour another malt. Some signal was received from me, somehow, through my sickness, and she dropped everything to see me. Then what? The red lady became the Red Lady.

How, exactly?

Spilt blood. Smothering, melancholy boughs.

The malt spills on to my cut, because my hand is trembling. My cut stings. I look at the lines on my palm.

My dead love gave
Lips warm with love though in her grave.

Your affectionate son,
Hugh

Fug. Musn't waste heating by opening the window. Have asked for a hand-held fan.

My dear Mother,

Malcolm is sitting in the middle of the hall on one of those chilly bucket chairs, like Krapp without his tape recorder. St George is a chinless, very plain man from the new estate, called Chris; the Turkish Knight is one Bruce, holding a file with his name and his role in big black Letraset on the cover. His Knight's boast sounds like a contribution to a sales meeting. Gary and Mark are without Beelzebub. Before the big duel there is a fight between the Fool and the Old Witch (Sally and a wheezy Jenny, both giggling), in which the Fool sees his own death in the mirror of the locked swords of some Morris dancers and draws up his will. He's killed and revived several times. Malcolm tells me that the Fogbourne Morris Society are invited for the real thing. The duel between the Turkish Knight and St George will weave in and out of the dance, dead leaves flying about in the air. 'How did you cut your hand, then?'

Mrs Pratt comes in with dog and younger son and I am shocked to see the latter in the bright-red hooded blouson that followed me up the lane into the garden. His eyes are as red-rimmed as his coat, and he keeps sniffling. Drugs, I think. Mrs Pratt invites me to supper on Tuesday. I quite fancy the kind of stumpy English fare she will no doubt heap on the porcelain, and thank her. Someone asks where the leopard skin's gone and Malcolm mumbles something under his breath. He glances at me guiltily. Lost? Stolen? Left out in the rain? 'Haven't seen it at all,' I say, 'perhaps John Wall's got it.' Malcolm stares at the floor. There's something strange about him, tonight.

I do the best I can with the duel and its aftermath. Afterwards Malcolm scratches his beard and asks if I want a 'jar'. I invite him to have dinner with me in the Old Barn, in case he thinks I'm in a huff. Anyway, I need company. Mrs Pratt's sons are now humping in dolmen-sized speakers with the help of an orange-haired man with a crucifix in his ear and baggy camouflage trousers. 'I'm Ed,' he says. 'I'm Disco Night.' I say I'll come if he's playing some *Venom* and he says of course he is. Malcolm's jaw drops. 'It'll be a gas,' says Ed. 'See you when I see you.'

Gas. Mad rats. That's when the dormant tendril started to uncoil in my head, Mother. Maybe Ed started it all. Maybe I should blame Ed.

Malcolm's nervous about meeting Jessica, who's serving tonight – some old history to do with his wife and Roger. But there's this something else, too.

'OK,' he mumbles, studying the menu, 'the skin's missing. Your skin.'

'The leopard skin?'

He nods. He's actually blushing. It was in the hall's big walk-in storage cupboard along with the old W.I. banners and card-tables and a few of their own props and then it wasn't. I knew the cupboard well, helping with things before the war. Big bolts on the door, but not stiff. Now they're stiff, you shoot them with difficulty. Somehow I know this, Mother, before he says that it was really safe there, it's hardly ever used, the bolts are rusty, you have to practically hammer them free. It could have been a kid, it could have been Wall, it could have been anyone. Nothing else missing, that he could see. He looks at me over the menu.

I tell him that I don't mind at all.

'But I do,' he says. 'Maybe someone didn't like the way it was being used.'

What does he mean by that?

Jessica does seem a little strained in his presence. But then so am I. She tells me she popped over to my garret this evening, with a tub of blackberries. I don't tell her that I've temporarily gone off hedgerow fruit, since the Ray débâcle. Tim and his bog bodies. What a sweet kind person she is, I think.

Scooping out his avocado, Malcolm tells me that he's finally got hold of a copy of Nuncle's little tale. Which tale? *I, Nubat, of the Forest People*. He wants to turn it into a musical. A youth thing, really relevant, with African rhythms. What can be relevant, I say, about a 1930s fantasy on Creswellians, Maglemosians and early Neolithics in prehistoric England? Amazonian Indians versus McDonalds, he replies. Shell in Nigeria. Agribusiness, forest destruction, all that. By the time his daughter's his age, he says, there won't be a shred of rain forest left.

He even peddles Nuncle's line about war starting with agriculture: hoarded grain, the owning of land, sources of water, fences, fortresses, the inevitable seeds of rivalry and slaughter. 'Your uncle was right, you know. *Reflections on Windmill Hill* is a great work. We're all more Stone Age than anything else, deep inside us. We're all Maglemosians, that's what he said. The Forest People, living in harmony with the forest. Dug-outs and bone fishing spears and roasted hazel nuts. It all went wrong with the farmers, the owning of land, these bloody nationalisms. I stuck an anti-McDonalds sticker up on Windmill Hill, after reading that.'

But, I point out, it's Nubat the Maglemosian who wipes out the poor little farmers at the end with his sorcery, paralysing them all in a rather horrible act of vengeance.

'It's not sorcery, it's nerve gas.'

He said so in an interview in the *Listener* not long before he died, apparently. Prophesying the day we'd use nerve gas on our own food, Malcolm suggests, like they do on strawberries in California. It paralyses you. I point out as best I can, without sounding superior, that we knew absolutely nothing about nerve gas until after the war. It was the Nazis who developed it, not us. And *Nubat* was published in the 1930s!

'Why didn't they use it, then?'

'I have no idea, Malcolm. I'm glad they didn't.'

Malcolm then virtually whispers to me that Jack Wall was poisoned, not by his own ratsbane, but by arsenical agri-chemicals while badger-baiting. The stuff leaches into the groundwater; we're poisoned even when we drink from the head of a stream. He's making me very gloomy, as Nuncle used to do. Can he be right about the rain forest? Ours seemed as infinite as starry space, Mother. Me in my miniscule bush clothes, and the rearing trees.

He's talking on, excitedly. There'll be a final performance of *I, Nubat* on the top of − guess where? − Windmill Hill! A sort of authentic midsummer fayre with real politics and real theatre. Oh dear. I must sound enthusiastic. His eyes are shining over the *crème caramel*. You, Hugh, have the rights. I know, I know! The apostate guarding the sliver of the True Cross (fake, but still a relic, still worshipped). I say of course he can do whatever he likes with it.

But frankly, my thoughts are elsewhere: not in starry space but on Aunt Rachael's rheumy eyes, thinned hair, hoarse voice, the gas-tight blinded cocoon of the house. I am not my usual self. I am getting bigger and bigger, Mother.

Night night, Malcolm. Splendid evening.

The tub of blackberries sits like a discreet offering to some nature god in front of the door, but there's a foul smell in my garret, of burnt pan and sour smoke. A note on the table: *To Hugh Arkwright Esq. You nearly burnt my pub down!! Yours Sincerely, Ted. P.S. Switch gas off at night, please.* Words to that effect. I toasted a muffin just before going out, feeling peckish. Careless. I'll have to see him, apologise. If he spots me sneaking away without apologising that'll be worse. I pocket my torch and the heavy claw and go down to the bar, trying to remember which gas smelt of garlic. Either lewisite or mustard. No, lewisite was geraniums. Odd smell, geraniums: scruffily chemical, sweet-sour, almost nasty. I notice scurf on my dark coat and brush it off in the corridor. The bar sounds packed. I sneak past the open door straight into Ted's sight line. He waves.

Bleach. Aunt Joy was a stickler for hygiene, but not that much of a stickler.

Mustard gas smelt of garlic. Iridescent patches on dry roads, like

Castrol piddled from motor cars. Insidious, penetrating, absorbed by skin and by tar, but not water. Rubber boots and oilskin clothes stop it but like oven, service respirator stifling. Gas-drill dreaded, stumbling about like gargoyles over the moor, tropical in freezing winds. Cloud blown downwind and mixing with air grows bigger and bigger, still able to blister and inflame until thins into harmlessness. Like crop-spraying, I suppose.

Nuncle and his apocalypse. Gog and Magog on the heath. The great gods finding out their enemies. Blow, winds.

Nick of the pony-tail appears in the door. 'Ted really wants to see you,' he says. 'You're not his favourite customer.' I enter the din. The hag's face appears through the smoke. Muck and John Wall are both at the bar. Wall's arguing with Ted about the condition of the flights on his darts. Why don't they have their own? Because they are scavengers, that's why, a pair of mound-pickers, twin fishers of flotsam! Muck perches on his stool like a Rackham goblin on a mushroom, smoking. To my horror they are hallooing me and nudging each other and attracting people's attention. Ted advances to my end, pushing his heavy specs up. 'I'm terribly sorry about that, Ted!' He's telling me how close it was, he's telling me off. But the pint he's drawing dribbles its head in front of me: propitiation, Mother. Otherwise I'd have left.

Muck and John Wall are separated from me only by the kick-wrestling man. I will take my drink to the bentwood chair in the corner occupied by Fatso, the resident tabby, having a friendly word as I pass. The priority is to smother the disaster yesterday morning in the field with a blanket of ignorance: make them think in the end that they'd misheard things, that it was all their own invention. I'm quite cool about all this: I'm not heated at all, not at this point!

A hiccup. The friendly word – something rambling about the weather – is met by a grotesque wink from Muck. Have I mentioned that his eyes bulge and that his eyelids close over them like a crocodile's?

'You've got a mote in your eye, Muck,' I say, pointing at it and slopping my drink on his boots.

Hag's face. A terror visiting me at night, even here.

'Watch out there, Mr Arkwright. Folk'll be thinkin' I've missed.'

'Like you missed them pigeons, boy,' said Wall.

'Here, you watch y'mouth or she'll be losin' a tooth or two.'

John Wall turns to me with a crumpled smile, as if the teeth have already dropped out.

'Do you reckon all mouths are fee-male, Mr Arkwright?'

'In French they are, but purely by linguistic chance. *La bouche*.'

John Wall peers at me through drifts of his friend's smoke.

'Your mouth,' he says, slowly, 'goes all funny when you does that, Mr Arkwright.'

Muck makes kissing noises, thrusting his lips out and towards John Wall's cheek in a spittly lunge. Wall reacts with wide-eyed panic – yes, it's definitely panic – flinging his hand up so abruptly that Muck loses his glass and almost topples from the stool. My trousers are wetted. Definitely panic.

'Whoa, boy, now look what you've done,' says Muck, with the lassitude of someone drunker than he seems. The glass is intact. I pick it up off the rubber floor mat and place it on the bar. He was referring to my trousers. I brush them uselessly and make non-committal noises as Ted peers over.

'What's up then, you load?'

One of the nearby drinkers makes a reference I don't catch, which switches John Wall's panicked eyes into post-box slits. Ted chuckles and turns away. The ripples the little accident has created wash through the pub and fade within the minute. The two men are staring at my trousers.

'Now you're up a gum tree, Mr Arkwright,' says Muck. 'Folk'll think you weren't whipping it out in time.'

'I'll clean 'em for you, if you want, Mr A.,' John Wall says. 'Send this fairy-turd the bill.'

'And this turd'll send you to bill, cunt,' growls Muck, over his shoulder.

Words to that effect. You've heard worse, in the sanny.

'People wash their hair in beer,' I remark, and start to move away. Muck grabs my arm. Strong grip. Almost painful.

'You're gettin' on a bit now, aren't you, for that lark, Mr Arkwright?'

I swallow involuntarily. Play the innocent, though I could do such unspeakable things.

'Lark, Mr Petty?'

'Don't you try to hide it, Mr Arkwright.'

I stare at him. His expression is not malicious, however. He's prodding my chest with his finger, grinning conspiratorially. His smoke stings my eyes.

'Arn time 'ee gets tired of Mrs Marlow, send her along to yere, boy.'

Jessica must have come to my room through the bar. The thickening into dialect, the use of the familiar 'ye', the realisation that it's not Rachael at the bottom of his cajolery, makes me almost want to hug Muck, at that moment. Is that so extraordinary, Mother? A dab of mustard in the corner of his mouth, his breath sour and hot, the worn front teeth making an elegant arc, like a pack-horse bridge, under which his tongue gleams like bloodied water: but he is suddenly of the old days, the bits of them that still echo or lie low in my soul. Drink turns us into fools before it turns us into demons: Muck's foolishness is pitiable, like Caliban's.

So I smile.

'I feel most flattered, Mr Petty, that you think my visitor this evening was there for anything other than an old man's advice.'

'Turn you into a toad, see.' He belches, horribly.

'Fee-fi-fo-fum,' murmurs John Wall.

My costume of patient civility serves also to avoid a scene. I continue to smile cheerily.

'I don't think I'm ready to croak yet. Would you mind releasing my arm, by the way? The blood's gone out of my hand.'

Muck looks at it, his own hand treating my bicep as he no doubt treats his gun. The thumb stroking the wool of my sweater. He's considering something, tinted glasses tucked into his top pocket. Clearly been drinking all day – a habit that the filigree of purply fissured veins beneath his dark skin suggests is chronic and old. If I try to tug myself free, I'll pull him off his stool. John Wall seems to be elsewhere, staring at the wet floor.

'Sing afore breakfast, cry afore night,' murmurs Muck, with a sphinx-like intensity, as if I have travelled the length of the desert to hear it. Perhaps I have.

　Your loving son,
　　Hugh

Awful carols, much too early. Mucky weather.

Dearest Mother,
　He lets go of my arm.
　'Thank you,' I say.
　As I am turning away, he sings, very softly, in a soft drawly harshness, 'Tiptoe . . . through the *raamsons* . . .'
　What? What's that? Na whatee dat ting dere?
　The hair on the back of my neck tingles. The kick-wrestling veteran is blocking my way. Stupidly, I glance back, still bearing my cheery comedy mask. Something more than a leer on his face. Intimacy, mutual knowledge, the veil of smoke and chit-chat and beer fumes torn away along with aged skin and flagging flesh, the years shredded to a green and tingling time. Our time! Oh yes! He's hauled me back there and I might wrestle with him as young men did once, stripped to the waist, bare-fisted, bleeding noses and mouths and ears. I might not even finally pummel his face to pulp. Smoke comes out of his nose, misting him, as if he's looking through glass, squashing his face against glass. But that's his normal face.
　I glance at John Wall, who's still dreaming. Wall was not yet born, of course. Most in this room were not yet born, or were still children. How long has Muck known? Yes, of course, long before Ray Duckett talked to him over the fardels. From the very day Wall's father spied on us, probably. The two would have been the same age, lads together, poaching cronies. Frank Petty, Jack Wall. My God – might Jack Wall's crony have been there, too, stuck up in the tree, sniggering between the boughs? Might Muck have actually *seen* it all? He's impaled me, like one of his pigeons. I'm hovering without the power either to alight or rise. The smoke shrouds him. Aunt Rachael peers through it, as she always did. They talked to each other, bleary-eyed, his cup smeared black

with his fingers and mouth, hers concealed in her trembling hand. Chortling chit-chat in the damp dark kitchen, years and years of it. God knows what he knows.

The one becomes the other in my dreams, Mother, over a mug of tea. That's the true horror.

>Your loving son,
>Hugh

Cold and wet. If I close my eyes, Christmas will go away.

Dear Mother,

Now the man is pointing up with jabs of his finger, discreet little jabs – his head thrust forward, his expression flatly stupid, like a bad puppet's.

I look, of course, automatically, as one does: the bulgy ceiling, jaundiced by decades of tobacco smoke; the black-and-red flex of the light bulb; the dwarfish plastic shade. Nothing, in other words.

Hands up like claws either side of his nose, face towards his lap. Pilot. Goggles. No, binoculars. Harpo and Chico's old charades routine! His face appears again. He points down, this time, and I look. His boots on the bar stool's cross-piece. Short man. Stub ends. Lost crisps. Wet pool. Now there's a discreet little movement close to his chest, private, between us only. A man in braces blocks us for a moment, his back dark with sweat, holding a pool cue. Why do I want to see? I could turn and walk away and never know. But it is like a game, after all: the word isn't finished, the title, the well-known phrase. It's not a film or a novel or a play, either. Braces has passed. The claw, close to the chest, now rounded. A cup. A well. The other hand's forefinger poised and now bouncing in and out of the well or the cup. Pipe. Me filling my pipe, when I had one. No. I'm so slow, Mother! Don't you remember?

John Wall's father up in the tree. Binoculars. Down there, oh no. In and out, in and out, his finger goes. The man's huge face like a god's above, florid and slightly frowning at me, as if all this takes thought and concentration.

Filth.

I have not moved. I would like to leap but I have not moved. I am frowning back at him. The pub's din has hollowed out, it's a sort of roaring silence. Then the face melts, alters. I am frightening it, yet I have not moved! He's flinched. Now there's an ear. The face has turned away, flinching. It worked, though my eye did not deliberately spit.

Let me explain, Mother. It's my work. I am going to write a book about it just as soon as I'm up and running again. My notes are lost, but it's all in my head. I have read and re-read Bacon, Gayton, Heywood – I know it by heart! They mumble to me in my sleep! Listen. Our passions stir our spirits, they ripple through the aether, they enter the spectators by the eyes, they agitate their spirits. Actors knew this, once. Sweet Shakespeare knew it. The force of imagination can stir a corpse – Francis Bacon said this! Up in Eilrig, we have struck each other with an emanation at fifty feet over gorse and heather, so that we all but stagger. It took years of repetition. Passion drill, I called it. Yet that passion is only what our Elizabethan masters would call 'counterfeit', Mother. Real, and also unreal! Like masks or fetishes or words, words, words! After five years we had got back to something like it, blown the dust off, cleared the centuries' cobwebs. Five years up in the heather, behind the whitewashed walls, learning and learning and learning! The sweet exile years of Eilrig. This was my work – is my work! Rigorous scholarship drives it. We do not call our acting 'authentic', but 'apt'. How I love that little word, 'apt'! How free of pretension, and yet what howls of change inside! For I have changed the face of British theatre, Mother. Oh yes. I am highly respected. I have done rather well. And it is all getting bigger and bigger.

I did not counterfeit my passion in the pub. It was tested on my teeth. It spat through the air and burned, and went on burning. You can't lave the burn of the evil eye. For that is what it was! The acid spittle that sends a man to his doom. I have worked on such things for the sake of art, aptness, the honouring of genius. I will work on them again, just as soon as I'm up and running, which will be soon, oh yes.

The room blurs into noise and I stare at the floor. My

312

emanation slips back into my eye and snakes towards its home in the entrails.

Revenge, I murmur.

I murmured the same word after reading Rachael's letter in my perspex nutshell, our blockbuster flaming somewhere in the shells of houses behind us. I murmured it as I walked back down the bomber's corridor, bruising my shin against one of her bulkheads, tumbling over another so that her ribcage and my ribcage met; murmured it as I dropped on to the concrete and walked under the fuselage, a tiny hot fellow with a hotter metal belly over his head, noticing the others in a group at the rear, their hair astray in the cool dawn wind. And there we stood, studying the dangling tank and rivet of what had been the rear turret, of what had been Reg's place. The wind through the rivet still fluting softly.

Whatever tune it was, it soothed my private furies.

But I never ever forgave them. Nuncle and this new Rachael, I mean, not the Germans! I just said nothing: no reply, nothing. Nuncle wrote to my superior asking if I was still 'upright and walking'. Another letter from Rachael, full of mystic rubbish about stars, platonic types of love, the fact that she knew – for certain – I had been her brother in a past life (another lonely only child, you see). Silence is a privilege, isn't it, Mother? The shield's glassiest polish: it threw back their own snake-crowned ugliness. My hatred for Nuncle went on sharpening itself, as Father used to sharpen his cut-throat by leaving it in a certain compass direction. Just by leaving it.

Then the silence was broken when a tuneless whistle stopped. I'll explain. London, a cold autumn evening, '44, on my way to the theatre. Over the rumble and natter and car horns comes this horrible sound, somewhere between a moan and a kettle on the boil. It's a doodlebug. (If it cuts out, pray hard.) It's keeping going, it's overhead, it's come a long way and it's keeping going –

Lamplit faces looking up, astonished, into a silence. Where's it gone?

We all start to run. We're off! I'm opposite Thresher and Glenny's, the gentlemen's outfitter's – remember Thresher and Glenny's? The big plate-glass windows start to move outwards. Everyone crouched, clawed at by a gale of ice. A pram is shredded. A hairnetted woman grimaces at her naked legs. A spiv holds his face and rolls gently into the gutter. A couple are crawling about as if looking for a coin. There are detached arms, legs, heads – but they're mannequins, oh good. Heat and bits of bright ice. A man stands with a tweed waistcoat over his head, the price-tag still attached. Blood appears in ridiculous quantities, as if swollen bags of it have been dropped from very high up. A lot of it appears on my torn trouser-leg. My best pair, too.

I don't consider for a moment that the blood comes from inside me. I cradle a man's head as he's dying, wondering whether to pick up his bowler with its silk lining, to adjust his tie above the mess. 'Don't let me go,' he keeps saying, sobbing away, 'don't let me die. I don't want to die. Oh, God. Oh, fuck. I don't want to die.' Then he wants his mother, though he's grey and balding. 'She's coming,' I say, 'she's coming in a minute.' 'Mummy,' he keeps saying, 'Mummy.' Then he says, 'I'm fine, now,' in a very firm voice, looking straight at me. A little shudder, as if he's smelt something unpleasant, and his soul flies away too far from me to bring it back.

I fainted in the ambulance, and came to with fifty stitches in my thigh and just enough blood to keep the valves going. Flesh is a liquid but a very thick one, Mother, too thick and slow to recover itself like water after the steamer's split it: Quiri would have much to say about my thick white mark. I limp ever so slightly – a certain stiffness on damp days. But that's all.

Father was contacted, I received visits. Father shuffled in and out every evening, tapping my hand but saying almost nothing, as if it was all his fault. I was under pain-killers – morphine, I think – when Rachael called. I see her face there in the hospital, the flowers she's bought, her hands crossed on her skirt. Her hair now cut and curl-ironed, in the fashion. Happy, she seems. Pale, a little dreamy. But happy. And I'm looking at her through binoculars again, from behind the spindle-tree. I shake my head, bring her nearer and into focus. The moment was exquisitely embarrassing, as if she found me on my knees, over my Meccano or Lotts Bricks. The morphine dulled my hurt but made me think of witty and hurtful things to say, or made me think they were witty and hurtful.

'Take dictation, Mrs Prendergast.'

'Sorry, Hugh?'

'Did you hear about the wife who was hurt while cooking her husband's breakfast in a horrible manner?'

I lobbed them like cricket balls in a game without any other players, or happening in a mist. Herbert E. Standing pretended to be a doctor in the distance, smiling.

'That was a close shave.'

'It was, Hugh.'

'No, it was me. But anyway I don't like beards. I'm glad to see you've got gloves. Are they made from your own skin?'

She looked around her, I suppose for a nurse. She was a nurse. Or used to be. She was living at Ulverton now, doing her bit locally. Typing out his work, his letters, pasting up the *Scarab*.

'Births, deaths and mirages. Play a straight bath. The fire brigade could not distinguish the flames. I just hope you've got an up-to-date road mop.'

'I want to talk about things when you're better, Hugh. Not to explain, but to be friends. No, relatives. That's what we are now, isn't it? My children will be your cousins.'

'Very well, Auntie. Or should it be plain Aunt Rachael, Aunt?'

She sighed, laid a Vanity Fair assortment on my blanketed feet, and left. I kicked my feet and the nurses had to scrabble after them. Ha ha. In doing so I tore a few stitches. The pain was somehow right, if severe, particularly in the first few minuets. Nurses on their hands and knees for ages, like polar bears ready to bounce. All I wanted to do was giggle, or maybe goggle, and I think I did.

As for Nuncle: I was hobbling about when he dropped by, my mind no longer gibbering, no white lint to unstick from it or the wound. A grin from behind a carton of books from his library.

'Hello, Hugh my boy. Glad to see you up.'

His deep, ringing voice turned heads. I had planned to riddle him with sarcasm, but I wasn't on morphine now and the jokes wouldn't come. Faces watching, so I sat on the edge of the bed and behaved civilly, on the surface. As he emptied the carton, commenting on the titles (books he didn't want, hopeless books of Aunt Joy's, forgotten novels and dull travelogues), I knew that my

315

secret weapon was to curve away from him for ever, the link severed. My strength would be in absence, the silence of a doodlebug, the whistle cutting out when it was time to drop: chilling, that. Much more than just not replying to their letters. I could even visit them, be civil over dinner, eventually. Anyway, I was fond of Ulverton, the garden, the woods, the downs. But set firm on my own course, as firm as the ruts in ancient marble roadways, carved merely by the to-and-fro of countless wheels, I would have the power and dignity to cope. That's where it really began, Mother. A crowded ward. Late wartime. North Kensington under black wraps.

He was shocked when I showed him the puckered wound stretching from the knee to the groin. In a poem written by him a little later, it appears rather ungraciously as *My own thin stocking-flesh, laddered by war's thorn*. Not that I minded. Why should I have done? That was the very least of it. He's done worse since, Mother. You'll see what worse he's done.

'I had to go on leave,' I said, 'to be hurt.'

'They say, old boy, that your AA chaps and their falling shrapnel rip up more of us than their cottonwool does the Boche.'

'It's Jerry these days, but they are quite right. What do you propose to do about it?'

He frowned, ignoring my question, and laid his hand on my arm.

'Hugh – are you, you know, *intact*? Your baggage down there ship-shape, and all that?'

I snorted. My metal brandy flask saved all that, but I wasn't about to tell him.

'Packed with nowhere to go, Nuncle.'

I looked at him steadily. He blinked and stroked the new thing, the beard – more brindled than his walrus moustache, which was old.

'I never forced her hand, Hugh. I really didn't,' he murmured.

'Well, that makes me feel *much* better,' I said, tapping my stick against the bed end so that it hummed at the other. 'Congratulations, Nuncle. Now I'm going to forget the whole business. Please don't think it frightfully awful of me not to attend the wedding, whenever it is. I have a life to lead, and it's mine, once the war's done with. I'm not cutting myself off, but I am going to be delicate with myself. That means coming round to it slowly. That means seeing you on my own terms, probably infrequently. I'll get my things at some point, when the leg's healed.'

Or words to that effect.

He clutched the raincoat on his knees, kneading it as he looked around him nervously. He's out of his pond, I thought. He's gasping like a fish. Then he turned his eyes back to me. I was wrong: he wasn't nervous. He was excited. Sated.

'Would you like me to lay a hand on it, old boy, speed it up with some magnetism?'

'If you mean my thigh, you must be joking.'

'Certainly wasn't pulling your leg, what?'

He laughed, happily – ever so happily. I think it is that laugh I hear again as Muck makes his obscene gesture, so discreet that no one else sees it – not even John Wall. A happy, light laugh – a laugh you always liked, come to think of it. It had always been the same laugh, you said, even when he was a boy, playing silly tricks on you in that big house, in that big garden, in that big wild-wood. (Was it so wild, then, such a lush tangle?) My mask drops, something tears in me very deep down, a sound like someone hawking down an alley, our minds made up of so many secret alleys, unventilated basements, fusty attics!

I've turned away now and with my pinched face I make it to the cat's bentwood chair, lift the horrible beast off and am rewarded with a scratch on my wrist. Nothing serious, scarcely puncturing the skin, but my drink spills. Fuck Fatso, I mutter. My neighbour in a green parka, with a face lost in its own mournful longitudes, grunts a greeting. 'Our furry relatives,' he says. 'Did you know that we share an almost identical DNA with 'em? Just one code thingummy reversed, that's all. True. Honest. Really.' He's twitching his thumb and forefinger, showing the reversal of the thingummy. He was on his own before I came along, has a rotten cabbage secreted somewhere on his person. I sit anyway, exhausted. I feel a fear of being alone, Mother. I like this man's wanderings through popular science, it means I don't have to talk, just nod. Like flicking idly through a magazine at the dentist's or half-listening to the radio. Something comforting in it. These amazing facts, devoid of fuzz and blur. Did I know this, did I know that? It means I can ponder, safely.

God knows how long I'm stuck there. Nearly an hour, maybe. I think I had another pint, on Green Parka.

'Night night, Mr A.'

It's John Wall, by the door, Muck swaying next to him. He purses his lips, as if about to blow a kiss. Then the wretched tune comes out again, the ditty, tiptoeing around my heart, needling it. They go out together, Muck still whistling. Fatso is warming my lap. Fatso leaps off. Green Parka's discourse on the two hemispheres of the brain fades as the door swings shut behind me.

They are standing in the street, under the orange lamp opposite the pub, as if waiting for me. A creak above my head and the Green Man grins down, a gooseberry-faced lion vomiting dandelion leaves.

'Listen –'

'Say that Frenchie word again, Mr Arkwright.'

'Shut up. This has got to stop.'

Muck hiccups, his head wobbles. He's looking straight at me, seeking his centre of gravity somewhere to his left. He finds it. He's absolutely sure he's found it.

'What's the chappie on about, John boy?'

The wine at supper, the strong beer – we're all in it together. Amongst the fumes.

'That song. It's got to stop.'

John Wall drags his foot forward.

'We like singin', Mr A.'

'It's got to stop. If it doesn't, I'll – I'll –'

'What's he on about, John?'

Then he snorts and collapses in giggles, on John Wall's shoulder. John Wall breaks away, as if disgusted by touch, and drags himself closer. He stands very close, in fact. His face is glistening, as if covered with oil.

'I'm not being funny, Mr Arkwright, but I'm owed summat, seein' as what I've lost.'

'Lost? What have you lost?'

He blinks.

'My mum's never got over it, acksherly.'

'If you're on about your father —'

Muck is swaying about behind, whistling again though about as tunelessly as a doodlebug, doing his best to tiptoe through imaginary flowers. Ramsons, of course. Crushing them. My head appears to contract to teeth and bone.

John Wall's small eyes, so very watery, even in the awful orange glare of the street lamp.

'We might claim damages, you see.'

He's both apologetic and vicious. Impossible to explain the effect, Mother. Impossible for the finest of my actors to imitate.

'Damages? What rubbish. What was he doing in the wood, anyway?'

'Eh? Well, takin' a short cut. Everyone has the right to take a short cut. From A to B. You can't deny ordinary folk takin' short cuts where they needs to —'

'I know what he was doing. Like the other time.'

The small eyes slide off.

'Health hazard, that's what that wood is,' he says. 'Could have been a kid. You can always put one of them electric fences right round. I can get one at wholesale price, from my mate in the Army —'

Muck is urinating loudly against a wall beyond, head thrown back, going la-la-la. I look back at John Wall. He is a mixture of guile and innocence, now.

'I am not about to put an electric fence around a perfectly harmless tangle of old trees —'

'Your uncle did.'

'Want a pigeon, Mr Arnold?'

Muck's stubby body is arched back, doing his trousers up behind his friend. They both stare at me as if I am about to perform a little turn.

'I am not my uncle,' I say.

'But it's your property,' says John Wall, scratching his bad leg.

'Cursed, that's what it is,' says Muck. His head's wobbling again, his eyes are runny. They're horribly like Aunt Rachael's eyes. Why did she blind the house, seal it like that?

'It ent *cursed*,' snaps John Wall, over his shoulder.

'Bloody is,' says Muck.

'Bloody is *not*,' snaps John Wall.

'You won't catch me going in there, any road,' Muck mumbles, pulling a long face. How can he see anything at night, through those tinted glasses?

'Good,' I say. 'I'm glad to hear it. And just to make sure, I'll put big KEEP OUT signs all around it. NO TRESPASSERS. VERY PRIVATE PROPERTY. Do you understand what I'm saying? I'm speaking *metaphorically*. In other words, the joke's over, or I might get very very *upset*.'

The two stare at me, apparently aghast. I realise that I have been spitting, and not only metaphorically. My lips have drawn back to reveal my gums – a thing you never liked, Mother. I have the sensation that my head has turned into a skull, and is lifted about an inch from my body. I have to wish them a hasty goodnight. I think I've made my point.

Your affectionate son,

Hugh

Midwinter. Rather miserable weather, but we're all well heated. Very low sky.

Dearest Mother,

I have just got back from a rather jolly walk around the grounds. Muddy underfoot, but I mostly kept off the lawn. Sap so down one feels it will never come up again, without a bit of encouragement. Awfully slothful air about this place. I so hate sloth. No one shaves properly. Tufts under the nose.

I walk away and my head returns, fleshed again, to my neck. Malarial, almost. A wolf whistle follows me, blowing me along. It might not have been them. Agamemnon killed his own daughter for a fair wind.

Did I know this? Did I know that?

Thump thump thump, from the village hall. There are youths dotted about everywhere, girls in dangling sleeves, boys in baseball caps, cropped hair, long hair. It'll be a gas. I make straight for the phone box by the old well in the middle of the square. I'm dialling my friend Morris.

'Impress me with your Internet thing. Gas. Mustard gas, nerve gas, the lot. Everything there is.'

'Gas?'

'I used to know but I've got holes. Particularly nerve gas, because I don't think it was around. Before the last war. Everything. Its history, who invented it, when, everything.'

'You're going to sniff it or something? You're missing London that much?'

I growl and give him the number and wait outside, sitting on a low wall by the old well and its seized glossy pump. This is my revenge, Mother.

The disco children wander past and giggle. One of them says, 'Ha haar, me hearties.' Their laughter is like a shout. I feel much like I did when I was a boy: frightened of them. I wish I'd had friends at home. It wasn't normal to do what I did: read, walk, bicycle about, act Shakespeare in a wood, not talk to anyone except Mrs Stump and Susan, the Jennets, the odd tradesman or farmhand or the dotty friends of Nuncle's. Nasty, dotty friends. Nazis. Jolly Nazis. I'm so excited! Oh, I've waited so long!

Sometimes he did actually speak to me.

'Hugh lad, did you *personally* hear of relatives of the deceased being killed before the burial?'

'Of course,' I would say, just to impress him.

Off back into his study, nodding and humming.

I stare at the defunct well and its potted flowers, sickly in the lamplight. It's all coming together. I'm walking through the wood and the pieces of the puzzle are being carried to me by tiny helpful elves. Avenge you, avenge Rachael. Deep roots pulled out screaming like the deadly mandrake, that sends all who hear it mad. But afterwards – what love-balms of mandragora, what healing and soothing follows that awful shriek!

The disco thumps and thuds, forms emerging to bright flashes from the hall's door. Torture while a girl with a lurid face calls her mother, the mother's voice a distant duck, the girl's petering out to a whine, revealing not even anger. 'Oh Mu-um!' When she emerges from the booth she jumps, noticing me only now, scurrying away on clapping heels. Wait. Wait. Then the phone rings and it's Morris, pleased as punch. The phone box is fetid with cheap scent, crawling with ugly words that have stayed with me, Mother, as these things do while the sweet ones fly away.

Morris tells me nothing I don't know already about mustard gas – nothing *you* wouldn't know, either.

'One to a million particles of air can scald the skin, hey, that's something.'

'Has it got arsenic in it?'

'No. That's lewisite. You have to prick the blisters, yuk. Doesn't lewisite ring a bell? Or am I thinking of some actor? Jerry Lewis! Didn't we all think they were going to slug us with it? Hey, did you ever do gas-drill? Wasn't it kinky in those rubber boots and oilskins –'

'Hot, Morris. Boiling hot in a freezing wind on Mam Tor.'

'Stumbling about like gargoyles, yeah. There was this paranoid sergeant called Watts, he thought every piddling rainbow puddle of Castrol was mustard – that the hour had come, O Lord!'

'We were all paranoid, Morris. We thought London was going to end up looking like a sugary pancake.'

'How many were killed here in the end, Hugh?'

'London lost 250,000 in about nine months.'

'Wow, that many? You haven't added a zero?'

'No.'

'How d'you remember?'

'Because I lost people I knew. Tell me about nerve gas. My card's running out.'

He tells me that in 1936 one Gerhard Schrader, working on chemicals for agricultural use, discovered a pesticide so lethal it was reserved for military use only: human beings instead of ants or slugs or beetles. *Suck Me Rob.* A minuscule dose was sufficient to block nerve transmission and bring on rapid death via uncontrolled twitching and paralysis. *Samantha's Tits Taste Nice.* The Nazis produced thousands of tons of this nerve gas in the late thirties and called it Tabun. Spell it, Morris. (I'm writing it down on my palm, along with the rest: TABUN.) *Ross and Mandy Shag Here.*

'It was never used. Amazing.'

'Why not, Morris?'

Wish I was Ross.

Sigh, like the sea.

'OK, I'm scrolling. The Nazis, poor deluded fools, were kind of convinced that British scientists had discovered similar agents and would zap back in kind. Isn't that Mutually Assured Destruction before its time? The British hadn't in fact discovered a bean. Correction. I'm scrolling up some more. Click. OK. They'd isolated the chemical that transmits impulses across nerve junctions. But that's all. Big deal.'

My palm is a mess, like a stone covered in runes. Why didn't I bring some paper? Why do I have this obsession about keeping my pockets clean?

'But the Germans must have *known* they didn't know, Morris. They only had to keep up with things, with developments over here. They must have gone to conferences before the war, asked questions, snooped about.'

'The glaring gap in British scientific papers was interpreted by the Nazis as censorship, it says here. That's called projection, in my book. It also says that if they had known the truth, we'd have been mincemeat.'

'Not mincemeat, Morris. Twitching horribly to death all over the place, maybe, but without a single scratch. A sort of mass lockjaw. Paralysis and agony.'

'I was speaking figuratively. We'd have been cooked, anyway. The end of civilisation. Apocalypse.'

'So things ran that close. Saved by a blank.'

'Yeah, a supposition extrapolated from a blank. I guess there weren't very many good spies in those days. I guess they didn't have Internet. Anyway, why do you want to know, my good friend?'

'What's the antidote, Morris?'

'Ah, um, atropine. Whatever that is.'

Remember, Mother?

Jason Scalehorne Wanks.

'Atropine? Are you sure?'

I'm blushing furiously, though Morris doesn't see that. There are lurid faces pressed up against the phone booth's glass, ugly and orange in the lamplight.

'Not bleach, Morris?'

I turn my back on the disco louts but they've started tapping and banging and calling me names.

'Hang on, Hugh. I seem to remember bleach being around. Chloride of lime, wasn't it? Don't crowd me. I'm scrolling right now. Yeah, bleaching powder for neutralising the stuff. You only take atropine if you're poisoned but it has to be quick. So you're too late. Anyway, in your case it's probably just nerves.'

I thank him very much and hang up. I open the door but can't say anything to the louts. They're waiting for me to say something but I can't, the mention of atropine has made me too small. I glance at my scrawled-on palm as I hide it: TABUN like the name on a tombstone, or a writer's big idea. I see it as a drum booming through the forest – and then I gasp, I see it, I gasp. 'Oh my God!' The door thumps shut. The louts gawp around me, mere kids again.

'Hey, he's having one of them heart attacks.'

I stagger forward a few paces, collect my stride, and walk away quickly. Faces on my back, as if they're up close breathing on it hotly. They jeer and wolf-whistle and one cries, 'Yo ho ho and a bottle of rum!' while another shouts, in a strong village burr, 'You've forgotten your pacemak*urr*,' but feebly, as if I might come back and clout him. Laughter like a single shout.

Of course you remember atropine, Mother. You and Aunt Joy would pronounce it to rhyme with 'sin', Nuncle to rhyme with 'whine', Father as if it was Latin. Horrible taste, humiliation in a sticky green bottle. You thought I did it deliberately, in protest. It dried my mouth out and I drank more and the problem got worse. The sheets flapped on the line, including the rubber one. I think that's why I never invited anybody to the house. Up until I went to Randle, beaten for it three times at Flytings. If the Dorniers had dropped nerve gas instead of H.E. and incendiaries, I'd have probably been the one person to have survived.

Nuncle with his bleach and atropine, and myself. Among the trees. With the jolly von Thuleites. What a fine start to paradise.

Your loving son,
Hugh

324

Not terribly good weather. On and on. Mud where they've introduced football.

Dearest Mother,

I'm doing fine.

We have to go back to that symposium of 1937, just for a bit: the copies spread on the table, for sale at some outrageous price, illustrations by an Eric Gill acolyte without the talent, Rachael turning the pages languidly. The cover features Nubat himself, looking like one of those bead-tressed derelicts who hang about Netherford clocktower, with huge dogs.

There were a few Germans still present – not jolly Thule types but the eminent academic sort with prissy smiles imitating that horrible *gauleiter* Heidegger. And the odd German kept on coming until just a few months before war was declared. Tabun must have been mentioned before then, obviously. Top secret, but they would have fished a bit, tried to find out whether the British bods at Cambridge and places had really (as they'd assumed) stumbled on the same.

Ted gives me a little wave with his drying-up cloth as I slip past the bar's back door for a steadying nip of my malt.

The next thing I remember is standing by the wildwood. I can't remember everything, can I?

Have you clicked yet, Mother? One of your favourite Father Brown stories started with that comment about dogs – that they're all right as long as they're not spelt backwards. Well, Nubat is all right as long as he's not spelt backwards.

I see it all, standing by the wildwood's moonlit tangle. The knowledge must have enthralled Nuncle. No wonder he had this apocalypse fetish! The silky thread of salvation is so fine, spun out of the belly of the white worm: he knew people on the fringe of the top science bods, must have discovered that no one had the foggiest, that there wasn't so much as a milligram of nerve agent outside Germany – and might so easily have passed this on to the likes of von Sebottendorff, or someone even more rabidly Nazi.

But he didn't, or none of us would be here, or not like we are. The tale of Nubat and his mysterious paralysing powers did not come true. The Stone Age did not come round again. The country of the trees, the smoking huts, the abandoned fields.

But *why* didn't he tell? Perhaps he couldn't bear the prospect of the emptiness being filled by strutting, Teutonic vulgarities, the nationalism he so detested – he didn't even believe in countries! It can't have been the anti-semitism: he was anti everyone who didn't think a Mesolithic bone-prong was the ultimate in technological progress, wasn't he? Even in your day, Mother! God's mistake after the Flood being to spare Noah and his kin. He would even chide you for being a nurse, for trying to interfere with the natural 'decay' of things – 'People should have the same rates of survival as a little oak sapling, my dear!' You would laugh. But I knew how irritated you really were.

My fists are bunched: a minatory gesture. Bulwer's *Minor*, perhaps, as used by all our Lears against the storm, though mine are dangling by my hips. Ah yes. I am in a kind of enthralled rage. An owl hoots. Not even birds in his poisoned Palaeolithic paradise. Perhaps Nuncle preferred the idea of just holding us all in the palm of his hand, the whole shebang rolled around in his palm like a ball of earth. Each morning he got up and thought: all I have to do is to tell my German friends that *we don't know of this*. And whoosh. Or crump. Or whistles – yes, probably whistles, like kettles on the boil, like that wretched man!

Then silence. No, screams. Then moans. The whole island twitching, all of us helpless in our puddles of piss, blind and incontinent, along with the animals, maybe the birds, probably even fish belly up in the rivers, don't know about the plants and trees, maybe as after Chernobyl, maybe not, maybe hitting only sophisticated nervous systems after all, cockroaches continuing to scuttle, flowers to bloom, birds to chirrup, rats squeaking – while the minutes of twitching subside to paralysis and peace, the Third Reich waiting with the ovens, the hoovers, the meticulous cleaning-up plans, and Nuncle with his bleach ready to greet them, like a cleaning-lady before the conquest-flesh'd prince and his scaly troops. *In poison there is physic.* Oh yes.

Greeting them with *what*? Just a lot of Vim? Now that's where I get very very clever. I walk up and down by the wildwood, sniffing, on the scent at last. Literally on the scent, Mother. Ah, what if I could prove all this! What sweet revenge, to shatter a reputation, however minor! Nuncle's is big enough for me. Always some mumbo-jumbo or other in print, the flame kept flickering by the Edward Arnold Society, letters from nut-roast types requesting some piddling piece of information sent on to his nephew, who tears them up into pieces. Even here!

I sniff the night air, the length of the wildwood along the lawn. There!

Garlic. That lingering garlic smell, pungent somewhere but thinned out here so that it vanishes after a few minutes. Always the danger of gas, that – getting accustomed to it when it can still scald and blister.

It's there, then it vanishes.

It was so delicate, it might have been imagined. It might even have been imagined as something sweetly vegetal, like ramsons.

I stride back up the garden and enter the house by the front door for the first time, the door shrieking as I push. A thorn from Wall's slicing, caught and shrieking over the tiles.

I flash the torch over the crates in the cellar, then prise off one of the lids with violent jerks of the jemmy's claw: tins labelled *Vanco*. White bleaching powder. Bleach and nothing but. I smell hospitals and the swabbed insides of bombers. *Vanquish armies of germs with Vanco*. Only one of the crates is different in any way, a little smaller: this contains several large bottles of Optrex eye lotion and some metal eye-baths. Soothes the eyes when attacked by gas. Gas goes for the eyes first. *It is suitable for young and old alike*. No date anywhere, though. That would have clinched it.

I sit among the crates and close my eyes and try not to think of the stiff rags in the shadows. I imagine the stuff crawling under the door and down the steps, heavier than air, invisible, a whiff of garlic and then nothing though still deadly, still penetrating, still persistent. And what does Tabun smell like? Can anyone ever know, if it's so deadly? Odourless, I expect. Did Nuncle sit down here when he, and only he, knew what thread the world hung by from his finger, balancing the pros and cons, smiling at the possibilities? Something large scuttles at the back, a flash of eyes, then silence. A cat, or a living rat. I hurry out without looking back.

Facing again the steely gropings of the massed trees of the wildwood, the moon now clear of the tops. Mad rat, my foot. Why do grown-ups lie all the time? How do these lies manage to linger on with their sharp little teeth, even unto old age, Mother? Why did Nuncle want to do such things to me?

I'm speaking of the other thing. The bundle on the table, here. We'll come to it.

I'm inside the wildwood before I know it – the effect of Wall's strimming, because I'm half-expecting the unkempt edge of nettles and brambles. I never even felt the springiness of the fallen chicken wire underfoot.

The moonlight carves and probes its way deep into the interior, scattering silver doubloons behind it. The wind's sorting them out. It's more like a forest, now, more like the bush. How does moonlight manage such nothingness in its shadows, such black nothingness set among the bright bones?

I manage to go twenty, thirty yards without scratching myself, until the glare of the lawn is shut off by the growth behind me. Mostly lime trees, wasn't it? A few oaks, alders, birch. Maybe it is a tiny patch of the original bush, after all. Maybe not. Does it matter? I stand, sniffing for the wild garlic smell, waiting for my eye to smart. This time, nothing. Either I'm accustomed or the wind's dispersing it. No pungency or even hints of it, no sensation of poisoned air. Yet the wind is not cold, and gas rises in warm air, blowing out to the fringes of the village, creeping in under doorways and over window sills, even in these double-glazed times.

Then I remember the cows, how they'd stood in a line away from the garden's wire. I should talk to the Jennets – go up there tomorrow, ask them if their cows wheezed and wept. I'm still on the scent. The stockpile must be somewhere in here. Waiting for them. The victors. The scaly-flesh'd, unsuspecting troops. The reptilian survivors.

And then? After Nuncle had dealt with them? Like a thane killing his guests in the mead hall? The lowest trick?

Nothing but this, of course. Trees. As it was. Silent. The little wildwood spreading like algae, silently. The animals slowly returning as after the Ice Age but not for a long time.

This.

I hear rustles ahead.

Speckles of moonlight. Not a breath of wind for a moment.

Then I definitely see something move, or flit, between the trees about ten yards or so to the side. Twigs snap above the blowing gusts and the pitter-patter of the falling leaves as the shadow, then the light, is clouded by movement. As if a piece of the cross-hatched moonlight had detached itself and shifted a few yards, no more than that.

It might have been a deer, it might have been a woman. It might have been the Green Man. Might have been the wine at supper, the beer. Stand stock-still. Only the monotonous, mechanical, hoarse whistle of some owl or other, I never remember which one, disturbed into its drill. The wind gusting about a little, but that's all. On and on the call goes, as it always used to do, audible from my window on sleepless summer nights. I think the presence might be you, Mother. After all, you could be very close, if my detestable thick wet lump of a thought holds any water. I'm hoping it's you and not Nuncle, or Aunt Rachael, or Aunt Joy, or Sir –!

No. Not him.

Stillness. Breaths of wind. Stillness.

I make a sudden, jerking movement with my leg; no response. Gone to ground, perhaps. Perhaps a badger. Yes. Where does the wildwood end? I have never thought of the wildwood as ending. Nuncle's fault, going on about the great original wildwood, rolling unhindered from cliff to cliff. Yet I know it slopes to a freshet, to a boggy place of bright moss and tangled alders, before the rise of Jennets' field – but that end was never drawn in my head. And on the other side, towards the village? That was where the army camped, on that rough field where the gypsies used to camp before them – where you once found a rare orchid among the iron bits and bobs, Mother. Gypsies frightened me. Their dead return to avenge themselves.

My hands are bright, the skin like milk just starting to boil. It's the leaves sifting the moonlight. Like Jekyll's changing hands in that old film we watched in the village, a draught billowing the sheet – old Mr Belcher shouting at Mr Linzey to look lively and hang on to the picture, stop her blowing out that blasted door, look. Hands billowing!

I retract my own into my own sharp shadow. They come out again as if not really mine – as they did in the brighter moonlight of Africa, when I'd turn them into claws, frighten myself with myself. And after that film in the village, I spent a long time gumming the horse-hairs collected from the farm, until my hand was hidden behind a swart mass, more like a gorilla's than a man of evil. Aunt Joy was dead by then, or I'd have teased her with it. Instead I made Mrs Stump shriek, creeping my fingers around the back door. I can't remember being punished.

I retract and advance them again, let them come out of the moonlight again. They're not mine any more. They have their own life. Like that story of yours you told us on your last leave. Father was away on a bush tour and I was away in England, you went into the chop-shed one night, bright moonlight, and you reached up for a tin and instead of your hand coming out of the blackness into the ray of moonlight, there was a small monkey's paw, covered in a sort of transparent porridge –

'Protoplasm.'

That's Nuncle. He has to have his say. The hearth's crackling, throwing our shadows against the spotty wallpaper. You're wringing your hands and your cheeks twitch. They always twitch when you tell us this sort of story about home, about some close shave or other. Nuncle smiles knowingly behind his pipe, hooding his eyes – but you say that whatever it was, it was most disagreeable and you couldn't go back in the chop-shed alone for weeks.

I'm turning back, now. My eye-patch and cheek are scratched by a bramble I don't even see. A thicket, as if just grown up! Gathering my bearings (it's like one enormous X-ray, if you know what I mean), my fingers close on the clawed jemmy in my coat pocket. Of course! What luck! I bring my sleeve up to the knuckles so that only the claw of the jemmy obtrudes, flashing in the moonlight, and slash. Slash again. The brambles catch my sleeve. I tug it free, the stems falling back with a snigger.

A snigger?

It wasn't the brambles, I think. I grip the jemmy and silence my breathing. I must really look the pirate, now: Captain Hook, perhaps. Or Black Dog. Wanting two fingers of the left hand. Blade loosening in the sheath. Give Bill a little surprise. Pieces of moonlight. Blind Pew in the frosty fog. Croaking of the crows in the wood. My mother almost entirely exposed. Flint's fist –

A snigger. A human snigger.

Get some lead in him. Pieces of eight, pieces of eight. All that.

I move forward towards the snigger, waving my hook to clear the scrog out of the way. A figure rises. Hooded, dark. Bright nose in a slash of moonlight.

Then more of the face.

'What the *hell* are you doing here?'

I'm spittling. Oh, I'm in such a rage! Terror straight into rage! I wipe my mouth. Well, I'm old. Mrs Pratt's son's looking terrified, now. It's my face, I realise. I'm showing my gums, my teeth must be so unnaturally white.

'Just sitting,' he says, in an unintentioned falsetto.

'You know it's private property.'

'Is it?'

Another snigger and a crash. A friend emerges next to him. Something flashes the moonlight – good grief, it's the claw – my upraised arm holding back leaves, the metal at the end of it. Hook. The two pale faces are so soft, like the faces in the war moving through London or through the sky or wherever metal might shred them. Metal doesn't flinch. Flying metal and glass are as free of mercy, Mother, as a leopard's eyes. You'd be wasting your breath, pleading.

Your affectionate son,
Hugh

Aconites in the snow. Or sweetpapers.

My dear Mother,

I've had quite a few visitors. One of my finest actors and his little boy, for instance. The little boy didn't like my patch.

I lower my arm, let the leaves rustle back.

'Get out.'

They don't move.

'Are you on drugs?'

Silence.

'Did you know that this wood has a mad rat?'

A glance at each other.

'Does it?'

Mrs Pratt's son is the age I was when gazing on Rachael through binoculars. The owl has stopped. Then starts.

'Mad owls,' I say.

'We like it.'

The other boy doesn't speak, but nods. Then it's a girl, her face moving into the light. Her jaw is large, the rest of her face balances uncertainly on top of it. Their youth touches me, Mother. My blood is already cooling.

'If you're not doing anything chemically harmful to yourself, then carry on, but not in here.'

They nod. I follow them out, they seem to know a path. We emerge on to the lawn.

'Em, are you really famous?'

'Yes. Horribly. But it makes no difference, in the end. When you're prime minister you will remember the pirate in the woods as if you're not prime minister. The moonlight. The owl. The mad rat.'

The girl draws in her breath, sharply. I ask if they've been coming here long. Yeah, at least two months. I ask the girl if she's had runny eyes, a stingy throat, after being in the wood. She giggles and shrugs. Her eyes look bleared in the steely light, her face a white mask with dark little spots on the chin. Sloppy sweater hiding her hands. Mrs Pratt's son lowers his hood. It must be the same bright red blouson, but the moonlight makes it a dull brown, like old blood. Where the shadows are, it is pitch black; not even the brightest colour can escape night's scissors. No wonder I never saw it back there. Was I talking to myself, then, out loud? Annoyance rises again.

'You're supposed to be in bed, aren't you, David?'

'Dominick. I'm not ill. It's just boring.'

'What is?'

'Oh, mothers. Bye!'

332

They leave me, moving sedately over the lawn. Perhaps they were talking, petting, nothing more. I'm an old irascible bully. I shout after them:

'Tell him to play some *Venom*, next time!'

Laughter, then friendly shouts of 'All right!' They run off, leaving the stale and hoary to itself. I could have ticked them off, torn a strip off them, but what a dreary residue to leave after I'm dead and gone! Residues are important, aren't they, Mother?

Your loving son,

Hugh

Frosts. Misty all day. A throat. I don't want to grow vegetables.

My dearest Mother,

They thought the last one or two a bit short.

They're terribly good, on the whole.

There's blood on my face.

The spots of it are almost black on my fingers. The lawn is empty, too big to cross.

My legs ache rather a lot.

The dead grass gleams where John Wall cut it. The moon is so lovely, chasing its shreds of cloud, a halo of mist around the gawping face. Or screaming face, mouth wide open. Or laughing. Big flat-faced man in it.

He isn't where he was.

The second moon was a dream, because the third moon has not shifted as far, yet it has moved. My forehead's encrusted with blood, some of it in my ear.

Way after midnight, I should think. I don't carry a watch. The owl has started up again, like a wind-up toy or a very slow metronome.

Blackness, the black moor and the starry firmament. Orion's Belt. It has four stars, now. Moving in formation. Well spotted, shine a light on it, angle 18. Sheep everywhere bleating, shoving me as I struggle with the searchlight. It's switched on but the damn thing's tipped over, it wants to roll its huge black drum down the slope. The others wave their arms at me, they're just like moths in the great cone of light. I'd better get it upright because the light of the universe is gushing out of it. All roaring and booming out of this plug-hole and the light going down everywhere, all over the universe – the stars fading, the sun shrinking, the moon not bright enough to see itself in any of the lakes. There's a raw smell of darkness, even Sirius can't hang on. The night air's shrivelling up and getting terribly cold. Oh, bother. Nuncle's flying around laughing at me, so I throw myself on the hole. I'm swallowed in light. I've saved the universe. The population of the world is clapping, it's nice but terribly loud. Right overhead. I'm awake now, that's the trouble. Very cold with this light engulfing me, clawing me into bright pieces and this terrible monotonous clapping. Pieces flake off my clothes as I try to stand up, with the light pouring down so I think perhaps the moon is crashing towards the earth, the apocalypse, the end. This is the end. Heart attack. This is death! I'm awake and this is death!

Then the light swings away like a huge tent. It billows over the lawn and across the house, the house rears up like an hallucination of what it ought to be. Stripped of its dimness and dark-ness, startled because never has it been stripped like this before – the eyes blind shocks of light, the porch gaping in surprise, then black.

Away the light goes, and I see it thinner, sucked up into the belly of a helicopter. A little blue insect devouring every little gleam and sliver, sucking it all up in a cone of sheer glare, leaving only a black deadness. Bursts of leaves still flying and scattering where the helicopter's blades took them, sheering low. Violet after-images hovering in front of my nose. I'm crouching in absolute terror, crouching as if a shell's about to land.

Someone missing? Am I missing?

An upside-down searchlight, that one. I stagger to my feet. I'm cold to the bone, numb with it. What on earth was I *doing*, sleeping out?

Back in the pub, I wash my scratch, just a little tear in my bag of juices. It's no more than that. A lot of blood in the forehead, Mother. I have to clean the ceramic with a sponge. Ted's fussy about that sort of thing.

Bad night. Too much light in my head. I unscrew the bulb but another one swells up. Disagreeable faces I know.

Your loving son,
Hugh

Too warm.

My dear Mother,

I must write more, they suggest. No one does anything here but suggest. I now have an electric kettle.

'Who's missing, Ted?'

He grunts, topping up the teapot, clearing away my kippers' bones.

'That Pratt boy and a girl, the Walters girl.'

'But they left the wood.'

'Eh?'

'They were in my wood. They definitely left it.'

'Were they now? Nasty scratch, that. Not Fatso, I hope.'

He's holding the teapot against his cardie, shaking it gently. I ache in various places.

'I can tell someone, if it helps.'

'I wouldn't bother. Too late.'

A chill seizes me.

'Oh God. How?'

'Eh?'

'Both of them, was it? Oh no.'

'Wasting our taxes. Imagine what that chopper costs. No one gets a wink of bloody sleep. All out on the square with poles and torches at five this morning, getting our brief. Then where do you think they were found?'

I picture them at the bottom of the pond, for some reason, holding hands with weeds about their stark-white staring faces.

'Sneaking in to her place. Oh, were we missed, Dad?'

He chortles. The teapot's spout dribbles tea leaves on his cardie, but he doesn't notice. 'His mum didn't half give him a drubbing, apparently. That Lizzie Pratt.'

He bends closer, whispering.

'Known as Dizzy Prattle, to everybody but her.'

After breakfast, I undo the oil-paper package and take out the

335

letters. It's sunny today. I will bicycle out to Windmill Hill. Nuncle thought Windmill Hill was evil. If there are people, there are people. I quite like reading with something else to look up at: families, cheerful and wind-blown. Do my headache good.

Aunt Joy's rusty machine serves me well, properly oiled: I walk the rougher part of the path from Avebury Trusoe, leading the bike, its tyres whitening on the chalk. The swarms dwindle in the two miles to the hill, apart from a walking group of my own vintage. Some recognise me and stare as they pass, nudging their companions. Twenty or thirty of them. On and on but in the opposite direction, away from the hill, thank goodness, towards the Avebury stones and tea. Last time I was here, the only people I saw were working in the fields, which are now empty. No haystacks to roll off, these days. A few sheep hanging on.

Rustling low beech hedge to my left. Ignore it.

Just a handful of roamers on the hill itself. The noticeboard is blank apart from Malcolm's sticker. It's tiny, like a self-adhesive label, not a big bold thing at all – 'Stop McDestruction', with something about cattle ranchers destroying forests and wildlife, 'People and Nature before Profits', or words to that effect. I feel a sudden pang of affection for Malcolm, looking at it – the fact that it's so small, stuck on crookedly. Perhaps he lifted up his daughter to do it, on one of her visits.

A bit breezy now and again, but the views clear and sunny, Silbury Hill as always like the grass dome of some interred cathedral. I settle on a hump, children running about around me, squealing. Then I'm left pretty well alone. Vague ripples and bumps, can't recall which was what, enclosures, barrows, different times overlapping, Neolithic, Bronze Age, different needs and desires. Nuncle gesticulating in wind, his big coat flapping, hat pressed to his head, showing me where the short-horned cattle were brought up, where the first fields of England were dug and sown on the slopes below, where the bulge-skulled dwarf was sacrificed that Keiller unearthed. Me bored stiff, cold in my long shorts. It didn't strike me as being the navel of evil, the inner circle of our hell. It was too chilly for that. But at least he was taking me out.

I'm unwrapping the bundle, Mother.

Now, I mean. Here.

I will proceed in my account as if I didn't know what I now know.

I unwrap the bundle and trap its oil paper under the bike's weight. The letters take a minute to sort chronologically, since there are only ten, but each one is several pages. Must be some lost, lost to ants or mould. The drab stuff – orders, accounts, lists – are to do with your job. Optrex eye lotion, rolls of lint, compressed absorbent wool, jaconets, gauze, peptonised milk, dressing scissors, thermometers, a request for a Surgical Pocket Case for Field Work. All those arms against the sweltering air! The residue of all that effort – just these crinkly carbon copies – the only faint proof! Imagine!

Skeletal ants in the folds, who once crawled about in Bamakum. A pin, rusted. A *Vogue* cover, tightly folded, its thin plumed girl in a leopard-skin shawl (truly!), her blue dress flowing out from her like water. Scrawled in ink at the bottom, below the name of the artist: *Plain gauze for poultices 6 yards, 10d. Gamgee tissue?* A childish scribble of a tree or a green monster that might have been mine.

I read the first letter again, the others kept in place under my picnic box. Such joy, such energy. This is not really what I remember. Arrival in Africa, stalled at Buea, but still happy, still singing the bright glee of your marriage. The sense of someone more daring than me, at your age, better equipped for outlandish things, far from family and friends. Your voice, Mother, so young and bright and funny, not at all the voice I remember. You were wearier, when I knew you. You had always been part of Africa. You had a pink mask, that was all.

Yet here you were just arriving, dew-fresh, knowing nothing about it.

A toddler in a postbox-red jumpsuit, staring at me, open mouth dribbling, standing astraddle as if about to draw his guns in a Western. I'm on the third letter. Still vivid and amusing. Your letters to me were never like this – you ran out of steam. The toddler won't go away, it looks mentally subnormal and has what Aunt Joy used to call a green nose that bubbles as it breathes, but someone must love it.

And then I want to weep, seeing how much you wanted to show me what you were like once, tucking these in with my clothes and toys, keeping Father out of it. The toddler toddles up with a sort of bouncer's waddle and flaps the oil paper about, tearing it. I should be telling this poor monstrous dwarf off but one has to be very careful these days. I look about and see a couple of women chatting on the slope below. There's no one else around, now. Perhaps it's nearing lunchtime, pub time. Yes, it is: it's after twelve-thirty.

'Go to Mummy,' I say. 'Go to Mum. Go on. Scat. Din-dins.'

The toddler gawps, dribbling more profusely than ever from its lolling lip. The bulge of nappy makes it look like a red pear on legs, its incontinence detectable on sweet-sour wafts. Very blonde hair, almost transparent and plastic-looking, sticking up and pulled about by the slightest breeze. The Neolithics were dark, I think; they came up from the Mediterranean, into our cold and fog. The toddler is now clawing at the letters, bending double only at the waist, right down like African women picking millet outside Ikasa, whose backs were always straight.

'No!' I say, firmly.

It takes no notice. There was never anyone else here, before the war, except the odd shepherd in a felt hat and string to keep his trousers up. Oh, the odd lusty hiker or amateur digger in shorts and long socks. But I want to laugh: your first letters have filled me with your joy, your youth, your hope. The toddler actually has one of your letters in its hand now, flapping it about as if it's stuck there, perplexed by its persistence. No, it's enjoying the noise. The carbon copy paper makes an interesting noise. It's the last letter in the bundle and in two pages. If I try to snatch it, it'll tear. Now the toddler's grinning, eyeing me as if I should be appreciating this too. I'm on my feet, encouraging the creature to hand over the letter. I have no idea how to speak to toddlers, really. I'm not even sure of its sex. I'm holding my hands out and bending down, back aching, saying, 'Give it to me, come on,' and glancing at the women, wondering whether to call them. It flaps the pages about violently now, closing its eyes as if firing a gun. Dust swirls through the air.

The toddler holds my life, my happiness, in its chubby hand. Pale violet marks on a page, flapping about.

Bent low over it, starting to tickle it, I'm stunned by its finger jabbed on my eye-patch. The letter is now hovering in the light breeze, on its own, like an enormous butterfly, turning over and coiling and separating into its separate pages before they descend and quiver on the grass a few yards off. I chase them as they're wafted another few yards through the air. The toddler's now at my picnic box, the other letters ruffling – such light paper, almost like rice paper. This is ridiculous. The last letter crinkling in my fist, loping back, my Achilles tendon tweaking for some reason. All I do is pull the toddler away and tap it ever so very lightly on the wrist. Such a tiny wrist, such a very tiny tap. More a touch than a tap. It instantly wails, of course. Wails and wails.

Bringing the mother. Head swivelling in instinct, blood calling. I stand helplessly, as if I've dropped a vase and the owner's running at the smash. She's not cross with me, exactly, more embarrassed, suspicious too, apologising and burying the toddler's face in a handkerchief but also wondering what might have happened – which I am explaining but also rubbing away, not wanting to blame a toddler for something, not wanting to sound peevish so sort of chuckling about it, crumpling the letter in my fist, making a paperweight of my foot.

'Oo, you're niffy,' she says, lifting the wailing thing to her face so that its midriff bulge is at nose-level, then snuggling her face into it. 'That's the trouble. She wanted to be changed.'

I'm glad it's a she, for some reason. The mother takes her away and she's changed there and then on the slope below me, the second woman glancing back as if I've done something wrong, not softening the glance with a smile. I feel too exposed on this hill, and the breeze is getting up. Silly decision. A Sunday, different in the week. Everybody disgorged on Sunday. I leave the letters for a moment, tucked back in the pannier, and eat my sandwich. Take time. Relish Mother's new voice.

Tabun. Nerve, nervous, what a nerve. Picturing Malcolm's musical up here, I, Nubat – awful songs probably, drizzling on the equipment, audience huddled on the slope in anoraks, usual thing. Fire-eaters, jugglers, shouting you can't hear, crackly guitars, a

339

dog running amok amongst the costumes, the cables. Should I tell him about Tabun? Only increase his enthusiasm. Edward Arnold saved the day. Have everyone dropping dead and twitching, twitching and dropping dead I mean, like that Ionesco play or the end of *Hamlet*. Awful lyrics about nerve gas, slides probably, Hiroshima sneaking in, the Gulf War. Multi-media. The arts bods loving it because it's a pot-pourri of sensations and terribly accessible, a floor-show for flounderers.

The letters I've read and not read rustle in the pannier. Mother in the bush, on the steamer. Those old names. Herbert E. Standing as the real person, not in cricketing togs at all. Gallantry as he left for the bush, to die. Tarbuck's stammer. Chief Ibofo, still young. Hargreaves, though haven't met him yet, haven't got to Bamakum even. Maybe we'll get to the bottom of the Lyle's Golden Syrup mystery. Maybe not. Not easy to read, have to read slowly: pale violet carbon, smudged, stained. Faded, of course – but the voice as fresh as if it was talking to me. No Quiri yet.

The toddler goes off between the two women, like a prisoner. No, that's unfair. Maybe the mother's sister or sister-in-law. Aunt Joy. The family in rings rippling out around it, to the furthest cousin. Not it, it's a her. Never learned her name. Could have been my granddaughter. Loneliness of no kin. But then think of Ray Duckett: not much help, his sons. Family after family after family, here, with their shorthorn cattle at first, then maybe goats, then countless generations later it was sheep, sheep and more sheep, and now each one arriving for an instant with woofy dogs and their little worries, incomes, recreational hours, growing memories like sponges on a reef. That time that man with the eye-patch. Can never be too careful.

A crow passes, sounding a couple of alarming croaks, as if a great ratchet in its throat is turning. The little toddler is a red blob now, way down where the big field's ploughed to the road half a mile off.

A lark, at last. Plain when they come down, brown and plain, they're noble and tiny and so very ecstatic when they're Shelleyising, as Rachael called it. Instead of shrilling. Rachael. Rachael. That scene in *Twelfth Night*, a Clown with a tabor, talking to Viola. What does he say? Something about sentences like gloves, turned inside-out by a good punning wit but then they're wrong, they're wanton. Not wanting his sister to have a name because a name is a word and to dally with that word might make her wanton. 'Rachael', with its secret entrances and nobbly bits, its openings into paradise. We might have had children, then grandchildren. Family lines. Viola and the Clown with a tabor have family lines. I am the last. After me, I suppose, it's a blank, not even a squiggle.

I can still see the red blob, now really a dot, as I munch my apple. When she's seventy, I'll be a hundred and thirty-eight. Doesn't sound so much older, put like that. Her red dot like the complementary dab Cézanne or Constable or maybe all of them put in to off-set the blue-green, like now. Puffs of turning trees, straw light in the air, autumnal. A poppy or a streak on a roof or just a red something, a splotch of red shadow, or the whole painting would go soft.

Then I freeze, the apple at my mouth. Oh my God. Oh my goodness.

Mrs Pratt's son, last night.

Oh my God.

With the apple at my mouth.

Your loving son,

Hugh

Sopping dullness. Wind cuffing the glass. Been like this for a fortnight. Cheers me up.

My dearest Mother,

I bite the apple. Sounds just like a burst of ack-ack.

I now know who Adrian S is. Why that bedside scribble out of *Macbeth*, a few nights back.

Adrian Samoiloff. The legendary lighting wizard from the 1930s. Converted a Henley Regatta scene into a Turkish harem at a touch of the switchboard. *Richard III*, Nottingham Rep, 1949 (Hugh Arkwright as Rivers); the whole cast turning from royal purple to funereal black on the death of Henry the Sixth, without moving a muscle. The complementary of red is blue-green:

moonlight has blue in it, its albino steeliness has blue in it. Dominick's blouson turned the colour of old blood. Without red light waves, redness cannot exist: nothing to bounce back into our eyes, Mother. Enter ten ladies in bright red gowns. Blue-green flood, up full. Ten red gowns snap into ten black gowns. They're ready for the funeral.

Now I understand that scribbled note in the night! *Making the green one red.*

So concentrate, Hugh. Finish your ack-ack apple and concentrate.

What had Gracie Hobbs said? She'd been singing carols, had an Aladdin lamp on a chain but she didn't need it. Then walking back, afterwards, after the drinks, saw the Red Lady in the lane. We had Aladdins in Africa – the moths swaddled their gentle light each dusk. God, I didn't think twice, when she said it: she didn't need the lamp not because she knew the words but – *because it was a bright night!* As bright as last night. A clear, full moon, as described in the *Netherford Weekly News* I looked at only a few days ago.

The snow shone, twinkling. A night brighter than a leaden day. Perhaps the cocks crew, confused. Perhaps even I noticed, sick in my darkened room.

Gracie Hobbs could not have seen a cherry-red coat that night – no, not with the snow and the full moon! It would have been the umbrous brown of old blood, wouldn't it?

I eat the core, pips and all.

Oh dear, Gracie. Oh dear. Anyway, that night has gone and for good. Like trying to hold a piece of light in your childhood hand, pretending it's a diamond. But the letters have brought you so close, I'm not all that upset, more embarrassed. I wipe my hands on the grass and read on, about other days and nights before my time.

Have you ever been to Pisa, Mother? Just after the war I met an American bomber-pilot who had bombed the railway junction there in 1944. He'd dropped incendiaries but messily, too high up, like the Americans did. The leaning tower, the cathedral, the old sun-warmed mossy roofs, all shrunk to a pale patch in olive green beneath him. Now he was shrunk and pale, too: it was his incendiary shell that had bounced on to the roof of the Campo Santo, he reckoned. Set it alight. Six centuries of rich bequests dabbed and stroked on to the cloister's walls – gilded horses and blue-winged angels and soft lumps of hills speared by cypress trees, the hundreds of faces spread either side of the sun-striped walk, all so busy. A kind of miracle, an alchemy of faith and grace and sheer zest!

Blistered to nothing in an hour. The only painting to survive was the Day of Judgement, full of leering devils shovelling sinners into flames and boiling oil, tweaking their noses with giant pincers, all that. He told me that on balance he'd rather not have been born, if by not being born the paintings could have remained.

Mother, up on Windmill Hill, putting the last letter down, I think of him. I think of that surviving painting. I think of myself looking at that painting in the ante-room a few years later and thinking of him. Then of myself looking at the scratchy old black-and-white photographs of all those lost frescoes in another room and thinking of him. Then of myself looking at the petroglyphs of nail holes and awl holes on the scorched brick of the cloister's walls and thinking of him. And how I'd heard by then from a friend that he'd killed himself, soon after our meeting. An eye for an eye, and all that. Shovelled down into the boiling oil and searing bunsen-burners of hell, clutching his Air Force cap. So much alarm and dismay in that painting; I stood and pictured the flames of his bomb throwing huge shadows upon its terrible liveliness, as if the painted flames had escaped from themselves. It had rippled and blistered in places, around the grimaces and grinnings and even around the benign smiles of the saved on their celestial escalator – some of them surprised no doubt, but not showing it. It had survived, prevailed over the damage, over the smouldering debris of the rest.

Isn't it extraordinary, Mother, that I should be thinking of him, up on that English hill, on a quiet Sunday in October some five decades later, the pile of rice-papery letters at my feet, ruffling in the rising breeze?

All their words read. Every single one in its pale violet. Violation.

343

Some cackling abstract thing pressing a branding iron against my mark, clutching my neck with an ice-cold hand. His slow drawl over the Martini.

'Hey, y'know what I feel? I feel those pictures against my life are no goddam contest. I feel like it might've been kinda better if I'd not been born. Ever feel that, Hugh?'

Please, please, please. No primal exhibitionism, no hysterics. Most of all, no Shakespeare quotes.

(I didn't realise then, Mother. Please bear with me. I am to go with the pain, they said. Think of it as one of your plays. *My* plays? I have never written a play!)

I stay on the hill an hour, maybe two. Perhaps three. People are around but they pass quickly. No one asks me if I'm all right but one doesn't these days and they probably think I'm drunk, a drunken vagrant, lost an eye in a brawl. One pulls away his kid who's come over to see why I'm crouched in a huddle, hugging myself, rocking to and fro. I'm the same shape as that curled-up rosewood Buddha paperweight on the mantelpiece over there – see it? My actors brought it back from Tokyo recently, so kind.

Mad. Mad rat. Don't touch.

Paperweight. The rice-papery bundle such a dreadful weight.

Rocking and moaning. Why shouldn't I? Everyone has the right to self-expression once in a while. Outside doesn't exist for me: I'm very very drunk but on something terribly bitter – quinine, that's it. You always forced me to drink my quinine! If I rock far enough I'll probably roll all the way down to the bottom. But I always rock back, like a clock's weight. Tick tock. People. Voices. Gauche voices. Awkward.

Then there's a moment when I stop, clear my throat, stand, pick up the letters, pick up my bike and walk as if nothing has happened but stiffly, achily, down to the gate. *Stop McDestruction.* That all seems so far away and yet possible, suddenly. Deliriously possible because there's nothing else left to do. When one has no life, no core, sucked of one's blood so one is undead but not alive, one can see how, there being nothing else left to do, all that Malcolm's little sticker says is possible, and I am probably the one to do it. I shout *YES* in a sort of roar and make the family threesome near me jump. Then they walk quickly away under their bobble hats. I wheel my bicycle down the path towards the vast field the other side, where the red blob went and where the Neolithic herdsmen sowed their harmless little plots. I can't go back the way I've come. Not ever again.

The path cuts across the field like a hair-parting. There is no one else. It only leads to the road, way off. It's a long slog. On either side, the dark and stony field. Seagulls scattered over it, but moving, not impaled. A plain of brute matter, the hill rising behind it, eye-catching, its top a place of safety and comfort – I can see this, yes, I can see why they chose it, Nuncle. Comfort? Big hard muscles and thick necks, coughing away in the smoke, dying wrinkled and still young, squawls of babies, fever, damp bones. Ten minutes, and I've still got half the field to go. Why do we live, why all this effort? The package bounces about in the pannier as Aunt Joy's bike bounces on the path. It's like a joyous little animal, in there.

You see what a state I'm in, Mother, after reading all about us.

It takes me years to cross that field. My head keeps lagging behind my body.

'You all right, in there?'

It's Ted, through the door. I'm back in my room, you see. I tell him that I was gargling. There isn't even a tap in my room, but he plods back down anyway.

Sleep.

Black pudding for breakfast. Ted has dry tea leaves stuck in his cardie. I want to get back to when they were wet, freshly slipped from the spout. When I was someone else entirely.

'You ought to see to that scratch.'

It does sting, yes.

'Bed all right, is it?'

Fine, massa, fine.

I'd dreamt it was a coffin, the sheets sliding off with a crash. And the other one, the nightmare. Uncurling from my bed, padding about the pub, seeking all the sleeping faces and giving them a quick claw. Even in the empty numbered rooms below, one face in each, ready for me, all soft. The pub was the house and I slipped into your old room, Mother. You were asleep, like the rest. The art of it in the swiftness, to do it before you screamed.

But no one ever woke up, I was so quick. Working methodically, padding this way and that, my bony supple body so light on its paws, the claws so white and strong. I entered the dark, silent bar and there was Fatso, on his bentwood chair, flat cat's face staring at my flat cat's face advancing towards him but his claw flashes and finds me first, finds my eye! Ohhh! Waking up to a stinging forehead, my blind socket sore – from not being able to make tears, I suppose, like its partner.

Scoundrel! Why did you engender me?

What does Nagg reply?

I didn't know.

> Your loving son,
> Hugh

Sunny intervals. Everything sopping.

My dear Mother,

Not been wonderful recently, but on my two feet again now. Ted hands me more toast.

'Anyway, there was a message for you. Barry phoned. If you want to talk to him before the meeting.'

In five minutes' time. I phone Cliff. He gets me there only fifteen minutes late. He nods at my scratch. 'Tried to be nice to Fatso, did you?'

The council building's all dazzling lino and sick cheese plants. Meeting place like a classroom, same dank smell, looking out on the concrete lump they call the Post Office. Their heads turn and there is a collective gasp. My scratch livid, my eye red, my patch scored, my hair full of woodland flora, my clothes rumpled. The heads are topped by greying or absent hair and set off by loud ties. Jackets stretched on the chair backs. A few rolled-up sleeves. A map of Netherford pricked by red pins just behind me, showing *Sites of Pedestrian and Vehicular Conflict.* Never realised the town was so big, like a hereditary birthmark worsening with each generation.

Brian Padmore eyeing Barry suspiciously, country mouse and town mouse. Barry's tie is thinner, jacket snappier. He looks nervously eager, ready for the kill, the Hugh Arkwright Centre idea sewn up legally. We're told that the Council are to give a start-up and maintenance grant to something called Green Shoot, which gives disturbed youths a second chance. How are they chosen? By their disturbed backgrounds. What is the definition of disturbed? Broken homes, adoption difficulties, 'negative' environment, neglect, mild but unrecognised autism, little contact with adults, loneliness. 'Dysfunctional,' someone says. That's the very first time I heard it, Mother, in that unpleasant room.

'I would,' I say, 'like to do whatever I can to encourage your project.'

Barry's mouth drops open, as if on a ratchet, the longer I don't add a 'but'. The founders of Green Shoot – a fortyish couple with hair almost as wild as mine, sporting lumberjack shirts and ties that look strained – thank me tenderly and suggest I have a place on the charity board. I accept. Barry now frowning at me. The others glance at him as if he might, at any moment, squeak like Piglet. He must have warned them, in my absence, of his client's 'alternative proposal'. Brian looks nonplussed, the comfortable countryman. I avoid Barry's eye as the overhead projector hums into life and an ink drawing of Ilythia wobbles on the white wall.

'Ah, the House of Usher,' I say.

A few laugh. The young but balding architect, in a black waistcoat and fob-watch, taps each image merrily with a stick, as if pointing out anticyclones. Dainty Venusians stroll between immaculate shrubs and converse before the glassed extension, where the growing of plants will drive the chlorophyll of tenderness into those troubled hearts. He wants to be 'sympathetic' to the original house. 'Gut it, go on,' I growl. Titters. The meeting continues in a fog of acronyms and in-words. The Green Shoot people are talking about the woodland, so I raise my hand.

'There's a problem there,' I say.

'A problem?'

Barry perks up, starts shuffling his notes.

'The wildwood – the wood to the left of the beechwood – is poisoned.'

'Poisoned?'

'I have reason to believe that there is an old stock of poison gas

347

there, and it's leaking. Probably mustard – mustard gas. Maybe also lewisite.'

Murmurs and gasps of disbelief. Barry scratches his head.

'First World War, wasn't it?' someone says.

Someone else starts droning on about their grandfather. 'I think we should have it checked,' I interrupt.

Further questions, so I explain: the garlic smell, the dead poacher, the thing about a curse, runny eyes, the diffident cows. The fact that Edward Arnold was rather 'disturbed'. More titters.

'And just to make sure, he fenced it off. I was not allowed in.'

'Was your uncle planning on *using* this stuff?' asks one of the Green Shoot people.

'Of course,' I say. 'He had the messianic touch, you know. All in the cause of a greater good.'

'Which was?'

'To kill everybody off.'

My right bottom eyelid and the upper muscles on my cheek start twitching. A tic so venerable that I am quite fond of it, but it afflicts me only in moments of extreme emotion – and it's not the same as yours, Mother. A thoughtful, slightly amazed silence.

'He liked trees,' I add, pathetically. 'Under the melancholy boughs.'

I keep nerve gas out of it. Anyway, my tic's worsening. I stand, make my apologies, and hurry out into the corridor. To a passing pair of stilettos' amazement, I am sobbing quietly. I don't know if they're amazed, really, but they've certainly swivelled and stopped.

'I'm quite all right,' I sniff. 'It's an allergy.'

Heartily relieved, the stiletto-woman claims she has the same thing, it's the cheese plants – and tic-tocks off over the dazzling lino, her huge, ungainly figure moving me rather deeply. Murmurings through the door, like rumour. I blow my nose and go back in. It all goes better than anticipated.

Afterwards I have to explain to a disgruntled Barry that I've had a change of heart. 'A triple bypass would've been better,' he jokes. 'Must be the country air.' The woodland can't be dug up, but 'a bod' from Environmental's going to check it over. 'You haven't been digging around in there yourself, have you? You look a bit mustardy, if you don't mind me saying.' 'It's been weighing on me, Barry.' Like Midas's servant, I do feel a certain relief; my secret's not dotty any more! Then the letters gush over my head and I have to sit down. My frontal lobe is bare bone and tinted with ochre. It makes me feel very self-conscious, but I mention it to no one, because I know it's not real.

When I'm back, I head straight for Ilythia, pausing only to buy a bottle of paraffin, a packet of bin liners and some matches at the shop. I check Wall isn't about, go up to the attic, open the trunk, and stuff five bin liners. Carrying them one by one down to the garden, I disgorge them near the wrecked summerhouse where Wall has already charred a circle, tuck in a few little stray sleeves, splash most of the paraffin on the heap, and set the thing alight.

   Your loving son,
   Hugh

Fitful sun. Hail has dashed the daffs.

My dear Mother,

The smoke is awful – thick, black, noxious – but a deal of prodding and poking, and the rest of the paraffin, keep the flames at work. After an hour, there's nothing left but a residue of black fibrous material on a pile of ashes, and part of a baby legging that refuses to catch. My scalp and eye itch, my face is greasy with smoke, my hands are black, my clothes stained – but I am terribly happy, terribly happy! Lighter, lighter, much lighter. I ought to burn the letters too, I suppose – but I have never been able to burn words. Anyway, I can't burn my own brain, can I?

I tell those whom I encounter on my way back (Mrs Pratt with her dog yet again, Jenny collecting her children from school in a swarm of mums bowing to little heads, Roger Marlow touching-up the hotel sign in a vile scarlet) that I have been firing leaves. They look quite concerned by my appearance, and I'm too light-headed, it's not normal. I make a strong mug of tea and take it into the bathroom where I run a very hot bath and throw in some bath salts found above the basin. The bath and tea are equally delicious. Lazing in the steam, I congratulate myself. I am a

349

cavalryman, not a foot slogger. My bottom grates on the salts, not quite dissolving as they should. Life, I think. I can still hug life!

I have dealt with the house, yes. I have a clear conscience. I must start afresh, cleanly diving into my new self. For my self is new. I am not who I thought I was, am I? No. (Mother, please forgive me for being so naive. Bear with me. I had not yet begun to realise.) No. No, not at all. Green shoots are springing up all over me, millions of tiny soft warm shoots. Ah yes.

I am, in one way, my own enemy. I must learn to − to respect him. Did the natives not find the crocodile worthy of worship, even as it dragged them to the deeps in its chops?

To love him, even.

Ancestors. Appease them but do not petition them.

I leave a Plimsoll-line of dark, greasy scum on the bath's sides that takes me quite a time to remove with no sponge, no Vim. Ted is in the corridor, to my surprise, when I emerge − a towel around my waist and my eye-patch off. He talks to me with his eyes circling my bared blindness: this looks, to those who don't know it (almost everyone but you, Mother), like a dried date flattened by a sharp heel, though the skin grew successfully over the hole.

'Muck's gone missing,' he says. 'Vanished. Frank Petty. The police are involved. Here we go again.'

Whether it is my exposed left eye, or the mention of the police, I don't know, but he's shifty.

'When you say vanished, do you mean run off, following some misdemeanour?'

'Vanished,' he says again, as if that curtness supplied the answer.

'Oh dear. Well, I'm sure he'll turn up.'

I feel much sympathy towards my fellow human beings, in whatever shape or size, but Muck has strained it, hasn't he? That obscene mime, that awful tune still tiptoeing through my head − it starts up again now, like a hurdy gurdy. I am feeling the chill in the corridor. I nod at one of the locked, numbered rooms.

'Perhaps he's in there, staying for free. You'd better check, Ted.'

Ted doesn't laugh, but quite the contrary: he looks offended. 'Anyway,' I go on, 'if I see him, I'll let you know.'

'Let the boys in blue know, you mean,' he murmurs, rubbing his chin thoughtfully, but really because he is hiding something.

I wait a few seconds. As if proving the truth of oratorical gesture, of theatrical decorum, of everything I have striven to reintroduce, I find my hands in the perfect posture of Bulwer's Gestus 11: *Innocentia ostendo*. Can you believe it! It is the same gesture Mrs Siddons would use when playing the sleepwalking Lady Macbeth – and familiar from all my own productions, Mother. The back of one hand rubs in the hollow of the other, as if you are trying to wash them. You would do this, sometimes.

'The thing is,' he says, 'they've found blood.'

My hands freeze.

I must be betraying my discomfort, because Ted backs away, mumbling something about seeing to the eggs. I want to ask him where they'd found the blood, but the wet chill in my gut makes me cough instead. I mount the steps and enter my room with what feels like the beginnings of belly palaver. As dusk falls, I wonder whether I should leave, for a week or so.

When I look in the mirror, I don't see my face, but someone else's. Neglected and hairy, despite the bath. Teeth bared like a wolf's, showing the gums. So very anxious. Well, all the parts of me I have treasured, like shining pieces of eight, only because I saw your face in them, Mother, have vanished.

Knock knock knock, after a light tread up the stairs. The police. Always the same felon's mask immediately gripping your face. A bulky freckle-eared one and another, a woman. I am only half dressed. Because the male one didn't mount the steps at first, sniffing around in the corridor, I thought the cautious knock was Ted. Very embarrassing, because she is embarrassed. I make sure she realises I do have my underpants on, under the shirt-flaps. (At least I was strapped into my eye-patch.) Looks as if she was born in her uniform some twenty years ago: even her large teeth look officiously regular. A lumpish tread and the other one joins us. 'Hello,' he says brightly, as if he knows I'm odd or too old.

They want to know what I did after leaving the pub 'with Mr Petty'. I did not leave 'with Mr Petty', I tell them. The witnesses are mistaken. I *followed* him out. *Them* out, I should say. He was with Mr Wall. We had a little chat. I presume you've made enquiries with Mr Wall?

She nods rather dismissively, scribbling with great alacrity as her boyfriend sniffs about in my room. Not actually lifting things, but snooping all the same. I am digging a hole and stepping in it. One does, even when reporting a theft. I tell them exactly what happened – that after our little chat, really about nothing, I said goodnight and took a little stroll around my property. Checking the house. I–L–Y–T–H–I–A. Why did I 'follow' Mr Petty out of the pub? To say goodnight. That sounds so feeble that I blush. My hands are trembling. I'm sure she notes the trembling. They refuse to answer any of my questions (when did he go missing, who reported it?), and leave after ten minutes. I'm hungry.

Jessica has learnt from someone who has learnt from someone that foul play is suspected. I've forgotten it's Monday, but she's kindly rustling something up in the microwave. Roger comes in and says that someone has just been told by someone that Muck's woolly hat has been found. Where? Cobblers Way. Never heard of it. A piss-smelling path connecting Bew's Lane with the beginning of Crab-Apple Lane, Jessica explains. I see it now – never knew its real name: walled and dank, yes. No one's quite sure when he went missing, exactly. A Mrs Stenton reported hearing something suspicious at midnight on Saturday. What's defined as suspicious? We amuse ourselves with suggestions – blood-curdling screams, the rattle of a machine-gun, the dragging of chains. I want to know who reported him missing. Roger thinks it was his mate, John Wall. Ah yes, of course. Muck has no missus. I suggest dredging the pond, since Muck was four sheets to the wind on Saturday night.

'Do you think he's really dead, then?' says Jessica.

'No idea. But he could be, couldn't he?'

Back in my room, I switch Ted's lamp on and watch the waxy globs rise and fall, remaking themselves but never into anything recognisable. This is what the universe did for billions of years. Sheer tenacity. That's all God is. My face looms in the glass cylinder, stretched out to a scream. Even the man in the moon can be screaming, at times. Have you noticed that, Mother?

Of course I dream about Muck. Who isn't dreaming about him, in this blighted village?

The next morning, a scribbled note at breakfast. Elizabeth Pratt cancelling dinner. She says she's sorry, but no reason given. This is the first crack in the wing.

'Is Mrs Jennet still alive, Ted?'

'Mrs Jennet up at the Jennets? The old farm? Oh yes. Just about.'

A headwind, full of wet but not raining. Buffeted, I'm feeling strangely jolly. Elated, yes. This is what grief does, before it drops you. Even the changes at the farm don't wreck it: the humming metal hangars, the Belsen huts. Looks like one of my old aerodromes! A withered old thing greets me from her chair as if I have not been anywhere at all since 1940.

'Mornin', Master Arkwright,' she says. 'You sit down here, make yourself comfortable, then.'

Yes, the same nose, forehead, jaw. I hand over a W.I.-made sponge-cake, purchased at the shop, and she identifies it as one of her daughter-in-law's.

'Coals not just to Newcastle, but to the colliery,' I joke.

Scuffed plastic-cushioned chairs around the same big table; worn lino hiding the brick floor; some crummy melamine kitchen units; a tomb-like freezer; a couple of trade calendars featuring farm machinery and topless girls; the usual bric-à-brac of electric gadgets and gew-gaws. These are the only material changes, Mother.

I went there more and more after you'd left us, you see. Mrs Jennet was a strapping young woman, then. She seemed to do everything herself. I gave her a hand bringing in the cows to be milked, a few times, enjoyed holding up the odd vehicle on the lane. I'm sure I swaggered, making clucking and whooping noises like her. She'd give me an apple pudding or a rhubarb pie to take home in a bowl; I'd treat it like my pay-packet, and eke it out. She was motherly, in her strapping way. Smelt of cows and hay. One evening I saw her with a baby at her breast, milking the cows at the same time. The milk spurting into the bucket and the milk dribbling from the baby's mouth. 'You'll be swallowin' flies in a bit, chit, stood there like that.'

I got to know her farmhand, too. Raymond lived in bachelor squalor in a tied cottage beyond the cruck barn. He was genial and a bit dim, with one buck tooth, but he taught me the essentials of farm life. I'd hold up a ladder on a hump-backed field when he was ploughing, so he could line up straight below the brow. Freezing and bored, I was – but the ladder towered up into the crisp air like the expectation of my life ahead. I saw the steam puffing up for ages before I saw the horses, then they broke tinkling over the crest and I'd cheer. Each time I would cheer, to myself.

She coughs and wheezes and taps the table with her cork-screwed fingers and tells me that Raymond died last year. Her sleeves are still rolled up, like yours would be, but her once-tight brawn flaps from each arm like a brown, fledgling wing. She'd pick up brimming churns as if they were full of air.

A woman with a bone-white hairdo comes in with four swollen Sainsbury's bags and frowns uncertainly when she sees me. It's the daughter. She was the infant dribbling the milk at the breast.

I identify myself and there is warmth enough, but of a diffident kind; the years between seem to flatten out. No scarps of achievement, no dark coombs of despair; just earth and lines and the upper rungs of a ladder over the brow, held rigidly. She asks me no questions, thank goodness. Does she even know of my fame, my success?

As she unloads box after box into the freezer, I pose the question about the cows' health, and she screws her face up. There is only this 'staggers' business, a bit hush-hush. Nothing remarkable about the herd keeping away from the fence: they do all sorts of funny things, do cows. 'Don't they, Mum?'

Mum nods, and says that cows know more than we think. She wants to make me a cup of tea, but I refuse. My head's floating again. I take her hand to say goodbye, and hold it for too long.

On my way out I pass the old concrete milking-parlour, with its tiny grates of windows; the frenzied gabble of a radio sounds over the odd thump of metal from inside. I don't want to meet the sons: they're responsible for the industrial look. About the only drolly original thing Nuncle ever did was write out choice extracts from *Fream's Elements of Agriculture* and stick them on the wall next to relevant passages from various sacred or literary texts, for the delectation of visitors. The yellowing sheets were still there after the war. I recall none of the sacred or literary texts but their wicked doubles have embedded themselves quite firmly. My favourite was: *Whereas the dairy cow is adapted to milk production the beef cow must be correspondingly adapted to the production of flesh. This must be laid on the skeleton in the correct places.* The right-wingers laughed, the left-wingers didn't. The flesh on my face feels incorrectly placed as I pause by the pig battery – its door's open and a couple of dim light bulbs glow in the snuffling blackness. Surely there's a moral drop between the old muddy pen full of black Berkshires and this hangar. Later, Jessica tells me that they slaughter the pregnant sow to have the piglets clean, as one pods beans.

>Your loving son,
>Hugh

I wish I was in Africa.

My dearest Ma,

Do you remember the Allenbury's Diet? It provides a convenient and light nourishment for Motorists and Travellers. A cup of Allenbury's Diet and a Biscuit relieves any feeling of Exhaustion.

It came with the tins, Joseph pinned it up. I close my eyes and I can see it, rippled next to the meat-safe. An open motor car paused in front of a whitewashed cottage on a Cornish cliff, the chauffeur in goggles like Father on the motorbike: A Light Repast. You liked Allenbury's but you stayed Exhausted. Some beastie ate it up from the bottom.

I close my eyes and unfortunately I can see the other thing. The rather dreadful thing. They say I have to tell you, as you'd want to know. Can't imagine why.

Here goes. There shall you find the wondrous ship wherein the spindles of King Solomon are laid. Please tell me where that comes from, when you have a moment. I think it's verse.

'The local environment bod's coming this morning, to check the wood, if you want to be there. Ten o'clock. They only told me ten minutes ago. Typical.'

Barry's annoyed with me about Monday's meeting. The bar is empty but for Ted wiping tables. He keeps having to push his spectacles up. 'No news,' he says. I don't know what he's talking about for several moments.

I arrive a few minutes late on Aunt Joy's bike, both of us wheezy. A blue Granada Ghia parked in front of the gate, with its door open. Inside, a dead body tipped right back with its stockinged feet on the dashboard, mouth wide open. 'Hello?' It gulps and gawps and climbs out, becomes Rob something – Garnett or Gardner, rumpled pin-striped shirt. Gardner, I think. He taps a badge on his tie: I AM 3. 'Sorry about this. From the wife. I was thirty yesterday. Into the small hours, I'm afraid.' Blinking as if he's squeezing out tears. He changes into a pair of shiny green gumboots and white cotton gloves, like a surgeon going fishing. That's it. No respirator, no oilskins. He has the usual array of portable contraptions, including a rod with a claw. One of them bleeps, of course. He stuffs them all into a haversack.

He has been told to expect gas, but not what type. 'Mustard and lewisite,' I say. He's never heard of lewisite. 'Arsenical, smelt like geraniums. Never actually used, thank God.' He asks about the wildwood's 'history'. 'My uncle reckoned it was a relic.'

'A relic?'

'Of the primordial forest.'

'I was talking about modern times,' he says, with a chortle. Do I look batty? Perhaps I do. A batty scruff. He's heading for the beechwood. I have to correct him with a touch of the elbow.

'Ever been Army?' he asks. We're peering into the tangle. John Wall's cut stuff is now yellowing. I think he's talking about me at first. I tell him that the Army set up camp during both wars on common land the other side of the wood. The gypsies had to remove themselves.

'Then we might have us a lost depot,' he says. 'There were loads of them in the war. Both wars, in fact.'

'How can you lose depots?'

'Like you lose little girls on the beach,' he grins. 'Sheer

356

carelessness. If this one's mustard or the Carl Lewis, it'll kick start the funding.'

He fiddles with one of his contraptions, making it whoop, tick and growl. 'It's not a lost Army depot,' I say. He checks his massive watch. The thing whoops again. There's a dim whoop from within the wood, like a mating call. He raises his eyebrows.

'Only the elves,' I murmur.

'Lead on, sir.'

He follows me with the detector thingummy held out in front. I'm in walking boots and trousers and we make reasonable headway. 'A badger track,' I explain. 'It's always been here. Creatures of habit.' He nods, studying the thingummy, murmuring figures to himself. Up on Mam Tor we had discs painted yellow dotted about on poles. If they turned red, we were being sprayed by blister gas. Otherwise it was just a matter of sniffing, like beasts. I tell him this but he's not interested. Maybe I should talk model trains, or frogs.

We go further along the meagre path, through the broken ferns and on into hip-high nettles, holding our arms up as if we're being body-searched. There's the odd bird, this morning. The sky's the whitewashed sort, very bright through holes in the canopy; each gust frays these bigger for a moment, then stitches them up. Leaves fall or sport about and hit our faces. We pass the spot where I caught Dominick and his friend. Then we step into a small clearing. This was where I had my picnic at the weekend. On my own. Strictly private. Lots of overgrown blown stuff, past its prime, finished for the year. Dank, an autumn dankness in a dark old wood. Not terribly prepossessing, even a bit derelict. Not a sunny glade, anyway.

No carpet of wild garlic, though the tangle of mould must be its remains.

Gardner looks as if he's sleepwalking, with his detector thing held right out. He stumbles on a fallen branch.

And then, as if on a gust, the faintest hint of it.

Has he noticed? I don't say anything, I just crouch down and all but bury my nose in the mould. Gardner's a bit bemused.

'Mustard? Lewisite?'

357

I rise stiffly. Just dankness, just sweet mould. And then the gust again, that dim hint. It's teasing me. That's what it's doing!

'Smell it?'

Gardner sniffs, holding his detector up. He's standing right on the spot. I shouldn't have brought him here. I shouldn't have brought anyone here. And then, Mother, I have this rather odd thought. Less a thought and more a picture, like the pictures I had as a boy, which were real and not real. Not storybook pictures, or pictures of spirits like Herbert E. Standing, but pictures like memories. Knights, for instance. Knights passing like gusts, clattering and shouting. A danger about them, as if they were drunk. And I wasn't me, but some lowlier person embedded in their time. Absolutely embedded, in all my squalor and filth. Not only knights, don't get the wrong idea: anything, anywhere, but not of my time and I wasn't always lowly. Just like gusts. And this picture I have is of Muck, Muck standing where Gardner's stood, right on the spot. He's tiptoeing about, like a clown would. But he's not enjoying it. He's looking at me and shaking all over, his face sweaty in the moonlight. I'm going to make him do this until he drops.

'Can't smell a thing untoward,' he says. 'And we're not getting a register on the dial.'

That's not Muck, that's Gardner, in a mottle of daylight. He's looking at me as if there's something wrong with me. I find my skin is drawn back from the teeth.

Gardner goes over to a trunk and scratches it. Bits of dry silvery lichen break off. 'Air pollution,' he says. 'General air pollution, that is. Lichen's our canary down the mine shaft. It needs fresh air to live. The buzz word's *bio-remediation*, by the way. Make your fortune by cleaning up the mess.'

The end gallops up before you've had time to adjust or get it right. Look at this wood. The wildness is frightening me. I much prefer lawns, these days.

'Here, take this,' Gardner says.

I look at him, puzzled. A mask dangles from his hand, a throwaway type with plastic eye-pieces. 'Lachrymation,' he says. 'Something's getting you in the eyes. I'm excited.' His own eyes

358

are blinking, a little red. But that's the nervous tic and a night in his cups.

'You've found something?'

He nods. I wipe away a tear and take the mask. He switches on the machine. A little red light flickers and it makes noises like a dreaming puppy.

'We're registering something untoward,' he says. 'Mask yourself up, if you would. We're in a hazardous area – I'd be the one to get the rap.'

He kicks at the mould with his heel and claws out a soil sample with the rod. Now there's a small. black hole just where –

We leave the clearing, advance deeper in. Is it deeper? I'm not sure. I need one of Father's coloured maps, names in whiteclay.

A bright pelt of moss on a log. 'Moss is an ace absorber of poisons,' he yells, peeling it off. His voice is now muffled by his mask. He looks like a deep-sea fish, white and ghastly in the gloom. I suppose I do too. He points to where the wood descends and the undergrowth is mainly the low, matty stuff of boggy ground, straddled by webs. A fallen log sprouts razor-strop fungi, and a something – a boot? a hoof? – has kicked a deathcap off its stem. Trees lean as if the ground is too soft for their roots.

'What happens in that direction?' he yells.

'The freshet,' I shout back. 'A little sort of stream. Then a big field.'

His mask nods and a jabbing forefinger indicates we should go there. Then there's another whoop, to our left. Our masks look at each other. And a panicky shout – but far-off shouts always do sound panicky. As we walk over the slubby ground, I try to picture the surveyor's map shown in the meeting. My breath's sour inside the mask, and rather loud. The freshet's a trickle in a tunnel of fern and brambles. I tell Gardner that it's the venerable county boundary – described in a tenth-century document where it's called a *merfleot*. I was with you, Mother, when Mr Fergusson showed us a copy of the document – and he died not long after I arrived. Yet I learnt it by heart, for some reason!

The boundary creek, hard by the wood known by the villagers as wulvesheafodwudu.

'Come again?'

'Wolf's Head Wood, in old English. Maybe Ulverton used to be Ulvesdun. Wolf Town.'

He looks around him a little nervously. 'It probably wasn't full of wolves.' I add, 'but Anglo-Saxon robbers and murderers. Malefactors, anyway. No-gooders, on the run. That's what someone like that was called then. A *wolf's head*.'

At that very moment a policeman appears out of the mist, out of the gloom. He's approaching with some difficulty over the undergrowth next to the stream. Of course this is odd, but I mix him up with our own investigation. He hails us at a little distance. He's got a stick. There's a patch so boggy between us it's pretty much a pool, with reeds sticking out of it and a few late gnats, the dark-green water covered in what looks like dust. I imagine his boots filling up. We slop over to him through a spongeous tract of dying hemp agrimony and browning meadowsweet. He has a short mac on, spotted with wet leaves and the remains of webs. A squirrel ripples up a tree trunk behind him, crashing through the branches overhead. Gardner pushes his mask up on to his forehead but is panting too much to get in first.

'Morning, sirs,' says the policeman. 'You're in the wrong place. We're back there.' He indicates upstream with a hitchhiker's thumb. 'And remember to look up,' he adds. 'Follow me, if you will, please.'

My companion looks at me as the policeman trudges back the way he's come. I push my mask up and say, 'They aren't to do with you?' He doesn't think so, he thought maybe they were to do with me, with this thing about my uncle. I honestly have no idea what's happening, Mother. None of this means anything. But I do have a vision of a sort of bunker full of rusting drums, and on each drum is painted a grinning death's head. I never once thought about the other thing!

On our way we pass quite close to the wood's edge, where the Jennets' burned field shows through. There's a lot of rubbish here, it's horrible, it's a sort of tip tumbled into the bed of the freshet: black fertiliser sacks and plastic demijohns, mainly. The more I look, the more I see. An empty drum labelled *ICI Teat Dip* in a tangle of chains and blades and barbed-wire, big tractor batteries –

even an old upturned freezer on the slope. Gardner turns round and taps the side of his finger with his nose, which I don't understand. He looks unhappy.

We follow the policeman to a bright red ribbon that runs from tree to tree. He lifts it up for us, but I still have to stoop. Age, Mother, is unavailing. Here are more policemen, amidst the crackle of walkie-talkies: all of them standing around, desultorily chatting with arms crossed, as if waiting for someone to take them on a nature walk, point out the squirrels, the scars of lichen, the badger toilets, the obscure ferns, the pond beetles. One or two are taking measurements with white tape. They look at us uncertainly as we break from the depths, our clothes wet, covered in streaks of webs, shaking leaves from our hair. Gardner's mask is looking upwards, as instructed, but his face is looking at me.

'I think I ought to tell them it's a Hazardous Area,' he says, blinking hard.

He sounds as though he's seeking my advice. But I've never been here before, not even in my youth! Never! We're inside an area cordoned off by the ribbon. The wood's much thinner here – I can see the brighter edge of it, and the blue and white of police vehicles. I have no idea what is going on, Mother: whenever I see a lot of police activity, I always think of it as an exercise. I feel damp and I stink of bogs and am somewhat out of breath. My shins rankle from nettle stings. A burly type with a more senior air approaches us and shakes our hands.

'Good morning, gentlemen,' he says. 'I hear you got lost.'

Gardner mumbles something but the senior type tells us to tiptoe. It's a sort of joke, but it makes me flush. Now we're near a silver birch, the only one here, very white and peeling. He's pointing upwards, into its branches. He's saying something, I'm not sure what he's saying. A leaf falls on my face. I blink and see a pair of boots. I know those boots. They're on legs that are growing out of the tree. And then the face a bit below them, spying on us with one wide eye. The Man in the Moon came down too soon and burnt his mouth.

Your loving son,
Hugh

Dull. Wet, windy. It has been nice, though.

My dearest Mater,

'We're leaving him up there until the snaps, of course,' says the senior type. '*When* they come. Traffic. Most inconvenient, whoever did it. Watch this.'

He gives the tree a kick and a piece of it hums off. Greenbottles. They like dead meat and living toads, you see. One bumps my forehead, swooping low. There's also a shower of tiny winged nuts, fluttering, not nearly as frantic as sycamore seeds. Gardner could be his mask, all aghast and white. The police officer rambles on behind his big red face.

'If you want a cup of tea, there's one in the van. The path lab said Jim Reed's on his way. Everyone's on their way. The fingerprint people are by the caravan, if you want to have a word. Caravan's empty, by the way. Has been for a year. But you never know. I'm new at Reading, or I'd know you by name, gentlemen. Detective Sergeant Fagg. Two *g*s, and I don't smoke. I'll fetch the ladder, if you want a peep. Not the most convenient place to take samples from. Not much on the ground, I don't think – two days, a bit of rain, predators. Talking of predators, there aren't wolves in this wood, are there?'

He's looking at Gardner, not at me.

'Not that I know of,' says Gardner. He ought to be in bed, really.

'Can't be dogs that ripped him up. Foxes don't climb trees, do they? What about foxes?' He's looking at me, now. 'What about foxes? They don't climb bloody trees, do they?'

'Leopards do,' I say.

'Who?'

Every movement we make on the dead leaves drowns our voices in ack-ack. What a hopeless idea of Malcolm's, to spread these over the stage. No one'll hear a word. A hand up there, too, picking a fresh catkin. Almost picking, but not quite, just hovering. Impaled up there. Oh, I know that hand. I'm good on hands, I know Bulwer's books of rhetorical gesture backwards and forwards and sideways. *Invito*, that one is. The Ghost beckoning on the battlements. Come and join me, it's not so far.

Bits of browned cloth hang like dead vines, or a knotted rope to bring him down.

Have you seen enough, Mother? Blood never bothered you, though. Only bad blood. Or old blood.

The detective sergeant is talking again. Very nasty, it is, but a friend has identified the boots as belonging to the missing chappie in the village, one Frank Petty, retired coalman among other things. Village character. A pity.

Gardner is finally getting through. The detective sergeant stoops to the poor man's mumble. I'm numb. It's too real and it's not real enough. The birch is made of flat painted wood. Sir Toby Belch and the others are behind it and I'm Malvolio in yellow garters. A couple of pink-red sickeners have sprouted from the leaf mould under the birch: I'd like to bend down and run my finger over the gills, hear the tell-tale rustle. If not for the dim pungency of something cadaverous, I'd be all right. Maybe I do start to bend down, but the ground comes towards me too fast. My face is in enemy fire. A hand is thrust under one of my arms and then under the other, pinching the flesh as they tug me up. I'm between two policemen and the wood circles slowly, one way for a little then the other way for a little, as if eyeing me up before pouncing. *They're not forensic, you silly bugger* I hear someone – perhaps Fagg – shout, apparently from high in the sky. Someone who's using my head is insisting that *I'm fine, now.*

I'm being fine in a police van, but it's not moving. I have a mug of over-milky tea. The mug says *On Probation* and has a busty girl stretched naked beneath its lip stains. A police officer with a form tells me to take my time. A colleague in the front seat is checking up on Gardner. *Hallo, darling. Morning my love. Good morning sweetheart, could you tell me?*

'Farewell, dear heart.'

'Whassat, sir? Not your address, is it?'

Now I'm picking my way over the rubbish and burnt bits strewn over the muddy grass. I pass the other police van and spot Gardner smoking inside, hands all a-shake. My mask is on the top of my head too, it's watching the sky. I step into weeds and a big rusty gridiron springs up, like a man trap. The grease on it brands my trousers, and yet the caravan's sprouting old man's beard from its roof. People are dusting it with tiny brushes. I'm on a path now, cutting up behind Herbert Bradman's place and the Manor. High old walls of soft brick. There's a marble slab further along, under tentacles of wild clematis and sprayed graffiti. An inscription. Do you know what it says, Mother? Not the graffiti! That is very rude! Look – underneath *Foreskins army*, there's this:

> Cease! drain not to its dregs the urn
> Of bitter prophecy.
> The world is weary of the past,
> Oh, might it die or rest at last!

Shelley, probably for someone's dog.

Well, it does make me cry. Once Nuncle told me to bang my own drum and I thought of that drum I'd had in Victoria, and broke down. I was ill, though. I find myself outside the last bungalow in Gumbledon Acres, studying its low wall. Plop plop, into the faded pinks. Malcolm's face.

'You look ghastly,' he says. 'Shall I get someone?'

He's carrying a drum over his shoulder. It's a big African one. It's my own, blown right up. It must be full of seeds because it rustles every time he moves.

'Before I forget, they'll make a noise.'

'What?'

'Dead leaves. Like your drum. Unless they shut. I mean shout.'

'I'll get someone.'

But I walk, with his hand under my elbow. We pass the primary school and then I tell him I want a brandy. Really, I want Jessica. She's all woolly jumper and tender heart, her hair is in ringlets and everywhere. Malcolm's just finished discovering music with the infants, and looks rather flushed and happy. Pink and orange tubes stick out of his knapsack. We steer towards the Old Barn. The bar is empty and a little cold. My clothes are still damp, my feet wet. Roger sets up an electric radiator. Thoughtful chap, if otherwise useless. The two men appear wary of each other: Malcolm's wife had a fling with Roger Marlow, of course. I can't hope to remember all these overlaps! Too many pebbles chucked in the pond! Too many circles! Their two ripples do not overlap with Muck's, though. I knew him better than they did. Roger can't believe that one person alone could drag somebody up into a tree. 'A leopard could,' I point out.

Malcolm freezes.

Perhaps he did it, I find myself thinking. I knock back my brandy in one go. Haaaaaa.

Jessica doesn't turn up. Outside, whoozy but upright, I am invited to Malcolm's for lunch tomorrow. Oh, he does seem shifty.

In a nice hot bath, I find myself sorrowing for Muck. Nobody loved him, either. Perhaps John Wall. Muck stamping the floor so the dart fell out, John Wall accepting it. I shave carefully and go upstairs to check myself in the wardrobe's mirror. Not bad, Mother! Then I do what I have done every so often throughout my life: I pick up my old battered Complete Shakespeare, still with shreds of beechmast in it, and turn to a photograph of Miss Lilian Braithwaite as Anne Page. She stands against painted blossom and a high wall of canvas brick. *Merry Wives* is froth, of course, Mother, but Miss Lilian Braithwaite uncannily resembles Rachael. Dark eyes, long nose, full mouth, the same curls of midnight hair. On the other side of the canvas wall is Aunt Rachael, but she's back stage, she's someone else, she's safely cut off.

Rachael as Anne Page. The lovely hand in a perfect upside-down *Invito*, the last gasp of the old ways –

'Will't please your worship to come in, sir?'

I wish I was in *Merry Wives*. I wish I was playing opposite you in a play that went on for ever because it was real (not you, Mother, I'm talking to Rachael, here, please don't be jealous). But I'm in a lot of different plays, that's the trouble. The hand is picking a catkin. No it isn't! Yes, it is! It's so stiff and cold and utterly utterly dead dead dead! I slam the book shut and hurl it at the door. It falls in a broken heap on the rug. Then the truth flashes so fiercely that I screw up my eyes. The genie came out of the broken book, it stole into my ear and bellowed inside my head. I'm yanking my bedside drawer and it falls right out on to my toes. The pain is nothing as I hold the bundle and thump it.

False letters!

Thump it.

The plays are awash with false letters!

Thump it.

People are made fools of and broken and even killed by false letters, in play after play after play! Thump it thump it thump it.

'What, frighted with false fire?' I think I shout this several times. I want to gnaw this bundle like a fleshy leg. You see, Mother? How close I come to madness? I hurl open the wardrobe door and scrabble for the fetish box. The mask rolls out, snarling at my ankles. I have the fetish box – but, oh horrors, where is Nuncle's scrap of paper? The cinders scatter across the floor behind me with the skull bits, the metal bobs, the nobs of redheart, the big white talons – I'm an animal digging out its hole! The red-tinted forehead lands on my knuckles and I feel disgusted, suddenly – and I flap it off, I'm afraid, Mother. I'm hunting for a scrap of paper, not your touch!

There it is, in among the cinders, oh sweet heavens. To think I might have thrown it away. My lifeline, Mother! All that keeps me who I am! This little scrap with its wonky message, bashed out one day long ago when I was having my hair yanked at school, probably!

> The centre
> Never gives
> Seven answers

I hold it in my teeth, leaving my hands free to tear open the bundle's oil paper. And there's a knock at the door.

A tentative trying-out little knock.

I stand there. I admit I feel a sort of dread. My towel has fallen off. I'm naked. I'm gripping the scrap of paper in my teeth and holding the bundle against me to cover my nakedness. The door stays shut. I say it quietly through gritted teeth:

'Mother?'

> Your loving son,
> Hugh

Light breeze, scudding clouds. Pleasant. Too many crocuses.

Dearest Mother,

A rat-a-tat-tat, now, like a drum.

'Mr – Mr Arkwright? You in there?'

A man's voice. Fagg's voice! I ask him to wait until I'm decent. I have to blow my nose. I stuff everything back where it should be and dress as fast as I can, falling over my trousers. The scrap of paper is sodden, because I forgot it was between my teeth, but the typing is still legible. I slip it back into the fetish box. The wardrobe door shuts as the other one opens.

'Not in your fancy tights, Mr Arkwright? We reckoned you were changing for a show. Plumes and all.'

My pullover's on back to front. The label scratches my Adam's apple.

Fagg's with a spotty minor in a suit who turns out to be his senior. Fagg does the interrogation while Detective Inspector Shaw, or Shore, or whatever his name is, leans against the wall, smirking. He keeps sliding his eyes to the side without moving his head, as if studying a fly on his cheek or keeping tabs on someone I can't see. This puts me off. At one point he leans down and picks up the broken Shakespeare, putting it on the table without glancing at it. A couple of pages fall out, and he tucks them back in – any old how. They've made a Darby and Joan between the killing and the fact that I haven't paid for some fruit. What fruit? I was spotted nicking fruit by some lads from outside the shop, Friday. Good grief, I never paid for it! Two measly apples and a banana! Shoplifting! I say that if I did, it was sheer carelessness, old age, call it what you will, I know Marjorie, Marjorie knows me. She certainly does, they say. (What's that supposed to mean? What have I done to upset her? Moved away, probably.)

They ask me outright if I was anywhere near 'Pry's Wood' on Saturday night. I haven't heard it called Pry's Wood in years but what a fitting name. (I know, Mother – pry is another name for the small-leaved lime. But all the same.)

I deny it. Why shouldn't I? I'm still feeling exhilarated. Nuncle almost had me, back there, but now I'm bounding off again. Be terse, they'll be gone soon. 'So,' says Fagg, 'you went straight from the public-house here to the gate of, er, your house, er, Eyelie –'

'Ilythia, yes –'

'Yes, and subsequently returned, having not entered by said gate, am I right?'

'Spot on.'

'I see.'

The other chap's eyes are not sliding any more. Fagg looks as if he's solving an algebraic problem in his notebook. He has the heavy breathing of a drinker – and from the smell of it, he's made enquiries down below. What's Ted told him about me? With a rush of blood I realise that they've trapped me, they know I'm lying. They'd have talked to Dominick Pratt! Fagg's telling me about his daughter's acting, now. Star appearance in the school's *Annie Get Your Gun*. I nod as if fascinated. Shore has gone into the bedroom. He emerges with a talon. I must have missed it.

'Been paring your nails have you, sir?'

'Of course not. *Let not him that plays the lion pare his nails, for they shall hang out for the lion's claws.*'

'Eh?'

'*And, most dear actors, eat no onions nor garlic, for we are to utter sweet breath –*'

'The Bard,' Fagg explains to Shore, without looking round. 'All right, all right,' mutters Shore. He's glaring at Fagg's back.

I explain that it's an African fetish.

'Fetish, eh?'

Shore passes the talon to Fagg. 'Looks clean enough, sergeant. Cinders all over the floor, in there.' Then he looks at me. 'Been having a barbecue in the bedroom, have you? A bit mucky.'

'Just been sorting through. Old things.'

The talon rolls around in Fagg's palm. 'African, is it? Africa. What a mess. We should never have left 'em to it.' He does something clever with his fingers and the talon pops up between his knuckles. He makes a clawing movement and hisses. Then the talon jumps back into his palm again. He offers it to me like a cigarette. I meet his eyes briefly. I take the talon and hide it in my hand. I must not speak first. I must keep my head still and my eye must not swivel about. I have a very delicate crown balanced on my frontal lobe. I am a prince.

Fagg breaks the silence.

'We may be required to do a search of both your room here and the house in Crab-Apple Lane,' he says. 'Don't have blood on any of your clothes, do you?'

My mouth drops open, I'm afraid. He waves his biro at my forehead. 'How did you come by that scratch, sir?'

'The struggle. He put up a savage resistance. Strong chap, even when drunk.'

A little pause. They might be waxworks.

'Gardening,' I sigh, eventually. 'There's a lot of clearing to do in the grounds.'

Fagg comes back to life with a sniff. 'These are routine questions, sir. Our job's to ask what's pertinent. And the thumb?'

I look at the filthy plaster. I can't remember for a moment. The fretsaw, cutting through the string on the bundle of letters. So long ago!

'The same.' I manage to say. 'Sawing old branches.'

They look as if they don't believe me. Sliding Eyes jerks upright and goes over to the door.

'Thank you, Mr Arkwright,' he says. 'If we have to search your room and the property, we might be in need of your assistance. We'd be grateful, therefore, if you have any travel arrangements in the immediate future, to let us know. It may be that we require your presence at very short notice.'

'In other words, I can't go to London this evening.'

'Was that what you were planning, sir?'

'I was.' I wasn't.

'Would it be inconvenient to you to cancel said trip, sir?'

'Inconvenient, but not impossible. I can put it off for a day or two.'

Sliding Eyes nods at Fagg and the big red-faced man rises with a grunt. 'Age,' he says, by the door, looking at the door handle. 'Creeps up on you, doesn't it? Back, memory, all that.' He turns round and studies me for a moment. Then he waves his biro at me again, almost in my face. 'Don't go burning any of your clothes in the next few days, will you, Mr Arkwright?'

Somewhere between counsel and threat. I snort. 'I have never burnt any clothes in my life!'

As soon as they've gone, I scrabble again for the letters. I place the first one next to the scrap of paper from the fetish box, like so.

Look, Mother: look how meticulously and with what care Nuncle plotted my destruction. Look how close we came.

Your affectionate son,

Hugh

Clouds slapped up there like grout.

Dearest Mother,

My new friend Malcolm is not quite Malcolm: he's shaved his beard. His chin looks like a small rodent unearthed from its den. Comes and goes, he says. But there's something else: he's even shiftier, almost wary of me.

I've been thinking hard in the night – I've had very little sleep. When I did drop off, I had the silliest dreams – more like flashes than dreams, dreams seen out of a hurtling train. In one of them, I came across Muck with his eyeball hanging out, but otherwise unharmed. He was collecting fardels on Mam Tor. I asked him whether Aunt Rachael ever wore a coat as red as any blood. He grinned and handed me a little picture in a gaudy plastic frame. It was a present. The picture was a photograph of Aunt Rachael in the last years, all eye bags and fag and stricken mouth. 'Just to say sorry,' he said. 'It's for your bedside table. Fancy, like.' I looked at him. He was smiling, shyly. She was wearing your red coat in the picture, Mother. I started smashing him over the head with it and woke up in a boiling rage.

But I'm still elated. I share some of my thinking with Malcolm, when the Subject comes up. He's overboiling the spaghetti.

'A big cat,' I say.

'Sorry?'

'Which big cat drags its prey up into a tree?'

Malcolm ladles out the spaghetti in tortured lumps. He seems to be prodding the answer into life. 'The one with spots. You already said, in the Old Barn.'

370

I'd forgotten. And Malcolm had frozen. 'Well. A certain spotty skin has disappeared.'

He gives me a dark glance. His chin is actually grey, like dead flesh. I nod discreetly towards the party wall.

'What are you saying?' He sounds annoyed, as if John Wall is his best friend.

'Ever seen his sitting room, Malcolm? It's full of animal skins. He's obsessed by skins.'

Malcolm looks at the wall as if he can see through it. Very faint persistent muttering of a telly. He shakes his head. 'No proof it was him who nicked it. Anyway, the boys in blue have had a word. Cast-iron alibi, apart from the fact that it was him who reported Muck missing, and that Muck was his best friend. Only friend, probably.'

He plops on the sauce, red and trickling.

'Thank you. Well? What's the alibi, Holmes?'

He doesn't smile. He sits and pours out some green home-made cider with bits in. Did he hear me? The spaghetti looks unpleasant. I wonder if they've taken him down. I can't believe the man's dead. Loneliness is the worst thing and you go into death alone. Quiri told me that the dead can take the living with them, by the hand; they can come for you at night through a hole in the winding sheet. I wouldn't mind if *you* did that to me, Mother, I really wouldn't. Really.

Malcolm comes back to it a few minutes later.

'He was with me.'

'With you? Oh. What was he doing with you?'

'Having supper. Wood-pigeon pie. I'm good at pies. He brought a couple of birds round on Friday, a sort of peace offering. So I said I'd make a wood-pigeon pie at the weekend. I invited him along.'

'Must have been a late supper. He was in the pub until about eleven. I saw him, with the murdered man. Not yet murdered, of course.'

'I'm talking about Sunday.'

A fleck of sauce has spotted his forehead. I swallow too much of the spaghetti at once and cough.

'Sunday? But Muck was dead for a day by then.'

'No he wasn't. He was killed in the early hours of Monday morning, apparently. Whatever made you think he was bumped off the night before?'

'I don't know. I just assumed. Seeing them go off together like that.'

I'm glad Malcolm didn't serve me wood-pigeon pie today. He leans forward. 'If I were you, I would let the police get on with it. My marriage was destroyed by rumour and supposition.'

I mop up my spaghetti sauce with a chunk of his home-made bread. It has grits in it. I recall Keiller going on about grit off the grinding-stones wearing down prehistoric teeth. Mine are mostly false. Malcolm has just been rather rude to me, I think. I'm almost upset.

'Well, I thought it was Saturday night for two reasons. First, I saw them leaving the pub together. Second, the police were very keen to know what I was doing that night.'

'They've seen you, have they?' This is almost a mumble. He's avoiding my eyes again, staring at his plate. Then he adds: 'John's not so bad, really. Heart of gold. Poor bloke. He might help with the sound for the mumming play. He's quite good with electrics.'

Something amiss.

'Not had our opportunities, has he, Hugh? You're famous and successful, he's at the other end. Lonely, rather pathetic.'

'He's got his mother.'

He snorts at this, of course, but I don't know quite what else to say, Mother; Malcolm's not really talking about John Wall. The party wall might as well be a mirror. Then he does look at me, very dark eyes and the grey snout of chin: 'I mean, if someone like you thought John Wall had done this thing, the police might listen. And who's going to stick up for the likes of John Wall? That's the point. If it were between someone famous and successful and powerful like you, and someone like John Wall, we know who'd go down. Fruit?'

'Thank you, Malcolm.' He fiddles about in a basket, washes some apples in the big old porcelain sink with its green stain. I don't like this at all, I feel threatened. Is it just the thing about Nuncle that's annoyed him? But if he knew my reasons! The care the man went to! So meticulous! Then the guitar's tuned and I have to hear the first song he's written for the *Nubat* show. It's called the 'Song of the Boners'. The Boners stand for the Cresswellians, in Nuncle's silly tale, Mother. Because we know nothing about the Cresswellians except that they were here before anyone else and lived in caves, Nuncle could do what he liked with them. Soppy words: 'We are the True People, We are the Boners, We are the Few People, We are the Loners,' or something, going on and on and on. I suppose 'Cresswellians' wouldn't sound very good in a song. His voice is feeble but the tune's catchy. This worries me. It's quite African, I remark. But of course it is, he replies, Africa's important in the book.

'Nubat, and all that.' What's Nubat got to do with Africa? 'Well, it's an anagram for Bantu, for a start.'

My face goes white. Feels like that, anyway.

'How do you know?'

The interview in the *Listener*, of course. 'We all started in Africa, he said. No one was saying that, not then. So Nubat is a sort of noble African warrior in the original jungle of England – what we now call England, anyway. Before it was even an island. Stone Age happiness.'

I can't bear it. Such fraudulence! I hear a cackle in the air. Fiends, probably. Or flames. Like the flame-like rustle of the letters as I turn them here in my room. The old way we theatre people used to do a fireplace, Mother, crouched behind the false hearth, strips of paper in front of the amber-red flood for the flickery shadows on the opposite wall, jiggled by the prompter, screwing up newspaper for the crackle. Ah yes. Half-empty halls. Cold back rooms smelling of mops. Truculent, squint-eyed janitors. Gorgets of size-stiffened felt, tin-lid armour bosses, Gertrude's brocade from an old armchair. Telephone speeches pasted into the phone book that no one can find minutes before curtain up. Blinded by the lights coming up on resistance before they short. My temple was built upon such draughty wild beginnings, as Nuncle's was upon poisoned mud. Ah yes. But Nubat can be Bantu *and* Tabun, surely! It is, it is! Nothing says it isn't! As Malcolm can be bearded, then beardless! As you can be

living and dead! As an actor can be a king or a fool or anything, anything! As I can be a man and a beast!
Your loving son,
Hugh

I'm sure there are bluebells in the woods, if I could get to them.

My dearest Mother,
I am very calm about all this.
'What Edward Arnold most admired about Africa,' I reply, 'was its prehistoric mortality rate.'
Malcolm's chin slightly flushes, the rest of him stays pale. But we talk about other things over coffee, which is much too weak. His little daughter; children in general; schools; ecological collapse. When I tell him about Nuncle's vision of the wildwood sort of bubbling over and spreading across the land, like the steaming porridge in the nursery story, smothering everything, his eyes brighten up. I don't mention my detestable thought, because the letters have somehow thrust it away, let alone the new blood soaking into the mould. Plop, plop.
On my way out, in the porch, feeling a little fumed by the drink, I ask him if he knows how the body was found. Was it the helicopter, in the end? He says yes and no, respectively. He's shifty again. He adds in a sort of mumble something about being a convert to reality, Marxist now Marxism's out of fashion. I say I don't see the connection. The narrow shelves in the porch are full of *objets trouvés*: pottery shards, hand-hewn nails, twisted sticks, flints with holes, a craquelured majolica door-knob. He's turning one of the big old nails over and over in his hand, staining his palm with rust.
'OK, she located the body.'
'Who?'
'My ex-wife. Maddy. She dowsed him. The police are into hokery-pokery, sometimes. They'll be using broomsticks instead of squad cars, soon. Ray Duckett taught her. He's a water diviner, mainly. You put a finger on the map and trace a line, as if you were walking it, and you hold his arm with the other hand. When the rods swing up or out or whatever it is, there's your water. Theoretically. It's never failed. He also does it with standing

374

stones, the auras around standing stones and barrows and all that. Impresses the tourists. And Maddy got roped in to do it for a ripped-up corpse.'

He gives me one of his dark, piercing glances and then passes a hand across his face, sighing. It's hot in the porch, even stifling, like a sweaty hand at the throat. Though divining is to do with long and boring afternoons in my youth, I express my amazement. 'It's not all that amazing,' he says. He hesitates, and then mutters something about them already having a pretty good idea.

About what? Its location? That it was up in a tree in the wildwood? But I don't ask him to repeat it. I can hardly breathe in the porch. Such an odd man: dismisses such mystic tripe at the same time as he worships Edward Arnold.

We wander out into the front garden and look in his shed: wooden music stands stare blankly back at us in various stages of completion – period copies of eighteenth-century originals in redheart and ash. Rather lovely, erect and raw in their heaps of shavings, but also like the old road signs with pointy caps. He says ash is a nervous wood but with a lovely grain. Like his ex-wife, he adds.

'Hey, it'll make my fortune,' he goes on. 'Can't you hear the rush? W.H. Smith's, I'm thinking. Free Big Mac with every five purchased, indigestion included.'

His stick savages the shavings at our feet, raising sweet smells. I tell him how much I like the music stands. We walk to the front gate. The mist of the last two days has lightened, but the sky's now an oppressive blind of white, like the reflective sheets photographers set up. Even the autumn colours look bleached out.

'By the way,' says Malcolm, undoing the latch and then standing there with the gate half-open in his hand, as if afraid I might bolt, 'if you want to tell me anything, you know, anything, I'm right here.'

He's chewing his lip. A horrible sensation of fear in my stomach. Heart-rate up.

'Tell you what?'

'That's the thing. Whatever.' He's run out, his batteries have run out. Out of the corner of my eye, through a tear in the ragged hedge, I see John Wall standing in front of his porch, looking our way. His face is a pale oval, from this distance. His hands in his pockets. Unusual, that. Not someone who stands about, slouching. Certainly slouched now. John Wall didn't do it, I have to remind myself. Dreadful of me even to think it. Then who on earth did? Perhaps the leopard skin has nothing to do with it. This is what happens in books, in thrillers, in murder mysteries. Red herrings, false trails. Have the police contacted zoos, safari parks, eccentric pet owners? Maybe Muck was savaged by a real beast, after all. I mean one with a leopard heart and lungs and brain.

The gate squeaks wide. I'm free to bolt. I say, quietly, 'I think you're right. I think it was wrong and even dangerous of me to start pointing the finger at anyone.'

'At John Wall, you mean.'

'Ssssh. He's just come out of his front door.'

'That's an event,' he murmurs. 'First time he's used the front in living memory.'

On my way back I pass Dr Johnson, standing by the house in the square that used to be the barber's; he wishes me a mournful good morning, studying the new paving stones tinted with sand that the council men haven't bothered to sweep off. He presses something into my hand and says, 'No need to say thank you.' He wanders away, towards the pub.

It's not an apothegm but a blue marble, chipped and soiled. A treasure. A great gift! I give the man a wave as he hovers under the oak in front of the Never Fear. He doesn't wave back.

Passing the shop, I notice ovals of faces through the window, as if hovering beyond a new display of dog chews, bloody Hallowe'en masks, black lacy tights, rocket fireworks. Are they all turned to watch me cross the road? Why do I feel, walking between the street's lacy windows, that I am on stage again? I don't like that business about the dowsing rods. They'll have a sorcerer in the mortuary soon, rubbing one of Muck's teeth with scented leaves and then waiting for the tooth to whisper the name of the killer. Father tried to stamp that out, didn't he? Because the killer was always a good man with a hard-working young wife much desired by his rich brother-in-law, and the sorcerer was always known to the brother-in-law, and the young man was always put to death just before Father arrived.

Lots of people in my room. The contents of the fetish box spread on the table, including the various skull bits – even the red-tinted skull-bit, Mother, though I'm not so sure it's yours at this stage. My brief diary on the floor. Ted by the window, hands in his pockets, not really apologetic.

I project my voice like a missile into the nape of the one fiddling in the table's drawer. '*Good* afternoon.' His head jolts, as if hit by a brick, and he turns, rubbing his neck. Eilrig exercise, Mother, based on Noh practices and arcane Elizabethan pamphlets. How to soar above the cracks of hazelnuts, the whine of orange-sellers, the groundlings' chatter, the rustling of gowns like bearded barley in a wind!

Like so.

Now they've come running in, the people here, to see what on earth's going on. Maybe I've said something!

Your affectionate son,
Hugh

Daisies on the lawn. I do love daisies. But the mower's getting nearer and nearer.

Dearest Mother,

Now the man's turned and being winded by my eye and he steps back, knocking the table. His surprise turns to fear. I've melted his guts, you see. Arcane techniques have their use off the stage, in certain extreme circumstances!

The other three, not in uniform, nod minutely and carry on plundering. Since there is little to plunder in my room, they're into the lifting and peering stage. Sliding Eyes appears from the darkness of the bedroom, holding the Babinga mask. He puts it over his face.

'To be or not to be, that's the question,' comes his muffled voice.

The glistening bit of his mouth, like animal tripe, like a man's insides, works between the jagged teeth. He's grinning, as are the others – even the frightened one (not Ted, I'm glad to see).

377

Something tears in me, I'm afraid. I leap forward, seize the mask by the edges and jerk it off his face. He lets go of it immediately.

'Never do that again,' I say, so steady, oh yes. 'Never do that again.'

A silence, except for my breathing. Sliding Eyes removes his aghast expression with a twitch of his head. No idea how the others look: I've an eye only for the oaf in front of me. My gut's sourness eats into his face like acid on an etcher's plate. Pure choler with a lashing of hate, by my reckoning.

'Only a jest, Mr Arkwright. If I –'

'Did you give them a key to get in, Ted?'

Ted nods.

'They showed their search warrants,' he adds, as if impressed.

'On what grounds, young man, are you wasting your time in my room?'

'I suggest you sit down and catch your breath first, Mr Arkwright. This isn't helping you, nor anybody else –'

'Give me a straight answer, please. On what grounds?'

The twine padding around the edge comes away in my fierce grip and the mask bounces heavily on the boards and clatters towards Ted's feet, rocking on its face. Almost more frightening from the back, like that – the scooped wood roughly hacked at and cindered black between the eye-slits and square mouth, as if someone's looking from the other side. Ted gapes as if it's a mad rat, about to bite him.

'I'll bet that's worth a bob or two,' says Sliding Eyes.

'I'll charge you for any repairs,' I say, my anger giving up on me. For an awful moment, I can't for the life of me think why these people are here, or what exactly has so infuriated me. Sliding Eyes goes over to the table. He tells the others to check the rooms. Ted goes out with them. There's a burly one left, in front of the door, taking a notebook and Pentel out of his top pocket. The inspector lays a thin white hand on the darkest cranium. The black hairs between his knuckles are a very realistic touch.

I've sat down with a sudden headache. The cider is rolling around like bilgewater.

'Why do you keep skulls and various items pertaining to black magic in your wardrobe, Mr Arkwright?'

'It's an African souvenir,' I say. 'From my childhood.'
My childhood!

In a gush like the pouring light of the open dream-sluice, the letters empty themselves upon me. I leap to my feet, shivering from head to foot.

'Letters. Personal letters. Private, absolutely private.'
He's startled.

I point at him. The scribbling bruiser behind me stiffens, I can sense it.

'Where are they?'
'Letters, sir?'

For the life of me I can't. Can't remember.

'Some private letters. Older than me, just. Don't take them away.'

'Come across any letters, have we, George?'
'Might have. I can ask the boys.'

With the socks, bedside table. I go over and pull at the drawer, the bundled socks making it stick. The cargo-label pops up, bent double. Feel with my hand, rustling, the dreadful rustle. Like putting my hand into the mustardy river from the dug-out, feeling a croc's skin. How I'd imagine it, being eaten. Like reaching your hand into black night and touching the moon.

'It's all right. It's all right.'

Sliding Eyes indicates to bruiser that he should take a peep –
'No. They're old. Strictly private. They're not even real.'
'Not real, sir?'

'They're pretend. Forgeries. *Fakes!*' Spittle shoots out of my mouth. They're frowning, they roll their eyes at each other. I end up in the easy chair, rubbing my thighs, holding my kneecaps. Loose bone. Bag of gelatine. Dripping for sale!

'Had these forgeries long, have you sir?'
'No. Yes. Anyway, I forbid you to look at them on pain of – killing myself – with an instant *fit*.'

'Fit' also spittles across the room, just missing the inspector. He thinks for a bit, tapping his tongue on the roof of his mouth. Then he makes this minute gesture to the other one – who relaxes, stays where he is. *Silentium postulo.*

'Can we resume, sir?'

I nod once, slightly crick my neck.

'Why was the, er, package in your wardrobe, sir?'

'I think I need to call my solicitor.'

'That's up to you, but these are preliminary questions, that's all. Designed to clear certain matters up, not an interrogation. Casting a bit of light in the murk, I call it. The reason we're searching your room is quite straightforward. You have, in the past few days, burnt some clothes in your property's garden. Also, the wood known as Pry's Wood is actually part of that property. Therefore the victim was picked up, as it were, on your property. You were seen in the wood on Saturday night. You were seen by many people looking dishevelled and not quite yourself on Sunday evening and Monday morning. In addition, it appears from the pathologist's report that the victim was in fact attacked by some form of animal, as the wounds conform to those made by large claws and there have been animal hairs found on the body. However, no animal drags its victim up into a tree, does it?'

Steady eyes on my face. He knows, Mother. Another trap. The Pentel is poised at the door. He might be about to sew something.

I win.

'Know anything about a leopard skin, missing? Belongs to you, apparently.'

'What I was going to say. A leopard does exactly that.'

'Sorry, lost you.'

I look at him. He's playing the dullard, low-status, ready to pounce. Bounce.

'A leopard drags its kill up, up into the tree.'

'Does it now? Ah. I should've asked my son. He's very keen on world animals. The one with the spots, isn't it?'

'World' said almost derisively, as if being whirled around. As if it's a notion he has to live with. He'll be keen on football, probably cricket too. Has a prize yucca on his lawn – like the one in the garden here, Mother, which I so dislike.

'A cheetah has spots,' says Pentel man, suddenly, sounding as if he's playing somebody acting stupid with great deliberation. '*Sherlock Holmes and the Speckled Band*. It was on telly the other day, with that actor who's divorced. A baboon, and a cheetah, with speckles. Saw through it before the first adverts –'

'At any rate,' interrupts Sliding Eyes, 'your leopard skin is among the items we would like to have a look at —'

'Good. I hope you find it — and the thief. Find the thief, and you find the murderer.'

He's fazed by this directness, I can see.

'You think so, Mr Arkwright?'

'I do.'

'That's very interesting. A very interesting deduction indeed. Wish I'd thought of it myself.'

I'm beginning to feel feverish, malarially so. It usually starts with jokes, Mother. That postcard in Bexhill, an Illingworth probably, Father chortling as I purchase it at the seaside kiosk: *Mother, do you know anything about Kipling? Naughty boy! I have never kippled in my life!* It's chortling through my head so I close my eyes, which doesn't help. Then there's Reg on that little stage in the troop canteen, doing his Arthur Askey thing: 'Now here's one for Mrs Bagwash!' Applause, whistles, whoops. 'Are you sure you didn't have the leopard skin in your possession between Saturday morning and Monday morning?' Oh, good old Reg, but I never really got his jokes. Everyone around me does, they're roaring, they can't have enough, they're in fits. I'm managing to say *No* through the din. It's so like a rumbling bomber, when I put my fingers in my ears. 'Here's another one for Hugh!' Good old Reg. Jeers now, though. 'Why did you burn some clothes?' Sudden, complete silence. My little voice. I'm being asked to go up on stage. I hate that. I can be an actor on a stage, but I cannot be a member of the audience on the stage. Oh, I so hate it! 'Personal reasons. The attic of my property is full of junk. Among that junk were old clothes. I burnt them.'

'Not good enough for Oxfam, then?'

Oh, Reg, you should have been a pro. Concentrate through the roars and whoops, the frenzied clapping. Boos, even. Some of these chaps won't be alive tomorrow. 'The attic hadn't been touched for a very long time.' That gets them. I'm winning. Reg looms very close. He's milking it. 'OK. Why were you in the wood on Saturday night, sir?' Silence again, except for this thin flute. It's Reg, playing his rivet. 'It's my property.' Now Reg stops dead and grins. 'You told us you came straight back here after leaving the pub.' So quiet they can't be breathing, out there.

'I forgot.'

Somebody coughs, but nobody laughs. 'Do you forget many things, sir?'

'Anyway, he wasn't murdered then, was he? He was murdered on Sunday night, apparently.'

Sliding Eyes ignores me and reaches behind him. He produces the claw-thing, wrapped in polythene.

'It's a tool,' I explain. 'A sort of jemmy, like burglars use. But it's not. Can't remember its proper name.'

'What my old Dad used to call a pry,' says Pentel.

'Really? How extraordinary.'

I'm in the room again. Reg is long dead.

'Why?'

'Pry's Wood. Pry meaning a lime tree. Prying on a pry in Pry's Wood.'

I flush. They might not know I had it that night, that anyone had seen me. Dominick, the girl, the helicopter. No sign of these, yet. Both men look stupid, for a moment.

'Anyway,' I go on, offering information rather than waiting for any forced entry, 'I used it to open things in my attic. Locked things, the old keys lost.'

'Could do quite a bit of damage with this,' says Sliding Eyes, reverently.

'I was careful how I used it,' I say.

The tool is put away again.

'I think that'll do. Sergeant, if you could tag this lot for the station –'

'What?' I expostulate.

'We'll be taking the African material temporarily for examination, Mr Arkwright. It's all covered, and we'll be very careful –'

'I don't wish to be alarmist, but these were once very powerful and sacred objects. In fact, to my knowledge, the box has never been opened up until now.'

Only after the words have left my mouth do I remember the fetishes are about to be examined, presumably for fingerprints as well as for microscopic bits of Muck. Sliding Eyes speaks before I can correct myself.

'I think you're wrong there, sir,' he says, taking a scrap of paper from a clear-plastic envelope. It's the scrap of paper upon which my life depends, Mother! 'Unless they have typewriters out in Bongo-Bongo Land.'

'Don't take that, please don't take that,' I want to say – but don't. I am in enough trouble as it is. While I watch from my chair, everything from Bamakum is tagged and wrapped in polythene and zipped up inside a holdall and taken away.

Your loving son,
Hugh

Hot.

Dear Mother,

About an hour later I am standing in front of the nursing home holding two long hazel sticks cut from a hedgerow. I tell Cliff to return in an hour. Inside, the good news is that Mrs Stanton-Crewe's sailing up the Nile. And Ray is 'a bit better today'. The sweet nurse eyes my hazel sticks as if they're unusual flowers. The end of one of them catches the strip of cardboard requesting old stockings for draught excluders, knocking it off the table. She doesn't mind at all. 'Whoops, that's all right, she passed away ages ago,' she says, folding it up and dropping it into the bin.

I go straight up, by myself. A good sign, I think. I knock on the door and enter, the sticks catching on the lintel. My mouth's open to say hello but instead I gurgle; Ray's so much better that he's become his son. The door returns on its heavy spring and catches the sticks so that they leap out of my hand. The son ducks, I dive after them. One stick, caught in the door, springs up and quivers at head level, horizontally. I almost take my eye out on it.

'Planning on taking dear old Dad out for a spot of fishing, this time?'

There's a growl from the high-backed chair: Ray emerges from it as if from a tomb. Piers, that's it. He's got the same suit on. I can't think of anything clever to say in reply. I feel very silly, holding the sticks. The whole idea feels very silly. The father and the son look at me: I'm an intruder, I've burst in on family. Ray asks how I'm doing, rather anxiously. But that's what I wanted to ask him, Mother! Piers is holding a box with a picture of a mobile phone on the top. I need to find an excuse for the sticks.

'I'm very well,' I lie.

'Not come to magic him away again, I hope,' says Piers.

Another remonstrance from Ray, but it ends in a cough.

'Just visiting,' I say, taking a bag of liquorice allsorts from my coat pocket. 'See how things were going.'

I stand like the third spear-holder in *The Kingmaker* (with whom I opened my professional career, Mother), handing a bag of gold to Robert Eddison. Piers looks quite like a pudgier Eddison, come to that. He places the box on a stool and takes the allsorts and gives them to his father, who has sat down on the edge of the bed, wheezing. These movements are complicated, as if we're in a complicated blocking rehearsal.

'My favourite,' says Ray, scratching at the plastic wrapping. 'And Piers thinks I need a mobile phone.'

'It's modern,' says Piers, 'can't have anything modern, can we?'

He looks at me brightly and suspiciously at the same time, then at the sticks.

'And I think your father needs a climbing plant,' I say, looking up to where the sticks end above my head. 'But I left the plant in the taxi, and the taxi's gone off.'

Piers looks up at them, too.

'Hope it's unusually vigorous,' he says, in a quiet voice.

Ray is blowing his nose and wiping his mouth in a kerfuffle of stained handkerchief. Anyway, his ears are bad. Ray's lucky to have children, I think. Even if they turn out to be rockers and evangelicals, he's damn lucky.

The son looks at his watch. He has very small ears. Tim said the Cheshire bog man had very small ears. It doesn't matter who we come from: we come from everyone. Then the miracle: Piers announces that he must leave, that it's the Get-Friendly-With-God bash over at Luton in a couple of hours and he's organising the coaches' car park. He says he'll tell the nurses about the phone but Ray coughs and splutters, insisting he take it away. Piers taps the box thoughtfully then goes to the door, the box tucked under his arm. He puts his hand out and I shake it. His hand squeezes my hand as if wringing it clean.

'Difficult sod, but we all love him,' he murmurs, keeping the door open with his foot. 'The Lord be with you.'

'And also with you,' I say. He doesn't take it as mockery. The door strains to close him off, as if it's under my influence. Then I'm alone with the father.

'Modern my foot,' he says, chewing on an allsort.

He's looking out of the window. The word 'modern' hovers for a moment in the grey sky, above the spidery antennae and white dishes. Then it evaporates into its own dullness. I feel a bond. The hazel sticks have purpose again, leaning against the wall.

We talk about doctors for a bit, as far as I remember. Then I sit down next to him, on the edge of the bed. We work through the allsorts like two small boys. 'Have 'em before the nurses do,' Ray jokes. I try to ignore the smell. We ramble around the subject of long-vanished sweets, the way certain brands fizzed or crumbled or shattered in the mouth. And the horrible counterpoint of the daily dose.

'What I need,' says Ray, 'is a flagon of Clarke's Blood Mixture.'

'Good grief, yes. Clarke's Blood Mixture.'

'Vampire medicine. Food for the undead. That's why I need it.'

He eyes me, wheezing under his baldness. I get up and go over to the window. Now or never!

I ask him if he has heard about Frank Petty. He has, yes. Awful business. Yes. Mr Petty was not only one of his 'chief sources', but the 'last proper village character'. 'Mr Petty' sounds different, a different person, Muck with front teeth and wearing a tie, not like a village character at all – they're always toothless. Well, I was never called 'Arkwright' until I went to school – was I, Mother?

He's shifty now, like Malcolm. I ask him what else he knows. He looks out of the window. 'Jessica tells me things.'

There's a little silence.

'But we both agree they've got it wrong,' he adds. 'Don't worry.'

'I'm frightened of them. They're incompetent. I've always been frightened of incompetence.'

'You can hide under my bed,' he says, grinning. 'It'll be like *The Thirty-Nine Steps*. You can pretend to be me. You don't look that far off. Now, what are those sticks doing there?'

I bring them over to him and clear my throat.

'Ray, I want you to do something for me. I will always regard it as the greatest favour anyone has ever done for me in my whole life.'

He says he owes me. Well?

'It's divining time.'

He looks at me as if I've told him that I did do the awful thing.

'But I can't, I can't,' he says, quietly, seeming to wither in front of my eyes, sitting back in his chair.

I wither, too, and sit down opposite him. The window wavers a little. A hunchback in a zimmer frame crosses the lawn with the sweet young nurse. Our lawn is much bigger here, Mother.

'Why not, Ray?'

'Too feeble. I need a pint of Clarke's Blood Mixture.'

Then he asks me what I want him to look for, and I tell him.

'Never done leopard skins before. You need a dog for that. Woof woof. Oh look, here's one. Fancy that. Woof woof.'

Bless his dying heart! I've brought along an AA map and I unfold it on the bed. It's a motorist's map, and the area's too big. It's all towns and too many roads. Ray shakes his head. 'That's not a map,' he says, 'not what I call a map. Look in my top drawer.' I open it and find a pink Ordnance Survey lying on crisp white linen. The eager contours, the little green woods, the winding lanes – how they wash through me! I'm a boy again. I'm planning my day-long bicycle trip, wiping crumbs from the crackly folds –

'Give me one of the withies,' Ray says. 'You should have found a forked one, but I'll do what I can.'

He starts to bend it, but its green strength is too much for him. With the help of my pocket knife, I force it into a V-shape. He sits forward with a grunt and holds it out flat in front of him. 'Bring the map nearer so you can touch me and it at the same time, please.'

I do so. I hold his forearm – sheer bone, it feels like, through the sweater – and place my forefinger on Ulverton's fawn sprawl. What a vast size my finger is. Albert Speer walked round the world in Spandau Prison Yard, using maps.

'Now, think of the leopard skin. Count its spots.'

He closes his eyes, gives a brief sigh, sticks his chin out, and tells me to work grid square by grid square. I should start in one corner of each square and spiral in. I move my finger up to the tiny fawn speck that marks Ilythia and spiral in slowly. The leopard skin spirals with me, but I can't fix its size or shape: it's minute and then it's enormous, blurring out of sight. I try to picture it lying on the tanning table in Bamakum; its hide is facing up, gleaming from its bath. Father, in a cloud of green flies, scrapes at it with his brush. The head is upside-down, hanging over the edge. I can even smell it, smell its dirt plopping off with the suds on to the copper earth of the yard, hear Father swearing softly as he scrapes and flicks, scrapes and flicks. I don't know where you are, Mother. Through this picture the map all but disappears, or seems to drop to somewhere very far down.

I move to the square below, taking in the upper quarter of the village, Ulverton Hall, the beginning of the scarp, the white horse, the long and supple lines of Frum Down. Nothing. I stroke the square, the church, the Old Barn, the shops, the pubs. I sidle past the mill and over Saddle Bridge, wondering if the water might twitch the rods, but it doesn't. I slow over John Wall's tiny black dot, hover over his roof, feel myself duck under the washing-line, afraid of being spotted. Cross on to Malcolm's lawn, past his woodworking shed, splash down the lane.

Nothing, nothing!

Everybody in Ulverton can feel my finger pass over them as a shadow, a little chill. This is the kind of thing I did in the war, Mother, as an observer, bent over huge maps of German towns and cities, of forests and fields and limber rivers; the maps swapped for photographs, my finger passing over roofs, streets, parks, no more than scores and scratches on splotches of grey until the open country appeared and the cross-light of dawn pulled trees, hedges, walls and even hay stooks up and out of the white fields by their shadows – those thousands and thousands of hay stooks and hay ricks like little houses that have gone now, Mother, along with wattled sheep folds and the white chalky roads!

Did they feel a chill as well, those who were to die in flames the following day, as our fingers passed over them?

Nothing.

I pass to the right, to the east, to the grid square of open downland, of rolling fields of corn, a tumulus or two, and Five Elms Farm. I remember the walk there with Rachael, the fields alive with butterflies and the air with love's nectar, the sky marred only by a silver speck, the vapour-trail of war. Deep, cool bluebell woods. The mighty undulations of the bare open downs. There. My finger has finished with it.

Nothing. Then, conscious of the time this is taking, I jump to the square, two to the left, in which the wildwood lies. I look up at Ray before setting off. He's unchanged, like a statue, as if made from wax. Only his eyelids are alive, the wheeze like an old pump. The V of the rod is rigid in his knobbly hands. He looks both very old — too old — and very young, still the boy with his toy. Put away childish things. But what remains, Mother?

I start to track the garden with my huge finger, bringing again the leopard skin and its cloud of green flies into my head.

Something. Something caught. The rod twitching up.

I am staring at the map, at the tip of my finger, but I don't think I stopped in time. A grunt from Ray — the rod's flat again now. I retrace my route, the pad of my finger like a sharp point — I am only just touching the map's surface, you see, shadowing a few square yards on the ground. I see the grass of the garden as I glide in front of the house. The faint line of the grid square is like a wall between the house and myself. But we have done the house before: it is not in the house, is it? I pass easily and slowly through the wildwood, with a bit of a shudder when I touch the part where the corpse hung, up in the tree.

I haven't been picturing the leopard skin. I go back and pass through Ilythia again. Scratch scratch scratch as Father swabs the hide. Quiri is in the door of the kitchen, beyond. He's crouched as if someone is trying to shoot him. I go up to him. Quiri is terrified — not of me, but of what we are doing. He tells me that the leopard spirit will return and avenge itself.

Then I see the skin in the main room, as a rug. Its eyes agoggle, as if the body has been winded by your weight. Why did you sack Quiri, Mother, as soon as my back was turned?

Something, again.

I am not in the garden at all, not now. I've moved out, over the beechwood, to the middle of the scorched field behind. Jenny has told me of the crop-circle here in the summer, a bit like a brain. Nothing again. I glance at Ray. He's looking at the map, at my finger.

'You're in two places at once,' he whispers.

What does he mean?

'Your thumb's the one,' he adds. He's wheezing, as if he's been walking with me.

Yes, the thumb on the same hand is poised very close to the sheet, I hadn't noticed. I lift my finger clear and drop my thumb as a needle is dropped on a record. The rod's pulled upwards, as if by a thread in the ceiling, until it is vertical, trembling in Ray's hands.

I am over Fierce End. The furzy, acid basin of Fierce End, where Rachael wobbled on the witch's stone. Where I told her that the lines of turf between the heather were scars made by giant claws. Where the clean galloping turf of the open downs has a bit of a tumble into heath!

Flying through the air as if pouncing, that's how I see it. And then realise how ridiculous this image is, since the creature weighs too much to be flung in that way. When it was wet, Father could hardly carry it from tub to table, could he?

The rod hits my hand. Ray has dropped it. He's fallen asleep, his head slumped to one side. No, he isn't asleep, he's murmuring something through a slow, heavy wheeze.

'Phew,' he is saying, 'I need a drink.'

'What kind of drink?'

'I'll thank you for some water.'

I fetch some and he drinks it with difficulty from trembling hands. The whole operation has been too much for him.

'I feel wobbly,' he says. 'I need my injection.'

I squeeze his arm and thank him profusely, fold up the map, and return it to the drawer. The white nightshirt, I notice, has a hood. It is more a monk's cowled habit than anything else. He's watching my quizzical expression with his mouth open, drawing breath with difficulty.

'Ask Cliff Trindle about it,' he whispers.

I nod, and fetch the nurse. She seems surprisingly concerned. Half-jokingly, administering the shot, she asks me what I've done to him.

'I think he needs a shut-eye,' she adds. 'Visit over.'

She smiles sweetly. I squeeze Ray's hand and he gives me a feeble smile.

'I'd go up in scale if I could, but it takes it out of me.'

Of course – we might have used one of his parish maps to find the exact spot. But Fierce End is not huge, and any disturbance of its surface would be easy to see. I tell him not to worry, it's fine as it is. The nurse is frowning at me, holding her syringe up – just like they hold it up here, Mother! I take the bent hazel withy, squeeze Ray's hand again, and leave.

Cliff draws up in the car just as I emerge from the gate.

'You look happy,' he says.

'I am.'

'How is he?'

'Better. But he needs a rest.'

'What else is he doing in there, then? Aikido?'

On the way back to the village I ask him to tell me about the monk's white habit in the drawer. A pause.

'We're both members of the local branch of the Most Ancient Druid Order,' he says, as if admitting to being a Rotarian.

'Gosh. I thought Ray Duckett was down-to-earth, for all his dowsing skills.'

Cliff gazes at me wistfully in the mirror.

'That, if you don't mind me saying so, is a rather ironic remark.'

He goes on about earth power and earth currents while half my mind is circling about the little patch of heath. It's dusk outside. We're passing the out-of-town shopping centre, with its prefab hangars and giant hoardings. There are lights on, lots of cars.

'Ray only does it because of Stukeley, I admit to you. Stukeley is Ray's hero. The guy pretty well invented us, you see. The Druids.

Eighteenth century, most of it. But that doesn't put me off. I like the ceremonial bit. We've got this huge horn, about ten feet long, and blow it at the solstice.' A giant, moaning sort of raspberry, the car wandering all over the place. 'Turns you inside out, takes you out of yourself, like the ships' hooters. Like a sort of aural sauna. That and the sun coming up between the menhirs. You know what Stukeley said about the bods that built them? *You've got to admire the vast size of their minds.* That's what he said.'

I pay him way over the odds, I'm so excited. Ted is standing by the back door when I arrive in the yard. He's sweeping leaves off the mat in the last of the light. His face is drawn and white. He seems surprised to see me.

'Back from the dead,' I say, too heartily.

'It's all right for some, then,' he mutters.

He went to the police mortuary yesterday, identifying the body.

'Definitely Muck, then?'

Ted nods. 'Horrible sight,' he murmurs. 'One eyeball hanging out. You'd think they'd have popped it back in or something, knowing I was coming. Couldn't sleep last night. Can't stop thinking about it. One eyeball sort of resting on his cheek.'

He stares at my eye-patch. There's a shape in the doorway, which turns into Fatso. Ted notices that I've noticed. 'Might have to take him to the vet,' he says. 'Doesn't normally fight, that one.' Fatso's flat face is mottled with dried blood, and a bit of his ear is missing. The animal pads off across the yard, still nervous. I think to myself: I must go now. I must bring it back before it's too late. But of course it's already too dark. I go to bed rather early, setting my alarm for dawn.

I wish the heat here was African heat.

Your loving son,
Hugh

Even hotter. Lawn yellow. Sputtery useless sprinkler.

Dearest Mother,

Morris has just visited. He calls me Mr Mime. I'm leaving him the bundle, with instructions to burn it ceremoniously, if anything should happen to me. Some idiot might want to publish its contents, Mother. The whole world prying.

A lovely crisp dawn stroll, in normal circumstances. Deer, rabbits, touches of mist. But I'm rather het up, of course. I have to wipe my brow quite frequently. Now I'm on the rim of the heathy patch, by the stand of beech. The sun has just risen enough to light them. They were there when you were with us, sixty years ago; one of them has fallen, but the others look much the same, except that the earth has worn away around the roots. The sarsens won't have changed, that I know for sure. Their Ice Age rubble stretches along the frosty coomb in the dawn light. The long limber waves of the open downs are more sky than earth, at this time, especially while the mist is still in the air. I could go for a long walk into those empty spaces.

Instead I walk down to the bottom. It's quite a bit colder, down here. Gorse and heather and waist-high bracken. I catch my breath and look about me. I'm nervous, Mother. I half-expect to see the skin sprawled behind a stone, or draped over the gorse thorns, and scan the bracken for a paw or a savage grin.

Nothing.

I look at the slope with the downy claw marks. The bracken has not crept over them at all – not in fifty years! I bend the hazel rod as Ray instructed, then walk up to the far end, where the easterly incline sweeps up to the dark brow of ragged pines. Turning round, making a dent with my heel, I start to dowse at a steady pace. One two, one two, the hazel rod held out before me, the ground passing under it, still grey and shadowy. My breath whirling in the air.

The leopard's hide, sprawled on the table in the yard, Father grunting over the suds of borax, soap and sulphuric acid, his panama shielding his face from me, the leopard's eyeless head bobbing slightly, hanging off the edge, as if it was agreeing with every point put, its long whiskers silver in the sunlight. I'd touched them, and Father had ticked me off. Not a whisker must be bent or broken. Think of them as piano strings, he said. Do you remember, Mother? How annoyed he was, how anxious.

Nothing, the whole way along that side. I do feel a bit

ridiculous, Mother, with my hazel rod. At one point I think I see a figure standing high on the crest above the stripes, and whip my head up to look. Nuncle, I was thinking about Nuncle: and it has the same stocky shape. It merges with the silhouetted bracken fronds – and might have been the bracken itself, moved by the early morning breeze.

I make my breathing shallower, with a couple of Eilrig exercises. I don't think it works if you're worked up. Aunt Joy could never dowse, anyway, and she was always worked up. I try to remember how it felt. Was it like a pulse, a current? A warmth, a chill? Or was it moved like a puppet by a thread hanging from the sky, or pushed up by an invisible hand? Did you ever have a go, Mother? I don't recall you having a go.

I think it just happened, at the time. I was waiting for the cakes, or for the chance to slip away and turn the boring, long-coated crowd into marauding pirates glimpsed from the trees, invading my coral island, desperate to lay hands on my treasure. I had my homemade bow and arrow but I never actually shot at them.

Nothing on the return, one pace to the north.

I think you have to let go. Not think about it.

My lines wiggle between the great lumps of sarsen. I'm not even sure whether the sighting I make each time on a distant tree, as the ploughmen used to do on a whitened branch or Raymond on my ladder, is enough to keep me on the right course.

Then I spot the witch's stone, the stone Rachael stood and wobbled on. It's the only one that rears up like that, like a stag beetle's armour. I lifted her off and hugged her, just there, between the scrubby gorse. How slow-growing is gorse? The peopled world vanished, when I hugged her here. Now there's no one to hug, so it stays: a bright vapour trail, distant blast-furnace of traffic, some snarly saw or other. But no people, at least.

Now I'm standing by the great stone and my hand is on it. The surface is cold from the night. There's lichen on its puckered flanks, green and crisp and perhaps dead. There are little holes scattered over it; I know what these are, these are where the roots of palm trees poked, when the climate was African, when the stone was not yet a stone. Before it was rolled by the ice and smashed up. Oh, that was only yesterday, it's saying. Or maybe the day before. This is not a witch, but a god. No wonder they set them upright.

And the little cupping heath becomes a slurry of ice again. The tundra stretches away, the graveyard of all those warm woods and ferns and African beasts. Hippopotamus, even! Crocodiles! All gone – only the tundra now, the wild icy wind and the sheets of scurrying white.

For the moment, anyway.

I climb onto the top – it'll give me a good view of the whole coomb. The effort of climbing it is age, not the stone. It doesn't wobble, anyway – it's no longer the wobbling stone. The little hollow in its top is filled with rainwater, with a few drowned rowan berries, dropped by birds. The rowan is called the witch-wood, isn't it? Nuncle's most famous essay was about the rowan berry, Mother. The berries germinate in the birds' excreta – their seeds are protected from the stomach's acids by a special skin. So he concluded that birds and rowan trees had made a pact, because rowan trees would not grow without hungry birds, and that this proved nature's vital intelligence.

I roll one of the berries around in my hand and think of Nuncle as a flint-blade buried deep in my vertebrae: when I am exhumed they will find it. A figure on the crest – head and shoulders – pops into the corner of my eye up by the oak copse, then is gone. I'm sure it dived out of sight. There again, it might have been a shadow on the bracken. It had a flat cap on its head, like Nuncle did for a time. I was once mildly rude about Aunt Joy long after she was dead; he told me that if someone ever thought of him badly after his death, he would know and respond, like a dead gypsy. 'This is why I only have good thoughts about Aunt Joy, d'you see?' I tell him in a whisper to go away. Then his presence seems to flood backwards from the future that lay before me when I was last here – and sweeps away the memory of Rachael, standing in my stead, arms out on top of this stone, her lovely black hair tumbling down and down.

Your loving son,

Hugh

Everything shrivelled.

Dearest Mother,
So I have to kneel, or fall off.
I kneel.

Oh, the stone is looking up at me. The trapped witch is pressed to the surface, staring through a chink. Her eyeball boggles up at me through the rowan berries in the little basin of water. At first I think it's the reflection of my own eye – but when I move, it stays.

A perfect eyeball.

Wisps of cloud float over it. Muck didn't actually lose his eyeball, did he? Oh, how horrible. When I've calmed down, I persuade myself to dip my finger into the water and touch it.

It's not gristle, but glass. They call sarsens 'bridestones', locally. At least they did in your time, Mother. Maybe Bride was the old goddess's name. The old goddess, the witch, the ill-wisher, the evil eye. Or perhaps this is one of her miracles. Perhaps she is giving me sight in my blind eye. So I scoop the thing out.

The big glass marble rolls in my palm, almost the companion to Dr Johnson's. Flecked hazel, ordered from London in a pair by Father, with instructions for insertion from a Mr Platting, Taxidermist to the Crown. The things you remember. The things you forget.

Of course I'm happy. If it takes me five, ten, fifteen days, I will find the leopard here. The one-eyed leopard. I even picture it with an eye-patch on. Imagine that, Mother. A snarly leopard with an eye-patch!

In the bracken, probably. Oh, I so like the eye's glassy hardness. Good old Mr Platting, Taxidermist to the Crown.

But why was it placed here? Now there's the funny thing.

I stand up, thinking hard. Oh, I can't remember exactly what I am working out. I don't think any of them were right. I can just see the two barrows poking above the crest, bright in the new light. Keiller once told me they were capped with chalk when they were new, gleaming like white rainwashed skulls in the green turf. Huge albino graves dotted all over the bare green roll of downland. Deathcaps, Nuncle called them. Then I think I see a figure standing on one of them. I shake my head to clear it. It's gone.

But I feel so vulnerable, Mother, up there on that rock. The sun blinds me, shafting over the crest of this place. That means I must be brightly lit, as if I'm on my own little stage. But this very peculiar fear grips me, when I think of climbing down. I think I'll be taken, you see. By the leopard men. Men who know they are leopard men, not men with leopards so deep inside them they don't know they are men. Men with big claws, stalking me. I fancy the whole little furzy coomb is surrounded by leopard men, that if I climb down and stand on the ground they'll leap up from behind every sarsen or rise in a ring from the crests. This strange idea seizes me in the belly, turning my guts liquid with terror. Real terror, Mother. It's so great I can't move. It's like the terror Father felt once, when he thought he heard the growl of a leopard on one of his bush tours. It saves you because it makes you stay absolutely still, gripped by a paralysing fear. I find myself on all four paws on top of the stone, unable to move. At least I'm higher than them, up here! Then this even stranger thing happens. My lips start to draw back from my teeth. I like this sensation, I like exposing my teeth, my gums. You hated me doing this but I'm doing it anyway. I'm doing it now. It requires effort, it's a strain, but I can just about expose my lower gums as well as my upper gums. It makes you feel very fierce, your whole face stretches and becomes one with this snarl, all teeth. It's very satisfying. You see? It protects you from all those leopard men, all those huge metal claws hidden under their skins. You can't argue or plead with a leopard man, you have to frighten him off – even if you are paralysed with fright yourself. You have to be more leopard than a leopard man, like Fatso was more cat than I was in my nightmare on Sunday night. And up there on that stone I feel more leopard than any leopard man, even without the skin. My body becomes limber like the lines of the open downs, and covered in fur like turf, and as strong as the chalk depths are strong. I recommend this sensation, Mother. It does away with the nuisance of being a mortal, fidgeting about with human matters. The only drawback is that you can't speak words. In my book, that is its advantage.

Then I see my first leopard man, for real.

He's disguised as John Wall, that's the trouble. I can tell it's John Wall by the way one leg drags as he makes his way up the coomb. He has a shotgun over his shoulder.

My leopard head is huge, it takes time to find my own little head inside it. I don't want to lose my own little shrivelled human head inside the cavern of the leopard's. But I have to find it in order to talk human words. Because it occurs to me that John Wall might be just John Wall, not realising the danger he's in, with all these leopard men about. On the other hand, he might be pretending he's John Wall so as to get near enough to rip me to ribbons. He's coming nearer and nearer, sort of determined but not hasty, not rushing. I'll stay up here for the moment. I manage to sit, crossing my legs. My leopard head is a sort of phantom cloud around my little human head. My whiskers gleam clearly, though, and are surprisingly long.

He stops at a little distance.

'Mornin', Mr A.'

'Morning, John. What are you shooting?'

'You look like Humpty Dumpty up there, Mr A. Oughta be careful you don't have a great fall.'

He's tempting me to step down.

'I used to come here as a boy, you see, John.'

His face is against the light, pale but shadowy. Otherwise I could judge his expression. I don't like the gun.

'Bad things have happened, Mr A.'

'I know. I'm very sorry about your friend, John.'

'Bad things followed by bad words. I hear as you've been usin' some very bad words, Mr A.'

He's taking the gun off his shoulder, tucking it under his arm. It's pointing at the stone – not exactly at me, but near enough to be worrying. Now my height is a disadvantage. I'm like a tin on a rock, ready to be peppered. He's just too far to be leapt on. You see my difficulty, Mother? I glance down to see if I can jump it on the other side and there's a neat tuft of grass which I think at first is a big clawed paw.

It is a paw.

It's sticking out of the rock, as if the rock is growing the paw. John Wall is carrying on as I look at this paw, but I'm too shocked to reply. Why should I be shocked? I expected to find the thing somewhere around here. The claws on the paw are like bulbous roots, exposed to the air.

'It ent polite, in fact it's bloody rude, what you've been sayin', Mr A.'

I manage to twist my head round. Now I'm sure he's John Wall, but that is no comfort.

'What have I been saying, then?'

'You know what you've been sayin'. Say it again, now.'

The gun is actually pointing at me. There are no boys behind us – it's pointing at me, and only me. He's threatening me with it. My leopard head has vanished, now. He's come to get the skin, I think. He's hidden it here and now he's come to destroy it.

'I would say whatever I said, if I knew what it was. I don't like you pointing that gun at me, John.'

'You bloody well know what you said. Bloody smart-ass toff, comin' down here an shoutin' your mouth off.'

He's savage. He would like to kill me.

'I honestly don't know, John.' But I do, of course. I know exactly what he's talking about. I should have kept my thoughts to myself.

'You're a bloody liar on top of bein' a bloody slanderer. But I know why, see. It's to cover yourself, innit? Blame a bloke what's innocent to get the dogs off of you. You'd have me inside for life just to save your neck. Bloody fuckin' toff.'

His pale, shadowy face is seething with hate for me. He drags himself a few steps nearer.

'Why, Mr A? Why me? Why the fuck get them dogs on me?'

He's almost crying.

'I don't know, John. I'm awfully sorry. I got everything wrong. The whole lot. I suppose I thought you'd stolen the skin, you see. All those skins in your house –'

His head jerks at that.

'Who showed you 'em?'

'No one.'

'Snoopin' again, eh? Snoopin' an pryin' again, eh? Private bloody property, eh? You wanna look in my bed, do you? Look at my sheets, do you?'

The shotgun's waving about, but always in my direction. I've never had a gun waved at me before, not like this, not so that I can actually see its tight snout. I'm so frightened that I have broken through to somewhere calm.

'Did you follow me here, John?'

The gun stops waving about.

'So what if I did?'

'Or were you unlucky, finding me here?'

He breathes so I can hear it. The day advances pace by pace. There's a little more light each minute. The stone's so used to this. It's had millions of days already, breaking over its flank. Something might have its head blown off on top of it, but the rain will wash the bits away, the blood. The stone won't notice.

Your affectionate son,

Hugh

Rain, at last. But not quite enough.

Dearest Mother,

John Wall then says, 'I reckon I'm bloody lucky, findin' you here, Mr A.'

The muzzle of the gun is pointing firmly at my head. Perhaps Nuncle sent him. Perhaps he heard voices.

'Do you hear voices, John?'

The gun wavers.

'Why should I?'

'Voices can make you do the most awful things.'

He starts to sing.

'Humpty Dumpty sat on the wall, Humpty Dumpty had a great fall.'

I sing with him.

'All the King's horses and all the King's men, Couldn't put Humpty together again!'

The strange thing is, Mother, I start to cry. I sit up there on that rock with the most uncomfortable bottom, tears rolling down my face and my mouth all loose and trembling. It's not just because you used to sing this to me in Africa, it's because I can see myself in little pieces on the ground. It's already too late. I always felt so sorry for Humpty Dumpty.

John Wall comes right up to the rock. His head is where I begin. The gun rests its snout like a dog on the top of the stone. Why hasn't John Wall got a dog? Has he skinned that, too? I don't care that he can see me crying. This is because he's been so rude to me, calling me names, as brothers can be rude to each other. It makes me feel close to him. He's my brother.

'Why don't you just tell 'em, Mr A? Tell 'em you come over all queer an didn't know what you was doin'? Before they collars you? Before they collars you an it's too late?'

'I didn't kill your friend, John. I don't know who did but I didn't.' I wipe my nose on my sleeve. Everything goes when you're in this state, Mother. 'Actually, I do know who did it. Whoever hid the leopard skin under this stone did it, you see. That's why the stone doesn't wobble any more!'

I laugh through my tears. The new fresh sun's blinding me. I let it. Nuncle forged the letters, I think. I have to think this to myself because I keep hearing your voice reading out phrases from the letters, as if you wrote them yourself. John Wall's laid his hand on my knee, stretching up.

'It's you as hid it there, Mr A.'

'Don't talk rubbish, John. Leave me alone. I need to think on my own. Why doesn't anybody leave me alone?'

'You were seen, Mr A. You were seen with it. That's why they knows you did it.'

I look down at him. His hand is lying with its dirty broken nails on my knee. His lips are drawn back from his teeth, like mine. I've let him get too close. I stand up and step backwards, almost falling off the stone. My heel splashes into the basin.

John Wall's eyes are wide, almost boggling. I think he thinks I didn't like him to touch me. 'He saw you, Mr A,' he hisses. 'He saw you with it, the day it were took out the cupboard.'

'Who?'

'I can't say, but it's someone as don't lie, Mr A. All you has to say is you weren't in possession of all your faculties. It happens. You're gettin' on, Mr A. You ent quite yourself, is you? You talks to yourself. You walk about at night. Maybe you need treatment.

Go along an tell 'em, tell 'em now before they tell you, Mr A. That's my advice.'

His face is savage again. It's screwed right up, desperate over the lip of the stone. Now I know everything. Now I know who did it, for certain. He's climbing up on to the stone, grunting because it's the sheer flank, because his leg is awkward. His hands are at my feet, gripping the rough surface of the stone, hauling the rest of his body up, his gun next to them, free to grab. Silly man. He must think, because I'm crying, I'm beyond decisive action.

He's wrong, Mother. I pick up the gun and point it at him. He looks up at me with a startled expression.

'Get down, or I'll kill you quicker than you killed Muck.'

He snarls and grabs my ankle – both my ankles! I try to kick free but his grip is tight as iron, there's a kind of equilibrium in our position, and I'm on the edge of the stone. I lift the gun and bring it down on his wrist – the right one, I think. He grunts and swears but his grip tightens even more. He's pulling me over, now. Then he'll kill me. So I have no option, I bring the gun down as I was taught in the war – on his head, the butt on his head, on his skull. But it all goes wrong because I'm toppling already. I end up on top of him, my face in the crook of his bad leg. The cloth of his trousers smells of fox, of vermin, of hung game. In disgust I scrabble free of him but he's caught my coat by the front, twisting it and pulling it towards him. 'You fucker,' I can hear him say, 'you rich murderin' fucker.' There's blood dribbling down his face from a welt on his forehead. I must have struck him, after all. I've half slipped down the shallow slope of the stone on one side, near the paw. The coat is going one way and I'm going the other, we're panting, I'm held only by the coat, by the fist bunched at my collar, the rest of me sprawling downwards nearly to the ground, dangling. His breath is in my face, foul as hell. So I bite his fist, sinking my old teeth and my new teeth as far as their looseness will allow. I taste blood, anyway. He yowls and I find myself spreadeagled on the grass. The gun has fallen off with me. He's up there, sucking his fist.

'You're a fuckin' animal, you are!' he's shouting.

I'm tugging at the leopard skin, holding it by its paw and tugging. If I leave it here, he'll destroy it. I was seen with the package on my bicycle and they all think it was this – I'm in deep trouble. I'm yanking the bulky skin with one hand and waving the gun with the other. There are bits of sausage in the claws. The stone is on top of the skin. How did anyone move something that hadn't been moved for millions of years? Then the skin comes and I tumble with it. The gun goes off. It goes off but I only hear its echo and a ringing in my ears. The leopard skin is on top of me, the huge head eating me up with its half mouth. I'm screaming because it's the agonised rat's head in the cellar, giant. People are running. I can see them running along the side of the world just as I saw Mr Allinson running along the side of the beach so long ago. Arms pick me up, no, pin me down. I'm being impaled like the ring dove, the skin is being tugged away, I'm being stripped of my fur. Africa leaves me, I'm raw like the open downs. Instead of the leopard's great head, there's Malcolm's little rodent chin. Above it, his mouth is moving. Words come out of it.

'Don't fight them, Hugh. Just don't fight. Just don't, OK?'

Your loving son,
Hugh

Chill snap. Leaves tumbling and getting raked.

My dearest Mother,

Fagg's face emerges from its silhouette.

'Morning, Mr Arkwright.'

I'm standing up, now. There are men around him with funny vests on, holding guns. Others are dressed as ordinary policemen. They all stand rather casually, in a haphazard circle around us. Some of them have thin poles. Two or three look around as if spotting a place to lay a picnic tablecloth, the eyes of the rest shift between my face and the leopard skin. Malcolm is rubbing his hands, looking down at the big black hole left by the skin.

'Thank God you came, Sergeant.' I can't remember his name for a moment. Only part of me is actually saying this, the rest is panting, bruised and crouched. 'Just in time, I'd say.'

'Detective Sergeant Ronald Fagg, even to my wife and the cat. You have a habit of forgetting things, sir.'

'Titles have always been my weak point. I'm sure even you have your weak points.' I clear my throat and point to the skin, my hand trembling away. One of the policemen is covering it in a sheet of plastic. Into the plastic goes the great snarling head. My voice sounds muffled, now. 'The murder weapon, I think you might call it. Very cleverly hidden, using what I think is a badger's sett. This stone is known as the Witch Stone. It used to wobble. Hiding the skin under it took away its wobble. That should have alerted me.'

I slap the sarsen rather heartily and end up leaning on it. One of the policemen blows his cheeks out, as if bored. 'Just in time, yes,' says Fagg. 'An early riser, you are. Disturbed my beauty sleep. You've got to be careful with guns, you know. They have a habit of killing people.'

I look around for John Wall. He's having his fist and head dealt with by the man I nicknamed Brut. 'I didn't kill him,' I point out.

'Knocked him about a bit, Mr Arkwright. An active man for your age.' Then he turns to Malcolm. 'That'll be fine, Mr Villiers. We'll call you if we need you.' Malcolm gives me a little furtive nod and walks off. I don't understand, Mother.

John Wall is holding the gun, having his head dabbed and holding the gun.

'He's got the gun,' I manage to say.

'It's his. He's got a licence,' Fagg says. He nods at someone and they stand next to me. He sets his weary eyes on my face. 'Come along now, Mr Arkwright. We've got a bit of talking to do. I have to warn you that anything you say —'

'He's got the gun and you're not going to take it off him? You're not going to arrest him?'

'It's you we're arresting, Mr Arkwright.'

John Wall limps up to Fagg, avoiding my eyes. 'Took your bloody time, didn't you? He nearly had me, there.'

'Looked like you were coping, from where we were, Mr Wall. Didn't want to leap too early, did we?' Then he turns to me and tells me again that I am under arrest. John Wall nodding, but not smiling, not catching my eye.

'Detective Sergeant Fagg, you have gone completely mad.'

The circle is closing. The young men look thuggish, suddenly, their faces pale and unappetising, with pimples. Their hats don't seem to fit. I have a tremendous desire to knock one off and run, run until their grasping hands tear the clothes from my back, run on until the last one falls behind me and I am free for ever, with nothing but the deep, wild woods behind and beside and before me, running with the wild deer and auroch for ever and ever.

Fagg is smiling, his head bent to one side.

'Mad, eh? Pot calling the kettle black perhaps, Mr Arkwright?'

Perhaps. Yes, perhaps.

Your affectionate son,

Hugh

First frost yesterday.

Dearest Mother,

You know how many days I spent in the cell? Because I don't. I was in a white space smelling of damp mops and fresh paint, with a small barred window through which the light changed from day to night at regular intervals. I had a lot of pork pies, their pastry's crinkles made by cellophane. The tea was awful, really awful. Always too much milk. You know how I hate pork pies and milky tea.

I was questioned many times. It was Malcolm who 'shopped' me. He passed me when I was on the bicycle, carrying the oil-paper package. He thought it was the leopard skin. It all clicked together in his head. I had scratches on my face, leaves in my hair, I looked generally under the weather, I'd burned my clothes, I was spotted with a metal claw. You can't blame him, can you?

Sitting in the white cell, I had lots of pictures. The wall cracked like the church's plaster cracked after the bombs fell, showing the pictures underneath. The freshly painted walls of the cell were covered in pictures. I saw Muck and Aunt Rachael giggling together. I saw Jack Wall up in the tree in the wildwood. I saw the Red Lady floating across the lawn. If Muck hadn't told me about the Red Lady, I would never have fiddled about in the attic, opening the trunk. So it's really your fault, Mother. You should never have bought that coat. You should never have gone off like that.

They even had my motive worked out for me: they seized my diary, you see – and John Wall had fed them with stuff about Rachael, my threats, all that. The only sticking point was how I managed to get the dead man into the tree. I didn't tell them that a man, even an old man, can have the strength of a leopard if he's a leopard man. I didn't tell them anything. Barry was useless, even though he did a lot of the talking. Morris and others gave excellent character references but sounded panicky on the radio and television news, in between shots of Alan G's Hamlet saying he was only mad when the wind was southerly. Imagine, Mother!

The pictures grew worse day by day. Some of them were actual nightmares. I saw Muck's terrified face and my clawed hands tearing at it. I saw Malcolm's chin turning into the agonised rat, forcing his mouth up into his eyes. The tinted frontal lobe positioned itself securely just here, tap tap, drilled in by Nuncle. The cell became your room, full of munching ants. Crocodiles bumped their snouts against the window's reinforced glass. But the very worst thing, Mother, was that Sir Steggie finally found me. After all that time, all that searching, he tracked me down. He did something very clever: he pretended to be Herbert E. Standing, in the same white cricketing togs. That's why I let him come close. Then off came the mask and it was Sir Steggie. His lips were right off his teeth, as if eaten away, but it was only a smile. He was sweaty and dirty, as if he'd come a very long way. He was holding your letters – I mean, the letters Nuncle forged in order to destroy me. Sir Steggie put a finger out and touched me on the cheek. His finger was sticky.

'Hello, Hugh,' he said. 'We meet at last. Yum yum.'

I was screaming – it was my only defence, Mother! Now they tell me that there was no one in the room at all – that I was screaming at my reflection in the window glass! If only they knew! I don't wear dirty spectacles, do I? I don't have fingers covered in Lyle's Golden Syrup, do I? I don't have a head like an armadillo, do I? And how do they explain the dab of Lyle's Golden Syrup on my cheek? Eh? I kept showing it to them, but no one would listen.

But the very worst thing, Mother, was that I began to believe the letters were not forgeries. The police found the grass-cutting rota for Effley parish church in my back pocket (I can't think why it was there, right now, but it made things even stickier, of course) – and its crooked type looked just the same as yours, and Nuncle's, and half the old typewriters in the world, I should think! So I began to believe that it *was* you who'd bashed out the letters –and all that that must mean for me! As I began to believe that I had sallied forth at night with the leopard spirit in me, and settled an aching score!

I'm getting worked up again. Enough to have them popping their heads round. I'm fine, now, I tell them. They need reassuring, you see. Poor souls.

Then one day they open the door and tell me that I can go home. Isn't that amazing, Mother? I ask them why. Because John Wall has come down to the police station and told them. Although he's very drunk. Told them what? That he did it, he did it, he did it. 'I dunnit, I dunnit, I dunnit.'

Do you know who told him to tell them? His mum.

Your affectionate son,

Hugh

Bright and breezy. Lovely colours.

My dear Mother,

I'm doing rather well.

Fagg isn't around to apologise. A minion hands me a holdall with the bits of Africa they had taken away. 'Tell Detective Sergeant Fagg that leopards stalk baboons in the trees, so he'd better watch out.' The minion smiles, funnily enough.

Most of my stuff is still in Ulverton, so I have to return to that wretched village. I take the bus, this time, but there is no one I know – there is almost no one, in fact! Ilythia turns as we pass, behind her Scotch pines; next to the gate there's a fluorescent planning-permission poster. Not quite a green shoot, but it'll do.

Ted thinks he's seen a ghost when I walk in. 'Hello, Ted. I'm to be hung tomorrow but they thought I ought to do a few more murders, starting with you.' Or words to that effect. Ted, you see, phoned the police when I crept out at dawn. He was asked to do this. Community service, I suppose. He stands me a double whisky in recompense, but in the back room. I do need a drink. His spectacles are right on the end of his nose as he tells me all. John Wall got the skins and Muck took them to the taxidermist. There's a roaring illegal trade in skins, you see – badger, fox, rabbit, even otter. And then your leopard one comes along. By the caravan next to the wildwood, on the old gypsy plot, Muck made a pass at John, that's what they think. 'If you know what I mean, Mr Arkwright. *Hands*, y'know.' He flutters his hand, grips his own thigh. 'Always something a bit corkscrew about Muck. John hits Muck, slightly too hard. Couldn't stop hisself, that's what he says to Scott-Parkes, this morning. Put the boot in, over and over. Horrible, really. Sort of frenzy. Then he, he rips him up with the leopard claws to make it look as if, as if it was an *animal* as had done it, see. Hides him up the tree. Inhuman strength, I call it.'

Now I see!

'An animal, Ted?'

'That's right. Cunning bloke.' He knows damn well what I'm thinking. He's still got the odd dry tea leaf in his cardie. I make a growling noise – I'm acting, it's an act. Then I point to myself. Ted frowns and shoves his spectacles up.

'This is the animal he was thinking of, Ted. He knew I'd been seen with the missing leopard skin just the day before. Malcolm Villiers told him, over a wood-pigeon pie. It's called framing someone. But I didn't have the leopard skin, did I?'

Ted shrugs his shoulders and offers me another whisky. I refuse.

'What time did the murder take place on Sunday night, Ted?'

'Oh, the early hours. John was going on about rough cider what had made his head go round and round, or summat, this morning. Poor bugger. You ask Doc Scott-Parkes. It was him as got the confession. God knows why.'

'Oh, I expect I'll read all about it.'

He thrusts his spectacles up his nose again, goes over to the door, hovers. 'You know you've been in the papers quite a bit already, don't you? We told them journalist buggers you were in the clink, you wouldn't be coming back here. Put 'em off the scent, anyway. All they did was drink, if you ask me. And there's a bit of post upstairs.'

The post goes straight into my bag along with everything else. I open only one letter, the one with a District Council stamp, from Rob Gardner. He confirms that the freshet, and the soil it floods into, has been seriously contaminated by a long-term leaking of arsenical pesticides and other 'agricultural products of a chemical nature'. The Jennets have been contacted. No mention of gas or corpses.

I pop into the shop. Marjorie pretends nothing has happened, that she knows nothing. I go over to Gracie in her basket chair and take her hand and kiss it. She has a bowl of redcurrants in her lap. Her hand is even lighter, like a sticky red fledgling. 'God bless you, Gracie,' I murmur. There are tears in my eyes.

'Don't folk gabble!' is all she whispers, as if it's something only she and I can share.

I go across to the Old Barn. 'Goodbye Jessica. In another age I would have married you.' She kisses me on each cheek and says that she never thought I'd done it, it was that creep Malcolm's doing and of course that weirdo John Wall's. 'Blame no one,' I say, 'but a ghost.'

'What ghost?'

'The Red Lady. Ghosts are will o' the wisps, they lead you off the path into bottomless bogs.'

'Do you believe in ghosts, Hugh?'

'Of course not. That's the trouble.'

The local headlines flap inside the grilles of the two hoardings outside the newsagents. Not changed since last week, I suppose: HORRIFIC MURDER SHOCKS VILLAGE, shouts the *Netherford Advertiser*. But the *Netherford Weekly News* has chewed its pen to shreds, clearly: THE LION OF THEATRE SPOTTED WITH KILLER SKIN. And the nationals ran even harder with it, Morris will tell me. Now there's egg on their filthy faces – but my reputation is dead. I am the Tate & Lyle lion, now, with bees making a hive in my head.

Buzz buzz, they go – even here, even as I'm writing to you, Mother. Reminding me that John Wall sits in his cell saying he didn't do it, these days. This is what I've read. He always was a liar, I tell myself. I dunnit. I never dunnit. One of these is a lie.

One of these is a mask. It's all his mum's fault, to my mind. (My head is such a hive of these sticky thoughts!)

People I pass stop in shock, or hurry across to the far side. Not everyone's heard! Then I spot Mrs Pratt, busy nattering to someone by the antiques shop. Rollo scampers up as I walk towards her. She turns her head and actually squeals. 'Mrs Pratt,' I say, 'you have nothing to worry about – even a leopard has taste. But watch out for the crocodiles. They eat anything, at any time. Crocs are not fussy at all.' She gives a little swallowy gulp and invites me to tea. I laugh.

On a whim, I enter the phone box in the square. 'Mr Gardner? I'm out. I didn't do it.' Rob Gardner sounds unwell. I ask him if any of the poisons on his list has a garlicky odour. No, he says, he knows of no product that smells of garlic apart from mustard gas. He is personally very very sorry that no traces of mustard gas have been detected in the samples. 'You have done me a profound service, Mr Gardner,' I say. 'You see, a scent of wild garlic is all I have left.' Silence. His breathing. As if he's wearing his mask.

Passing the primary school, on my way to the parish clerk's house, I hear a drum. Bom bom bom. It's Malcolm's drum. So I tap on the window until he stops and turns. His expression is one of sudden horror, since I am leering at him. The children laugh and some of them burst into tears. My face squashes against the glass and I'm wiggling my fingers by my ears. His rodent chin is covered in stubble. He hides it behind his own fingers. Then I leave him to his fright.

Mr Quallington comes to his door and pales on seeing me. 'I've been let out into the community,' I say. 'John Wall has confessed.'

'I'm not surprised,' he says. He huffs and he puffs, full of apologies for not finding out about your plot, Mother.

'I'm leaving for ever this afternoon,' I say. 'It's now or never.'

The vestry's chilliness is stronger than the warm smell of wine and linen and beeswaxed wood. Mr Quallington pulls out a big leather-bound file containing half a century of documents relating to the graveyard. Your plot, Mother, was near Aunt Joy's, but is now someone else's. 'I want to know when it became someone else's,' I say. He huffs and he puffs and turns the big pages through the 1930s. Nothing. The war, but the gummed-in scraps continue as if nothing has happened. Deaths. Reclaiming of old plots. A small fee to tend it when there's no one else.

At last – an Arkwright! It's the copy of a letter to Father, dated late November 1944. From Herbert Hobbs, Gracie's husband. The winter is harsh, there are more deaths than usual, the churchyard is short of space. He wants to know whether Mr Arkwright might consider releasing his late wife's plot. Father's reply on the next page is tardy but terse, his hand shaky from drink. He is writing on the eleventh anniversary of his dear wife's disappearance. He can see no objection to annulling his reservation of the plot and thus freeing it. (He was broke, for one thing, Mother, but he didn't say that.)

The next letter pasted in gives me a little shock. It's from Nuncle. He objects to this annulment, speaking as the dead woman's brother, in sorrow but also 'eternal hope'. Mr Quallington smooths the page. The husband overrules the brother. 'A bit of a kerfuffle, it seems,' says the little man, gloatingly. 'Oh, it's par for the course in this book.'

Jessica will kindly drop me off in Netherford – but I will go, not immediately to the station, but to the library. I will scroll the microfiched pages of the *Netherford Weekly News* for the last wintry weeks of 1944. There! Owing to the wartime blackout, and the danger of waving bright lamps about at night, Ulverton Manor's carol-singing round took place *in the morning.*

The librarian will wonder why I am laughing so loudly, in a place of whispers. What I guess in the vestry will be confirmed, you see. The carol-singers crunched from house to house *on the same morning!*

I mean, Mother, the morning of the day Herbert Hobbs received Father's letter. The tea was an elevenses of hot mulled-wine and cake. It was all accounted 'a great success, despite the bitter temperatures'. Well, I am glad.

Their lamps swinging on chains through the grey gloom, but not for reading by, oh no. Gracie, dear Gracie, is neither a liar nor ga-ga. You weren't dead for her in 1933, were you? You were only dead for her when her husband mentioned, oh good, the Arkwright woman's plot is free. No longer waiting for Mrs Arkwright? No, she's gone for good, my dear. From then on, I

410

was the only one waiting for you, Mother. I was the only one keeping you alive.

So who did the tipsy Gracie see that day, in a cherry-red coat and raven hair, crunching over the snow in the noon light? That day you were officially extinguished, Mother.

Well, it could have been anyone. Mrs Rachael Arnold, for instance. Newly wed. Getting used to the country. The coat emerging with a rustle from its cellophane, now its owner was officially extinct. An expensive coat, wartime scarcity, the bitter cold. Father would've had no use for it, would he? Kept in the family, never used.

The effigy of you, from the back, in the days before she declined.

He's talking again, the huffy-puffy little man in that place of wine and beeswax and mothballs. He's turned to the next page, another typed letter on wartime paper under his finger. He sees his father's signature – it makes him very happy, this. Rambles on about the old times, about Len and Harry the gravediggers. Somebody's practising scales on a piano somewhere near, it wafts over the churchyard and enters by the open door, plink plonk plunk. Harry grew prize geraniums. Crumbled bone for fertiliser. Bright red geraniums. He's rambling. Rambling about rams. A ram. A ram's skull.

I open my eyes in the shadows, on my little wobbly chair. He's stabbing the book with his plump finger, looking at me expectantly. 'Isn't that funny?' he says. 'Never made the connection.'

'What connection?'

'Between your mum's plot and the ram!'

'What ram?'

He sighs. Where have I been just now? he's thinking. Goodness knows. Then he softens, because I'm old and the cassocks hang next to my cheek, reminding him to be charitable. He folds his hands like the people fold them here, not quite in prayer.

'They found a ram's skull, in your mum's plot. Len and Harry did. Nice big twirly horns. My dad was the replacement sexton, you see, it being the war, so I was there when he was shouted for. Me a little lad in shorts, next to him, peeping over. Frost on the ground, earth hard as nails. And these twirly horns at the bottom of the pit, in this sort of rotted sack. Horrible smiling teeth, big skull, just like you find them out on the downs. Now who would stuff a sheep's head into an empty plot?'

I continue to sit in the shadows.

'It wasn't stuffed,' I say, 'it was dropped into a pit secretly dug for the occasion.'

He clears his throat and puffs. He doesn't like to be corrected. Who does?

'Were there any other bones, Mr Quallington? Or was it just the ram?'

I'm tapping my frontal lobe, which still tends to be tinted.

The letter crackles under his finger. 'Not according to my old dad's report, no. Apart that is, from a pig's trotter and an ox tail – but we're always finding bits of lunch in the churchyard, Mr Arkwright. That's what Harry used to say: this place is one big lunch, he used to say. Gallows humour, see. All out on contract, now, of course. Oh no. No *human* bones, anyway.'

He chortles as I go to the door. Stand there, a bit dizzy: the churchyard, the trees, the open downs. The high-piled sky. He's talking behind me, huffing and puffing again. 'I hope I've not upset you, Mr Arkwright. I mean, with respect, even if there was a whole lorry-load of bones found in your mum's plot, there's one poor soul you can bet they wouldn't belong to, Mr Arkwright.'

'Who's that?'

'Your old mum, God bless her.'

He gives another little chortle, then thinks better of it. My hands are trembling. The cell did me no good. The pork pies. The shiny walls. The smell of bleach.

'God bless her indeed, Mr Quallington,' I whisper from the door, 'for you are absolutely right.'

Then I stride away, without falling over.

You see, Mother, it's only since I have come here that I have regained my faith. It's taken a long time to rebuild, piece it back together, bit by bit!

Nuncle's typewriter bashed away that little bundle of foul lies, oh yes. But why? That is the question. Why go to such trouble? Such invention? And so very meticulous! And then to tuck it away for the years to come. For me. For the one person he knew must happen upon it in time. Tick tock!

I am still working that one out, Mother. When I have worked it out, I will leave here and travel to Africa. I will steam up the river to Bamakum, of which I believe there is nothing left. Because when I close my eyes and travel there in my head, I see only tendrils and creepers hanging from tall trees and the dark swirl of water before them. Nothing else. Shall we go there together? We'll take a panga each and cut our way to Father's road. Do you think Father would come, too? The three of us should manage it, in silence of course, each as speechless as the trees. We'll keep cutting our way to Odoomi, and then take the ancient paths to your dark lake in the crater. This time, I promise I will try to swim.

And may I invite Quiri?

Yes, I'll start arranging it now: a certain long moment lost in Africa.

Our own, our own long moment, Mother.

Your ever loving son,
Hugh

5

Buea, November 2nd, 1920

Dear Joy and Edward,

Well! Here we are! And it is not nearly as hot as James implied. I'll tell you why in a minute. No, why not now? We are halfway up (at a guess) a most enormous mountain – a volcano, would you believe, and not in the least bit dormant. Don't fret about us: the lava flowed down the other side, last time, about fifty years ago. Isn't this, Edward, what Alex Keiller said things were like when we were all still apes? Except that in Buea there are fine tea-roses – and cups of tea to keep away the foggy *chill!*

The journey was awful. Three weeks of sickness in mostly rough seas (James said they were *not* rough, just 'lively'). I'll pick us up when we first saw Africa – *smelt* her, actually, great beast that she is. I don't mean the northern, sandy bit – that's not *our* Africa. I mean the point where the copper-green of the forest runs right down to the water under frightfully thunderous-looking cloud. Left and right it runs, on and on into eternity, with only a pencilled line of pale beach and the odd white flash of foam between. You can just hear the roar and crash of the breakers from the rail of the poop deck (you see how technical I'm become!), but the *smell* is the most remarkable thing. It is of things vegetable, rotting. James is saying (we're on the ship, remember) that the smell is of the mangrove swamps, stagnant waters between the roots, full of crocodiles.

Whenever the ship leaves the open sea, the stench is worse (no, not *worse* – simply thicker, like a steaming flannel pressed to your face!) and each tiny port we anchor off seems to be little more than a Turkish bath of tin roofs and bright red soil and a jetty that wobbles on big oil drums. James gives these places names, rather

417

grand ones that bring back lessons at school – in particular Miss Goodall slapping the oilcloth Empire with her ruler – but I won't bore you with them. Thinking of school makes me feel very far away from all my friends and family, as school itself used to do – but I only allow myself a little homesick weep in the cabin while James is drinking with some Gold Coast fellows (magnificent cummerbunds, of course). Then we see Mount Cameroon – the volcano. It is black and huge, finishing up in the cloud almost before it has properly got going. The cloud still sits over the coast like a giant kettle lid. (When there is a break, and the sun shines through, the vegetation turns from copper-green to silver and gold!) Instantly, I yearn to climb to the top, because James says there's snow up there. Mrs Kingsley did it – I'm reading her book on deck, when the sun's not burning. *Travels in West Africa*. What about *Nursing in West Africa*?

James wants to show me Duala, where he had his big naval battle. So we don't hop off at Victoria, like all the English people, but stay with the rather pompous and oily-haired Frenchmen (small hands, small feet – have you ever noticed?). The ship is now creeping towards the cluttered dock of the 'major' port, our great wake slapping at the chopped-out hulls of 'pirogues' rather arrogantly, and only meeting its match in the prisons of mangrove roots on the edge (not really an edge, since the creeks break it in a thousand places . . . I don't think Africa *has* edges, really). I'm casting pennies, like the others (well, they're casting centimes, I suppose), from the high side of the steamer into the khaki-coloured water, and glistening youths dive after them, dangerously close to our huge sliding bulk, and emerge like seals with the pennies on their noses.

'Look, my darling,' says James, pointing at something like an electricity pole sticking up out of the water, 'look at the gulls on that mast, look at its rust. Six years ago, it was riding high above a shining steel hull and twenty great guns.'

Edward: I'm afraid I made admiring noises. One can be the *generous* sort of pacifist, can't one?

Duala is really just a bigger version, in French, of those tin-roofed Turkish baths along the way. Cockroaches in the Hotel Akwa, but everyone *so* starched and dapper, despite their coarse, sunburned faces! (I'll ignore the unshaven drunks in the corner, whom James identified as up-coast traders, 'the worst sort'). One night showed me all, especially the mosquitoes. All the native waiters and bellboys had white gloves and starched collars more spotless than our own, and spoke a pidgin French reminiscent of mine.

Then a morning's drive to Victoria along the wide orange – no, red – dirt road. (Strewn, according to James, with uniformed corpses six years ago.) Trees, trees, trees, but so thick, like a wall. A ritual stop before the 'Hanging Tree': if anyone thinks the Germans did it better, then let them look at the polish on that big branch! (James was disappointed to see the rope gone.) At each scatter of huts – cosy, all thatched, with old men beneath the spreading tree, like our dear Ulverton – the villagers cried, 'White man! White man!' That told me we were in the British part. Then on and on, bumping and swaying, me holding on to my hat in the back, squeaking each time we hit a puddle. The puddles are ponds, here. Some are deep enough to drown a motor car, says James, only one can't tell which. They remind him of flooded shell holes, which is unfortunate (he goes very quiet, like you, Edward, when thinking of that time). The sky looked very low and rainy and dark, in fact, but it never broke. My own perspiration was quite drenching enough, thank you.

No, *it* never broke, but *we* broke into *it*!

That's to say, when we started climbing up the mountain to Buea, we had to put the hood up – and it *has not stopped since* (three days)! James says the heaviest rains are nearly over. Jolly good.

We are in the guest bedroom of Government House, which used to be von Puttkamer's residence, and there is a display of his favourite torture instruments in the lobby, though they look suspiciously like bits of iron bedsteads sawn up. The *real* HQ is in Nigeria, so Government House is as aptly named as the DC here, a very small and fat chap called David Tall. He is Welsh, but without any redeeming rhetorical fire. Africa bounces off him, he claims, thus he is invaluable.

What else can I write? Well, Africa is so full of great, exaggerated things, all borne upon a crowd of black, laughing faces and cloth bright enough for the cover of *Vogue*, that one thinks one cannot possibly match it. It is all I can do to breathe this air, so weighted with the heat and vitality of life! I feel like sobbing my heart out, overwhelmed by it all – by the thought that this country is to be our real home for the foreseeable future (may God preserve us both from ill).

We might be moving to our station in a week, or six months. Nobody knows!

Think of me. Keep well. A kiss for Natch, on his droopy ear.

My fondest love to you both,

Charlotte

Buea, January 5th, 1921

Dear Joy and Edward,

I now know where James acquired his permanent tinge of yellowness: it was not the yellow jack, but the climate. Also why his moustache droops. Did I ever tell you about the precise moment I fell in love with him in the sanatorium? I expended much care arranging a visitor's flowers at his bedside when he was slumbering – returning to find a card propped against the vase, with the word *Disqualified* written neatly upon it. Those grey eyes twinkling at me from the pillows, of course.

The eyes still twinkle, but we are both very tired of Buea and chilliness and cummerbunds, and eager to have our post in the bush. It is all wrong here. A particle of England deposited on a slope. (The other whites are neither interestingly eccentric nor quite dull enough to overlook.) We now have a house: it is a concrete square with tiny windows and warped furniture and a fireplace. There is no electricity or running water, so we live like peasants. Our toilet is behind a rose-bush (little yellow *banksia*), in a hole with a plank across it, unless we run through rain to Government House. I spare you no details, you see.

James has ordered two crates of gin, only to be opened when we are settled in his posting. One sweats most of it out, he says, and what remains kills unwelcome visitors.

He is kept very busy here, I am glad to say. All the rubber and banana and palm-oil plantations taken from the Germans in the war are to be auctioned this year, and it was thought fitting that a former member of the Cameroons Expeditionary Force should itemise them. He is knee-high in the Kaiser's metal chests, sorting a muddle of maps and papers. I hope someone buys them, after all this work. I am helping him by typing out the catalogue. I would love to be the owner of five billion trees, or whatever the total will come to.

The rain and the fog rolling off the peak stopped long enough for me to climb it. James accompanied me, with two African guides. It is only twenty-odd years since Mary Kingsley did the same, and not many women have followed her since, so I am very proud. The top was just like Scotland: driving mist and rocks and sprawls of snow. I sang 'Loch Lomond', James performed the bagpipes on his canvas pouch, and the guides chased after his panama. We now have feverish colds.

There has been a muddle of some kind, emanating from London via Calabar, which means we are not off to Bamenda, as the fellow there did not succumb to malarial fever after all! James is terribly disappointed. I keep myself busy, treating natives for all sorts of horrible conditions with little more than gripe water and Izal – and they only come to me after their own medicine men have wreaked havoc. For instance, their answer to a swollen or purulent eye is to put lime juice on it, or a hot pepper. I have had a score of newborn babies shuddering from tetanus, as the umbilical cord is cut with the nearest rusty knife. Circumcision is practised on both boys and girls, likewise. The poultice for open wounds is animal dung. Everyone is terrified of upsetting the local spirits, which live in everything, so the sorcerer is very important. There are chickens everywhere, but eggs are believed to cause sterility so are left to rot. I have stepped on so many bad ones that I no longer smell the coastal mangroves wafting up.

I am not yet disenchanted, but a state of limbo does not reconcile one to Africa's ways. The people (including our three servants) are perpetually cheerful, so that one thinks they are taking advantage of you. Perhaps they are.

I hope the frosts did not go too deep into the garden.
     With love and affection,
        Charlotte

Baptist Mission Station, Ndian River, April 13th, 1921

Dear Joy and Edward,
     As you can see, we are on the move – we are not converted:
this is a pause on the journey. A week ago, something came up in
a place called Bamakum. Rather worryingly, we couldn't find it
on any of our maps – even the ones spared by the ants. David Tall
assured us that it was on the Ndian River, west of here, and
marked the place with a cross – a spot where the blue river swells
on a page mostly left white. (This means that no one armed with a
plumb line and ruler has ever set foot in it.) He also assured us that
it was a 'one-man' station in a 'jolly remote' area. James leapt at it,
but Tall pointed at me rather rudely. James then went into
confabulation with him; they know something I don't. James
came back saying Tall was wiring the Big Chief in Lagos for
permission! Governor (or Guv'nor, as James puts it) said Yes,
'given the history'. What history? James just refers to a 'bad
pedigree'. We packed in three days.
     And over there is the mission steamboat, SS *Grace*, gracelessly
wallowing in the shallows, holed on a sandbar that wasn't all sand.
If we don't leave soon, and the rains start early, the stretch up to
our station will be too swollen to navigate without peril. The
overland trip is impossible from here. There is even a problem
with the road between Ikasa and Bamakum: James's predecessor,
by the name of Hargreaves, has let it grow over. The forest here is
steamy and dark and grows secretly every time you turn your
head.
     We left Victoria four days ago, in a cargo boat held together by
rust. I waved gallantly at our friends on the beach. At home I
would find them intolerable: here one puts up with all kinds of
discomforts, from ants to bores. Neither, like mosquitoes or
snakes, are in short supply. James says that they don't have intrepid
types in Buea or Victoria, only administrative types. The sun

broke between huge and gloomy clouds just as we hit the swell: the fine trees of the Botanical Gardens glittered, the flannels and Bombay bowlers glared, the huge shoulders of the mountain silvered almost white – and I wanted to cry, suddenly. The representatives of His Majesty's Government dwindled to a speck, the old boat swung north, and the impressive breakers became nothing more than a flicker against the shore. Had we really lived somewhere in those folds of forest, draped in cobwebs of mist, towering up to another landscape of horribly grim clouds? Remarkable, I thought.

You should hear the melancholy roll of the sea breaking upon this part of Africa, one day, Edward. Its dim booming must be one of the earliest sounds of our terrestrial globe, and the drumming that comes from the forest at night – even here – merely echoes it, and makes me hear the music as sullen, when it isn't at all.

I am now excited by what I have to do, and James has to do, in this extraordinary country. James is sure there will be a spare hut for my 'surgery'. I told Mr Tarbuck, the head of this mission, that I hoped to penetrate the loathsome unhealthiness of this country, and inject it with my own minuscule dose of serum, my little flicker of curing light. He answered that, while he admired my intention, he felt it incumbent on him to point out that many of the worst diseases (was he thinking of syphilis, among others?) had been introduced by the white man. I told him that he sounded like my dear brother, back home.

It is too late to go back, Edward. Africa is in a backward, primitive state, and we are here to coax her forward. Our ideal is noble, of course, and not mercenary. Let me quote Lord Lugard in James's copy of *The Dual Mandate in British Tropical Africa*, which is our new Bible: 'The British Empire, as General Smuts has well said, has only one mission – for liberty and self-development on no standardised lines, so that all may feel that their interests and religion are safe under the British flag.' What can possibly be wrong with that? And don't think things are the same as before the war, here. There is a new colonial thinking, of which James is in the young, vigorous vanguard: the African will not be won over by coercion or persuasion or the dreadful tyranny of the Maxim gun, but *by example*. Purely African things such as chiefs, having lots of wives, telling fortunes, queer methods of administration and religious practice and so on – all these will be allowed to continue, as long as they are not cruel. And some of them are (and were) horribly cruel. Our colonial hand will be light. 'Indirect' is the official term. We are to supervise, that is all.

James, by the way, is almost as interested in the anthropological side as you are, and even dislikes the term 'pagan'. Neither does he approve of the missionary movement as an ideal – while deeply admiring brave and selfless individuals like the Reverend Tarbuck. You see now why short Mr Tall reckoned James had 'gone bush' on his last posting, up the White Volta in a place I cannot spell.

This is my first taste of what James terms 'backwoods' Africa. The Mission is a few miles in from the mouth of the Ndian estuary, and dates from German times. It is thoroughly British, of course. We were greeted very warmly. It is like a grander foretaste of our own station: a scatter of thatched huts, a few concrete buildings (including a chapel and a dispensary), a shady iron bench under the tropical version of a horse chestnut (where I am sitting next to James, writing this), all animated by a cosy bustle of activity presided over by Mr Tarbuck and his daughter. She is a very pretty fair-haired girl of eighteen, called Grace (the boat is named after her, of course). Grace was mostly educated in England, but has 'answered the call' and returned to help her father. Personally, I think this as admirable as it is foolhardy, since the Mission is notorious for its unhealthiness. It faces a wide expanse of purulent-looking brown water, is surrounded by a steamy swamp of mangrove brimming with disease and flies, and backed by the wettest of equatorial forests. It is no consolation to know that this forest continues, without a break, to our own station, and for hundreds of miles beyond that. I took a little excursion into it – only a few hundred yards along a wriggling track – and found it frightfully dark. The creepers took on the shapes of the goblins and monsters said to dwell in it. Also dwelling in it are (a small selection only): man-eating leopards, bloodthirsty gorillas, and snakes who drop on you from the branches armed with a venom that can kill an adult inside a minute.

I have seen two grinning crocodiles, sunning themselves on a sandbank.

The Reverend Thomas J. Tarbuck has a face like a ball of brown paper creased up, with a crooked pince-nez perched above a huge white beard. He has a tic which twitches the pince-nez when he talks, so that I think of it as a tiny golden bird about to fly from its nest. He is famous as an explorer and is very outspoken against colonial 'excess'. He told James all about his last trip to the Congo, which appears to be little better than in the terrible days of King Leopold – especially in mining and rubber work. He believes it will take a century for the country to recover, were we to purchase it from the Belgians tomorrow. Though he is rather bent and shrivelled, with a painful stammer and a very sour breath from his teeth, I believe him to be one of the most selfless individuals I have ever met.

James says I must give you the technical details of the vessel by which we hope to reach our destination, because you will find them interesting. He doesn't understand you, does he, Edward? He is dictating this. The SS *Grace* is a flat-bottomed twin-screw, 70ft in length but a mere 10ft wide, which draws only a foot of water. It is thus able to carry physical, mental, moral and spiritual salvation up reaches previously accessible only to canoes (James said that with his tongue in his cheek, I think). Have I said it's a steamer, with a black funnel in the middle? I will get covered in smuts, but the smoke will keep away the mosquitoes and flies.

It was sent out in bits from England four years ago, and took two years to reassemble. Why so long? The Reverend Tarbuck said, as if it was obvious: 'Because we kept losing our young engineers.' I thought of that line in Oscar Wilde, I'm afraid. 'No sooner had one chap stepped ashore,' the good man went on, 'than he would leave the scene of his earthly labours, and we had to wait for another. Still, one musn't be in the dumps about it. God has been very good to us here, generally speaking.'

The cemetery is certainly stocked generously. Is it just faith that keeps him going, I wonder?

I was heartbroken to hear about Natch. I hope you buried him decently.

I am in reasonable health – which means excellent, here.

  With all my love,

    Charlotte

SS Grace, somewhere up the creek, April 24th, 1921

Dear Edward and Joy,

Where to begin? Well, at the beginning. Every day in Africa starts at the beginning. I mean, right at the beginning. It is like whoever-it-was rolling that stone uphill, only to see it rolling down again, for ever and ever.

Our crates are 'steeved' beneath a cargo of Bibles, and four new recruits joined us on our journey – along with the Reverend Tarbuck and pretty young Grace (she kept telling me how pretty *I* am, but she is eight years younger and in full bloom). On land, the four new recruits buzzed about Grace like bees around nectar. On water, they have no choice, since the boat is, if you remember, a thin rectangle 70 ft by 10 ft. She finds this attention charming, while I find it tiresome – that is, none of them is yet buzzing about me, and I feel married and old. Their conversation, however, is frightfully chapel, so maybe I should be grateful.

You will be interested in our living arrangements for these seven days on the water (for which I am dressed fashionably in the season's nautical neckline, I might add). Two cabins, the bigger fore cabin (the men) bearing trunks and cases on its tin roof, the little aft cabin (the women) rattling a collection of thin poles for tents. An awning spreads the length of the boat, with the funnel poking up in the middle, and the pilot house perched high at the back. A flag droops at the prow, behind which is set a table and five canvas chairs. This is where the bees buzz. Three chairs in the stern. This is where the older members drone – and (right now) cough in the smoke.

The Africans in the Mission lined the shore and waved.

Tarbuck's white deputies waved, less boisterously. We waved back from the rail. The steamer 'throttled up' and I felt instantly nauseous. The river became less like a lake, and more like a tunnel, and lost its sea-borne swell. In fact, it became like a tunnel without my noticing. Then it opened up again, and I felt happier. Then it closed, behind and before and all but overhead. Edward: you must come to Africa. It would cure you of your trees obsession. One can have too much of anything – even God's own vegetation. The tropical forest has the same yearning as the mangrove – to carpet the water. However, the forest has a hem which stops at a precise line about two feet above the brown surface, in case it wets its skirts. It looks as if someone has taken a ruler and scissors to it. It means that there is no proper edge, only the blackest of shadows. I asked James why this was. He said it is the flood-line: the lowest boughs indicate the upper limit of the river's rise in the wet season. So there.

Because of this hem, and the wraiths of mist that hang in the trees like fairies' washing, the forest is not of this earth. It floats in the air, like a wall hung from the sky. The sky is very low, of course, and utterly grey. Once or twice, for many hours, we have seen nothing either side but vague phantoms. Then we chug along, very slowly. Horrible. The forest is altogether decadent, much too lush. It drips with heat and moisture and perpetual fertility. Into this fearful domain we deliver these pimpled, pale young men from places like Barnsley and Birmingham, one by one. They stand on a primitive jetty with a green canvas valise, a hurricane lamp, and a waterproof case full of Bibles, and wave merrily from a group of perplexed-looking natives. Then a shaggy bend hides them. There is one left: a cricketer! He has a complete cricketing set, anyway; he hopes to win the pagan tribe over with that infernal game. I have no doubt that he will be successful, out here. The men's cabin is now less like the Bakerloo Line in the rush hour, James says.

Animal life: the chief fear is the hippopotamus, which I had thought utterly harmless. They have canoes for breakfast, it seems, and mission steamers for lunch. Or rather, they might capsize us for the benefit of their friends, the crocodiles. Many a hippo turns into a sandbank, many a croc turns into a log. Also vice-versa, unfortunately. The three black crew (they sleep where they can) are granted pot-shots at the crocs with a rifle that James claims was last active at Waterloo. I can't blame them for trying: people have been snatched by these reptiles all along the river – especially children. In the day the forest is quiet. As soon as night begins to fall, it is worse than Gala Night at the Lyceum. But its inhabitants, animal and human, are very shy. Yelps and screeches are its speciality. The goblins talk to each other in whistles – particularly when I am just nodding off in the stifling darkness of my cell, Grace breathing gently opposite. I hope God is Baptist, I think, for all His cruelty.

We stop at dusk, when the mosquitoes come out and we retreat to the main cabin. We can't retreat there during the day since the rattling funnel makes it uninhabitable (I type or sew or read or doze under the awning). We hardly ever go ashore – there are no clearings, and few settlements. We sit in the cabin around a small table, on which stands a hurricane lamp. The Reverend is surprisingly keen on cards, and there is a small warped backgammon set. The river belches through the window, and its last meal was of something putrefying. Mingled with the sweat from our bodies (it runs down and tickles my ribs), these evenings are rendered scarcely endurable, to put it politely. Herbert Standing – the cricket man – disapproves of card games; he spends each evening oiling his bats in the darkest corner of the cabin. The sickly linseed smell overwhelms everything else after an hour, and will stay with me for life. He is sure his bats are beginning to bend. They think they are bananas, I say. (Bananas here are quite delicious, and the mango is Eden's own fruit.) He is inscribing each one with his name, using one of my needles heated to redness in the lamp. *Herbert E. Standing.* He is too tall for this vessel, and has almost knocked himself out twice. I, not Grace, rubbed camomile lotion on to the bump.

The next day: Well, it might as well not be. It might be tomorrow, for all we know. The forest wall is broken by creeks: their vista is further gloom. James thinks the scene is romantic. I feel as if I am trapped between two stage canvases on rollers, for ever returning to the same point. If I close my eyes, sitting here at the table in the prow, the same moss-hung tangle fills my head.

When I open them again, five minutes or half an hour later, it is still there – the same drapes, the same branches and leaves, the same moss. I am sure the vessel has stopped, its chuggy rumble just this second started up again. The water barely laps at the mangrove roots as we pass; it seems too viscous to carry a wash. We create a foam, or a froth, like dirty suds. It curls and bubbles yellowly and sinks behind us. I have a horror of picturing the submerged part of the hull creeping along above the putrid bed – so I immediately picture it! The intense stench makes me [*wish?*] to expectorate – it cannot be healthy. I feel as if I am perpetually slipping in a stagnant bog; I'm sure the stench must be increased by our disturbance of this prehistoric calm.

James relishes it all, even while he loses at cards against the Reverend. He says I will adapt, like the chameleons in Victoria on the chess set, to this most demanding of places. Personally, I never saw a single chameleon grow chequered.

The next day again: I now have a terror of not knowing what day it is. There is nothing to tell you. If one lost track, one would lose it for ever. I now understand Robinson Crusoe's notches.

We are nearly at Ikasa, however. I am learning to discriminate, as I learned to discriminate between patients' similar conditions. I'm talking of my surroundings. There are creatures flitting about, if one looks long enough. I'm not sure what type, but they are more than leaves stirring, or shadows. Herbert Standing thinks of the wall as a face, full of thought and expression. The trick is to keep staring until one's eyes adapt. Scientifically, one's eyes do adapt enormously, as we know when we take our candles to bed from a gas-lit room.

Gaslight! Electrical light! What dreams *they* already seem!

I am training myself under young Mr Standing's tutelage (he went to drawing school, until he saw the light). The trees are of many different types and even colours. One is crimson, but I didn't notice it until he showed me. The hanging vegetation, the loops of creepers, are like Raphael's drapery, apparently. The chaotic and suffocating tangle is beginning to look contented, at ease with itself, even merry (once or twice, when a bird breaks

429

from it, or a huge trumpet-shaped flower shows). I am seeing the clues.

Standing and even James agree that the mosquitoes are appalling. I wear my veil and gloves if I venture out in the cooler air of late dusk. It has rained on and off, but not heavily: the air is already quite soaked enough, it cannot be sponging up more. The books I have brought for the cabin evenings have curled and grown mould, or ripple like the page I'm typing upon. (I wonder if it will unripple by the time it reaches you?) Spots of slime have appeared on my clothes. I spend much of the evening cleaning these off with pure alcohol, as Standing cleans his bats and bails, and Grace takes notes from her Bible, and the other two play cards.

The last day: We were becalmed by something hitting the engine, but it is now repaired. Herbert Standing has been delivered to his Raphael drapery, his intelligent face. He said, for some reason, as he took my hand to say farewell, that he would never forget what I was. What was I? I have no idea. Anyway, there he stood, with his misted spectacles, droopy collar, and sweat-clamped shirt, making love to me in the most endearing manner. Tarbuck grinned away behind his beard, the black crew secured the gangplank, and James was somehow already on shore, taking this brief opportunity to 'make contact' with his Responsibilities – these being a dozen bush-dwellers with not a stitch between them, looking cautious. I cannot blame them. They gave us a basket of yams, and I thought them (the natives) quite beautiful, in their diminutive way. They were not strictly Pygmies, though. I am disappointed.

Grace is ill in her cabin, but has only a mild fever.

I will give this to someone in Ikasa, to post in Victoria. There must be someone about to go back there, though we haven't passed anything but a few dug-outs.

>   With all my love and affection,
>   Charlotte

P.S. I am well. James has a headache from not wearing his hat for two minutes when the cloud broke yesterday.

Bamakum, May 3rd, 1921

Dearest Edward and Joy,
Your January letter has only just arrived, half-obliterated by damp. Remember to use indelible ink. Better, chip it out on stone: one page was holed by ants, or maybe rats. But I have the gist of your news. I am glad the snowdrops were on time, and the frosts not too hard. Does England really exist? It is like a penny picture, all in black and white, seen through a pall of tobacco smoke.

The smoke in Africa is spicy. Ikasa was spread beneath it, merely a larger sprawl of huts with a dishevelled trading station. This was constructed from iron girders, crate-boards and palm leaves – 'optimistically', as James put it – with shelves holding a variety of tinned foods and grubby bottles. It was just like Hobbs's Stores during the war, only this one gave credit. A pair of florid rogues smoked and grumbled inside it, the worse for the rum. Hargreaves, the current DO, had abused them for running out of whisky two months before. They had seen 'not a bloody blink of him' since, despite the row of Claymore tucked at their feet. 'He's gone savage, I reckon,' said the balder one, and his colleague spat out his quid in agreement.

James and Tarbuck reckon they are here for gold or diamonds: the impenetrable range rolling for hundreds of miles to our north is said to be a plunderer's paradise, openly seamed with both. Tarbuck added that they were doomed to disappointment. I have a horror of our territory becoming overrun by such gold-rush rascals, but the Reverend reassured me that the legends were as hoary as those of the local monster. (Anyway, were they not so, Cap'n Flint himself couldn't map a hill of doubloons out of that tangle.)

The chief is a heavily scarified, pleasant man of about thirty, and was quite drunk when we met him. (Power and alcohol, like poverty and alcohol, seem to go together, do they not?) We spent the evening in the sober simplicity of his clay-walled compound. The sixteen palace wives danced in a shuffling circle to the pounding of huge drums, and a goat's throat was ritually slit. 'It

431

used to be a human throat,' Tarbuck murmured to me. Should I believe him? We drank palm wine out of gourds. Wine is the wrong word: phenol is better. Whatever, I was instantly woozy. A male dancer came on and made movements that would have shocked Paris. The Reverend is a keen recorder of traditional customs, and looked on benignly or chatted with Chief Ibofo. He has a handsome face topped off by a broad plume of feathers bigger than the Governor's. James was in a creased white dress coat and 'evening' flannels, and mostly listened. He was marble next to the Chief's ebony, both equally noble-looking in the firelight. James has 'bags of ideas' but insists on the 'indirect' approach (in the manner approved), so he hardly opened his mouth. Neither did I.

We stayed in a Public Works Department rest-house, first-class. That is, four concrete walls under a tin roof, netting instead of glass in the one tiny window, and a warped door. No furniture (it was all eaten by termites). Our camp beds were fetched off the boat. Mine yielded a slim orange snake which, on being battered to death by James, turned out to be a quite harmless type.

Ants. Have I mentioned ants? They come in all colours and sizes, and there are too many of them. I no longer *see* the little red ones. 'They even eat through our tins,' moaned the stubbled rogues. 'But it is you who eat through your bottles,' I replied.

The next morning, we chugged a further two hours up-river and passed a delightful, clean-looking village with conical roofs. Children waved and shouted. One knows a village is coming by a smell of smoke and (thinking of my sanny days) sharper whiffs of 'natural secretions'. It is not unlike some of Ulverton's back lanes – pissiferous, I think you call them, Edward. Tarbuck pointed at a gleam of water ahead, all the more brilliant for the dark, narrow reach it lay beyond. 'That's the bay,' he called. James rustled a map, and said that the station should be on its northern flank. I assume his heart quickened as much as mine, at this point, even though I did not know where the north was, and was too shy to ask. I would look where James looked. We settled in the prow, craning our heads forward. It made no difference to the steady screws of SS *Grace*. (Her namesake, by the way, was by my side, quite recovered.)

We worked up the tight channel of the reach. A half-mile of deep-looking water, with large muscles, like our African pilot's arm. Then into the broader, calmer waters. In this natural amphitheatre of primordial forest, both James and I missed the stage. Our sense of scale had been worn down, perhaps, and we were looking for something larger. The boat started to turn towards the far bank, and we saw our new home simultaneously. I'm afraid I clapped my hand over my mouth, or I would have shrieked. I had a hand spare for James to squeeze, which he did. Tarbuck, who had never steamed beyond Ikasa, hummed a madrigal. He is very fond of madrigals, and hums them when he is excited, or miserable. I think he was excited.

After that, I was quite calm. The boat moved frightfully slowly over the waters of the bay, made slower no doubt by my impatience. Let me try to set down my impressions while they are still reasonably fresh, and not [rest of sentence made illegible by a mould stain]. At any rate, I will try to describe as Mrs Kingsley does.

The water between us and the station was as still as a mirror, only shot across with blinding patches of reflected sky. The dark streaks faithfully reflected our home. The bright patches shifted at the slight gust blowing down the creek, and made the bank difficult to discern: I had the impression that the five or six squat little buildings I could see would at any moment float out towards us. The main house seemed right on the water, which was rather alarming (an optical effect only).

The trees behind were extraordinarily tall, with very slender trunks of a creamy bark. Their high foliage looked quite ready to pounce on the buildings, and I could not see for the life of me how these latter all fitted in to such a narrow space. There were two dead trees in the front, bone-white to the topmost branch, as if the merest touch of the river had [killed them?]. They were so perfectly reflected that it looked as if each had grown a single thin root to the very deeps. I felt, in other words, that the station was squeezed between hostile water and malevolent forest, and felt momentarily terrified at the thought of setting my foot, let alone living, in such a place. It seemed almost insulting that such a thin scrap of civilisation had been handed to my husband, like gristle to a dog.

433

In the next minute – and not just because I saw, as we approached, that there was a decent space between the buildings and the trees, colonised with a large hut and some fencing, as well as a high bank at the water's edge, with steps and a jetty – I felt an extraordinary *contentment*.

What a wondrous place, I thought, to live with the man you love!

What a gift we have been given, this union with nature at its most innocent, this happy loneliness far from the teeming masses, with nothing but good to perform!

Edward – I reckoned myself the luckiest woman in the world!

That emotion stayed with me a full two minutes (which is rather long for Africa). Until, I suppose, I saw Mr Hargreaves.

'There's Bamakum,' said Tarbuck. 'Home sweet home. And there, from the look of it, is Hargreaves. Quite brilliant in his day, it must be said.'

I couldn't see Hargreaves anywhere, but my sight was a little blurred from sweat. The air was very heavy – leaden, I think novelists call it – and through this leaden air came a strange wail. The crew had described to me a monster who lives in the forest: Mary Kingsley actually *saw* it, said Tarbuck. It has long hair, bloodshot eyes, is extremely smelly, and sits in trees. Its legs dangle down and its feet – whatever the height of the branch it is perched on – always just touch the ground. If you walk into these legs you are no better off than a fly in a spider's web. It wails, but faintly. I held on to James, I'm afraid.

There was a little white post on the jetty, with some sort of cap. This turned out to be a man, wailing. No, not wailing: singing. Light operetta, it sounded like. The man's face was shielded by a large straw hat, but as we drew closer I saw that his hands were moving. Sharp claps came over the water, but none of us commented. This is rather fun, I thought. Churning the shallows on its lee side, the vessel released a particularly thick stench, as if suffering from severe dyspepsia. We breathed through our mouths. The whole of equatorial Africa is ill ventilated and full of tainted matter: it would cause Miss Jenkins, our ward sister at the sanny, nightmares. She was never happy unless a fresh gale was blowing through, and was very keen on the Hinckes–Bird plan, which meant closing the lower sash on a thick board. These boards would always fall on my toe. For some reason, this is what I thought of when I saw what I saw, and I burst into laughter. The District Officer of the Bamakum region, and many regions adjoining (almost the size of Wales, when totted up), was dressed in a khaki cotton shirt, a lightweight dress coat, a pair of tropical puttees and creamy canvas shoes – but between his puttees and the shirt's hem lay a large area of pink thigh. He had omitted his breeches.

On the bank behind him stood a young black boy beside a table, and on the table was a huge horn gramophone. This was the source of the light operetta.

'Oh dear,' said James, 'he's gone doolally.'

'Not the first time it's happened,' said Tarbuck. 'Caruso, I think. I like Caruso.'

I was unable to contribute. The Hinckes-Bird plan was forcing giggles into my throat. Grace was still, very still. So very sober and contained.

'Stay on board until I've dealt with it, if you want, dearest,' said James.

Mr Hargreaves brought his hand up to his head and saluted us. He was standing to attention on the jetty. The jetty was a series of boards lashed with algae-covered ropes to six rusted drums. These undulated as our wash slapped against them, but Mr Hargreaves kept his balance by straddling his pink legs.

Then our steel hull bumped the jetty.

Mr Hargreaves wobbled manfully – and fell on his back. Like the Scotsman, he had nothing under his shirt but his pride. My trained eye spotted a livid rash on his buttocks. I blushed. Edward – naked men do not turn a hair on my head, but Mr Hargreaves was representing His Majesty's Government, and I felt all Africa staring at him (and thereby at us).

He scrambled upright and resumed his former posture, as if nothing had happened. A sudden misgiving seized me. I had felt we were on the verge of a great adventure, in those patient days at Buea: flying like the hornbills did, breaking from the treetops below and gliding for ages over the valleys. Now I saw our time here as more like the lumbering whirr of one of the

435

coleoptera, its wings scarcely carrying its heavy body from twig to twig. Mr Hargreaves was getting me off to a very poor start, in other words.

As the gangplank was set down, James and Tarbuck had a hurried confabulation, under their breath. The best course of action, Tarbuck decided, was to humour the fellow. James, discarding 'indirectness', decided to adopt a middle course. He stepped off the boat and held out his hand.

'Hello, Hargreaves,' he said. 'James Arkwright, your successor. Trust you're in good health. You've forgotten your breeches, by the way. Bad form.'

James did it very well, however silly it sounds on paper. Officially, he was now the District Officer. I don't know what that made Mr Hargreaves.

The fellow took the proffered hand limply and frowned. 'Sorry,' he said, 'but I simply can't wear them.' He wore thick, round spectacles, with a cracked right lens. He peered through these at James. I wished James would say something. It was awfully silent, apart from the clucking of water under the jetty.

Then Hargreaves turned his head towards the boat. His skin was a mass of sweat, and somewhat soiled, so that the drops made stripes over his cheeks. The effort to see screwed his face up so much that his top teeth, yellow as old ivory, showed their gums.

'Company?' he said. 'Isn't that old Tubby Tarbuck?'

'Yes, and –'

'Who's that with him, skulking in the shadows? Don't say they've paid for a damn clerk, the money-pinching buggers! And there's another! Two bloody aide-de-camps, as it were?'

'Mrs Charlotte Arkwright, my wife. Grace Tarbuck, the Reverend Tarbuck's daughter.'

Hargreaves blinked and peered again. His teeth shot back in and his hands became tight little fists, his body beginning to curve into a pugilist's crouch.

'Dear God,' he said, 'oh dear God.'

'She's a nurse, Hargreaves.'

The silly man started to back away, gripping his shirt tails and stretching them almost to his knees. It now makes me think of some of our shell-shock victims, but it didn't then.

'Protocol!' he moaned. 'They'll kill me for this!'

In the same posture, he backed up the first dilapidated flight of steps beneath the main building and paused before the tin-covered staircase leading to the veranda. 'I'm awfully sorry,' he shouted, 'but the damn buggers didn't tell me!'

He disappeared up the staircase and into the building. James turned as Tarbuck, Grace and myself joined him on the jetty. There was an odour of alcoholic vapours above the river-mud's stench.

'Welcome to the circus,' said James. 'All we need is a few buckets of flour.'

The boy, no doubt obeying some previous instruction, had replaced Caruso with – 'God Save the King'! The record was so warped that the gramophone needle bobbed up and down like a sewing machine's. We were forced to remain respectfully at attention with the jetty swaying under us, and I felt a perfect fool as well as seasick. I wondered if this was all expressly designed to make us feel that – foolish, I mean. The record came to an end in a great hiss and the boy removed the needle.

There was a moment of peace, then. None of us wanted to move or to say anything. Well, we were home, James and I. Home at last! Our first proper home, Edward. A rather marvellous moment. The first creature stepping from the primordial swamp and setting its print on the sand . . .

'Poor man,' Grace said. 'Poor, poor man.'

That broke it completely. Perhaps nursing has dulled my sympathies. I used to disagree with the instruction (in our training and our manuals) that chronic alcoholism should be treated as for lunacy. Now I concur. But I am writing a little from hindsight, for Mr Hargreaves has very little sympathy from me, owing to his deleterious character and the problems he has caused us already in just a few days. I will write about these in my next letter, when I am feeling less weary. I have 'come down' as they say – and anyway, James is being paddled off to Ikasa for urgent supplies at any minute. The post leaves there every week, I have now discovered, by carrier to Kumba. He has very little to carry, it is said, but a lot to sell. One of James's first projects is to give the poor fellow a motorcycle. Tarbuck claims that this will hold him up, as he will have to wheel the cycle as well as carry his pack.

I am never sure when someone is being serious, here. It is just as you say of gentlemen's clubs, Edward. But it is hardly Africa's fault if she is too much of this world to be thoroughly real.

I am very well, though very tired – and so is James (very well, not very tired).

> With much love,
> Charlotte

Bamakum, May 15th, 1921

Dear Edward and Joy,

It is raining fat balusters, not stair-rods, outside. Tarbuck and daughter have done their exploring up-river and have just stopped for the night. He will take my letter in the morning.

If it were not for the wetness, it would not be as hot as the hottest day in London. However, I am adapting to the stiflingness. There is a little respite when the storm starts, from the moisture-laden gusts, but the sponge quickly fills up. Goodness knows what germs must be swimming around in every intake of breath I draw. So far, I have not been ill. I am too busy to be ill, and too far from help.

You will be wondering why a married man was given such a far-flung post. Or, indeed, why the post is here at all. The first is because Mr Hargreaves's predecessor as well as Mr Hargreaves himself were both bachelors, and both went dotty. I am to keep James from going dotty. The Colonial Office never considered who was to keep *me* from going dotty. The second is less easily answered, but to do with blank spaces on maps pinned on London walls, and the wealth that might lie in the virgin forest around us. This wealth could be anything from tin through manganese to (of course) gold and diamonds. James says he thinks timber is the real wealth, but no one is interested. Also, there are numerous inhabitants – whole tribes, apparently – who do not yet know that they have the British flag (or any flag) flapping above their heads. They probably do not even know that there is such a thing as an albino who is not an albino. It is James's job to let them know. This means, unfortunately, that he must go 'on tour' every so often. I stay to look after the servants, of which we have several too many (of which we have several, I meant to say).

Alas, the story of Hargreaves is not only depressing, but horrible and even tragic. I find I have recorded it rather minutely. I will try to be brief (for the carrier's sake, who still awaits his motorcycle!), but I know you like this sort of thing, Edward. There is not very much magic in it, of the African kind, however.

I need to go back to our arrival. Well, finding our way about the compound took no more than a matter of minutes: a chop-shed, a cookhouse, a thatched privy, a simple guest bungalow, an overgrown cemetery, a ruined construction of rusting girders at the edge of the bush, and a lot of spotless red earth in a yard full of chickens between the cookhouse and the main building. Someone had erected a solid wire fence around all this, now bent double under creepers. The servants emerged and shook their new *massa*'s hand and that of his *missus*. They seemed shy, even cowed. The forest was even taller, close to. It cast all into shade (James said we will be grateful for that *when* the sun comes out). The river lapped at a slippery bank on which, at various times, concrete lumps, iron posts, and even sandbags had been arranged and forgotten. They are still there, and shall remain a little longer, for there is never enough time!

Now for the interior description. The main building is as simple a construction inside as it is outside, being divided into four rooms, two each side of a narrow hallway. However, we could hardly move through it for tea-chests, broken chairs, legs of tables, rolls of canvas, empty whisky bottles, shards of glass, books – even half-finished paintings done on planks of wood. Our first task, then, was to clear a path, not through African vegetation, but through European dross. We found Hargreaves in the gloom of the shuttered main bedroom, apparently insensible on the bed, a sheet pulled taut up to his chin.

'He might be feverish,' I whispered.

'Deal with it, nurse,' said James.

Welcoming host was transforming into guest-who-falls-sick-on-you with each additional box unloaded from the vessel. James directed operations by the jetty, hoping it wouldn't collapse. The second bedroom was condemned and filled with the dross. The afternoon sky turned cindery-black, and the figures started to scuttle seconds before the devil's tattoo was tapped above my head and water drew its shiny gauze curtain across the scene. (The house, being roofed entirely in corrugated iron, is a tin rolling down a pebbly slope when it rains. We all have to bawl at each other.)

My patient's temperature was only slightly higher than normal. I'm sure mine was rocketing: the heat in the bedroom was infernal. I treated the rather pustulent rash as for severe bedsores, since it seemed to resemble the latter. The main difference being that it wasn't on his back, but extended from his buttocks to his navel. I mopped it with spirits of wine from my medicine chest and dusted it over with dusting powder. Grace was an excellent assistant. She dealt with the filthy bed covers, and helped me improvise a bed cradle from a tea-chest (removing the lid, bottom and one side) to let air at the rash (what air there was). I am quite sure he was awake the whole time, with a queer little smile, but the odd man made no attempt to communicate. Odd, or crazed – I am not sure which.

From the paintings propped about the place, I came down on crazed. They were mostly a portrait of something between a knight in a helmet and a rhinoceros. It stared out through piggy eyes in front of a lot of lurid leaves, like tongues of patients with interesting diseases. The oil paint was as thick as dried mud, and half of it had ended up on the walls. Some had a name neatly printed at the bottom: *Sir Steggie*. The Reverend suggested a good dose of Gospel light might drive away the shadows, and so Grace read bits of the Bible aloud in each room. I forget which bits. She then sat with Hargreaves while I supervised the placing of our luggage. Then the rain stopped, and everybody was splashing out again.

Have I mentioned the veranda? It runs around the front and side of the house, reached by the covered steps that look alarmingly like Sir Steggie's plated nose. At the back of the house there is another flight of steps, so warped and half-rotted as to be unusable. These go up to an equally uncertain little veranda before a locked door which is discovered, from the inside, by lifting a tatty muslin curtain in the narrow hallway. This makes the back of the house look like the front. James has therefore christened it 'Janus Mansions'.

My patient remained unstirrable, but not insensible. We had to sleep the first few nights on mattresses in the main room. This contained a worn sofa, two heavy wooden tables and a crooked sideboard, but no chairs. Tarbuck slept in the guest bungalow, on a hammock of green canvas. Green canvas is the only material apart from glass and corrugated iron which ants do not eat. It is all that stands between the white man in Africa and utter disintegration. Ants are swept off the beds and tables and walls, pour from the tap in the kitchen before any water gurgles out (brown as rust, and tepid, from the rain tank at the back), drown in old tins scattered outside, wind like an electric flex to the chop-shed (wherein they do indeed appear to pierce the tins), or the palm-thatched bathing hut of a privy with its tea-chest of a seat and its flowery pudding bowl (I spare no details, you see). In the end, the smaller variety are treated as dust is in England.

In the smoky cookhouse we discovered a lot of bright blue stains on every surface. According to the servants, this was 'magic powder' for killing the ants. I must write to the manufacturers of Reckitt's Blue to tell them of this second role. 'The real answer,' I informed them, 'is to keep everything absolutely spotless, which means swept and scrubbed.' The cook told me that it was Pa Hargreaves's idea, so I will need to do a lot of persuading.

When I returned to my patient, at dusk, the door was locked. We left his portion of supper outside it (fresh yams and cooked bananas from our stay in Ikasa) covered with a bowl. It was quickly consumed – by the ants. We were too tired to bother with him, frankly. But it was not at all comfortable; we felt like intruders. Most bothersome, and quite without justification. This was our home now, I thought, as yesterday it was his.

Tarbuck and Grace (she was lodged in the hallway, at her insistence), retired early. James and I chatted around the table, and after a while we moved out on to the veranda; the night air was gusty and almost cool. The holes in the mosquito nets are patched with varieties of pretty but ineffective lace curtain. Here, on the river margin, we are a brief and very welcome intrusion on the world of the mosquito. They have been at it for hundreds of millions of years. I wish we did not know that. To believe one is younger than the mosquitoes by half a week is much more manageable. James's pipe spared him much of the slaughter.

Anyway, we donned our mosquito boots and sat it out by the hurricane lamp. I quote from the diary that I started typing there and then. Sorry if it is a bit flowery. I have always believed that good diaries are written in a literary manner. You know I have plans for a book.

'The view from the veranda is so lovely tonight, now the storm's mist has cleared; the near-full moon has risen high above the river, turning it to molten silver (or mercury, as James has just suggested. But that reminds me of thermometers). Even the boat's funnel, to the left side, looks like a castle's turret. Tarbuck called the forest "awfully inconvenient", at dinner, but right now it is jolly romantic, tall as two houses on the far bank, looped with elegant creepers and washed in blueish hues that make it dream-like, fantastical. Added to this are the flickering fireflies, the usual "scree-scree" of the cicadas, the million burbling frogs, and the ever-changing talk of the bigger beasts concealed around us – whooping, shrieking, giggling and grunting, or mournfully repeating the same note. "Macrological", James calls it, but I dare not show my ignorance. We think we can hear lots of methodical tom-toms, too, but we cannot distinguish the beat from that of our own hearts. (Well, James will insist on taking my hand and kissing its knuckles.) It is all much noisier than in Buea, which makes me think how I am at last in real Africa, the Africa James talked so much of at Hetherington's. How far away seems that place, now! – those neat lawns, the doctors rattling up the drive, the cheeky young chaps on their crutches or in their bath chairs, smiling through their "fags", and the bland skies of England over it all. I can't bear to think of those carbolic corridors, now – down which I might still be perpetually moving were it not for my darling James!'

There, Edward – is that not proof that I am not at all disenchanted with my husband, as you veiledly suggested in your last letter!?

We talked of improvements, as if we were in a villa on the Metropolitan Line. Some had been brought with us: a tin hip bath with a lid (it doubles as a trunk on tour); a tin bucket with a wooden seat (no guesses); a muslin-curtained meat safe; and bolts of patterned cloth for curtains, tablecloths, napkins and so forth. James sited the croquet pitch, I sited the shrubbery, flower, and vegetable garden. Against the mouldering voraciousness of this place, we set our standards.

We called the houseboy and interrogated him. The facts about John Simkins Hargreaves, BA Oxon, were these.

'Massa DO' had drunk through the stocks of sundowners some time ago, and set out for Ikasa in an old, half-rotten pirogue, hauled from the sludge. It had sunk, and for some time they all thought he was drowned. Like a miracle (or a restless ju-ju spirit!) he had returned a few days later, much the worse for wear – found, at any rate, sprawled in the cookhouse one morning, his clothes in rags, his face covered in ants.

'We done look um. 'E go get craw-craw too much in dis place –' The man (a small, tubby fellow called Mr Henry, with rheumy eyes and a light white stubble) patted his loins. 'Craw-craw' is a sort of African ecthyma, encouraged by starch and severe humidity. I wasn't far wrong. If it had been smallpox, or rubella, the pustules would have appeared on the face.

James nodded – grimly. If we are to set by example, then what an example was here! James was wonderfully philosophical about it.

'One hopes to get vital info out of the chap one's relieving. Now we've got to begin from scratch.'

'Well, God managed it,' I quipped. 'What do we do when the poor fellow wakes up?'

'Rub gin into him,' James replied.

'No, quite the opposite. Total abstention, forced if need be.' No comment from James!

My few exposed parts (knuckles, a bit of the neck) were turning into a butcher's slab. The holes in the netting were big enough to

443

let the moths in, too. They plastered themselves on the glass of the hurricane lamp so thickly it was considerably dimmed. My first task, as usual, would be a bout of sewing. James lit his pipe and the whining thinned from choir to principals. A satisfying number of them were crushed by my tapping keys: my diary, if written in the evening, is splattered with blood. Since most of it is mine, this does not perturb me.

You only have your first evening in Eden once, so we dragged it out until well after one o'clock. The sublime satisfaction of not having the boat underfoot was part of it, and the fact that we had not yet had our 'own' home until this moment. Never mind that James might be moved on in five or seven years! And, dear Edward – this *is* our Eden: at least, it eerily resembles the engraving in the old Arnold Bible, if you remember it. It certainly has serpents as big.

Eventually, yawning, I stood up to go to bed. Then I froze, and not from cold. James asked what the matter was. I pointed to the river. The moon had moved, of course, but the bay is so wide that the water was still a silvery glare. At one point in the middle, it had been interrupted by a considerable shadow, like a long log.

'The Big Beef,' came a voice from behind. I hadn't even said anything!

Mr Hargreaves was standing in front of the open double doors. He was dressed in a linen suit, rumpled but clean, and an open-necked shirt. He had canvas shoes on, but no socks.

'Hargreaves!' said James. 'You've forgotten y'socks, this time.'

'Look here,' said Hargreaves, 'I'm awfully sorry. I seem to have misbehaved myself.'

'Not at all,' I said. Adding: 'We were on the point of retiring.'

'We've commandeered the main room for a few nights,' said James, 'until we sort things out. Feeling our way about, y'know. Hope you don't mind.'

The wretched man asked if it was late, consulting at the same time a rather grand fob-watch fetched from his suit pocket. Perhaps time had indeed stopped.

'Rather late,' I replied. 'It is already tomorrow.'

444

'It is never tomorrow,' he replied, pedantically. 'By the way, what's the month?'

'We are the third of May,' James said.

There was an edgy pause, during which Hargreaves tapped his watch almost thoughtfully and then pocketed it with a grunt. I felt *exhausted*, now. All I wanted was my bed and our mosquito net.

'What's the Big Beef, then?' James asked, just as I was about to move.

The man snorted. This either meant: No Idea, or God, Don't You Know? (Clue: 'beef' means animal in pidgin.) The moonlight glared off his spectacles, so that one couldn't see his eyes. I turned away and studied the river. The long, humpy log had gone, leaving a ripply wake. The forest was plunged in shadow now, quite black. It seemed to be set back further than the brightly massed stars above it.

'A remarkably clear night,' said James, 'and possibly the last.' He is *so* good in these situations!

Hargreaves pulled up a chair, tweaked his trousers, and sat rather gingerly.

'Aaah,' he sighed. 'The pleasures of the night, and of solid company.'

Protocol and myself struggled, and protocol won. I sat down again. (Disconcerting, though, being appreciated for one's solidity.) I was about to ask after his medical complaint. He was looking up at the veranda's rusting sheets. 'I built this, y'know,' he said. 'With my own hands.'

'Very impressive,' I lied.

'Took me six months. Northcott –' He waved his hand about, as if dismissing someone. 'My predecessor. Giles Northcott. Cambridge man, so never knew him. Northcott was bloody hopeless. Hadn't done a thing. All the improvements you see, were my doing. I leave them to you, with J. S. Hargreaves's blessing.'

'Thank you,' said James.

'Who's that lovely creature in the hallway?'

'Tarbuck's daughter. Grace Tarbuck.'

'Ah yes, that's right. Lovely creature.'

445

I had the strange notion that he'd studied her while she was asleep. Possibly for ages.

'I'm most awfully sorry about this morning,' he went on. 'Or was it actually the afternoon?'

James gave a little snort.

'Between the two, old chap. We call it noon.'

Hargreaves's sigh told me that he had been drinking. In the light of the hurricane lamp, his face looked flushed and congested, not pale at all. We would have to remove all offending bottles from wherever they were hidden, I thought. (I also thought: there is little difference between those ill-fed wretches who beg for alms in London and spend it in the public house, and this official of our august Colonial Service!)

'Enjoyed the music, Hargreaves. Nice thought,' said James. (What a kind, decent sort he is!)

The wretch looked confused. Did James realise how drunk he was? If he'd been pretty well starving, a mere drop would have an effect. To fill the awkward silence, I asked after his complaint. In those starched trousers, he must have needed no reminding.

He looked at me with a most sinister leer, and I instantly regretted bothering.

'My dear Mrs —'

He was struggling to remember his successor's name, showing his gums again. He bore a remarkable resemblance, with his round spectacles, to the Wolf dressed up as Grandmother Hood. (I *loathe* drunkenness, don't you?) He gave up the struggle, or the struggle gave him up. His eyes must have closed behind the glare of his glasses because his head lolled like a puppet's, and he started breathing stertorously.

'Is he asleep?' whispered James.

Sweat was running off the man's face like drops of rain; one gleamed on the end of his nose. I felt his pulse at the wrist (very feeble) and asked James to hold the lamp close to the unconscious face. I lifted his eyelids to check the pupils were dilated equally (they were), and pronounced him to be collapsed from drink, not from an apoplectic fit. However, none of these activities stirred him, so I went into the main room to fetch my smelling salts. One of the crates stacked at the end had two of its boards levered out of their nails. Blades of straw were scattered on the concrete floor. Enough of a gap to pass a bottle through. Temptation had come via Messrs Griffiths McAllisters' habit of marking their crates' contents. The ants were already inside, their little polished bodies barely distinguishable from the glass. I have to say that the crate smelt of England, of course: of dry little offices and fields stooked with hay. *There* was James's favourite sherry! I fervently hoped that Hargreaves hadn't pilfered one of those; we had carefully calculated the amount, as with everything else.

There were an awful lot of crates. I felt quite dwarfed. There was nothing of ours that was not in a box. I thought: this is how I might be taken out, were the worst to happen – and the worst is as likely to happen as not! Isn't that a morbid thought? I am only going by statistics.

Grace is saying to me: the rain is lessening, we are going. As you might gather, I had to take this up again in the morning, but I have run out of time. I will relate further in my next missive. I hope you find it interesting.

I am learning so much. Partly I am writing all this to you in case there are unforeseen consequences, and a defence is needed. Explanation will [*indecipherable*]. I am keeping copies, but everything here is subject to Africa, and Africa swallows everything at a gulp – sometimes without chewing it first.

With all my love and affection,
Charlotte

P.S. Please write with all your news – however tiny. (The tiniest is best, in fact. I prefer it to your 'large concerns', I'm afraid, Edward. We are already too large here!)

Bamakum, June 13th, 1921

Dear Edward,

I am addressing this to you alone just in case Joy finds the enclosed a little 'vapourish', as she puts it. I know that she doesn't like the sordid in life. Neither do you, but for different reasons. We used to share our secrets, did we not?

I have discovered two things about dear James that are new to me. 1) He likes gin. 2) He cannot father children (medically speaking). Both are the result of his last tour in Africa, before we met. When I say he likes gin, I mean that he likes it a little too much. He drinks nothing before sundown, but makes up for it between that hour and bedtime. He sees the habit as necessary to health – like the taking of one's quinine grains. I wouldn't mind if it didn't make him so crabby, like Father got towards the end. But that was port, and Mother's death.

I did hope to bear children one day, before I was too old. However, I had already accepted that having children and living in the tropics do not go easily together. The knowledge that the yellow jack had fatally enfeebled James's reproductive capacity, if revealed before our marriage, would have changed nothing. He is the man I love.

It is fate, or God's will, or whatever, this. I can now concentrate solely on my life's mission. It is almost like being a nun.

As if to seal this acceptance, my dispensary or 'bush hospital' is thatched and stocked and already running. It is merely one of the huts on the edge of the compound, but is as grand to me as any sanny in Hampshire. Slowly, it is becoming known about, and the patients trickle in from the bush. I am teaching mothers some sensible habits, such as: coming to me *before* rather than *after* seeing (and paying) the medicine man – avoiding rusty blades – and not, when a woman is in labour and having difficulties, pounding her abdomen like a tom-tom. I could tell you other things but they are messily medical and womanly. I am not yet sure if my advice is being taken up: all they want is shots of serum for everything. But don't think yourself superior to these ignorant people. All any human being wants is a shot of serum for everything: James regards his glass of gin in that light. If there was a serum against white men slaughtering each other in their millions, I would inject all your sex immediately. Instead we put all our faith into bits of diplomatic paper and gold reserves.

Mr Hargreaves has finally left us, thank goodness. We are now on our own, with the servants. Let me recap the last four weeks.

I had a few revealing conversations with the poor man, while he recovered with us, waiting for Tarbuck's return. One in particular would have interested you. We were in 'his' room, where I was treating his craw-craw (its complications are only interesting to a nurse). He congratulated us on being given Bamakum. I asked him what there was to be congratulated about. He said Bamakum was the Garden of Eden. I replied that such a comparison had indeed come to me as the steamer approached, but that brief acquaintance had quickly banished it: the Garden of Eden was without mosquitoes, servants, gin, rainstorms, and craw-craw. I nearly added 'bibulous predecessors'. Instead I stressed that I liked it here. After Buea. In the way that hell would be more stimulating than limbo.

'Is it hell, then?'

'No. Not at all. I was merely being amusing. But it certainly isn't Eden, Mr Hargreaves.'

'What three classes of sin are possible, my dear Mrs Arkwright?'

He was sitting on the bed in his towelling robe. I was packing up my equipment. He looked at me in a most forbidding way. I thought hard for a moment.

'Original, deadly, and a third one, less important. Trivial, I think.'

'Venial, Mrs Arkwright.'

'Ah. I'm sure you're right.'

It was so *very* hot and humid in the room, even with the shutters put to. All we have here are primitive cloth fans without the punkah-wallahs to operate them. I felt as if Africa was taking a mould of my face. I was about to leave the room with a tray of soiled swabs, when he asked me if James had had 'a good war'. I said that there was no such thing – but that Africa, for all its discomforts, had not been as horrible as the trenches. He nodded furiously. Then he stood up, as if on parade.

'Flanders was in the second class of sin, Mrs Arkwright. Deadly. Deadly sin. All seven, actually. Even sloth. Sloth let it carry on and on and on and on and on. I have never ever felt such sloth. I watched a man sink into the slime of a shell hole, and couldn't do a damn thing about it, I was filled up with so much sloth.'

Every time he said 'sloth', he expectorated a little, making him

449

look even more deranged. I replied that I had treated dozens of poor young men with the same listless condition, and that it was called shell-shock, or battle weariness. He snorted rather rudely. He was leaning against the wall. This is inadvisable. (When you visit us for the weekend, I will inadvise it.) The walls have all been painted in creosote, which the climate has prevented from drying properly. As the fellow pushed himself off, he lost a few strands of hair and some flock off his cherry-red robe. He didn't seem to feel the former, but came right up to me. I tried not to grimace at his sour breath – he was talking straight into my face, with only the soiled swabs between us.

'There never was any unfallen garden, Mrs Arkwright. No damn fall to make, you see. I've studied crocs, for weeks, for months, for years. And they should damn well know, having been around a sight longer than us, what?'

'I'm not sure what point you are making. Don't touch the swabs, they are purulent.'

'Original sin is original sin, Mrs Arkwright. It was there before the great round gourd itself. It was there before the water trickled down the sides of the gourd to the earth. It was there before the lightning crackled and the first green shoot grew. It was there before any ancestor smiled by the light of his fire. Everything else is icing on the cake, Mrs Arkwright.'

'You welcomed us with some light operetta, Mr Hargreaves. I was glad for that particular icing.'

He grinned, but pleasantly. Actually, he would have a rather pleasant, lively face, if it wasn't for his diseased gums and his general look of derangement.

'Protocol, Mrs Arkwright, protocol.'

He stood to attention again, perhaps mockingly. As I was going out he called after me, 'Grateful to you for your care and patience. Your fingers are very cool, Mrs Arkwright.'

Edward – do you find this little discussion useful, with your ideas of civilised decadence and so forth? I found it oddly distressing.

I have wandered out several times to the cemetery. It's from the time of the German traders. James had the gardener 'tidying it up'. Apart from poor Northcott's modest affair in stone, cut by the

Baptists, it's all bumps beneath crosses made out of iron joists and bed rods. They're already rusted and ancient looking, with the odd blank name plate. Whatever names were painted on have long disappeared, yet the traders only left during the war. This fact combined with that little discussion brought my spirits down for a full week.

I told James that I thought Hargreaves had become an out-and-out pagan.

'As long as he isn't in any secret society, darling, it can be classed as professional interest. Most of the old Coasters have a bit of them that's gone that way. Like wearing robes and smoking hooglies in Arabia, or putting your hands together and bowing in India. Helps one understand the people.'

A secret society, Edward, is exactly like the ones we have at home, only the problem out here is that it can end up very nastily. You must have heard of the Leopard Society business in Calabar, which was like the Masons with spots – those spots being slavery and murder-by-leopard (someone disguised, with horrible claws). Tarbuck's lot stamped it out, and they all sing hymns now. But around here, and even deeper in the forest, no one knows quite what goes on. There are even Crocodile Societies, apparently, which makes me physically shudder. James showed me the local map he'd found in a drawer. It's from trading days, and covered in mould – but that makes no difference, since the mould can stand in for the forest, and most of the forest is uncharted. Even the Germans have nothing written in that ugly Gothic script, north of us, except *Der Wildnis*. We are a little red hut on the thicker one of the wiggles, and Ikasa is three red huts. I don't think we deserve to have a hut, if Ikasa has only three. The ends of the map dropped off the ends of the table, which was very fitting.

James is going to rebuild the veranda. Don't ask me how, but it involves a lot of concrete. Mr Hargreaves was very proud of it, but every time it rains the tin roof not only rattles but lets in quite a number of the balusters. I am astonished, in some of these storms, that we are not all washed away, let alone the veranda. Every time the concrete floors are scrubbed, little pebbles come away with the bristles. James blames the PWD. I blame the weather.

The second conversation happened one evening, after supper, on one of the rare occasions Hargreaves joined us (he only left a week ago). Normally he stayed in his room, or went for little strolls around the compound. For dinner, he would dress up – in soiled evening jacket and trousers, but no tie. He would make fun of James wearing a tie. One doesn't wear a tie in the bush, but James is a stickler for etiquette. Anyway, we were all three smoking on the veranda. It was not raining. (In Buea, I would have had to retire. Here I do not.) The subject of ju-ju came up. Fetishes and spirits and such-like were discussed. Hargreaves thought Tarbuck's trip up-river was putting Grace in great danger. He paused to pull deeply on his cigar, crackling the tobacco. He nodded to himself. Then he announced that he had seen a man pierced through the heart with a spear. James, who has seen the same done with bayonets and other horrible manly things, wondered what that had to do with ju-ju.

'Everything,' came the reply, with that rather lunatic look in the eyes again, exaggerated perhaps by the glow of the Tilley lamp and all its flickering beasties. I puffed on my cigarette, feeling rather nervous.

'He lived, you see,' murmured the fellow.

'Trickery,' said James.

Hargreaves smiled.

'No. Saw it myself.' He indicated his eyes. Personally, I wouldn't take them as reliable witnesses. 'Arterial blood and all. The spear went through and stuck out the other side, about an inch to the left of the vertebrae. It was a jolly hard thrust.'

'Ugh,' was my contribution.

'Oldest trick in the book,' said James, tapping his cigar in the ashtray. I do respect his phlegm.

'I know, Arkwright, when a man is pierced through and when he isn't.'

Mr Hargreaves had gone rather hoarse.

'Go on,' James said.

'It's the seventh, and final, test. I am not permitted to tell you the first six, each advancing in degree of severity and risk to life. Only the seventh is not a secret. Once passed, only old age can claim you. You are immune. Not even the tsetse fly dares bite.'

He was staring straight into the lamp, as if he was blind. I had the feeling he was considering telling us something more: his eyes flitted for a moment between us. But then he sighed, and leaned back, his face relaxing, saying we would find out for ourselves. I'm sure I won't, unless I go deranged!

He started snoring a few minutes later, falling insensible again, and James and I made a two-handed seat and carried him back. He is not heavy, and I am not weak. War does teach you some useful things, apart from how to kill people. On subsequent occasions, we made sure he sat in the same chair, which was easy to slip a couple of brooms through and use as a carrying chair (you know, like a sedan). He never asked how we returned him to his bed each time. Thank goodness the servants never saw us!

If there was ever any further discussion of the local superstitions, it got Hargreaves terribly excited. A few nights later he didn't go to sleep in the chair, but paced about the compound, smoking furiously and muttering to himself. We watched him before going to bed, standing in the veranda's shadows in our nightgowns. The fireflies were fantastic, and the frogs very loud indeed, and the forest full of whoops and shrieks and chatterings. The night air was freshened by the day's rain – that is, the world didn't feel like one great vapour bath or a giant steam inhaler. Although he was muttering to himself, we couldn't catch his words. He simply splashed right through the puddles, and we were afraid he might fall down the steps.

James murmured that he'd be eaten alive by various little beasts, and wondered if he was taking his quinine. I told him that I was adding the grains to his water. James told me that I was a wonderful nurse. I told him that, in my capacity as a wonderful nurse, I thought his daily intake of Gilbey's to be medically ill advised.

I'm afraid, Edward, that he stormed off, as if I had said something very rude.

As a man, how do you advise I proceed? I thought perhaps that the presence of Hargreaves was partly responsible, but now I realise that it is an old African habit, masked in Buea by his being beholden to his superiors there and quite frequently out of my presence, hobnobbing at the Club. Also, something in the loneliness of this place, and the terrific difficulties of matching his ambitions with their realisation, has triggered it, I think. He has nightmares in which he again sees poor Bailey in that tent with black bile pouring from his mouth and screaming with pain – which turns into himself, licking the last of the calomel from the bottle before plunging into a coma. Into wakefulness, in reality. I reiterate that yellow fever can never be caught twice, and read him the passage in my copy of *Tropical Medicine*. Bailey was a first-tourer, by the way, also from Merton. But James drowns the apparition with another dose of his wretched gin.

If I had the courage, I would throw every bottle into the river and send the crocs to sleep instead.

Everything about Africa *touches* one so – the body, then the mind. Do you remember when you read me *Dracula*, all those years ago, and I said that I would like to dissolve into mist, like those awful red-lipped vampires? Well, here one nearly does. I have been too used to crisp sheets, carbolic, boric lint and spica bandages. My little bush hospital looks helpless against the enormous weight of vegetation behind it, which insists on creeping forward while one's back is turned. I dream of jumping into the river to get out of the tendrils – only to be gobbled up by a crocodile. I'm not sure if the Big Beef is a big croc, or hippo, or something sinister and unknown. I lie awake at night and stare at the ceiling: the lathes have apparently warped, and the plaster is cracked and has smoky patches of damp. Nothing will persuade me that it won't fall on my head in one of these storms.

As for Hargreaves's spearing business: I had to read Professor Clifford's books before nursing shell-shock patients, and he would call this an *eject* – a thing thrown out of one's own consciousness. Not quite trickery, but not quite ju-ju, either. Do you know what Dr Symons used to say to us, in his lectures? No broken crockery, however skilfully mended, ever looks quite the same. The most hairline of cracks can come apart, quite suddenly, when heated.

A thought that bothers me, I don't know why: the river here will never, ever freeze – not in a million years.

I am a little girl in a big wood. I'm not sure how Northcott finished himself off, but I prefer not to ask. Perhaps he did it in this very room (the sitting-cum-dining-room). I need not have ended up here. I refused Dr Symons, Edward. I might have carried on in Hampshire, risen to Sister, helped him with his lectures, even giving my own. He was popular, good-looking: the junior nurses giggled in his presence. But I fell for a patient. We were warned about that. James enthralled me with his stories, as I wheeled him about those big, soft, velvet lawns. His neck was thin and yellow, like a fluted column. It has fattened up, now.

As long as we boil and filter the water, wash vegetables in potassium permanganate, and take our quinine, I do not expect to succumb to anything more than the odd dose of malarial fever. The point is – I don't regret a thing. I am in a perpetual state of excitement and wonder, only now and again I feel myself stiffening into depression, as if my skin is made of plaster of Paris.

Please write more frequently, Edward. My love to Joy. I am glad her cuttings have taken. Here, everything takes and all the time. Apparently it is cooler between November and February, but the forest does not stop growing as it does not stop dying. I think of it seething, sometimes. Its floor is a sort of rich molasses, full of decaying matter. There are fungi the size of my head, and the oddest sort of tubular flowers stuck to tree-trunks. It will help when James has the 'road' that goes into it properly cleared. I can only venture in about a hundred yards (though my patients find a way in and out). After that it is a struggle, but in the odd dry moments he has Baluti the laundry boy and Quiri the handyman – or handylad, as he is all of twelve or thirteen – cutting and advancing by a few more lianas. He plans to do the whole thing when the rains slow up, in November, with a large team of the Chief's fellows from Ikasa. Jolly good. A few miles in, the road is said to fork – one way Ikasa, the other way the forest interior and some villages Hargreaves claimed he had visited, where they go without a stitch.

Head Office have promised James a fleet of clerical assistants, but I think they alighted at the wrong bank. I'm sure Northcott and you-know-who were promised the same thing. Maybe the lost fleets will found a city, full of typewriters and ink pads and refusals-to-sign-papers-until.

I will tell you more about Hargreaves in the next letter, *only*

455

when I have received something from you. It is better than *Dracula*.

    With all my love and affection,
       Your sister, Charlotte

Bamakum, July 18th, 1921

Dearest Edward,

It has just arrived. Your letter, I mean. I would like less of your 'grand scheme' and more of gossip. Maybe Joy should also write. She notices the little things. There is quite enough 'grand scheming' here to keep me happy for eternity. I'm talking of the natural order, from ant to gorilla. You would say that I have understood you, in that case.

Here is our gossip. Our servants are called Baluti, Mawangu, Joseph, Mr Henry (the houseboy), Mr John, Augustina and Quiri. Mawangu is the second houseboy. Remember his name.

No Tarbuck or Grace on the expected day. Not surprising: Africa does not run to timetables and clocks. We were only as worried as one is when anyone is late. However, Hargreaves moved out of his room into the guest bungalow, as planned. The guest bungalow is a hut a little separated from the servants' huts. James had it cleaned up and kitted, I hung a sign on it saying *Mon Repos*, James took it down (a Position and a sense of humour do not go together).

The bedroom was thoroughly cleaned and aired (if that's the word) the same night, before we moved in. Mawangu found the whip under the bed. It's a *bulala* – a big thing of hippopotamus hide, used by the police. The wooden handle had termite holes. Hargreaves was not in his hut – or anywhere. Joseph, our white-haired cook, pointed at 'dat big wildnis dere' (he was cook's mate in the days of the Germans!) and said, 'Massa Hargreaves, he gone aus for small-small time with panga.' The man had left a note: *Dear Mr and Mrs Arkwright, I will be back for dinner. Ever yrs, John S. Hargreaves. SL to be applied, of course!*

SL is 'in-house' code; it stands for 'Sumptuary Laws'. These once prevented court extravagance, back home. In the colonial circuit out here it means Dress Informally and Don't Put Out the Silver, and so forth. Rather cheeky of the man, we thought.

I was very glad to have our bed at last. It is a solid PWD affair with added ends of fancy brass (poor Northcott's touch, apparently). The room was filthy. There were dirty dishes the ants had not tackled, and lots of screwed-up papers and scraps in the wardrobe and under the dressing table. The *bulala* was a shock. The other side of Hargreaves! David Tall had found far nastier things rusting in the old German headquarters at Buea, but the whip disturbed even James. He said it might be the chap's fetish.

'Are you serious?' (That is me talking, by the way.)

'Well, you either guard against the evil eye with magic or you take it out with this.'

'How horrid.'

'But he's taken himself off this morning, without it,' James noted.

We looked out of the window. The wire-netting across the glass is just about eaten away by rust, this side. We could see the beginning of the path: the fellow had slashed it a little wider. A very beautiful bird was picking about in the debris: not large by African standards – about the size of a jay. Jet-blue head, yellow wings, and a tail of malachite green that splits into a curve, like a swallow's. I asked James if he knew its name. He thought it quite likely that it didn't have a European one – or even a taxonomic one in Latin. Isn't that extraordinary? We might be the first white people to have seen it. I'll play Adam – no, Eve – and name it. *Edwardia Joy*.

Baluti came out of the cookhouse with a bucket and the bird flew off, absolutely brilliant against the trees, which are mostly a sort of coppery-green. Baluti didn't seem to notice it – or if he did, ignored it. I wondered if James, looking out, holding that horrible whip, saw the forest as his own, as a king does. Of course, Cameroons is a sort of halfway house, a mandate from the League of Nations – though not yet officially ratified, James has just said, when I asked him for further details. Even His Majesty wouldn't go so far as to say it was part of his Empire, quite in the way he might of Nigeria. There is a resentment felt by the Cameroons officers towards their counterparts in Nigeria, from where the mandate is exercised. One does feel second class, here. First Lagos, then London. It is somehow crushing. But the forest is neutral. At least, it is itself.

Being not at all nosy, I couldn't help glancing at some framed photographs of Hargreaves's family, face-down on the bedside table: a matronly Mama in a flowery hat, a timid-looking Papa hiding behind a beard, and either a very pretty sister or a romantic attachment. The climate had spoiled the faces. They all looked drowned. I'm quite sure he gazed on them every night, in his befuddled way. I never noticed them out, though.

We asked the servants about the whip, but they were awfully evasive. However, Joseph showed us his back. It was covered in long scars. For a horrible moment we thought this was Hargreaves's work, but it was not. Joseph had worked here for the Germans, and the Germans had savagely whipped him for various minor misdemeanours. Far worse went on, apparently: there were many hangings here, and shootings, and a lot of deaths from starvation and disease among the African workers. It all seems like very ancient history, but it is only a few years ago. However, I do think things have changed so much since the war, everywhere. Feeling young and thoroughly modern is not easy here, but I intend to stick to it. I have brought out some jazz records and the station gramophone has been scaring the wildlife. James shuts himself away while I have a little dance – I do the Vampire and the Shimmy very well, and perspire no more than one does in a London night-club. Before you groan, Edward, I'll have you know our Nurses' All-Night Jazz Dance Marathon raised £125 towards the War Memorial Fund, two years ago!

Two years ago? It seems like ten. This place is so very good at covering tracks. I hope I don't grow old and decrepit as quickly as everything else does. According to African beliefs, let alone English ones, Bamakum must be teeming with ghosts. Joseph has a particularly large fetish hanging around his neck and several more round each wrist. Frankly, I'm not surprised. My own fetish is a Bible – old-fashioned, I know, for a modern girl, but it reminds me of my room at home. I read from it each night, and murmur one of those little prayers Mother taught us, while James is having his last cigar and 'nightcap' on the veranda. That should keep any stubbled rascals away, phantasmal or otherwise.

We were having lunch at the table (where else?) the same day when Hargreaves appeared at the door. He was stripped to the waist and holding the panga (like a machete, Edward). It was all gleamy with sap.

'Not dressed for luncheon, old boy?' said James. (Calm as a cucumber, of course. The perfect DO.)

'Tinned sausages, plenty of them,' I added. My voice was a little shaky, which was hardly surprising since I honestly believed the fellow was about to carve us up. He had the most filthy, torn shorts on, his legs were scratched and dirty, and his boots were clogs of mud.

'Look, I'm awfully sorry to interrupt,' he said, 'but do you have any honey, or treacle, on you?'

I summoned my thoughts. His eyes were hidden behind his dirty lenses, so I couldn't gauge the extent of his derangement.

'Would Lyle's Golden Syrup do?' I asked.

'Perfectly,' he said. He then drew a chair towards him and sat, a little way from the table. He looked immensely relieved. The panga had dropped to the floor with a clatter, just missing his foot. He'd already ruined the rug, but it was a dull one.

There was an awkward silence. It needed our big clock to fill it, but our big clock had already decided that the equator was not to its liking. My face was sweltering. I felt terribly irritated.

'Is the condiments crate open, James?' I asked. 'If so, Mr Hargreaves can have his golden syrup straight away. On bread, Mr Hargreaves?'

'Just as it is, Mrs Arkwright. Just the tin, and a big spoon.'

James commented that he must have got dashed bored with millet cake and plantains, when the stock ran out. Hargreaves replied that he didn't eat. (Almost true, I suppose.) I told him that there's nothing to be proud of in that.

Mawangu took the plates away and brought clean ones for the mangoes. In Africa, so the old Coasters say, chatter is not a prerogative, and silence a blessing. Anyway, mangoes are too messy to allow talking. (They grow by the ton, and I love them as much as the monkeys do.) I told Mawangu to bring the tin of golden syrup and a big spoon. I wanted to make sure that Mr Hargreaves didn't use it all up, but he followed the servant out. That was the last we saw of the fellow for two days, and the very last we saw of one of our precious golden syrup tins. I have never been sure whether the lion on the label, with the bees around its head, is dead, or sleeping. We felt the same way about our difficult guest, during those two days. But I found myself filling up with sloth, when I began to worry about him. Isn't that awful, for a nurse?

I will take this interval in my narrative (from Hargreaves, I mean), to tell you about my Typical Day. This might encourage *you* to describe the little things in life.

First thing, I might take a little stroll to the river's edge. The river is terribly brown and sombre, as if permanently in uniform, or smeared in mustard when the sun shines, but I'm fond of it. James wants three decent canoes – two large, one small – chained to the jetty, available at all times. There is so much to do! I have seen only one crocodile here but that is quite enough. It was in the middle of the 'bay' and rolled its eyeball at me. They are very toothy – the teeth stick out like an Oxford aesthete's. Otherwise there is no comparison. I hope. It would be awful to come all the way here and find oneself suffering that.

I am kept very busy telling the servants what not to do. The wash-house is a tin hut by the water tank, and Baluti the laundry boy leaves the laundry on the line after dusk. This is much-much bad-bad, or 'nyama-nyama': there's a fussy fly that lays its eggs only in clean linen after sunset. Then you don this clean linen and the eggs use your flesh as a nest, popping up as worms out of your thigh, or somewhere equally unexpected. As it is not raining for a minute, Baluti is hanging out the washing this morning: my elaborate gestures exhaust me. I know that tonight, if the rain holds off, the washing will still be there. One day, I will master pidgin.

To the cookhouse, now: outside it, the cook's assistant, Augustina, is pounding yams for foo-foo. She is enormous, with slender ankles, fat brass ringlets on her arm that clack, and an orange calico dress. I ask her where Joseph is.

'Chop-shed, Ma.'

She shrugs all the time, I don't know why. I enter the kitchen (or cookhouse) and look around it discreetly, while Augustina comes in and slops the foo-foo into a big pan. It is horribly close in here. Flies wriggle in past the netted door. Our meat safe hangs in the darkest corner. It has a pretty curtain of pink roses. The linoleum is peeling off the concrete floor. The cupboard, which I have personally scrubbed inside and out only yesterday (thus upsetting Quiri, whose job it really is), swarms with tiny ants, as does the floor. The tap dripping melancholically into the tin sink makes me think of prisons. But it *is* like a prison, this room: tiny windows, a door with a heavy spring, the minimum of conveniences. How typical of the PWD to separate it from the main building!

Under the eaves of the chop-shed, in a spot always out of the sun, stand five huge water jars from the time of the Germans. The water tank was installed, in 1919, by Northcott's predecessor – a notoriously rough fellow called Harvey-Lewis. (It has *HL 1919* scratched into it by some awful claw, I should think.) The jars are empty. I would like to use them again, as coolers for butter and so forth. The metal tank keeps the water *warm*, which is hopeless. I hear a grand crash and clatter through the brick walls of the chop-shed and open the door: Joseph stands in a heap of tins, rubbing his head. The shelves run along either side, and the Tilley light swings on empty spaces. These gleam with fresh cobwebs. There are still two chop-crates to unpack, thankfully. The organisation of the chop-shed requires my presence, so I stay an hour with Joseph. We put back the tins of peeled pears and apricots and remove the Ovaltine from the savoury sauces department. The chop-shed must seem a very eccentric place to someone who eats only what grows out of the ground here, but I would die if I lived off nothing but millet, cassava, sweet potatoes, plantains and tiny fried fish. And so forth.

I drop in on James in his 'office': this has been carved out from the (diminishing) jumble of crates in the second bedroom. He is studying maps, or typing letters, or sorting his scratch box, or staring into space, imagining that cleared road. And maybe the fleet of lost clerks. (Where will they sleep?) We have tea together, mid-morning. Then I spend time in my little bush hospital, patients or no. (I write letters in the evening.)

Mawangu brings the tea, usually. But on the second day of Hargreaves's absence, he failed to. Now this is the horrible and exciting bit, Edward. Hold tight.

On that particular day, then, we wait, discussing you-know-who. I imagine the blighter sitting in the forest like a little bear, tucking into my golden syrup. Actually, we are worried. I heave myself from the chair and return to the cookhouse. I ask for Mawangu. They all shrug, now. Then young Quiri runs out.

'Where kuku-matey fly to?' I ask.

I open the door and spot Mr Henry crossing the yard. I ask him about Mawangu. He looks concerned.

'He run away too, like massa DO?'

'Massa DO is my husband now,' I reply, forcefully.

I walk sedately back to the main building. YCHA, or You Can't Hurry Africa.

'Mawangu's gone,' I call over my shoulder, checking the veranda.

Muffled utterance from the office. I go back in.

'How about up here? With another toilet behind it?' says James. He is holding up a sketch map of the compound, tapping it with his pencil. He wants to build a brand-new guest bungalow, for VIPs, out of homemade bricks. (He doesn't think the clerks, or even one clerk, are ever going to come. VIPs first, anyway.)

'Mawangu', I say, 'is absent without leave. Is this normal?'

I catch sight of myself in the mirror. I am bright red in the face, and my hair is awful. I fall into the chair and wipe my top lip with my finger. I am one moist exudation from head to toe.

'They do this from time to time,' says James.

After lunch, and the compulsory nap (only Wallis-Gore, Tall's assistant, flogs himself through the day without one), I decide to venture beyond the compound's perimeters. It is that very rare thing at this season: a nice day. The cloud has thinned, and the sun shines. I put on my bush-boots. These are frightfully ungainly things of dubbined leather — they will be all the rage in Mayfair soon, I'm sure. I take Quiri with me as guide and moral support, and my shooting stick for same.

'Come, my small-small boy,' I say, and we set off, side by side, up the forest path (James calls it a road, the maps call it a track, I call it a path).

For the first hundred yards or so, there is a something Joy would have kittens about: an utter untidiness. Either side is a mess of broken stems and branches, all entangled in vines and creepers. A real jungle, without rhyme or reason. Then the tall trees begin, the glare dies away, the sunlight slips from one's shoulders, one feels a momentary cool – even a chill, just like in an English beech-wood, and the path is nothing more than a trail of mud. Quiri is dragging behind, one hand in his shorts' pocket, looking about him carefully. I have, of course, read Mary Kingsley's *Travels in West Africa* at least three times. I have even tried to describe things here in her vivid style (and failed dismally). Now I feel, for the first time, the exhilaration of the explorer. A curious mix of solitude and action (it involves the *reclusive* part of the soul, Edward). Such virgin realms before one! I look back: the forest has screened the compound from me. I worry about gorillas, momentarily. To right and left I glimpse pools, with vermilion flowers and onyx-winged butterflies. The huge trees soar, as bland trunks, until they reach the light, where they seem to burst into smithereens. It makes me giddy to look up that high. Creepers much bigger than my arm have followed them up. They look uncomfortably like fat snakes, wrapped around the trunks, but only for a moment. There are thrashings and squealings and whoops up there: monkeys and birds, but I see nothing – nothing more than shadows flitting, anyway. Leaves twirl down. Then there is silence, which one imagines might continue for ever. There is a thick carpet of leaves on either side, and ants galore now that the sun is screened (sunlight kills ants – did you know?). There are huge ferns and curving bamboos and palm-like growths that seem to start halfway up the trees. I wish I knew all the names.

The path darkens even more, into a sort of tunnel. My eyes adapt very well. The tiny spots of light that have survived down here seem quite brilliant, independent of the shade. There is a very thick smell, quite different from the smell of the river. It's a little like old cupboards left out in the garden for the hens – times ten. I will keep going for as long as the panga has done its work: fresh stumps are shrouded with bees, sipping the sap. An enormous beetle whirrs past my face, into its own domain. Yes, the Garden of Eden. Watery bird calls, clearer in here, remind me of nightingales on summer evenings in childhood, in a *real* twilight. I find English cousins for the flowers, too: viper's bugloss, yellow rattle, wolfsbane, marsh orchid – anything, really, with tongues, though there is something that looks exactly like a tiny poppy, and creepings of cinquefoil, and a goldeny eggs and bacon.

For many minutes I walk in a daze, dazzled by the beauty and the ease of meeting it. Puddles bother me as little as do thoughts of gorillas, snakes, or leopards; they (I mean, the puddles) lie like tawny ribbons along the path, fringed by bright fungi and ferns and blooms that up and flitter away. My bush-boots slap straight through the mud, spotting my dress. I have never seen, even on the slopes of Mount Cameroon, such enormous leaves. Like an ogre's aspidistras. A brief recollection of the Palm House in Kew Gardens intrudes: the same luxuriant odour, the same smotheringly hot moistness, yes. But not the immensity! I thrust back the iron-and-glass walls and stop for a moment, smiling at Quiri as he appears around the bend. Easy to imagine this bigger than the scrap of it at Kew, but not so easy to make it bigger than the Botanical Gardens in Victoria. Surely it can't go on, like this, for as much as the maps show it does! All of England was once a wilderness of woodland, Edward, I know. You have told me so many times. But that, too, is hard to imagine. I keep seeing little red-brick villas and Esso signs just when the woods are at their thickest.

I notice a lump of black rock, glistening in the mud a few yards in front of me. The rock on Mount Cameroon is black, because it is really hardened lava. This must be old lava, too. Odd in this wonderland of soft green growth – but the range, James has told me, is also volcanic. As Quiri comes up I try to tousle his head but he ducks, as if he thinks I am about to hit him. Perhaps Hargreaves did.

We look at the rock. It's not a rock but a swarm of ants, massed in the shape of a cross. Like the X that marks the guest bungalow on James's map. I want to giggle (you know me, Edward). I am about to poke the nest with my shooting stick when Quiri shrieks and runs off, back down the path. This makes me jump. Something rattles away from my boot. It is the tin of Lyle's Golden Syrup, cleaned to a shine. I think I see, out of the corner of my eye, a branch shake vigorously a few yards away, where the foliage is very dense. Something snorts tubercularly. I step back, looking around me, having mild palpitations. Then I look down at the nest, noticing something different. The molten ants have parted at one spot, revealing something yellow.

I think to myself: if I'm not jolly mistaken, those are teeth, still set firmly in their gums.

I don't want to scream. I'm used to horrible sights. But the black, moist horror of the rainforest seems to close around me, wanting to swallow me up. How the Garden of Eden can turn in a second to a dark hell I don't know, but it did. The toothy leer crawled all over by ants is actually the place itself, about to eat me. I set my own ears abuzz and some hidden birds go flapping away with a decent imitation, high up. Then, muttering furiously to keep myself from fainting, I absolutely *hurtle* back.

As I splash blindly through the puddles, I have the very curious sensation of hearing my scream answered from somewhere, like a long echo.

There, Edward – I hope that impressed you. I don't think it comes near to describing what *wildnis* of this sort can really do to you, but I tried. James was typing out a list of Urgent Things To Be Done when I burst in.

'That silly man,' I shrieked (apparently), 'that silly silly man!' Then I was sick all over his scratch box.

James was marvellous. He ordered the servants to bring as many debbies of water as they could manage and strode up the track. I followed, against his advice, with the servants. I am a nurse, after all! We both knew from David Tall (Tall Tales, I call him) that one of the methods of execution in certain parts was to peg a man down for a night in the forest, his face and limbs smeared with honey or palm sap. It had sounded too like a *Boy's Own* tale to be thoroughly believed. But this was James's first thought, wondering what on earth old Hargreaves had got himself mixed up in. His second was that he was completely deranged, and gone the way of Northcott.

'Are you quite sure it's Hargreaves, darling?' he asked.

'No one else has such stained teeth, James.'

We reached the horror at last. It wasn't like a rock, now, but a discarded overcoat. James has seen many a fresh corpse strewn about – not only in the war, but on his last tour, when there was a bad bout of cholera in his area. All my corpses were tucked up nicely in bed, looking as if they were waiting for Mother's goodnight kiss (you know how young some of you were, Edward). Did you know that one's chief dread out here is to incapacitate oneself in the bush, far from help? The flies and ants get to work with admirable thoroughness, starting with the eyes. I have seen lizards crawling along with little ants pouring out of their sockets. What went on in Eden, I wonder?

James had brought along the ceremonial switch of leopard hide, given to him by the Chief in Ikasa. He brushed at the ants vigorously, but they merely crawled up the strips to the handle, and thence towards his glove. They were also advancing up his mud-spattered puttees. He stepped back and said that it might simply be a local type of nest. There was no odour, for a start – not enough, anyway, to intrude on the general fetor. I was about to protest when the ants thinned, and something hollow but peach-like showed. I felt nauseous and so did James – he had to expectorate, at any rate, with his hands on his knees.

'Oh dear,' he said. 'Judicial enquiry. DO as detective, jury, judge – and executioner.'

Quite true, too. It's what DOs most dread, after blackmail.

The servants were instructed to pour water on the spot where I thought I'd seen the teeth. The debbies' original contents – petrol – would have been better, but it seemed callous. Anyway, enough of the ants were washed away into the path's gullies to show a human form, rather like a worn Jesus on the Cross, with a face like one of those outlandish masks in Government House. It was still grinning. The ants had been very busy: they would make the Gourmand Society look like prissy vegetarians. Short work had been made of the torso, but in patches, like one of your

466

archaeological excavations, Edward. Where the skin survived, it was cindery black above the pink chitterlings. James put his hand on his helmet.

'Oh dear God – Mawangu!' he murmured. 'Hargreaves has done this to Mawangu. The repercussions, oh my God, the repercussions . . .'

'Pull yourself together, James,' I replied. 'Mawangu's teeth are filed sharp and are white as snow.'

'Are you sure?'

'James, they terrified me. I have only just got used to them.'

'They're not meant to be terrifying. They're meant to be beautiful.'

James seemed rather lost. He had always dreaded dealing with murder.

'Anyway,' I said, 'Hargreaves might have disguised himself.'

I told him, Edward, how the Ulverton Mumming Team would rub their faces with soot and lard or burnt cork, and became quite unrecognisable. What a pity this horrible sight was not dear Ernest Shadlow the schoolteacher, turned Turkish Knight, ready to be revived by Henry Fergusson or (in the old days) Harry Dimmick, surrounded by a circle of delighted village faces! (And what a pity such innocent entertainment is now deemed old-fashioned. You should revive it yourself, Edward, as part of your grand scheme.)

James seemed not at all convinced, but he wasn't about to test my theory on his finger. Apart from anything else, the ants looked quite vicious. Another debbie was emptied, glugging unpleasantly. There seemed to be a ceremonial mantle of fur over the shoulders, the thickness of my boa (left behind in England, of course!), and exactly like the one the Chief wore in Ikasa. Extraordinary, what the ants could do in a matter of hours. The teeth grinned, bigger than in life. The eyes were gone. Despite the foraging pits in the flesh, the nipples were intact.

I heard laughter: the servants were laughing.

'Who done dis ting?' James demanded.

Best to start with the ones you knew, of course.

They didn't stop laughing, however. Mr Henry in particular was enjoying himself, pointing and slapping his head, the side of his face, as if he couldn't believe the madness of it. In a hundred years, I thought, the native sense of humour will be colonised, and we will understand each other.

James was flushed and furious. He took off his helmet and mopped his brow.

I said, 'People laugh from shock, darling. It's medically proven, and quite normal.'

He gripped my arm and took me aside. 'For God's sake, Charlotte – whether this is Hargreaves or some other poor fellow stuffed with ju-ju rot, *we* provided the murder weapon –'

'James, a tin of Tate & Lyle's Golden Syrup can hardly be classed as a murder weapon –'

'Can't it?'

He shook his head slowly and sadly from side to side.

'Absolutely anything can be classed as a murder weapon, Charlotte,' he said, very faintly. 'Anything. Even a word.'

He was thinking of poor young Bailey, of course. He came out to Togoland when James was about to go on tour up north, beyond Yendi. Bailey had asked to go with him and James had said yes. The fellow wasn't properly acclimatised. James has always blamed himself, especially as he knew they'd be passing through a yellow fever belt. I don't think, frankly, James will ever get over the horror of watching Bailey vomit himself to death in the tent, while feeling seedy himself.

But to see James in that state, now, was doubly awful. It was as if he had never got physically better: his face went quite pale and bony again, and even his bald patch seemed to expand.

Astonishingly, young Quiri then gave the corpse a kick.

James positively exploded.

'Stop dat!' he shrieked. He hit the little fellow with the leopard-skin switch, across the shoulders. 'Stop dat! Stop dat ting!'

I held James's arm very tight. To be sued by an African is run of the mill, but it is awfully tiresome and potentially damaging.

'Sorry,' said James. 'Sorry.'

Mr Henry was now brushing the remaining ants from the top of the head with a large, stiff leaf. There was a furry, black cap. The face was frowning. The nose had actually gone, eaten to the bone, exposing great nostrils. Something huge crashed through the trees fifty yards from the path. There was that curious, hooting sound. I felt my scream welling again. Even Mr Henry looked frightened, now. He ordered us to stay put in a sharp, hissy voice.

'Hey, no move atall! Bad-bad beef! Dis beef big an' strong too much! A man move one finger, 'e go chop um!'

We froze for at least a minute. I was sure the 'beef' in question was a snake. Since all snakes are regarded as venomous to the natives, it did not need to be a black mamba, or a puff adder, or something equally frightful – but it just might be. Birds trilled and burbled in the echoey pastures, high up. A lizard snaked across the path, with horns like worms on its head. The ants were struggling in the mud at my feet. The corpse's half-eaten arms were ridiculously long, with calloused hands. I remembered, in London Zoo, a certain large beast scratching its fleas in the corner of a miserable cage, with surprisingly long arms and just such calloused hands. I leaned towards James.

'It's not human,' I whispered.

James blinked for a moment. Then he, too, saw it. He struck his palm with his fist.

'Good God,' he said.

Mr Henry looked about him and sniffed. 'Dat beef done go now,' he said.

We relaxed.

'It's smaller than it should be,' said James. 'Maybe it's a baby.'

Baluti shook his head. 'No Pa, dat dere be a big-big old chap. Dat be a chief.'

The wrists and ankles had been tied carefully to tent pegs, but these came out of the soft earth easily. It took all of us, however, to turn the animal over. (Except Augustina, who had her face in her hands, grinning through her fingers.) The back of the poor creature was silver-grey, like the hair of a dignitary. It had calluses on it, and fat white ticks.

'What a frightfully repulsive act, James,' I said.

'It's an animal,' he replied. 'A fierce, bloodthirsty one. Think of it as a wolf.'

But I couldn't, Edward. A gorilla is simply too human-looking, even ravaged as this one was. I absolutely insisted that it should be buried, and only just prevented Baluti from hacking off the head. He claimed that the white traders paid five shillings and sixpence for an adult skull. They are turned into ashtrays, would you believe! We did allow the servants, however, to take a tooth each, as protection. The teeth were extracted easily: it was evidently an old specimen. Quiri (or Quicksilver, as I prefer to call him) had run back for a shovel and several pairs of gloves. We dug a rough hole a few yards from the path, which instantly welled up with swampy water. Gloved and with much grunting, we carried the gorilla to its final rest. James reckoned it weighed thirty stone. Its devourers floated up, settling like a skin on the water. We then covered it in humus, branches, and leaves. I wove a simple cross out of twine.

The servants now only use the path if they have one of those teeth in their pocket, or hanging around their neck. A fetish, Edward, to ward off the gorilla's ghost.

The wretched man appeared, just before dinner, covered in insect bites and dirt, creasing up his panama in his hands. A sheepish Mawangu was in tow. I'm afraid I rose and retired to the bedroom without a word of greeting. His very presence made me feel sick. But I heard the interchange through the wall, the walls being paper thin (Edward, that is unfair – I am not at all nosy).

'Listen, Hargreaves, she's jolly upset by something we found on the path. Next to the tin of golden syrup.'

There was a mumble I couldn't quite catch. Something like, 'Oh, the gorilla, I wondered where it had gone.'

The bedroom, if I wasn't mistaken, was filling up with his smell, both sour and sugarish.

'Yes, the gorilla,' said James. (*Stronger, be stronger*, I was thinking.) 'Waste of golden syrup, dear chap. Hoping it's not a dry run for another. One of life's necessities, golden syrup. Only nineteen left, now. Under lock and key, of course. Safe from sticky fingers, as it were.'

James had rehearsed this approach over tea. I, being of the gentler sex, had wanted a violent rebuke. James had said that it never pays to go overboard, in Africa. Humour works best. A chap in that state can't cope with humour.

I think James had miscalculated. My ear was now pressed to the wall. There was no mistaking the content, now.

'God, you do cheer me up, Arkwright old chap. As does your lovely wife. Quite the best fetish a fellow could have, out here.'

I heard James dismissing Mawangu sharply, then there was a sort of shuffling noise, a thumping sound, a cry – and I immediately rushed around and into the room. Hargreaves was crumpled up against the wall, looking astonished, with blood on his lips. There was glass glittering on the rug: the cracked right lens of his spectacles had now shattered. The frames lay at his feet. James was in a sort of half-crouch, nursing his fist. Hargreaves picked his spectacles up, held his hand across his mouth, then studied his hand.

'Your husband's cut my lip,' he said, looking at me.

He then pulled out a canine, holding it up like a magician. James stood straight, looking rather anxious, or perhaps pained. I've never understood this hitting thing between men, but now I felt rather satisfied, I'm afraid. However, I kept my mouth shut.

'A stitch in time, Hargreaves,' James said.

(I thought: what a wonderful pun! Did he mean it?)

'The next time I might send you packing,' he continued. 'Put that thing under your pillow. Your spirit friends might leave you thruppence.'

'It was only a bloody animal,' growled the wretched man. He had quite forgotten the insult towards me, which had actually triggered the blow. 'You've bust my glasses as well, damn you. What did you think? That I was planning to do it to you or something? No such luck.'

'You can dine separately tonight,' said James, not quite as steadily as before. 'You're a stain on the Colonial Office, and therefore on your country. Unless you apologise, and start behaving yourself, I will be writing a full report on the matter, for Headquarters. There's creosote in the office, for the lip.'

Hargreaves began to smile, then winced. 'Do what you bloody well like, Arkwright. And keep your bloody creosote. I don't need it. That's the whole point, you idiot. *I don't need it.*'

He walked out of the double doors on to the veranda. The night was terribly loud – full of the usual frogs and cicadas and so on, but almost painfully cacophonous now. He dragged open the netted veranda door (it sticks) and backed down the steps carefully, dabbing his chin with his wrist. At the bottom he looked up, grinning crookedly.

'It *was* quite dead, wasn't it?' he called.

James nodded, but that was all. I think he was speechless with rage. From my position at the window, it looked as if Hargreaves was peering blindly, holding his spectacles to his face, genuinely eager to know. Muttering to himself, he then wandered off in the direction of the cookhouse.

James pointed out to me, in weary disgust, what I had just missed: Hargreaves's question implied that they had pegged the poor creature down alive. But in that case, I pointed out, its legendary strength should have made escape simple.

Without further comment, he went with me into the office and checked in the old school tuck-box of his that serves as our personal medical case. A syringe and one of the morphine bottles had gone. James sat down, drawn and slightly trembling.

'If Tarbuck doesn't get back in the next day or so,' he said, 'I'm going to put that fellow on the first canoe that passes. I don't mind him pilfering our drinks cabinet, but I stop absolutely at theft of medical equipment. That's the absolute rottenest.'

'I haven't seen any canoes pass,' I pointed out. 'But I'm sure he'd be happy with one of his crocodiles.'

'Like Adonis on the blasted dolphin,' sighed James. 'What a smasher of a notion, darling. Meanwhile, everything has to be kept under lock and key. He only has to take our quinine bottles and we're finished. It nearly finished Livingstone, you know, having his medicine box cabbaged. Saved by Stanley.'

The Reverend Tarbuck and his daughter steamed into our bay the following afternoon, to our immense delight – and theirs. They had met with some impressive adventures, which he is to add to his book. The natives they had met were astonished at their whiteness, and considered them phantoms. The very pretty phantom was Grace: I heroically insisted they stayed more than one night in order to recover their strength and a bit of weight, positively pouring my extra-strong beef tea down their throats (we have it in powdered form, of course) and persuading both of them that the stimulating properties of my White Wine Whey were medicinal, not bibulous. (In case you don't know it, Edward, I merely add sherry to boiling milk and cream off the resultant curd. A peptonising powder is optional. All our milk is condensed, it goes without saying.)

Grace spent most of the time in bed – a camp bed in our own room (James slept in the hallway, Tarbuck on the sofa in the main room). She was utterly exhausted, but not ill. I treated her as an invalid, however. Hargreaves stayed in his hut, scowling at the world. He reminded me of a dog in the kennel, tail thoroughly between his legs. James and I spent a lot of the time talking with the Reverend about many matters, not just Hargreaves. It was most useful. Grace joined us for most meals, but was very quiet. Sharing a room, we talked a little before going to sleep. This should have been a great pleasure, but was marred by her inability to sound interesting, whatever the topic. I coaxed out of her a pale account of the journey up-river, but it might as well have been a day's outing on the Thames, for all it stimulated me. I think she is a kind of saint, very pure and selfless and of course young. Perhaps saints are a little dull, in the end. One wants to plump her up, like a pillow, to give her more character. I felt thoroughly stuffed with selfishness in her presence, anyhow.

You would say she was a prig. I would not go that far. In twenty years she might be, but right now she is too innocent. I fear for her, here.

She talked of Hargreaves as if he needed saving. She went out to see him when she should have been resting, one afternoon. I kept an eye on them through the bedroom window. He seemed to be smiling and talking with her pleasantly enough. She returned quite flushed and animated, saying that he had taken a copy of one of her Baptist tracts. I think of them as the Devil and the Angel – they will still be together on that wretched little steamer, a day away from the Mission Station, as I write these words. I feel I have failed with the fellow, as I have quite failed to wrest James from his gin.

That is all the news. Hargreaves said goodbye perfunctorily and didn't bother to wave from the poop, by the way. It is terribly moist today, so please send us some of your drought. The keys stick and the paper is all corrugated. This morning I found a couple of jiggers in my toes. I'm too tired to explain what that means, but it is nothing to do with the one-step. All right – if you don't remove the blighters, your legs eventually drop off.

With much love to you and to Joy,
Charlotte

Dear Edward,

Either you have forgotten your poor, far-flung sister, or your letter has been lost somewhere between Ulverton and Bamakum. Or eaten by ants. Or swallowed by a mamba. Do not put anything with it that might be construed as treasure: even a snapshot of an English country garden can be framed prettily in carved mahogany and sold in the market for two shillings.

We do hear, however, that England is so dry and hot without us that people in London have been choked in a gale by clouds of dust, the Thames is a trickle, and silk-hatted pedestrians are measuring 107 degrees under their black hats after ten minutes' exertion! I know this because we have just received our month's worth of *The Times* – to the end of July. Maybe September is full of wet and cold, but I am still in July, I'm afraid. Here we do not have to have black hats in order to have our brains boiled, of course. I read also that the West End is full of girls taking cocaine. Here my servants all chew something called a cola-nut, which I'm beginning to believe is just as efficacious, though James tells me it's no more potent than powdered coffee.

So much has happened that I am forced to write anyway. Here, the chief complaint is a chronic malady called rainitis. Its effects are the same as over-prolonged sea-bathing in the summer: exhaustion, depression, palpitation, loss of appetite, lassitude, and sleeplessness. This is no coincidence: the air is so saturated with water, whether actually falling in curtains or no, that one swims through it all day. This is why *our* heat is not to be measured in degrees but in ripples. Today I measured a million-and-one ripples per inch of air, so there. At dusk and at dawn we are shrouded in mist. A palpable miasmic mist, I'm afraid. I have had a touch of fever and passed with flying colours. I feel thoroughly baptised, now: I was worried when Africa would choose to bless me with her hot hand.

Events are more jagged, as it were, elsewhere. James has learned that the auction of the plantations went off very badly. That is, no one wanted to buy them. They are probably to be returned to the Germans, who will have to be kept an eye on. Let us hope their defeat in the war will have caused them to lose their appetite for massacres and assorted cruelties. There is a vein of natural justice in the world, but it always arrives *after* the crime.

The canoe that brought the bundle of our *Times*, three *Vogues*, and a single veteran *Tatler*, also carried a letter from Tarbuck, with unwelcome news.

Mr Hargreaves left the Mission Station just before the cargo boat arrived, which was to return with him on the final leg to Victoria. When I say 'left', I mean disappeared. One of the fresh cadets thought he had seen a white fellow in a battered panama paddling furiously in a dug-out, up-river – which means this way. I do hope he isn't thinking of 'dropping in'. I keep glancing up at the window, thinking I see his face leering in, one eye hidden behind a dirty lens, the other horribly clear. He really did resemble a pirate, standing there in the steamer as it moved off. Now he must resemble Ben Gunn, the maroon.

Grace is grief-stricken, apparently. I really think Hargreaves had some devilish hold over her. Perhaps she finds missionary cadets lacking in spunk, as you find modern girls lacking in profundities.

James has drawn up all the necessary plans for the making of the road. His grand project is to link Ikasa with Kumba. We hope to have a small generator soon, just enough to drive a wireless, or whatever generators do. Then we can wire the world our news.

I have some hens. Augustina cooks the eggs reluctantly, since she insists that Pa Arkwright will be made sterile by them. I say nothing, of course. Whether it is the rain, or the isolation, James's problem (I don't mean the gin) weighs on me now, and makes me feel sad.

Once the sky stops moving its pianos about, the path-track-road will be cleared to the nearest village, which will then open up the interior to us. I expect my bush hospital to flourish. It languishes in puddles, now.

I wish I lived under thatch. Tin and rain are made only to come together in noise.

> Please, please write,
> Charlotte

Bamakum, May 1st, 1922

My dear Edward,

You say you found my last two letters full of domestic trivia, that I should be plumbing the depths of this ancient continent. I am not sure which two you mean: I have sent at least three since Christmas. You have written once in November, and now yours of April 3rd. Are you annoyed at my pestering you to reply? Or at my suggestion that Joy should tell you how to write of the little things? I don't want to fall out with you, not from this far.

I cannot write about Africa but in the way that I do. I am proud of being a 'modern girl', if that's what I am. Dancing on my own to my jazz gramophone records does not make me 'shallow' or 'flippant' or 'facetious'. I know you were saying this of society in general, but it came like a tract, and hot on the heels of your doubting whether my 'mental life' was sensitive enough for 'the wholesome wisdom of natural Africa'. I don't take Africa like a cup of Oxo, I can assure you. Africa takes me. You wish me to listen to her 'occult rhythms' and report back, so that your masculine reason can 'synthesise and give it shape'. But if I did that, dear Edward, Africa would gobble me up like a crocodile, or an army of driver ants. You would find me (if you bothered to come out here yourself instead of singing your folksongs *im hintersten Berkshire*, or at least out on its wildest frontier) engulfed by psychological creepers, too heavy for my slender trunk. I admire some of your views, and wish your books good wind, but my job out here is to do with serum and calico and disinfectant and decent, womanly advice.

Anyway, I have quite another 'interference' than a warped rag-

476

time record. I have a baby. This baby is not mine, of course. I hope what I am about to tell you will not be judged by you as vulgar, or trivialising, or 'de-bunking'. But I must explain how I came about adopting this child. Probably for good.

About a fortnight ago, a message was wired from the Mission Station: poor Grace Tarbuck, who had been ill for some time, had died. The great shock was that she had been delivered of a child the day before. Apparently, this was a surprise to everyone, including her father. James agreed that I should make the trip straight away, which I did. Down-river, this takes only four days by canoe. I took two servants with me, Quiri and Baluti. Baluti paddled, and we rested in villages on the way (James has organised all this very well). Poor Tarbuck was in a hopeless state, completely stricken with shock and grief. Grace had been weakened by a recent bout of enteric fever, and the crisis of the birth itself had resulted in a severe haemorrhaging from an internal typhoid ulcer which had not yet healed. (Is there time for these details in your Nature worship, Edward? They are very common out here.) If it hadn't been for the baby, she would have lived, I am sure. She is buried in the Mission cemetery, under a small acacia tree. The whole station had the most extraordinary atmosphere, as if a great light had gone out.

An African *ayah* was nursing the baby, and I asked Tarbuck what should be done with it. (The baby is fully white, by the way.) By asking this, I was also hoping to find some clue as to the identity of the father. Unless Grace really was holier than even we realised, and God the Father was to blame again, then I reckoned some fresh-cheeked cadet to be responsible. Tarbuck was stricken as much by the shock of finding his angel fallen, as by her death. He had no idea who the culprit might be, at first. I asked him who had been present at the Mission nine months ago (the baby was born full-term). He ran through four or five names, dismissing all of them in turn as 'quite beyond the bounds of credibility'. Looking at his present lot, terribly young and pimply and almost vulgarly pure, all apparently from Macclesfield, I found little to disagree with there. His white assistant, Mr Horace Wilson, is fifty-five, with a limp, severe smallpox scars, and no hair.

You will already be on to it, I am sure, dear Edward. I was a little slow, I'm afraid. Mr Hargreaves had not come into my thoughts since young Quiri claimed he had seen him lurking in the shadows behind my hospital hut one evening, some months back. We locked everything up for a while, after that, but have by now returned to our easy bush ways.

Tarbuck groaned when I mentioned the man's name; Grace had fluttered about him, tending to his various needs, like a moth around a candle. He had remained surly and charming, in equal quantities, all the way back. Tarbuck had retired early each night on the boat, exhausted by the long trip up-river, and suffering from a mild recurrence of his malaria. Whenever he woke up, he would hear voices. These were the voices of the other two, coming to him on the night air as they talked under the stars (figuratively speaking – it rained buckets).

I cannot explain to you, Edward, if it needs explaining, why a young girl like Grace should fall into the arms of such an ill-looking, weak-minded rotter. At least he was not dull and pimply and pure. Perhaps his rottenness was the result of his drinking too deeply of that beef-tea natural wisdom of yours, let alone the fermented variety.

Whatever, I am left holding his baby. (Or the *ayah* mostly is. I struggle to feel some maternal affection for it. This will come, I am sure.)

James and I feel partially responsible, of course. We treated the whole matter wrongly. We should have warned Grace, or packed Hargreaves off in a canoe, earlier – and so on and so forth. James is really quite content, of course. He has a son, now. Tarbuck hardly blames the child but has difficulties in even looking at it. Time will bring him round: it is the sole souvenir of his own child.

However, I fear that Grace's physical wanness was no match for her lover's vitalities: her pale features have not so far appeared in the infant face. *His*, however, strike me from the cot each day, with more and more force. Thank God the little creature has two good, bright eyes. After James had broken the lens in those smeared spectacles and revealed an eyeball of singular glitteriness, I have always seen Hargreaves as part-blind. The thought that I might be literally haunted by that one-eyed visage every day makes me shudder.

Meanwhile, you must grow used to thinking of yourself as Uncle, and Joy as Aunt. I hope you do not think *that* a trivial responsibility, or in any way irksome. James and I have both agreed that the little chap cannot stay long in this feverish climate. Apart, perhaps, from a few plucky youngsters bearing it up on some of the Mission Stations, I am certain that he is the only white child in the whole of equatorial Africa. I think he might, by being born out here, become as immune to certain rigours as the native. But one cannot educate a child off natural wisdom for ever, Edward.

Oh – I almost forgot. His name is Hugh. His middle name is yours. I hope you don't mind.

Please do write, and more kindly, to your sister.

With love and deep affection,

Charlotte

P.S. We plan to treat the boy as our own, and have instructed the servants not to speak of his origins, under pain of instant dismissal. Tarbuck is agreed. If – and when – the moment comes, I might well use these letters as proof. Please do not destroy them, though I have copies. And if anything were to happen to us here (God forbid), they at least provide the gist.

Acknowledgements

Among the many who have helped me with this book, I am particularly grateful to the following for their help and advice: John Lucas, Jenny and Nick Moore Morris, my editor Robin Robertson, Philip Stevens, Margot Venus, Richard Wistreich, Paul Wright, and my children Joshua, Sacha and Anastasia for reminding me how the young see things.

With a special thanks to my wife Jo Wistreich, whose unerring eye, sure judgement, and long-suffering support have guided this book from start to finish. Also to Niek Miedema and my agent Bill Hamilton for critical support at critical moments throughout.

For the methodology of seventeenth-century acting and its link with ancient medicine, I am deeply indebted to the first chapter of *The Player's Passion: Studies in the Science of Acting*, by Joseph R. Roach (Ann Arbor, University of Michigan Press, 1993). For the lines from Patrice Kayo's poem 'The Song of the Initiate', I am grateful to the *Penguin Book of Modern African Poetry* edited by Gerald Moore and Ulli Beier (Penguin, 1984). Other books that have travelled with me all the way: *Prehistoric Britain* by Jacquetta Hawkes (Pelican, 1943), *Four Guineas: A Journey through West Africa* by Elspeth Huxley (Chatto & Windus, 1954), *African Creeks I Have Been Up* by Sue Spencer (David McKay, New York, 1963), *La Puissance du Sacré: l'Homme, la Nature et l'Art en Afrique Noir* by Clémentine Faik-Nzuji (Maisonneuve et Larose, 1993), *The History of the British Countryside* by Oliver Rackham (J.M. Dent, 1986), *English Downland* by H.J. Massingham (Batsford, 1936).